Steel ☆ Tiger

ALSO BY MARK BERENT

Rolling Thunder

STEEL
TIGER

☆ ☆ ☆

Mark Berent

G.P. PUTNAM'S SONS/NEW YORK

G. P. Putnam's Sons
Publishers Since 1838
200 Madison Avenue
New York, NY 10016

This is a work of fiction. All of the characters in this book are
fictional and bear no resemblance to real-life personages either
living or dead. (Sometimes I think the Vietnam war bore no resemblance to real life.) However, in striving for authenticity, some
of the organizations and public figures exist or existed at the time.
Note that not all actual events occurred in the exact chronology
presented.

Map illustration copyright © 1989 by Lisa Amoroso

Library of Congress Cataloging-in-Publication Data

Berent, Mark.
Steel tiger / Mark Berent.
p.   cm.
1. Vietnamese Conflict, 1961–1975—Fiction.   I. Title
PS3552.E697S7   1990   89-70151 CIP
813'.54—dc20

ISBN 0-399-13538-3

Printed in the United States of America
1 2 3 4 5 6 7 8 9 10

This book has been printed on acid-free paper.
∞

*This book is dedicated to the KIA, MIA, and POW
aircrew from Air America, the U.S. Air Force, the U.S. Army,
the U.S. Coast Guard, Continental Air Service, the U.S. Marine
Corps, the U.S. Navy, the Royal Australian Air Force, and to the
men of the U.S. Army Special Forces.*

"We stand to our glasses ready."

And to MB.

"No guts, no glory. If you are going to shoot him down, you have to get in there and mix it up with him."

—Frederick C. "Boots" Blesse, USAF
10 victories, Korean War

"The fighter pilots have to rove in the area allotted to them in any way they like, and when they spot an enemy they attack and shoot him down: anything else is rubbish."

—Baron Manfred von Richthofen, German Air Service
Leading Ace of WWI with 80 victories

"I love the vertical. Why? Few know how to use it. It's not just geometry. It's mental. And you've got to think in four dimensions; time, both horizontals, and the vertical."

—Bill Sakahara, USAF, Fighter Pilot Instructor

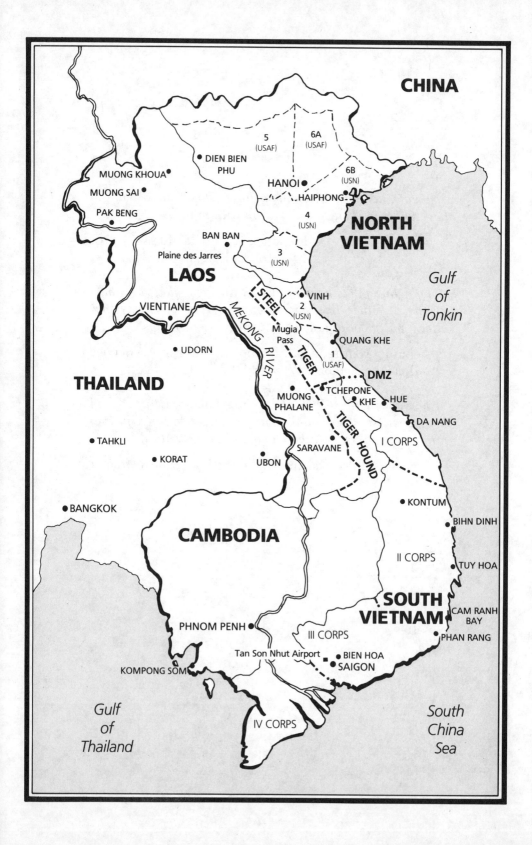

Prologue

☆

He would kill the American. Secure in the cockpit of his MiG-21 jet fighter, Lieutenant Colonel Vladimir N. Chernov of the Soviet Air Force stalked the lone F-4 Phantom 6,000 feet below. His face was hidden behind his oxygen mask and buglike rounded sun visor. The light blue of his helmet matched a scarf knotted at his throat.

Chernov had positioned himself in the glare of the sun to hide from the searching eyes of the crew of the two-man Phantom. He carefully checked the sky around and behind his own airplane. From his vantage point, he saw no other evidence of the large American air fleet that had been over the Bach Mai Cement Works just moments ago. Black and white smoke drifted up from the ruined buildings that had been smashed by a strike force of F-105s protected by F-4s.

Four of Lieutenant Colonel Chernov's North Vietnamese students had tangled briefly with the Americans using the carefully briefed radar-controlled sequence he had taught them. Under control of the ground intercept radar, they had shot down two of the American pilots by using a one-pass, high-speed stern attack, firing K-13 missiles from behind and below. Then they had turned and dove away before they could be seen and chased. Two of the four MiG-21 pilots, Toon and Van Bay, had scored one kill each. The two American planes, an F-4 and an F-105, had never known what hit them. The missiles had blown them into red and black streaks that had arced into the rice paddies. The other two students, lower-ranking wingmen, had not gotten into missile-firing range. After the attack, Chernov had directed them to land. He remained aloft to do what he was forbidden to do: fight American airplanes.

Chernov monitored the American's emergency radio frequency of 243.0 megacycles, the one that warned of MiGs. He was surprised their C-121 airborne radar airplane had not called out his position to the F-4. Maybe it was too far away. *Hara sho,* so be it. Worse luck for the American fighter.

"Good hunting," his North Vietnamese ground controller said in passable Russian.

"I'm not here. I am not on your screen," Chernov shot back, momentarily furious at the controller's breach of security. The last thing Chernov wanted was for anyone to know he was actively flying combat. If his superiors knew, he'd be disciplined by exile to air base Chita up in the Siberian wastes, where the mechanics drank brake fluid to get drunk.

If the Americans knew he was flying combat with the North Vietnamese Air Force, it would give them a propaganda coup that could seriously erode Soviet aid to North Vietnam, not to mention damage international Soviet credibility. Either way, Chernov thought, I lose. I'll just credit honor-pupil Toon with my victory, same as before.

He took one last look around, lazily rolled to an inverted position and, never taking his eyes off the enemy fighter, pulled the nose of his MiG-21 down so the glowing round dot of his gunsight was pointing into the black smoke emanating from the engines of the jet. Ridiculous, he said to himself, the way this big American Phantom had engines that smoked so badly they left trails in the sky pointing to them like Thor's arrows.

The smoking jet engine was just one of the many things that hampered the Americans' efforts to bottle up North Vietnam, Vladimir Chernov thought. He had often discussed the Americans with his Russian ground crew. They had laughed about how easily and safely they could fly Soviet fighters and transports into and out of the Gia Lam Airport near Hanoi, because the Americans were not allowed to strike the field. They couldn't even strafe the MiGs parked on the ground. Only if they were shot at, could the Americans shoot back. And that was almost a joke. Many times Phantom pilots had been in good firing position, yet did not shoot. Or, if they did, many times the missile either fell off or went wild.

All the better for me, Vladimir Chernov thought, and concentrated on his pursuit curve. He rolled out and slowly pulled the nose of his airplane up to place his gunsight dot on the heated tailpipe of the Phantom. His visibility directly forward, like that to the rear, was not good, and once again, he cursed the thick bulletproof glass directly in front of him that restricted his forward observation to a mere three miles. Sighing, he flipped up the cooling switch for the guidance system of his missile. Just inside three miles, the missile's heat-seeking system awakened, and began to growl its lock-on to the heat of the

Phantom's tailpipe. Chernov pressed in. He wanted to get close enough to fire one missile, then break away. If successful, it would be the second U.S. jet fighter he would have been able to down with one missile. Yet he would rather be using a gun. It was a romantic throwback, he knew, to the Yak and Stormovik fighters of the Great Patriotic War. Chernov hoped his request to headquarters for a 23mm gun pod he could sling under the belly of his MiG would be approved. He much preferred the swirling of the classic dogfight to this reliance on an impersonal heat-seeking missile.

The missile tone reached its highest pitch, indicating it had a solid lock. *Zashel v hvost,* I am on his tail. He checked his airspeed, bank angle, and G-load; and made sure he wasn't too far away or too close. Everything was within tolerance, which meant he was well within the missile-firing envelope. He lifted the cap that protected the firing button on his control stick grip, and pressed down. With a swoosh and a great trail of white propellant smoke, the K-13 missile dropped from its rails and homed in on the fleeing jet. It guided perfectly and flew up the left tailpipe. The Phantom disintegrated. There were no parachutes.

Chernov's radar controller saw the Phantom disappear from his screen and couldn't restrain himself.

"Congratulations, Comrade Chernov. You have scored again."

Chernov swore. Would these imbeciles never learn? "You are mistaken," he responded, barely keeping his anger under control. "It was Comrade Toon who scored the victory. *Comrade Toon.*"

"Acknowledged. Comrade Toon," said the controller.

Shaking his head in disgust, Vladimir Chernov headed back to base.

1

☆

It was to have been a normal flight, in which the student test pilot was to have practiced his newly learned ability to perform a simple stall check. But deep in the bowels of the sleek jet, a wire had been chaffing for the last six flights. The final thread of Mil Spec W5086 PVC/nylon insulation was about to separate, which would allow the 12-strand copper wire to ground out on the electrical motor that moved a trim tab. This tab relieved the pressure on the pilot's control stick, enabling him to fly hands-off, by positioning a flight control, called an elevator, up or down at the rear of the plane. The elevator was more formally called the horizontal stabilizer.

The pilot, Air Force Major Court Bannister, was in his fifth month of training at the Test Pilot School at Edwards Air Force Base (AFB) at the western end of the Mojave Desert in California. He was well into the Stability and Control phase, which taught him how to evaluate aircraft handling characteristics. An hour earlier, Bannister's instructor had given him his final guidance. "Fly the card," he had said, meaning Court was to conduct a routine stall check exercise following the climb test, as outlined on the flight test card on his knee-board.

Today's project airplane was a Lockheed T-33A jet trainer. Nicknamed the T-Bird, it was the two-seat version of the venerable F-80, America's first jet fighter. This particular T-Bird, number 29846, had been a mainstay of the school since 1959.

Bannister's test card called for him to climb the plane in a sawtooth profile to 35,000 feet and trim it for hands-off straight and level flight.

Then he was to reduce power and record the speed, stick forces, and aircraft warning signs as he approached a stall. To actuate the trim, he used his right thumb on a little coolie-hat-shaped button on the top of the control stick. Thumbing it forward or back actuated the electrical motor that moved the elevator trim tab; thumbing it left or right moved a tab on the left aileron that moved the wing up or down in the same manner. Bannister began to perform the stall check.

Right hand on the stick, left hand on the throttle, Bannister cleared the area with two ninety-degree turns and made his check-in radio call to Test Control.

"Eddie Test Control, Test Four Six beginning stall check."

"Test Four Six, Edwards Test Control. You're cleared. Report completion."

"Four Six. Rodge. Out."

Bannister eased the throttle back to the idle position on the quadrant. He wiggled contentedly in his straps and harness as he watched the airspeed bleed off. He hummed as he increased back stick pressure to hold the airplane level. This was the last and, surprisingly, the simplest test of the stability and control series. The sky was clear and blue and the visibility was so good he could easily see beyond the dirty yellow haze over Los Angeles to the flat slate of the Pacific Ocean.

This is a great life, he thought to himself. A bachelor fighter pilot with a combat tour of Vietnam behind him, and an astronaut position in front of him—if all went well, that is. First, he had to complete the twelve months' course at the Test Pilot School, and get selected for the astronaut corps. He thought he had a good chance, though. He loved the school and the challenges and rewards it presented. He loved being in the United States Air Force, but most of all he loved flying jet fighters. This was his second appointment to the school. He had turned the first one down a year ago, because he felt he should spend a year in combat first. He almost hadn't gotten accepted the second time, but things had gone so well since, it felt like smooth sailing.

As the airspeed neared stall speed and the T-33 began to buzz and vibrate, Bannister thumbed in enough back trim to remove the pressure from the control stick. When it felt right, he relaxed his grip on the stick and, in a moment of bravado, to show himself how well he had trimmed the plane, he held both hands in the air while behind his oxygen mask he flashed a look-Mom-no-hands grin. But abruptly the grin was gone.

The first indication of the disrupted airflow over the wings of the T-33 as it slowed to a stall was a slight buzzing and a small vibration. All perfectly normal, but the onset of the stall vibration was enough

to cause the insulation on the 12-strand wire to part and the wire to
ground out. The trim motor hummed briefly as it ran to the full up
position, then stopped with a screech and began to smoke.

The jet trainer pitched up abruptly, hung in the sky for an instant
like a great shotgunned bird, then began to tumble toward the earth
seven miles below. Its motions were like a badly punted football spiraling around its longitudinal axis while tumbling end over end as it
fell from its apex. First, positive g-forces crushed Bannister into the
seat, then negative g-forces threw him up into his straps toward the
canopy so hard the blood vessels in his eyes began to gorge. Left and
right pitching moments cracked Bannister's helmeted head against
each side of the canopy with the jolting smashes of a jackhammer.
The cycle repeated itself every four seconds.

Abruptly the 4,600-pound-thrust engine flamed out with a loud
bang. Its compressor had stalled due to the interruption of airflow
into its intake caused by the wild gyrations of the airplane. Unless
Bannister made a quick recovery, the out-of-control jet would smash
into the ground in a matter of seconds. Already it was showing signs
of disintegrating. Small blue flames began to dance around the over-
heated electrical motor.

Slowly, the surprised and dazed Bannister began to struggle feebly
with the controls, instinctively placing them first this way, then that,
in vain efforts to recover the fiercely tumbling jet. Both his mind and
body were viciously assaulted by the sudden and brutal departure of
his airplane from controlled flight.

He saw neither up nor down, merely the blurred flashes of the vivid
blue of the sky, the straight line of the horizon, and the brown of the
Mojave Desert flashing past the plexiglass canopy like bits of blue
and brown glass in a madly rotating kaleidoscope. Nor did he feel
upness or downness as the plane plunged madly toward the hard
desert floor. He struggled not to lose consciousness against the bat-
tering. Not even his flak-filled flights over North Vietnam had beaten
up his body like this.

He knew only one thing: He had to neutralize the flight controls
until he could determine exactly what the airplane was doing and
then assess what placement of them would effect recovery. He did
not, however, think of his predicament in exactly those dry classroom
words. His reaction was more like, "Holy Christ, what happened? I
gotta *do* something."

As the airplane fell lower, flashing silver in the sun like a tossed
coin, he barely noted the sound of the wind rushing first one way,
then the other, past the whirling cockpit. Slowly, the creaks and
groans of the airplane structure subjected to unplanned stresses began to penetrate his consciousness. Unless he recovered or ejected,
he didn't have long to live. Yet he wasn't really afraid of crashing.

Like all fighter pilots, the thing he feared most was making a mistake and being grounded.

Then he saw the first thin wisps of smoke beginning to penetrate the cockpit.

It was as if he had been jolted by an electrical shock. Deep down in every pilot's consciousness is an almost unreasonable terror of fire, particularly fire in the cockpit, slowly burning him as he struggles vainly to escape. But the good pilots know how to make fear work for them, and so it was with Court Bannister. Adrenaline exploded through his body. His whole being suddenly came to a clanging alert, and time seemed to slow, as his mind became pinpoint clear and sharply focused. He knew exactly what to do as if it had been taught in a class. He released the stick and throttle, jammed his elbows on each side of the canopy and put his hands on his helmet to brace his head. His vision cleared. Through the front of the canopy, he saw the brown horizon line was slanted, rotating, and pitching up and down. Glancing down to his instruments, he saw the low engine revs and low tailpipe temperature that spelled flameout. He knew what had happened.

He was in the worst possible phenomenon a T-Bird could experience. In the old days, this type of departure from stable flight was called The Thing. It had been cured by minor modifications to the leading edge of the wings. But this school T-Bird, besides being rather bent and twisted by scores of student test pilots, had just now gone beyond design limits when it had stalled, and pitched up and over into The Thing. Now it was a collection of junk with a dead engine and—according to the increasing smoke—on fire.

Court Bannister knew he could raise the handle on his ejection seat, and squeeze a trigger to blast himself out of the airplane to descend by parachute. But such an ignominious end to a supposedly normal flight was not to be contemplated, unless he still had not recovered by 10,000 feet above the ground, the altitude at which school regulations demanded separation from an out-of-control aircraft. No pilot as yet had followed that particular guidance to the exact foot. To abandon an airplane merely because it was momentarily out of control, while two miles of recovery airspace remained, was unthinkable. Many productive seconds remained for an enterprising pilot to try various recovery methods. There was always one more trick to find in the aeronautical bag so crammed full of lessons and stories and experiences. Of course, if the airplane was in the process of breaking up, or clearly on fire with no chance of extinguishing it by side-slipping, then stepping smartly over the side was considered the intelligent and prudent thing to do.

Bannister saw the altimeter needle pass through 20,000 feet as it unwound like a clock gone berserk. His rate-of-descent needle was pegged down at 6,000 feet per minute, which meant he was falling faster than a mile a minute. He knew he had to perform several actions at once.

He had to jettison the partially filled fuel tanks on the end of each wing tip to change the airplane's center of gravity, which would stop the whirling-dumbbell effect. Next was to pull the throttle full back, report his problem to Edwards Test Control, and turn off the master electrical switch to stop what he was sure was an electrical fire. Then he would recover from the normal spin the T-Bird would enter once he halted the tumbling—if he could.

"Test Four Six, Edwards Test Control. Report state." Test Control had noted his rapid descent with no forward motion. Court didn't register the transmission.

He took his arms down from the canopy and, fighting the whirling and flailing, punched the red emergency jettison button on the instrument panel that released the wing-tip fuel tanks. Centrifugal force flung one tank straight away from the airplane. The other one rolled up the wing and smashed the plexiglass canopy into jagged shards that blew away like shattered ice. Bannister flinched as the huge 400-pound tank narrowly missed his head before flying off into space.

The release of the tanks caused two things to happen at once; the tumbling stopped and the T-Bird fell into an inverted spin. And the draft caused by the missing canopy caused an eruption of white smoke to gush past Bannister's face. The altimeter unwound relentlessly past 14,000 feet.

Upside down, and resisting an urge to unstrap and just drop out of the airplane, Bannister fumbled with both hands on the right console for the electrical master switch. He found it, and nearly tore it loose turning it off. Immediately the smoke thinned, then stopped. Somewhere back in his mind, he logged a dispassionate note that the circuit breaker for whatever electrical circuit that was burning had malfunctioned. It should have tripped long ago. Now, without electrical power, he could not report his predicament to Edwards Test Control.

He grabbed the control stick. Stopping the inverted spin should be easy. He centered the stick, then shoved it forward a few inches. Simultaneously he tried to push the rudder against the direction of his spin, only to find his legs and feet were floating a few inches above the rudder pedals. He could feel his vision dimming from the inverted spin as he fought his feet down to the pedals and pushed. At first nothing happened. The altimeter spun through 10,000 feet. He was breathing in short fast breaths now. The roaring airflow through the broken canopy was buffeting and tearing at his head. Had he not fastened the chin strap before takeoff, his helmet would have been torn off long ago. There was nothing between the top of his helmet and the brown desert sand over a mile below.

Slowly, almost lazily, the T-33 stopped spinning. It was now merely falling upside down in a forty-five-degree nose-low attitude. He released the rudder pressure to center the pedals, and eased back on the stick to pull the nose of the T-33 straight down. This should gain him the forward speed necessary to control the aircraft. He saw the altimeter unwind through 6,000 feet.

For the first time he thought seriously about ejecting, though he knew that, hanging in the straps the way he was, the rising seat would probably compress and fracture something in his back as it slammed into him. Further, the seat would propel him even faster toward the ground as it blasted him out of the upside-down airplane. His eyes fixed on the airspeed indicator. It was beginning to creep up from the 60 knots it had been registering since the plane had gone out of control. It quivered and passed 65, then 70; it moved faster to 80, then 90. By now the altimeter had gone under 3,000 feet remaining. He knew by feel he would need at least 120 knots before he could pull the plane out from its dive. At that low speed he could not pull many Gs to level the airplane before it dug a hole in the desert. The airspeed needle jerked past 100 and Bannister started to ease in some back pressure on the control stick to bring up the nose of the T-33.

At 120 knots, the airflow started forcing the runaway trim tab to pitch the nose up. Bannister had to push forward on the stick to overcome this force, yet still position the elevator to let the nose come up smoothly and as fast as possible to stop his downward plunge. Now the ground was too close to risk looking in the cockpit. He had to pull back on the stick without snapping the plane into another stall, while completing what in effect was the bottom half of a loop. He raised his head to fasten his eyes on the horizon. Below him was the blur of brown desert. There was absolutely nothing he could do except hold exactly the amount of stick pressure against the conflicting forces. His years of flying experience told him he was on the thin line on the graph between high-speed stall and the lesser amount of g's which would increase the amount of altitude he needed for recovery. No chart or performance curve depicting g's versus airspeed and altitude would do him any good at this point. It had to be by feel alone. This used to be called seat-of-the-pants flying in the days when barnstormers flung their bi-winged kites through vaulted clouds. He wished he dared put the electrical master switch on long enough to transmit an emergency radio call to Edwards Test Control—maybe transmit some last cool message that he was putting it down.

The T-33 neared the ground at the bottom of a graceful low speed arc. There was no thrust from the dead engine. His speed came from the kinetic energy of his fall, and he was losing that speed by pulling g's to break the fall. The only question now was what would happen first: a low-speed stall or a smashing impact with the desert floor.

His mind's eye unrolled the film of an F-100 in Vietnam he had seen hit the ground because the pilot had recovered too low from a strafing pass. Like Bannister, the pilot had sat there asking the airplane for as much up-elevator as it could give him. When it had become apparent there wasn't enough, the doomed pilot had pushed the radio transmit button on his throttle and transmitted the words usually said by all pilots who are about to die due to their own error: "Ah, shit." The F-100 and its pilot then rolled into a huge, boiling, red-and-black ball of flames.

The air rushed by the open cockpit, tugging at Bannister's helmet and mask. Less than four hundred feet below was the flat desert and the dry lakes area that most of the year was so firm an airplane could land on it. He rapidly checked his altitude, attitude, and airspeed. With a thrill of excitement, Bannister knew he could pull out of the dive safely and land on the dry lake bed. He resisted the urge to try an airstart, because putting the master switch on long enough to go through the entire airstart procedure would re-ignite the electrical fire.

With that awareness came the realization that he had to use the emergency system to lower his landing gear. A dead engine could not operate the hydraulic pumps that gave him both the pressure to lower the landing gear and the aileron boost he needed to control wing rock. It was like trying to recover a car from a high speed skid without power steering or power brakes because the engine was switched off. As in a car, the backup to a T-33's hydraulically boosted aileron flight controls was a manual system that required a lot of muscle, which didn't allow for much delicacy or finesse. The landing gear was a separate problem. There was no manual way to put the wheels down. Nor were there any manual brakes.

As he pulled the plane up level from the dive, he saw he had 300 feet of altitude and 130 knots of airspeed to play with. He burned up 10 knots and 100 feet finding a rolling tumbleweed to determine from which direction the wind was blowing. Now Bannister had only seconds to get the nose wheel and two main gears down and locked. He reached down with his left hand and slammed the landing gear handle down, which mechanically released the locks holding the three wheels up in the belly of the T-33. The gear doors opened, the three wheels and struts partially extended. To get them fully down and locked in place required electrical power to operate a hydraulic pump.

Now the T-Bird was only 200 feet in the air and the airspeed was fast bleeding off. Bannister was too low to eject. Crunching down with no landing gear, or on wheels and struts partially extended, could tear the jet apart. Flying with his left hand, he quickly reached to the right console and turned on the emergency pump switch, then the master electrical switch. White smoke from the re-ignited electrical fire immediately started boiling up between his legs. He held the switch on just long enough for a few pounds of hydraulic pressure to push the main gear into position. Because of the heavy smoke, he had to flip the master switch off before the cockpit indicator showed the nose gear was down and locked. He had felt the mains thudding into place. The smoke dwindled, and swirled in strips from the smashed canopy.

Now the desert floor was just 20 feet below. He could feel the T-33 near a stall as the airspeed bled below 110 knots. Without electrical power, he could not put the flaps down to help him land at a lower speed. Grasping the control stick with both hands, Bannister wrestled the plane down to merely inches above the ground, then rocked back and forth on the stick in a cadence to bounce the main gear on the hard desert. For once, he was thankful that neither the elevator nor rudder controls needed hydraulic pressure to operate. On the second bounce, the nose gear snapped into place, just as the airplane ran out of flying speed. Brown dust puffed up and away from the tires, as the T-33 slammed hard on the ground with 100 knots forward speed still on the indicator.

No engine, no electrical power, and no hydraulic power meant no brakes to steer and stop with. Bannister was now strapped into 12,000 pounds of runaway airplane moving at 115 miles per hour across a desert floor as flat and firm as a bowling alley. The area was smooth and clear for 20 miles in all directions except dead ahead, where he saw a weathered one-story farmhouse surrounded by trees. Directly in his path, just before the oasislike setting, was a deep irrigation ditch.

Rain on the western Mojave in late fall and winter months turns the dry lake bed into a gummy quagmire totally unsuitable for use as a runway. Whereas the dry desert is a light brown, the wet or drying portion of the floor, or a dried-up water hole, is dark brown, almost black when seen from certain angles.

To his right, at his one o'clock position, Court saw a black patch. A fighter pilot knows there is always one more trick; that one more last-ditch maneuver will present itself if he remains calm and knows how to find it. The black patch was it. He punched the right rudder pedal with all his strength. There was still enough airflow past the rudder control surface on the vertical stabilizer of the T-33 to cause the nose to head to the right.

At just over 70 knots, the T-Bird shot into the shallow depression full of drying desert mud. A huge carpet of brown splashed up from the nose wheel to cover the top of the airplane. Underneath, the mud splashed up in undulating waves and sticky sheets to coat the entire underside and fill the wheel wells with hundreds of pounds of the gummy substance. The sticky and clinging effect was the same as if the speeding jet had engaged the nylon barrier put at the end of runways to stop runaway airplanes.

The T-33 slowed abruptly and stopped. In the sudden silence, Court sat back, drew in a deep breath and slowly let it out. He held his hands in front of his face and noted with satisfaction they were not shaking. He methodically took two four-inch pins with the red tags from the map case and pushed them into the proper holes to secure the ejection seat mechanism. The mud on the windshield prevented him from seeing anything more than a blurred image in front of the airplane. He thought he saw movement. Not wanting to use the electrical switch, he found the handle and manually cranked open the broken clamshell canopy. He looked out, and found his hands starting to tremble.

Twenty feet away at the edge of the mud pool, a woman sat astride a big bay horse. She wore dark britches and boots, a gray flannel shirt and a wide-brimmed man's hat, and had a grin on her face that scrunched up her too big nose and raisin eyes into a happy clown's face. Black curly hair escaped from under her hat. She had large, man-sized hands that held the reins in a light and experienced grip.

"It's none a my business, sonny boy, but if you're looking for the goddamn air base, it's way ta hell over yonder." She pointed toward Edwards. "But if you're looking for Pancho Barnes, you done found her."

Pancho Barnes pressed another Mason jar full of scotch and ice into Court Bannister's hands. He took a sip, then pulled some crushed Lucky Strikes and a Zippo from the pocket on his left sleeve and lit up. The Zippo had a rubber band wound around it. They sat at a weathered wooden table in the shadow of a giant willow next to her mobile home. Pine and palm trees and rows of eucalyptus shut out the desert. Two fat Labs sprawled in the dust at their feet, tongues lolling. Court had telephoned the base and told the relieved Test Control he and the airplane were on the ground in one piece. They said a helicopter would be there in minutes. That was half a pint of scotch ago. Court was tearing into the second half with gusto. He was pleased the trembling had stopped in his hands.

"So I told them sumbitches," Pancho said, continuing her story of her lawsuit against the United States Air Force, "they damn well owed me four hunnert Gs for my land. The land they extended that Edwards runway over. My club had burned down, so what the hell. Mought's well get some cash in hand." She waved her hand expansively at her rundown complex, containing a mobile home and a few sheds with sagging chicken-wire fences.

Court knew the story of this famous woman pilot and of the Happy Bottom Riding Club she had operated for so many years, the club where all the famous Edwards test pilots had hung out. Pancho would be the last to complain, but the years and the breaks had not been good to her. No lady of fortune had stood by her side as she'd first lost her club to fire in 1954, then her land to Air Force expansion. But rugged old Pancho Barnes loved pilots. Anyone who flew an airplane was special, she knew. She just didn't know how special she was herself.

"Hey, Pancho," Court sang out, buzzy on both scotch and the rush not only of having cheated death, but taking the old bastard by the horny scaly tail and flinging him clean into the next galaxy. "Wahoo, Pancho, wahoo." He stood up and yelled at the sun. "Hey, we did it. We did it in 'Nam and we did it here."

"Shut up, Bannister, and siddown." She had read his name from his flight suit name tag. "You're scarin' the goddamn dawgs."

"Pancho-Pancho, I love you." He leaned over and gave her a hug and a boozy smack on her leathery cheek. She was over sixty and her lived-in face showed every minute of her years.

"You goddamn Air Force guys are all alike. Do ya a little favor an ya wanna play grab-ass." Her grin was magnificent.

They heard the whine and hiss of the Hillman Husky helicopter from Edwards coming to pick up their wayward student test pilot.

1830 Hours, Friday, 19 May 1967
Officer's Club
Edwards Air Force Base, California

☆

"Hey, great job, Court. Now all you got to do is go out there and wash all that mud off that T-Bird," a tall captain with a mustache said. Court Bannister and most of his thirteen classmates were standing at the bar, drinks in hand. They were having a brief get-together celebrating the end of the classroom day and Court's recovery from his unusual flight. All wore the green cotton K-2B flight suit, the one with thirteen zippers. Some had scarves representing their previous fighter squadrons around their necks. Normally they wore the school scarf, but occasionally, out of a sense of loyalty to their old squadrons coupled with a sense of independence from the school solution, they took to wearing their old ones. Court always wore the red, white, and blue scarf he had been awarded by the Third Corps Mike Force commander, Tom Myers, in Vietnam. Myers had awarded one to him and one to Lieutenant Toby Parker for the air support they had provided under some very hairy conditions.

"Yeah, and then fly it out of there," a second man said.

"Fly it, hell. That bird's going to have to be towed out of there if they want it back before the mud dries," the tall captain, Ken Dwyer, said. He was a student and the acknowledged leader of his class in both academics and flying. He was the only man in the test pilot school—staff, faculty, or student—to sport a mustache.

They all laughed. Court signaled another round from the bartender. He was feeling good. He had told the story of the wild T-Bird problems and his countermaneuvers to the provisional investigation team upon his arrival back at Edwards. He had been told to write it up and evaluate the flight as an extra assignment; this would further his ability to write a technical report, they told him. He had already, as had the rest of his class during the previous five months, written scores of performance reports. No point in being a hotshot engineering test pilot if you can't tell anybody what went on inside the airplane you were testing.

The men laughed and joked easily. They had well survived the rigors and shock of a heavy academic load and the long hours of seminars, study, and flying. One more drink and they would leave the Club to prepare for a long weekend of hitting the books. So far, they agreed, all that time spent getting up to speed on differential and integral calculus and thermodynamics, then applying those skills to viscous flow, supersonic aerodynamics, and maneuvering flight stability, had been a bitch. And there was no release. All of them knew that, instead of the usual Friday night beer bust that went on with fighter squadrons in the rest of the Air Force, they would all be in the school library tonight, or buried deep in the books in the BOQ or at home.

"You knew Ted Frederick, didn't you, Court?" Dwyer said. Of the thirteen in the class, only Court and Ken Dwyer had seen combat in Vietnam. "Didn't you and he shoot down a MiG? What do you think of his court-martial?"

Court had flown with Ted Frederick several times in the back seat of an F-105F from the USAF base in Tahkli, Thailand. On a particularly hairy mission near Hanoi, they had attacked and shot down three MiGs. Court had been credited with one of them. A few months later, the Russians claimed a USAF fighter had, without provocation, strafed an unarmed Soviet cargo vessel in a North Vietnamese harbor. A Congressional aide, who had refused to give his name, had leaked to the press that the pilot was Ted Frederick. A media storm had evolved, demanding Frederick be court-martialed for making an attack on a peaceful vessel.

"Well," Court said, "the court-martial wasn't really for Ted's straf-ing the ship. The ship fired at him two days in a row, so he shot back. Quite accurately, I might add. Under the Rules of Engagement allow-ing return fire, he was legal. The court-martial was for destroying government property. It was a big mess."

"I don't get it," Dwyer said.

"Few people did," Court replied. "The 'government property' in question was forty bucks' worth of gun camera film. Seems Ted's boss tried to protect his troops by exposing the film that might or might not have shown the strafing. Since they couldn't nail Ted on the strafing, they nailed his boss for destroying the film. Like I said, it was a mess. Everybody involved wound up eating dirt. And now Ted's MIA."

Dwyer shook his head. "As the captain said, 'It's a fucked-up war.' So here you are, hero first class, going through test pilot school. Where do you want to go when you graduate—MOL or Apollo?" Dwyer was referring to the two space programs available to graduates selected for astronaut training. In 1961, the school at Edwards had been des-ignated as the Aerospace Research Pilot School, much to the dismay of the students, who much preferred the earlier and more down-to-earth name of the experimental Flight Test Pilot School. The school had taken on new dimensions when it had become an adjunct to the NASA astronaut training program. At that time the course had been divided into two six-month halves: the experimental test pilot course and the aerospace research pilot course. Those who finished the aer-ospace course could volunteer for the Air Force Manned Orbital Lab-oratory (MOL) or NASA's Apollo moon flight program. Though NASA was harrumphing that they wanted scientists in orbit and fly-ing to the moon, wiser heads convinced them that it was a lot easier to train a pilot to pick up a rock, than train a scientist to land on the moon.

"I'm not sure I want either, right now," Court replied.

"What do you mean?" Dwyer asked.

"Well, maybe as long as the war is on, I should be earning my fighter pilot pay. I'm not sure I'd feel all that comfortable shot up in space knowing my buddies were still being shot at in Vietnam, or POWs in the Hanoi Hilton."

"How tall are you?" Dwyer asked.

"Six-one. Why?"

"I heard they won't put anybody over five-eleven into space, that's why."

Court nodded. They fell respectfully silent as two of the academic instructors, Majors Fred Derby and Flak Apple, walked by the group. Both wore their Class-B khaki uniforms. Derby was medium-sized with dark hair, thin lips, and piercing gray eyes. Algernon Albert Apple, on the other hand, was as big a man as the USAF allows in a fighter cockpit, and quite black.

Major Algernon A. Apple, known as Triple A, Trip, or Flak, but never Al, much less Algernon, was the Chief of the Operations Division for the Test Pilot School. He and Derby had been on the debriefing team when Court had returned earlier that day. Apple had been sympathetic, even laudatory. Derby had not.

"Glad to see you gentlemen are preparing for your weekend study load," Apple said with a wide grin. He stopped to talk. "Me, I prefer a more leisurely approach. While you guys are sweating to improve your testy little minds, I will be up in the mountains in the cool waters of a river I refuse to name, on the prowl for the wily golden trout."

Apple, the top graduate in his class two years before, had won the Honts trophy for academic achievement and flying excellence, and had been chosen as an astronaut candidate. He had achieved this success by natural ability and by spending every hour off the flight line buried in books. At that time he hadn't even known his secret river existed. He claimed he'd burned up two Batori slide rules and an E-6B computer getting through the test pilot school. Apple had lost his astronaut slot, however, when a slug of cold water injected into his ear for a balance test had thrown him sideways. He had had a hard time convincing Congressman Dwight from New York it wasn't a racial slur that had forced him out of the astronaut program. The USAF happily brought him back to Edwards as an instructor in the test pilot school, but though he loved his job, he had quickly volunteered for Vietnam and was soon to go.

Flak Apple was bigger than most fighter pilots, much bigger. Properly measured, he would stretch up to six foot two and a half, which was one and a half inches taller than the USAF height limit for pilots allowed to squeeze into fighter aircraft. But Flak Apple knew how to fake out the measuring devices by using what he called his "saddle slump."

"When I'm in those flight surgeons' offices taking my annual physical, I can't afford to be tall in the saddle," he had told his confidants. "In the airplane, sure; but not under that prong sliding up the back of those medical scales."

Flak always wore the baggiest flight suit he owned to his annual flight physical. When it came time to step up on the scale to be weighed and measured, he would unlock his knees, curve his spine, pull his neck down, and settle his head lower, while tilting it back so the prong wouldn't rest on the crown. The fact that his head wasn't massive and his features were fine aided in the deception, especially since he kept his hair cut short. Occasionally the technician would make some surprised comment about how well he carried his weight of 190 pounds.

The Air Force had a valid reason for limiting the height of its fighter pilots. Not only would a bulky person, six-one or over, have a difficult time in the small cockpit of a fighter, but his knees could hit the bow of the windscreen as the seat shot out of the airplane on ejection. Flak had gone from F-86s to F-100s, where that might have happened. Now he flew airplanes such as the F-4, which had roomier cockpits and an ejection seat that would rocket back at such an angle that Flak's knees would probably clear the forward canopy bow. At least Flak hoped so.

The group slowly broke up. Bannister and Ken Dwyer remained. Derby had stood by while Flak Apple and Court bantered. Now, off to one side, Derby spoke to Court.

"You got off easy today, Bannister. If I had my way, you'd be out of the school for exceeding the student test card and for improper and sloppy control of an airplane. You damn near lost one of our T-33s. You were just lucky to get it back on the ground in one piece."

"Hey, hang on, Fred," Flak Apple said. "He did a pretty good job getting it down."

Derby ignored him. "I know about you, Bannister. I know you threw away a slot for the school last year so you could run off to Vietnam and be a hero. And you probably had some pull to get back in here."

Bannister's face flamed. "Listen, Derby, you may be right about today's test card, but by God I didn't use any pull to get back in here. I don't have any. I re-applied and took my chances like everyone else. I won my second slot just like the first one—fair and square."

Court Bannister walked up to face Derby, who, though three inches shorter, did not flinch. Derby stood five foot ten, but was stocky and powerfully built. He looked a match for Court. They knew one did not yell or fight in an officer's club. They also knew they were on the edge of something that maybe neither could stop. Derby flicked Court's Mike Force scarf. "School scarf not good enough for you? Or do you always wear your Boy Scout scarf?" Court glared, muscles tense, fists clenched. Both men were at flash point.

Flak Apple stepped in between them. "Shut up, you guys. You are among the better people I know, and I'll be damned if I'll stand around here and watch you go at it. You guys got enough tough stuff to do around here without getting all stupid and riled at each other." He placed a big hand on each man's shoulder and squeezed none too gently. "Knock it off or I'll punch the piss out of both you dummies."

Major Fred Derby glared with narrowed eyes at Bannister. "You don't have it, Bannister. You won't make it through the school. You're just a flashy hotshot who thinks he's Hollywood's gift to the Air Force." He spun out of Apple's grip and stalked off.

"What in hell is his problem?" Court asked Flak Apple.

"Take it easy, Court," Apple said. "He's a good guy. Just a little testy once in a while."

"That Hollywood comment was a cheap shot," Court said, and snorted in disgust. This wasn't the first time something like that had happened. When he'd first joined the Air Force he'd had to face the fact that being the son of a well-known movie actor both intimidated and put off his squadron mates. That, coupled with his own natural aloofness, had made his early days difficult and solitary. During his combat tour, however, especially after he had received credit for shooting down a MiG, his reputation as an able and dedicated career fighter pilot had spread in the fighter pilot community. Yet Derby's actions and comments seemed more than just a reaction to his Hollywood background. He looked at Apple. "Something's riding that guy," he said.

Ken Dwyer spoke up. "Maybe it's because you've been to Vietnam and he hasn't. He had a volunteer statement in, but pulled it when he was selected for astronauts."

Apple looked surprised. "How did you know that?"

"I date lovely Rita, one of the civilian admin clerks at Wing Headquarters," Dwyer replied.

"Maybe what you say is true," Apple said. He put his hands on his hips and looked at Bannister and Dwyer. "I guess you guys think you're pretty hot just cause you've flown combat in Vietnam."

Bannister and Dwyer looked at each other. Between them, they'd had hundreds of combat missions. Before they could answer, Flak Apple broke into a broad grin.

"Well, you *are* pretty hot," he said quietly. He reached for his hat. "I'll get my crack at it soon. Finally got my orders to F-4s at Ubon." He waved his hand. "See you all Monday. I'm off for the wily trout. Study hard." Apple walked out of the bar.

Court and Ken Dwyer walked out of the club toward the library. "Say, Court," Dwyer said, "you better double check that 'fair and square' business about your re-appointment."

Court stopped and grabbed Ken Dwyer by the arm. "Just what is that supposed to mean?" Still riled over Derby, his blood was running hot.

"Take it easy. Rita told me she heard the Commandant talking about you to a Pentagon general, a Lieutenant General Austin. Seems Austin didn't want you in the school, but another general named Whisenand did." He saw the look on Bannister's face. "Do you know these guys?"

Court relaxed. "Whitey Whisenand is my dad's cousin," he replied, "but I haven't any idea why Austin was against me coming to the test pilot school."

Dwyer looked concerned. "I think I know. Rita heard something else. Maybe you can find out about it. Austin will be flying out here every month or so to ramrod the NF-104 zoom program."

"You mean she heard something about why Austin seems to have it in for me?" Court asked.

"Yeah. He thinks you killed his son."

2

☆

John Walker studied the two messages again. It was something he had already done several times in the last six months, as though to reassure himself they were real. He was a full colonel and had been commander of a flying training wing for two and a half years. During that time he had earned outstanding ratings in all areas. Because of his fine record, he had been selected above all others to start up the 3510th Flying Training Wing at Randolph. The USAF was expanding its pilot training program to fulfill the increased requirements for more pilots for the Vietnam war.

By working 18- and 20-hour days, and nearly the same on weekends, Walker had brought in the training wing reactivation and expansion on time and on budget. If he continued doing as well with this wing, he would make brigadier for sure when his records were due for review by the promotion board in five months. His flying safety record, student pilot graduation record, maintenance record, wing administrative record, and re-enlistment record were the best in the Air Training Command, and he knew he could maintain them that way. There was just one problem. That problem had presented itself in the form of one not-so-bright-eyed or bushy-tailed first lieutenant named Toby Parker, who had about as many hero medals as Audie Murphy. Colonel John Walker reread the messages. The first was addressed to both his boss and himself. It was directive in nature.

280832Z DEC 66
FROM: DEP CHIEF OF STAFF USAF
TO: COMMANDER, AIR TRAINING COMMAND, RAN-

DOLPH AFB, TEXAS
COMMANDER, 3510TH AIR TRAINING WING, RANDOLPH AFB, TEXAS
INFO: DCS PERSONNEL, MPC, RANDOLPH AFB, TEXAS
S E C R E T AFPTRF 88390 NOV 66
SUBJECT: (U) INCREASED PILOT PRODUCTION

1. (S) SECDEF ON 25 NOV 66 AUTHORIZED USAF TO INCREASE UNDERGRADUATE PILOT TRAINING (UPT) BY THREE THREE PERCENT. EFFECTIVE IMMEDIATELY, YOU ARE AUTHORIZED TO TAKE ALL IMMEDIATE PRACTICAL ACTIONS TO INCREASE UPT FROM 2307 PER YEAR TO 3000.

2. (S) FY-67 (SUPPLEMENT) AND FY-68 BUDGETS ARE BEING ADJUSTED TO REFLECT NECESSARY RESOURCES FOR THIS INCREASE.

3. (U) WHILE THE MOTIVATIONAL BENEFITS OF CEREMONIAL FUNCTIONS ARE APPRECIATED, THEIR ACCOMPLISHMENT TO THE CUSTOMARY AND DESIRED DEGREE UNDER THIS INCREASE OF FLYING TRAINING MAY RESULT IN THE LOSS OF FLYING TIME. THEREFORE YOU ARE AUTHORIZED A PERIOD OF AUSTERITY IN WHICH YOU WILL JUDICIOUSLY CURTAIL CERTAIN CEREMONIAL ACTIVITIES USUALLY HELD IN CONJUNCTION WITH GRADUATIONS. WHILE A MINIMUM PROGRAM OF FORMAL PRESENTATION OF WINGS AND DIPLOMAS PLUS A SOCIAL FUNCTION SUCH AS A RECEPTION OR DINING-IN IS EXPECTED BY THIS HQ, OTHER TRADITIONAL ACTIVITIES SUCH AS A PARADE OR FLYBY ARE NOT.

4. (U) 1/LT TOBY G. PARKER, USAF, SSN FV41296248 IS ASSIGNED TO RANDOLPH AFB FROM CURRENT SOUTHEAST ASIAN (VIETNAM) ASSIGNMENT REPORTING NOT LATER THAN 2 JAN 67.

5. (S) PARKER IS TO COMMENCE UPT COURSE NUMBER 111103 IMMEDIATELY. DUE TO THE EXIGENCIES OF THE SERVICE HE IS TO COMPLETE THE COURSE AND GRADUATE AS A RATED PILOT (USAF SPECIALTY CODE 1115Z) NO LATER THAN 29 SEPT 67. AT THAT TIME HE IS TO REPORT TO GEORGE AIR FORCE BASE, CALIFORNIA, FOR UPGRADE INTO THE FRONT SEAT OF THE F-4 AIRCRAFT FOR SUBSEQUENT REASSIGNMENT TO A SUITABLE FIGHTER WING IN VIETNAM AS AIRCRAFT COMMANDER.

6. (S) CSAF RECOGNIZES THAT PARKER IS TO RECEIVE ONLY 39 WEEKS OF UPT INSTEAD OF THE NORMAL

52 WEEKS. YOU ARE AUTHORIZED THE FOLLOWING
ACTIONS: A) HIS TRAINING WEEK WILL BE SIX DAYS,
B) ALLOW HIM TO PROGRESS FROM ONE ACADEMIC
AND FLYING PHASE TO THE NEXT ON A "QUALIFIED
PROFICIENT" BASIS AS HE DEMONSTRATES HIS ABIL-
ITIES, C) FLYING TRAINING TIME MAY BE CUT AS
FOLLOWS: T-41 AIRCRAFT FROM 30 TO 10; T-37 AIR-
CRAFT FROM 90 TO 80; T-38 AIRCRAFT WILL REMAIN
AT 120, D) 168 HOURS OF GROUND TRAINING TIME
MAY BE CUT BY ELIMINATING ALL THE OFFICER
TRAINING SUBJECTS WITH THE EXCEPTION OF
COUNTERINSURGENCY.
7. (S) SINCE NO T-41 AIRCRAFT ARE ASSIGNED TO
RANDOLPH, PARKER IS TO RECEIVE HIS T-41 PHASE
UNDER CONTRACT WITH HALLMARK AVIATION AT
STINSON FIELD, SAN ANTONIO, TEXAS.
8. (U) FOR EXTREME HEROISM AND VALOR IN SUS-
TAINED COMBAT WHILE PARTICIPATING IN AERIAL
FLIGHT, PARKER HAS BEEN AWARDED THE AIR
FORCE CROSS, THE DISTINGUISHED FLYING CROSS,
THE ARMY BRONZE STAR WITH V FOR VALOR, AN AIR
MEDAL, THE VIETNAMESE CROSS OF GALLANTRY
WITH STAR, AND THE PURPLE HEART. IT IS MY DE-
SIRE THAT COMMANDER ATC PERSONALLY PRESENT
THESE AWARDS AT AN APPROPRIATE CEREMONY
(PARAGRAPH THREE THIS MESSAGE WAIVED ON A
ONE TIME BASIS FOR THE OCCASION). MAXIMUM LO-
CAL PARTICIPATION BY SAN ANTONIO OFFICIALS AND
NEWS MEDIA IS ENCOURAGED.
9. (U) HE IS IN THE PRIMARY ZONE FOR CAPTAIN.
HIS PROMOTION ORDERS WILL FOLLOW.
10. (S) CSAF REALIZES THERE IS A CERTAIN CALCU-
LATED RISK INVOLVING THE ACCELERATION OF
PARKER THROUGH UPT. HOWEVER, HE HAS DEMON-
STRATED PHENOMENAL INNATE FLYING SKILLS
AND SUPERIOR JUDGMENT IN A COMBAT SITUATION.
ASSIGN HIM YOUR BEST INSTRUCTOR PILOT, MONI-
TOR AND REPORT HIS PROGRESS TO THIS OFFICE.
BACK CHANNEL EYES ONLY TO CMDR ATC. MESSAGE
REFERENCE 280830Z DEC 66 FOLLOWS. GP 4.
NNNNNNNNNNNZ

The second back-channel message had been given to Walker by
Commander, ATC, for his personal records. It was to the commander
from the USAF Chief of Staff.

280830Z DEC 66
EYES ONLY
FROM: CHIEF OF STAFF USAF
TO: COMMANDER, AIR TRAINING COMMAND
SUBJ: 1/LT TOBY G. PARKER, SSN FV21296248 REF
MSG 280832Z DEC 66 DEP CSAF
JOHN: GO WITH THIS ONE. THE ADMINISTRATION IS
TAKING SOME HITS AND SO ARE WE FROM THE PRESS
RE AIRCRAFT LOSSES IN SOUTHEAST ASIA. THE PRO-
TEST AND DRAFT DODGE MOVEMENT SEEMS TO BE
HEATING UP. WE JUST MAY NOT GET ENOUGH AP-
PLICANTS TO MEET OUR INCREASED PILOT TRAIN-
ING QUOTA. WE NEED ALL THE FAVORABLE
PUBLICITY WE CAN GET. PUT PARKER IN FRONT. PUT
HIS DECORATIONS ON HIM NOW AND HIS WINGS IN
9 MONTHS. HE IS A BRIGHT AND IMPRESSIVE YOUNG
MAN WHO DID A WHALE OF A JOB IN VIETNAM. READ
THE CITATIONS ON HIS AWARDS. THE PUBLIC INFOR-
MATION PEOPLE WANTED TO PUT HIM ON A RE-
CRUITING POSTER BUT I NIXED THAT. ONCE HE IS
UPGRADED IN THE F-4 I WANT HIM SENT TO VIET-
NAM TO WHATEVER BASE HAS THE MIG MISSION,
PROBABLY THE 8TH TFW AT UBON, THAILAND, AND
WATCH HIM MAKE ACE. MEG AND I SEND OUR BEST
TO YOU AND DOROTHY.
NNNNNNNNNNNNNNZ

Colonel Walker had checked the records. It turned out that Parker had single-handedly saved a Special Forces unit under heavy fire while flying a small plane, an 0-1 Birddog, from the back seat after his pilot had been killed. Parker's duties at the time had been as a courier. He was not, and had never been, a rated pilot. Only his natural ability to fly coupled with some training given him by his pilot, Phil Travers, had pulled him through.

So John Walker had done all that was required for Parker. He had pinned captain's bars on him, and had been present when Toby had received his medals from Commander, ATC, at a full parade, for which the whole base had been turned out. (The press had thought him "handsome, winsome, all-American." They could not, however, bring themselves to use the famous World War II phrase "authentic war hero." To use the word "war" would give the lie to the term they had already coined, "conflict." There was no way the press would give an honorable title to a war they were declaring to be immoral.)

Walker had personally tailored Parker's flying curriculum per CSAF instructions. He had selected his best young instructor, Chester

Griggs, and forwarded appropriate messages as he monitored Parker's progress. Beyond doubt, Parker was eating up the course as no student had ever done before. Also beyond doubt, Parker had an attitude problem that rivaled that of Frank Luke, the World War I ace who had received the Medal of Honor posthumously. Like Luke, Parker simply didn't respond well to authority or regulations. Both displayed a tendency to run off and do things by themselves. While, overall, this is a normal fighter pilot tendency, training and sense of overall mission responsibility shape and form this vice into a controllable virtue. Walker sighed and looked out the window at the training airplanes landing and taking off from the runways. He knew Parker was flying at this very minute. He hoped he was behaving himself.

1045 Hours Local, Thursday, 8 June 1967
In a T-38 Training Aircraft Letting Down in
the 14L RAFB II Penetration
Randolph AFB, Texas

☆

Due to sheer boredom, Captain Toby G. Parker was about to perform an unauthorized acrobatic maneuver. At the moment, Parker didn't know he would do this. He merely scanned the gauges on the instrument panel in front of him. He flew, quite relaxed, in the back seat of a twin-engined Northrop T-38 jet trainer. His instructor pilot, First Lieutenant Chester Griggs, sat, not quite as relaxed, in the front seat. They had been shooting touch and go landings over at the Sequin auxiliary base. Parker's had been perfect.

"OK, read 'em off," Griggs said over the intercom system to Parker. Both men wore full helmets with oxygen masks and sun visors. The microphones were built into the oxygen mask, the earphones were in the helmet. A switch on one of the throttles activated the radio. The cockpit was spacious. Though a wide plexiglass canopy provided good visibility, Parker could not see out. He had a white canvas hood fixed inside his cockpit in such a manner that all he could see were the gauges on the instrument panel. This was the way student pilots practiced to fly in bad weather. Parker sighed, and began the litany for the instrument letdown he was making using the TACAN navigational beacon at Randolph.

"The engine's RPMs are at 82 percent, speed brakes out, ten degrees nose low, we are tracking outbound from the Randolph TACAN holding three two zero degrees, at an airspeed of 280 knots, descending at five thousand feet per minute out of twenty thousand feet. We are passing through sixteen thousand now. At eight thousand, I will turn inbound to the TACAN and commence a low approach to runway One Four Left at Randolph." His readings were precise because his gauges were right on the money and had been the entire flight. Such excellence was normal for Parker.

"Very well," Griggs said. He marveled at Parker's innate stick and rudder ability. The man was an absolute virtuoso with an airplane.

Parker stared at the gauges. There were three long minutes remaining before he had to begin the penetration turn back to the runway. Without hesitation he smoothly fed in left bank and, against Griggs's startled protests, made a perfectly coordinated descending barrel roll.

A barrel roll is a beautiful but complex maneuver. To be performed correctly, the pilot must constantly change his altitude, airspeed, and aircraft attitude as he makes a graceful roll around a point. He must reach the inverted position with wings parallel to the horizon, then, without pause, continue rolling to the upright position on his initial heading and attitude. Anything but a yank-and-bank maneuver, it is an operation of grace and style which can demonstrate exactly how coordinated and skillful a pilot truly is. Few student pilots in UPT master it before their 50th hour in the airplane, and then only after practicing the maneuver over 100 times with full outside visibility. To perform one on the gauges during an instrument letdown was unheard of, not to mention quite contrary to ATC regulations.

Regarding the breaking of regulations, Parker's barrel roll was on a par with flying under a bridge; regarding skill, it was on a par with flying under the bridge inverted. To perform either maneuver would be to invite instant washout due to lack of discipline and lack of flying safety considerations; but mostly certainly for lack of judgment when performed with an IP on board. That's the ultimate stupidity. Captain Toby Parker was guilty of all of the above. The obvious course for Chet Griggs would be to recommend Parker for elimination.

"EEEEHAH," Parker yelled into his mask at the end of his roll. Griggs acted as if nothing had happened.

Parker made a perfect penetration turn and started inbound to the TACAN beacon. Swapping hands on the stick, he unzipped his left sleeve pocket, pulled out a package of Luckies and a Zippo with a rubber band around it. He never took his eyes off the instruments as he shook one from the pack, unhooked his mask and lit up. He inhaled deeply.

"Enjoy your cigarette," Griggs said. "It's your last one flying an airplane in the United States Air Force."

1530 Hours Local, Thursday, 8 June 1967
Office of the Commander
3510th Flying Training Wing
Randolph AFB, Texas

☆

Colonel John Walker stared at the pink ATC Form 861, Student Dis-
crepancy, the paper that formally records transgressions by hapless
students. Three pinks and a student is up for a progress check by a
more senior instructor. It is the first step toward elimination if the
student does not shape up. The pink slip Colonel Walker held went
well beyond just the first step. It was accompanied by a formal statement by First Lieutenant Chester Griggs, Instructor Pilot, 3510th
Flying Training Wing, ATC, that Captain Toby G. Parker had ex-
ceeded the bounds of disciplinary propriety and judgment by such a
wide margin that said transgression called for immediate dismissal
from UPT on grounds of gross lack of judgment.

Colonel Walker had received a call from the squadron as soon as
Griggs's operations officer had received the fateful write-up. After a
moment's hesitation, Colonel Walker had said for Griggs to report to
him ASAP. Griggs now stood at a position of attention in front of
the colonel's desk, his eyes fixed on a point in space six inches over
the colonel's head.

"At ease, Chet. Sit down," Colonel John Walker said. "Cigarette?"
He offered one from a box on his desk.

"No, thank you, sir," Griggs said.

"Don't smoke, eh? Good boy." The colonel put the box down. He
didn't smoke either, but used the offer of a cigarette as a ploy to see
who would dare light up in his presence. "I've been meaning to talk
to you for some time. You've been doing a good job. I know teaching
Parker how to fly is a tough job. That's why I picked you."

He re-examined the pink slip. "What exactly do you mean, 'un-
precedented lack of judgment'? Isn't it more a case of a spirited young
man feeling his oats and knowing he is outstanding in his field? Didn't
you ever do a roll or two at altitude just because you were feeling
good? Don't you think perhaps you are overblowing this just a bit?"

"No, sir, I don't. And, yes, I've done a roll or two in my day, but
always when legally planned under controlled and safe circumstances
in clear air, and then only after making clearing turns." Griggs set his
jaw.

Walker sat back in his chair. He looked thoughtful. "Well, then,
how did Parker come to the conclusion he could do a barrel roll
during an instrument letdown and get away with it? You must have
given him some cause to think that."

"Well, maybe I did, sir." Griggs paused. "Maybe we both did. You remember the pink I gave him for the landing problem he was having in the '38?"

Griggs had pinked Toby Parker once before for having difficulty landing the T-38. It had been a minor thing involving rollout on final approach that had soon been cured. Griggs had really given the pink slip more to get Parker's concern and concentration rather than to call attention to a real deficiency. His ploy had failed in two ways: it hadn't gotten Parker's attention, and it had brought a request to Griggs to drop by his wing commander's office at his earliest convenience. "What do you mean, he has trouble landing?" the colonel had said. "We've got nearly one hundred students here and less than five percent have trouble rolling out on final. Here you've got a proven pilot and you tell me he can't fly. Are you sure it's not you? Perhaps you have some sort of a personality conflict with Parker?" There had been times after that session when Griggs would have pinked Parker but did not. And he had always felt guilty about not doing so. He had consciously not tried to square these omissions with the honor code he had learned as a cadet at the Air Force Academy.

Then there was his responsibility as an instructor pilot. It made no difference that Toby Parker was a captain and Griggs a lieutenant. An effective IP has knowledge his student does not. His job is to pass it on correctly, safely, and quickly. Outside of a "sir" at the proper time, rank hath no privileges. First lieutenants or captains upgrading full colonels to a new aircraft or leading them on area checkout flights is an accepted and common practice. No quarter given, no quarter asked. The upgrading pilot, regardless of his rank, must learn what the IP has to teach him. He must pass the proper written and flight exams before being signed off as competent to fly that particular airplane on those particular missions. The IP who is intimidated by the rank or notoriety of his student, and consequently does not perform his job of transferring information from his head to that of the student, is not an effective IP.

"Sir," Griggs began, "every time Parker goes up solo, he's wearing my wings. Every minute he logs by himself in training is logged with my wings riding on his judgment and maturity. I don't think he has the basic judgment to be a pilot, and I am no longer going to jeopardize my career on some whim of his. How can I place my career on a line drawn by a man, a boy really, who doesn't care one bit for his own career?"

Walker ignored Griggs's question. He sat forward. "Do you realize how many phone calls I get about Parker from Commander, ATC, or how I'm required to send regular progress reports to the Deputy Chief of Staff of the Air Force?"

Griggs didn't answer. He sat expressionless, his eyes fixed on his commander.

"You're from the Academy and a plow-back now, aren't you?" Colonel Walker said, more as a statement than a question.

"Yes, sir," Griggs answered. He was an Air Force Academy graduate who had come out of pilot training at the top of his class. He had always wanted fighters and a chance at combat in Vietnam. Instead, being so stellar, he had been put back into the training system as a plow-back, a first-assignment-instructor-pilot, called by the acronymic term FAIP.

"Randolph is the showplace of the Air Force," Walker continued. "You well know that excelling here guarantees your choice of aircraft and assignments. Let's see," he examined an open file on his desk. "You want F-4s at Ubon Air Base in Thailand, don't you? Want to get over there with Robin Olds and his 8th Tac Fighter Wing, eh? Where all the fighter pilots go to become MiG killers." Walker was referring to a folder on his desk containing Griggs's USAF Form 90, called a Dream Sheet, because it contained what an individual desired for his next and subsequent assignments. Griggs knew he probably wouldn't get fighters without a favorable recommendation from his wing commander, Colonel John Walker.

"And you want Phantoms with the 8th at Ubon, right?" Walker said again, this time looking up for an answer.

"Yes, sir," Griggs had said.

Colonel Walker fixed Lieutenant Griggs with a fatherly smile.

"You help me with Parker, and I'll guarantee you Phantoms at Ubon." He handed Griggs his pink slip and report on Parker.

"Colonel, I'll accept this only on one condition."

John Walker looked startled. Lieutenants don't make "conditions" with colonels. "All right, Lieutenant, suppose you tell me the one condition."

2030 HOURS LOCAL, THURSDAY, 8 JUNE 1967
BACHELOR OFFICER'S QUARTERS
RANDOLPH AFB, TEXAS

☆

Toby Parker sat in the easy chair with his feet up on a hassock. He had bought both, and several other items of furniture, including a small refrigerator, to spruce up his 16-by-17-foot BOQ room on the second floor of the students' BOQ. He was wearing a rumpled USAF flight suit that had reddish brown stains on the chest and legs. It was unzipped down his chest, revealing a piece of jade hanging from a gold chain. On his feet were scuffed jungle boots stained with the red mud of Vietnam. He was drinking by himself. When he'd first arrived at the base, he had hung around the Auger Inn, the stag bar at the O-Club. He'd given that up when he'd found he was too snarly and uncommunicative with the younger pilots, who wanted war stories from their famous classmate.

Now he preferred the privacy and solitude of his room in the BOQ. There was a highly expensive hunt scene by Herring on a wall and a few prints, but no decorations or memorabilia from Vietnam. He never pulled out photos or tape recordings of his time in Vietnam for what few visitors he had. His only outward reference to Vietnam was the flight suit and boots he wore on certain solitary occasions, and the jade earring hanging from the gold chain.

Cigarette smoke curled up from a stand-up ashtray next to his chair. He took manly swigs from a double scotch as he listened to a tape of Piaf's "Non, Je ne Regrette Rien" ("No, I Regret Nothing"). The tape wheels spun slowly on the Akai deck he had bought in the big PX at Tan Son Nhut Air Base next to Saigon. He leaned back and closed his eyes as the rich nasal tones of Edith Piaf swept over him with vibrations and pulses that seemed to resonate in his groin.

Once again he was back in Saigon holding Tui in his arms. She was a tall and straight-shouldered Eurasian with long brownish-black hair that hung straight past her shoulders and curled in wings by each side of her face. Her teeth glistened white and perfect in a half smile, her eyes closed as she burrowed her head into Toby Parker's shoulder while they danced. She wore an *ao dai*, the traditional Vietnamese dress of white blouse and black flowing silk trousers and long white wraparound apron with long slits up each side of her legs.

"I love you, Tow-bee," she said, as she shook a wing of hair to one side and leaned back to look up at him with eyes brown and soft and deep with adoration. "I love you so much." She took a jade earring from her ear and gave it to Toby as a symbol for love eternal. Piaf's rich and melancholic song swept over Toby Parker as he danced once again with his beautiful girl, her body firm and curved in his arms, her perfume filling his head, sweeping his mind, tingling his very being with love and desire like he had never known. The image began to blur.

Like a movie screen gone wild, discordant and tragic images swept just behind his eyes. Phil Travers once again died bloody and bent in his arms; Haskell's eyes drilled into his as he embraced an exploding grenade; and Tui danced into death as the bullets tore her body apart.

"Aaahhhh, aahhhh," Parker moaned. He sat slumped for a long moment, immersed. Slowly he sat upright. Then, with a quick gesture, he gulped the rest of his scotch, and hurried over to snap off the tape deck. "Got to stop that," he muttered, knowing full well he would not. He was addicted, and to more than the scotch. He was addicted to the memories and he knew it. He didn't feel complete without them.

He had been a floater for all his college and early Air Force years, just a frat boy floater looking for another party, another meaningless adventure. He had volunteered for Vietnam as a lark for his third and last year in the Air Force, and there had been an administrative officer who'd wound up flying in the back seat of the little 0-1 puddle-jumper with Phil Travers as pilot. They had flown around South Vietnam delivering classified documents to remote Special Forces camps. Many times they had controlled air strikes in support of U.S. ground forces, and, as Travers had felt Parker's keen interest and natural ability to fly, the two of them had become close.

Now, Toby Parker couldn't shake Vietnam and he didn't want to. There had been no meaning to his life before his tour and precious little since. Now he just wanted to be with the people he loved most; lovely Tui, who induced a depth of feeling he never knew he possessed. And solid Phil Travers, the forward air controller pilot who'd showed him the glory and thrills and fun and mystique of combat flying. And the Special Forces men with such easy professionalism about living and dying. The exhilaration of being shot at, and doing something about it. The camaraderie. Rich emotions. He missed it. He missed it all.

But the people who had brought him to life, who had put meaning and depth and purpose into his life, were dead. Blown away, gone forever. Travers had died in his arms, his blood staining the flight suit he had just given Parker a few hours before, as a tribute to Parker's eagerness and ability to fly. He had seen his lovely Tui cut down by American guns, his name on her lips as she died. Now they existed only in his mind and memories and he intended to keep them alive there forever. Until the glorious day he joined them.

There was one man still alive from those days, Wolf Lochert, a Special Forces lieutenant colonel. In Vietnam, Lochert had taken an interest in the young Air Force lieutenant. Toby would get drunk and call him up. But Lochert wasn't accessible anymore. He had left Fort Bragg and was back in 'Nam. His last words to Parker had been to tell him to get the hell off the sauce and the memories, and get to work learning how to fly airplanes. And to come back to Vietnam where the big boys were.

There were a few others: Court Bannister—but he was up to his ears at the test pilot school—and Tiffy Berg, a Braniff stewardess he had met in Vietnam. They had had several days together in the Philippines, where he had flown up from Vietnam. He had called her a few times and drunkenly rambled on. She was a direct link to Vietnam. Once she had flown out on a pass to see him. It hadn't gone well. She wouldn't drink with him and talk about the war. And he wouldn't—said he *couldn't*—go to bed with her; said he just didn't function well anymore.

But it was all over now, Parker thought. He had let them all down. He was being tossed out. He would never fly, never go back to Vietnam as a pilot. He was through. Griggs had told him he was out.

The phone on his desk began to ring. Parker finally picked it up on the eighth ring. It was Chet Griggs.

"Parker, we've got to talk," he said.

"What about?" Parker said to Griggs ten minutes later, as Griggs, dressed in a white polo shirt and light blue cotton trousers, stood in his room. "What could we possibly talk about? You said I was through flying. You said you were washing me out. What the hell do you want now?" Parker took a swig of his scotch. He felt agitated and mean. "You got a new lecture about discipline I haven't heard? You want to maybe preach about responsibilities? You're a real puke, you know that, Griggs? You don't drink, you don't smoke. You probably don't even come. I'll bet all you do is pee through your pecker. Isn't that right? You only know how to pee through your pecker?" He pushed his drink toward Griggs. "Here, take this. Let's see you drink some down. Maybe then I'll talk to you."

Griggs waved it away, an expression of exasperation on his face. "Come on, Toby," he said. "Ease off. You can do better than this. Be a gentleman."

"Ease off? Be a gentleman? Oh, I get it. You're one of those, those Latter Day morbids from Salt Lake. Aren't you from Salt Lake? Oh yeah, and you're a zoomie from the Academy, aren't you?"

"Yeah, Toby, I'm all of that. But I'm also your friend. Or I want to be. Look," he said, "I understand. I know you had it rough over there. I know you lost—"

"What the hell do you know what I lost? What do you know about it, you weren't even there. Go log some combat time, then we'll talk. Go get some blood on you and we'll talk all you want." Parker turned away to splash more scotch into his glass.

Griggs walked over and took Parker by the arm. "Toby, hey man, I just want to be your friend."

"I don't need you," Parker said. With a sudden motion he tossed the scotch into Griggs's face.

Griggs grabbed Parker's outstretched arm and, rotating, bent it behind his back to double him over. He stood wide and braced as Parker tried to kick back his shins. Parker groaned and swore as he tried to wrench free. Griggs held Parker's bent arm tightly and reached forward to the back of his collar, pulled him upright and marched him toward the bathroom shower.

"Hey, ouch, goddamn, stop it. What the hell do you think you're doing?" Parker struggled unsuccessfully in Griggs's expert hold as Griggs stuffed him into the shower stall and turned the cold water full on. Both men got soaked as Griggs held Parker sputtering and choking under the thrumming of the needle spray. They grunted from the force of their struggle, but Griggs had the edge both in size and sobriety. He held Parker firmly under the stinging water. Some of the old blood dissolved from Parker's flight suit and swirled down the drain along with red mud from his combat boots. Parker saw it and began to shout in a voice made hoarse by scotch and a tightening throat.

"No," he yelled, "oh no. Oh God, Phil." His voice cracked. He struggled and slammed about, but couldn't break Griggs's hold. He relaxed and slowly slumped down to sit on the floor as Griggs turned him loose. Water beat on his bowed head and ran in rivulets down his face, off his chin, and down his bare chest to swirl past the jade. Griggs stepped out of the stall, water streaming down his polo shirt, cotton pants stained dark. His blond hair was plastered to his head. He looked down at Parker. Toby had cupped his hand over the drain and was letting the reddish water flow through his fingers into the drain. After a few moments, Griggs turned the water off. Parker continued sitting there, watching the last of the water go down the drain.

"Okay," he said, his voice hollow and echoing. "Let's talk. I'll listen."

Ten minutes later, toweled off and dry, the two men sat across from each other, Griggs in the chair, Parker on the hassock.

"I said I would wash you out," Griggs said. "But it seems that's not what Colonel Walker or the Commander of the Training Command, or even the Chief of Staff, desire."

"You mean you aren't going to wash me out?"

"I suppose I could if I made a federal case out of it, went to the Inspector General and all that," Griggs said. "I could eventually get you out of the program. But that's not what I'm going to do."

"But I signed the pink. I admitted what I had done." Parker looked surly.

"You're getting a second chance. Your *last* chance," Griggs said. "I had a long talk with Colonel Walker, or rather he had a long talk with me. I've withdrawn my report. You're still in the program."

Parker looked up. He studied Griggs for a moment. "Do you mean that?" He reached for his scotch, thought better of it and put it down. He looked contrite. "Hell, I don't know what to say. Thanks, I guess. And after all that stuff I said about you . . ." he trailed off.

"Don't thank me, Parker. I don't want to hear it. I still think you should be out of the program. Any other student would be. I've washed them out for far less than what you did." Griggs sighed. "You've got some serious problems, Toby. I don't know which came first, your drinking or your lack of discipline. But you are a first-class problem drinker, maybe an alcoholic, I don't know. I do know I like you, Toby, but, drinking aside, I honestly don't think you have the discipline to be a pilot in my Air Force." He shook his head. "It's obvious, I can't be your IP anymore. Starting immediately you will have a new instructor pilot."

Parker absorbed the information. "Well, thanks anyway. You've given me some good news." He paused, then added hastily, "But it's bad news you won't be my IP anymore."

"You haven't heard the really bad news, Toby."

"What is it?"

"You lost your fighter assignment. You are not going to F-4s when you graduate. I am, but you're not. I'll level with you. I kept you out of fighters on pain of my resignation if Colonel Walker didn't approve. It went all the way up to the Chief of Staff. I'm telling you, you don't have enough discipline to be trusted with something hot like the Phantom. Not in my book. Instead, you're going to Hurlburt Field in Florida to learn how to be a forward air controller so you can fly all over Vietnam entirely by yourself and run your own war."

3

☆

The olive-drab Army HU-1B slick (no guns) whop-whopped its way across the jumbled hills covered with triple-canopy jungle. The sky looked gray and desolate through the early morning mist that rose in wisps and torn banners. The helicopter cruised at an altitude of 4,500 at a true airspeed of 100 knots. The pilot preferred this higher altitude to avoid ground fire and to take advantage of the upper air that had cooled two degrees for each thousand feet above the ground. Both side doors were open. The chilled air swirled around the compartment, cold-soaking men and machine in preparation for the heat of the earth below.

As is normal in helicopters, the pilot sat in the right seat and the co-pilot in the left. They wore jungle fatigues and olive-drab flyer's helmets with earphones and boom mikes. Three other men in jungle fatigues sat on the pull-down red canvas seats behind them in the center of the cargo compartment. Strapped to the floor of the compartment were resupply cases of ammunition and radio batteries, C rations, and clothes for the Special Forces Forward Operating Base (SF FOB) at Lang Tri. The helicopter crew chief sat in the right rear canvas seat facing forward. Like the pilot and co-pilot, he wore a helmet with a boom mike pressed to his lips. Next to him sat two passengers. They wore green berets with the distinctive flash of the 5th SFG.

The younger of the two passengers, a thin sergeant first class, was from the Special Forces C Team that serviced the men at the Lang Tri FOB. He was responsible for their aerial resupply. He carried a two-foot dark-orange nylon mailbag with a padlock through the metal bands at the mouth. Inside were classified documents and mail for the twelve Americans at Lang Tri.

The older passenger had a rucksack and an aluminum carrying case at his feet. The case was dented and heavily scratched. In his lap he held a small book with gold-tipped pages and a tooled black leather binding. The book was open, but he was not reading. Instead, he was staring at the jagged horizon line. His eyes were dark, his skin tone brown, and his cheekbones were high with a hint of Indio blood. His jungle fatigues, thin and faded from too many in-country washings, were neat and pressed. On the right collar of his blouse was the black stitching and thin white border depicting the silver oak leaves of a lieutenant colonel. On his other collar, stitched in black thread, was a chaplain's cross. Sewn above the right slanted pocket of his blouse was his name tag, Sollivan. Stitched in black thread over the other pocket was the wreathed rifle of a combat infantryman's badge.

The SFC leaned over to shout against the wind and blade noise. "Hey, Padre. Kind of a small place to be going for your Sunday rounds."

Chaplain Sollivan turned his head and looked at the young SFC. "One of many," he said, with a faint Puerto Rican accent. He stretched his mouth into a smile that exposed white and even teeth. The SFC nodded and looked back outside the speeding helicopter.

The tone of the whirling blades increased as the pilot pushed forward on the collector. The blades slapped air as he entered a steep descent to the east of the Lang Tri landing zone. The pilot, a 20-year old warrant officer, kept his helo back-lit by the morning sun as long as possible. At the last minute he scooted the slick over to the LZ and, nose high, touched down with a finesse born of hundreds of combat takeoffs and landings.

On the ground, between the landing helicopter and the camp, a half-circle of pot-bellied brown children stood giggling and pointing with pudgy fingers. Some wore a narrow dark cord around their waist, others nothing. Their nakedness was as natural as the surrounding jungle. They held their hands up to shield their eyes as a wave of red laterite dust thrown up by the whirling blades engulfed them. The blades made "sweet sweet sweet" sounds. Three Special Forces men from the camp carrying bags and boxes ran crouched to the helicopter. They helped the crew chief and the two passengers offload the supplies, then loaded their own boxes on board. The pilot had not shut down the turbine engine, and the hissing exhaust, combined with the whoosh of the big blades, reduced communications to hand signals. The SFC swapped bags with one of the men and reboarded the helicopter. Two of the men from the camp went behind the children and picked up a stretcher that carried something inert and oddly positioned in a green rubber body bag. The bag protruded at such odd angles it looked as if a thick tree limb with branches sawn off at varying lengths was inside. The men hustled to the helicopter and gently placed the bag into the cargo compartment. Engine noise covered the hollow thumps the protrusions made when they thumped on the deck.

Chaplain Sollivan quickly made a sign of the cross in the general direction of the rubber bag, threw his ruck over his shoulder, picked up the aluminum case and walked hunched over under the blades toward the edge of the dust circle. The helicopter turbine hissed louder and the skids were five feet in the air by the time he reached the edge of the cluster of children. In seconds, the noise was an echo and the dust was settling.

The children swarmed around the visitor. They had seen many rough-looking men come and go. Almost always they carried something for them. The chaplain did not disappoint them. He dug into the flapped pockets of his blouse for bits of rock candy. He also gave each child a folded blue bandanna from a supply he had bought from the PX. The children danced with delight, then silently ran up to a large sideless dirt-floor hut. Inside, their parents, a Nung fighting force, rested on hammocks and woven mats. City kids would have been screaming with delight. Not so these little ones, who had been taught the rigors of jungle life since before they could walk. They disappeared in with the families to show them what they had been given by the American.

Back at the LZ, the larger of the camp men, a captain, walked over and shook hands with Sollivan.

"Good to see you, Padre. Welcome to Lang Tri." He was in his late twenties and wore his green beret tilted forward upon his closely cut blond hair. His name was Janosik, and he was built like a tall and rangy college fullback. He had heard of Sollivan, that before becoming a priest he had been a 17-year-old dogface in the Korean War.

"Carry that for you, Padre?" He nodded at the case.

"Thanks, I'm okay," Chaplain Sollivan said. They walked toward a low rectangular wooden building with screen doors at each end. Next to it was a bunker covered with earth and logs.

The captain held open the screen door. Inside, several bare-chested men wearing only the camouflaged pants of their striped olive-drab-and-black tiger suits were sitting around rough wooden tables. Behind them in a corner sat a slender Vietnamese with watchful eyes. He wore a complete tiger suit, and appeared to be about forty. The Americans stood up.

"Hey, Chaplain Sollivan," one of the younger men said, recognizing him. "How ya been? It's me, Burton. I heard you were running around the AO [Area of Operations] giving church services. Hear confession, say Mass, save souls. Stuff like that." He remembered

Sollivan from the 1st Special Forces Group at Okinawa, where he had been known for his ability to jump out of airplanes and put away beer with the best of them.

"Right. But I've given up trying to save your immortal soul, Burton. It's far too late for that." He slung his ruck into the corner and set the case next to it.

"Yeah," Burton laughed, "ever since I went SF." Soldiers in the Special Forces refer to themselves as just that, Special Forces, or the abbreviated form, SF. Regardless of the publicity since "The Ballad," they never said green beret in any other way than as a reference to a type of hat. They might refer to a helicopter pilot as a rotor head, or a nonparatrooper as a "leg," from the term "straight leg," but no one could refer to them as Green Berets, for the beret was a hat, and only a hat.

Captain Janosik, the team leader, spoke. "There's a place out in back where you can hear confessions and say Mass, Padre. A couple of the guys here and a few of the Viets set it up. Nothing fancy." His troops called Janosik the *Di Uy,* the Vietnamese term for captain.

"Nothing fancy required," Sollivan answered. He had many times said Mass in the jungle in pouring rain with no more protection than a poncho and a floppy-brimmed jungle hat. Based now at 5th Special Forces Group (SFG) at Nha Trang, he tried to make the rounds at least once a month of the scores of SF camps scattered throughout Vietnam. He particularly liked Lang Tri. The base was unusual, because it was one of the three FOBs from whence clandestine missions originated that, among other things, searched for downed American pilots. Chaplain Jaimie Sollivan's younger brother, Luis, was a Puerto Rican Air National Guard pilot on active duty with the USAF flying F-4s. Jaimie truly appreciated any ground support available for pilots in trouble. You never knew.

Outside the team house, Sollivan followed Janosik to a ten-by-ten structure that was nothing more than a thatched roof set on four thick posts over a dirt floor. Enough wooden benches for 20 people were in front of a narrow five-foot-high altar carefully fabricated from halved sections of bamboo.

"Not bad, not bad at all," Sollivan said in admiration. He placed the aluminum case on a bench close to the altar and began to unpack. From the case (Kit, Chaplain's, Catholic, NSN 9925-5206), he placed on the bamboo stand the chalice and its paten, the communion paten, and a crucifix. To one side he placed the tube holding the communion wafers. He hoped and prayed that God had a special place for soldiers of any religion, of any country, of any age, who trusted so much in their leaders and their cause. He wanted to do the best he could for these young men, because they were among those dying and killing and he was doing neither.

In a matter of minutes there were eight Nungs and four Americans gathered for Mass. Sollivan was just about to ask if anyone wished to serve Mass as an altar boy when he saw a figure approaching from behind the benches. It was a squatty man with sparse black hair shaved close to his skull, and almost Neanderthal bushy black eyebrows overhanging dark brown eyes. He was bare-chested, with burly arms and a pelt of black hair, and wore a pair of cut-off tiger suit pants. He was carrying a folding-butt Avtomat-Kalashnikova-47 assault rifle, and around his right leg, just above his knee, was a bloody wraparound bandage. He favored the leg as he walked up to the chaplain.

"Jaimie, you spic soul-saver," he said in a gravely voice, "welcome to Lang Tri." The two men pumped hands and embraced.

The heavier man, Wolfgang Xavier Lochert, was an SF lieutenant colonel assigned to the Military Advisory Command Vietnam Studies and Observation Group, better known as MACSOG.

The innocuous Studies and Observation Group name was a cover for MACSOG's classified mission. The group was a joint service unconventional warfare task force engaged in clandestine operations throughout Southeast Asia. MACSOG had the assistance of certain USAF (the 90th Special Operations Wing) and Navy SEAL units. The MACSOG troopers, of which Lieutenant Colonel Wolfgang ("The Wolf") Lochert was well-known, conducted highly classified sabotage, psychological and other special operations in North and South Vietnam, Laos, Cambodia, and Red China.

MACSOG men were tasked with many other special operations, as well. They had been known to kidnap, assassinate, plant booby-trapped ammo in big enemy supply caches, steal enemy documents, and other such venturesome and risky behind-the-lines business.

Wolf Lochert had returned a few hours earlier from a snatch mission in which he had bagged an NVA division commander just as the man was making his weekly visit to his girlfriend's hootch. The division commander had been a man of habit, and punctual, which had made the snatch rather easy. Wolf had had only one other man with him on his mission, Buey Dan, the watchful Vietnamese who had been in the team house when Sollivan arrived.

"Hey, Jaimie, welcome back." Wolf slapped the chaplain on the shoulder.

"How are you doing, Wolf? You've come a long way since Maryknoll," Chaplain Sollivan said, holding Lochert by the elbow.

"Too far, maybe," the Wolf said, his grizzled face serious. He had been in the same seminary class as Jaimie Sollivan, late of the New York Puerto Rican barrios, after a stint in the U.S. Army. At the time, each had known he had the calling to be a Roman Catholic missionary priest. But, after 18 months, Wolfgang Xavier had realized he simply was not the type to stand by and passively watch events take place around him. He was a participant, and that was all there was to it. If another seminarian made a mistake in class or on the sports field, Wolfgang was right there to correct him. And it had been like that in high school. More than once he had been dismissed from the practice field for telling his coach exactly what he, Wolfgang, thought the coach was doing wrong. It usually involved some hard-hitting tactical strategy and Wolfgang was usually correct. And woe to the man who uttered profane words around Wolfgang. "You don't take the Lord's name in vain in my presence," he would say, while backing the hapless curser up to a wall.

During a tour of duty at Bad Tölz in Germany, he did pick up the term *scheiskopf,* shithead, which he dearly loved to use on those who merited it, particularly those who swore. "Don't swear, *scheiskopf,* or I'll bust you one," he would say when necessary. Even among the collection of what the regular army called the snake-eating maniacs, the Wolf was considered unique, not so much because of his anti-swearing campaign, but because he rarely drank. And when he did, his rampages were of herculean proportion.

So young Wolfgang had dropped out of the Maryknoll seminary in upstate New York, convinced he was a failure in the eyes of Almighty God. He had dropped out because he could not submit. The devastating truth, as Wolfgang Xavier Lochert saw it, was that since he was old enough to comprehend the world about him, he could not be submissive to anything that happened to him or around him. At each Mass and in his evening prayers, he sought and prayed fervently for humble submissiveness.

"O Holy Spirit," he'd prayed thousands of times, "soul of my soul, I adore Thee. Enlighten me, guide me, strengthen me, console me. Tell me what I ought to do and command me to do it. I promise to be submissive to everything Thou permittest to happen to me, only show me what is Thy will." Only when he could submit to the forces around him, Wolfgang knew, would he be worthy to wear the cloth of a Maryknoller. So far nothing had worked. He still questioned, argued, and ultimately resisted anything about him that he didn't agree with or approve of, whether the matter was physical or moral.

After dropping out of the seminary, Wolfgang Lochert had joined the United States Army. He had been 19 years old at the time. Since then he and Sollivan had seen each other every few years, more often now that Sollivan had been assigned in-country to the 5th SFG at Nha Trang.

"Got a message for you, Wolf," Chaplain Sollivan said. "It's from Al Charles. He wants you to drop by MACSOG ASAP."

Lochert raised his eyebrows. "Did you come all the way out here to tell me that? Why didn't Al just tell me on the daily commo check? Or send me a note in the mail sack?"

"Dunno. I'm just telling you what he told me to tell you," the Chaplain said. The Wolf nodded. Sollivan regarded him kindly and pointed to the altar.

"You'll serve, won't you?" he said, more as a command than a question.

"Yeah, sure," Wolf said. He went into the team house and came out with his shirt on and a fresh bandage on his leg. He leaned his AK against a pillar. The Chaplain handed him a paten, and turned to the group that had assembled on the wooden benches. "I need one more to serve Mass." There was a slight stirring. Before anyone could volunteer, the slender Buey Dan stepped up and said in a quiet voice that he would be honored to serve Mass that day.

"It has been a long time," he said, "perhaps too long since I served as an altar boy in the Catholic church in Hanoi. You will permit me?"

Both Wolf and the Padre stared at the Vietnamese. The Wolf was the first to speak.

"Beedee, you never cease to surprise me. You're a *chu hoi*, an ex-VC, one of the greatest jungle trackers and night fighters I've ever seen, a former tennis club manager at the Cercle Sportif in Saigon, and now I find out you can serve Mass." Wolf Lochert looked at Buey Dan with undisguised respect and admiration. Seven months earlier, Buey Dan, or Beedee, as the Wolf liked to call him, had saved the Wolf's life in a surprise encounter with an NVA patrol.

Chaplain Jaimie Sollivan handed the Vietnamese a card with the Latin Mass responses. As he did, his eyes narrowed and became mere slits from which reflected obsidian blackness. He didn't speak. He turned and began the Mass. Wolfgang Lochert and Buey Dan began the familiar responses in Latin. Lochert loved the words the priest spoke:

"*Introibo ad altare Dei. Ad Deum qui laetificat juventutem meam.*" I will go unto the altar of God, to God who brings joy to my youth.

When it was time, Chaplain Sollivan's sermon was short and to the point. As usual.

"It's very easy to become fatalistic when one's role in life, for a while, is to kill or be killed. What a terrible role, but now is not the time to whimper over it. We will do what we have to do. But we must reflect once in a while how close we are to enormous evil. The killing of people is no good, yet we find ourselves in the damnable position that we must do it as the lesser of two evils. Pity is, if we stop to ponder in time of crisis upon what we are doing, then we are dead ourselves. Yet God expects us to have hope. Hope . . . hope is the virtue by which we trust in God. Trusting that God will ultimately do the best for us. In the meantime, we must try to do our best. And God bless you for trying."

Chaplain Sollivan had to force himself to look away from the men in front of him. He wanted to memorize their faces. He wanted to look into their eyes, and draw part of their souls to him so they would always be a part of him. He loved them so, these young warriors, and he wanted to give them life everlasting, even if only in his memories.

After communion, during which Buey Dan solemnly took the host on his tongue from a stone-faced Chaplain Sollivan, the Mass drew to an end. As Sollivan was performing the final rituals, his thoughts turned to his brother. He had offered the Mass for Luis, and for the dead soldier in the body bag, and for all the men in the lean-to. At the final blessing, *"Benedicat vos Omnipotens Deus,"* he made a larger than usual Sign of the Cross over his jungle congregation, hoping this symbol of power over evil would extend out through the jungle and protect his brother. *"Pater et Filius et Spiritus Sanctus."* He stopped for a moment and looked at his charges. "Go," he said in Latin, "the Mass is ended . . . *Ite, Missa est."* A shiver ran the length of his spine. He didn't know why. It happened sometimes.

Burton never knew what hit him. He slumped with a cry, fresh blood staining the back of his shirt. Then came the echoing pop of the sniper's rifle.

"Hit the dirt," someone yelled. He didn't have to.

Instantly, every man, including Chaplain Sollivan, dropped to the ground, eyes searching the area from where they thought the round was fired. A Nung crawled over and tended to the groaning Burton.

"Anybody get a line on it?" a voice shouted from the team house.

"Yeah," Lochert growled back, his face barely five inches above the ground, "I got a line on him. I saw some smoke." He crawled forward to get his AK and bring it to bear on the spot in the tree line from where he was sure the round had been fired. It was a finger of jungle, barely five feet wide and ten feet long, pointing at the camp. Wolf estimated the distance at nearly 200 yards, about two football field lengths away. He again saw smoke rise next to a particular tree in the finger as two more slugs thudded into the dirt followed by two pops from the same place.

"That's a mighty heavy caliber he's firing," the Wolf said. A series of rounds zinged back toward the sniper from several fighting positions around the camp perimeter on that side. Wolf put in the proper elevation and squeezed off three rounds which he knew were of no value at such a distance. The captain sprang out of the team house door and dove into the dirt next to Wolf.

"Something funny about this," the Wolf said. "Why hose off in the middle of the day?"

"What in hell do you think is going on?" Janosik asked. "We never draw fire into the camp during daylight."

For a moment Wolf thought it might be a daylight ambush. Maybe the purpose of the sniper was to draw troops down from the camp to investigate. If there were an ambush, they could be trapped and chewed up. He looked closer at the sniper's site.

"I don't think it's an ambush. That finger of jungle he's in is too easy to cut off and too narrow to hold any significant amount of enemy troops." He looked at Buey Dan. "Come on, Beedee, let's go get that dummy," the Wolf said. He started to get up, then turned to Janosik. "Ah, if that's okay with you, Captain," he said, acknowledging the protocol of the team leader, who ran the camp. Wolf was a transient at the FOB and hence should follow the orders of the man, regardless of rank, who was responsible for the security of the Lang Tri camp. He was pleased he had remembered to ask, even if it was rather pro forma, because, as the Wolf knew, he rarely asked anybody's permission to react to a combat situation. Invariably, he reacted first and sorted out details later.

"Be my guest," the captain said.

"Where's your path through your mines?" the Wolf asked.

"Go to the left of the brown post and head toward that tall broken palm tree to the right." The captain gave the visual clues to provide safe passage through the minefield he had planted around the perimeter. There had to be a path for patrols that was easy to remember, though one not obvious to the enemy. "Be careful, it's only two feet wide," he added.

"Got that, Beedee?" the Wolf asked. When Buey Dan nodded, Wolf sprang to his feet and dashed zigging and zagging in a low crouch from cover to cover to the wire. In an instant he was through, bare knees scrabbling in the red dust, then out along the safe path. Buey Dan, who had his own AK, followed in the same manner. When they were deep into the jungle, Buey Dan trailed Wolf by whatever distance it took to keep him in sight. Sometimes three feet, sometimes ten, depending on jungle density.

Buey Dan permitted his lips to tighten once when the muzzle of his AK swung within range of Wolf's back. The Vietnamese saw again the scene in front of the shattered church, when this hairy long-nose had killed his son after his son had set the blast. Though his son's death had been for the glory of the revolution, Buey Dan had sworn he would take his blood revenge—but only after he had extracted all the usefulness possible from his military comradeship with the long-nose. Until then, he would serve the Front, who knew him only by his code name, the Lizard.

Back at the camp, the team captain ordered everyone to hold their fire while the two men worked their way toward the sniper. Wolf crouched and walked silent and slow. He had to favor his sore leg.

When he knew he was close, he signaled with his hand for Buey Dan to move right, putting him deeper into the jungle, while he stayed left to parallel the tree line. Both men were bent low, barely moving, carefully lifting and placing their feet, slowly cocking their heads from side to side listening for telltale sounds of enemy activity. Each sensed the position of the other beyond the green wall.

Suddenly from close in front of them, they heard a shot muffled by jungle growth. Both men froze in a crouch. Wolf pointed his finger at Buey Dan, then made a "stay" sign, spreading the fingers of his hand and making a push down motion. The Vietnamese nodded and slowly crouched lower.

Down-and-dirty time, the Wolf thought. The sniper knows we're here because everybody from the camp is holding their fire. He got down on his elbows and knees and moved slowly and precisely in the direction of the sound. He no longer favored his wounded leg. He was particularly alert for wires, bent twigs or grass, or any other sign of a booby trap. He was vibrant and alert for odd or out of place objects. Ahead of him, he spotted a small bit of color not consistent with the green jungle surroundings. He crawled closer until he was behind the base of a giant palm tree. He peered around the base and saw the back of a lone man, a Vietnamese he was sure, in torn and raggedy black pajamas laying prone behind a fallen tree. Well-concealed by underbrush, he was aiming an ancient rifle at the camp. Wolf looked cautiously around, determined the VC was by himself, and called in Vietnamese from his position behind the tree.

"*Hands up, hands up.*"

For an instant, the figure froze, then slowly turned to bring his rifle to bear on the Wolf. His face was contorted, his eyes wild.

"*Drop that gun. Don't move. Don't move,*" the Wolf cried in Vietnamese.

As if controlled by wires, the man continued swinging his rifle in jerky motions toward Wolf.

The Wolf aimed his rifle directly into the face of the man, who was barely ten feet away. He yelled again.

"*Don't move.*" When the man did not stop his inexorable movement, the Wolf shot him twice between the eyes. The man fell back with an odd clanking sound.

"Okay, Beedee, come on up, but slowly. Something funny here."

With Buey Dan covering him, Wolf Lochert advanced to inspect the corpse. Checking for booby traps, he held the AK with one hand like a pistol, pointing at the head of the man, while he carefully turned him over with his foot. Bile rose in his throat.

"This is terrible, Beedee. Come here and take a look at this." Wolf pointed down at the body as Buey Dan came next to him.

The dead Vietnamese was an emaciated boy of about twelve years of age covered with ants and angry red bites. He was chained to a log, and his ancient rifle was strapped into his arms. Under his body was an anthill.

1430 Hours Local, Tuesday, 4 July 1967
MACSOG Headquarters, rue Pasteur, Saigon
Republic of Vietnam

☆

MACSOG operations was run from an unpretentious four-story villa situated on the tree-lined rue Pasteur in central Saigon. Two pedicabs churned down the street and stopped in front. Wolf stepped from one, toting his ancient mountain rucksack and his folding butt AK. Chaplain Jaimie Sollivan climbed out from the other carrying his black satchel. They were both dressed in jungle fatigues, sleeves rolled up, and wore their green berets. They returned the salute from the villa guards, tiger-suited Nungs who wore thongs and carried AK-47s, and who opened the wide steel gate for them. They walked through and past the giant tamarind tree on the right.

"How come you were staring so narrowed-eyed at my buddy, Buey Dan?" the Wolf asked.

"There's something behind his eyes I don't like," the chaplain responded.

"Yeah? Like what?"

"Death."

Wolf stopped and turned to the chaplain. "That's in all our eyes," he said. Jaimie Sollivan shrugged, and they walked on.

After a few paces, the two men entered the door of the villa that housed the headquarters team of the Studies and Observation Group assigned to MACV (Military Advisory Command, Vietnam). As a secret directive so dryly spelled out, MACSOG's six primary duties included:

☆ Conducting regular cross-border operations to disrupt enemy intentions;

☆ Keeping track of all captured and missing Americans and conducting raids to find or free them;

☆ Training and sending agents into North Vietnam to run resistance movements;

☆ Conducting black psychological operations, such as establishing false radio stations inside North Vietnam;

☆ Conducting gray operations, such as the Hue-Phu Bai radio
transmitter;

☆ Conducting other operations as deemed necessary to disrupt
enemy plans.

"Ah, it was terrible, Al," Wolf Lochert said to Lieutenant Colonel
Al Charles, his boss, the MACSOG commander. Lochert and Sollivan sat in cheap vinyl lounge chairs in front of Charles's battered
wooden desk. Charles wore the standard jungle fatigues.

"The kid had been chained to a log placed over an anthill. He
couldn't get away. The ants were all over him. The gun was strapped
lengthwise to him in such a way he couldn't shoot himself. All he
could do was shoot at us and hope we'd kill him. His face was all
twisted. He had gone crazy."

"Did the camp commander know anything about him?" Al Charles
rumbled. He was a burly black man with a huge chest.

"As a matter of fact, he did. The kid was a local who used to shine
shoes for the GIs and run errands for money. He was a nice kid, they
said. He had told one of the guys he was being pressured by the local
VC cadre to spy on the camp. The commander figured he was staked
out to make an example to the others about what happens to nice
kids who won't rat on the Americans."

"Hell of a war," Al Charles said.

"But it's not a war, Al," Chaplain Jaimie Sollivan said. "As our
congressmen and senators say, 'It's a conflict.'"

"Nuts," the Wolf said. "If somebody's shooting at me, it's a war.
And if it isn't, I'll declare one." He slung his good leg over the rusty
metal arm of the lounge chair and motioned toward a calendar.
"Happy Fourth of July," he said in a voice thick with disgust. "Let's
start another War of Independence. This time let's separate from
Washington."

"Right on, brother," Al Charles said.

"Here, here," Chaplain Sollivan said.

The Wolf leaned back. "Okay, Al," he said. "What's up? Why send
Jaimie all the way to Lang Tri to deliver the message to come see
you, when you could have sent it on the commo net? Or sent a
written message up with him?" Wolf's face suddenly brightened. He
sat forward. "Is the MACSOG rescue committee on? Do we finally
have the green light for some full force POW rescue attempts?"

Late last year, Wolf Lochert had been sent first to Fort Bragg, then
to the basement in the Pentagon, to help conceive some large-scale
rescue attempts of American soldiers and pilots held in prison camps.
When the JCS rescue committee had gone forward with the plans,
they had been told that small forages into South Vietnam were authorized. They had also been told, by the civilians who staffed such

answers for the Secretary of Defense, that rescue attempts in North Vietnam were absolutely out of the question. Such efforts would be seen worldwide as further American aggression. Further, the efforts would be interpreted by North Vietnam as an overabundance of interest in Americans held prisoner, therefore increasing their value. Lastly, it might just start World War III with Russia, or Red China . . . or both. The rebuttal white paper that had demolished the rescue ideas had implied that the JCS was not only impertinent in requesting such foolishness, but that their judgment was in question. Didn't they know there was a war on? When the dismal response had been received, a boom had echoed up Pentagon Stairwell 71 from the spook area in the basement, causing passersby to wonder if an explosive device hadn't just detonated. It had. Wolf Lochert had just punched a metal locker.

"No, Wolf," Al Charles said, "I am sorry to say that is not why you are here." He sat forward, his black face uncommonly solemn. "You are here because what I have to say, I don't want anyone else to hear. And better you hear it from me first." His words resonated from his deep chest cavity.

Concerned at the tone of his voice, Lochert leaned forward.

"What is it, then?" he asked.

Al Charles cleared his throat. "Wolf, I think you are going to have to go to jail."

"What the hell for?"

Al Charles stood up and put his hand on Wolf's shoulder. He looked down at his friend and best warrior. "Well, now, we're going to have to talk about that."

1030 HOURS LOCAL, TUESDAY, 5 JULY 1967
THE BUTTERFLY BAR
TU DO STREET, SAIGON
REPUBLIC OF VIETNAM

☆

The fight started suddenly and violently, like a thunderclap on a clear day. The Butterfly Bar, a long narrow place with a bar to the right and tables to the left, was a known SF hangout, and woe betide the "leg" who accidentally entered for whiskey or women. Occasionally, cocky paratroopers from an airborne unit would enter looking for trouble. They'd find it. Usually in quantities they could not handle, because by the time they were drunk enough to have the courage to challenge the SF men on their home turf, they were too drunk to swing more than a feeble fist.

The Wolf had been standing at the bar, drinking a fizzy French orange soda, minding his own business. He wore khaki civilian pants with cuffs and an atrocious Hawaiian shirt. He needed a shave. The mama-san and two bar-girls sat patiently behind the bar. The Wolf had made it clear he wasn't springing for any Saigon Tea, the amber water the GIs bought at outrageous prices for the B-girls so they could talk and play kissy-face. It was early in the day. The bar was cool and dark. The only other occupants were two SF men on pass from a remote up-country camp. Several large bottles with the red number 33 stood on the small table in front of them. All GIs swore that Bamuiba, which meant 33 in Vietnamese, contained formalde-hyde. The Wolf had shaken off their greetings and inquiries about what he was doing in the bar so early. Wolf had muttered and snarled something about the United States Army being ungrateful and stupid about the way it was treating him. This wasn't like the Wolf, they said to themselves.

Three tall and well-built paratroopers wearing jungle fatigues en-tered. They were staggering slightly and joke-talking loudly among themselves. They blinked in the darkness, then selected places at the bar close to Wolf. The mama-san immediately filled their order for Bamuiba and dispatched the girls to sit with them to cadge Saigon Tea.

For twenty minutes, the men fondled the girls and drank beer. Twice they asked the mama-san to turn up the volume for the coun-try music on her tape recorder. Several times they looked contemp-tuously at Wolf. Finally, the bigger of the three made a remark about green beanies drinking orange piss. The Wolf's head came up and turned slowly like a tank turret to face them. There was a lurching jostle, and the fight erupted.

The mama-san quickly dialed MP headquarters. The bar-girls fled screaming to the safety of the back room to peer through the beaded curtain at the fight. The two seated SF men sprang up and joined in with whoops of glee.

In the beginning, it was really an unfair engagement. The Wolf, equal to two or three troopers on any given day, today seemed pos-sessed of a powerful rage that turned him into a maniac. The six men were soon in a tangle. There were groans and thuds and curses. Much of the cheap furniture was smashed. The melee boiled out into the street. Vendors and passersby screamed and crowded around to watch. Unexpectedly, the burliest of the three troopers got the Wolf down and started kicking him. A second pulled a switchblade from his pocket and snapped it open with a flick of his wrist. He crouched and held it low, knuckles down, thumb up along the handle, sharp edge up. He moved the tip in small circles and lunged at Wolf.

Before either of the two SF men could tackle the man, the Wolf rolled away and reached under his right pant leg for his social weapon, a Mauser 7.63mm, and shot the knife-holder in the chest. The man dropped the knife and flung his arms up. He went down without a sound. A red blotch appeared and spread on his chest.

Sirens were sounding in the distance. The trooper's buddies ran away. The two SF men lingered just long enough to ensure the Wolf was okay, then took off. He sat up and looked at the dead man. He slowly bowed his head and carefully unloaded his Mauser. "Aww," he said out loud, "aww, why'd you have to go and do that?"

Two police jeeps screeched to a halt and six helmeted MPs wielding nightsticks dismounted and sized up the situation. Two tended to the wounded man, four swarmed over Wolf and snatched his gun. He roared and fought, but Saigon MPs were picked for size and aggressiveness, not civil rights affirmation. The raging man went down. The MPs bonked his skull a few times, handcuffed him, and dumped his battered body into the back of a jeep. The two MPs next to the bloodied man on the sidewalk looked up.

"Radio for an ambulance," the senior said, "but tell 'em to take it slow. This guy's dead."

The two SF men had circled back to watch the Wolf being taken away. "Hey, man," one said to the senior MP. "It was self-defense. We saw it all." The MP paid no attention. He pointed at Lochert. "Take him to the station and book him for murder."

The jeep with Lochert and the MPs sped off for the Saigon station of the 92nd Military Police Battalion. The two SF men watched.

"You know something?" one said to the other, as the MP jeeps disappeared in the heavy traffic. "That trooper, he wasn't too smart."

4

☆

In 1954, Lockheed built the F-104, the fastest jet fighter in the world. It was the first Mach 2 fighter, and the first to break the sound barrier in a climb. To help it slice through the air, the leading edges of the stubby wings were as sharp as a dinner knife. Although it was faster than an artillery shell or a .45-caliber bullet, nobody really knew its top speed, because it would start to melt after it passed Mach 2.3. Naturally, the hierarchy at the Test Pilot School at Edwards Air Force Base thought that, with a few design changes, it would be a grand vehicle for high altitude and high angle-of-attack training for future space vehicle pilots. So they acquired a couple and attached a 6,000-pound thrust rocket to the rear end of one of them to make it go even higher, farther, faster. They called this modified Lockheed F-104 the NF-104.

The most famous—and most dangerous—of NF-104 flights at the Test Pilot School was the zoom maneuver. The object of the flight was to provide training to test pilots and future astronauts in the operation of aerospace vehicles at altitudes above 20 miles. One of the three birds configured with the rocket engine and hydrogen thrusters had already crashed in 1963. The thrusters were to provide the pilot with attitude control since the NF-104 zoomed so far out of the atmosphere the air wasn't dense enough for normal flight controls to act upon. The zoom flights were to introduce students to rocket-powered flight; extended zero-G conditions, as they arced in a parabola over the top of the zoom maneuver; high-altitude, low-dynamic-pressure flight; and, finally, experience using the hydrogen thrusters mounted on the wing tips, nose, and tail to control the attitude of the craft. An NF-104 sat poised and ready for flight in the purple dawn.

Court Bannister was scheduled for his third ride in a T-38. In this phase of the program, the student learned properly how to fly and position a chase plane following an important test aircraft through its maneuvers. Chase Three, as today's flight was called, consisted of advanced aerial maneuvers while pursuing an airplane that might well outperform the chase plane in speed, altitude gained, and maneuverability. Major Flak Apple was Court's IP, the Instructor Pilot in the back seat of the slim, dartlike T-38 supersonic trainer built by Northrop. Both wore flight suits. They were in a small briefing room, one of four in the building by the flight line that housed the school. The walls were covered with local area flight maps, chalk boards, and aircraft cockpit pictures and data. The two men were sipping coffee. Flak had asked Court please not to smoke in such confined quarters. "I don't want anyone but myself ruining my lungs," he'd said, tapping his massive chest.

"Okay," Flak continued. "First we rendezvous with an F-105 doing weapons delivery on the range. He'll be doing loft and over-the-shoulder maneuvers. In loft, he pulls smartly up from level flight to about forty-five degrees, where a computer will release a bomb. Over-the-shoulder means he'll come smoking in on the deck and pull up into a four- or five-G Immelmann, a half-loop over the target. He releases the bomb going straight up, then rolls out down the backside of the loop facing the direction he came from and going like hell to get away from the burst." He sipped his coffee. "We'll follow the Thud through a couple of those, then get into some diving, high-G spirals to loosen up. From there, we will do some out-of-plane maneuvering—that's a fancy test pilot term for the old high and low speed yo-yo maneuver you use to cut across a turn to catch up and join up with another bird. Finally, as the PDR . . ."

"PDR?" Court interrupted.

"Yeah, PDR, *pièce de résistance*. As a PDR, we'll join up with the zoom chase and watch him intercept the NF-104 when it comes down into the atmosphere and restarts its engine.

"You see," Flak continued, "the way the NF-104 climbs to twenty miles, 100,000 feet, is to nip along at top speed of about Mach 2.2 at 35,000 feet. That J-79 engine is delivering nearly 16,000 thousand pounds of thrust to the 20,000-pound NF. Then the pilot flips the switch igniting the rocket, which kicks in an extra 6,000 pounds of thrust. He then pulls the nose up to a 70-degree climb. As he zips through 60,000 feet, his jet engine flames out from lack of oxygen in the thin air, so he stop-cocks the throttle. As the engine unwinds, he loses hydraulic pressure to move the flight controls. That doesn't make much difference, since there isn't enough air where he's going to make any difference, anyhow. When his flight controls lose effectiveness, he uses a hand-controller on the instrument panel to spurt hydrogen peroxide out of nose, tail, and wing tip thruster nozzles to control his attitude. Without thrusters, any disturbance would toss him ass-over-teakettle, and there wouldn't be anything he could do about it. He'll top out of his upward arc at about a hundred grand, then tip the nose down for reentry. He has to get his nose down and wings level, so when he gets down to about 40,000 feet where the air is thick enough to flow properly into the intakes, the airflow will windmill the engine enough so he can perform an airstart. That's where the chase pilot meets him. The chase pilot has to know where and when the NF will appear. Radar can give him a steer to the rendezvous point." Flak stopped and peered closely at Court. "You okay? You look a little tired."

"Yeah, I was up most of the night with a sick paper," he said.

"Which one?" Flak asked.

" 'Frequency Response Method of Determining Aircraft Longitudinal Short-Period Stability and Control System Characteristics in Flight,' " Court answered.

"POC. I did mine on a Sunday morning," Flak said.

"POC?" Court said.

"Piece of cake. Have another coffee and let's get to work."

After they finished the briefing, the two men walked in the early morning coolness along the ramp to their T-38. They were wearing parachutes on their backs and carrying cloth bags decorated with patches from prior squadrons. In the bags were their helmets, gloves, and kneeboards with flight cards clipped to them.

"Who's flying the NF today?" Court asked.

"Your old buddy, Fred Derby," Flak said.

0720 Hours Local, Thursday, 6 July 1967
Airborne in a T-38 over the Rogers Dry Lake
Edwards Air Force Base
California

☆

An hour later, the two men were airborne over the Rogers Dry Lake area talking to Edwards Test Control and Zoom Chase. Zoom Chase was an F-104B with a flight test photographer in the back seat. His job was to record as many phases of the NF-104 flight as he could point his camera at. There was always the possibility of something going wrong, and a film record would prove invaluable. Court and Flak, call sign School Test Two One, had already spent 35 minutes flying with the F-105 weapons test bird. Now they were in a long arcing left cutoff turn to keep the F-104B chase bird in sight. They were to fly 200 feet to the rear and to one side to keep out of the way, yet still go through all the planning and gyrations necessary to meet the returning NF-104. Both planes were at 42,000 feet, where abrupt maneuvers could produce stalls.

"Zoom Chase, Edwards Test," the ground station radioed.

"Eddie, Zoom Chase, go ahead," the pilot of the F-104B answered.

"Zoom Test is at your one o'clock high coming through eighty thousand," Ground said.

"Eighty thou, rodge," Zoom Chase said, then added, "Uh oh, I, ah, got a little problem here. My oil pressure is falling off."

"Zoom Chase, Edwards, are you declaring an emergency?"

"Negative, but I guess I'll have to abort and bring this beast back before it locks up on me."

"Roger, copy, Zoom Chase. Break, break; School Test Two One, you copy Zoom Chase?"

"Edwards, School Test Two One copies," Court transmitted.

"School Test Two One, do you have Zoom Chase in sight?" Edwards Ground asked.

"Affirmative, you want me to escort him back to base?"

"Negative, Two One, I want you to meet Zoom Test. What's your fuel state?"

"Hey, hey, hey," Flak Apple said on the intercom from the back seat. "Think you can handle it, Court? I can't see much from back here."

"No sweat," Court said on the IC (Intercomm). He punched the radio button on his throttle. "Eddie Ground, School Test Two One, no problem, glad to oblige. I've got forty-five minutes of fuel until bingo at this altitude. Will maintain this orbit." Court had just told the controllers he had forty-five minutes of flight time remaining if he stayed at the same high altitude at a constant throttle setting. Jet engines burn less fuel the higher they go.

Zoom Chase transmitted. "Eddie Ground, Zoom Chase, I'm breaking it off now and heading back. Oil pressure low but stabilized. Switching over to Approach Control."

"If you guys are done bullshitting," a new voice broke in, "I got some real problems up here," Fred Derby, the Zoom Test pilot, radioed.

"Zoom Test, Edwards Ground. What is the nature of your difficulty?"

"The nature of my difficulty is I can't get the frapping nose down. Stand by to copy data."

Like all good test pilots, while looking for a solution to his problem, Fred Derby wanted to make sure the ground station was recording everything he was saying, in case he didn't make it.

Edwards Ground said the recorders were on.

Derby gave his angle of attack at the top of the parabola, the indicated air-speed, engine RPM, tail pipe temp, peroxide tank pressure, and peroxide remaining. He spoke on in a flat, unemotional voice, detailing the information vital to a crash investigation even before there might be a crash. The last F-104 that had crashed had buried its engine and airframe thirty feet into the desert floor, making reconstruction of the burnt, dime-sized pieces of gauges and flight recorders impossible. All they had found of the pilot in the exhumed wreckage was a thumbnail.

"We got a good copy, Zoom Test," Edwards Ground said. "Break, break, School Test Two One, Zoom Test is at your twelve o'clock high for two miles, descending rapidly through six zero thousand. You got a tally?" Edwards Ground had all the airplanes on its height and directional radar. A "tally" was short for "tally ho," meaning, "I have him or it in sight."

Court strained forward. He saw the silver speck glistening in the sky nearly three miles above him.

"School Chase Two One has a tally on Zoom Test," he transmitted.

"You have negative overtake speed, Two One," Edwards said. That meant the NF-104 was not only ahead of Court's T-38, but going faster and pulling away from him. "Go Buster for 100," Edwards ordered.

"Roger, Buster for one hundred," Court replied and pushed the twin throttles of the two J-85 engines to engage their afterburners. "Go Buster" meant increase speed as fast as possible; the 100 stood for 100 knots. He was to increase his speed by 100 knots on his airspeed indicator, enabling him to overtake the returning NF-104. Unfortunately, pouring raw fuel into the flaming exhaust, as the afterburner ignited to increase thrust, also increased fuel flow by over 30 percent.

Slowly, Court's T-38 drew up to the flight path of the descending NF-104. It was difficult to see the needle-nosed fighter whose wing span was only 21 feet. It was descending wings level, but in a nose-high attitude so extreme that air could not flow into the intakes to windmill the engine.

"Passing through fifty thousand and still can't get the nose down," Derby transmitted. "The nose-tail thrusters just aren't working . . . oh God," he transmitted in a strangled voice, "here we go. It's departing."

Court saw the nose of the NF-104 suddenly pitch up even higher, then the airplane fell off on the right wing into a flat spin. Each revolution of 360 degrees lasted about 10 seconds.

"He's in a flat spin to the right," Court yelled to ground control. He felt his pulse shoot up.

"No engine RPMs, no thruster action, controls are all locked up. I'll try the drag chute," Fred Derby transmitted quietly from the cockpit of the spinning aircraft. It was spinning flat, almost straight down, with no forward speed. The drag chute was a twenty-foot parachute attached to the rear of the jet that the pilot would normally deploy on touchdown by a handle in the cockpit. The chute would blossom out to slow the fast-landing fighter to a manageable speed on the runway. Now, in this situation, it might just jerk the tail up and dump the nose, allowing air in to windmill the engine.

"Roger, pull it, Zoom Test," Ground said.

Court pulled his two throttles inboard to cut off the afterburners, as he slid into a diving spiral just outside the radius of the spinning aircraft. As they shot through 40,000 feet, he saw the housing door in the tail section spring open, and the drag chute pack fly out to the end of its 15-foot cable. It deployed briefly, jerking the tail of the spinning jet outward, then shredded like a dandelion puff in a windstorm. The bare cable streamed, following the circle of the revolving tail. The pull of the chute had been enough to place the NF-104 into a lazy, skidding right turn, yet the nose was still too high to take in enough restart air.

"It blew out," Court transmitted. "The drag chute blew out."

"No good," Derby said after a moment, his voice sounding resigned for the first time. "I'm not much better off than before. I am in a slow descending right-hand spiral. I'm just above stall. There is not enough airflow to windmill the engine. My controls are still frozen. Passing through thirty-five thousand feet."

"Okay, copy," a new voice said, deeper and with obvious authority. "You're going to have to get out, Zoom Test. Get out, eject. Rescue chopper scrambled. This is General Austin, eject now," the man who had taken over the microphone at Test Control said. His voice was cool but authoritative.

"Roger, getting out," Derby said, equally as cool. "Hate to leave this beauty, though."

"Two One, stay with him, follow his chute down," Austin ordered Court Bannister.

"Roger, with him all the way," Court said. He had taken up a position just outside of Derby's spiraling aircraft and, by holding a diving tight turn, pulling three Gs, he was able to orbit around the stricken aircraft.

"Now you'll see what a real ejection looks like," Flak Apple said from the back seat.

"Saw a couple in 'Nam," Court said. "One was really bad." He had seen a burning Marine F-4 from Chu Lai, from which just the back-seater had gotten out. The front-seater had been torched after the back-seater had ejected; the fire had sucked into his face and flowed out the back canopy like a blow torch.

They watched Derby position himself in his ejection seat, head back, torso erect. He wore a full-pressure suit and a spaceman's helmet. He reached to pull the upper ejection device, a face curtain, to begin the ejection sequence. The canopy would blow off, then the seat would rocket up the rails at a peak speed of 90 miles per hour, shooting the pilot well clear of the high tee tail. The early F-104s had had downward ejection, because the rocket seats that would build up gradual Gs (if a tenth of a second can be considered gradual) had not been invented. The cannon shell that had been used in the old days to blast a seat out hadn't been powerful enough to loft the pilot and seat clear of the high tail. Famed jet ace and test pilot Iven Kincheloe had been killed when his F-104 had flamed out just after takeoff. He'd tried to roll inverted and eject "up," but couldn't make it. A shell with a strong enough charge to blast the pilot up and clear of the high tail would have also broken his back. The accelerating rocket seat that had replaced the hard bang of the shell had ended the problem.

Derby pulled the face curtain down. Nothing happened. Court and Flak saw Derby quickly lower his arms to grab the other ejection handle between his legs. They saw his body jerk as he pulled up on it. Again nothing happened.

"Seat failed," Derby transmitted, his voice one pitch higher and many times faster. "I'm blowing the canopy and going out manually." They saw him bend over as he tugged at the manual canopy ejection handle. Nothing. They saw him beat on the canopy with his fists, then stop and put his arms down.

"I have complete ejection system failure," Derby transmitted, in a voice now slow and laconic. "Guess I'll just have to ride it in."

"Fred," Court transmitted, "if I can get your nose down, can you get a restart?"

"Damn right, if you can get it low enough to get air flowing through it. But there ain't no way," Derby said, excitement abating.

"Just let me try," said Court, tightening up his turn and pulling in closer to the spiraling NF-104. "I'm going to try to tip your left wing up, so maybe your nose will slice down. Jettison that cable. I don't want to get tangled up."

"Nothing to lose as far as I'm concerned," Derby said, "but screw it up and you'll go in with me." He pulled the handle to jettison the drag-chute cable. It flew off and disappeared in a blink of an eye, writhing like a thin black snake.

"Court," Flak Apple said from the back seat, "are you out of your mind? You can't keep this thing steady enough or close enough to push his wing up. And we barely got enough fuel now to get back. This guy's gone."

"Two One, Bannister, isn't it?" General Austin transmitted. "Stay clear. That's an order. You don't have the experience. Return to base."

Court ignored him to talk on the IC to Flak. "I'm going to try it, Flak. I think we can do it."

"What's this 'we' shit, white man? I have my very own ejection system back here, you know." He took a deep breath. "What the hell. Let's try it. Screw it up and it'll be more my ass than yours. I'm the IP in here, you know."

The problem Bannister faced was pulling his plane around in a steep bank, tight enough to stay just outside the circumference of turn of the downward spiraling NF-104, while diving at the same rate of descent. This meant pulling six to eight Gs in a diving spiral with a downward velocity. While doing so, Court had to fly around the circumference of the spin with the NF-104, while placing his right wing tip under the tip of Fred Derby's left wing to force it up. So far, he had been flying several hundred feet outside the circumference. Now he had to reef it in and match his turn radius and speed with that of the NF.

"Aerodynamically, what you're trying to do is impossible," General Austin at Edwards Test Control radioed. "The engineers here say it can't be done. You can't pull enough Gs to maintain such a turn without stalling. I order you to break it off and return to base."

For a split second, Court started to say something about how, aerodynamically, the bumblebee shouldn't fly either. Instead, he jammed the two throttles full forward and into the afterburner range. He had to have maximum thrust from the engines to counterbalance the terrific G-load he was already imposing as he reefed it in to the NF. He pulled his turn tighter and tighter.

"Watch it, Court. You're going to over-G this thing," Flak grunted against the strain where, now at six Gs, his 200-pound body weighed over half a ton. Just the helmet alone of each man became a 15-pound weight on his head and neck. Both men wore G-suits, the zip-on chaps like cowboys wore, except they were filled with inflatable rubber bladders. A hose from the suit plugged into a valve in the airplane that metered air under pressure into the bladders proportionate to the number of Gs being pulled. Air expanded the bladders, compressing the thighs, calfs, and abdomen to help force blood to the head. As the G-load increased, blood would drain from the head, first out of the thin capillaries behind the pilot's eyes, causing him to gray out, then black out. Sustained loss of blood to the brain would make the pilot unconscious. The G-suit was really an aid to the pilot, who was already tensing his thigh and stomach muscles and grunting to keep the blood with its life-giving oxygen in his brain. It was exhausting work and couldn't be kept up for long periods, unless the pilot was in excellent physical condition.

Derby's airplane was spiraling to the right, requiring Court to bank sharply to the right to stay with it. Fighter pilots prefer a left bank, maybe because it's easier to pull the right arm to the left, maybe because the throttle is on that side, or just maybe because that's the way their mother said was best. Regardless, banking tightly to the right was difficult for Court.

"You're . . . too . . . far . . . out, you'll . . . never . . . catch . . . up," Flak grunted.

Court didn't answer. He reefed it in tighter, then had to snatch the throttles back as he began to overshoot. In an instant, he fell too far back. Got to leave one throttle in burner and just play the other one, he thought to himself.

"Break it off," Derby said. "No way you're going to catch me." His voice sounded remote and far away. Derby began to bang on his canopy with what looked like his kneeboard in a futile attempt to break through. Should have that heavy, short-bladed canopy buster we had in the F-100, Court thought.

Again he started forward, trying to place his right wing tip in position under the left wing tip of Derby's airplane to push it up. They were plunging through 30,000 feet. He inched up, his wing tip within two feet of the plunging NF-1-4, then inches, then he hit too hard. The tip housing of Derby's plane crumpled and flew off.

"Watch it, my God," Derby yelled, as the two planes plummeted downward. "Get the hell away from here."

"Low . . . fuel, low . . . fuel," Flak Apple gasped against the G-load. Court had his head turned full right as he looked down over the smooth surface of his wing. He could not afford to take his eyes from the wing tip to look at the fuel gauge.

"Land . . . dead-stick . . . okay," he grunted. They passed through 25,000 feet. Three more turns and both airplanes would dig deep holes in the desert floor.

He eased up again to the wing tip of the NF, playing the throttle of his inboard engine with two-fingered delicacy. He had to match precisely the angular rotational rate of the wing tip with his turn radius and rate of turn.

"Bannister, break it off, BREAK IT OFF," General Austin yelled.

"Shut . . . up . . ." Court gasped, concentrating so hard he was barely aware of what he said. He didn't need any distraction at this critical point. The sweat was pouring off his body. It ran down from his soaked hair, stinging his eyes and making him blink.

Derby, the quintessential test pilot, began dictating the conditions of his spin to Edwards Ground. He had plenty of battery power to operate his radio.

In the back of his mind Court marveled at how calm Derby sounded. The doomed pilot had even timed his rate of descent with a stopwatch and the altimeter because his vertical displacement needle was pegged down at its limit of 6,000 feet per minute, and the plane was dropping at 21,000 feet per minute.

Court finally had his wing tip under that of Derby's airplane. He gave just the slightest jerk to the left on his control stick to tap the spinning jet's wing up. It didn't work. Drops of sweat slid into his eyes. He overcontrolled, and his wing tip slid up toward the canopy. He saw Derby duck.

"No way, no way," Derby yelled. "Get outta here."

"Flame ... out ... one ... minute," Flak struggled to get the words out. Fuel consumption by the thirsty afterburners and the lower altitude had all but emptied the tanks of the T-38.

"Flame ... out," Flak said again, then slumped forward in his harness, unconscious.

That fact registered with Court. He knew that unless he unloaded the G-force on the airplane in a matter of seconds, Flak Apple would die at worst, or suffer brain damage at best. Then Court began to feel fuzzy and his vision dimmed from the sustained Gs.

"Yaaaahhhhhhh," he yelled into his mask, forcing more blood up into his brain. "Yaaaaaaahhhh," he yelled again, in a last-ditch effort to remain conscious. His adrenaline and pulse rate, already high, shot up even more. He held his breath like a shooter preparing to squeeze off the decisive shot. With a final effort, he slid his wing tip directly under that of the NF-104. Then, with an overlap of two feet, he raised it to contact Derby's wing, then gave a sharp jerk on the stick to the left. It worked. Derby's left wing came up, slicing the nose of his airplane almost straight down. Court frantically snatched his T-38 away and rolled left, as the NF-104 suddenly gained forward speed and pitched down into a normal dive. They passed through 9,000 feet.

"Hey, my God, I got air. I got RPMs. I GOT RPMS," Derby yelled across the airwaves. "It's starting." The relief bubbled his normally cool voice to a fever pitch.

Flak Apple came to just as the T-38 flamed out.

"Bannister, you bastard, are we still alive?" he blurted into the sudden silence.

"No brain damage there, I see," Court said. He blew out a lungful of air. He didn't realize he had been holding his breath. "The bad news is, we ain't got no gas. The good news is, a couple hundred square miles of Rogers Dry Lake is right beneath us. I'm going to dead-stick it in."

He actuated the ram air turbine and the auxiliary pumps to supply hydraulic pressure for the controls and landing gear. Everything functioned as advertised. He had just enough altitude to circle and set up his flameout pattern for the four-mile length of the runway marked out on the hard, dry lake bed. The NF-104, having power, was there ahead of him, already set up on final approach for landing. Court heard the mobile control, Lake Bed, clear him for landing.

After a few S turns to lose altitude and get pointing in the right direction, Court set up the silently gliding T-38 on the final approach, heading for the parallel lines that depicted runway 25. He could see a blue USAF ambulance and a red fire truck waiting for him. At the far end, off to the north side, was Derby's NF-104 surrounded by crash and rescue vehicles. A rescue helicopter orbited off to one side of his own plane. It followed him down to the runway. He eased over the approach end, careful to maintain 110 knots, the correct forced-landing speed for a T-38, plus a few extra knots for the air disturbance caused by the bent right wing tip. He started his flare. Dust spurted from the mains, and then the nose gear, as they smoothly touched down. The chopper flew parallel to his left side, the ambulance and fire truck sped down the runway through his dust following him. He rolled to a halt one hundred feet short of Derby and his NF-104. Court saw the firemen ax open Derby's canopy and help him out. Court and Flak sat in silence for a few moments, then thumbed the switches to raise their canopies. Fresh air blew in. Though hot, it still cooled Court, whose flight suit was black with sweat. He unhooked his mask and slipped his helmet from his head. He used both hands to wipe the sweat from his forehead and face. Flak Apple did the same in the back seat. They sat for a moment and breathed deeply.

"Sweet Jesus, that smells good," Court said, and ran his hand through his short-cropped blond hair. The desert air was quickly drying it to a salty stiffness. He felt drained and limp, as if enmeshed in molasses. He looked out as the arriving crash crew propped egress ladders against the fuselage.

"Better stick the pins in and safe our seats," Flak said in a quiet voice.

With hands that felt heavy and swollen, Court pulled the safety pins from his G-suit pocket and stuck them into the safing holes to prevent the seat from accidentally ejecting on the ground. Flak did the same. They climbed down the ladder from their two-seater jet. The ground crew surrounded them, congratulating them on the rescue. Both men nodded and grinned.

"Gut check," Flak Apple said. Both men held their hands out in front of them. Both pairs showed barely perceptible trembling.

"Not too bad," Flak said.

"Not for government work," Court answered. He pulled his cigarettes and lighter from his left sleeve pocket. He lit up and sucked a deep drag into his lungs.

"Those things will kill you," Flak Apple said.

"I hope to live that long," Court said. They watched as three men detached themselves from the cluster around the NF-104 and headed toward the T-38.

"Oh, oh, here comes trouble," Flak said.

General Austin and the commandant of the Test Pilot School, Colonel Chuck Hunter, were in the lead. General Austin was a sparse man with thin features. His brown hair was flecked with gray. He wore the 1505 khaki uniform with several rows of World War II and Korean War ribbons set beneath his command pilot's wings. Colonel Hunter, sturdy and tanned, wore the green K-2B flight suit. They were followed by Fred Derby, still in his full pressure suit minus the helmet.

"Bannister," General Austin said as he stomped up, "you're through here. You disobeyed a direct order and jeopardized the lives of two other men besides yourself, and almost destroyed two valuable airplanes. You might as well turn in your school patch right now, because you'll never fly here again." He had thrust his face up at Bannister, his anger obvious. Although Court had been prepared for a chewing out, he was shocked at the finality of the statement and the anger in the general's voice. Too much, perhaps? Bannister wondered.

"General," Colonel Hunter spoke up. As Commandant, he was responsible for the school, its students, and its curriculum. "With all respect, sir, I think I am the judge whether or not Bannister finishes the course. And he certainly didn't jeopardize the life of Major Derby, nor almost cause the destruction of the NF. They were already as good as lost. Isn't that correct, Major Derby?"

Derby nodded, his face thin and pale above the round metal collar that topped his pressure suit. He stepped forward and held his hand out to Court Bannister. His mouth twisted into a grin.

"Thank you, by God. Bannister, I don't know how you did it, but you did it. If it weren't for you, I'd be at the bottom of a smoking hole out there." He jerked a thumb toward the desert. He looked Court Bannister straight in the eye, his face at once stern and uncompromising. "But I agree with General Austin. You don't belong in the School. He ordered you to get away, I told you to get away, but you did not obey. It all leads to one conclusion. You don't have the discipline or judgment to be a test pilot." He turned to his boss,

Colonel Hunter. "As one of Bannister's instructors I recommend he be washed out for lack of judgment." There was a silence. The wind was picking up and starting to swirl sand around in miniature tornadoes.

"Gentlemen," Flak Apple said, stepping up, looming over them all, "you have just witnessed some of the most unbelievable flying you will ever see in your entire lives. Flying that saved a man's life. Flying that saved an expensive test aircraft. And you are standing here telling the pilot who did such superb flying that he is not worth a shit. This is crazy." He looked from Austin to Derby, hands on hips, shaking his massive head.

"Cool it, Flak," Court said, and took him by the elbow.

"Look, Apple," General Austin said, "you're not exactly clean in this. You are an experienced instructor pilot who flew in the back seat of this airplane," he patted the T-38. "That means you were in charge. Makes no difference that Bannister was in front, you were responsible for the flight. It's your signature that's on the school flight plan and on the Form 175. Seems to me you could have taken control of the situation before it developed, and stopped it."

"What," Flak Apple said in mock surprise, his eyebrows raised, "and missed being in on some of the most unbelievable flying I've ever seen?"

General Austin looked grim. Apple's response was not what a lieutenant general expects from an officer five ranks beneath him. "I want you two in my office at Test Control this afternoon"—he glanced at his watch—"at two o'clock." He spun on his heel and walked to his staff car. Colonel Hunter and Derby remained behind.

"Apple, you've got a big mouth," Chuck Hunter said. "But you're dead right, that *was* some shit hot good flying." His eyes twinkled. "You guys come see me after your visit with General Austin and I'll see what damage control is needed." He turned to Fred Derby, put his arm across his shoulders and drew him along as he walked back to his staff car. "Fred," he said, "you are one of my top instructors. Your point about Bannister's judgment is well taken, and, going by the book, totally accurate. But there are a few things that aren't quite spelled out in the book that you and I need to talk about." They climbed into Hunter's staff car and drove away. Flak and Court rode back in the flight-line van.

Flak spoke first. "Court, ah, about calling you a bastard—look, I really didn't mean it. It just sort of popped out. You know, it's so easy to say. It rolls so nice off the tongue . . ." He spread his big hands in a gesture of futility, a rueful grin on his big black face. "Oh hell, I'm sorry," he said.

"Apple, you big bastard. You didn't try to stop me, and you laid your career on the line for me with your smart-ass remarks and now you are apologizing. You're too much." Court slapped him on the back. "You're too much. I love you, you big bastard."

"You do?" Flak Apple said, and beamed. "Well then, kiss me, whitey."

Court studied him. "You know," he said in a serious tone, "I could probably trade you for a bale or two of cotton any time I wanted."

Promptly at two minutes to two that afternoon, the two majors presented themselves to General Austin's temporary secretary at his away-from-Pentagon office. They were decked out in 1505 silvertone khakis with ribbons and badges. Flak Apple had senior pilot wings and a row and a half of peacetime ribbons denoting faithful service, good shooting, and a commendation. Major Courtland Esclaremonde de Montségur Bannister had all of those plus the Silver Star, the DFC, a Bronze Star, the Vietnamese Cross of Gallantry with Palm, and numerous Air Medals. He had been eligible for a Purple Heart, but, in a moment of misguided false modesty, had turned it down. He had considered his wound "too piddly" compared to what routinely happened to his Special Forces buddies. He also wore senior pilot wings and a parachutist badge he had earned going through the 10th Special Forces Group jump school at Bad Tölz, Germany.

"Major Apple, the General wishes to see you first," the secretary said. Flak winked at Court, knocked twice at the closed door, and entered when bidden. He closed the door softly behind himself.

Court sat stiffly in one of the yellow vinyl lounge chairs in the secretary's office. He smoked three cigarettes, holding a red butt can for his ashes. The secretary, a slim brunette, coyly peeked at him from behind horn-rimmed glasses, a puzzled look on her face as she typed. Suddenly, she sat upright and squeaked, "I know who you are. You're ... you're Silk Screen Sam Bannister's son."

Court smiled and nodded. This had happened before. He knew what she was thinking, saw it in her eyes. "If the son was like the father ..." she would be musing. He saw her eyes stray to his left hand, looking for the wedding ring that wasn't there.

She looked up at him, boldly. Then she took her glasses off and softly spoke the rhyme that half the world seemed to know: "Silk Screen Sam, the ladies' man./If he can't get it in, no one can.

"Oh," she said, and giggled, "did I really say that?" She flushed and put her hand to her mouth. Court Bannister nodded and smiled. He knew better than to say anything and get involved in a prolonged gambit that could only end that evening in pneumatic and lubricious maneuvers. It had happened many times before and the ending was always the same. The girl would try to hogtie and wrap him, and call him her very own. He smiled again and looked away.

He thought of Nancy Lewis and Susan Boyle, two stewardesses he had met in Vietnam. They'd flown for different airlines and didn't know each other. Nancy was quiet, with soft brown hair. Her husband had been an Army advisor who had been killed in the Delta region of Vietnam. Susan, blonde, sun-bleached, and boisterous, had never been married as far as he knew. He had been seeing both of them, but sleeping with only one.

"Maybe Ken has told you about me," the secretary said.

"Ken Dwyer?" Court asked, focusing on her.

"Yes. My name's Rita. We've been dating, He talks a lot about you." She quickly put her glasses on and turned as the door to the general's temporary office opened and Flak Apple walked out.

"He wants you now," Flak said to Court.

"How did it go?" Court whispered as they passed. The door was still open to General Austin's office.

"I'm not exactly court-martialed, but I'm sure glad I've got that F-4 upgrade and Vietnam assignment locked up. Otherwise, I think I'd be permanent range officer at Tonopah." Tonopah was a secret test site out on the Nevada desert miles from nowhere. "That'll teach me to wise off to a two-star—maybe."

Court entered the office and saluted.

"Major Bannister reporting as ordered, sir," he said in the stylized ritual he hadn't used since he was a second lieutenant. The fighter squadrons he had been in didn't go for much formality. He stood at attention in front of the general's desk, eyes drilling straight ahead. Lieutenant General Austin did not see fit to tell Major Courtland Edm. Bannister to stand at ease.

"Bannister, I've been on the phone to NASA. They don't want you." The pleasurable malice was obvious in his voice. "And, frankly, I don't think you belong in the United States Air Force. You certainly don't need the money." He tapped a 201 record file in front of him. "I see you are up for a Regular commission. Why don't you just get out and make room for someone else? Why don't you do like your father did and go back to Hollywood with all the other phonies?"

Bannister broke his locked military stance and looked down at Lieutenant General Austin.

"Sir," he began, voice and eyes steely, "I don't know what in hell you've got against me, but you damn well keep my father out of this." He could feel his face flushing and his ears burning. Steady, boy, steady, he said to himself. It was too late.

"Don't you swear at me, boy. You hear me?" Austin stood up, his face red and swollen with a rage out of proportion to his words. "Bannister, I could run you up on charges so fast you'd be out of the Air Force in a week, if not in jail."

"Jail," Bannister said. "What for, disobeying an order?" He had abandoned his position of attention, but stood stiff with bewilderment and concern.

"Murder," Austin yelled. He leaned across his desk. "You murdered my son," he said, in a voice that sounded close to the breaking point.

Suddenly, Bannister understood. He had seen Major Paul Austin crash his F-100 on a combat mission in Vietnam, due entirely to Austin's ineptitude. There had been ground fire that day. To spare Austin's wife and children anguish and shame, Bannister had taken it upon himself to report his death as a shoot-down. He had had a small twinge over the lie, but had assuaged his conscience by thinking that maybe Paul Austin *had* taken a round in the cockpit, thus causing him to pull out too low.

"General Austin," Court began, in a voice thick with sudden compassion, "I didn't murder your son, sir. I didn't murder Paul. He was hit by ground fire on a ground attack mission and went in with his airplane."

"That's just it. There was ground fire and you didn't call it out. You didn't warn him." The general leaned heavily back into his chair.

"General Austin, the FAC had called out the possibility of ground fire. Your son was leading the flight. We were spread out in the attack pattern. If I had seen muzzle flashes, I'd have called them out. We all do. But I didn't see anything except his crash." Involuntarily, behind his eyes, the film rolled of Paul Austin's nose-high crash, afterburner kicking up a rooster tail of rice-paddy water. What was he going to do? Tell this pitiful man that his son had fouled up? That he had rolled in too low and slow to ever pull out? That he had punched the mike button and died with the words "Oh shit" on his lips when he'd realized what he had done?

"General, listen to me. You have no case. There is no fault or deficiency here, unless it was your son . . ."

"What do you mean?" the general raised his head, eyes bright.

"You know your son was a cargo pilot all his life and new to fighters. He died because he . . ." Court hesitated.

"Go on," the general urged, eyes narrowed.

"He died because he was . . . a hero who brought the fight to the enemy." Court just couldn't tell this father, who had once changed the diapers and loved and raised his only son, that said son had splattered himself all over the battlefield because he couldn't fly fighter aircraft worth sour owl shit. "He was a hero who paid the highest price for his beliefs," Court concluded about a pilot who should never have been passed through the F-100 upgrade program.

The general had his head down and was silent for a moment. Finally, he looked up.

"I didn't tell you to stand at ease, Major," he snapped. Court popped to attention, eyes straight ahead.

"You are lying and I know it," Austin said, in a voice thin and hard. His eyes were narrow, and too bright. "But you are right on one thing, there is nothing I can do about it."

"General Austin," Court choked out, "I'm not lying, goddammit." Oh shit, Court thought, I *am* lying, but not the way he thinks.

"I know you're lying and I can prove it. Your own operations officer, Major Harold Rawson, told me about the ground fire, and that you could easily have warned Paul. Instead, you let him fly directly into it." The general spoke with distinct triumph in his voice.

"General Austin, I am not lying, but Major Rawson was. He wasn't there, he saw no such thing, I told him no such thing, and the FAC on the scene reported no such thing. In fact, the FAC will totally support me, because that is what happened. There was no ground fire for me to call out to Paul."

"How dare you say that? Men who are mighty enough to win the Medal of Honor, as Rawson did, don't tell lies," the general grated.

"General, I'm sorry about your son," Court said in a loud voice. Forgetting military protocol, he pounded on the general's desk. "But I didn't kill him. That's a preposterous idea."

Austin jumped to his feet and leaned over his desk, his face red and contorted. "Get out, get out of my office. I don't want to see you again. Get out. You haven't heard the last of this. Get out," the general shouted again. Tiny bits of spit dotted the corners of his mouth.

White-faced and furious, Court spun on his heel and stalked out of the office. He did not salute.

An hour later Court Bannister sat in Colonel Hunter's office and, after sincere encouragement by the Colonel, told him the whole story. He omitted nothing, not even the part about Paul Austin saying "Oh shit" just before he crashed. And he told them about Harold Rawson.

"Major Rawson was a lying little wimp and coward who damn near killed me and a lot of other people at Bien Hoa because of his actions. He was the only guy in theater who could miss with napalm by 1500 feet . . . to one side. But he did receive the Medal properly because he picked up a satchel charge that was thrown into a bunker full of people and ran out with it. It vaporized the little shit."

"Sumbitch, Bannister," Colonel Hunter began, "I've heard some stories in my day, but yours sets all records for sheer unbelievability. It's the most improbable, outlandish, and . . . and . . ."

"Outrageous," Flak supplied.

"Yeah, that too. As outrageous as a drunk fox in church," Hunter said. Colonel Chuck Hunter, a double ace from World War II and the first man to break the sound barrier, loved his metaphors. He'd grown up with them in West Virginia and dropped them in his daily language like birds in a corn field. He looked at Court.

"Outrageous, but I know it's true. I know your old boss, Jake Friedlander. He was the wing commander at Bien Hoa at the time you're talking about. I called him at TAC headquarters today and he told me the whole story. Seems you left out one part; you pulled a gun on Rawson."

"That's because he was lying about some airplane problem and wanted to abandon some of our guys out in the jungle," Court said, starting to heat up again, not noticing the twinkle in Hunter's eyes.

"Cool off, hotshot. I know that. Jake told me all about it. You got more sides to you than a piece of coal." Hunter leaned back and put his hands behind his head.

"Austin talked to NASA all right. He fixed you for good there. They don't want you under any circumstances. My man on the scene, Joe Engles, the only one of the active-duty military guys in the astronaut program, by the way, who wears his uniform, says that Austin's wired in with Senate appropriations and Johnson's space budget like honey in a comb. One word and they can lose a million here or a million there. So if Austin says you're out, you're out. Remember, Bannister, Austin is a three-star who you cussed out and told to shut up. There are wiser things to do. So, you tell me. Do you want to stick around for the aerospace portion of the course and hope when you graduate you can ride around in the USAF MOL program like Spam in a can? Or do you want to graduate at the end of the test pilot phase with your test ticket and join the real world of plain old flight test?"

"I'll take my test ticket and run," Court said. "I don't fancy orbital mechanics, anyway."

Hunter nodded. "Thought you'd feel that way. I already canceled your last six months here," Chuck Hunter said. "Anything else?" he asked.

"Yes, sir. Rather than go right into testing, I'd like to upgrade into the F-4 and get another tour in Vietnam," Court said.

"Thought you'd feel that way, too. It's all arranged. You graduate from here next week, take a week of leave enroute, and report to the 479th Wing at George Air Base to check out in F-4s. From there, you've got orders to the fighter wing at Ubon. That means MiGs over Hanoi and the Steel Tiger mission over Laos. Think you can handle that, boy?"

☆

"You bet I can handle that Ubon assignment," Court said to Flak Apple. They had decided to have two beers only—it was, after all, a school night. Each man still had work to do; Court finishing up some papers, Flak grading tests and reviewing the next day's curriculum. They stood at the makeshift bar in Court's room in what was laughingly called the Desert Villa in Housing Area "D." The spider-and-scorpion-infested cinderblock Bachelor Officer's Quarters was more pre–Pancho Villa than anything else. Court had a tape of Puccini's *La Bohème* on his Akai 250SD.

"Well, I'm off to George and Ubon as well," Flak said, "only I get the quickie course at George 'cause I got previous time in the F-4. So I'll get to Ubon before you. Got to get me a MiG or two, you know. You got a MiG from the back seat of a Thud the first time you flew it, didn't you?"

"Not exactly, well, yes. But I never pulled the trigger. Ted Frederick, the front-seater, did. I just spotted the MiGs and put him in position."

"He's the guy who shot back at that trawler and is now MIA?"

"The very one."

Flak took a pull, and hummed a bit along with Mimi. He looked at Court. "At least you've already had one combat tour. This will be my first. Did you, ah, I mean before your first tour, ever feel, well, nervous or anything?"

"Oh, hell yes," Court laughed. "I had done pretty well on the gunnery ranges, but I didn't know if I could hack it when someone was shooting back. It worked out okay. Although, I'll tell you, seeing your first, or any SAM shot at you is the most puckering experience you'll ever have. And it doesn't get any better with practice."

"Then why are you going back?"

Court looked out the window. There was little besides sandy desert and Wherry housing to see. A few mountains in the distance broke the monotonous horizon. "I just am. It's what I do."

"You know," Flak said, "I knew there was something wrong with you. That's not much of an answer."

"Listen, I want to go back for the same reason you volunteered. The war is on, our guys are still over there. We should be with them. I feel that more than any political motivation. Besides, there's a lot of MiGs to kill. I want to make ace, and I'm antsy to get going."

Flak Apple studied Court. "Look, every fighter pilot wants to make ace. And we all have a variety of reasons. What are yours?"

Court looked at the picture of an F-4 behind the bar. "I was your usual dumb-shit fighter pilot, having a good time flying airplanes, chasing girls, tearing around the world with my hair on fire. Then several things happened. I got married, and I decided to be the first man on the moon. I worked my buns off getting my engineering degree at Arizona State so I'd qualify for Edwards. I made it. I got my degree and qualified for the test pilot school. My wife thought that was so great she asked for a divorce. About then the Vietnam war started." Court sighed and turned to face Flak. He shrugged. "I asked to slip my appointment one year so I could go to Vietnam." He thought he saw a flicker in Flak Apple's eyes. "They said I had to reapply. So I took my tour in Huns at Bien Hoa, reapplied for the school, made it, then came here." Court looked back toward the F-4. "But I didn't get everything I worked for, did I? After today, I get my test certificate, okay, but I don't go through the aerospace portion. Lack of discipline and judgment, I believe is the phrase. Where do you go from here? Back to Vietnam. For me, anyhow."

"That doesn't tell me why you want to make ace."

"Anybody ever tell you you were relentless?"

"Yeah. And cruel, too. Tell me why."

"It's obvious."

"Maybe. Tell me anyhow."

"Apple, you're really pressing. It's because I flunked marriage, I flunked the moon, so what's left?" Court's voice was very flat. "I want to be the best goddamn fighter pilot there is."

Flak Apple nodded. "Ah, ego," he said.

"Damn right, ego. I believe in ego as a strong force, a great motivator if used correctly. Ego can help you, or it can kill you. A fighter pilot has to have the right mixture. Enough ego to get into the card game confident he can whip the shit out of anybody, but not so much he won't throw his cards in on a bad hand and, equally as important, not so much he isn't afraid to learn what he did wrong so he won't do it again."

"Couldn't have said it better myself," the black man said.

Court took out his cigarettes and offered one to Flak, who shook his head no. They listened to Puccini's opera. Flak moaned a few lines along with the man singing Rodolfo's part, revealing a passable baritone.

"Not bad," Court said.

Flak grinned. "Thanks. Say, that was quite an article on your dad today," he said. The *Palmdale Press* had run a half-page society spread on Sam Bannister, who, besides being a famous old-time movie star, owned the Silver Screen Hotel and considerable real estate in downtown Las Vegas and Palm Springs. "Is he really everything you read about?"

"Yeah," Court said, "he is that. He's quite a guy. He was a B-17 gunner in the big one."

"Any other relations? Brothers? Sisters?"

"One, Shawn Bannister. He's my brother, half brother, actually. He's a newsie for the *California Sun*." Court swirled his beer bottle. "We don't get along so well. We tangled in Vietnam when I was on my first tour."

Flak looked surprised. "Sure. I remember. He's the guy who wrote that article about some jock napalming a bus full of civilians. Made quite a spread."

Court rapped the bar. "Goddammit, that jock was me, and what he wrote wasn't true! We had a shot-up M-113 armored personnel carrier, and it was real, live VC that blew it up and they were who I dropped some napalm on. He saw the pictures of the track, but he chose to lie anyhow. No, we sure as hell don't get along."

Court thought back to the last time he had seen his brother, just a few weeks ago, when he'd gone to Las Vegas to see his father. They'd been sitting together at dinner when Sam poked Court.

"Look who's coming," he said.

Court looked up as Shawn Bannister walked to the table. With him were two long-legged showgirls, one on each arm. He looked down at Court.

"So, why are you going back to Vietnam? To napalm some more women and children?" Shawn was nearly as tall as Court, but younger and more slender. There was a resemblance. His face was tanned and astonishingly handsome. He had blond hair brushed to his shoulders, and wore expensive slacks and a heavy gold chain with a tiger's tooth and a gold clip shaped like an alligator. Although his smile at Court was wide and dazzling, he didn't put out his hand. The buzz of local conversation was momentarily interrupted as women at nearby tables gave muffled little shrieks and tried to appear unconcerned. They were sure they had recognized the young man as Sam Bannister's son.

"Dad said you were in town," the blond man said. "Thought I'd stop by. No, don't get up. I'm just passing by." Court hadn't moved to get up. Shawn swayed slightly, tightening his grip on the girls' arms. "I'm on my way to the Coast, Berkeley. Then I'm off to Saigon, as a matter of fact. Seems the *Sun* wants me to look into all the military corruption and smuggling going on over there."

"Shawn," Sam Bannister said, "you're tight. Sit down, talk nice."

"Not tonight, Dad. Say goodbye to big brother here. I got places to go and things to do." He waved a hand to his brow. "Cheerio." He moved off with the two girls. Every eye in the room was on the trio.

"Court, I didn't arrange this. I'm sorry, old man." Sam Bannister had a rueful smile on his face. He held his hands palms out. "But you know Shawn."

"Yeah, Dad. I know Shawn."

Flak looked at Court, who seemed lost in thought, and decided to drop the whole subject. It had to be painful as hell to be attacked by your brother like that, for all the world to see.

"Fuck it," he said. "Drink up, Court. We got a war to get to."

5

☆

Ever since Premier Kosygin's visit to Hanoi in February 1965, Soviet Air Force aid to the Democratic Republic of Vietnam had increased dramatically. Besides older MiG-17 and MiG-19s being transferred to Hanoi, fifteen of the latest model MiG-21s had arrived in September 1965. Initial training and combat clashes with the Americans had been disastrous. By the 6th of January 1967, all of them had been shot down. The loss of the fifteen in less than a year and a half had been very bad indeed. But what had caused head-rolling all the way into the Kremlin was the fact that seven MiG-21s had been shot down in one day—the 2nd of January 1967.

Pod-Palcovnik (Lieutenant Colonel) Vladimir Chernov smiled grimly to himself. That raid on the 2nd of January was why he was in Hanoi and not teaching advanced fighter tactics at Fruenze. That devastating raid had been conceived by the fighter pilots of the 8th Tactical Fighter Wing over at Ubon in Thailand. It had been led by their commander, a full colonel named Robin Olds. Only after the raid had Soviet intelligence supplied all the details—names, tail numbers, weapons. Soviet intelligence had completely missed the ruse Olds and his men had used that day. The raid idea had been quite simple, and simplicity, Chernov knew, was not always the Americans' strength. Ever since the Korean conflict, American planning had gotten convoluted and complex. Yet in this case, simplicity itself had made the final tally of the day seven MiG-21s shot down at no cost to the attacking Ubon F-4 Phantoms.

Olds and his men had simply masqueraded as bomb-laden F-105 Thunderchiefs. They'd used the same call signs, flown in from the same direction, used the same speeds and altitudes. The MiG-21s had been sucked in. Chernov seethed. It was at that time he had been hurriedly detached from his position as chief of MiG-21 instruction for international pupils at Fruenze and sent to the People's Air Force at Hanoi.

There was a puzzlement, though, about that day; and other days when the Americans were fighting MiGs. Sometimes a Phantom would be in perfect firing position but would fail to fire. Either the plane was out of ammunition—in which case it should depart the battle scene—or for some reason the pilot had decided not to shoot. More likely, Chernov thought, it was equipment failure of some kind. That might be a weakness to exploit. He made a note to ask the GRU to investigate this matter by whatever means they had.

Problems with the Americans aside, there was further disaster for Soviet equipment on 5 and 6 June, this time in the Mideast. With a loss of only 26 airplanes, the Israeli Air Force had destroyed 428 Egyptian, Syrian, Iraqi, and Jordanian airplanes on the ground on 27 different airfields. Of those destroyed, 269 were MiG fighters, of which 136 were MiG-21s.

The ultimate irony was that Soviet Air Force Colonel General Kirsanov had seen the whole thing. He had been airborne in an Ilyushin transport the first two hours of the strike with the Egyptian Air Force Commander in Chief, General Mohammed Sidki, and the Egyptian Chief of Staff, General Amer. It was ludicrous. They had been forced to remain aloft until cleared into Cairo International because all the military airfields had been under attack.

Now Kirsanov was in Hanoi. Kirsanov, once an impressive man— now gray and coughing—still retained an impressive title. He was the Deputy Commander in Chief for Combat Training, Chief of the Training Department, and a Merited Military Pilot of the USSR. He had fought with distinction in the Great Patriotic War, avoided purges, and had risen rapidly through the ranks as he trained pilots for various wars of liberation. Once a handsome and hearty man, Kirsanov had turned into a doughy replica of his former self. Things had gone well for him through the decades as he carved a comfortable career for himself. Until this year, that is. This year, things had gone sour very quickly for Kirsanov. First the Mideast disaster, now Hanoi was in trouble. Something had to be done.

Kirsanov had arrived on an overnight trip to Hanoi, slipping into Gia Lam Airport in an IL-18 transport with Aeroflot markings. He'd immediately hammered the entire Soviet advisory contingent for three hours about Soviet equipment and training. He said Soviet prestige and excellence were on the line in the eyes of the world. He was agitated and angry. He said the honor of the entire Soviet Air

Force rested on their shoulders. The Air Force men in the contingent stared at the ground. They couldn't understand why this pompous air bladder was blaming them. When Kirsanov had finished, he told Chernov he wanted to see him privately.

They sat in Chernov's tiny office in the embassy. It was after three in the morning, and the air was cool and damp, like that from a Lake Baikal icehouse. The general was due to take off shortly before dawn for Moscow. He took off his tunic and loosened his tie, and from his oversized briefcase produced a flask of vodka and two silver cups. He and Chernov each tossed one off. The general took a second, then lit a Marlboro, which provoked a heavy coughing fit. Chernov sat quietly until he finished. Kirsanov wiped his lips with a handkerchief, then gazed at Chernov with kind eyes. He liked Chernov.

"Volodya," he began in a hoarse voice. "I knew your father, you know. We were flying sergeants for a while. In Stormoviks." Chernov knew this. Kirsanov had mentioned it many times before, as if he wanted to establish the same sort of bond he had had with the older Chernov. Maybe it brought back pleasant memories, maybe Kirsanov was trying to impress him. Chernov didn't know. He did know that in addition to setting his own record as a crack pilot, the contact did not hurt. Kirsanov had no sons of his own.

"Things were clear then," Kirsanov continued. "Now they are not. Now we are running around the world giving sophisticated equipment to peasants who barely know how to put on shoes. It's bad, it's bad." He coughed. "The Arabs. They don't listen to what we say. They are obsessed with killing Jews. I'm not a Jew-lover, but Thor's balls, you don't plug a meat grinder with your own hand just because you hate pork. But of course, Headquarters says it is all my fault." He shook his head in disgust, quickly downed another shot. He coughed a bitter "Hah."

"There we were, that ass-wipe of a pilot, Sidki, and me, in an old tub of an Ilyushin 14 at eight o'clock in the morning. I had told Sidki the night before our intelligence had said there would be a preemptive strike. So he put his patrols up in the wrong place at the wrong time, and said let's go look at the slaughter. When his pilots landed for breakfast, as they did every day at eight-thirty, the Israeli Air Force struck at eight forty-five. Oh, it was funny, I tell you. We saw the whole dirty show. Couldn't do a thing about it." He lit another cigarette and went into a paroxysm of coughing; "Ah-hee hee hee, ah-hee hee hee." He rumbled and spit into his handkerchief.

"So it comes to you, Vladimir Nicholaevych. You are the chief instructor of the most visible contingent of Soviet equipment in the world today that is actively in combat—and with the Americans. This is it. For sugar or for vinegar, this is it. The Premier wants results, superlative results. We must prove the superiority of our equipment and tactics. Prove it, or we will all share a little cardboard dacha in Siberia."

"I understand fully, Comrade General," Chernov said. He thought of the disastrous second of January. "Perhaps we could have better intelligence input to help us provide those results. It is inconceivable how F-4 Phantoms could take off from the American base and change into F-105 Thunderchiefs in midair. We need better intelligence about enemy air bases."

"Something is being done, Volodya. There are plans to exploit the American newspapers' love for printing anything, even military secrets." He started to laugh, but again it degenerated into a hacking cough. "Ah-hee hee hee, ah-hee hee hee." When he was through heaving, he leaned forward, a serious expression on his face.

"But listen carefully to me. This is a bad, bad time. Air Force Headquarters is after the heads of the entire Combat Training Command, starting with me. You can show them we are doing our job. Train these little people. Teach them to use our airplanes to their fullest, Volodya. The Soviet Union cannot have the reputation of its equipment sullied. When it is used by incompetents, we are laughed at. We cannot stand by and let this happen. Do whatever it takes. I've read the reports. We need victories. We must have revenge for the Ubon attacks," Kirsanov said. He bit off a cough. "Our agents say it was called 'Bolo.' "

"Our agents read the American magazine *Aviation Week*," Chernov said. "That's how they know what it was called. It was printed out in some detail."

"The Americans like to congratulate themselves too much," Kirsanov said.

"Yes," Chernov replied. "I also think they need heros and battle triumphs. That is what the American people need to read about."

"It is not only the American people who want victories, Volodya. I too am under pressure. We must have victories." He paused. "I mean, of course, our equipment must *provide* victories. It must be superior to that of the Yankee imperialists. I see in the reports the names Toon, Van Bay, Vong. They are doing well. Make sure they fly at the proper time in the proper places to get victories—victories without risk. I'll see the reporters from sympathetic newspapers and journals come to Hanoi to record what they do. The world must know our equipment is good. We cannot rely on those Arabs to prove it. Those Arabs—pah."

The general paused. "Of course," he said in an oily voice, "we must help our Vietnamese friends in their struggle for liberation." He looked around, as if to spot the microphone to take in those obligatory words. Then he rapped the table. "Do whatever it takes, I'll back you on anything, Vladimir Nicholaevych. Anything," he repeated. He puffed himself into another coughing spell.

Chernov studied Colonel General Kirsanov. He wondered how far he dared go in telling him about his flying combat against the Americans. He decided Kirsanov knew all about it. He had just made his instructions clear, and didn't want any further talk. Do what you have to do, but don't let on what it is you are doing. Yes, Kirsanov's instructions were clear: Defeat the Americans, even if it means you fly every day.

Pod-Palcovnik Vladimir Nicholaevych Chernov smiled at Colonel General Kirsanov. They understood each other.

More than one Vietnamese pilot was about to become an ace.

6

☆

LBJ was the nickname for the Long Binh Jail, the huge stockade in the middle of the sprawling Long Binh Army Depot 20 kilometers northwest of Saigon on Highway 1. Prisoners the U.S. Army particularly wanted to impress were locked in metal Conex shipping boxes at LBJ.

The huge Long Binh complex was the headquarters of USARV, U.S. Army Vietnam. Hundreds of tents, one- and two-story buildings, barracks, and huge warehouses were set in neat, orderly rows on an enormous flat plain of 300 acres of red dirt. Interspersed midst the rows of barracks were community latrines with showers and sheds containing soft-drink vending machines. Just outside the main gate were dozens of Vietnamese concessions housed in lean-to structures made of plywood and hammered beer-can tin. There were short-time play sheds, tailors, barbers, and tiny two-table bars that sold iced Bamuiba and soda. Inside the gates on the sprawling post, concession privileges had just been granted to selected American and Chinese businessmen who were frantically building and opening shops to sell furs, diamonds, and clothes. There were even automobile dealers selling American cars to GIs for delivery back in the World, as the GIs called the States. Madame Tang's Steam Bath and Laundry Emporium did a landslide business cleaning both bodies and clothes.

USARV wasn't even close to performing the duties its name implied—a field army headquarters overseeing combat operations, as was done by similar organizations in World War II and Korea. Rather, it was an enormous supply center incorporating administrative and logistical headquarters where rather dull jobs were performed mostly by people who had originally thought they were being assigned to an important post. In addition to the support groups (and a huge ammo depot) at Long Binh under USARV were an engineering command, a security agency and intelligence group, an aviation outfit, and a medical brigade with a huge evacuation hospital and Dustoff helipads. At one side of the complex was the 18th Military Police Brigade, whose men tended the USARV Installation Stockade on 10 Hall Road.

Lieutenant Colonel Wolfgang Xavier Lochert, hands handcuffed together in front of him, sat in the right front seat of the MP jeep as it drove up to the stockade gate. He was wearing rumpled prison issue fatigues with painted white stripes and a white "P" on the back of his shirt. He was bareheaded. The stubble on his face accentuated the lines of exhaustion and indignation. The sign over the stockade gate, WE WELCOME COMMAND FAILURES, was flanked by the crossed pistols of the provost marshal.

Inside, Lochert was signed over to a beefy MP lieutenant named Hartigan, who roughly pushed him to a table where he held each handcuffed hand to roll his fingerprints. Then Hartigan jerked him to a position in front of a camera.

"They done all that to me in the Saigon MP station," Lochert growled.

"Got to make sure it's the real you I'm signing for," Hartigan snapped.

"That's not how you talk to a superior officer, Hartigan," Lochert shot back.

"In here, there's nothing superior about you, *Colonel*," he said, lacing the title with heavy sarcasm.

Lochert held up his cuffs. "Must you?" he said.

"You're lucky a wild man like you isn't in leg irons." The lieutenant went to his desk. "Come over here, *Colonel*, I got to read something to you." Lochert walked over, eyes smoldering, as the lieutenant picked up the charge sheet and began reading.

" 'Charge One: Violation of the Uniform Code of Military Justice, Article 118, Murder. Specification: In that Lieutenant Colonel Wolfgang Xavier Lochert, United States Army, 5th Special Forces Group, Nha Trang, Republic of Vietnam, APO 96240, did at 122/3 Tu Do Street, Saigon, Republic of Vietnam, on 5 July 1967, murder John Charles Stevens by means of shooting. Charge Two: Violation of the Uniform Code of Military Justice, Article 128, Assault.' " Hartigan paused, then looked down at the paper.

" 'Specification: In that Lieutenant Colonel Wolfgang Xavier Lochert, 5th Special Forces Group, Nha Trang, Republic of Vietnam, APO 96240, did at 122/3 Tu Do Street, Saigon, Republic of Vietnam, on 5 July 1967, commit an assault upon John Charles Stevens by striking

John Charles Stevens with his fists and did thereby intentionally inflict grievous bodily harm upon him.' " Hartigan cleared his throat.

" 'Charge Three: Violation of the Uniform Code of Military Justice, Article 133. Specification One: In that Lieutenant Colonel Wolfgang Xavier Lochert, 5th Special Forces Group, Nha Trang, Republic of Vietnam, APO 96240, did at 122/3 Tu Do Street, Saigon, Republic of Vietnam, on 5 July 1967, commit murder to his disgrace and compromise his standing as an officer of the United States Army. Charge Four: Violation of the Uniform Code of Military Justice, Article 109. Specification: In that Lieutenant Colonel Wolfgang Xavier Lochert, 5th Special Forces Group, Nha Trang, Republic of Vietnam, APO 96240, did at 122/3 Tu Do Street, Saigon, Republic of Vietnam, on 5 July 1967, willfully and wrongfully damage by breaking and smashing furniture, the amount of said damage being in the sum of about 14,500 piasters, the property of Madam Lien Van Loc.' Quite an accomplishment, *Colonel.*" Hartigan stood up. "It is my duty," he said in an officious voice, "to order you placed in pretrial confinement here at the Long Binh Installation Stockade. Do you have any questions?"

"Yeah, why don't you unlock these cuffs so I can rip your face off?" Wolf Lochert rasped.

"Oh no, *Colonel,* no fancy games so you can call for a mistrial. But once you are sentenced, I'll be more than happy to accommodate you out back of the Conex boxes." Wolf just glowered.

Hartigan took Lochert down a hall past several cells occupied by figures in prison fatigues, standing or sitting, all smoking cigarettes. He stopped at the last cell on the right. It was empty. The cell next to it held a man lying on his steel bunk smoking and reading a lurid pocket novel.

"Turn around so I can take your cuffs off, Colonel Lochert," the MP lieutenant said in a quiet voice. Lochert turned, eyes widened in curiosity. He held his wrists out for Hartigan to unlock the cuffs.

"Chaplain Sollivan sends his best and says he will be up to see you soon, sir," the MP lieutenant said, in a low but respectful voice. He had positioned himself so the man in the other cell couldn't hear him. Then he released the cuffs, locked Wolf in his cell, and walked away. He trod the freshly shined linoleum as if he wore metal parade taps on his boots.

A metal GI cot without bedding was welded to the bars of the end wall. On the bed was a rolled-up mattress. It was thin and stained. Wolf stood next to the bed and looked around. He estimated the cell to be six feet by seven. Fluorescent light shone from the ceiling. All the walls were made of one-inch steel bars. The cells, he noted, were fabricated within a large room in the building like animal cages in a laboratory. There were five on each side, furnished identically with a GI cot, a wooden chair, and a narrow metal locker with no door that opened toward the cell door. His cell, like all the others, had a ceramic wash basin fixed to the back bars. Next to it was a toilet with no seat. Bare pipes were visible behind and under the fixtures. Wolf walked to the barred window and looked out at an exercise yard, where prisoners were slowly walking or performing in-place exercises. A few were lifting weights. Wolf smacked his fist into his palm, again and again.

The man reading in the next cell looked up. He was about thirty-five years old, had dark hair, and measured five foot eleven. Unlike the other prisoners in military fatigues, he wore civilian black pants and a white sport shirt.

"Welcome," he said from his cot. "Welcome, Colonel Lochert. I've heard good things about you." He stood up and held out his hand through the bars. Wolf Lochert looked but made no move to take it.

"My name's Bubba Bates," he said, "and you sure look familiar." He pulled his hand back. He wet his lips. Lochert looked at him without speaking. Bates stared, then spoke.

"Why won't you shake my hand, Colonel?" he asked. "It's not wise to make enemies in this place. You never know who has connections."

"How do you know who I am?" Wolf asked over his shoulder, as he turned back to the tiny window.

"Word gets around fast, once you're connected," Bates responded.

Wolf knew exactly who Curtis ("Bubba") Bates was. They had met over a year before at the Tan Son Nhut Officer's Club. Bates, the civilian station agent for Alpha Airlines, had brought a beautiful young Vietnamese girl named Tui to the Club. When Bates had become abusive to her, Air Force Lieutenant Toby Parker had intervened. In the ensuing fight, Parker had knocked Bates down, and Wolf had stopped two of Bates's civilian companions from beating up on Parker.

Bates knew him by name, but did he remember him by his face? He fingered his beard. He hoped not. He looked at his reflection in the small window. The black wire stubble on his face made him look piratical. He turned to face Bates.

"Yeah, you're right, let's shake." He did his best to conceal his disgust at the limp paw Bates presented as they shook hands. Bates peered at Wolf, obviously puzzled.

"I still think I've seen you somewhere before," he said. He cocked his head, then his face lit up.

"I've got it," he said, and snapped his fingers. "I know who you are. I mean, I know where I saw your face."

Wolf Lochert imperceptibly bunched himself for an attack. It wouldn't do to be recognized as the man who had helped Bubba Bates be vanquished in the Tan Son Nhut Officer's Club.

"I know," Bates said. "Last Christmas. You had your picture in the *Stars and Stripes*. You and three other guys. Some hippies had splashed blood on you in the L.A. airport."

"Yeah," Wolf said. He relaxed. "Yeah. That's it. We had our pictures plastered all over the stateside papers and the *Stars and Stripes* over here. Even made *Newsweek*. Some photographer in the terminal caught it just as that hippie broad threw red dye on us. She was screeching and saying we were murderers."

"And you said you were a killer, not a murderer," Bates said. "Yeah, that's it. I remember now." He stared at Lochert a long moment with hard eyes.

"How come you're all of a sudden in jail? From an all-American hero to public enemy number one. Doesn't make sense."

"It does if you look at it from my standpoint," Lochert said.

"Which is?"

"Which is I've had it with those ungrateful bastards. Give your all for your country and what do you get? Some punk kids wearing the American flag on their ass throwing stuff and spitting on you. It used to be if there was a war and you *weren't* in uniform you got spit on. The hell with 'em." Wolf waved his hand in dismissal.

A guard unlocked Wolf's cell door and threw some bedding and a towel on the floor. He kicked it toward Wolf, and walked out. He carefully locked the door. Wolf and Bates watched him walk down the hall.

"And to hell with the United States Army, too," Wolf said. He walked to the far side of the cell with steps that thudded onto the floor. He turned to face the man in the cell next to his.

"What are you in for, Bates, and why don't you have prison fatigues on?" he asked.

"It's like this," Bates said, his voice thin and reedy. "I'm a civilian, see, and the MPs got me on a little smuggling charge. You seen that Viet civilian jail in Saigon?"

Wolf shook his head.

"Well, it's rats and sewer shit and real downtown shakedowns. Nobody speaks English. You know what I mean?"

Wolf shook his head.

"It ain't fit for a civilized man," Bates replied. "Now, me, I got some connections. Instead of serving my time down there, I fixed it to come here to the LBJ. I've got some clout."

"How come you didn't get sent back to the slammer in the States?" Wolf asked.

"That was handled by a legal technicality involving extradition or something. I don't have to go. Besides, this here jail is considered federal territory. So I'm serving federal time, see?" Bates looked smug. "Like I said, I got *connections*."

Wolf rolled out the bare mattress on the springs and stretched out. "I gotta rest," he said. "I got a lot to think about." He closed his eyes. Bates looked at him for a moment, shrugged imperceptibly, then turned back to his book.

1830 HOURS LOCAL, SATURDAY, 8 JULY 1967
USARV INSTALLATION STOCKADE
LONG BINH, REPUBLIC OF VIETNAM

☆

Wolf was finishing his sit-ups. He was on his third set of the day, doing sixty repetitions each set. He had already finished his push-ups and squats under the same regime. He did pull-ups on the bars, but not as many. He had only been allowed out for ten minutes of exercise in the morning and ten in the afternoon, always under guard. No one spoke to him. He had been taken to the small mess hall to eat by himself. The food was not good.

A guard brought Bubba Bates a plastic bag with Vietnamese lettering on it. From the bag, Bates extracted a sealed white envelope and read the contents. Then he pulled out two beers and a bag of peanuts. Through the bars, he offered a can to Wolf, who took it and downed a deep draught. He looked appreciatively at Bates.

"One man says I ought to be in leg irons, and here you are giving me a beer. Yeah, I guess you got clout, all right." Wolf shook his head in admiration. He leaned forward. "Do you think your clout can help me?" he asked in a low voice.

"Maybe. I was wondering if you would ask. Say, you sure we haven't met before?" Bates grinned. His teeth were tobacco-stained.

"No, I don't think so. But you know how it is around Saigon. You can easily run into the same people at a bar or some club. It's probably just those pictures you saw of me." Wolf tensed again. For Bates to remember the old animosity would not be good. He might go for revenge, and right now Wolf needed Bubba Bates's good feelings.

"Maybe so. That's probably it. But I do know all about you," Bates said.

"You do? How come?" Wolf seemed surprised. "What's going on?"

"What's going on is you killed a man, scragged him good, so I hear. For that you're going to spend the rest of your life in Leavenworth prison in the middle of the Kansas nowhere," Bates said.

"Maybe not," Wolf said. "I'll get off because it was self-defense."

"That's not quite the way it works. You used excessive force to defend yourself. Force far beyond what would be considered reasonable and prudent. Furthermore, you could have walked away. And further than that, you struck the first blow." Bates nodded emphatically as he ticked off each point. For an instant, he no longer seemed the sleepy-eyed bumbler.

"How did you know all that?" Wolf asked, his eyes narrow.

"Colonel, you haven't been listening. I'll put it another way. I'm wired in at a very high level, very high indeed."

"Why are you telling me all this? It isn't just to impress me, is it?"

"No, it isn't just to impress you. I think we can help each other. My, ah, connection thinks so, too."

"If you are so well-connected, why are you in the slammer in the first place?"

"It was a planned fall," Bates said. He lit a Marlboro and blew the smoke toward the ceiling.

"Tell me why you took a planned fall," Wolf growled.

"My, ah, *patron* needed to establish his credentials. We worked up a little scenario where he could, ah, *capture* me. The charge was rather trivial, so my time is about up. I'm due out in three days. Meantime, his record looks good. And I have been paid quite handsomely, quite handsomely indeed, for my time spent locked up."

"What are his credentials?"

"I'll have to wait until he tells you himself."

"Doesn't he trust you?"

"Of course he trusts me. Maybe it's you he doesn't trust," Bates said.

Wolf fixed Bates with a narrow-eyed stare. "We're getting no place. Why are you telling me all this?"

"Because you need us. You need our help so you don't go to Leavenworth for life."

"What makes you think I need you?" Wolf thought of Mahoney and Spears who would spring him with a can opener, if need be. Of course, they were NCOs, and that made the difference. Outside of Al Charles, there was no officer he could rely on for such immediate help. "There's any number of men I could call who would spring me from here in a heartbeat," he said.

"You're joking. You are here under charges legally presented because you scragged someone. You think they would risk their careers—more than that, risk going to jail—to help you get out? No way."

"I could find a way to get out of here and be free," Wolf said.

"Forget that. You'd be a fugitive and a deserter. Somebody would be looking for you all the time. After all, you are a murderer, Colonel Lochert."

0830 Hours Local, Sunday, 9 July 1967
USARV Installation Stockade
Long Binh, Republic of Vietnam

☆

The next morning, on Sunday, Wolf lay stretched out on his sweat-soaked cot. Except for being allowed out a total of 20 minutes a day for exercise and for the latrine, he hadn't been out of his cell nor seen anybody except Bates and the guards. He had refused to shave with the giant seven-inch bar that cleverly held a dull blade such that it could never be used as a weapon. It had been provided along with other toilet articles. He lay, half-dozing in the sweltering heat, day-dreaming of a cool glen bordering a stream he knew in northern Minnesota, his home state. His thoughts wandered. He wondered what his buddies would think, seeing the great Wolf Lochert jammed up in a cell. He thought of Charmaine, the ex-wife of the fighter pilot Court Bannister he had known since Bad Tölz. Charmaine of the green eyes and long legs; Charmaine who had given him smoldering glances and little else when they met in Las Vegas at a week-long party last December thrown by Court's father. He started to doze, but was abruptly roused when the steel door was unlocked and thrown open with an echoing clatter. Lieutenant Hartigan stood there.

"Someone here to see you, a big wheel," he said, and handcuffed him. Hartigan was wearing fatigues with sidearm. He carried a night-stick. From his cot, Bates watched the scene with hooded eyes. He had a small enigmatic smile on his face.

Hartigan led Wolf Lochert out of the cell area into the hallway. He stopped before an unmarked door.

"We'll have to wait in here, *Colonel*," he said loudly, using his customary sarcasm. "Your big-wheel visitor will be along soon."

The room was sparse and set up for interrogation and law-yer/prisoner visits. A two-way mirror was set in a wall. From the other side, victims could see a lineup without being seen, or military police officials could view an interrogation. Two scratched and dented gray steel chairs stood on each side of a battered gray steel table. A large electric clock with a white face hung on one wall. An old air condi-tioner braced in a rectangle cut out of the wall clattered and chugged. Cold air puffed from the broken vents, condensation dripping yellow map outlines on the faded green wall. In a far corner was a humming water cooler. The brackish liquid in its tank denoted water heavily laced with iodine and chlorine. Hartigan winked and shook his head slightly to discourage conversation. The two officers sat without speaking for twenty minutes. At ten o'clock, the door opened.

A slim Army major general entered. He was of medium height, and had a light and sallow complexion. His eyes were light blue and watery. His khakis were pressed knife-sharp. His right collar point held the two stars of his rank, on the left were the crossed pistols of the provost general.

Hartigan jumped to his feet and saluted. "He's all yours, General," he said.

"Thank you, Lieutenant. Take the cuffs off him," the general said, and dismissed him.

"Colonel Lochert, glad to meet you." The general extended his hand. "Please be seated. I'm Major General Joseph Wohler, the Provost General for all of Vietnam. I'm so sorry to meet you under these conditions. I have heard so much about you. You have set a fine record, which none of us can hope to follow." He used a self-deprecating tone. On his left breast he wore ribbons showing he had served in World War II and Korea. There was a DSC, two Silver Stars, and several commendations, along with a Legion of Merit and a Bronze Star.

The general spoke in a soothing voice. "We will attempt to convene a board of court-martial at the earliest possible moment, rest assured. It's easy enough to get a law officer to act as judge, but it is difficult to get a jury, that is, a court of your peers, together all at once. Your little problem in Saigon was, well, rather unwise. I simply cannot understand how you of all people could do such a thing." Provost General Wohler seemed genuinely interested, perhaps even sympathetic.

"Look, General, as far as I'm concerned, I didn't do anything. I was *defending* myself, and no court-martial board will convict me for *that*." Wolf slammed his fist on the table, his face angry, thick black brows drawn together. "And where is my counsel? Why haven't you appointed me a military lawyer? I'm entitled to one. He should have been here long ago. Where is he?" He stood up, working himself into a smoldering rage.

"Take it easy, Colonel," Wohler said. "We're working on that. Most of the young men are quite busy out in the field. Rest assured, we will get you one soon. In the meantime, wouldn't you feel better if you shaved?" The general pulled his lips back in a movement that was more a horizontal rictus stretch than the smile he thought it was. Nor did his eyes crinkle.

"I was *defending* myself. I will be *acquitted.* Then I'm getting *out of the army,*" Lochert bellowed. "And I'm not going to shave until *I get out!*"

"Colonel Lochert, please, relax," Provost General Wohler said, his eyes watching Wolf Lochert closely. "Maybe that's just the way it will work out. Maybe you will be let go. The military criminal justice system in Vietnam is eminently fair and impartial."

"Oh yeah? You can take your 'eminently fair and impartial' *and shove it!*"

"Dod rot it, Lochert, relax, I tell you." The Provost General seemed to make a decision. "Look, I'll make better arrangements for you here. More yard time. Better food. And if you don't like the food here, I can arrange for something to be brought from the Officer's Club. Now what is more fair than that?" Wohler made his rictus stretch at Lochert, then suddenly pulled out his handkerchief and sneezed twice. "Allergy," Wohler mumbled.

"Why are you being so *eminently fair?*" Wolf asked when he was through.

"Because you are a worthy man, Colonel. And I want to help you." He put his handkerchief away.

"Aren't you afraid of conflict of interest or prejudicial conduct before a trial?" Wolf asked.

"No, I don't think so," the general said. "Besides, it may not even go to trial. First there has to be a preliminary hearing. Maybe, if things work well at the hearing, there won't even be a trial."

"What do you mean, 'work well'?" Wolf asked.

"Dod rot it, don't ask so many questions. Let's just say you have friends and let it go for the moment." He stood up. "We will talk about this later. Can't talk you into shaving?" He saw the look on Lochert's face. "No, I guess not." He stuck his head outside the door and called for Hartigan. "No cuffs, more yard time, take him back," he told him. Wohler nodded goodbye and walked down the hall. Hartigan locked Wolf Lochert back into his cell.

Bubba Bates had a strange, almost smug look on his face. "Well?" he said.

"Well what?" Wolf asked.

"How did it go?"

"What do you mean, 'how did it go?' How could it possibly go? He said he would be fair with me. As if the system could possibly be *fair.*" He spit the word out like a piece of bad food.

Bates looked steadily at him. "What if we get you off? Completely off. All charges dismissed."

"How can you do that? After all, I did shoot the guy, even if it was self-defense." Wolf knitted his brows. "What would you do? Produce some witnesses who said I didn't do it? That wouldn't work, because there are too many other people identified who saw me do it."

"We'd do better than that, Colonel, far better. We would produce a man who would say he shot that GI. A man who looks very much like you. Then you would be freed on your own recognizance until the formal hearing which would completely exonerate you. How does that sound?"

Lieutenant Colonel Wolf Lochert stood up and walked to the tiny window. He watched two stockade prisoners watering some wilting potted plants next to the wooden latrine. He spoke without turning.

"Okay," he said, "it sounds good. When do I get out? What do I do?"

"Right now, you do nothing. We'll get you out in a matter of days. Then, at first, you would also do nothing. We will help you make sure you get some obscure job in Saigon so you will have plenty of spare time. You just go around as normal and keep your eyes open and your mouth shut."

"All right, so your people get me out of here," he said. "When can I get out of the Army?"

"You don't get out of the Army. At least not right away," Bubba Bates said.

"Oh, yeah? Just what am I supposed to do? Where do I fit into whatever it is they do?"

"Well, there is one little thing," Bates said.

"What's that?"

"You'll have to prove yourself."

"What do you mean, 'prove myself'? Seems to me you've gone through quite a bit to get me to this point. Now you want me to prove something to you. Prove what?"

"Prove your loyalty."

"How?" Wolf snapped.

"By killing someone for us. You do that for us, Colonel, and we will cut you in on the whole thing. We need a man of your skills and connections as a planner and an enforcer. But you must prove your loyalty."

"That's not proving my loyalty," Wolf said in a disgusted tone. "That's setting me up so you've got a hook into me for life. Nothing doing. No deal." He moved suddenly, reached through the bars and grabbed Bubba Bates by the shirt front and jerked him close.

"*You* prove *your* loyalty. You and your people get me out of here, then we'll talk about what I will or will not do for you." He pushed Bates back, causing him to stumble and fall to the floor.

Bates's face was red. He struggled to his feet. "Lochert, you just dealt yourself out of the best card game in town."

"Bates, I didn't deal myself out of anything. You don't have any say-so. When I get out of here, *I'll* tell you and your boss whether or not *I* want in."

"It doesn't work that way," Bates protested.

"You want me, it's got to work that way."

1715 Hours Local, Friday, 14 July 1967
Randolph Air Force Base
San Antonio, Texas

☆

Captain Toby Parker tapped the steering wheel of his Corvette in time with the strong beat from The Doors' *Light My Fire*. His flight suit was stained with sweat, but he was happy. He had aced an early morning navigation test, and had just landed from the smoothest formation flight he had ever flown. Now he had the whole weekend to be by himself, and maybe go someplace and drink; maybe Corpus Christi.

He wheeled into the lot next to the BOQ, parked near the main entrance, and took the steps two at a time. Quick shower and he'd be on the road. He flung open the main door and started through the lobby. He skidded to a stop and stared at the girl seated on a couch. An overnight kit and garment bag were next to her.

"Hello, Toby," Tiffy Berg said. She was a firm and chunky brunette. She wore light gray slacks and a white blouse. She had a soft smile on her generous lips.

"My God, Tiffy, what are you doing here?" In an instant, memories of her and Vietnam flooded back.

For two hours they sat and talked in the dining room at the Officer's Club. After two cups of coffee, Toby had ordered beer. He finally asked her why she had come. "I didn't think you were interested," he said.

Tiffy covered his hand with her own. "Chet Griggs called me, because he was worried about you. He's so sweet," she said. "He sounded so sincere and so worried I'd take it wrong when he called. Said that although he was no longer your instructor, he was concerned. He said you really needed someone around you that cared. I had some time off due. So here I am, all yours for ten days." She smiled uncertainly.

Toby wasn't exactly leaping for joy. "So, what did he say he was worried about?" he asked in a flat voice.

Tiffy tried to brighten her smile. "Why not pack and we'll take a weekend drive? I'm all packed, so let's just hit the road. It's a lovely time of year to see the Gulf."

"Tiffy, answer my question. What did he say he was worried about?"

She stood up. "Let's talk about it in the car. You get us on the road and I promise to tell you all about it." She shoved his beer away from him.

☆

They made Corpus Christi just after sunset. Toby drove in silence and seemed to be enjoying the trip. They drove with the top down, letting the wind and sun tousle their hair and crisp their faces. He had not repeated his question about why Chet Griggs had called. They took a room with twin beds in the Gulf Ramada, and ate seafood on the dock overlooking the Gulf. When Toby ordered wine, Tiffy said she wanted only iced tea. Later they stopped by a beach bar. Toby drank beer and happily soaked up the raucous atmosphere. They were back at the Ramada by midnight, after an argument over who should drive the car. Tiffy drove, and calmed Toby by saying she had never driven a Corvette before.

"Hell, I don't care. Drive all you want. Enjoy yourself. Makes it easier for me, actually." He took a pull from the beer he had smuggled from the bar.

Once in their second-story room, Tiffy went into the bathroom. Toby splashed scotch into a silver cup from his traveling kit, and slid open the door to the Gulf. Salty humid air rolled in to replace the dry processed air from the vents. He stepped out onto the balcony. The low, oily surf rumbled softly. Toby stood at the rail and tried to clear his mind. He began to feel fuzzy and hazy, and slightly nauseated. He turned back to the room.

Tiffy came out of the bathroom wearing a sheer white chemise, firm breasts jutting. She had a small unsure smile on her face.

"Well, look at you," Toby said. "Here I am ready for the shack ... sack, to sleep, I mean, and look at you, all ready for fun and, and ... wha's the word? Oh yeah, frolic."

Tiffy's smile faded as Toby poured himself a scotch. He took a deep swallow, then stood, hipshot, absently tapping the silver cup against his lower lip. He shook his head.

"It's no use, you know. Sex, I mean. Why don't you just have a drink?" he said.

"Can I have yours?"

"Sure, here." He handed it to her.

"Thanks," she said, sniffed it, made a face, and quickly poured it into the bathroom sink. She returned and sat on a bed.

"Come over here," she said, patting the space next to her.

Toby shook his head. "It's no use. No use. That one time in the Philippines was just that, a one-time thing. I just can't do it. This is all a waste of time." He poured another scotch. "You never did tell me why Chet Griggs called."

"Well, he didn't call me because he was worried about any sexual dysfunctions you might think you have. He called me because you drink too much."

"That pompous ass. Who in hell gave him the right to mess in my life?" He sipped the scotch.

"You know, for a brand new Air Force pilot-to-be, you're really quite dim. He thinks you are a valuable person." She gave him a down-turned smile. "So do I, I think you are very valuable. But you drink too damn much."

"That's not true. I don't drink any more or less than any of the other guys." He waved his scotch cup.

"Toby, it isn't necessarily how much you drink, it's what happens to you when you do. You lose control. Your judgment goes bad. And it happens fast." She beat her fist on her thigh. "You are an alcoholic. When you're drunk, you get all strange. Admit it, why don't you? You get all funny. Do you know what I'm talking about?"

He snorted. "No, I don't. And you don't, either. You don't know what you're talking about." He moved to the chair next to the bed, and spilled his drink as he sat down. He cocked his head and smiled. "Well, maybe a little bit. Okay. So what happens to me? What do you mean, '*all funny*'?"

Tiffy drew her knees up under her and smoothed her chemise. "For one thing, you become morose and sullen."

"Nothing strange about that," he interrupted. "Besides, I didn't tonight."

"Maybe not, but you usually do. You usually start mumbling about Vietnam and Phil Travers and that girl. See, even now you have something of hers." Tiffy pointed to the pieces of jade suspended on a gold chain around Toby's neck.

"Leave that, and her, and everything else out of this. I don't even know what we're talking about." Toby scowled as he spoke. His face reddened. "You want to screw, or what?"

"Oh Toby, you look so angry and pouting. You're such a little boy. Your mood changes so fast. I thought you wanted to know what I meant about your drinking."

"Well, I don't. I changed my mind. I didn't ask you down here, you know."

"I know that. I'm here because, like Chet Griggs, I really like you and want you to be happy. You're quite a guy, but I don't think you know that."

He snorted. "My parents wouldn't quite agree with you. To them 'quite a guy' is someone who runs around Fauquier County, Virginia, in a Cadillac between horse shows and big real estate deals."

"Doesn't the fact that you earned the Air Force Cross, that you're soon to be an Air Force pilot, mean anything to them? My God, what do they expect from you?"

"I already told you. It's a world of Cadillacs and cul-de-sacs, and they want me to be a permanent part of it. Nothing less. Anything outside that world doesn't exist." He took another sip.

She looked at him, her soft brown eyes filled with tenderness. He stared back.

"Ah," he said. "I see more compassion in your eyes than passion. You look like a cocker spaniel that someone just smacked." He waved his drink at her. "What are you, big mamma for all the little broken-wing birds? Yahh, you shouldn't have come to see me. Waste of time. I'm not the guy you should tangle up with." He hunched over.

"Toby, don't be that way." She looked hurt. "Aren't you sleepy yet? Come to bed." She stood and folded the covers back.

"What do you want? Leave me alone." He stood up, weaving from side to side.

Tiffy got up and put her hands on his chest. "Toby, oh Toby. How can I get through to you?"

"You don't need to get through to me 'bout nothin'. I'm telling you, I'm not the guy you think I am. I'm not the guy for you."

She stepped back. "Look, I like you. Maybe I don't love you, but I like you, very much, and I want to help you."

Toby blinked at her, owlishly, trying to focus. His knees locked and unlocked as he struggled to keep his balance. He was fading rapidly.

"You're not getting a word of what I'm saying, are you?" she said. He didn't resist when she helped him out of his clothes and into bed with her. She held him, his head on her breast, until his breathing deepened, then placed him gently on his own pillow. She got up and went out on the balcony for a smoke. She stared at the distant waves without seeing them, her thoughts solidifying.

Berg, you are one dumb bunny. Leave this guy. Leave him now. You are starting to maybe love him? Bad, bad, bad. Get back to L.A. Fly, and date, and fly some more. This is a no-win deal. Get out. She nodded to herself. Do what he says, leave him. If she felt the same way in the morning, she would.

The next day, Saturday, Tiffy Berg flew back to her base at Los Angeles. Late Sunday afternoon, sick and dizzy, Toby checked out of the Ramada. He drove straight to San Antonio, stopping only for a six-pack of beer. On a particularly lonely stretch of the highway, he had the Vette up to 125 mph.

7

1130 Hours Local, Wednesday, 19 July 1967
Oval Office, the White House
Washington, D.C.

☆

The bathroom was larger than one in a deluxe room in a good hotel. Not gold-plated, but not cheap chrome, either. The predominant color was blue. Blue-and-white four-inch Scallezi tiles covered the floor up to the level of the towel racks, which held deep-pile terrycloth towels ranging in size from hand to bath. Double sinks were set side by side in Athenian marble. Kohler Goldflow spigots and single-flow spouts fed each basin. The shower, with sliding glass panels, was outsize. It had four four-inch swiveling heads which could be directed from three sides at the person showering. In the ceiling was mounted an eighth-horsepower exhaust fan between twin rows of inset 48-inch fluorescent lighting tubes. On the wall, within reach of the oversize toilet, was a pushbutton intercom system. Next to the intercom hung a black wall phone with four lighted line buttons and a hold button. The toilet was a dark blue Kohler with a large capacity tank. Between the toilet and the shower was a magazine rack containing the latest *Time, Newsweek,* and *U.S. News & World Report.*

At the sound of a discreet beep, the big man seated on the toilet pressed the intercom button. Dark trousers circled his ankles like leaves gathered at the base of a tree. His bare legs were white and hairless. They looked like two poles sticking up from the leaves.

"Yes, Ethel. What is it?"

"Mr. President," the crisp female voice with barely a hint of a Texas accent intoned, "General Whisenand is here for his ten o'clock appointment."

"Show him in, show him in," the President's voice boomed from the intercom box on Ethel's desk. If the faint echo indicated to her that the President was speaking from the bathroom, she gave no sign. She looked up at the white-haired, rather portly Air Force major general, her face and voice betraying no hint of where her boss might be.

"Right *now*, sir?" she said.

"Yes, goddamn it, right now," the President thundered.

Ethel's face remained expressionless. She had been with LBJ since the Senate, and was more than used to his temperamental excesses.

"You may go in now, General Whisenand," she said, and indicated the Oval Office door to the right of her desk. They were in the corridor anteroom of the West Wing of the White House. She noticed the General carried, as usual, his battered brown leather envelope-style briefcase. The *USAAF* imprint was barely visible on the flap of the Briefcase, Navigational Satchel Type, MB-1, that had been issued to Second Lieutenant Albert G. ("Whitey") Whisenand when he had been a student pilot in the United States Army Air Force at Randolph Army Base, Texas, in the thirties. Though his career started in fighters in the thirties, Whitey had been sidelined to intelligence after a near fatal crash in Korea. He still bore burn scars that made his face look as if he had just removed his oxygen mask after a long flight.

Once a week, Ethel had announced General Whisenand to the Oval Office, where he saw the President in his capacity as the Special Advisor for Air Support on LBJ's National Security Council. It was usually on Tuesday, just before the weekly luncheon where the President and his civilian advisors picked the next targets in North Vietnam to be struck by Air Force and Navy planes in an operation called Rolling Thunder. The general was never invited to the luncheons, not since the incident 18 months ago. The incident had revolved around the answer Whisenand had given to a question posed to him by the President. "Tell me," the President had asked, "how do you like my ability to run an air war?"

When Whitey had finished informing his Commander in Chief just how badly he was wasting American lives and airplanes, sending piecemeal attacks on North Vietnamese supply points, there had been stunned silence among those present, as they waited for the big Texan to explode. Instead, after narrow-eyed reflection, the President had thrown back his head in a big guffaw and said, "Whitey, you old fart, you don't give an inch, do you?"

The President had realized he had on his hands an utterly honest military officer who put integrity over career, who, regardless of what the President *wanted* to hear, would tell the President what he *should* hear. At that point, LBJ had decided to move Major General Albert G. Whisenand from his position in the Pentagon as Director of Operations and Planning Special (Detached) to the Secretary of Defense, to the position of Special Adviser to the President's National Security Council. LBJ had been vague about his new duties. The best Whitey could tell, he was to monitor and advise on the correct application of air power in the Vietnam war. He had not been used much in this capacity. He had become restive and discouraged, and had a faint suspicion he was a patsy, so LBJ could refute those who claimed civilians were running the whole war. He could point to Major General Albert Whisenand, a highly experienced military personage who was advising him.

General Albert G. ("Whitey") Whisenand opened the door and strode into the Oval Office.

"Whitey, come in, come in." The President's cordial voice echoed from behind the partially opened bathroom door.

"Good morning, Mr. President," Whitey said. He walked over to sit in the leftmost leather wing chair in front of the President's desk. He sat with his back to the partially opened bathroom door.

"Open the door, open the door, Whitey," the President said, "so I can see you. We have to talk."

Whitey stood, placed his old briefcase and hard-brimmed blue hat on the credenza to the left of the bathroom door, and pushed it open. He kept his face devoid of expression as he looked at his Commander in Chief, President Lyndon Baines Johnson, who sat on the blue Kohler, black trousers around his feet, white shirt tucked under his armpits, red necktie thrown over his left shoulder so as to not interfere with his duties. The seated man had a broad smile on his face.

Whitey returned to the chair and sat with his back to the President. "I hear you just fine, Mr. President," he said, raising his voice slightly. Whitey was aware of the President's ploy. He liked to assert his maleness and position of power by talking to certain people while seated on the "throne," as he called it in his Texas vernacular. As did King Louis XIVth, Whitey remembered, or was it the XVth, who sat on his large toilet box covered with heavy robes while conferring with members of his court. Undaunted, Whitey waited for the President's reply.

At 56, Whitey was old for a major general. He held his active-duty commission at the sufferance of the United States Congress. They remembered and appreciated him for his great ability as an intelligence officer; he had verified the Russian missiles in Cuba. They knew of his great integrity; he had warned Eisenhower, along with General Matthew Ridgeway, not to involve American forces on the ground with the French at Dien Bien Phu. They appreciated his straightforwardness in warning the DoD and Congress to stay out of Southeast Asia, specifically, Vietnam. Thus, most of the Congress had felt secure when Whitey had been assigned to Secretary of Defense Robert Strange McNamara as Director of Operations and Plans (Detached). His job had been to screen targets for air strikes emanating from the unwieldy chain of command from Vietnam.

Air operations in South Vietnam were directed by COMUS-MACV—Commander, United States Military Assistance Command, Vietnam—who was Army General William Westmoreland. COMUS-MACV directed air operations through Commander, Seventh Air Force, a USAF general. Both commanders and their offices were in the MACV compound on the sprawling Tan Son Nhut Air Base, outside of Saigon.

Unlike those for South Vietnam, air operations in North Vietnam were controlled by Admiral Grant Sharp as CINCPAC through his subordinates, the Commander in Chief Pacific Fleet (CINC-PACFLT), and the Commander in Chief Pacific Air Force (CINC-PACAF). CINCPAC received his targets from the President and his civilian straphangers.

CINCPACFLT relayed the orders to use naval air power to Commander Task Force 77, a flotilla of U.S. Navy carriers and supporting ships off the coast of North Vietnam at a position called Yankee Station.

CINCPACAF relayed his orders to Commander, 7th Air Force, located at Tan Son Nhut Air Base, Republic of Vietnam. This unwieldy dual-chain of command, the lack of a single manager for air power, cost lives and the loss of hundreds of airplanes because of duplication and lack of coordination. In the early years, Navy and Air Force fighters had even struck targets in adjacent areas, because they hadn't known the other would be there at the same time. Incidents such as that had led to the Route Pack system, which divided North Vietnam into seven geographical target areas assigned either to the Air Force or the Navy.

Whitey's task, along with two subordinates, USAF Colonel Ralph Morgan and Navy Captain Jim Tunner, had been to massage the list for targets that would not inflame the public, while inflicting maximum damage on the North Vietnamese Communists. They had immediately found the two specifications to be incompatible. In the long run, however, that made no difference. Regardless of their recommendations, the target list they rank-ordered and submitted to the President was mangled by the Tuesday civilian lunch bunch.

Now Whitey had just returned from his second trip to Vietnam made at the President's direction.

The first had been to determine why so many Air Force and Navy aircraft were being lost over North Vietnam. The answer he had given was simple. The losses were due strictly to the rules of engagement that prevented the Air Force and Navy from taking out the air defense system. They could not attack airfields or SAM (Surface-to-Air Missiles) sites, or destroy MiGs on the ground. Nor could they go after the supplies and SAMs sitting openly on flatcars in the rail yards. They were allowed to evade them the best they could in the air at any time, but even that was often a wash, because the strike scheduling, done by Lyndon Baines Johnson and his Tuesday civilian luncheon group, put the American attack airplanes in the air at predictable times coming from predictable headings.

Whitey had just returned from his second trip two weeks ago. He had been instructed by LBJ to report to him personally why all the American military might, with all its technological advantage, couldn't stop those little fellas from running a few rice bags and some bullets into South Vietnam down that there trail of Ho's.

"All I'm asking for," the President had said, "is some plain old everyday interdiction," pronouncing it "intradiction." "That *intradiction* thing is something you air power guys been telling us for years you can do so well. Look how well it worked in Europe in 1944. Why, ole Hitler couldn't move one boxcar 'cross France to his troops defending the Normandy beach."

"Mr. President," Whitey had responded, "the terrain was level, the countryside friendly, the air defense negligible. The case for the Ho Chi Minh Trail is just the opposite. The terrain is mountainous, the countryside full of the enemy, and the defensive guns massive. Furthermore, the roads in Europe were clearly defined, as were the rail lines. This is not true where the Trail runs through Laos and Cambodia, and on into South Vietnam. It isn't really a trail at all. It is a series of footpaths, oxcart ruts, and sometimes a dirt road not more than eight feet wide. There are hundreds and hundreds of miles of these, running like a twisted cobweb. They are rarely in the open. Mostly, they are under double and triple canopy. With them are switchbacks, cat's eyes, revetted truck parks, storage caves, and about four hundred thousand workers whose only job is to fill in the bomb craters in a road of sand. That, and sweeping up the aluminum of shot-down Air Force and Navy fighters. As primitive as it sounds, Intelligence estimates they can have 200 tons on that road any given day."

Weeks before, Whitey had patiently explained that the tons of matériel run down the supply network that fanned out from North Vietnam through Laos and Cambodia by thousands of trucks protected by hundreds of guns could easily be stopped by cutting them off at the source before they even got close to the Trail.

"You mean bomb Russia and China?" LBJ had all but yelled.

No, Whitey had explained. Just cut the two rail lines that come from China into North Vietnam, and prevent the supply ships from off-loading by such measures as mining the harbors, mainly Haiphong. That would stop the supplies into Vietnam.

"They would soon run out of the matériel to send down the Ho Chi Minh Trail. They would also run out of the antiaircraft-gun ammunition and SAMs they use to down American planes. That," Whitey had concluded, "seems a reasonable and prudent way to bring the North Vietnamese representatives to the negotiation table."

Attending the briefing that day two weeks past had been Secretary of Defense Robert Strange McNamara. McNamara did not much care for Major General Albert G. Whisenand, because the USAF general seemed unimpressed with the Secretary's ways. Black hair combed straight back, razor-eyed, in a crisp monotone, McNamara had told Whitey that what Whitey proposed—and the military proposed, for that matter—was impossible, because it was against the rules of engagement.

That the Rules of Engagement, ROE, as they were called, had taken on a life of their own hadn't occurred to, much less bothered, LBJ or his court. Men like McNamara and his staff members were convinced they knew more than the military. They weren't about to let those war-mongering generals engulf the great United States in World War III. Not one of those civilian men had ever seen combat. Those that had served in the military in WWII, such as McNamara and Johnson, had done so in supply and logistics positions.

The toilet roared. The President walked out, zipping up his trousers.

"I suppose you brought your 'black' board?" he asked. He was referring to the black-edged 8½-by-11-inch poster board containing POW information that Whitey Whisenand always carried.

"Yes, sir," Whitey said. He opened the flap on his ancient briefcase and dug out the acetate-covered poster board that he updated every day with a grease pencil. He carried it to all the briefings and meetings he attended, and made a point of bringing it out whether or not he was a participant, and whether or not such a presentation was appropriate. Whitey knew it was always appropriate to know how many airmen were sacrificing their lives while Washington bureaucrats debated the sanctity of command, or the efficacy of sending messages to Ho Chi Minh via the United States armed forces. No one dared tell him different.

Major General Albert G. Whisenand read the statistics to his Commander in Chief, Lyndon Baines Johnson, President of the United States, in a loud, clear voice.

	MIA/KIA	POW	AIRCRAFT
USAF	358	199	759
USN	197	102	326
USMC	24	11	193
USA	125	45	379 (Helios)
TOTAL	704	357	1657

"Nearly one thousand pilots are gone, Mr. President. And of those airplanes, Mr. President, two hundred sixty-eight are F-105s, one hundred sixty are F-4s, and one hundred forty-three are A-4s."

There was silence for a moment, then the President spoke.

"Goddamn, Whitey, you always sound like the man at the tomb reading the scroll of the dead."

"Mr. President, I feel like the man at the tomb reading the scroll of the dead." He did not tell his boss that because of these losses and his feeling of helplessness, he was a little more into the red wine each night than his beloved wife, Sal, thought wise.

The President walked to his desk and sat down. He put his big head in his hands. He pressed his eyes with his palms, then looked up at Whitey with eyes of infinite sadness.

"You hurt me," he said quietly. "You hurt me more than you know, every time you do that. And I get complaints about you. I get complaints that you do the same thing every damn time you get the chance. You show that damn board around. A thousand pilots. My God." The big Texan stood up to his full 6-foot, 3-inch height. "And you know what I tell those complainers," his voice resounded. "I tell the bastards that if they don't like to hear what's happening to our boys then they got no gawdamn business being in the govmint." He pounded the back of his chair. He was in possession of himself again.

Whitey judged the time right once again to bring up the subject of prisoners of war. "Mr. President," he began, "I believe you should consider plans to send in forces to rescue our prisoners of war. We both know that as long as Ho Chi Minh holds hundreds of our men, he has the upper hand for negotiations. It means nothing to him that we hold thousands of Viet Cong and North Vietnamese prisoners. He does not acknowledge their existence. He knows full well we value the life of each man he holds. Why else would we risk so many lives and airplanes to rescue them when they are shot down? Based on his record of not giving anything away, I urge you to consider and approve large-scale rescue plans."

The President looked out the French doors facing the Rose Garden for a long time before he spoke. "I cannot do it." He turned to face

Whitey. "You don't understand. Sending rescue forces into North Vietnam is the same as an invasion. I know, I just know, there are secret treaties between Russia and Red China to help North Vietnam if I cross a certain line. An invasion would bring Red China and Russia into the war. You don't know how many times I worry, when I pick the targets I let you generals strike up North, that this or that one might be the very one that triggers World War III." The tall man bent over his desk. His eyes flicked back and forth as he pawed among his papers, and he finally seized one.

"I am pursuing another course. Take this," he ordered. "Read it." He handed Whitey a letter on White House stationery. "This is why I called you over. I want your opinion. It's a draft, of course," the President said. "Take a good look, particularly paragraphs six, seven, and eight."

The letter was addressed to His Excellency, Ho Chi Minh, President, Democratic Republic of Vietnam. "Dear Mr. President," it began. After some platitudes about "a just and peaceful" solution, it brought up "direct talks in a secure setting." Whitey studied the paragraphs the President had indicated.

In the past two weeks, I have noticed public statements by representatives of your government suggesting that you would be prepared to enter into direct bilateral talks with representatives of the US Government, provided that we ceased "unconditionally" and permanently our bombing operations against your country and all military actions against it. In the last day, serious and responsible parties have assured us indirectly that this is in fact your proposal.

Let me frankly state that I see two great difficulties with this proposal. In view of your public position, such action on our part would inevitably produce worldwide speculation that discussions were under way and would impair the privacy and security of those discussions. Secondly, there would inevitably be grave concern on our part whether your government would make use of such action by us to improve its military position.

With these problems in mind, I am prepared to move even further toward an ending of hostilities than your government has proposed in either public statements or through private diplomatic channels. I am prepared to order a cessation of bombing against your country and the stopping of further augmentation of US forces in South Vietnam as soon as I am assured that infiltration into South Vietnam by land and by sea has stopped.

These acts of restraint on both sides would, I believe, make it possible for us to conduct serious and private discussions leading toward an early peace.

As to the site of the bilateral discussions I propose, there are several possibilities. We could, for example, have our representatives meet in Moscow where contacts have already occurred.

"Well, what do you think, Whitey? Will the old rascal meet with us? Do you think this is the best way to approach him?" LBJ took a cold Fresca from his small refrigerator and popped it open. Whitey declined an offered can with a wave.

"I have two questions, sir," Whitey said. "You mentioned statements by North Vietnamese public officials. I take it you have not received any formal communication from Ho Chi Minh or a deputy?"

"I have not. What is your second question?" the President asked.

"Based on the fact you have received no official communication from Ho, what makes you think he will even respond to this letter, much less in a favorable way?"

LBJ peered at Whitey over his glasses. His eyes were no longer friendly, his brow was deeply furrowed.

"Dammit, Whitey, why do you insist on putting my feet to the fire?" He picked up his appointment book, pretended to study it, then slammed it on his desk. "I *don't* know if he will answer. I *don't* know if he'll agree. I *do* know I haven't any other good ideas at the moment. I *do* have more pressure from the JCS to hit more targets in North Vietnam." He stood up. "And I *do* have the most pressure from these peacenik hippie people right here in the United States. From these people who want us to put our tail between our legs and run like a whipped cur." He shook his finger at Whitey. "Whisenand, if you've got a better idea, I damn well want to hear it."

Whitey sighed. "Mr. President. My ideas are, as always, either go all the way or get out. I'm sure you are bored with my repeating that."

"No," the President said, "I'm not bored with your line." He pointed outside. "But if I did either option, I could never be their President again. I do have a second term coming up, you know."

8

☆

"Oh, Shawn, Shawn. Oh, honey, oh, you're the greatest ..." They were sweaty and wet, and awkwardly joined. They were in her apartment, code-named House of Venus. She had taken him up to the edge, then down, then up again. Shawn Bannister had never experienced anything like this before, not even in Asia. He had met her, Becky Blinn, just two days before, at the office of the *California Sun.* She had told him she would introduce him to physical and transcendental ectasies, and she was doing just that. She had long fingernails on her thumbs and forefingers, and knew just where to touch and pinch and when to do it. Marijuana smoke hung heavy in the room. The pillows and bed clothing were steeped in the heavy, burnt-rope odor.

Becky Blinn collapsed face down on the mattress, then turned over and thrust her arms up. "Come here, baby, come to mama." She pulled him down to her breasts. He lay there, spent, happier than he had ever known. He felt far, far removed from Las Vegas and money. From this woman he had learned so much, so fast. Maybe now he would have a real purpose to his life.

He was on it, now. On life. He knew he was close to the big secret, the answer, the cosmic revelation of what it was all about. He would know soon ... very soon. He dozed, sated and content.

She reached over, lit a cigarette, and smoked silently, her long black hair tangled over her small breasts, her eyes light gray and wary. She watched the minute hand on the brass alarm clock resting on the dressing table.

After twenty minutes had passed, she woke him. "Okay, baby.

Mama has to go to work. Let's get moving." She massaged the back of his neck. He came around slowly, from a deep slumber, and smiled. His eyes weren't quite focused. She gently pushed him away. He sat up, stretched, and yawned.

"That's a good, good boy," she said. She stood next to him, naked and warm, and kissed him briefly. "Get going now. Call me tomorrow."

He dressed slowly, khaki pants and safari shirt, then put on his Italian shoes over bare feet. When he saw what he had done, he giggled and stuffed his stockings in his pocket. She put on a shift, and gently propelled him out the front door.

Shawn Bannister walked down the flight of stairs from the second floor. The hall was carpeted and quiet. He passed through the foyer of the old Victorian home which had been converted to expensive apartments, two per floor. He blinked in the sun, searched his pockets for his sunglasses, and ambled down to Telegraph Avenue. He felt light and amiable, and friendly. Now he knew he could contribute. Becky had instructed just what to do. Now he could contribute to . . . well, life itself. A better life for everyone on this planet. Yes, that's what it was. He made a mental note to tell his accountant to send them, say, a thou a month.

He didn't notice the two men in the tan 1961 Ford sedan across the street. When he was a block away and out of hearing range, the driver, a fellow with long brown hair tied in a pigtail, pushed twice on the horn ring. Becky Blinn opened the heavy glass door of her apartment building, walked down the steps, and got into the back seat. The driver started the engine. With nimble fingers on the steering wheel, he pulled out into the street, headed in the opposite direction from Shawn.

"Did it work? Have we got him?" the man in the passenger seat asked. He was a slender black man with long frizzy hair and a comb stuck in back. He wore an ornately embroidered dashiki, faded Levi's, and sandals.

"I've got him," Becky Blinn said, "hook, line, and pecker. He'll do anything, say anything, write anything. He's ours."

The man, whose name was Alexander Torpin, laughed. "Becky, love, you are not exactly Ann-Margret. How did you compete with those Vegas showgirls he runs around with?"

"Easy," Becky Blinn said. "I gave him something they can't."

"What's that?"

"Dirty sex, and a cause."

1630 Hours Local, Wednesday, 26 July 1967
Cholon District, Saigon
Republic of Vietnam

☆

Cholon was a city within itself, a Chinese city, located on the south-eastern edge of Saigon. Ninety percent of the inhabitants were ethnic Chinese, the remainder were East Indian, Burmese, and Vietnamese. A contingent of American deserters there was rapidly growing. A combination of things made Cholon a haven for the unsavory: Any quantity or quality of sin and drugs was on sale for modest prices; the area was so dangerous for Vietnamese Quan Canh (QC) and American Military Police (MPs) that a deserter, American or Viet-namese, could hide out forever; and bribes up to 100,000 P were common from males wanting to avoid being drafted into the Viet-namese army.

The man who held this disorderly and notorious ghetto together was the Chief of Police of Precinct Five, Y. Lim. He had paid fifteen million piasters, about 127,000 American dollars, to buy his post. By ruthless control of pimps, drugs, the black market, and visas, he was able to bring in triple that amount each year into his personal coffers.

Lim was a contented man. He kept an armed enclave at his pre-cinct house in the depths of Cholon. There, he maintained his com-mand post for all his activities—legal, illegal, and pleasurable. For pleasure, he kept concubines for his use, and for the use of his fa-vored friends. When he needed to travel, he and his three bodyguards were chauffeured around in one of his three black Mercedes 260Ds. For security purposes, the other two Mercedes were kept moving at the same time in diverse places with shadowy figures that could have been Lim and his guards.

To appease his deep-rooted Chinese sense of family, and because he wanted to perpetuate the family line, he maintained an eighteen-room villa on rue des Trois Fleurs in the exclusive northeastern sec-tion of Saigon. He kept his wife and four children at the villa, along with his mother and two uncles. A staff of nine tended to them. They knew little of his work in Cholon.

But Lim was unhappy. He had a problem: how to move 175 tons of valuable goods. At five tons per truck, he needed fifteen trucks to carry the Portland cement, ten trucks for the corrugated tin, and ten trucks for the GI clothing. Even in these loose times, thirty-five truck-loads of stolen goods was hefty and highly visible booty. These valu-able items had to be moved from the Saigon Harbor docks within two days. Failure to do so would result in their rightful owner, the United States Government, claiming them when the paper trail led some clerk to discover the goods had already been unloaded and were just sitting on the docks. The United States Government had been told by the Saigon Port Authority that the articles were still on some of the 19 ships waiting in the crowded harbor to off-load. When, or if, the mistake was ever discovered, the official involved would merely shrug his shoulders and smile.

The Saigon harbor was a great boon to Lim and his cronies. It was from the rackets he ran there that he had made the money to buy his police chief post in Cholon. Lim and Chung Duc Mai, the vice-director of the Port of Saigon, had an arrangement going. Chung would tip off Lim what vessels and cargoes were the most valuable. The United States, as "guests" in the Republic of Vietnam, had to pay all harbor, docking, demurrage fees, unloading, stevedore, and warehouse fees. At any of these points Chung could hold up the process until he had made the proper arrangements via Lim. He could just about guarantee two-week delivery on any item "ordered" by a customer, ranging from typewriters to ten-ton trucks. One of his lesser-known customers, Israel, happily paid exorbitant prices for 81mm and 4.2-inch mortar shells. Sometimes Chung was able to divert whole shiploads to client countries. By and large, however, their main customers were the Viet Cong and the thousands of black marketeers who were cheerfully selling out their country. They would pass their money to Nguyen Huu Co, an ex-minister of defense who had found it more lucrative to be a banker in Hong Kong. After skimming his fee, Co funnelled the money to their Swiss bank accounts.

Unfortunately, Lim had overdrawn his Hong Kong limit to finance the hijacking of a supply ship. He had gotten the ship, a medium-sized freighter under a Panamanian flag, but lost it to pirates in the Straits of Malacca. Naturally, it was not insured. Lim needed money fast, or he would start losing pieces of his body. It made no difference how big Lim's guard contingent was. The Chinese tongs in Vietnam were controlled from Hong Kong. They were financed well enough to buy or bribe their way into anyone's court. No one reneged on money. Not for 5,000 years had anyone gotten away with such a transgression. Even if revenge cost triple the missing sum, it was extracted—usually in inventive ways involving selected body parts, one piece at a time.

Lim could commandeer only twenty-three trucks with U.S. military markings. He needed twelve more, and he needed them rolling by Friday morning. He had just 48 hours. The trucks must have U.S. markings and proper papers to ensure uninterrupted passage through American and Vietnamese checkpoints. Then they would proceed on their way for delivery to the Viet Cong buyers at Nan Pi near the Cambodian border. Lim sent a message by courier to arrange a meeting with one of his ranking American cohorts.

☆

They met at Lim's villa on rue des Trois Fleurs in a teak-paneled back room Lim kept as an office. The red-tiled villa was hidden behind trees and armed guards.

"How is your allergy?" Lim inquired politely of his guest. He poured tea. "I have some herbs that might subdue the sneezing."

"Dod-rotted fumes. It's the exhaust from the motor scooters." The guest sneezed twice into his handkerchief. "The castor oil mixed with gasoline. My doctor said I should wear a mask." The man was tall, and as thin as a man with a tapeworm. He wore brown slacks and a short-sleeved white shirt open at the neck. His blue eyes were faded and aqueous. His color was bad.

Lim handed him his tea and resumed his seat. He wore a black silk mandarin's robe with fiery red dragons. "My friend, drink this. Tea, true Chinese tea, is the balm of the soul and the body." He leaned forward and patted the man's arm solicitously. "I do hope you are well enough to discuss business."

"It's why I'm here," the man said.

"I'll try not to take too much of your time. First, my gate guards report you were followed here." Lim's voice, while soft, was edged in steel.

"I know that," the man said impatiently. "They are my men."

"In a military police jeep with full markings and pole-mounted machine gun?" Lim raised one thin eyebrow.

"Of course. I am, as you are so well aware, a major general in the United States Army and the provost general for all of Vietnam. It is only natural I should travel with protection."

"This is new," Lim said. "You did not do so in the past."

"There are some people—deserters, drug addicts, common Army criminals—that I pursue who might like to see an accident occur." The general interrupted himself to sneeze twice.

"Might not your men become, ah . . . suspicious when you visit here?" Lim inquired.

"No," the general answered. "They would not. My men are hand-picked. They are reliable, trustworthy, and do not talk. They know I investigate many aspects of crime and fraud within the American forces in Vietnam. It is not unusual for me to appear at various places at various times. They rather like it, in fact, that I am not a deskbound general."

"My congratulations, then, dear friend, on your resourcefulness and caution."

"Thank you, Lim. What is more natural than for me in my position to visit you, a police chief, at your own home?"

Lim nodded, and blinked his turtle eyes. "For which I thank you.

I recognize you came on short notice. There is a problem that requires a man of your contacts to resolve," Lim said. He explained about the twelve trucks he required to move his dockside goods in a mere two days.

"This seems a rather trivial problem in which to involve me," the general said. "We meet here rarely, and then only on matters of policy or cooperation. I prefer meeting you at your precinct. Therefore, I do wonder at this meeting over such a small matter as trucks."

Lim's eyes flickered. "My dear friend, nothing I do is a small matter. I require help, you are here to help me, therefore you will help me. A friend helps a friend, even in small things. If you must know, these goods are part payment to an individual who even now prepares to move west. I owe him. Time is of the essence. What are good friends for? You will be well taken care of, I assure you." Lim paused to pour more tea. When he looked up his eyes were mere slits. "Of course you will not refuse such a simple request. Indeed, you cannot."

The general drew his head back. His sigh was just short of a moan. "No, I cannot. Give me the instructions."

"The trucks must be at the Newport loading area of Pier Fourteen by seven-thirty Friday morning. There must be twelve of them, with current United States Army markings. You must supply drivers."

The general snorted. "I can't do that."

"General, I dislike repeating myself, particularly with such a valuable friend as you, but ..." Lim leaned forward, *"you will supply drivers with those trucks."*

The general nodded slowly. His frown was thin and prominent. Lim would get what he demanded.

"More tea, dear friend?" Lim asked in a solicitous tone.

"No, dod-rot it, no." The general stood up. Lim escorted him to the door.

"One last thing, dear friend," the Chinese said. "Neither the trucks or the drivers will ever be seen again."

1430 Hours Local, Thursday, 27 July 1967
Camp Goodman, Saigon Military Command
Republic of Vietnam

☆

"I told you we could get you out as quick as we wanted," said the black-haired Caucasian driving a Mercedes convertible.

"Bates, I admit I'm impressed. Where are we going?" Wolf Lochert had exchanged his prison clothes for jeans and a denim work shirt.

His beard was now quite heavy. It was deep black, flecked with gray. It gave him a wise simian look.

Bubba Bates was driving his new Mercedes 250 convertible down Highway One from Long Binh to Saigon. The top, crisscrossed with silver duct tape, was up. He had been so very pleased to take delivery of his $22,000 car, but quickly became so very disappointed to find that every time he drove with the top down, people threw things into it. Old garbage, dirt, rocks, dead animals, once he found a horribly decomposed dog. The first time he had parked with the top down, two people had sat on the door ledges and shit in it. If he parked it with the top up, people slit the canvas. Top up or down, people ran knives and keys along the side, deeply scoring the paint. He had concluded, correctly, that new Mercedes convertibles were not *de rigueur* in Saigon, or anywhere in Vietnam for that matter.

"I wish I had my old 240D sedan back," Bates said.

"Where are we going, Bates?" Wolf rasped.

"Like I said, it's an emergency. I don't know what the problem is. All I know is what you must get for us."

"Well then, tell me. You acted mighty mysterious. You said you wouldn't talk until we were in the car. We're in it. Talk."

"Ah Wolf, we need . . ."

Wolf swung his head left to stare at Bubba. His lip curled when he spoke. "Bates, you don't call me Wolf. I'm Mister Lochert to you."

Bubba Bates ground his teeth. "You're not making it easy for yourself."

"This isn't exactly along the lines of the 'obscure job' you talked about. So shut up and tell me what you want with me," Wolf commanded.

"How can I shut up and still tell . . ."

"Bates, you're a *scheiskopf*." Wolf Lochert had to keep Bates off-balance. He didn't want him to question too closely how he had managed to clear the stockade so quickly on just a verbal request from the Provost General. Particularly, he didn't want Bates and his people to know that he was now wearing his Mauser 7.63 and ankle holster, thanks to a surreptitious move by Lieutenant Patrick A. Hartigan as he had picked up his personal gear.

"Here it is then, *Mister* Lochert. You must get us twelve two-and-a-half-ton Army trucks and twelve drivers."

Wolf Lochert interrupted with a barking laugh. "You're nuts," he said. "Why not ask for an aircraft carrier while you're at it?"

Bates ground his teeth again. "And they must be at the Newport Army Docks by dawn tomorrow," he concluded in a rush.

"You're nuts," Wolf Lochert repeated, his mind already working on the problem. He was intrigued both by the enormity of the challenge and about whatever the reason for the request might be. This might be a way to wrap this case up in a hurry and get back to what he did best—jungle fighting. He looked at his watch. Nearly fifteen hundred. Got to move fast, he said to himself. He nodded at Bates.

"So you need a specialist, and I'm it. Sure you don't want me to prove myself first? Kill somebody? You, for example?" Wolf was clearly enjoying himself.

"Please, Colonel Lochert, do . . ."

"Bates, you aren't even authorized to call me Colonel. Now shut up, and take me to Camp Goodman," he snapped. "Let me off a block away. I don't want anybody to associate me with this kraut atrocity."

Twenty minutes later, Wolf showed his ID and was admitted to Camp Goodman on Hai Ba Truong near Tan Son Nhut Air Base. He walked quickly past the stately three-story French-built buildings shaded by towering trees. Deep red flames offset the cool green plants. The lawns and drives were immaculate. Behind the main buildings was the home for the labor force that kept Camp Goodman, and a few high-ranking officers' villas, spotless and manicured.

Wolf entered the prison that kept the fifty or so Nung soldiers. They had committed crimes in the service of the Special Forces that didn't quite require tiger cages on Con Son Island, or death. They were trustees and, as such, available for menial outside labor for those who knew how to tap the system. Wolf Lochert knew.

"My God, it's Wolf Lochert," SFC John Bertucci, the Non-Commissioned Officer in Charge (NCOIC), cried.

"Watch your language, *scheiskopf*," Wolf replied.

"Sure, Wolf. I mean, Colonel." He took a look at Wolf. "At least, I think it's you. A beard? You look awful." He brought Wolf into his office, air-conditioned and plush, and handed him a soda from his refrigerator. Bertucci was dressed in neatly pressed and starched fatigues. He had a Combat Infantryman Badge and jump wings over his left pocket. He also had a left leg that was so defective he could barely walk. He had walked eleven months of point for a platoon of the 173rd until he had triggered a mine. A grateful commander, an old friend of Wolf's, had asked for help. Wolf had arranged to hide him administratively at Camp Goodman so he wouldn't be processed out of the Army, medically or otherwise, until he was good and ready to go. Once in a great while, things like this could be done.

"Damn, Colonel, good to see you," Bertucci said. He smiled. "I know you want something. You don't pay social calls. Got any more of those homemade VC flags to trade?" Wolf's Nungs used to turn out by the dozens fake VC flags stained with chicken blood.

"Not a one, Bertucci. You're right, I need something. I need something bad, and I need it quick. Can't pay you now. I'll catch you someday."

"I'm intrigued. Can't figure out how I can help you, though. Forget pay."

"I need twelve truck-driving Nungs this afternoon for a couple days," Wolf Lochert said, as nonchalantly as if asking for a loaf of bread.

"Christ, Colonel . . . oops, sorry," he said when Wolf glared. "That's half my jail."

"You loan more than that many out to police up various villas around town and you know it. And they gotta speak English."

"Yeah, but that's legitimate Army litter control. You want . . . " He stopped, as Wolf pulled an eye down with his middle finger.

"Okay. Say, you still in the Army?" Bertucci said, eying Wolf's beard. It just dawned on Bertucci that Wolf's status might be altered. "I heard something about you wasting a guy in front of the Butterfly. That true?"

"Does it matter, Bert?"

Bertucci thought for a moment. "No, I guess not." He got up slowly and with obvious pain. "Let's go look at the crop."

Wolf and Bertucci faced forty-two Nungs standing at attention in ranks. "At ease," Wolf called in English. All the Nungs slouched. They wore ragtag mixtures of uniforms; tiger jackets, fatigue pants cut-offs, black slacks, T-shirts. Several wore the red, white, and blue Third Corps Mike Force scarf. Some had missing limbs. Two wore eye patches.

"Everybody knows what 'at ease' means," Wolf said. "Now let's get complicated. Let's find out who really speaks English," He raised his voice and spoke very slowly. "I will give a carton of Salems to every man who raises the correct foot to push in a truck clutch."

Four men, hesitating and looking about, raised their left foot a few inches off the ground. There was some rapid-fire Nung-talk, then three more raised their left foot. Wolf spotted the man talking rapid-fire Chinese. He was one of the men with the Mike Force scarf. His left arm was missing below the elbow, and his left foot was firmly planted on the ground. He looked about and spoke again, in a commanding voice both guttural and singsong. Two more men slowly raised their left foot, a look of fear on their faces.

Wolf counted nine Nungs standing wobbly-footed and fearful. He looked carefully at the one-armed Nung that had been calling out what were obviously instructions, and strode in quick steps to stand in front of him.

"Vong Man Quay," he said in disbelief to the leathery little man. "You're Vong Man Quay."

"Sure, Thieu Ta Wolf. I Vong Man Quay, sure. You wait. I get more people for you. You want drivers, neh? I get you drivers." Vong Man Quay turned, looked with a gimlet eye at the shirkers. He selected three and slapped them. Immediately, every man in the platoon raised their left foot. Vong Man Quay snapped and rattled out some words that caused twelve foot-raisers to dash to the front and stand at attention in a ragged semblance of a military formation. Vong Man Quay slowly strode to their fore, made a perfect about-face, and saluted Wolf.

"Cam-pan all pree-zant, sar," he said.

"Can't believe you're still alive," Wolf said to his old friend. "Why are you here?"

"I kill one too much. No talk of it, please."

Nodding, Wolf changed the subject.

Wolf and Vong Man Quay squatted in the shade of a palm tree. "I'll pay a carton of Salems and a quart of cognac to every man who drives for me," Wolf said.

"I get halb the Salem and co-nack, Thieu Ta. Hab," Vong Man Quay replied.

"Okay, Quay. You'll get 'hab.' But not until the job is over."

"I truss Thieu Ta Wolf," Vong Man Quay said. He gave Wolf his best, and toothless, smile. Wolf clapped him on the back. "Settle your men, down, Quay. I got to talk to the *trung si*." He walked into the building.

"Okay, Bert, here's what I need now," he said to Bertucci in his office. He looked at his watch. "By midnight, anyhow." Wolf quickly wrote on a sheet from his green field notebook and handed it to the sergeant. Bertucci studied it for several minutes before he spoke.

"Thirteen international drivers' licenses ... ho, ho." Bertucci squinted at each entry. "Enough black paint to cover twelve deuce-and-a-halfs ... ho, ho, and ho. Current nine-digit CORDS ICEX bumper numbers ... ho, and hah hah. And white paint for bumper ID. Gosh, Wolf. We're fresh out of white paint. You want I should maybe throw in the Brooklyn Bridge?"

"Who's got the Motor Pool these days?" Wolf asked, ignoring Bertucci's attempted sarcasm.

"You want that, *too*?" Bertucci asked in mock alarm.

Wolf stared.

"You have a compelling way about you," Bertucci said. He made a wry smile. "Santarelli has it and he owes me a bunch."

"Then tell him to get the paint and spray guns ready. We'll have the trucks here just after dark. You call your buddies at the ID section and arrange for the drivers' licenses." Wolf Lochert got up. "Oh yeah, one more thing. Get Santarelli to rustle up something big enough to drive me and the troops to the PX and commissary compound at Cholon. Have it here in an hour. And have him send over some spare steering wheels, distributor caps, and bolt cutters. Meanwhile, I got to teach these guys how to hot-wire an M35 deuce-and-a-half."

At any given time, more than two hundred Americans, Koreans, Filipinos, Thais, Aussies, troop entertainers, and selected Vietnamese shopped the huge PX and commissary facilities just outside Cholon. Country-wide, yearly grosses were in the billions. An estimated $75 million a year was stolen Vietnam-wide by the over 5,000 Vietnamese, Korean, and Filipino clerks and managers. No one did anything about it. "We are guests in their country," said MACV, when quizzed about the terrible losses that no civilian company would permit.

Wolf drove the motor-pool truck into the Cholon commissary compound. Quay sat up front with him. The other Nungs were under the canvas cover in back. He slowly toured the giant parking lot, crawling along in low gear. At selected points he nodded to Quay, who barked a command through the rear opening. A Nung would drop off and start wiping down a truck with a rag, as if paid for the service while the owner was inside. In one pass they found ten deuces and three Dodge D500 stake-beds. They used their spare steering wheels and distributor caps where necessary. In minutes, the trucks were started and moving out.

One Nung nearly jumped out of his skin. He was in a cab upside down under the dash, when he heard and felt movement from the rear. He stayed motionless upside down for seven agonizing minutes while a GI finished screwing a practiced round-heeled, scrip-taking truck-hopper from the Armed Forces Exchange Service shipping department.

By nightfall, nine irate truck owners were complaining to the Saigon Military Police about their missing vehicles. The other four drivers let the theft go unreported. Three had stolen the trucks in question, one was a deserter. Wolf gave the extra heisted truck to Bertucci as part payment of his debt.

Wolf and Vong Man Quay kept the Nungs in the Camp Goodman Motor Pool to help paint the trucks. Even at a turnaround of twenty-five minutes, the spray jobs weren't going to be completed by dawn. To meet the deadline, they parceled out brooms and rags, and buckets of black and olive-drab paint. They did not, however, skimp in either time or paint when stenciling the bumpers, fore and aft, with the indispensable nine-digit CORDS ICEX numbers.

The Civil Operations and Revolutionary Development Support (CORDS) program deployed civil/military teams throughout Vietnam to neutralize VC infrastructure. CORDS had combined with

CIA's ICEX (Intelligence Coordination and Exploitation) program to really pile it on. There was so much classification and spook work involved, the members ran around with "get out of jail free" cards, special ID, and equipment authorizations that almost rivaled, but not quite, the black market. Their nine-digit CORDS ICEX numbers were a known and common sight on vehicles that were not to be trifled with at MP posts or barriers. Wolf had to have them on his trucks.

Toward dawn, Wolf had some private words with Vong Man Quay, causing discreet modifications to be made to each truck as they were parked in the darkness. Wolf had also made certain Bubba Bates stayed in the motor pool and worked.

0720 HOURS LOCAL, FRIDAY, 28 JULY 1967
NEWPORT ARMY FACILITIES
SAIGON RIVER PORT
REPUBLIC OF VIETNAM

☆

At exactly 0720, the caravan of trucks lead by Wolf Lochert and Vong Man Quay in a Dodge stake-job were in position at the waterfront to on-load their cargo. Bates had followed in his Mercedes. It took each truck twenty minutes to be filled at one of the three loading docks. By 0900 hours, Wolf's contingent was ready to roll. He waited for the other trucks to be loaded. Wolf had purposely beat them to the site.

Wolf never let Bates out of his sight. Both men were splattered with paint and frazzled from being up all night. With Quay, they squatted in the shade of the Dodge and watched the loading.

"Where do we go?" Wolf asked Bates.

"I don't know. We're just supposed to deliver the loaded trucks and drivers. That's all."

"That's all?" Wolf rasped. "Nothing doing. These are *my* trucks and *my* men. I don't just turn them over and walk away. Who's running this show?" Vong Man Quay's head snapped back and forth as he watched the two men talk. He was not smiling.

"I can't tell you," Bates said. He looked nervously around as Wolf nodded at Quay. The two men pulled Bates to his feet and backed him up to the side of the truck. Quay pulled a pair of eight-inch vice-grips from his pocket with his one good hand. He tucked them under his stump, and grabbed Bates by his belt.

"That's a Nung nutcracker, Bates. Quay just loves to use it. He's kind of sloppy, though, what with only having one arm." Bates's eyes bulged as sweat popped out on his forehead. He started to stammer.

"Slow down, Bates. Just take it slow and easy. Start with who your patron is, and how he's tied to these trucks and stolen goods."

"My God, they'll kill me," Bates stammered.

"Maybe so, but that's later. We'll do it right now, right here, slowly. Nobody around here is going to see anything," Wolf sneered. Vong Man Quay caressed Bates's belt.

Bates swallowed. "There's a Chinaman," he began.

"Names, Bates, names," Wolf interrupted. Quay glared.

"Lim. His name is Y. Lim," Bates squeaked.

"Positions, Bates, positions," Wolf interrupted again.

Bates swallowed. "Oh, God, he'll kill me. I can't, I can't."

Wolf nodded to Quay, who took a shop knife from inside his shirt and sliced Bates's belt.

"Okay, okay. Jesus," Bates screeched.

"And don't swear, *scheiskopf*," Wolf said.

"He's the Chief of the Precinct Five Police in Cholon. I think this convoy is going west to Route One, to, ah, the Cambodian border," he said in a rush.

"How you going to get through the American and VC checkpoints?" Wolf asked.

"Lim arranges it with the VC, and his American partner arranges things with the Army," Bates said. He mopped the sweat on his brow.

"American partner? I want names and positions. I won't tell you again," Wolf said.

"I think Lim is tied in."

"Think?" Wolf said.

"He is tied in with General Joseph Wohler, the Provost General for Vietnam. That's his partner." Bates licked his lips. "Why do you want to know all this? You're not going to tell anybody, are you?"

"Bates," Wolf Lochert said with heavy disdain, "I don't do anything, go anyplace, or get anything without knowing who, why, and how much. Now you tell me exactly where this convoy is going or I'll let Quay here see how high he can make you jump and flap your arms." He had known the Provost General was deep in the cabal, but he needed a direct and provable link.

"I swear, I don't know. I don't know. Out Route One, that's all I know," Bates said. He was wringing with sweat; fear contorted his face into a grotesque mask. "I don't know where else," he moaned.

Wolf peered into his eyes. "I guess you don't," he said. Bates sagged in relief. Wolf looked around.

"Quay," he said, "take two men, find the convoy leader of this mess. Persuade him to tell you where he is going and anything else he knows about this."

In five minutes, Quay was back. "He not know. He start west on Route One. Jeep meet him at city edge with RFPF license plate. He tell where convoy go. I believe him." Quay showed his toothless mouth. "But that man, he say not to touch him. He hab powerful,

powerful friend. Mister Y. Lim has powerful friend who fix all things. Mister Y. Lim, yes."

Lim has a friend, all right, Wolf thought. The Provost General of all Vietnam. That's about as high as you can go. He spoke to Quay.

"Tell your men to fall in line and go with the convoy. But tell them to fake engine trouble, tire trouble, whatever they can come up with so they don't pass Cu Chi by 1700 this afternoon. Go with them, make sure they do what I say." Quay bared his gums, and joined his men.

Wolf watched the convoy get under way, engines roaring, black diesel smoke gushing from the stacks. All the time, his mind was debating the next action he should take. Just like combat, he said to himself. Be bold and act; carry the fight to the enemy.

He drove back to Camp Goodman in the stake-job and gave it to Bertucci in return for a jeep. Then he drove to his quarters to shave and put on a fresh uniform. After that, he drove to the small PX near the Freedom Pool, bought a pair of small brigadier general stars, and pinned them to his collar. On his chest he wore a name tag, "Smith," that he had lifted from a floor mannequin. He wore no other decorations or badges. When he walked past the American military policemen at the villa gates of the Provost General, they popped to and saluted with a great snap and crackle. No one questioned his identification or authority to be there.

Once in the villa he brushed past the protestations of the *thi-ba,* the number one housemaid, as he searched for the provost general's private office. He found it on the second floor, forced the lock, and entered. He figured he had about ten minutes before the *thi-ba* would rouse somebody to get serious and investigate his presence.

The paneled room was hot. He switched on the overhead fan, then took a thin metal bar from inside his waistband and forced the locks on each of the two four-drawer legal-sized filing cabinets. He wasn't sure what he was looking for exactly, but knew he would know when he found the one piece of admissible evidence tying the general and Lim together.

I suppose, he thought, we should let "due process," with all its warrants and red tape, handle this. He grimaced at the thought. That was not the Wolf's style. He had been given the task to infiltrate the smuggling ring. He had not been given any particular instructions how to go about it. No one had said he couldn't break the case himself, probably because no one dreamed he could.

He found nothing in the files or taped under a drawer. He went to the big teak minister's table the General used for a desk. A black Tiger Switch military phone rested on one end. The wide center drawer was unlocked. It contained nothing of interest, nor was anything taped under it, or to the table itself. Wolf began to pull the books down from the shelves that lined two walls of the room. They tumbled like fluttering birds, but revealed nothing. Nor was there anything behind the large map of Vietnam he jerked from the wall. He stopped for a moment, sweating in the close air, lowered his head and looked at the thick Oriental rug on the floor. He followed it around the room. It was a 12 x 16 hand-knotted Kashan and in one corner, behind a chair, there was a faint crease. Wolf moved the heavy chair, knelt, flipped the rug back, and studied the exposed floorboard. He saw faint scratches at one end, took out his penknife, pried up the board, and lifted out a thin white envelope. He straightened up when he heard the click behind him. The envelope was still in his hand.

"I can shoot you right now as an intruder," Major General Joseph Wohler said. He held a .45-caliber service automatic in his hand, pointed steadily at Lochert's chest. One slug from that weapon would slam him against the wall. As it exited, it would make a hole the size of a grapefruit in his back.

"But you haven't," Wolf said. "That means you want to know something." He didn't raise his hands. He held the envelope in plain view.

"Give me the envelope," the General said.

"No, I won't," Wolf said. "Go ahead and shoot if you want it so bad." He was gambling that the General didn't want to have to explain a shot in his house and that, in any case, the General needed some information before he needed Wolf dead.

The General raised the heavy gun. He aimed it directly into Wolf's face. "Give me the envelope," he said, in a voice so strained his jaw quivered. His eyes flicked down to the envelope Wolf held. He spoke again in a monotone. "Why did you come here? Why?" He looked at Wolf through distraught eyes. "No matter, I am going to kill you. I have to, now. Not here, though. No, not here." His forehead was knotted and lined.

Wolf recognized the facade of a man who had lost control. He knew now the general had passed the point of no return. He would kill for the envelope, regardless of the consequences.

"Yes, sir, General Wohler," Wolf said in obsequious tones. He started to walk toward him as if to hand over the envelope.

"Put it on the table, and back off," the general said, waving his .45 at the minister's table.

Wolf eased sideways to the table, never taking his eyes from those of the other man. He flipped the envelope onto the top of the table in such a way that it slid off the edge at the General's end. As Wohler stepped sideways and knelt to pick it up, Wolf slammed the table into him and rushed him. As soon as he reached the struggling man, he pushed on the muzzle of the .45, activating the mechanism that prevented it from firing. He followed up by grabbing the gun with his other hand and twisting it from the general's fingers, at the same time throwing him over his hip to the floor. Wolf pushed the man flat on the floor and knelt on his chest while he searched him. His chest was bony and fleshless. There were no other weapons. His struggles and twisting seemed strangely weak to Wolf.

"Oh no, oh dod-rot it," the General moaned in a voice that was so thin it sounded like a small child. "Oh, oh, oh . . ."

He raised his head and looked about until he saw the envelope. He made a frantic lunge that almost unseated Wolf. Wolf backhanded him, grabbed the envelope and, keeping the gun leveled at the general, stood up and sat on the edge of the desk.

A thin trickle of blood started at the corner of Wohler's mouth. He tried to hold his face of ruined anguish steady. He blotted his mouth with a silk handkerchief, and looked at Wolf. Then, as if he had put on a whole new personality, his face assumed authority and his eyes cleared and focused on Wolf.

"I don't know how you got in here. I don't know who you work for. I don't know what you want. But I must ask you, as one officer to another," the general regained some timbre in his voice. "As one officer to another, I implore you to give me that envelope. There is nothing in there of any importance to you," he continued. "Nothing." He eyed the stars on Wolf's collar. "If you are a general officer, you will give me the envelope."

Wolf tucked the general's automatic into his belt behind his back. He pulled the star from his collar and dropped it into his pocket. As he started to thumb open the envelope, the General rushed him, all authority and composure gone. Wolf easily held him off and pushed him into his chair behind the desk. His earlier search had revealed no hidden weapons there. The general's face was ashen. He slowly lowered his head to his arms. "Burn it," he croaked.

Wolf stared at the clear and focused pictures from the envelope. "Aghh," he choked in disgust. He couldn't bear to look further at the image of the naked man and two children. There was a piece of paper, a note in perfect script written on thin rice paper.

"More pleasure of even greater tender succulence await you anytime," it said. There was a Chinese chop impressed with red ink on the bottom.

The General slowly raised his head and turned his back to Wolf to stare out the window.

"You are a man of honor. Burn those." His voice thinned. "They . . . they made them available," he whined. "Then they took pictures. I didn't know . . . if I had known . . ." His voice became firm again. "I will sign any statement you desire, just so you burn those . . . now."

"Burn them?" the Wolf said. "Nothing doing. There are GIs who are dead because of you. There are GIs who are dead and mangled because you took ammo and military equipment to sell to the enemy. You're going to face every bit of this." He waved the envelope.

"I never received any money, I swear to you. Check my books, my bank accounts." His voice was becoming high-pitched and frantic. "I didn't do it for money."

Lochert snorted. "It would have been better if you had," he said, "Better than *this*. I won't take a statement. You would claim duress." Wolf's voice was harsh with loathing. "Oh, no, I'm turning these in, and you are going to spend the rest of your life in Leavenworth where everyone will know about you and how you like little boys."

"Ahh, ahhh, no, noooo," Wohler moaned. His voice trailed off. He raised his head, then jerked and sat upright. He spun around in his chair, more alert and alive than Wolf had thought him capable.

"Colonel Lochert," he said in a deep and commanding voice only slightly tinged with madness. "You must look at what is best for the service. These are times when the reporters and the film crews are out to destroy the United States Army. One suspicion of this, and irreparable harm will be done to us."

"Not 'us,' filth, you're not one of 'us.' Not anymore," Wolf spat out the words.

The General continued as if he hadn't heard, his eyes once again clear and focused. "Therefore it behooves us to act in a prudent way such as to minimize the hurt upon the innocent. There is, after all, the Army to consider. We must do some damage control." He paused. His voice thinned once more. "I do have a . . . a wife. She's from an old and respected military family." His jaw quivered only slightly. He stood up, proud and tall, remembering parades and snapping flags from his past. He spoke again, his voice clear.

"Remove the magazine from my weapon. Give me one cartridge," he commanded. "Wipe your fingerprints from it, then give it to me. I will give you five minutes to go down the stairs to start a conversation with one of the guards to prove you are blameless. You are a man of honor. Later you will burn those pictures."

"Who has the originals?" Wolf asked.

"Y. Lim, chief of the Fifth Precinct Police in Cholon."

"Do you have solid evidence that will hold up in a trial implicating him in smuggling, dope running, black marketeering, anything?"

"I do not. I tried to collect proof. He knew I would try to counter . . . what he has on me. I found nothing. Even the meetings between a Vietnamese police chief and an American provost general would be viewed as normal."

Wolf Lochert studied the man. "It doesn't matter," he said. He hesitated barely a second, then took a cloth from a chair and began to wipe down the General's .45. He removed the magazine and performed several one-handed cocks to clear the chamber and snapped the trigger each time. "Do you know where the convoy is headed?" he asked.

"I think out Route One to Nam Pi." The general spoke in a professional voice, as if he were head of an investigating team.

"Pick up the phone," Wolf ordered. "Call the CID. Identify yourself. Tell them the entire convoy is loaded with stolen military supplies and must be intercepted. Tell them all trucks with nine-digit CORDS numbers are driven by friendlies. Tell them those friendly trucks also have an X painted on top." He waited while General Wohler made the call the way he wanted.

"I'm not going to talk to any of your men," Wolf said. "I don't want them to see me. I'm going out the back way. Call them up here on any pretext. Say you want to tell them goodbye. Then dismiss them. As soon as they are out the door, use this." He handed him the .45 still wrapped in the cloth. He removed all the cartridges from the magazine of the big automatic and put them in his pocket with the photos. He removed his military shirt, rolled it, and tied it around his waist. "Use that weapon or I'll use these." He slapped the photos. He moved toward the door, stopped, and flipped the general one cartridge. "Use it and I'll burn these, and the others," he promised. He slipped out the door.

Three days later, Wolf Lochert sat in Al Charles's office at MACSOG. He wore clean fatigues and was freshly shaven. Each man was silently reading that day's edition of *The Pacific Stars and Stripes.*

USARV PROVOST GENERAL FOUND DEAD

Saigon—Major General Joseph Wohler was found dead in his quarters before noon on the 28th of July. Preliminary investigation states death occurred due to a gunshot wound, apparently self-inflicted.

CHOLON PRECINCT CHIEF SLAIN

Cholon—Y. Lim, chief of the Fifth Precinct police in Cholon, was found shot to death along with two bodyguards in his Mercedes. The car was then burned. Although there were passersby, no one saw the attack.

STOLEN CONVOY RECOVERED

Saigon—Helicopter-borne U.S. Military Police, apparently acting on a tip-off, intercepted at Cu Chi a 35-truck convoy consisting entirely of stolen goods, headed west on Highway 1. State Department officials claim there

> was a misunderstanding, that the convoy had merely been misdirected due to faulty paperwork. When quizzed by journalists why American goods were not unloaded by Americans and placed in American trucks driven by Americans to American-guarded warehouses, State Department officials said that such a procedure would ". . . be insulting to our host country. We are, after all, guests here." When the official was told it was reported that large white Xs had been painted on the canvas tops of the trucks, he appeared flustered and had no comment.

Wolf threw his paper to the floor. "How could you accept such an assignment, Al?" he asked. "Since when are we an arm of the CID?"

"You know in our charter, that sixth directive that says 'conduct other operations as necessary to disrupt enemy plans'?"

Wolf's eyes narrowed. "You mean what I think you mean?" He grasped the armrests of his chair as if he were going to spring over the desk at the throat of Al Charles.

Al Charles's black face broke into a wide grin. "I do indeed. Yes sir, I do indeed. Listen up, Wolf. Too many of our guys are getting greased by our own equipment funnelling through that miserable bastard's hands. Busting that outfit up is disrupting enemy plans, don't you think? Not to mention ridding our Army of a real traitor."

Wolf laughed back in his throat like a large animal grunting in a sepulcher. "You're one devious guy, you know that, Charles? One devious guy."

Charles barked back at Wolf Lochert. "You should talk. You the one who had half the MP corps convinced you really killed that guy on Tu Do Street, and the other half believing you hated the Army."

"How about Hartigan? What does he believe?" Wolf asked.

Al Charles laughed. "He believes you're the greatest thing since J. Edgar Hoover."

9

☆

Late summer in Hanoi is particularly uncomfortable. The southwest monsoon season is at its most humid. Daily rain, followed by bright sunlight streaming between towering cumulus, sends steamy vapor rising from the streets throughout the city. *Pod-Palcovnik* Vladimir Nicholaevych Chernov waited in the shade of the giant willow tree in the courtyard of the Soviet Embassy in Hanoi. He wore dark trousers and a gray shirt with rolled-up sleeves. A light blue scarf was knotted at his neck. Major Toon, still his prize pupil, with six victories now (three of which belonged to Chernov), was to pick him up for a visit to the Hoa Lo prison, where many of the captured American pilots were being held. Another advisor, at least Chernov thought him an advisor, a Cuban, was to meet them at Hoa Lo. The Cuban had promised to conduct what he told Chernov would be a "most informative" tour. Chernov had never met the Cuban, Ceballos, and was sure he would not like the prison tour. Seeing pilots in captivity was not his idea of a pleasant way to spend his time. Yet he felt he had no choice. Part of his job was to know every aspect of the lives of American pilots.

Chernov looked at his watch. It was just after five in the steamy afternoon. He glanced up as two MiG-21s on a training flight streaked overhead beneath a sky rapidly darkening and filling with clouds. It was quite safe. The Americans never attacked after three o'clock in the afternoon. Certainly not when the cloud cover was complete, as was about to occur. Chernov shook his head. The number two MiG was not flying in good formation. Obviously he had not been trained at Lugovaya or Fruenze. He remembered from the schedule he had set up that morning—the man was weak to begin with. Yet most of the North Vietnamese students had been surprisingly good, and thoroughly inclined to accept and follow the Russian way of total central control.

Very good, Chernov thought, but real fighter pilots preferred *voz-dusny boy*, a tooth-and-fang air battle, not these ground-controlled shoot-and-run tactics. How are we to extract our revenge for the Bolo fiasco if we cannot innovate? The Americans can innovate, why can't we?

Still, we are having some success here, he mused. Most of his students weren't quite ready yet to meet the Americans in combat, but soon they would be. He was teaching them to maneuver in the *po-lupetlya* as well as the *viraz*; the vertical as well as the horizontal.

Chernov had studied American tactics long and hard at Kharkov, and later, when he had been assigned to a fighter squadron. His foreign language assignment (no one had any choice) had always been English. He could easily read American and British aviation journals and pilots' handbooks. He even had several copies of the *Fighter Weapons Newsletter* from the American fighter training base Nellis in Nevada. They were not classified and easy to obtain. Air base Nellis was located just northeast of Las Vegas, where all the women and whiskey and gambling in the world were centered, he mused. Must be the only way to keep the decadent sons of the ruling class in hand. It wasn't that way with him. He was patriotic. He loved the *rodina*, Mother Russia. And he loved flying. He just had no time for bureaucrats.

His father had been a Stormovik pilot killed fighting the Germans. Besides the tall build, brown hair, and blue eyes, Vladimir had inherited his father's love of flying. Volodya, as his father called him, had been ten when his father had disappeared over the Sevastopol front in 1944.

From then on, Vladimir lived to fly. From his first days as a sixteen-year-old in the *Tula Airi Klub* as a member of DOSAAF, to his years as a student at the H.Av. military jet fighter college at Kharkov, he'd known he was destined to spend his life as a fighter pilot. It was all he lived for. He'd taken top honors in academics and air instruction in the beloved propeller-driven Yak-18 at Tula. He'd graduated second in his class at Kharkov, flying the MiG-15 and the new MiG-17. The number one man had been killed the night they graduated. Full of vodka, he'd drilled a motor pool Moskvich auto into a large beech tree. One companion had been killed, another crippled for life.

It was at Kharkov that his classmates had realized Chernov was a real *Chekalov*, a super pilot. Later, in the fighter squadrons, he was known as a *laitchik* of the gods; a magical fighter whose skill rivaled that of the gods; whose skill was so high he could do anything. Life was good for Chernov in the Soviet Air Force.

Now, at 33, Vladimir N. Chernov was a *Pod-Palcovnik*, a lieutenant colonel, and commander of the MiG-21 air advisory detachment to the North Vietnamese Air Force. As a pilot instructor, his duties were to see that the NVAF pilots were not only current and proficient in the latest version of the fighter, the MiG-21PF, but were able to use the delta-winged airplane as a successful weapon against the Yankee aggressors. The Soviet Union had supplied the MiG-21PF to supplant the MiG-17s that, although maneuverable enough, were simply too slow to fight American jets. While the Soviet Union was upgrading the NVAF into the MiG-21, the Chinese were building, and would soon supply their variant of, the MiG-19, called the F-6. This version might prove a most valuable opponent against the Americans. It would carry two 30mm cannons, plus air-to-air rockets. The Soviets very much wanted to demonstrate that the MiG-21 was far superior to any Chinese-built upgrade.

Much to Chernov's disgust, the sole air-to-air armaments that his MiG-21 carried were four ten-foot K-13 missiles that, like the Americans' Sidewinder, was a short-range heat-seeker. It could also carry an advanced radar-guided version of the K-13, the K-13A, but it was not proving out reliable. His request for twelve of the Gsh-23 gun pods to attach under a dozen MiG-21s had been in the logistics pipeline for nine weeks, with no hope for a quick delivery. He doubted the imperialistic forces with their unlimited money had such a faulty supply system as the Soviet Air Force. But, he really shouldn't complain, because using a gun was supposed to be against the current attack philosophy, as propounded by the Kharkov school of tactics. To complain would be to draw attention to himself and his upcoming violation of current Soviet air tactics doctrine. In the Soviet Air Force, individual initiative was not encouraged.

Hara sho, he sighed. Still, he had an excellent arrangement here in North Vietnam. Away from the Motherland and the strict central control of the Soviet Air Force, he could do certain things with no one the wiser—although that fool of a political officer, Anatoly A. Ignatov, sometimes questioned his reasoning on certain nonpolitical subjects. He fingered his scarf.

One trouble with Ignatov was with the MiG-21, number 054, that he had modified for his use. Chernov wanted to monitor what the Intelligence people had told him were the Americans' strike frequencies. Normally, Soviet military aircraft were not allowed to have radio equipment that could listen or communicate on Western frequencies. But now in a hardship post, away from Russia and heavy-handed leadership, Chernov could do pretty much as he pleased. Two things that pleased him were having his airplane modified to receive American UHF frequencies, the other was actually flying air defense missions with the students he was only supposed to be advising.

Ignatov didn't actually question the flying, for he really didn't know what Chernov did in the air in his single-seat fighter; it was the inclusion of the radio set that bothered him. In the past, certain East Bloc defections had prompted the Soviet Air Force to remove all such radios. Chernov didn't know how Ignatov had learned of his radio modifications. Maybe through a technician. The system was such that everybody was supposed to report on everyone else. He sighed. Maybe Ignatov wouldn't feel the modification so important that he had to file a report. He looked up at the sound of a vehicle pulling up in front of the embassy.

Toon arrived in the passenger seat of a UAZ-469, a Russian-built version of the famous American WWII General Purpose vehicle called the jeep. Chernov climbed in back and held on, as the driver, a sergeant in the NVAF, lurched through Hanoi traffic consisting of a few oxcarts, many more pedicabs, and bicycles; all vehicles that didn't have engines requiring gasoline. Though many of the streets of Hanoi were broad, they were devoid of powered traffic, and many of the shops were boarded up.

Once in the middle of Hanoi, they drove down Tran Hung Dao Street past the giant government shopping center. The walls were old and crumbling, and in desperate need of at least a new coat of whitewash. In great contrast was the freshly painted, nearly block-long sign that hung along the second story of the shabby store. TAT CA DE DANH THANG GIAC MY XAM LUOC, it read, ARM FOR THE VICTORY AGAINST AMERICAN AGGRESSORS.

They had to bypass a kilometer of the wide Hanoi Boulevard that ran past Hanoi Lake in the center of the city, where workers had rolled out tens of thousands of meters of freshly dyed black cotton cloth to dry. Each long band was one meter wide. The cloth was for the black pajamas used by both peasants and guerrillas.

They turned down Hoa Lo Street to the D-shaped Hoa Lo Prison compound that occupied an entire block. They drove parallel to the massive gray stone wall that stood sixteen feet high and was topped by barbed wire and six-inch greenish-blue glass shards set in concrete. Guard towers rose up at each corner. They turned into the main entrance and, after their papers were examined by two guards, the huge iron gates were opened. Chernov estimated the walls to be two meters thick. Once through the gate, they drove across a cobblestone alley that circled the prison like a dry moat, and up to another massive gate. After being inspected, they were waved through the gate and into an underpass beneath a prison administration building. At the end of the underpass, they gained access through a third iron gate into a large courtyard.

The Hoa Lo prison had been built by the French years before to house Viet Minh and other Vietnamese who fought French colonialism. Hoa Lo meant "fiery furnace" in Vietnamese. It was now North Vietnam's main penitentiary and administrative headquarters. The sergeant braked the UAZ at the edge of the courtyard.

As Chernov and Toon climbed out, a well-built Caucasian man in a khaki safari suit strode up to them. He stood 5-foot 10, had dark brown hair worn short, sideburns, a full mustache that appeared waxed, and hard eyes that were so murky Chernov couldn't tell if they were brown or black.

"Colonel Chernov, Major Toon, comrades," the man said in unaccented American English, extending his hand. "Welcome to what the Yankee criminals call the Hanoi Hilton. I am Comrade Alvaro Ceballos of the Direccion Generale Inteligencia, the DGI, as some say." His hand, surprisingly big even for such a large man, felt moist yet hard to Chernov. His safari shirt was dark with circular sweat stains. He appeared to be in his mid-thirties.

"I know you both speak English," he said. "Far better than I speak Vietnamese or Russian. I hope you don't mind conversing in this language. It is good practice, is it not?" Chernov and Toon agreed.

They followed the Cuban to his office on the second floor of the administrative building, a structure whose ancient whitewash was streaked with mold and stain. Two ceiling fans barely stirred the heavy air. On a table between two windows were arranged soda, tea, and vodka in plastic liter bottles; biscuits, nuts, and freshly sliced apples were on separate dishes. Two freshly opened packs of Marlboro cigarettes lay next to the vodka.

The windows overlooked the courtyard and the one-story buildings in the compound. Chernov saw a few figures, dressed in ragged blue and white striped pajama-like clothes, being prodded by khaki-clad guards wearing green pith helmets and carrying bamboo batons. Occasionally a guard would yell at a prisoner and strike him with the baton. Prisoners meeting guards walking toward them had to bow or were beaten, Chernov noted.

"Help yourself, comrades," Ceballos said, waving toward the table, "and be seated." Toon poured some of the tepid tea into a cup. Chernov selected the bottled soda. He and his Russian contingent had learned to drink liquid only from bottles or cans, not anything that might be from a water tap. The Hanoi water system was anything but safe. Chernov and Toon took chairs next to the desk where Ceballos had seated himself. He took out a box of Havana cigars and offered them with an expansive gesture. Both visitors declined. Toon did not smoke; Chernov dug out his own Russian cigarettes. He had taken a dislike to this hot-spit Cuban and did not want to give him the satisfaction of accepting his Cuban cigars or his American cigarettes.

"Why did I ask you here?" Ceballos said. "I will tell you. Because it is in the spirit of mutual cooperation between Havana and Moscow to aid Hanoi in its heroic struggle"—he nodded at Toon, who did not acknowledge—"against the Yankee imperialistic forces. We can be of communal aid to each other. Now, how can we be of communal aid? I will tell you." Ceballos took a scratched Austrian lighter from his pocket and inhaled long, satisfying draughts from his cigar after he lit up. The smoke drifted sluggishly along with the downdraft from the fans.

"How can we be of communal aid?" Ceballos repeated. "By the exchange of information. Now, what information can we exchange? I will tell you. It is quite simple. Do you know what it is?" He looked expectantly at the two pilots.

Buckets of bullshit, Chernov said to himself. Who is this pig's blow-hole?

"Comrade Ceballos," Vladimir Chernov said, "I truly appreciate your invitation, your hospitality, and the idea that you wish a communal interchange. Would you be so kind as to get to the point?" He looked at his watch. "Major Toon and I are due at the field in an hour," he lied.

Ceballos eyes slitted. "All right, Colonel Chernov. Perhaps I had better show you. Come with me." He seemed to have forgotten Major Toon was even in the room. Chernov motioned to the Vietnamese. They followed Ceballos out the door and down the stairs. Ceballos led them diagonally across the compound past two large flower beds that had surprising color, as if the guards and administrators needed to show vitality in the grim surroundings. In a mustard-colored one-story building, they entered an office where they were met by two Vietnamese men, one in an officer's uniform, the other—a man with little piglike eyes—in loose-fitting khakis with no insignia. The Cuban introduced the officer as Colonel Nam. He was thin, gray-headed, and held a cigarette in fingers yellow and wrinkled by tobacco.

Colonel Nam nodded. "We ready," he said, his accent heavy. "Follow, please." It was obvious he had been expecting Ceballos and his party.

They fell in behind Nam as he walked from his office across a narrow corridor, through French doors with opaque windows, into a room numbered 18. The stench almost made Chernov gag.

The room was, Chernov guessed, seven meters by ten, and dizzying to the senses. The walls and the ceiling were covered with white plaster covered with symmetrical sound-absorbing knobs protruding from all the surfaces. The knobs and walls were stained and evenly splashed with red up to eye level, as if painted by some bizarre artist. Chernov looked up. Some spurts dotted up to the ceiling. A meathook was firmly attached to a supporting frame on the ceiling. At the far end of the room, he saw a long conference table covered by a blue drape. At first glance, he thought a long, bulky package lay in front of the table. When he focused on it, he felt the bile rise in his throat.

It was a naked man grotesquely bound with green straps seated on the concrete floor. His arms were lashed behind him, one against another, palms together, all the way to his shoulders, which looked dislocated. His arms protruded in the air behind him, like a handle to his upper body. His torso and head were pulled and tied so far forward over his straight legs that his toes were jammed into his mouth. His position was so rigid he couldn't even smash his head on the floor to induce unconsciousness. The man, who had voided from every orifice in his body, appeared dead. As they walked closer, Chernov saw he was alive, although rags were stuffed into his mouth, and his eyes were bulging in an effort to breathe.

"He surrender thirty minutes already," Colonel Nam said proudly. "But we leave him for you to arrive. He talk to you now."

"I have been working on this criminal for some time," Ceballos told Chernov. "He is a navigator from an electronic B-66 airplane. He wants to tell us how his equipment is supposed to decoy the Hanoi air defense missiles." He squatted by the man.

"You are ready, now, aren't you, Bomar?" he said in a soothing conversational voice. "Tell me you are ready." He drew back. "You poor fellow, you can't talk, can you?" Ceballos winked at Chernov and jerked the rags from the man's mouth. Instantly, Bomar sucked in great draughts of air and exhaled in rapid wheezing and cracked moans. "Tell me you are ready, Bomar. Tell me."

"I . . . am . . . ready," the bent figure said in a voice so cracked and faint that Chernov barely heard it.

"What did you say, old chap?" Ceballos said. "We can't hear you. Are you truly ready?" He got to his feet and, balancing carefully, stepped on the man's neck. He had to wave his arms like a tightrope walker to keep his balance. Chernov's skin crawled as he heard the crunch of bone and cartilage cracking, and a continuing croak broken only by sobs for breath from the twisted creature beneath Ceballos's feet.

"Ready . . . ready . . . reaaaaadEEEE," he heard the man scream with a massive effort.

Ceballos stepped down and motioned the pig-eyed guard to free the man. It took the guard fully five minutes to remove the tightly wound straps. When free, the man could not move. He lay on the floor and breathed in hoarse, rattling gasps.

Chernov could see he was white and purple and bloody over his entire body. His arms were almost black where they had been wrapped by the straps. He looked like a partially decomposed corpse. He was smeared with blood and dried excrement. He smelled worse than a decomposed pig in a barnyard, Chernov thought. What type of human could do this to another, he wondered, repulsed beyond anything he had ever felt. He slowly untied his scarf and put it into his pocket, as if it would be sullied by being at such a terrible and degrading spectacle.

"Sit up, Bomar, sit up, for God's sake, man. Sit up so we can see you." Ceballos went to sit at the far side of the conference table. "Over here," he said to Chernov and Toon, who took chairs behind him, each with an impassive face. The wretched navigator raised himself from the floor and swung slowly and painfully to a sitting position.

"On the stool, on the stool. You know what to do." The man crawled and inched his way to a low three-legged stool in front of the conference table. In great pain, he rolled and jerked himself up onto it.

"We've spent a lot of time together, haven't we, Bomar?" The man swayed on the stool, his eyes half-closed. "HAVEN'T WE, BOMAR?" Ceballos screamed so suddenly Chernov thought he had gone insane.

"Yeah," Bomar croaked.

"And I'm tired of fucking with you. Today is the day you talk or I will put you back in the ropes and throw your body in the latrine pit. You said you are ready. It is your choice. LOOK AT ME," he suddenly screamed. "WHICH IS IT?"

Bomar's head came up. From a long way out, he focused his eyes on Ceballos. They seemed to clear. Chernov stared, torn between revulsion and pity for this creature who was so obviously in unbearable pain, who was obviously facing more unbearable pain and even death, and who was struggling to say something.

Chernov turned to Ceballos and spoke in a low voice. "I do not think he is in any condition to tell us anything. Let him rest. He can talk tomorrow."

"Not tomorrow. Oh no, NOT TOMORROW," Ceballos screamed. "Now, Bomar, NOW. TALK TO ME NOW!"

Bomar's head came up. He painfully pushed words through his crushed and dried throat. His pain-racked eyes focused first on the Cuban, then on Chernov.

"Up ... yours ... Fidel, ... you ... too ... Russian ... prick." Then he fainted and fell backwards off the stool, his bowels involuntarily voiding a trickle of black scum.

1815 Hours Local, Monday, 31 July 1967
Hoa Lo Prison, Hanoi
Democratic Republic of Vietnam

☆

"Some of these criminals are crazy," Ceballos said when they were back in his office. "They don't understand. They are losing the war. The protest movement back home will blow their fucking El Presidente Johnson to hell. They even send people here to wish us good luck in our righteous struggle. Even now there is a Quaker Friends boat in the harbor come to bring good wishes and crates of whole blood for our hospitals. Swedish and British ships bring us goods. American senators and doctors condemn the war. Bertrand Russell holds condemnation trials in England. The whole world is on our side." Ceballos walked to the window and stared at the courtyard as rain swept down from the north. "What is the matter with these criminals? Can't they see they can go home if they cooperate?" After a moment, he turned to Chernov.

"Here is how you can help. I told you I would tell you. Help me quiz these criminals, that is how you can help. You know technical things to ask. Do it correctly and we do not have to use ropes and straps. Even now I gather articles from influential American people to show these criminals how their own countrymen hate the unjust and murderous bombing they have been conducting on the peace-loving peoples of the Democratic Republic of Vietnam." Ceballos sounded like he had long rehearsed his speech.

Chernov noisily cleared his throat. "Comrade Ceballos, we must go." He stood up.

"A moment. Hear me out. We hold over two hundred sixty American criminals here at Hoa Lo and at six other prisons. Don't you know we can get any information we want? It is not difficult. We already have one gringo—you know what a gringo is? It is what we call Yankees, gringos. We have one gringo Marine lieutenant colonel who quickly saw the error of his ways and is being very cooperative. He supplies letters and broadcasts of great propaganda value, and some tactical information which is valueless, although he doesn't know it, because it is what we already know." Ceballos examined his cigar. "But you see, how you can be of immense value? You your very self, is by asking these Yankee air pirates questions of a technical nature. Questions about their airplanes, and their tactics, and their radar, and their weapons." He laughed. "But you know what to ask. Who am I to tell a man of your stature what information he needs to know of enemy capabilities? Indeed, who am I?"

He leaned forward, chin outthrust, eyes rolling. "I'll tell you who I am. I am a simple soldier in the great socialist army, the vanguard of communism that someday will liberate the entire world. That's who I am." He sat back and inhaled happily. "And you, who are you? I'll tell you who you are. You are a soldier in the same army, struggling for the same goals, devoted to the same cause—the same grand cause. A cause for which you will help in whatever way you can. And one of those ways is to help me extract information from these gringo air pirates. Let us examine the value of this information. Not only can you pass it on to your students defending their cherished homeland, but you can send it direct to Moscow. Would not they be happy with current information about the Yankee air fleet? And wouldn't they reward you appropriately? I'll tell you they would." Ceballos took another cigar. He spent a moment lighting it.

Chernov had heard fragments of the long, droning speeches of Castro and thought it must be something all Cubans liked to do. Then he thought of his inquiry to the GRU about the apparent failures of the American missiles. So far there had been no answer. He could not conceive of telling this to Ceballos, for it would provide the Cuban with a natural opening with which to prod him.

"Of course," the Cuban said, "Comrade Ignatov would also be most appreciative of your assistance. Not so much for helping me accomplish my mission, but for gaining the information so vital to the defense of Hanoi. Information which would also be vital to the knowledge of the great Soviet air fleet." Ceballos slowly streamed smoke from his lips as if he were gently blowing out a match. He suddenly leaned forward.

"Diametrically, Comrade Ignatov would not be appreciative of any lack of endeavor on your part, would he now, Colonel Chernov? As the head of the political directorate for the Hanoi detachments, he reports directly to the Leninist Central Committee, does he not? Of course he does. Is it not true that favorable or unfavorable communications from the Committee bear heavy weight on both your promotions and assignments? Of course it is true. How do I know all this?" Ceballos sat back and smiled. "I have studied your *spravochnik*, your officer's handbook put out by *Voyenizdat*, the publishing house for the Soviet Ministry of Defense. Each officer must have one in his library. Oh, yes. I have done my studies." He sat back and looked hard at Chernov.

2145 HOURS LOCAL, MONDAY, 31 JULY 1967
SOVIET PRIVATE CLUB SWALLOW
HANOI, DEMOCRATIC REPUBLIC OF VIETNAM

☆

Vladimir Chernov poured another vodka and returned to his seat in the overstuffed chair. The room was large and crowded with worn furniture that was sodden with humidity. The floors were cool marble. It was on the second floor of the Russian Cultural Center. The magazine racks held issues of *Tekhnika i Vooruzhenie,* the technology and armaments magazine, the *Voenniy Vestnik,* the military herald for officers, and one or two untouched copies of *Sovietskii Voin,* a dull book of military pulp fiction and pinup pictures of pretty Russian girls in heavy folk costumes. The most sought after military magazines were the East German *Armee Rundschau* and the Polish *Zolnierz Polski,* both of which ran photos of bare-breasted girls that rivaled the forbidden and decadent American *Playboy* magazine.

Chernov thumbed through a new copy of *Aviatsiya i Kosmonavtika,* a magazine on current aviation and space subjects he considered quite readable. A record player was quietly playing some popular Moscow music. Polish air conditioners set high up in the whitewashed walls chugged and strained to reduce humidity in the room. Chernov had traded souvenirs from crashed American planes for the machines with members of the Polish embassy. Still-life paintings of forests and snow-covered mountain peaks adorned the walls. Cigarette smoke from four men playing cards hung heavy in the room. They laughed as they slapped cards down. Several other men, advisors and support cadre, were scattered about reading or writing letters. A large minister's table held plastic liter bottles of water, vodka, and orange soda. Several plates with crumbs from tinned snacks were scattered about.

Anatoly Alexei Ignatov entered the room, poured a shot of vodka and a glass of tea, spied Chernov and seated himself in the plump chair next to him. Ignatov, as the political officer, was a *sotrudnik,* meaning he was an employee of the state but with special Communist party privileges. He had a red stripe across his identification card that was a symbol of a high security clearance and permission to go anywhere. He could go through Russian customs without checks, board Russian planes free, enter Russian movies free, and enjoy unrestricted shopping privileges in Moscow. He used these privileges to his utmost.

"Health," Ignatov said, and tossed his vodka down. He smacked his lips and sucked on the tea.

"How was your tour with Comrade Ceballos to see the imperialist criminals?" he inquired conversationally.

"He is a zealot who uses vile methods to get the Americans to talk,"

Chernov replied, surprised at the sharp tone in his voice. It wasn't wise, he reminded himself, to be so truthful with the political officer. Everything he said might well be written down and filed in a dossier at KGB headquarters on Derzinsky Square in Moscow.

"Nonetheless," Ignatov said in a pedantic voice, "he performs valuable work for the revolution. You know full well Marxist-Leninist teachings clearly state that whatever must be done must be done to further the cause of true communism."

"You are correct, comrade," Chernov said, "but the Soviet Union is also a signer of the Geneva Conventions concerning the treatment of prisoners of war, as is North Vietnam. They are badly mistreating these men," Chernov said.

"And you are also correct, comrade. The *rodina*, Mother Russia, and the North Vietnamese are signatories, but this is not a war. The Americans themselves have not declared war, so . . . it is not a war. Therefore, those scum who bombed this country are criminals, war criminals, who have committed crimes against humanity and must be treated as such." Ignatov had a chubby face. When he spoke, his mouth opened and closed, Chernov thought, like the mouth of a fish sucking in water.

"Why must they be treated that way? They have no information of military value. Thor's balls, we probably have more of military value in forgotten files than these men will ever know. This is not a tactical situation where lives or territory can be saved by rapid intelligence acquisition." Chernov took a heavy pull at his vodka.

"There are other considerations, comrade," Anatoly Ignatov said in an officious tone. He looked somber.

Chernov turned to face him. "Buckets of bullshit. Other considerations. You mean propaganda value? What propaganda value is there in photographs of emaciated automatons who bow to the camera and say they are repentant of the grave crimes they have committed against the peace-loving people of the Democratic Republic of Vietnam. Everyone knows Americans don't talk like that."

"And you shouldn't talk like that, either, comrade colonel. Your tongue is sharp tonight. It might do for you to review the basic tenets of your officer's *spravochnik* as it regards the principles of conscious military thought and good discipline." With that, Ignatov excused himself and walked out, after saying he had some reports to study. Chernov saw with amusement the covert glances, as every man in the room watched the political officer leave. A collective sigh went up when the door closed behind him.

That's the second time today I've been admonished to study my officer's handbook, Chernov thought. Keep this up and I will be a candidate for a psychiatric examination.

10

☆

Major General Albert G. ("Whitey") Whisenand sat alone in his Pentagon office sipping black coffee from a thick mug. A late afternoon thunderstorm spattered soundless rain against the thick windows. All the lights were on to stave off the outside gloom. He picked up the black phone on his desk and dialed his home. His wife, Sal, answered.

"I'm going to be late, dear wife," Whitey said. He rubbed his left eye with the flat of his palm as he talked.

"Again?" she said with infinite patience. After twenty-five years of marriage, Whitey had yet to be a nine-to-five worker. Few career military personnel were. "You sound worried," she added.

"Things are brewing," he said. There was an air of tension in the upper corridors of the Pentagon. He couldn't tell her over the phone what he thought was about to happen. "I'll call you before I leave." They exchanged "I love you's" and he hung up, then checked his watch. It was time. He strode down the hall to the office of the Chief of Staff of the United States Air Force (CSAF), Room 4E924. One of the aides ushered him from the secretarial room into the large office.

"You look worried, Whitey," CSAF said. He walked over to shake hands, then they headed toward the couch and coffee table. Whitey sat down on the leather couch.

"Thanks. My wife said I sounded worried, now you say I look worried." In truth, beneath the brown matte of his burn scars, Whitey's face was pink and senatorially benign.

"I am more than worried," CSAF said. He sat in a deep leather-covered armchair and rubbed his forehead. "I'm sick of it. Sick of it all." He was an aviator, highly experienced in bombers and fighters.

Now he looked worn and bent with the burden of problems far more threatening than just his own death in combat. The loss of Air Force men in Hanoi showed in his face. Once a man of humor and grace, he now wore a perpetual frown, and his kind eyes were sad and wrinkled. His name was John McConnell. He rose to his feet and began to pace.

"I asked you to stop by for two reasons. You're close to the Chairman, and you're certainly close to the President." Whitey had been a West Point classmate of the Chairman of the Joint Chiefs of Staff.

"The Chairman is getting close to the edge," CSAF said. "He is shocked by what he considers to be McNamara's lies before the Stennis Committee yesterday. The Chairman was sure the testimony he gave to the committee himself, before McNamara spoke, would force Congress to act. When he told the committee the administration policy would fail unless the military was allowed to go to Haiphong to stop the flow of supplies into South Vietnam, that the conduct of the air war was all wrong, he expected the uproar would force the President to get things moving, one way or the other. Either prosecute the war properly or get out of Vietnam entirely. Now, I don't know what's going to happen."

Whitey remembered McNamara's words the day before. Hair slicked straight back, steel-rimmed glasses shining in the lights, his voice cool and in control, McNamara had said, "I welcome this opportunity to discuss with you our conduct of the air war in North Vietnam," and then proceeded to contradict everything the Chairman had said.

As USAF General Perry had remarked afterward to Whitey, "Now he's done it. He has broken the unofficial contract between civilian leaders and military officers. The military has always sworn to obey the civilians without question, in return for the civilian leadership not squandering military lives. But what does McNamara call this?"

The red line from the Chairman's phone rang once on the desk of the CSAF. He picked it up and identified himself, then listened with furrowed brows. "Yes, General," he said, and nodded at the spoken instructions, glancing at the clock on the wall. "Yes, sir, I understand. I'll be there," he said, and hung up. He remained standing.

"This is most unusual," he said. "The Chairman wants all the service Chiefs to his office immediately. You know what a stickler he is for procedure and precedence. We always meet in the Tank, never in his office." The Tank was the large windowless room in the Pentagon used for formal JCS meetings. "And he said no aides and no notes. Most unusual."

0145 HOURS LOCAL, SATURDAY 27, AUGUST 1967
QUARTERS TWO, FORT MYERS ARMY POST
ARLINGTON, VIRGINIA

☆

Very early the next morning, the call came to Whitey just after one. From years of practice, he surfaced quickly from deep sleep and was alert in seconds.

"Do you know who this is?" the deep and measured voice asked.

Whitey was astounded. "Yes, sir, I do."

"I would like you to come to my quarters . . . right now. Can you do that?"

Whitey nodded. "Yes, sir," he said. "I'll be there in less than thirty minutes."

He kissed Sal, who muttered something unintelligible, slipped into some old slacks and a pullover, and heated up some old Brenny's coffee, which he sipped as he drove to Fort Myers on the hill above Arlington Cemetery. The sentry at the main gate saluted and waved him on post. The late thunderstorms had cleared up, leaving the August night steamy and without a breeze. Minutes later, he pulled in front of one of the two large red brick houses on Washington Drive at the top of the hill overlooking Wright Gate and due east across the Potomac. Quarters One, with its two ancient cannons parallel to the walk, was traditionally reserved for the Chief of Staff of the United States Army; Quarters Two for the Chairman of the Joint Chiefs. Most Chairmen selected from the Army chose to live there. The houses were equal. However, the houses farther up on Grant Avenue had better views.

Inside, the Chairman of the Joint Chiefs of Staff waved Whitey to a chair in the study, the windows of which looked down on the Iwo Jima Memorial and the city. In the distance, the lights of Washington glowed with moist halos. He seemed impatient to speak.

"We all agreed, this afternoon," he began without preamble, "and I am to call a press conference this morning to announce our decision." He stood looking intently at Whitey. He was a tall man, and thin. His years of Army life and constant critical decisions showed on every line in his face. His brown eyes looked anguished and unutterably tired. He hadn't told anyone, but he had been suffering chest pains recently of a kind he had never experienced before.

"I am to announce that we are going to resign. All of us, together. All the service chiefs and myself. I am to tell the press that the reason is the unconscionable way Johnson and McNamara are throwing away American lives on a war we are not allowed to win." He spoke the words slowly and with great pain.

Whitey viewed him without blinking. He had known the general for years and had seen him rise in rank and authority, well past himself. The Chairman had been a young aide when Whitey had sided with Army General Matt Ridgeway and told President Eisenhower that supporting colonial powers in Asia such as France was not good policy. The Chairman had told Whitey then, and many times subsequently, how much he admired his honest and candid way of expressing himself.

"Do you want a drink?" the Chairman interrupted himself. "Coffee?" He indicated a carafe.

"Yes, sir, coffee," Whitey said. The Chairman poured. The action seemed to put the Chairman more in charge of himself.

"Now I'm on the fence, Whitey. I'm not so sure we should resign." He pursed his lips. "It smacks of mutiny. It goes against anything I've ever been taught. Or anything I've taught others, for that matter." He sighed, and turned to gaze out the window overlooking Washington. "And if we do resign, they'll just get somebody new." He was silent for a moment, then turned to face Whitey.

"By now, you've probably guessed why I asked you here," he said. "I know how the Chiefs feel. I need your opinion. You're close to the President, and I think you could predict how the Secretary of Defense will react. What will they do?"

Whitey walked to the window. He stood, looking out for a few seconds at the darkness that was Arlington Cemetery. He knew every man sleeping there, and in the hundreds of tended cemeteries and lost graves of American soldiers throughout the world. These men slept knowing that before they'd died they could trust their leaders. He turned to face the Chairman.

"You are correct," he said. "They would just replace you with someone new who would do what they say. And you would prove the protesters correct—even though for vastly different reasons. Further, you are, all of you, too knowledgeable about what is going on to pull out now. There are many subtleties, and you know them. Stay and fight."

The Chairman stiffened and managed a smile. "I thought you would feel that way. It's what has been on my mind these last few hours. I needed to be sure. I will reconvene the JCS first thing this morning and tell them I've changed my mind. There will be no resignations." With that, Army General Earle Wheeler looked more resolute than he had all week.

It was three in the morning when Major General Albert G. Whisenand walked into his house. He went into the music room, decanted six ounces of a harsh Chianti, flipped a switch and placed the needle at the beginning of the worn Gilbert and Sullivan record. The jaunty words of "A Modern Major General" spread through the room. He slowly rocked his head from side to side.

Sal opened the double door and walked in. She wore her old silk robe over her negligee.

"Oh, my dear, you look so sad," she said, her brow wrinkled with concern. "What is it? What happened?"

Whitey quickly outlined the events at the house of the Chairman of the Joint Chiefs of Staff. He took a deep draught of the wine.

"And then, my dear, I lied to my Chief. I lied to him." He finished the wine in his glass.

"What do you mean?" she asked.

"I would have resigned."

0800 HOURS LOCAL, FRIDAY, 29 SEPTEMBER 1967
PARADE GROUND
RANDOLPH AIR FORCE BASE
SAN ANTONIO, TEXAS

☆

In a brief ceremony, wings were awarded and class standings recognized for the graduating pilot training class. It was time now for the pee-rade. As with all parades at a military function, the "Pass in Review" is the most important command. When given by the senior officer, the band immediately strikes up a marching tune, usually Sousa's *Semper Fideles*, and wheels into proper marching order. The student wing commander shouts a mighty WING, foh-WAAAARD ... HARCH, which is echoed down the line to the squadron and flight commanders, and the parade begins. Each man starts out on his left foot, which he synchronizes to the beat of the drum. That is why the troops in the rear of a long parade are not in step with the lead element; they hear the drumbeat a split-second later.

The parade got under way. The marching band was in fine tune. When it swung into the last 32 bars of Sousa's *Stars and Stripes Forever*, the 134 officers and airmen immediately sang to themselves the familiar words about their webbed-footed friends. Same effect at the next piece, Bagley's *National Emblem:* They hummed about why the monkey wrapped his tail around the flagpole.

Colonel John Walker stood in the reviewing stand taking and returning the salute of the men leading the elements passing in review. July is extraordinarily hot in Texas, and by noon each day the drill field at Randolph Air Force Base would be blistering enough to melt an iceberg. Graduation ceremonies in the summer months were always scheduled early enough so that the field could be cleared no later than nine-thirty.

Ever since the austerity program that had been promulgated (Colonel Walker loved that word) by the Chief of Staff, graduation ceremonies had been held in the air-conditioned comfort of the base theater. But this graduating class had been special, so Paragraph 3, CSAF message 280832Z Dec 66, SUBJECT (U) INCREASED PILOT PRODUCTION, had been waived. Thus all the student pilots, in addition to the graduating class, were marching around the parade grounds.

The class was special because one Captain Toby Parker was a member, and he was off to the Vietnam war. Many of the rest of his class would be off to war also, once they completed the various upgrading assignments to fighters, tankers, trainers, or bombers. Although Parker's academic and military record in his class was deplorable, he did stand number one in terms of flying ability. The Randolph public affairs people, goosed by direct orders from their boss in the Pentagon, had invited as much of the local and national members of the press and TV as they could find in their handbooks. The results had been dismal. One national network, CBS, had sent a team, based on a rumor there would be a Vietnam protest sit-in at the main gate to Randolph, but that hadn't materialized. Texans take their wars and their military men seriously. No protester was anxious to test that disposition with the San Antonio police, the Texas State Highway Patrol, and the Air Police. One local radio station had shown up, as had a reporter from the *San Antonio Express-News*.

Toby Parker's parents from Fauquier County, Virginia (real estate—second largest holdings in the county), were there. They were planning a little write-up in the *Fauquier Democrat* and maybe a short piece in *Chronicle of the Horse* (Toby was a well-known horseman), but those little pieces wouldn't count as far as the Air Force was concerned. However, a documentary team from the Audio-Visual Service unit at Norton AFB, California, was on hand to film the event and interview Parker for the USAF's monthly "Air Force Now" programs.

"Congratulations," Colonel John Walker had said, and handed Toby his graduation certificate and his aeronautical orders.

HEADQUARTERS AIR TRAINING COMMAND
UNITED STATES AIR FORCE
Randolph Air Force Base, Texas

AERONAUTICAL ORDERS
NUMBER   314   26 September 1967
1. The following officer, 3510th Flying Training Wing, ATC, Randolph AFB, Tex, is granted the aeronautical rating of PILOT, effective 29 Sep 67, under provisions of

paragraph 4b (1) (a), Chapter 1, AFM 35-13 and CSAF message 280832Z Dec 66 (as amended) to Commander ATC, and is hereby required to participate frequently and regularly in aerial flight in such rating under provisions of Executive Order 10152, 17 Aug 50, and Chapter 2, AFM 35-13.

CAPT TOBY G. PARKER, USAF, SSN FV41296248

OFFICIAL: ROBERT J. GRAHAM
HEADQUARTERS AIR TRAINING COMMAND
USAF   Lieutenant General, Commander

David A. Anderson
Lieutenant Colonel, USAF
Adjutant

When the parade was over, the field cleared rapidly, as the Texas sun seared the grounds.

During and after the ceremonies, the Parkers had watched with momentary pride as Toby, resplendent in Class A khakis, was presented his wings. They had yet to get over being cross about the fact that their son seemed to have selected a life in the military. "Oh, dear," his mother had once said, "it's all so *dreary*, running around in uniforms and everything. Why don't you just join your father's firm and sell and ride and sail like everyone else?" (Toby had been a junior Star class champion sailor on the Chesapeake Bay.) The Parkers had enjoyed the local headlines when he had returned from Vietnam the previous December as an authentic war hero. They were, however, a little bewildered at his casual acceptance of it all. Particularly his graduating from pilot training.

"Mom, Dad, I appreciate your coming down, I really do. But it's no big thing," he said after the ceremony, as he drove them to the civilian airport. He packed them off on their return flight, his mother slim and fussy, his father permanently red-faced and heavy. Both were known as good riders in the Woodsford Hunt, which they had practically formed themselves. Toby had asked if they wished to stay in San Antonio a few more days. "Oh, no," his mother had replied. "We couldn't possibly. Our farrier, Lee Rose, is coming at nine Monday morning. If we're not there exactly on time, he will never shoe our horses again." Toby had grinned. He remembered Lee Rose as a grizzled combat veteran from the Korean War who brooked no nonsense from his clients.

At the airport, Toby turned in the four-door sedan he had rented the day before to drive his folks around, and retrieved his red Corvette. He remembered with great pleasure when he and his pal, Court Bannister, had bought Corvettes in Las Vegas last December, after they had returned from their tour of duty in Vietnam. Court's father had thrown a ten-day party that was still a blur in his memory. He smiled in recollection as he drove skillfully but fast back to his BOQ. He planned to start the 700-mile trip to Hurlburt Field at Fort Walton Beach in Florida that afternoon.

11

1815 HOURS LOCAL, FRIDAY, 6 OCTOBER 1967
DONKIN'S INN
MARINA DEL RAY, CALIFORNIA

☆

The floor-to-ceiling windows behind the bar at Donkin's Inn looked out over the forest of bobbing and rocking masts that flashed in the late afternoon sun. They belonged to the hundred or so boats tied to the marina piers. Inside, Donkin's was crowded as usual with the serious hunters of flesh. The men, mid-twenties to early thirties, were roaming, drinks in hand. Those dressed in expensive clothes, the blazers and yacht caps, could barely make the rent payments for their one-bedroom Santa Monica apartments. Those in dockers and worn jeans were usually the ones who owned the 40-foot Wheelers and the two-masted yawls that stretched out over sixty feet—and usually several apartment buildings in Santa Monica. The girls, early twenties to early thirties, wore inexpensive blouses and miniskirts. They were fun girls who worked hard and played hard, and who demanded and received respect.

Court wasn't interested in any of them, though. He was waiting for Susan Boyle. He had met Susan on his return flight aboard an American Airlines contract flight from Vietnam. She was bold, blonde, buxom, a sun-brown Manhattan Beach girl with sleek lines and a leonine mane of hair. And she liked to laugh. Court had been seeing her for several months.

He had just finished the three-month upgrade course at George Air Force Base, a two-hour drive from Los Angeles. He had learned to fly and fight the big F-4 Phantom, but not as well as he would have liked.

He took a table on the patio next to one of the marina docks. The boats moved gently and creaked as they rocked in the light chop. Two female joggers trotted by, breasts and ponytails bobbing, looking gaunt and intense. A few minutes later, Susan Boyle walked up the steps. Her contrast to the joggers was startling.

"My God, you look stunning. No, ravishing is the word. You look ravishing," he said. She did. She wore tan high heels with matching chamois miniskirt, and a form-fitting light cotton shirt with rolled-up sleeves and collar open to just above her breasts. He could see the white silk of her brassiere. Her wide, generous smile framed even teeth, though her two upper center teeth were just slightly larger than the others, which gave her a look of permanent eager interest. Her tawny hair tumbled down her back; her brown eyes were warm and shiny.

Susan Boyle had the special confidence of those girls who chose the California beach as a place to live. The unconscious competition among the lithe and leggy beach girls pervades their walk, the way they hold their head, their direct eyes; they are girls who achieve things. The beach doesn't make them that way, it draws them forward while the less confident hang back. Those who move close to the water without those instinctive talents become discontented and move inland. It's a process of natural selection for both achievers and beauty.

"Ravish me, then," Susan Boyle said, and leaned forward to kiss him, "or I'll ravish you. But whatever we do, let's get going quickly, beast. I've got all my night things in the car." She stroked his cheek, her eyes roguish and sensual. They had two white wines, a shrimp cocktail, and departed, Court in his Corvette, Susan in her golden Porsche. They were to spend the night at Court's beach place in Venice, then drive leisurely through the desert to George Air Force Base the next day. That night they were to attend the formal graduation dining-in for Court's F-4 upgrade class in the Officer's Club.

2045 HOURS LOCAL, FRIDAY, 6 OCTOBER 1967
OCEAN FRONT WALK
VENICE, CALIFORNIA

☆

The white-topped surf splashed soft thunder on the smooth sandy beach which lay between Marina del Rey and Santa Monica in the area called Venice. The foaming water glowed phosphorescent in the moonlight. Out to sea, small night thunderstorms were building. Tentative cloud-to-cloud lightning illuminated them like ghostly galleons of the air. Court and Susan parked their cars in the lot next to the two-story building fronting the ocean, then climbed the back stairs to his apartment. It stretched from the kitchen straight through the living room and bedroom to a sumptuous balcony overlooking the beach.

In the wide living room, Court lit two big candles, and turned on the FM to some slow California swing. They embraced, hard and breathless. Court got a jug of wine from the small refrigerator, and they walked forward into the bedroom. The farthest wall was all glass, long drapes, and a wide sliding door out to the balcony.

"Race you," she said. In seconds, their clothes were scattered on the floor and they were in the big king-size bed nuzzling and grasping, tangled in the black satin sheets.

It was close to midnight before they slept, damp and entwined in each other's arms. The thunderstorms, rumbling and mumbling as they dissipated, had decided to save their power for another time. The hypnotic surf beat continued. At five-thirty, they awoke. Court made coffee, and they shared a cigarette in the soft light of a candle.

"Ah, this is so great. Three days of you," she said, and hugged him. "When do you actually have to ship out, Court?"

"Soon." He looked at her. "I don't *have* to ship out, you know. I'm shipping out because I want to. I leave from Travis in four days."

She drew back, slightly. "You volunteered?"

"Yeah, guess I did," he said, remembering his problems at Edwards. "Sure, I'm a volunteer."

"Again?" she said. "Seems to me you said you volunteered the first time."

"That's true."

"But I don't recall you telling me you volunteered *this* time." Her mouth turned down. "What for? Why are you going back? You said yourself you didn't have to. So why?" She sat up, and hugged her knees.

Court propped himself on an elbow and reached for his Luckies. "This doesn't sound like your basic after-sex conversation." He lit a cigarette.

"Don't change the subject. Why are you going back?"

Court got up and padded to the open balcony door. The surf was low now, white and rhythmic; it was an old friend you could always count on to be there. The air was warmer than he expected. In the far right corner, next to the railing, was a round white wicker table and two recliner chairs. The railing shadowed the light from the street-lamps below. Susan got up to stand in the doorway next to him. He put out his cigarette and breathed deep of the damp and salty night air. It smelled of rain.

"I just have to, that's all."

"Hero stuff?" she asked. "I thought you were deeper than that."

"There's some of that, sure. Scratch the surface of any fighter pilot and you'll find many things. One is being a bit of a hero." He gave

her a half smile she could barely see in the dark. "That might have
been one of the many reasons the first time I went. And I suppose it
flavors a little bit of my feelings now, but it is more than that, much
more."

"What, then?"

"It's still going on. I thought it would be over by now, but it's still
going on. So I have to go back."

"You thought the war would be over? Why on earth did you think
that? Westmoreland is begging Johnson for even more troops to be
sent to him in Vietnam."

Leaving him, Susan walked out on the balcony and, still nude, sat
in the shadowed corner facing Court. She stretched her legs out,
crossed her ankles, then tossed her head so her hair hung down on
her right shoulder. She lit a cigarette. The flare of the match illuminated her body in red and gold. Black shadows danced beneath her
breasts, drawing attention to the dark vee of her thighs. The image
stayed in Court's mind as the flame died, and the odor of sulphur
blew away. He went and knelt next to her, and, cupping her face
with his hands, kissed her. She tasted salty, and he breathed her
fragrance from their lovemaking. He nuzzled her neck, and the curves
of her breasts. They were firm and moist, and cooling in the air.

She tried to push him away. "You haven't answered my question."

"All you do is come up with questions." He bent over her. "God,
woman, but you taste *good*, and smell *good*," he said, his voice muffled from the hollow between her shoulder and her neck.

Susan sighed, and shivered. "Ah God, Court. You're getting to me
again," she said. She quickly stubbed out her cigarette, and they
kissed, deep and hungrily. He crouched by her chair and slid his
hands under the curve of her knees and behind her back.

"Oh, I'm too heavy. Court, I'm too heavy." She laughed low in her
throat.

"Not tonight. Not here, not for me. I'm Superjock, remember?"
He laughed, and swung her up easily and started for the bedroom.
She put her arms around his neck and nuzzled his chest.

Later, they lay side by side, cigarettes glowing. The dawn was gray;
soft rain had started, straight down and gentle.

"Okay," Susan said, "so you have to go back. That tells me nothing.
You have to go back because you like little slant-eyed girls? You have
to go back because you like the sixty-five bucks a month combat pay?
You have to go back because you like flying airplanes while somebody
is shooting at you?" She thought for a moment, then pulled herself
up on an elbow. "Or is it the other way around? You like to shoot at
people?"

"All of the above," he said. He flicked his Lucky into the ashtray on his bare chest.

"Don't be a smartass," she said. She tossed her head. "Maybe you just like the combat. Maybe you like the thrill."

"All of the above," he said again.

She sat up. "That's horseshit, and you know it," she snapped. "You're just fooling around. I want to know why you said you *have* to go back as if it were some kind of a . . . a. . . ."

"Duty?" he said. "Some kind of a *duty?* Is that what you meant?" His voice became harsh.

"No, death wish. That's what I meant, death wish."

"Well, horseshit to you too, lady," he said, getting up. He carefully poured another wine and took a deep swallow. He put on a robe from the closet, and tossed her one. She put it over her shoulders and drew her knees up.

"Well then, answer my damn question," Susan said.

"What question?"

"Good God, Bannister, you're acting like a little kid who has to answer to his mother what he was doing in the bathroom so long."

Court laughed. "What an analogy." He shook his head. "You and Doc Russell. You're just alike, you know. He was our flight surgeon at Bien Hoa. Always asking the same questions you are. Why this, why that. Said he wanted to know what made fighter pilots tick."

"I know what makes *you* tick," she said, and flicked his maleness.

"Again?" he leered.

She sat back and crossed her legs with exaggerated movements. "Nothing doing. Absolutely nothing doing until you tell me."

"That's extortion."

"Okay, then, tell me and we'll screw."

"That's bribery."

"You don't want to tell me, do you?"

"No."

"Don't trust me?"

"Oh hell, Susan, of course I trust you. I trust you not to understand."

She jerked as if struck. She grabbed her pack, lit another cigarette, and blew an angry puff in the air. "Okay, Court, then let me tell you. I know exactly what it is you won't tell me." She got up and wrapped the robe around her, yanked the belt tight. She crossed her arms. "I fly, too, you know. I've been to Vietnam, too, you know." She waved away the wine Court offered. "You want to go back because your buddies are there, and you don't feel right being here fat-catting it on the beach. You feel guilty here." She snorted. "Now isn't that the truth? Hell, I know it is. Bannister, you wear guilt like a hair shirt. And you hide it about as well as knights hid their armor."

He turned toward her. "I like that analogy, about the armor, I mean, but I don't like its basic premise. What makes you think I feel guilty?" he asked, his voice becoming harsh again. "I don't feel the least bit guilty. You know, that's a helluva connection. I'll bet you didn't come up with that idea just flying MAC contract to Vietnam and back."

"I never told you? My dad was career brownshoe Navy. He flew Hellcats off the Lex in World War Two, and Panthers in Korea. He told me things. One night we got blitzed together down in San Diego. At North Island. He told me a lot of things that he said he could never tell Mom."

"What things? Why couldn't he tell her?"

"About volunteering. He always lied to her about volunteering. He always said he had to go. He never told her he was a constant volunteer." Her voice sounded tender and critical at the same time.

"Well, he was right. I understand that," Court said. "That's how it was with Charmaine. She wasn't even pleased I was working so hard at ASU to get into the astronaut program. By the time I went to combat, we were divorced."

"You haven't really said why, Court. Dad told me he volunteered, but it never occurred to me to ask him why." She sighed. "I guess I believed all those World War Two movies where the hero always volunteers. It's what you do, isn't it? No questions asked."

"You're making a lot of this," Court said.

"And you're being evasive," Susan said.

"Okay, I'll try to tell you." He blew out a huge cloud of cigarette smoke. "Yeah, it's what I do. I've been drawing flight pay all these years, flying Uncle Sam's best. And it's time to do what I've been training to do, and, incidentally, what I do best. I'm like an insurance policy. The government invests in me and a couple of hundred other guys so we can go fight if we have to." He almost said "so we can go kill people with airplanes," but thought better of it. But that was his job. He knew peace was not his profession. He picked up where he left off. "We have a lot of fun cavorting around the world learning, but there is always the possibility the day may come when Uncle Sam cashes you in for the return on his money. That's how it is. At least that's one of the reasons I'm going back. There's another reason."

"Which is?" she said.

"The guys are still there."

"What guys?" she insisted. "Tell me. What guys? Your brother? Father, maybe. Come on, what guys?" Her voice was harsh and insistent. He could see a glint of tears in her eyes.

"Hey, take it easy," he said. She twisted away when he tried to stroke her back. "The guys, just the guys. The pilots, the GIs, the people in the Hanoi Hilton. I want to be with them." He lit another cigarette. "They are the only people in the world I give a damn about."

"You don't even know more than a dozen, or so," she said.

"No, you're wrong. I know them all. And they know me. We know each other," he said.

"You sound just like my dad. Like a member of some big goddamn fraternity with secret signs and ways to recognize each other." She looked angry.

"Come off it, Susan." He tried to change the subject. "How about your dad? What happened to him? Is he still alive?"

Susan made an inverted smile. She walked to the sliding doors and looked out over the water. The rain had increased. Silver rose from the sand and the sea. "No," she said. "He's not alive. He crashed at night into the Med. Just flew into the sea behind a carrier while lined up for a night trap." Her voice cracked. "The dumb shit, he was just like you. He said he *had* to be with his guys. Oldest CAG in the Navy. No deep draft command for him. Fly, fly, fly. And that's just what will happen to you. You'll fly and fly and fly until you bust your ass." She whirled to face him, her face angry. "But you don't believe that, do you? Maybe the other guy will get it, but not nice old you. Oh, no, not sweet lovable pink-body you. You're just like him. You think you are invincible. So did he. So did my father, Commander Tug Boyle, You Ess fucking Enn, deceased." She tossed her head back, her lioness hair flowing. Her lips were white, and drawn back. She brushed hot tears from her eyes.

"Well," she said, her voice becoming stronger. "Nothing like a little cry to clear the air." She nodded to herself, lips pursed. "To hell with your dining-in. I'm going home. Don't follow me. Don't call me. Don't see me again. Go play war with your fly-boy buddies. I knew there was a reason not to start seeing you, and I just remembered what it is. You put it so nicely. You're an insurance policy running around looking for someone to cash you in. Well, Buster, I ain't gonna be around when you get cashed in. Nothing doing. I won't touch you or your dip-shit policy. So long, fly-boy."

He heard the refined snarl of her Porsche through the rain as she worked her way through the gears leaving the alley.

He took the rest of his wine and walked to the balcony door. He could still smell the tang of their lovemaking. He drank deeply from the thin crystal goblet, and walked out on the balcony. The rain plastered his hair. He felt lonely and morose. He shivered.

She is only half-right, he knew, only half-right. The other half, he could barely acknowledge or confront within himself, much less to her. Odd thing is, she had almost caught his secret.

He started to play the game he had invented a short time after returning from his first combat tour. A game where he could take out a well-buried thought from its compartment, examine it dispassionately, and stow it securely at his leisure. Now he let the thought, the secret, bubble up. Then it came, rushing out unchecked at full power, smacking him with an intensity for which he was unprepared. His teeth started to chatter. He couldn't control or diminish his emotion. He shivered as he was flooded with a punishing reaction.

Dominant was the unpleasant reality that he was beginning to like combat. To like it all. The flying on the edge, the troops, the heightened awareness. It was like a high. He had heard of adrenaline highs. Maybe that's what it was, maybe he was hooked.

His mind moved quickly to the next postulate: There was nothing in the stateside Air Force for him. Being an astronaut was out. The next thought marched into his mind in an orderly fashion. There is no one person in the States to keep me here. I am not in love. A tremor ran through him. Christ, what a realization. He surprised himself as he drew a choking breath. The rain streamed on his face. I am not in love, he thought. I'm not in love. A wave of loneliness almost buckled his knees. Loneliness for a mixture of things, he realized. On one hand, he wanted the deep love and sense of permanency, with a wife and children, which he had never had; on the other hand, he liked living on the edge and the sense of doing something important with comrades he respected highly. That sums it up, he thought. I have no reason to be here anymore. I want to go back. I *have* to go back.

I can't stop these thoughts, and I don't want to. Got to play this one out. There's more to going back to Vietnam than being hooked on combat and not being in love, he chastised himself.

Court shook his head, as if to clear away buzzing insects. Okay, admit it. Yeah, there is more than just that. It's the beast in the cage. I have this fucking beast in me. I have to let it out of the cage to do my job in combat, then try to stuff it back in when the tour is over. It's heady stuff, when the beast is out. You can get drunk on it; that's it, the high. Pretty soon, maybe that's all you want to do. Then you're lost, there is no coming back. The rain felt colder. He shivered again, in constant tremors now, yet he knew it was more from emotion than cold. His racing thoughts began to slow. He drew a deep breath, and realized with surprise that, as he calmed, he felt unutterably sad. Waves of melancholy swept him as he felt the rain beating down, straight and cold. He loved the rain and the raw energy of crashing storms. I'm going to die in the rain. Too much has happened to me in the rain. I'm going to die in the rain. He knew that would someday happen.

He shook his head once more, and forced a laugh through his shivers. He raised his glass to the sea.

"Bannister, old man," he boomed out, "here's to it, and the bloody hell with thinking about it." He tossed off the wine.

Deep down, he knew he was faking it. But there was no other way. You had to gut out moments like this. He'd seen it before, in other pilots who had felt a premonition. Too often it became a self-fulfilling prophecy. Such thoughts could leave a sour residue that might surface at moments of total danger, distracting one or, worse, making one give up. Time's up; life isn't worth such agony. Easier just to quit. So you had to fake it and not go too deep. You had to gut it out and be invincible. He laughed at it all. He had to.

At noon he called Nancy Lewis at her Manhattan Beach apartment. It was warm now, and sunny. Secret thoughts of the night before were safely stowed, and a temporary patch placed over the pain of Susan's walking out. He stood holding the phone at the end of the extension cord and looking over the water from the balcony of his Venice apartment. The rain was long gone, the sun high and bright. The sand had dried to virgin smoothness. He had some good Mamas and the Papas swing on the FM, and was doing reasonably well blocking last night; the rain, the thoughts, Susan Boyle. He tried to concentrate on Nancy Lewis.

"Hi, it's Court. How about going to the beach for a beer?"

She hesitated a fraction, then answered in a low voice. "Court, it would be good to see you, but I don't want to go out."

They had had some intense days together during his first tour. He had met her at Bien Hoa, when she'd been a stewardess on a civilian airliner with an engine problem that had landed at his military base. She had told him she had volunteered for the Vietnam flights, hoping the closeness would help her search for information about her Special Forces husband who was missing in action, but presumed dead.

Later, after her husband had been officially declared dead, Court and Nancy had met at Clark Air Base in the Philippines. For three days, they had talked and explored each other's feelings, then embraced in mutual trust and need. That had been last year. He had seen her a few times this year, but always just for a quiet dinner.

"It's not the same now, Court. I've started dreaming of Brad, and he's always calling me." She was silent for a moment. "I really do hear him, you know. Am I going out of my mind? That isn't the only thing that's been happening to me." Her words came faster. "I'm sometimes so sure he is just in the other room. Then . . . there were other things, horrible things, that used to happen when I flew to Vietnam. That's why I had to quit. I'm not flying MAC." Flying MAC meant crewing the Braniff flights chartered by the USAF Military Airlift Command to deliver GIs to and from Vietnam. "I just can't take it anymore."

"What do you mean?" Court asked.

"It's not like the front end crew," she said. "They don't get involved. They don't even see the kids. But we feed them when they're hungry and cover them when they sleep. We listen to them when they are lonely and sometimes . . . cry with them." He heard her voice catch. "All those boys, those young boys. I don't mind bringing them home. I like that. If that was all I had to fly, I would do it forever. Bring them fresh milk to drink on the plane, and talk to them. Yes, I could do that, I could bring them home. I just can't take them over there," she said, simply. "I just can't do it. Isn't that silly? It started on a flight out there two months ago. I looked down the rows of these young men, and . . . I saw who wasn't coming back. I mean I could tell who was going to die in Vietnam. Believe me, I'm not crazy. But I . . . I couldn't see their faces. One out of every three or four boys, I couldn't focus on their faces. It was all blurry and that meant they were going to die, don't you see?"

"Nancy, I'm no psychiatrist—"

She interrupted. " 'I'm no psychiatrist, but.' That was your next word, wasn't it? But."

"Yes," he said. He began to feel decidedly uncomfortable. Between Susan Boyle and her dead Navy pilot father, and Nancy Lewis seeing her dead soldiers, he was rapidly becoming depressed and—he didn't want to admit it—a little unnerved by it all.

Nuts, he said to himself. This is a typical Saturday morning after a boozy Friday night when I broke up with my girl. I'm just a little wobbly, that's all. All I'm trying to do now is fix myself up for Saturday night. He sighed inwardly. And it ain't working out quite as well as I had hoped. He brought his thoughts back to Nancy Lewis. He put what he hoped was a cheery yet comforting tone in his voice.

"Hey, you did right by getting off MAC contract. Don't go back. Your mind was trying to tell you something. It flat out was telling you to quit that kind of flying. That's all. So, you did quit that kind of flying. Now you'll be okay."

Court made it back to George in less than two hours. Top down on the Corvette, he yelled obscenities into the wind. He turned some Jefferson Airplane up so loud he felt it in his molars. Grace Slick belted it out.

"FEED YOUR HEAD . . . FEED YOUR HEAD"

Bannister, you are a bonehead and a coward. That woman needed your help, and you bugged out.

Yeah, he said to himself, I bugged out because there was death all over the place. A tremor ran down his spine. He clenched his teeth. He refused to admit to himself that he was afraid she might look at him and not see his face.

12

☆

The United States Air Force decides what to title their installations by dividing them into major installations called Air Force Base (large, combat-related, U.S. property), and minor installations called Air Force Station (small, not U.S. property). There are also support sites (radar or radio relay, missile tracking, etc).

The names of the bases, Randolph, Edwards, Hurlburt, are in honor of men who died performing an aerial task, sometimes routine, sometimes outstanding, for the United States Air Force. Those of lesser stature are enshrined by having streets named after them on various bases. In between are individuals who did great things and who are recognized by having a building or an auditorium or a barracks named after them.

The "Field" of Hurlburt Field is an exception.

Captain Toby G. Parker was assigned to the 4409th Combat Crew Training Squadron (CCTS) at Hurlburt Field, Florida, to learn how to fly the Cessna Model 337 Super Skymaster, which the Air Force designated the O-2A. He had signed in at Wing Headquarters two days before, on Saturday, the seventh of October. He had been given a welcome packet, and directed to Base Housing for quarters assignment. An hour later, he had found the Officer's Club across Highway 98 from the field, and was on the patio drinking beer. Two hours later, he was at the Eglin Beach Club farther east on Highway 98. With him were two new friends, captains, fresh from signing in for the same training course. They met at the O-Club.

There were girls there that afternoon, brown and warm, with flowing Southern accents. The three captains, full of beer and courage, went into the pursuit mode. They talked with many and danced with a few after the sun went down, trying out variations of their repertoire that just might lead to a friendly seduction. Among the jovial crowd were obvious pairings and re-pairings, and the shared laughter of well-known jokes and jargon as they danced and drank in the warm Gulf air.

The fighter pilots from Eglin Air Force Base seemed to have the edge, mainly because they knew most of the girls. To show their displeasure, the O-2 pilots gathered and howled at the stuffed marlin on the far wall. The tradition had started, it was said, as a pointless ritual exclusively for Hurlburt pilots. There was a bonus. This nonsensical performance never failed to induce one or more girls to inquire laughingly, "Jus' what is this all about?" The pilot's answer depended on the intensity of the girl's question and the interest level in her eyes.

Toby, neither dancing nor pursuing, attracted more female attention at the bar than his two hunting classmates. He looked boyish and wistful. His remoteness attracted a few girls who were just a little tired of eager hot rocks who talked so much of flying and nothing else. Toby bought the girls drinks and let them flutter and flash around him. His two new pals suddenly realized he was the candle to the delicate Southern moths, and came swooping in like night birds for the kill. Quickly accommodating to what seemed to them Toby's winning style, they adopted a morose and brooding demeanor and drank until their eyes crossed and they had to excuse themselves to go into the parking lot and throw up.

On Sunday, the three of them dried out on the beach, passed a football, and talked about their backgrounds and upcoming FAC assignments. The captains, Roy Thomas and Gerry Draper, had been B-52 co-pilots and were more than happy to fly something they were in command of—even something as small as the Oscar Pig, as the underpowered, prop-driven Cessna O-2A was nicknamed.

The O-2A had two Continental 210hp engines mounted fore and aft of the cockpit, a push-pull arrangement, and side-by-side seating. It had a high wing, retractable landing gear, and a control wheel instead of a stick. It weighed two tons full up with pilot, fuel, and armament. To improve visibility, the USAF had installed large plastic panels over the pilot's head. The wings had been strengthened to allow four hard points for the attachment of pods of marking rockets or light machine guns. The 2.75-inch marking rockets had warheads of white phosphorous, nicknamed Willy Pete, that exploded into a huge cloud of dense white smoke to attract the eyes of the fast, high-flying jet pilots. From that point of mutual reference, the forward air controller (FAC) pilot would give instructions as to where the strike pilots were to place their ordnance. When the strike was called to provide close support for American or Vietnamese troops, the FAC was in radio contact with the ground commander. Only when the ground troops were clearly located would the FAC place the ordnance where they wanted the strike. From tiny strips spotted all over Vietnam, the FACs flew over Vietnam and Laos, searching out targets, patrolling roads, and spotting ambush sites for advancing American troops. Other times, in a free fire zone, or on the Ho Chi Minh Trail, the FAC would seek out and destroy with strike aircraft what he knew to be enemy positions.

The O-2A was an interim replacement for the tiny O-1E, until the larger, faster turbo-prop OV-10 was ready to take over the FAC mission. The FAC airplanes carried three radios: UHF and VHF transmitters for talk between airplanes and air base control sites, and an FM set in the 25- to 75-megacycle range to talk with ground troops. They also carried an AM navigational set that received broadcasts in the civilian 540- to 1640-kilocycle range. The cruise speed of the Oscar Pig was 125 knots, about 145 mph. Cessna had a contract to deliver 346 of the O-2s to the USAF.

Though Thomas and Draper had heard of Toby Parker receiving the Air Force Cross for bravery under fire flying an O-1, they didn't bring the subject up. They lay on towels spread on the hot sand, talking aimlessly, never revealing their dreams to be a combat hero like Toby.

The next morning, Monday, at 0700, the three officers reported to the academic building for a welcome speech from the commandant of the FAC school. Following his words were a series of school orientation lectures. By 0800, still gingerly protecting a throbbing head, Toby Parker started the upgrade course for the O-2 Forward Air Controller program.

Five days later, he was arrested by the Fort Walton Beach police for speeding and drunken driving.

1330 HOURS LOCAL, MONDAY, 9 OCTOBER 1967
LOS ANGELES INTERNATIONAL AIRPORT
CALIFORNIA

☆

At the back ramp of the cargo area, away from the bustling passenger gates, the Boeing 707s off-load Americans coming home from the Vietnam war. There are no stewardesses. There are not even any passenger seats on these airplanes. The only stairs are up front, for the three-man crew. The returning soldiers are taken off the plane, a freighter, four at a time, by tall Case-440 forklifts.

Ramon tried to meet every plane. His friend, Stapka, who worked at the airplane wash rack, would get the schedule. The two of them would stand together, slick their hair back, arrange their clothes, and salute the men who had fought for their beloved country. Ramon, gatekeeper at the Braniff employee parking lot, was from Honduras; Stapka from Hungary.

At first, the tow tractor drivers and cargo handlers chuckled and made fun of them. Then one day a handler straightened up from his labors, and put his hand over his heart as a freighter taxied by. Another joined him, and another. In a few weeks, it was a ritual that was observed by all the ramp and line crew. Every air freighter bringing war dead home was met with reverence and salutes. Soon, pilots were taping small American flags and gold stars to the side window of their cockpits. The linemen never spoke of this among themselves when they had their beers in the local taverns after work.

Susan Boyle of American Airlines was exhausted. She had worked the grueling Boston–New York–Chicago trip Sunday. Her short layover at the Airport Hotel at O'Hare had been fretful and sleepless. She had tossed and pounded her pillow, and generally discomforted her roommate as she thought about Court Bannister. Damn him and his fighters. Then the double-leg from O'Hare to Memphis to Los Angeles had taken what reserve she had remaining. She sat now, weary and frazzled, in the crew bus, as it threaded its way from her 727 along the ramp to American's operations office.

She felt leaden and dispirited. Her head nodded as her eyes began to close. God, what am I going to do about Court? she asked herself for the forty-fifth time. I don't know if I love him or what, but I miss that big bastard. I want to be with him. He makes me feel so ... girlish and sleek. And I am so lonesome. But I won't call; nothing doing. Better, smarter this way. I'll forget him. Her eyes slowly closed. Her head snapped up as the bus stopped for a taxiing freighter. She looked out and saw the ramp people at attention, right hand holding work caps over their hearts. She had heard of this. The other crew members in her bus saw the tribute to the returning soldiers and fell silent.

Susan watched the freighter head toward the blocks by a large open hangar where other freighters from Vietnam had unloaded. Inside she saw the stacks of silver-gray aluminum caskets. She caught her breath as a chill ran down her neck. She tightened her lips. Court, oh God, I've got to talk to him.

1530 Hours Local, Monday, 9 October 1967
Penthouse A, Silver Screen Hotel
Las Vegas, Nevada

☆

Sam Bannister could never be mistaken for anything but what he was, and what he had been: a stunningly handsome sword-wielding buccaneer who had aged extremely well. He still looked as if he could fight pirates to a standstill after swinging to the deck from the yardarm. He stood six-foot-four. His broad shoulders tapered into a trim waistline and narrow hips. His nose and lips were thin, a millimeter short of being sharp. His blond hair was combed to one side in studied carelessness. The slight cowlick in back at the part was one of the many endearing things about Silk Screen Sam that brought out the motherly and protective instincts in women. He was well into his mid-fifties and looked a trim forty.

His white canvas slacks and white denim shirt open at the neck accentuated his tan. Around his neck, he wore a heavy chain of 18-karat braided gold from which hung a large curved tiger's tooth mounted in cheap brass, and a slender gold alligator with movable jaws. Court had sent him the tiger's tooth during the time he'd flown F-105s over Hanoi. It was a Thai talisman against shoot-downs, the common cold, and VD. Shawn had sent the alligator from Saigon. It was a roach clip.

During World War II, Sam Bannister had been a gunner on B-17s of the Eighth Air Force. Afterward he had picked up his acting career, made several highly successful adventure movies, and, with an old high school chum, invested this money in movies for TV and California and Nevada desert real estate. It had all worked out.

Court and his father sat on huge white chairs in the vast living room of Sam's twentieth-floor penthouse. Floor to ceiling tinted glass overlooked Las Vegas on one side, and the desert on the other. They drank scotch and reminisced.

Court was talking of Toby Parker and his red Corvette. He wondered how Toby was doing since a year ago when they had both bought their Corvettes at Geisen's here in Las Vegas. Toby had plenty of family income to add to his back pay to purchase the Vette for cash. So had Court. They had just returned from a year's tour of duty in Vietnam. Sam Bannister had thrown a weeklong party for Court and his two friends, Toby Parker and Wolf Lochert. Toby had been drunk most of the time, and Wolf Lochert had followed the dancer Charmaine around like a love-struck teenager. Whereas Charmaine seemed fond of Wolf Lochert—even attracted to him—she showed him nothing more than Las Vegas. Wolf didn't really expect more under the circumstances; Charmaine was, after all, Court Bannister's ex-wife.

Midst much laughter and nostalgia, Sam had given back to Court the old Stetson hat Court had bought for the unheard-of sum of forty dollars as a teenager when he had been riding in Grade B westerns. He was wearing it now, the Stetson Sun Ranger, brim pulled low. He finished talking about Toby and was silent.

Sam Bannister looked at his son. "Tell me why you wanted to upgrade into the F-4."

"That's obvious, Dad. I'm a fighter pilot, it's a fighter, I'm on my way to combat. What more can I say?"

"Say more."

"I thought it was obvious," Court said. "I want to fight the best way I can."

"And . . . ?"

"And the F-4 is the plane for me to make ace. Four more MiGs and I'll be the first ace in the Vietnam war."

"There's more to a war than just making ace."

"Not for me there isn't," Court said.

Sam Bannister looked reflective. He stared at his son for a few seconds. "I'll ask you the same question at the end of your combat tour. We'll see what your answer is then." He sipped his drink, and changed the subject.

"What time is your plane?" Sam asked. "I'd like to take you out in the Lear, you know."

"Never mind, Dad. I don't like prolonged goodbyes. I get Western from McCarran at six-thirty tonight to San Francisco, then up to Travis Air Force Base by bus for an early takeoff tomorrow. A day and a half later I'll be in Thailand."

Sam Bannister looked at his son. "Considering this is your last night in the States before a year in Asia, you aren't exactly whooping it up." He waved his hand expansively toward Las Vegas. "So many girls, so little time," he grinned.

The phone buzzed. Court was still chuckling as he picked it up. Earlier that day, he had thanked his dad for the offer of any girl in town over five-ten and under twenty-five. He answered the phone. Terry Holt, his father's major domo, said it was for Court, from a personnel officer of the United States Air Force. Puzzled, Court said to connect the caller.

"Oh, Court, I'm so glad I found you," Susan Boyle said in a relieved voice. "I'm so sorry for the other night."

"Good God, woman, how did you find me?" Court's voice was a bit thick from the scotch.

"Your Venice phone is disconnected, so I thought your dad

would know. I told the secretary it was urgent, that I was from the Air Force personnel office. It worked. Oh, Court, dammit to hell anyhow. I can't let you go like this without making it right between us."

Court looked at his watch. "Stand by," he ordered, then thought better of it. "I mean, hold on a minute." He punched the "hold" button. He looked at his father with a broad smile.

"Hey, Dad. Can I use the Lear tonight?" His father grinned.

"I'll pick you up at LAX, then you can go up to Travis with me," Court said into the telephone.

"Oh, Court, I can't. I go out early in the morning. I'll write. I promise. I'll write." The tears were just behind her voice, making it hoarse. She saw the caskets. "But I'll get over to Asia to see you. I'll get back on MAC flying. Count on it."

1730 HOURS LOCAL, 10 OCTOBER 1967
SAIGON—VUNG TAU HIGHWAY (QL 15)
REPUBLIC OF VIETNAM

☆

Lieutenant Colonel Wolfgang Xavier Lochert, green beret scrunched over his left eye, was singing at the top of his lungs. He was singing into the sixty-mile-per-hour wind streaming over the top of the flattened screen of the black jeep he was driving. Actually, it wasn't singing, it was humming, very forceful humming. *DEE DEE DUM, DEE DA DA DUM* was Wolf's way of rendering Barry Sadler's "Ballad of the Green Berets."

Wolf was singing/humming because he was very, very happy. The cause of his happiness was sitting next to him, handcuffed to the handhold bar on the panel in front of him.

"Colonel Lochert," Curtis Bubba Bates screamed, his words torn away by the wind. "My God, Colonel, why don't you answer me?" He twisted his hands against the bar.

Lochert gave him a casual backhand that made Bates's head loll. "Don't swear, *scheiskopf.*"

The jungle was closing in on the road. It was hardtop that had once been heavily traveled by wealthy Frenchmen as they drove to and from their expensive villas at the sandy cove of Vung Tau, which they called Cap Saint Jacques. Now it was far too dangerous to be on the road in anything other than an armed convoy—and then only during daylight. In less than an hour, it would be dark. Through a break, Wolf saw a high point off to one side that he was sure was a Viet Cong observation post.

Humming loudly, he pulled over to the side and stopped. He switched off the ignition, jumped out, and jabbed the point of his K-bar knife into the right rear tire. There was the sound of a vehicle on the road, from the way they had come. Then Wolf unscrewed the valve from the rear-mounted spare. Bubba Bates squeaked as the air began to hiss out of the two tires.

"Colonel, please . . ."

He stopped as Wolf Lochert removed the cuffs. "Out," Wolf commanded.

"Wha . . . what . . . ?"

"Out." Wolf pulled a package from the back floorboards, and threw it at Bates. "Put these on." Now his voice was flat and gravelly. He was not smiling. Sweat was soaking Bates's face. His hands trembled as he began gingerly to pull clothes from the package. They were the summer khakis of a major. The insignia and badges said the wearer was a staff intelligence officer with MACV.

A second jeep, driven by one man in jungle fatigues, pulled up behind. He stepped out, cradling an M-16 under his arm, and stood grinning. It was SFC John Bertucci.

"Quickly," Wolf snapped at Bates, who was struggling into the clothes. When he was dressed, Wolf took a black GI issue briefcase from the second jeep, then a pint of Jim Beam from the briefcase and handed it to Bates.

"Drink."

"Oh my God . . . oh, I mean, I'm sorry. Oh Jesus—I'm sorry, I'm sorry—are you going to shoot me?" His voice was frantic and high-pitched.

"Drink." Wolf's voice was like a slap in the face. Bates took a tentative pull. "More. Finish it." As Bates guzzled, Wolf examined the contents of the briefcase. It was half full of documents and folders, many stamped with red "Secret" and "Top Secret" labels. There was a set of GI dogtags on a chain.

"Hurry up, Wolf," Bertucci said. "It's going to be dark in less than twenty minutes."

Wolf leaned forward and tapped the bottom of the bottle, causing the last of the liquor to spill down the front of Bates's uniform shirt. Then Wolf unstrapped the jack and wedged it incorrectly under the jeep frame. He straightened up, took the dog tags and pulled them over Bates's head. The tags said Curtis was an OT Protestant with a regular officer's serial number. Wolf closed the briefcase and put it on the passenger's seat of the jeep. Bates held on to the fender to keep from falling. His eyes looked glassy, and his head wobbled. The jungle noise grew louder.

"You're not going to sh-shoot me?"

Lochert didn't answer. He turned his back and strode to the jeep as Bertucci jumped in and started the engine.

"Whersh . . . whash . . ." Bates started after them, wobbling badly. Ignoring him, Bertucci made a tight U-turn and started back toward Saigon. With a sickening shock, the awful truth dawned on Bubba Bates. He lurched after the jeep as it faded in the distance. He fell, his legs still pumping.

"Shoot me," he screamed in a hoarse voice. "Shoot me."

13

☆

Ambassador Boris Orlik appeared to listen intently, as he always did, at the briefing given by each member of his civilian and military staff. The eight of them sat around a long table in a surveillance-proof section called the *rezentura* on the third floor of the embassy building. Orlik was a portly man, with white hair and a square face covered with thick folds of dough-colored flesh. Although he was the titular head of the Soviet Embassy, control really belonged to the *rezidentura*, KGB Colonel Pavel Predvechnikov, whose power transcended that of the Ambassador, or any member of his staff. On his word, anyone, from the Ambassador on down, could be recalled to Moscow. Predvechnikov could, in fact, dispose of any Soviet diplomat, general, doctor, or specialist who worked in the Democratic Republic of Vietnam.

At the weekly briefing, each attendee had to outline for Ambassador Orlik what was happening in his area of expertise. Not that the Ambassador absorbed it all—he didn't. But it was a required protocol that, if not upheld, would cause deep grumbling from the KGB *rezident* and the communist party officer, Anatoly A. Ignatov.

The Naval attaché gave his five minutes on the disposition of the American Task Force of seventeen ships off the coast in the South China Sea. He reeled off the tonnage of military supplies brought into Haiphong harbor by Soviet and Warsaw Pact ships, and the tonnage of machinery and medical supplies brought in by ships of Swedish, British, and Japanese origins, and other countries trading with the North Vietnamese communists. "At any given time," he said, "we have ten ships in Haiphong harbor, and five in Cam Hoa. Fortunately, the Americans are not allowed to attack any of these vessels, nor place water mines in the harbor. Therefore, we expect this type of access to continue unabated, and the weekly tonnage to increase."

"How can you say that?" the Ambassador rumbled. "How do you know the Americans don't have a plan to sink the ships? Or at least the dredge. Haiphong is so full of river silt that it has to be dredged every day. If the dredge were sunk, or a few ships sunk at the harbor mouth, the harbor would be closed forever. Or what if they bombed the dikes holding the river? Hanoi would be under ten feet of water."

"Comrade Ambassador," the naval attaché said, "your military expertise is profound, as witnessed by your shrewd questions. Our analysts have asked the same questions. In fact, the first six months of this war, in 1964 and 1965, we fully expected these things to happen. It even seemed like it would happen when Johnson sent in American Navy bombers to attack after that stupid blunder by the Vietnamese Navy."

"Oh, yes," Ambassador Orlik said. "Some Vietnamese torpedo boats shot at some American ships, didn't they? Now why did they do that? I seem to recall our giving explicit instructions to the contrary."

"The answer, esteemed Comrade Ambassador, is that we cannot always tell Comrade Ho Chi Minh exactly what to do. In other words, he does not always take our advice."

"We control his supplies," Orlik said in a peevish voice. "We can stop them whenever we wish. That should bring the little man around."

"Were it that simple, Comrade Ambassador." The Naval attaché sighed. This was at least the tenth time he had explained exactly the same thing in exactly the same way to the Ambassador. The man simply was not capable of retaining what he was told. It was no secret that he started on his vodka by ten in the morning.

"It is a Party directive," the naval attaché continued, "that we supply all that is necessary, but not apply the type of pressure that could cause a split with our esteemed colleagues of North Vietnam. Personally, I don't think Ho Chi Minh gave exact instructions to the Navy to attack the American destroyers. I think the attacks came as a result of a local commander's decision to see how serious the Americans were in steaming off the coast." The attack in 1964, which President Johnson had used as a *casus belli*, set up the Tonkin Gulf Resolution.

Chernov was growing fidgety. He sneaked a look at his watch. He was due to fly early that afternoon. There was one more briefing before his turn, and it took almost half an hour to drive to Gia Lam, where the MiGs were parked.

The Army attaché rose and gleefully listed the tonnage of the matériel arriving by the two rail lines from China: 600 tons per week. New vehicles, trucks, artillery, and SAMs arrived daily to flood the city. They were even parked outside the Canadian and British missions. The attaché was positively gloating as he read off the figures for the matériel flowing south along the Truong Son route, which the Americans called the Ho Chi Minh Trail: 350 tons per week.

Then it was Chernov's turn to give the latest status of the Hanoi air defense system.

"Comrade Ambassador, and comrades," he began. "During a one-week period ending yesterday, there were twenty-two air strikes against North Vietnam. Each strike was composed of thirty to forty aircraft. Seven strikes were prosecuted by the American Navy, fifteen by their Air Force. Although our Vietnamese comrades claim seventeen Americans were shot down, the actual losses were five: six by antiaircraft fire, one by SA-2s, two by MiG aerial action, and one that appears to have gone out of control and crashed."

"What is the ratio, Comrade Chernov," the Army attaché began, "between the number of sorties our fighters fly and the number of Americans shot down?"

It was a point that Chernov did not want to address. It was difficult training the Vietnamese. Not that they weren't good pilot material, but bureaucracy limited their training. He could not requisition enough fuel or ammunition for sufficient training sorties to raise the Vietnamese to a level of competence approaching that of the Americans. That was why he had started flying on combat missions with the pilots he was advising. He needed the time in the air for further training. From there it had been easy for him to progress to actual aerial combat with the Americans. How could he "advise" his "students" if he did not partake in the actual sweat and strain of combat with them? As it was now, however, the ratio of sorties to planes was about thirty sorties to one American shot down. He was asked the next dreaded question.

"How many American aircraft shot down for each one of ours?"

"That is not a good subject," Chernov replied. "At this time it is barely one of theirs for one of ours." At least it was better than fifteen years earlier in Korea. Then, North Korean and Chinese pilots and airplanes had been blown out of the sky at the appalling rate of twelve friendly aircraft for one enemy American.

"How are these American pilots?" Predvechnikov asked.

Chernov took a deep breath. He was torn between telling the truth or merely telling what they wanted to hear. He decided on the truth.

"They are very, very good," he said. "Most have exceptionally high time in their aircraft, and employ them in an extremely professional manner. They seem to like to fight other aircraft, and do not run if outnumbered. Strange, though, sometimes they are in a position to shoot at one of our aircraft, and they do not. We are trying to gather intelligence on why this is so." The *rezident* made a note. Chernov continued.

"Their bomber pilots seem to be nerveless. Regardless of the antiaircraft fire we put up, they dive to the attack. Then there is the American mania for rescue. They will lose two pilots to recover one."

"How do you suppose such a decadent society produces such seemingly dedicated men?" Orlik mumbled.

"Salary," Anatoly Ignatov broke in. Chernov's accolades for American airmen had gone far enough, the political officer decided. "Americans will do anything if you pay them enough."

The chief military attaché spoke up. "About the deplorable shootdown ratio, you must do better, comrade," he said, as if it were Chernov's fault personally. "The victories of our Vietnamese comrades must be increased."

"You must understand, Comrade Chief Military Attaché," Chernov said, "the Vietnamese air defense forces cause the Americans to use from 25 to 50 percent of their aircraft on any one strike to protect their bombers by attacking our defense forces. This means they are not bombers. Furthermore, many of the bombers have to jettison their weapons when they are attacked before they reach the target. When intercepted properly, sometimes as many as half of the attacking force jettison. I would remind you, comrade, one does not have to shoot an airplane down to render it ineffective."

"I give that point to you, Comrade Colonel Chernov. But is it not better to destroy, than merely deter?" the Comrade Chief Military Attaché said. He continued before Chernov could answer. "What then of our SA-2 surface-to-air missiles? What results do we have?"

Chernov actively disliked this pig's blowhole. As the chief, he was also the head of the GRU, the Soviet military intelligence arm. He was a fat, arrogant man with a face like a rotting potato who, in Chernov's eye, sucked up to the Ambassador like a bitch in heat. Further, the GRU man obviously disliked the Soviet Air Force in general, and fighter pilot Vladimir Nicholaevych Chernov in particular.

"Let us go back two years when the Americans started attacking," Chernov said. "In 1965, the SA-2 shot down 11 Americans. Last year, 1966, it shot down 31. So far this year, we have shot down 42 Americans."

He hoped desperately they would not ask how many SAM missiles it took to bring down one airplane. The ratio was appalling. He remembered the air defense artillery classes he had attended before his posting as advisor. The instructors had said they were sure an SA-2 SAM would claim 70 to 80 percent kills. What a joke. A Soviet artillery lieutenant advising the SA-2 installations had told him the Vietnamese fired the big missiles like machine guns, that they had little discipline. Nor would they take advice from their advisors. It had taken exactly 3,691 SA-2 missiles to shoot down 84 American aircraft—a 2.2 percent kill ratio. Even that was going down as the Americans developed their electronic countermeasure systems to spoof the missile radar.

"What about the antiaircraft batteries? What is their score?" the Ambassador asked.

"Very high, over eighty percent of all Americans shot down are by the guns," Chernov replied. "Mind you, to achieve this score, about 25 metric tons of ordnance detonates in the air each month."

For safety, everyone stayed in their shelter for an extra four minutes after the all-clear sounded. During that time, the streets and buildings tinkled and rang with shrapnel pieces that fell from the sky like steel rain. Occasionally, a faulty SA-2 crashed back and exploded in a residential district or an enemy airplane fell in town. In those cases, the propaganda ministry had its cameras out to record the latest incidence of "indiscriminate bombing by the Yankee air pirates."

"That is a certainty," said the Ambassador, "that so many tons are blown up above our heads." The men at the table nodded as if his redundant remarks were of grave importance. The Ambassador turned to the chief military attaché. "I believe it is your turn to update the situation, comrade." The GRU man arose. He started his briefing with an admonition.

"My subject today is classified as Secret, Level Two. You must not repeat this to those who are not directly involved. Yet, in time, as the strategy I am about to discuss becomes clear, you may speak more freely, but only among yourselves."

It was what he always said before his current strategy briefings. Chernov kept a straight face as he listened to its inconsistencies. Classified, but you can talk about it ... but only when it became clear. Ridiculous, Chernov thought. Regardless, his face was without expression. He remembered hearing these types of lectures before with his old friend Igor Smirnov of his MiG-17 days. They had been friends since DOSAAF. They would look and roll their eyes and wink at each other when the bureaucrats tuned up. Now, there was no one in Hanoi he could confide in. Closeness was politically risky. One never knew who would report what to the political officer in an attempt to curry favor. The GRU blowhole continued.

"General Vo Nguyen Giap has released his current plan for an attack strategy against the imperialists. He has released it, I should add, after our study and approval. Although I suspect our approval— or indeed our nonapproval—is of little consequence to the man. His plan is in three phases. In the first, National Liberation Front guerrillas will make frontal assaults against enemy bases, such as the Marines at Con Thien and Gio Linh." He pointed to the positions in South Vietnam near the DMZ. "The purpose is to draw the imperialists away from their coastal positions and from populated enclaves. The second phase includes the righteous uprising of the peasant and city dwellers against the imperialists and their puppet government. The NLF guerrillas will equip and lead this spontaneous uprising. The third phase will see General Giap mounting one or more decisive battles in the northern provinces."

"What forces does he have at his disposal?" Ambassador Orlik asked. He wanted the truth, not the popular lie. He knew the official line perfectly: There was a civil war in the south of Vietnam, peasant against landowner and corrupt government; it was supported with a few supplies from the north. And, the North Vietnamese emphatically said to the world at large, there were no northern troops in South Vietnam. The National Liberation Front was purely a spontaneous group mounting a just struggle against their oppressors. The North Vietnamese and the Soviets had gone to painstaking detail to establish the ruse for international consumption. They had succeeded beyond their dreams.

"General Giap has thirty-seven battalions," the GRU man said, "which is about 18,000 men, and hundreds of artillery pieces, up to 152mm, for his use in the northern provinces. Giap reports his troops are well dug in and have not been discovered by either imperialist photo reconnaissance or ground agents."

"How does he know they have not been discovered?" the Ambassador asked. Even Chernov laughed inwardly at the stupidity of that question. It was well-known the communications networks of the Americans and their Vietnamese cohorts were riddled with the ears and eyes of the NLF. So much so, in fact, that the Soviet advisers referred to American communications as the *mezdunarodneay telefon,* "World Telephone."

"Comrade Ambassador," the GRU colonel said, not unkindly, "we know everything that goes on in the American camps and units. Our information comes from Vietnamese shoeshine boys and officers in the military, bar-girls, our Eastern bloc allies, and poor American communications security." He laughed. "What they cannot supply, we get from Western magazines and newspapers. Why, KGB and GRU subscription rates total hundreds of thousands of rubles. Of course, that saves millions in research work by our people." The Ambassador nodded. The subscriptions were actually paid for in western currency. Outside of East Bloc countries, the ruble was worthless.

When the briefing was completed, Chernov tried to slip out the door to make his flight line appointment. The usual afternoon American raid was due soon, and he wanted to be airborne to meet the attackers. He was barely out the door and into the hallway when Anatoly Ignatov took him by the arm.

"Ah, Comrade Colonel. Very nice briefing." His voice became almost conspiratorial. "I must see you. Can you come to my office now? It is quite urgent."

Chernov looked at his watch. "Comrade Ignatov, I am overdue at the airfield at Gia Lam as it is. I cannot stop."

Ignatov frowned. "You are a busy man, comrade. But you must never be too busy for Party affairs," he said.

Chernov felt his stomach tighten. "Party affairs" was the euphemism for subject matters that invariably involved detrimental information passed by a *stukach*. What did Ignatov know?

"I will see you now," Chernov said. He followed Ignatov down the hall.

Since the first grade in Moscow, Chernov had been brought up in a snitch and self-confession atmosphere. He remembered being an *Oktyabryata*, a child of the revolution. Octoberites had to live up to Party standards so as to join the next link in the training chain, the Young Pioneers. The thirty children in his class had been divided into "links" of ten, each with a link leader under command of the class leader. At the beginning of the school day, each link leader would dutifully report the failings of his link to the entire class. "Boris picked his nose. Vladimir sang in the march. Yelena wore dirty stockings."

After they grew up, the link leader snitchers entered into the vast, faceless bureaucracy that toiled away at impossible quotas. The good snitchers, derisively called *stukachi*, went into factories, the military, and the countless other places that needed paid informers. They were easy to spot, for they were the ones who got promoted even though incompetent; the ones who drove one of the few cars around and had high privileges. Chernov had never been a good link leader, but his outstanding academic grades and athletic ability combined with his perfect "New Soviet Man" looks of brown hair and blue eyes carried more than just the day for him. He was thought of as a model Communist youth, and was monitored and swept forward under ever-increasing scrutiny.

"Comrade Chernov, thank you for giving of your valuable time. I know you have a busy schedule," Ignatov said. He moved to sit behind his desk.

"I do, comrade. I must be at the airfield by noon," Chernov said. On one hand, Chernov was irked. It was a half hour's steamy drive from the Soviet Embassy to the Gia Lam airfield. On the other hand, Chernov had a healthy respect for the immense power wielded by this or any other CPSU official.

"What do you want to see me about?" he asked.

"I have here a document of interest to you, comrade." Chernov read the sheet Ignatov pushed forward.

"*Report on V. N. Chernov's Character in Hanoi, DRV,*" it was titled. "*V. N. Chernov was squadron commander of Field Training Detachment, MiG-21PF. He conducted training and development of Vietnamese Air Force pilots and radar tacticians. His activities in this direction should be regarded as of great value.*" It ended there.

"You will notice," Ignatov said, "the character report is not finished. It does not include my assessment of your Marxist-Leninist activities. It does not include whether or not you are upholding the standards of international communism." He looked sharply at Chernov. "It has come to my attention that you are spending too much time flying and not enough time conducting ground training. Further, Comrade Ceballos has stated you are not cooperative with his investigations of American air secrets." He paused, as if waiting for Chernov to protest. He continued. "You must ask yourself if your activities are in the best interests of the Party." He took the report back. "What I want you to do, Comrade Chernov, is to give deep thought to your feelings and actions. Are they truly in accordance with Party needs? Perhaps, Comrade Colonel, we need to have a self-confession session wherein we probe your innermost thoughts and beliefs." Chernov thought Ignatov looked and acted like all the *stukachi* in the Communist party: fanatically gaunt and zealously jealous. They were always the ones, as children, that had stood on the edge of things, picking their pimples and watching with cruel and envious eyes those who were active and achieved things.

Self-confession, pah!

1430 Hours Local, Wednesday, 11 October 1967
Airborne in a MiG-21 over Hanoi
Democratic Republic of Vietnam

☆

On the flight line, Chernov conferred with Toon and Vong. Instead of wearing his normal dark blue flight suit, he had requisitioned the largest of the Vietnamese dark-brown Chinese-made suits. He did not want to be visible as a Russian pilot, at least not from a distance. And, in a more practical sense, were he ever to bail out, he did not want to be mistaken for an American by the villagers. For prestige purposes, the Soviet Air Force had supplied the NVAF with full-pressure suits to fly the MiG-21 as if they were rocket ships. Since full pressure was only necessary over 63,000 feet, where the low pressure causes blood to boil at body temperature, no one wore them. The face masks were suffocating and the tight-laced coveralls uncomfortable. They dressed, instead, in the lightweight cotton coveralls made in China. Chernov did continue to wear his form-fitted blue helmet.

Chernov told Toon to lead their flight of three today. Toon smiled widely, and began his briefing to his two wingmen. He spoke a mixture of French and English because Chernov didn't speak enough Vietnamese to comprehend a technical briefing.

"We will take off under control of Hanoi Radar," Toon began. "They will position us west of the sector to await the enemy. This time, after we take off, we will fly very low and seek cover behind the hills. Hanoi Radar will pass us off to Victory Intercept Control, who will tell us when the Americans are in the best position for us to commence the attack. Upon my signal, we will advance power to the maximum, gain airspeed, then fly up and behind the Americans. From there, when your instruments give you the proper signal, you will fire your missiles all at once. I will then command you to dive away, to the left or right as I specify, to return to ground level as fast as possible. This entire plan is coordinated with the air defense batteries. There will be three more flights of three at two-minute intervals behind us. If your missiles will not fire or if you see they do not guide, you will not go in for a gun attack." Chernov had finally secured three Gsh-27 gun pod packages for him and his prize pupils to mount on their airplanes. "No gun attack. To do so is to get too close and risk taking a hit from either a ground battery or a missile from the flights behind us. You must be clear, so the flights behind you can fire their missiles." Toon tapped the map at the spots where the AAA guns were located. "We must be particularly careful not to fly in the cone of antiaircraft fire. After what happened to Lieutenant Thanh of the 26th Air Defense Battery, they will be shooting at anything. When the fire coordinator called for each battery to fire at once, Thanh would hold back his battery one or two seconds. That way when the Yankees dove in, they would see someone else's muzzle flashes to attack. Thanh was shot this morning for cowardice. His sector commander was censured for lack of vigilance in leadership."

Toon looked at his watch. It was 1430 hours. The American afternoon raid usually appeared at 1500. He nodded. The three pilots touched hands and went to their planes. Each of their MiG-21s, the PF model, was equipped with two K-13 heat-seeking missiles on wing stations and (thanks to Chernov) one GSh 23mm gun with 200 rounds of ammunition under the belly. Chernov still did not want his "students" to use the gun unless it was an easy kill, or a last-ditch maneuver. He, himself, could hardly wait to get into a gunfight. When the members of the flight had started and checked in, Toon called for instructions from the control tower.

"This is Ba Ch'in Hai flight with three airplanes. Request permission to taxi," he transmitted.

"Ba Ch'in Hai flight, you have permission," the control tower answered.

"Understood. I am executing," Toon replied, and advanced the throttle. Unlike American ground control, Vietnamese pilots are expected to know the prevailing wind and to pick the active runway. This method sometimes caused confusion. Once on the runway, Toon and his wingmen advanced their throttles and selected afterburner range. Their flight call sign, Ba Ch'in Hai, was Vietnamese for the big numbers 392 painted on Toon's MiG-21.

"Ba Ch'in Hai flight, you have afterburners. You are cleared to take off."

"Understood. I am executing," Toon said, using the Russian style of communication. At ten-second intervals, Vong and Chernov followed Toon into the air. Minutes later, they closed to fly in a loose trail formation on his airplane. Toon leveled at 300 meters above the ground and brought his throttle back to maintain 650 kilometers per hour, about 360 knots. He contacted Victory Intercept Control.

"I see you clear," Victory said. "Turn to one four zero degrees, Ba Ch'in Hai. Stay at your present altitude. *Mui lo* inbound at 8,000 meters. They will be over the river in twelve minutes." The controller used the slang term *mui lo*, meaning "long-noses," for the Americans.

Toon led his flight to the low hills, where they could duck into a valley and become invisible to the American airborne radar that bore the call sign College Eye. Chernov had turned on his modified radio to hear College Eye warn the approaching strike force.

"Bandits, bandits." College Eye's radio transmissions were much more powerful than Victory Control's. "Bandits airborne one four zero from the bull's eye. Gone off scope. Lost contact. Watch Banana Valley. Repeat, watch Banana Valley."

Chernov knew Banana Valley was the slang name the Yankees used for the very area in which they planned to orbit and await the strike force.

"*Hara sho*," he said to himself. It makes no difference. The F-4 Phantom patrol planes won't come down, because they don't have the fuel. If Toon attacks the bombers correctly, probably a mix of F-4s and F-105 Thunderchiefs, they may release their bombs early. Even if we don't shoot one down, we have kept the Yankees from attacking their target.

Under Toon's direction, all three planes had throttled back to burn as little fuel as possible. The MiG-21 was a great fuel guzzler, even more than most jets, especially at their low altitude of 300 meters. Chernov followed Vong and Toon as Toon set up a wide turning circle. In doing as Chernov had taught, Toon ensured that all three planes in the flight had sight of one another. If they were attacked, each could defend the plane in front of him. It was a standard defensive wheel tactic Chernov had developed for his protégés from a World War I ace called Lufberry.

Their fuel was down to twelve minutes remaining when Victory Control finally called them.

"*Mui lo* approaching your position from the southwest at 5,000 meters and descending."

Toon acknowledged, and slowly pushed his throttle up. Vong and Toon did the same to stay in position. Toon had to gain airspeed at the expense of fuel to climb up and attack from the rear of the American strike force at just the correct moment. Chernov looked up in time to see the American force passing overhead. There were four F-105 Thunderchiefs in two flights of two. His experienced eyes recognized the shapes of the cluster bomb units and bombs they carried to attack the missile and antiaircraft gun sites around the target area. Behind them were twelve more Thunderchiefs, each carrying nine 750-pound bombs for a hard target. The Americans flew in three flights of four each.

Chernov added more throttle to stay in position. He looked first north, then south, of the strike formation. It was standard American practice to place F-4 Phantoms nearby to escort the F-105s that carried the bombs. Now Toon was at full throttle, as were Vong and Chernov to stay with him.

"Ba Ch'in Hai, go to attack throttle," Toon transmitted.

All three pilots moved their throttles into the afterburner range and accelerated to Mach 1, the speed of sound. All three planes bucked and vibrated from .96 Mach to 1.0, a bad unsolved characteristic of the MiG-21, then smoothed out. Their airspeed indicators registered 1,200 kilometers per hour. The F-105s had passed overhead without seeing them. Toon had judged correctly when to advance the speed of the three MiGs. He started the flight upward. As briefed, each man would select a target, lock his missiles on, fire when five kilometers from the enemy airplane, then dive away.

Chernov looked past Toon and Vong to select a suitable F-105 target. Every ten seconds, he had to twist and throw a wing down to look behind him. The cockpit and canopy of MiG-21s was arranged such that the pilot had no rearward visibility. As he drew closer to the F-105s, he no longer had the time to do this, nor did he have a wingman protecting his tail, now that they were strung out in attack formation. All he could do was glance into the two rear mirrors mounted on his canopy bow to check his tail. Soviet philosophy at the time of the MiG-21 design had been to use only missiles against attacking American bombers; there was no reason to look behind, since they were not in a dogfight and no one would be there. The

United States Navy had felt the same way twelve years before about the fleet defense role of the F-4 Phantom. It would carry missiles only to attack bombers in straight and level set-piece radar intercepts.

He saw the four specks that would be the next flight of F-105s inbound to the target with a full load of bombs. Ideally, Chernov thought, all four Thunderchiefs behind him would jettison their bombs to attack his flight, then ignite their afterburners for extra thrust to catch him. It would be a foolish move, because he was already beyond Mach 1. Then, while they wasted their bombs trying to catch up, he and his flight would shoot down three of the four in front and dive away to safety. He looked at his fuel gauge. He had just enough to hold course for one more minute, fire his missiles, then dive away for the sanctuary of his air base, where he knew the Americans were forbidden to attack. He concentrated on the reticle of his gunsight projected on the forward windscreen. Again, he damned the Soviet Airplane Bureau. Why they had put thick bullet-proof glass in front could be known only to some obscure aero-engineer. The chances of it ever deflecting a shell fired at him from head on was nil, while the thickness of the glass reduced his forward visibility to five kilometers. Ridiculous.

He selected the far left airplane. He could see Toon and Vong behind the two on the right. His missile-tracking system gave a warning growl in his headset that it was starting to track the heat of the F-105 in front. He was closing rapidly. It was important to be at exactly the correct range and not have excess side loads or bank angles if his missile was to fire clean and stay locked on, and not wander aimlessly because it had broken lock. He made one last glance to the mirrors to be sure he was safe—and his heart froze. The four specks he had assumed were F-105s were actually four F-4 Phantom fighters that had sandwiched themselves between the attacking F-105 flights, hoping Victory Control would think they were bombers. The ruse had worked. Now the four enemy were attacking Chernov and his two pilots. Victory Control had not been skilled enough to see the difference on their radar scope. He shouted a warning on the radio. It was Bolo all over again.

"Ba Ch'in Hai flight, enemy behind, enemy behind. Left, sharp left ... *now*," he commanded. Immediately, all three MiGs broke sharply left to escape the four Phantoms tracking them. Chernov had seen enough to know they were D-model F-4s carrying heat-seekers and radar missiles. The high Mach number at which all three MiGs flew caused their turn to be wide, because the MiG-21 control system was set so the pilot could not pull the stick back far enough to cause a high-speed stall. That meant the pilot could not get the maximum performance from his airplane. The attacking F-4s, Chernov saw, were looking at free meat. From their position, the Americans could easily stay inside the turn radius of the MiGs and bring their noses to bear on each one.

"Get down," he yelled. "Fly at ground level to base airfield." The order was too late for Vong. He had started to trade his airspeed for altitude, which would have enabled him to turn sharper and meet the F-4s head-on. An aggressive but foolish move, Chernov registered. He and Toon hugged the ground with what remaining drops of fuel they had. Chernov kept checking his mirrors. He saw the long plume of rocket smoke as at least four, maybe five, missiles streaked toward Vong's airplane. The last he saw before they topped the low hills was a brilliant flash as Vong's airplane exploded. He knew the F-4s had lost sight of him and Toon in the excitement of chasing and shooting down Vong.

"Do you desire a vector to base, Ba Ch'in Hai flight?" Victory Control asked in a contrite voice.

Toon reeled off a string of Vietnamese at them that made clear reference to their illegitimate canine ancestry, and their cross-eyed inability to warn them of attacking *mui lo*s. He then demanded the controller tell him his number. It was *nam bay*—five three. Victory Control was silent as Chernov and Toon landed at Gia Lam with barely enough fuel to taxi clear of the runway.

"Quickly," Chernov shouted to the ground controller. "Give us fuel and we will fly again." He and Toon stayed in their cockpits while the refueling hoses were lifted to the three fuel tank openings.

Chernov had studied American airplanes. Ever since the F-86 fighter, they all had single-point refueling systems, which allowed the airplane to be filled up from one hose under pressure. He and Toon tried to remain calm as they waited for the outmoded gravity tanks of their fighters to fill. Yet theirs was an advantage. All well and good for the Americans with their fancy gear; it took a special refueling truck, hose, and nozzle, whereas the MiG-21 could be refueled anyplace by anybody, even by hand on a desert field from a barrel. That was an advantage of simplicity the Americans didn't seem to care for. Twenty minutes later, they were airborne, Toon leading.

"Two one zero degrees, Ba Ch'in Hai flight," a new and authoritative controller's voice said. "Climb to twelve thousand meters. The enemy is off target and heading west. You will intercept in six minutes. Confirm missile switches."

"Executing. Confirm switches," Toon replied. "Switches confirmed," Chernov repeated.

The F-105s had egressed several minutes before, but the last of the attacking F-4s were orbiting the parachute of a pilot downed by AAA fire. Chernov knew the F-4s had to be low on fuel. In any case, they never rescued their pilots this far north. No helicopter could get through the heavy flak. Soon it would be too dark to do anything, regardless.

The sky to the west was clear. Toon stayed low to remain in the shadows. They both saw the black smoke trails of the unburnt fuel from the Americans' J-79 engines built by General Electric. Small consolation, Chernov said to himself, but the telltale smoke did point like curving arrows to his American Air Force targets. He had long ago noticed the American Navy had almost solved that particular problem. Chernov reached up and turned his gunsight on, then lowered his hand to the right panel to put his missile switches on. He selected single fire, and checked that his coolant switch was on to prepare the IR head of his missile.

Toon and Chernov swept in on the two Americans just as they were leaving the downed pilot. The College Eye transmission was loud as it warned the two F-4 pilots about the approaching MiGs, but it was too late for the one closest to Chernov. His K-13 missile was at a high-pitched scream, telling Chernov it had locked on to the Phantom's tailpipe heat. Although the sun was in that direction, Chernov knew the tone was too loud to be locked on to the diffused heat of the setting sun. He pressed the firing button on the control stick twice to launch two missiles. The Phantom he had shot at must have spotted him, for it turned sharply into the attacking missiles. Chernov cursed in disgust as the first missile bored straight ahead and didn't try to turn with the American airplane. It had lost its lock. He quickly fired a third and fourth in desperation. Then cursed again at his wastefulness, as the second missile impacted the tail of the big Phantom, blowing off pieces and igniting a huge stream of white flame.

The American plane continued westward as the trailing flame got bigger. Then, as it started to roll uncontrollably, he saw two figures eject from the crippled airplane. Keeping an eye in the direction he knew the parachutes would be opening, he saw Toon turning back from chasing the other F-4. He hadn't gotten close enough to shoot and had had to turn back because he was low on fuel. Chernov and Toon orbited the descending parachutes. Toon radioed the coordinates to Victory Control. Chernov pulled in tighter as he orbited the chutes. He felt a sudden urge to look at the men he had just shot down. One man hung limp in his parachute, unconscious or dead. He slipped over toward the other, careful that his maneuvers didn't upset or spill either chute.

Chernov grinned when he saw what the second man was doing. He had a pistol out and was shooting at him.

"That is a fighting man," Chernov transmitted to Toon.

They were at 1,500 meters now. Chernov looked down. He saw the rice paddies below the two men. Villagers were gathered to capture the two flyers. They knew they were Americans, because the parachute canopies were white. All the Vietnamese canopies were either bright orange and white in a square pattern or a dirty yellow color. Over 700 American airplanes had been shot down up North. The villagers knew their canopies. Chernov had visions of the torture awaiting the men, if they survived the beatings at the hands of the villagers. He stopped grinning.

1915 Hours Local, Wednesday, 11 October 1967
Office of the Fighter Regimental Commander
North Vietnamese Air Force
Hanoi, Democratic Republic of Vietnam

☆

Dai Ta (Colonel) Nguyen Van Huu was the fighter regiment commander of the North Vietnamese Air Force. He was a tall man, thin and grave. His almond-shaped eyes were black and somber as he listened to *Pod-Palcovnik* Vladimir Nicholaevych Chernov debrief the events of the day. Major Toon was also present. They were in the colonel's office at regimental headquarters, and sat in dim light in front of the colonel's wooden desk.

The afternoon raid results were inconclusive. Two F-105s had been shot down by ground fire, one F-4 shot down by Chernov's MiG-21. One MiG-21, Vong's, had been lost to an attacking F-4, determined by its call sign to be from the American air base named Ubon Ratchitani in northern Thailand. Vong had parachuted out successfully, and was even now in a truck returning him to the Gia Lam air base. Colonel Huu and Chernov were discussing tactics. So far, Toon had said nothing.

"The Americans," Chernov said, "tried an old mischief today. They placed one flight of defending F-4s between the first two F-105 flights at the same altitude and airspeed. Victory Control did not break them out soon enough, even though they started to descend faster than the F-105 bombers. One of them shot Vong. The others disrupted an attack Toon and I were making on three Thunderchiefs. We had to disengage. They lost us in the ground clutter."

Colonel Huu fixed Chernov with a malevolent eye. "American tactics aside, you flew today," he accused.

"I fly most every day, Colonel," Chernov said respectfully.

"Do not throw dice with me. You do not fly to one side, observing. You fly combat. That is expressly against the agreement between our governments. If the Yankees were to find out, they would inflame world opinion against us. We have problems enough. You will not fly combat. I warn you."

"With the greatest of respect, *Dai Ta* Huu, may I be permitted to speak?" Toon asked Colonel Huu. Huu dipped his chin a quarter-inch in assent.

"This man Chernov has been of inestimable service to our air force. You yourself knew him as the best instructor at Fruenze. Here and now, there are nearly one hundred Soviet pilots 'advising' us, but this Chernov has taught us more by example than all the Russian long-noses who sit around and drink vodka and try to defile our women. Or those flat-faced North Korean imbeciles who barely know a pitot tube from a *pissoir*. Chernov is not like that. He helps us, *Dai Ta*. To ground him is to ground the hawk, it is to break the wing of the falcon."

Hara sho, Chernov said to himself in surprise. Toon is eloquent far beyond what I had imagined. He stopped a beginning smile.

"He is not 'grounded,' as you put it," Huu said. "Nor is it for you to tell me what I can or cannot do." His face was impassive as he stared at Toon, who at first kept his eyes lowered. Then Toon's face became rock hard. He stood up and assumed a position of rigid attention.

"I must make a confession," he began. "I did not shoot down all six . . ."

"You have no permission to make a confession," Huu interrupted in a monotone, his face without expression.

Toon tightened his lips. A thin veil of sweat broke out on his upper lip. "I respectfully request permission to make a confession, *Dai Ta* Huu," he said in a strained voice.

Huu sighed. "Sit down, Toon, have some tea and be quiet. I know what you want to confess, and I don't want the words spoken, now or ever. This is not a time for self-confession." *Dai Ta* Nguyen Van Huu leaned forward and poured fresh tea, starting with Toon. "We must relax," he said. "Perhaps I was imprudent to talk about your flying, Comrade Colonel Chernov. After all, you did have a victory. We will leave that subject for now." He sipped his tea. "Please," he said, pointing to Chernov's cup.

"We will discuss tactics only. My MiG-17 and MiG-19 pilots are doing better than my MiG-21 pilots, but all of them could be doing better. I want you," he said to Chernov, "to tell me what you and your government can do to make my pilots more able in our fighter aircraft."

Chernov took out his red notebook and outlined for the fighter regiment commander the ideas he had written down.

"Comrade Colonel," he began. "The men must fly more. They must train more with live missiles and guns. They must have better coordination from Victory Control. And they must know their families are safe from the Yankee air raids when they are in the air." He paused. "And I must fly more with them," he added.

Dai Ta Huu arose and walked to the window. He looked out over the darkened airfield. The dim light from the bulb on his desk lamp barely contoured his body. He wore a tan two-piece uniform made of thin cotton. The red rank badges on his collar were old and faded. He sighed, and lit a thick French Gaulois cigarette with a flaring wooden match. There were no black-out requirements. The Yankees never attacked at night. Huu sighed, and turned to face Chernov.

"You show an ignorance of your own logistics system," he said. "We can get barely enough fuel and ammunition to mount what few defensive missions we can. However, I can ensure that coordination with Victory Control will be better. I will assign Vong to spend one month there as punishment for his stupidity today." He puffed on his cigarette. "Family safety concerns us all. Yet there is nothing we can or will do. We must all drink from the same cup." He eyed Chernov. "And you cannot fly more. You fly too much even now. I cannot afford the fuel, much less the risk of discovery."

"I beg your pardon then, Colonel Huu," Chernov said, "since there can be no additional training, I have an airborne attack plan to suggest. Your pilots can get training while actually flying air defense missions against the imperialists."

Huu nodded. "You may speak of this plan," he said.

"In addition to the regularly scheduled training flights, I will fly in the defense missions as an airborne director. We have seen that even the best controllers in Victory Control can make mistakes. They have only their radar scopes to monitor. They cannot place the air battle into proper context. They cannot readily tell an American F-4 from an A-4, a fighter from a bomber, much less their intentions. As an airborne director, off to one side, I can see these things and direct the defending elements into proper position. Victory Control can, of course, keep me informed of distant threats."

Huu regarded Chernov steadily. Direct eye contact was not something that Vietnamese normally do. Yet Chernov had seen it practiced by combat-hardened Vietnamese military men as if they were beyond any cultural mores or protocol.

"I authorize you to try your system," he said, "but understand, I want no dueling, no prolonged fights against the Yankee air pirates." He scribbled some notes, then looked up. Once again, he fixed Chernov with a stern look. "Do not let me *catch* you flying combat," he said.

"There is another subject," Chernov said. "We must be permitted to launch attack sorties against the radar warning planes the Yankees fly over Laos and the South China Sea. They have slow, four-engined propeller C-121 airplanes that carry radar to warn the enemy as we try to intercept them. They also have B-66 airplanes over Laos to perform electronic warfare. It would be a simple matter indeed to eliminate these craft."

For the first time, Huu's eyes flashed. "You will *not* tell me what we will do. We have our own policies and our own reasons. It is not for you to dictate what tactics we will use to achieve our goals." He did something Vietnamese rarely do, he displayed emotion by slamming his fist down. Huu was, after all, a fighter pilot used to being obeyed. "If we attack these planes outside of our borders, then we can no longer count on world opinion to regard us as simple people defending our homeland from the Yankee juggernaut. It is for that reason we will not permit our air forces to strike and bomb Yankee bases close to the Demilitarized Zone." He leaned toward Chernov. "Understand, Comrade *Pod-Palcovnik* Chernov," he spoke in a deliberate voice, "we will do two things in our heroic struggle against the imperialist forces: we will maintain favorable public opinion, and we shall win the struggle. It is better we lose ten bridges, twenty MiGs, one hundred thousand people, before we lose the favorable opinion of the world. For that opinion is worth many regiments of airplanes, hundreds of ships sailing to our country with military equipment, many thousands of rail cars filled with supplies." He drew a thin smile across his lips. "Of course, it will be just the opposite with the *mui-lo* imperialist aggressors. They are already losing world opinion, and they will lose the war. If not soon, then later. No matter, they will lose. We can wait while they destroy themselves in their own country and in the eyes of the world. We can wait. We will win."

Chernov was silent. He knew the intense colonel was dead serious.

The ancient black telephone on his desk gave two short rings. Huu answered with his name, listened for a few seconds, and spoke a few words in Vietnamese. He held his hand over the mouthpiece. He looked at Chernov, his eyes inscrutable.

"Señor Ceballos is waiting for you downstairs. He wants to escort you to Hoa Lo to meet one of the American flyers shot down today."

Chernov went pale. "I do not wish to see him," he said.

Huu looked quizzical, but nodded. He spoke into the phone and hung up. "You do not like him?" he asked.

Chernov moistened his lips. "I do not," he said.

Huu spoke, his eyes veiled. "I know what he does. I said you were not available."

14

0730 Hours Local, Friday, 13 October 1967
Briefing Room, Headquarters
8th Tactical Fighter Wing
Ubon Royal Thai Air Force Base
Kingdom of Thailand

☆

By 1965, it had become apparent that more American aircraft were needed to engage in the air war in North Vietnam and Laos. The number of air bases in South Vietnam close enough to hit the northern targets were too few. To increase the number of strike aircraft located in Thailand from a token force, the State Department and the Thai government had met and hammered out the details. As a result, the Department of Defense had directed the USAF to enlarge and operate from seven Royal Thai Air Force bases. The five strike bases were Korat, Nakhom Phanom, Tahkli, Udorn, and Ubon; the two support bases were U Tapao and a section of the civilian airport Don Muang outside of Bangkok. At the request of the Thai government, command of the forces had to be by a USAF officer actually stationed in Thailand. This situation, of course, made the commander subject to the U.S. Ambassador, the highest-ranking U.S. official in the country. The USAF had complied and placed a major general at Udorn to command the USAF. He, of course, responded to orders from CINCPAC in Hawaii, who was in charge of all air campaigns against North Vietnam. The U.S. Ambassador to Thailand, as was the case in South Vietnam, did not assume operational control of the military. Out of range of rockets and sapper attacks, and in range of towns with calm and friendly Thais, the USAF bases in Thailand were considered good duty. If you must go to war . . .

Ubon Royal Thai Air Force Base at Ubon was one such base. Quartered there was the 8th Tactical Fighter Wing with 72 F-4 Phantoms built by McDonnell Douglas. For a fighter, the Phantom was the heaviest around. It weighed more than a World War II B-17 bomber, and it carried three times as much ordnance. Its two jet engines put out 700 percent more horsepower than the four piston engines on the B-17. Yet its crew was two men; the B-17 had a crew of ten. Of course, the B-17 cost 276 thousand in 1943 dollars, the F-4 cost 2.4 million in 1967 dollars.

"Fuck you, fuck you" sounded loud and clear. The cry startled Court Bannister and the other new crew members in the front seats of the briefing room at Ubon Royal Thai Air Force Base. The command came in a rising and falling high-pitched voice from the curtained wings of the stage in the big briefing room. Onstage, the Wing Weapons Officer, Major Algernon Albert ("Flak") Apple, briefing the newly arrived pilots and back-seaters, laughed and explained. Because Apple had previous F-4 time, he had gone through the short F-4 refresher course at George AFB, then straight to Ubon.

"That's George, our good luck gecko," Apple said. He was wearing his K-2B green bag flight suit, as was Bannister and the other air crew members sitting in the audience. "He's a six-inch lizard that has the run of the stage. His comments are not necessarily those of the wing commander, nor are they in any way to be construed as a critique of my orientation lecture. He's been here since the place was built. As long as he tells off the briefer, we have a good mission. If we don't hear from him, we get worried. Last January, for Operation Bolo, he read off everybody from Colonel Olds to the tech sergeant briefing the weather. Maybe you heard what happened that day. The Eighth shot down seven MiGs with no losses of our own. Two weeks later, George was out chasing a lady gecko or doing whatever gentlemen geckos do, and didn't make the briefing. We lost three that day to ground fire."

Apple pulled out one of several 8 × 4-foot chart sections resting on slotted tracks in the wings. "I am going to tell you about the base, our mission, and the town." He pointed to a map of Thailand. "Ubon is one of seven air bases used by Americans in Thailand. We are here at the sufferance of the King and the Prime Minister. Thailand has a military government that can toss us out anytime. Note that it was only last March they admitted we were here flying missions into North Vietnam. Remember, gentlemen, Ubon Ratchitani belongs to the Royal Thai Air Force. We are guests here. Conduct yourselves accordingly."

He pulled out the fighter wing composition chart. "Your chain of command is through your flight commander, your operations officer, your squadron commander, then the DO—the Director of Operations—and ends with the wing commander. Our Wing Commander is Colonel Delbert L. Crepens. He is flying right now. As soon as he lands, he will stop by to say hello. In case you didn't know, Colonel Crepens just took over the 8th last week when Colonel Pell was shot down up north. We've had some bad luck. Colonel Pell had just re-placed Colonel Olds, who had rotated back to the States to become Commandant of Cadets at the Air Force Academy. Pell was on his second mission when he got nailed stooging around at 5,000 feet looking for MiGs." Apple looked carefully at his audience. "Offering yourself up as a target is not the way to attack MiGs and be a hero. Particularly offering yourself as a low and slow target," he added dryly.

He pointed to the organizational chart. "Our DO is Colonel Stan Bryce. He and Colonel Crepens have about 5,000 people to oversee in this wing. We have four fighter squadrons. Three work in the day-time, one—the 497th Night Owls—is a dedicated night attack squad-ron." There were some puckered orifices when he mentioned the Night Owls. No pilot enjoyed dive bombing at night among karst mountains that rose a mile in the air around the target area. The new guys, FNGs, hadn't been assigned to a unit yet, and were fervently hoping it would be one of the day squadrons.

"Now, about our mission," Apple said. "Our mission is to gain and maintain air superiority over North Vietnam and Laos; to interdict enemy lines of communications, which is a fancy way of saying to stop supplies that flow to or down the Ho Chi Minh Trail; and to respond as ordered to certain other missions. Those other missions, gentlemen, are classified Secret. They can be anything from support-ing Laotian ground troops to providing air cover for extraction of clandestine American operations in North Vietnam or Laos." He stopped talking and pointed to the raised hand of a young captain.

"Those clandestine American operations. Does that mean we have Americans on the ground in Laos and North Vietnam?" he asked.

Flak Apple grinned. "That's a 'need to know' subject right now. You'll get more information if you are ever lucky enough to be fragged for one of these missions."

"Lucky?" the captain persisted.

"Sure, 'lucky,' " Apple said. "All of our missions are *against* enemy installations, supplies, rail lines, stuff like that. On these missions, you are *for* some real, live Americans on the ground. Kind of personalizes things." He leaned forward and spoke in a confidential manner. "I can tell you this. If you are ever unlucky enough to be shot down, you would be mighty happy to see one of those gentlemen offering you a ticket home. They could be Navy Seals; but most likely Green Berets."

Apple continued his orientation briefing. He outlined the mainte-nance, munitions, intelligence, and weather organizations that sup-ported the four F-4 fighter squadrons assigned to the wing. Flak Apple came from behind the podium to stand at the edge of the stage. He surveyed the new F-4 crew members.

"You are going to be very busy," Apple said, "busier than perhaps any other time of your flying careers. The war is a 24-hour operation. We fly or don't fly by the frag order that comes in every night from the Frag Shop at Tan Son Nhut. In case you didn't know, the 'frag order' is that fragment of the daily operations order that tells us what targets to strike, what ordnance to strike them with, and the TOT, time on target, meaning exactly what hour and minute to strike. The frag comes in by teletype and is broken out by our wing operations people—people like me, your friendly wing weapons officer. The frags are measured out to each squadron, then your friendly squadron operations officer assigns the aircrews to fly them. The schedule for the next day is posted in the Officer's Club. If the missions are big and hairy, and are scheduled to go up north with a gaggle of airplanes, we brief the mission in here. Individual flight briefings are held in the squadron buildings afterward. In addition to flying, you will pull extra duties that depend on your experience. You lieutenants pull squadron duty officer, which means you man the operations desk and help the ops officer keep every mission posted. Next level, the captains, pull mobile control out on the end of the runway or in the control tower. You report problems with the airfield, you make sure every airplane is buttoned up before takeoff, and you make sure every airplane has their gear down for landing. Next and hairiest, is SOF—Supervisor of Flying. You experienced guys pull that up here in Wing Headquarters in the Command Post. The SOF oversees all the flying operations and makes decisions such as who goes where in an emergency. It is not for the faint hearts. In the air you got your ass hung out. As SOF, your career is hung out a mile. One faulty decision, and goodbye fighters." He looked around. "You captains can relax. SOF is for majors and above." He pushed one chart board in, and pulled another out.

"Our navigation facilities are the Ubon TACAN on Channel 93, Lion is the call sign for our local radar control, and Invert is the call sign of the radar that will see you over the fence into the Steel Tiger portion of Laos. Over northern Laos in the Plaine des Jarres or North Vietnam, you will run into other call signs that will be briefed as the missions are fragged." He pointed to another chart.

"We carry a lot of bombs, not many rockets, Cluster Bomb Units, napalm once in a while, and air-to-air missiles and/or the pistol, depending on the mission we are fragged for. The pistol, which hopefully you all got a chance to use in your upgrade program, is the one-ton SUU-16 20 millimeter cannon we hang under the centerline. It carries 1150 rounds. If you're too close to get your MiG with a missile, stick this pistol in there and hose 'em down. It's made gatling-style, and can squirt off 6,000 rounds of twenty mike-mike per minute. We don't always carry it. Depending on the mission, we may carry a 600-gallon drop tank in the centerline position. Soon we will be getting the Electronic Countermeasure pod [ECM]. For missiles, we almost always have the radar-guided Sparrow in the wells." The F-4 had four slender recesses under its fuselage to house the AIM-7 Sparrow. He pulled out a chart of North Vietnam with many red circles around major cities, railheads, and bridges.

"About enemy defenses. They range from MiGs and SAMs—the surface-to-air missiles—up north, to kids with slingshots in the south. In between are 12.7s, 23, 37, 87, and 100 millimeter guns. Most are radar-directed. Some, like the four-barrel ZSU-4 23mm and the quad ZPU-14.5mm, can be manually controlled and the gunners are damn good. Give 'em half a chance and they'll stitch you from one end to the other. You studied MiGs during upgrade. Then there are the SAMs. You'll get special briefings on them."

He pulled out a photo of a two-seater F-105 bristling with antennas and weapons. "These are the Wild Weasels. They go in before anybody else to take out as much of the air defense system as they can. Primarily, they home in on the radar that directs the guns and the SAM sites. The Weasels, the Sandys, and the Jolly Greens are the ballsiest guys over here. The Weasels go after the guns that shoot at you; the Sandys, flying that old A-1 prop job, protect you if you are shot down; and the Jolly Greens come in with helicopters to rescue you. No Weasel, Sandy, or Jolly buys a drink in our club. You guys got any questions so far?" Flak Apple asked.

"Yeah, how do I get transferred out of this chickenshit outfit? And if I can't get transferred out, how do I get laid around here? What's the town like?" Heads turned to look at the questioner, a white-haired captain with the name Partin on his name tag. He was as leathery as an old Texas saddle. Apple ignored the flippancy of the question and gave a straight account of the town of Ubon.

"The town of Ubon is located just outside the main gate of the air base. It's a nice quiet town with many trees, paved streets, and industrious people. The housing runs the gamut. There are corrugated tin hootches on dusty streets that hold newly arrived peasants working for the Americans. Deeper in town, near the Mun River, are many nice houses and a few marble villas under palm trees. There are religious structures called wats. They are temples for the Buddhist monks. In the main section are several tailors for GI clothing, and some restaurants, ranging from pizza parlors to an old Frenchman's place. Also down there is a U.S. Government AID office and some Peace Corps people. There are even two small hotels. There are buses, some hard-packed dirt streets that stream water during the monsoon season, a large market, and the Mun River curving through town. And there are scattered beer joints and bars with girls for the GIs. We of the Eighth Tac Fighter Wing also help support the Saint Joseph Orphanage on Palochai Road."

Apple pirouetted his bulky body to show his well-tailored flight suit. "Rajah Wongsee makes these and your party suits for you. At a price, of course." Finished with his display, he turned and pulled out a large aeronautical chart of the entire Southeast Asian area.

"Back to business. We've two kinds of weather here," he said. "Hot and dry, and hot and wet. The weather in this part of up-country Thailand is either in the monsoon or dry season; six months' heavy rain, then six months of heat and dust. Gentlemen, the weather can kill you as fast as the guns and the karst."

A navigator raised his hand. "What's karst?"

"Before I answer, let me welcome you and the other navigator to the 8th. You guys are called a GIB, guy in back. Up until now, we have had pilots back there, not navs. It's about time we got some navs assigned here." Flak Apple smiled. The navigators did not smile back. They had been hastily recruited from the Air Defense Command, and were not at all sure what they had gotten into.

"To answer your question, karst is a limestone outcropping that juts up all over the northern part of Thailand, Laos, and western North Vietnam. It assumes bizarre shapes and is riddled with caves and guns. The bad guys are in 'em like fleas on a hog. Some have so many guns poking from them they look like battleships. When we go north over Hanoi or the Pack Six targets, we fly a couple of miles over the top of them. But when we are on the Trail, we're down among 'em. And that's bad, because they look down on the Trail and can give you a good hosing."

"What's Pack Six?" a lieutenant asked.

"The powers that be have divided all North Vietnam into seven areas that are assigned to either the Air Force or the Navy." He pulled out a large map of North Vietnam. "The DMZ is the Demilitarized Zone which divides North from South Vietnam." He used his pointer on the map. "The Route Package system starts at the DMZ with Pack One and runs north for about sixty miles. The Air Force is responsible for Pack One. Heading farther north are Two, Three, and Four, which belong to the Navy. The USAF has Five. The Hanoi area is split into Six Alpha, which the USAF is responsible for, and Six Bravo, which the Navy has."

"Why is North Vietnam so divvied up? Seems complicated," a major said.

"It is," Flak said. "Our illustrious Air Force and Navy have yet to agree to a single manager of air power. Unfortunately, this means there isn't always a combined effort against Uncle Ho. Our targets come from the President down through the JCS, who sends them to CINCPAC in Hawaii. There, they are split between 7th Air Force at Tan Son Nhut in Saigon, and the Navy's Task Force 77, which is composed of carriers and support ships at Yankee Station, here, and Dixie Station, there." Flak pointed to the two spots in international waters in the South China Sea where Navy carriers launched strikes against North and South Vietnam.

"Regardless of the problems the wheels have," Apple said, "we jocks make it work. It's simple. Our job is to fly and to fight, and don't forget it." He consulted a piece of paper. "One last thing, the personnel people want me to remind you to keep your Emergency Data Form 246 current, and the hospital people want me to remind you to take your malaria pills every day."

A tall man wearing the eagles of a full colonel walked on the stage from the wing next to Flak Apple. Apple called the troops to attention.

"At ease," the colonel said, "be seated. I'm Colonel Del Crepens, your new wing commander. I say new for two reasons—you are new here and so am I." Delbert L. Crepens had light brown hair cut short, a long, narrow face, and thin features. The lines on his face suggested he was always listening for a sound others might not hear. His eyes were pale blue, almost watery. His flight suit was stained dark with sweat where his G-suit had covered his legs and belly.

He continued. "There has been some bad luck here in the past. But that's over now. There is more to our job than just flying and fighting. I have been sent up here personally by General Raimer, the Director of Operations for 7th Air Force, to see that this wing regains its position as the top wing in Southeast Asia."

Court Bannister raised his hand. Colonel Crepens looked surprised. "Yes?" he said.

"Sir, I thought the Eighth already was the top wing in Southeast Asia. It's shot down more MiGs than any other wing, and has a higher in-commission rate for its airplanes than anyone else."

"Well, son . . . what is your name?" Crepens asked.

"Bannister, sir."

"Well, Major Bannister, there is more to having the best wing than shooting down airplanes. For example, our relations with the town of Ubon is not good. Too many of our people are creating drunken scenes. We have too many reports from the officer's and NCO's hotels in Bangkok about drunkenness and rowdy parties of our people." He frowned as he consulted some notes. "The base hospital reports the Eighth has the second highest VD rate in the Command. In our officer and NCO clubs, there is frequent damage due to drunken parties. Just last week, there was an incident concerning our pilots against two colonels from Seventh Air Force, who were here on an inspection tour. The colonels report several of the pilots were disrespectful and raucous in the Officer's Club." Colonel Delbert L. Crepens surveyed his audience. He tilted his chin up in the unconscious but unmistakable gesture of a man looking down his nose at something a bit rancid. His pale blue eyes darted over the seated audience.

"I am starting some new policies. Since you are new, you will hear them first. My first policy involves aircraft utilization. Based upon instructions from the Secretary of Defense, I wish to double up on maintenance men on each aircraft rather than request more aircraft from the States. This plan I call Rapid Roger. *Rapid* for the speed in which we will perform, and *Roger* for our willingness to do it." He made a benign smile, then took on a serious air.

"My second policy regards personnel. It is as follows; the Officer's Club and the NCO Club will serve drinks only between the hours of 1700 and 2000 instead of the current policy of twenty-four hours open bar. Regarding drinks, there will be a chit system such that no officer or NCO can have more than two drinks of hard liquor or three beers in any twenty-four-hour period." He paused and looked around as if expecting some dissension. The pilots and navigators exchanged glances and eye-rolls. No one dared voice their astonishment over such an outrageous restraining order.

In a combat zone, the NCO and Officer's Clubs were the family dining room, the lounge, the local pub, the living room, the corner drugstore, and the social gathering place for the troops. There was no other facility so all-inclusive. Everyone lived a bachelor's existence on a combat air base. Outside of work at the flight line, there was a hobby shop or two (wood and leather), a base gym (weights, basketball, racquet ball), the movie theater (hot and crowded during two shows a day), and that was it. The clubs were everything. It was taken for granted that people would get drunk and blow off the steam they had accumulated while flying long and hazardous combat missions, or maintaining the planes that flew those missions. To restrict the bar service was like removing the engine from an airplane and still expecting it to fly.

Whatever response Colonel Crepens expected from his audience did not materialize. There was only silence. Abruptly, George the gecko decided to let the world know what he thought of Colonel Crepens and his restrictive policies.

"Fuck you, fuck you," he said, then "fuck you, fuck you," again for good measure. Colonel Crepens's eyes widened. Up to this point in his short tenure on the fighter base, no one had informed him about George the good luck gecko. He turned to Flak Apple, whose black face was anything but composed.

"Ah, sir," Apple began, barely able to talk, "that's our good luck guh-guh . . ." Flak was losing it and he knew it. "Guh-CHOO," he faked a giant sneeze, and whipped out a bandanna to cover his face. The members of the audience bit down on fingers, pencils, even tongues, in an effort to be quiet. Each knew that if even one so much as tittered, it would spread and the whole place would come apart in a storm of guffaws.

Colonel Delbert L. Crepens made his first wise move since mounting the stage; he left the stage. Flak Apple called the auditorium to attention for the departing wing commander.

"What in hell have I walked into?" Court Bannister asked Flak Apple. Apple's briefing was just completed. They sat in his small office in wing headquarters. The green compa-board walls were covered with blowup pictures of F-4 armament and radar panels.

"I dunno, Court. This guy is an unknown," Flak Apple said. "As far as I can tell, he never was a DO in a wing, or even a squadron commander I wonder just how much squadron time he has. All I know is, before coming up here he worked in Blue Chip, the command post down at Seventh. His reaction to old George was not a particularly good indicator of his sense of humor. Ah, well, such is life in the service of our country." He leaned his chair against the back wall. "Do you have a squadron assignment yet?" Apple asked.

"No. I have an appointment with the DO, Colonel Bryce, at 1400. I guess I'll find out then. What's he like?"

"Stan the Man? He's a great guy. Everybody likes him. He's new. Only been here three weeks. Came in from a job in the Pentagon. He's got a great fighter background. Flew '86s in Korea. It's his first tour, but I think he'll be okay."

"Flak, how you been doing? Got any MiGs yet?" Court asked.

"Shit, no. All they want us to do is bomb, bomb, bomb. I've had only three knockdown fights. Got me one damaged and one probable. They got some new tactics and some new shit-hot jocks in MiG-19s and MiG-21s that are giving us fits. They've got GCI, ground controlled intercepts by radar, and some very aggressive people both at the scopes and in the cockpit. As you know, we don't have any GCI. We do have a couple big four-engined radar prop jobs hanging over Laos and sometimes the South China Sea trying to give us MiG warning. Their call sign is College Eye. The Navy has a destroyer out there doing the same thing, call sign Crown. But they have spots they just can't see. Anything under ten thousand feet more than fifty miles inland, for example. That's where most of the MiG bases are located." Flak Apple got up and walked to the large map of Southeast Asia. He indicated with the flat of his hand the area near Hanoi where U.S. radar coverage was available only when the USAF EC-121s were airborne. Then he pulled out pictures of the two types of air-to-air missiles the F-4 could carry; the radar-guided AIM-7 Sparrow, and the heat-seeking AIM-9 Sidewinder.

"We got missile problems," he said. "The parameters under which we must fly to successfully launch them are unrealistic. Pull too many Gs, be in the slightest slip or skid, be too close or too far to the plane you're shooting at, don't cool the seeker head enough; any of those and the missiles go nuts. Sometimes they just come off and don't do anything, even if you're in the firing envelope." He leaned his hip on the desk. "Thank God we got the pistol. Maybe we're not fighting as many MiGs as we'd like, but at least we got the cannon to back up the crappy missiles. Oh yeah, one other thing, you can't shoot until you have a positive identification on the bird you're attacking. That causes a lot of lost opportunities to fire radar missiles in head-on attacks from 30 miles. But until we get a positive way to instantly ID friend from foe—a MiG-21 and a Navy A-4 look alike—we've got to bore in close to get the Mark I, Mod O eyeball on the target. That's the way it is."

"What about the new MiG tactics?" Court asked.

"Let me tell you. When Olds had the wing, we got eighteen MiGs for a loss of only three F-4s. That's six of theirs to one of ours. Since he left here, things have turned to shit," Apple said.

"Why?" Court asked. He pulled his Luckies and lighter from his left sleeve pocket and lit up.

"The new MiG tactics, and bad intelligence processing from Seventh Air Force. Besides the six F-4s we've lost to MiGs, we've lost another thirty-one to ground fire."

"My God," Court said. "That's more than two squadrons of airplanes in less than a year. How many pilots did we get back?"

"Less than half. About thirty went down in Pack Six and we only got six out."

"How come?" Court asked.

"You just can't take those big Jolly Green helicopters into Pack Six. There are too many guns. Plus it takes a long time for them to get there at a hundred fifty miles per hour. They stage out of Lima Sites in Laos near the North Vietnamese border. But they can't make the Pack Six area fast enough. If you can't get a guy out in the first fifteen minutes he's down, you're going to get trouble. The bad guys close in, capture or kill him, and set up a flak trap." Flak Apple blew out a stream of air. "It's a bitch. By the way, Court, do me a favor."

"Sure, what?"

"Put that cigarette out. The smoke is bad for my lungs."

1400 Hours Local, Friday, 13 October 1967
Office of the Director of Operations
8th Tactical Fighter Wing
Ubon Royal Thai Air Force Base
Kingdom of Thailand

☆

Colonel Stanley D. Bryce had a twelve-pound, cast-iron bulldog on the shelf behind his desk. He had won it as the star football player at the University of Georgia in 1948. On his desk was a large teak plaque with his name and a pair of pilot's wings topped by a wreath around a star, which indicated Bryce was a command pilot. An Air Force pilot had to fly for 15 years and amass 2,000 hours as a fighter pilot before he was awarded command pilot wings. Stan the Man, as he liked to be called, was six feet even, had smooth black hair combed flat, gray eyes, and broad shoulders. His face was square and pleasant in the Slavic fashion, his presence commanding. He offered a cigarette to the man sitting in front of his desk, Major Court Bannister, who thanked him, and said no. Bryce smiled as he tapped Court's Form 5 Flying Records and his 201 Personnel file laying in front of him. He pointed to one order in particular. "Every fighter pilot worth his salt would like his name on this."

DEPARTMENT OF THE AIR FORCE
HEADQUARTERS SEVENTH AIR FORCE (PACAF)
APO SAN FRANCISCO 96307

SPECIAL ORDER G-1032   18 DECEMBER 1966

1. Announcement is hereby made to credit CAPTAIN COURTLAND EdM. BANNISTER, AO3021953, 531st Tac Ftr Sqdn with 1 MiG-19 destroyed in aerial combat on 29 September 1966. Authority: Minutes of Hq 7AF Enemy Aircraft Claims Evaluation Board, 15 Sept 66.

FOR THE COMMANDER	DISTRIBUTION
	PACAF (DPSP)
	7AF (DO)
	3RD TFW,
GEORGE D. WILLIAMS, Capt. USAF	531 TFS
Chief, Publishing Division	DASPO
Directorate of Admn Services	DPSA

"Mighty impressive, Court. One tour in Vietnam, one MiG to your credit, recently promoted to major, graduate of Edwards. We are glad you are assigned here to the Eighth. You'll be an asset, I know."

Bryce sat back and regarded Court with a genial expression. "I haven't quite decided where in the wing to assign you. I have open slots in the standardization and evaluation shop here in Wing Head-quarters and two flight commander slots opening up soon in the squadrons. But, regardless of where you wind up, I want to put you on flight test orders. We need experienced guys like you to fly and check the birds that come from our maintenance hangar." He leaned back, and smiled. "At any rate, I personally want to fly with you. Today. Now, in fact." He stood up. "Get your gear, meet me in front of Wing Ops in thirty minutes. I've got a bird standing by, a very special bird I think you will like."

Court wondered why Bryce wanted to fly with him. It was common practice for a DO to fly with higher-ranking people when they first arrived in a wing. The purpose was to evaluate the man's abilities personally before assigning him an important command slot such as squadron operations officer or squadron commander, or chief of a slot in Wing Headquarters. Prospective flight commanders, however, like Court, were evaluated in the squadron, usually by the ops officer.

An hour later, Court was in the front seat of a clean F-4D, tail number 753, climbing at 20,000 feet per minute through clear air toward the Laotian border. Clean meant no external fuel tanks, bombs, or racks under the wings. Fighter pilots love clean birds be-cause they are fresh and slick, and very fast and responsive to the controls. This airplane was right from a maintenance overhaul.

It was special, all right. Under the left canopy frame was painted Court's name, and on each side of the nose was painted a large white cowboy hat. On the big metal slab leading to the left engine was painted red star, signifying the pilot had a MiG kill to his credit. It was all a bit dazzling and discomforting to be singled out for what he knew was special treatment. Where was it going to lead? The cowboy hat, well, he did wear his old Stetson Sun Ranger once in a while, but, hell . . .

Court mumbled something about thanks, which Stan the Man brushed off with a big grin. Got to take care of our troops, he had said. Why me? Court wondered. He had a suspicion that if his name wasn't Bannister, it would be weeks before an airplane would be avail-able. Most of the other F-4s that belonged to squadron and flight commanders, and to the old heads, were assigned and labeled. He'd seen "Protester's Protector" and "Betty Sue" in the revetments on either side of him as he had taxied out. They, like all the other F-4s in the Wing, had WP painted on the tail to indicate that they were from the 8th Tac Fighter Wing at Ubon. The 8th was known as the Wolf Pack, WP was one of the few times tail ID made sense. But a cowboy hat?

On the ground, Bryce had explained that what he wanted him to do during the flight was perform an FCF, the functional flight check required after extensive maintenance had been performed on an F-4. Once in the air, Bryce, from the rear cockpit, read off the FCF checklist for each item.

At 40,000 feet over Laos, according to the checklist, Court accelerated to Mach 2, pulled back on the stick, zoomed to 53,000 feet, rolled inverted, and pulled it through in a dive back toward the earth. From that ten-mile altitude, the curvature of the earth was visible in the hazy purple. He filled out the flight card on his kneeboard as he made tight turns, exercised all the avionic and hydraulic systems, and pronounced the aircraft safe for flight. Bryce pointed out a few terrain features to the east that he said were prominent landmarks along the Ho Chi Minh Trail. Within thirty minutes, they were back on the ground, taxiing into the revetment for his big Phantom.

Several maintenance people gathered around as he shut down the engines. The crew chief, Sergeant Shanahan, climbed up the ladder he placed next to the fuselage. Court had noticed his name on the other side of the canopy. Court put his helmet on the canopy bow, unstrapped, and started to climb down.

"Hold it a minute, Court," Bryce said from the rear. "We need some pictures for this occasion." He motioned to two fatigue-clad figures standing against the revetment wall, away from the maintenance people. One held a large Graflex camera. He started snapping pictures as he came forward. Still on the ladder, Bryce grabbed Court's hand and shook it while grinning into the lens as the flashbulb popped.

"Now let's get a couple by the nose of the airplane," Bryce said. Court followed instructions without speaking. After ,the picture-taking, the second man held a microphone from a tape recorder to Bryce's face.

"We have made history for the 8th Tac Fighter Wing. I have just checked out MiG killer Major Court Bannister as a Wing test pilot. At the same time I instructed him on his first combat mission," Bryce said. He moved next to Court and put his arm across his shoulders. The flashbulb went off twice more.

The man with the microphone moved in on Court. "What's the significance of the cowboy hat, Major?"

While Court stood there with a dumb look on his face, trying to say something other than it was a gross embarrassment, Colonel Stan the Man Bryce stepped forward and said it was obvious. "The significance is that old Cowboy Court not only kills MiGs, he used to ride in western movies." The public affairs officer looked doubtful, but compliant. After all, this was the DO. One does what the DO wants.

In the crew van on the way back, Bryce told Court he'd flown a good flight.

"After you get checked out with the 433rd, I'd like you to work in Wing Headquarters for a while," he added.

Court nodded. "Yes, sir," he said in a low tone. No line fighter pilot enjoyed working in the headquarters section unless he was highly experienced and in charge of a tactics branch or something similar that required daily combat flying. "In what capacity?" he asked.

"I'll let you know," Colonel Stan the Man Bryce said.

"I'm not much of a paper shuffler, so if it's all the same to you, Colonel, it's got to be in a full flying capacity," Court said. He was pressing and he knew it. But, he rationalized, I didn't go to all that trouble to get back over here just to hang out at Wing Headquarters.

"It will be," Bryce replied. "It surely will be."

2045 Hours Local, Friday, 13 October 1967
Officer's Club, 8th Tactical Fighter Wing
Ubon Royal Thai Air Force Base
Kingdom of Thailand

☆

The word was out. Normally, over fifty patrons were in the dining room or at the bar of the Officer's Club. Tonight, merely twelve officers were present. The atmosphere was sullen and sour. "The hell with it," one of two captains said. "Let's make for the hootch." Two majors in for the night with a bent airplane asked what in hell was going on. The captains explained about the booze ban, and invited them to the squadron hootch for a drink.

It was custom, tradition, common sense, and just plain efficient to have a bar or two in the hootch area. In fact, each of the four fighter squadrons had fabricated their own bar in the covered patio and breezeway area joining their wooden motel-like barracks. Lieutenants were four to a room, captains and majors two to a room, one single for the lieutenant colonel operations officer. Community showers and toilets were down the screened-in hall. The lieutenant colonel squadron commander was allotted half a house trailer in another compound.

The bars they built between the buildings were elaborate affairs with refrigerators and quality stereo systems. In the town of Ubon, the pilots had bought tables, chairs, and couches, and rolls of mesh to screen off the breezeway. The walls and ceilings were loaded with memorabilia fighter crews like to keep around: flags, pictures, weapons. All of it humorous. Framed in bamboo was a quote made by de Tocqueville in 1835 that always incited favorable comment:

"The journalists of the United States are generally in a
very humble position, with a scanty education and a
vulgar turn of mind . . . the characteristics of the American journalist consist in an open and coarse appeal to
the passions of the readers; he abandons principles to
assail the characters of individuals, to track them in
private life and disclose all their weaknesses and vices.
Nothing could be more deplorable . . ."

Well-kept lawns maintained by battalions of Thai workers covered
the officers' quarters as well as the whole air base, making the community of five thousand American men and nine women very attrac-
tive. Were it not for the imminent death or capture of several of its
inhabitants each month, Ubon Royal Thai Air Force Base could almost be considered an exclusive country club.

The four men walked into the hootch bar complaining bitterly
about the ban on liquor in the officer's clubs. "Well, hell, the NCOs
don't like it any more than we do," someone yelled at them. "They're
still doing their job."

Flak Apple and Court Bannister sat side by side in deep lawn chairs.
They were talking as they gazed absently through the screens at the
lighted walkways and roads extending from the hootch area. The
overhead fan stirred the cool night air. Each had a cold bottle of beer
in his hand. On the stereo, the Mamas and the Papas sang convinc-
ingly about the joy of going where you wanta, wanta go.

"I've walked into some weird stuff here," Court said. "First, a CO
that doesn't believe in booze, then a DO that believes in logging a
combat mission just because you cross the fence into Laos on a maintenance check flight. The hell of it is, he hasn't assigned me to a
squadron yet. Said I'll be working in Wing."

"Court, let me tell you something," Flak began. "Stan the Man
Bryce is a great guy. He'll take care of you, you'll see. He's sharp and
he likes to have sharp guys around him."

"He's taking care of me, all right. You heard about that bird he had
all rigged up for me? I'm not so sure I want to be that close to him—
or let him get that close to me."

"Don't worry about it. Maybe I can get him to put you in my
shop," Flak said. "As far as Crepens is concerned, he'd better rescind
that no-booze order damn quick or there'll be war right on this little
old air patch."

Court sighed. "Yeah, I suppose so. There's another thing," he said.
"I just don't function well with a guy in back. A couple times in
training my GIB misread an altimeter or talked when he should have
been listening. Damned distracting." Court put down his beer bottle.
"There is something else, or maybe it's related, Flak. But I don't fly

the airplane quite as I would like. Something keeps me from pushing just a little farther. I don't feel like I really know the bird yet. Everything I've flown so far I've spun and stop-cocked at one time or another, just to practice recovery and airstarts." Court had just revealed a practice he had used, quite illegally, since he was a cadet. No fighter squadron taught or permitted such things; intentionally switching off an engine to learn the airstart procedures, or deliberately putting an aircraft into a spin to see how well it recovers. Had he been caught, he probably would have been grounded. Yet this practice, like his jumping out of airplanes with the Special Forces, he regarded as prudent kinetic and antipanic insurance against the day—that would most surely arrive—when he had to do it under unexpected and adverse conditions.

Flak nodded. "You've got to remember, you're a bomber pilot now," he said. "You have a crew to look after. You can't hang it out like you used to in single-seaters, because it isn't just your life at stake anymore."

"Shit," Court said. "You would have to appeal to my decency."

"I'll appeal to more than that," Apple said. "As far as a back-seater is concerned, you'll get used to having one. Try a night mission on the Ho Chi Minh Trail without one, and see how far you get. Or a MiG CAP without an extra set of eyeballs. You'll see. A GIB can make you a hero or he can make you a bum. He can save your life or he can get you killed. He is as important to the proper use of that airplane as your control stick. More so, in fact. You get your stick shot away, he can use his to bring you home."

Court shook his head. "Look," he said. "I've been around this fighter business a long time. I'm up from the single-seaters—the F-86 and the F-100. I'm used to doing my own planning, preflighting, airborne eyeballing, radio calls, and all the rest. Even my own panicking, without help from anybody else. If that guy back there wants to tune the radio and radar set for me, more power to him. But don't expect me to rely upon his superior airmanship to get me out of tight spots." Court laughed. "Come on, Flak. These guys are brand-new pilots. They came here directly from pilot training. They barely know how to fly, much less fight. While I'm at it, why in hell is the Air Force putting pilots in the back seat of the F-4, anyhow? The Navy doesn't, and that's who we got the airplane from. They put RIOs back there, Radar Intercept Officers. If we must have a rear pit, why not put a navigator back there? At least he wants to be the best there is in the back seat. All a pilot wants to do is get the hell out of there to a front-seat assignment someplace." Court shook his head in disgust.

"Maybe they put pilots back there," Flak Apple said, "because there's a stick back there. Who knows? The fact remains, you have an extra set of eyeballs, an extra pair of hands, and an extra brain to draw from. Use 'em. Use 'em all. It's plain dumb to only use half a fighting tool. You wouldn't fire an automatic weapon on just semi-auto, would you?"

"Point taken," Court said.

"Or deliberately not use your wingman."

"I would not. Another point taken," Court said.

"Besides, we are already getting navs." Flak finished his beer. "Another?" he asked.

"No. I've got an oh-dark-thirty get up and go," Court said.

"Who you flying with?" Flak asked.

"The 433rd. I'm going to fly two sorties a day for the next four days with them," Court said.

"They're the best, those 433rd guys," Flak said. "I'll get on the schedule with you. I can pick and choose, you know, since I'm the Wing Weapons Officer. I get to fly with anyone I think necessary. Maybe we'll run into Colonel Tomb."

"Who's he?" Court asked.

"Just North Vietnam's first ace, that's all. The intelligence on him is a little spotty. They think he's got three Thuds and two Phantoms so far. He and a guy named Van Bay or Vong something are supposed to be the twin terrors of the skies. They run two MiG-21s around like they were on wires, and saw anything in half they can get between them. The guys flying MiG CAP in Pack Six are getting a bit nervous. What did you say you were flying tomorrow?"

"I didn't. It's combat air patrol. MiG CAP in the only place that counts, Pack Six."

Flak looked at his friend, his dark eyes sober and concerned. "You ready?" he asked.

"Yeah," Court said. "I'm ready."

"Gut check," Flak Apple said.

Court held both arms and hands straight out, palms down. Flak examined them for tremors.

"Steady as a rock," he said, "steady as a rock."

Court's stomach twitched. "You expected less?" he said.

15

1130 Hours Local, Saturday, 14 October 1967
Okaloosa County Jail
Fort Walton Beach, Florida

☆

Toby Parker's first awareness was the sound of his own name. He blinked, and opened gummy eyes that felt swollen and full of tiny bits of sand. He found himself lying on a concrete floor against a wall painted a bilious green. His head throbbed, his mouth tasted like rotten fish, he smelled of sour sweat and vomit. He wore soiled khaki pants and a white shirt with rolled-up sleeves. Six other souls in various states of alcoholic disrepair occupied sections of the 12 × 12-foot concrete floor that slanted toward a drain in the center.

"Parker, Toby G.," the voice intoned once more.

"Yeah," Toby said. He pushed to a sitting position. In sudden concern, his hand darted under his shirt. He felt the jade piece, and relaxed.

"Over here," the voice said. A deputy in a brown uniform unlocked the heavy barred door, and motioned him out. Toby struggled to his feet, staggered to the door, and followed him down the corridor. The deputy walked with quick, clean steps. His metal name tag said his name was DuBois. Toby had to trot to keep up, causing his head to jangle and throb. DuBois led him through an office door.

In the administration room, Toby's two classmates, Roy Thomas and Gerry Draper, were waiting. Each wore Bermuda shorts and colored T-shirts. Their eyes were hidden behind USAF aviator's sunglasses. Toby initialed the receipt as the clerk returned his personal effects. He had no memory of being booked, searched, and relieved of his possessions.

"Over here," Deputy DuBois said. Toby walked to his desk. "Sign this."

Toby looked over the hold-harmless form that certified he had not been harassed or unfairly treated in any way. He signed it. The deputy handed him the recipient's copy of his tickets for speeding and drunken driving.

"See here," the deputy said, pointing with his pencil at a line on the yellow form. "Says you gotta be in court nine aye em Tuesday the 17th for disposition."

Toby studied the form. "Do I have an alternative?" he asked. "Can't I just pay a fine or something?"

The deputy looked up. "No. You were arrested and booked. These guys"—he indicated the two captains—"just paid your bail bond. You're lucky the judge has a light schedule, so you can get your hearing in court in two days. Gimme fifty bucks and I'll give you a receipt for your car. It's over at the Impound on Racetrack Road."

Outside, Toby blinked in the brilliant sunlight. Gerry Draper said he was headed back to the Club. Roy drove Toby to get his car. He filled out the paperwork, paid the fine, and drove away, Roy in trail.

At a filling station, Toby sponged himself and put on an old polo shirt and sweat pants he had fished from behind his back seat. They decided to go to the Sand Flea on Okaloosa Island for a late lunch.

"Bloody Mary?" Roy asked Toby when they were seated. Toby nodded, too shaky to speak. He felt better after he had drunk two in quick succession.

"What happened, Roy? The last I remember is being at Bacon's," he said.

"Good old Bacon's by the Sea. From there we started the usual Friday night races. All the guys with Jags and Corvettes were dragging on Highway 98, west of the town of Mary Esther. You did just great, until you said we should race east into Fort Walton. You won. You sprang every trap all the way into town. They must have radioed ahead. We dropped back and watched. Four with all lights on behind you, and one crosswise in front. You finally stopped. They locked you up right then. You were very dignified and polite." He stopped and looked past Toby at the door.

A man was striding purposefully toward their table. It was Deputy DuBois, still wearing his uniform from the county jail. His mouth was etched in a thin line. The other diners stared. Uninvited, he pulled over a chair and sat down. He threw some crumpled paper onto the table in front of Toby. Toby hesitated, then picked up the ball and smoothed it out. It was the administrative and court copy of his speeding and DWI tickets. He looked up in confusion.

"Captain," the man said, and removed his sunglasses. His face was stern and severe, his eyes hard and angry. He looked to be in his late twenties. "I know who you are. Your friends explained a few things to me, and my boss just now, he explained a few things to me. My brother was killed in the Air Force in Vietnam. Your friends told me how you helped save some soldiers, and how you lost a friend, Captain Travers. Because of that, I am tearing this ticket up." Toby looked stricken as the memory of the dead Phil Travers flooded his hungover and unguarded mind.

He poked the papers into Toby's hand. "I don't do it much, tearing up tickets like this."

Toby tried to thank him. DuBois brushed it aside. His face was stern.

"I didn't do it for you. I did it for those guys you saved. And your dead friend, Captain Travers." The deputy flicked the tickets with his thumb and forefinger. "But what would they think of this?" His voice became harsher. "What would Captain Travers think if he saw you in the drunk tank laying in your own puke? He'd think you were a disgrace to the Air Force. I know I do. I think you are a disgrace to my brother's Air Force. What gives you the right to disgrace my brother's Air Force? You didn't earn that right in the back seat of Captain Travers's airplane. Your Air Force Cross doesn't give you the right to do that. You have military ID in your pocket that says you are an officer in the United States Air Force. Start acting like one, Captain, or get the goddammit-to-hell out of the military. And you can bet if you come to the jail again, you'll spend a lot more time in the drunk tank. Do you copy, sir?" Deputy DuBois stood up. He nodded sharply, turned on his heel, and strode off with quick, angry steps.

Toby Parker's face was flaming red. He felt bile rise in his throat, jumped up, and barely made it to the men's room in time. For long minutes he racked and spat until nothing came up. Sweat poured from his body. His belly was cramped and knotted. After a while, he splashed water on his face, and returned to the table. He emptied both their water glasses, slowly and carefully. Roy Thomas said nothing. Toby wiped his mouth and pushed his chair back.

"I feel like shit," he said.

"You look like shit," Roy said.

Toby pushed away the now cold scrambled eggs.

"That's it," he said. "No more."

"Those eggs do look a little greasy," Roy said.

"No, I mean booze. I've had it. I quit."

Toby said he wanted to be alone. He took Roy to his car, then drove to a secluded spot on the beach. He locked his shoes and socks and wallet in his car. He walked to the shoreline. The waves rolled and crashed with soothing regularity. Seagulls swooped and called. He started walking east. The sand squeaked as his heels dug little divots.

He walked faster, and faster, then he was running. He ran and ran, leaping over driftwood and culverts, splashing in a wave that rolled up higher than the others. And he ran. He had no concept of time, he didn't see what was ahead, and he didn't care. When his legs felt leaden and uncontrollable, he slowed to a fast walk, then ran some more. Several times he stopped to retch. Then he would plunge into the water to wash away the stink and sweat. Soon there was nothing but spasms and pain, and looping spit. And still he ran. And when he could run no more and his world was red and gasping, when his lungs felt torn and shredded, when his legs finally gave out and he fell sprawling in the sand, he felt his first shred of self-respect.

He lay on his back until he could breathe normally. Then he arose, and took up an easy jog back the way he had come. Four miles later, he came to a long concrete-and-metal fishing dock that extended over the Gulf. He didn't remember passing it. The evening sun was low and fat on the horizon.

Still barefoot, he walked to the end of the dock. The metal drain bars hurt his feet. Seagulls soared and swooped, crying for food. He focused way out and for several minutes watched the waves make up and roll shoreward. Without taking his gaze from the horizon, he slowly took the gold chain and jade from his neck and curled it into a heavy mass in his hand.

He held it to his lips for a moment, then hurled it so far out over the water the splash was lost in the waves.

1600 HOURS LOCAL, SUNDAY, 15 OCTOBER 1967
CIVILIAN FLIGHT RAMP, TAN SON NHUT AIRPORT
SAIGON, REPUBLIC OF VIETNAM

☆

Shawn Bannister stood for a moment on the top of the steps to the Pan American Boeing 707. His khaki safari was wrinkled and limp. He needed a shave after his thirty-six hours enroute from San Francisco to Saigon via Honolulu and Guam. His blond hair was long and curled over his ears. He wore his gold chain with the gold alligator roach clip attached.

He glanced over the civilian and military flight ramp from which he had departed barely ten months ago. The dissonance and stridency of the noise was exactly as he remembered. The hiss of auxiliary power units, the tearing roar of jet fighters taking off from one of the dual runways, the throb of blades from Army helicopters landing to the east side of the base, these were the sounds he remembered. The oily kerosene smell of the jet engines was as nauseating as ever.

Now, he had finally returned to Vietnam both as a journalist and a man dedicated to the cause of world peace. Becky Blinn and her friend Alexander Torpin had spent many weeks teaching him. They also had smoked tons of some really good shit.

He started down the steps as someone from behind commanded him to "*Allez, allez,* go, go."

The 707 was parked in line with Air France and Air Cambodge airliners, an Air Vietnam DC-3, and a Braniff MAC contract Boeing 707. Extending in both directions, in rows of revetments made of corrugated steel and sand, were many types of military aircraft. Civilian airliners taxied and took off, intermingled with military fighters and transports. Civilian passengers saw helmeted pilots in the cockpits of their bomb-laden fighters waiting for takeoff to fly a combat mission.

A recent rain shower had left a thin film of water, which was quickly turning to a steamy vapor. Shawn Bannister walked across the concrete ramp to the two-story civilian terminal. Inside, after an interminable delay at Immigration, he crossed to the baggage pile and claimed his one suitcase. At customs, he watched the agent run his hand several times along the smooth and expensive brown leather. Shawn Bannister finally caught on and passed a five-dollar bill to the man. No one seemed to care about the obviousness of the transaction. It hadn't been so obvious before, Shawn Bannister said to himself.

He was happily surprised to see his name spelled out with grease pencil on a piece of cardboard held by a slender Vietnamese man with a badly scarred left arm. He wore black trousers and a white shirt with short sleeves. Maybe the *Sun* is getting organized, after all, he thought. He walked up to the man.

"I'm Bannister," he said, pointing to the sign.

"And I am Nguyen Tri from the Caravelle Hotel," the man replied in passable English.

"The Caravelle," Shawn replied. "I didn't advance book a room there. Aren't you from the *California Sun?*"

"I am to take you to the Caravelle," the man repeated. Shawn Bannister seemed to hesitate. "Alexander Torpin said to make you comfortable," Nguyen Tri added.

1530 Hours Local, Monday, 16 October 1967
Joint United States Public Affairs Office (JUSPAO)
Saigon, Republic of Vietnam

☆

The first stop for any newsie who wanted to be accredited and be issued his Wahoo card, also known as the JC card, was the Joint United States Public Affairs Office, known best by its acronym, JUS-PAO. The magic ACOI Form 3 was called the Wahoo or JC card because when the new recipients got one and realized the incredible freedom it gave them, they either belted out "Wahoo," or "Jesus Christ, I don't believe it."

JUSPAO was run by Barry Zorthian, a Yalie and ex-Marine. His organization had expanded to fill a six-story, French-style building (definitely not Le Corbusier) on the corner of Le Loi and Nguyen Hue streets. Next door was the Rex Hotel, used for officer's billets. JUSPAO's roster would do justice to a small American town. Fully six hundred people, American civilians and military, and Vietnamese, worked to spread the good word among the world's populace.

Shawn Bannister registered and was given his card. He looked at the handout he was given with his new credentials. It said that by March of 1967, there were 480 newsmen—which included newspapers, magazines, TV, and radio—with credentials in Vietnam. Of this number, 393 were Americans; the remainder were Vietnamese, British, Japanese, Koreans, and Filipinos, and New Zealanders. He didn't know it, but only about 30 percent of these men and women were hard-core newsgatherers who would hump the boonies and share foxholes to be with the troops, to see what was happening. However, so many of these hard-core journalists and photographers had been killed or wounded, that the news profession was taking losses proportionally far greater than the GIs.

When he was finished at 1645, Shawn decided to attend the official briefing at JUSPAO, the Five O'Clock Follies.

The Follies was the derisive name given to daily news sessions held in the JUSPAO 200-seat auditorium. Each day the United States embassy people, Zorthian's United States Information Services (USIS) people, and the military gave journalists briefings on how they wanted them to think the war was going. Each had his own distinctively marked podium on the stage. Shawn Bannister entered the auditorium.

It was 1800 hours when he exited the JUSPAO building, blinking in the late sunshine. The air was steamy from a passing shower. Shawn checked his watch. He was to meet Nguyen Tri, and he was unsure what was to happen that evening. The briefing had been terribly boring, and contained no information of substance. The crowd of journalists, he had noted, were unruly, and as boisterous as teenagers at a Saturday matinee.

He walked the short blocks from the JUSPAO building down Le Loi to the Caravelle. The scene hadn't changed since he had walked the same streets ten months ago with his godfather, USAF Major General Albert G. Whitey Whisenand. Women vendors in black silk baggy trousers and white short-sleeved blouses still sold black market and stolen goods from their storefronts, or from bamboo mats laid on the sidewalk. Consumer goods such as watches and radios, booze and boots were out front. In the back of a store, one could negotiate for an M-16 rifle, hand grenades, or even more lethal merchandise. In-between were shops selling tailor-made suits, cameras, Honda and Vespa scooters, and other commodities essential for the good life in a war zone. Little boys ran dodging and skipping through the crowd peddling their sisters or stealing watches from the wrists and pens from the pockets of unwary strollers.

"My God, Artie. You see that slope kid? He came out of nowhere running like a stripe-assed ape, and he ripped off my shirt pocket as he went by. Got two pens and a pencil. Cheap stuff, but my God, what a trick."

"Watch out for the ones on Hondas who snatch watches right off your wrist," Artie said as they passed out of Shawn's earshot.

The castor oil exhaust fumes from the thousands of scooters in the street piled a layer of blue smoke and noxious vapor up to waist level. Strident taxi and cyclo horns added a discordant layer of sound to the thrum of traffic. Saigon was no longer the Pearl of the Orient. Saigon was now the forsaken courtesan, reduced to making her living in the streets.

Shawn wasn't in Vietnam for the money. He didn't need it. Even if he was giving one thousand dollars a month to the movement, there was still plenty left over from the five-thousand–dollar trust his father had set up for him. It was the same with his half-brother, Courtland. He knew Court didn't need his Air Force salary. In fact, in Shawn's mind, it didn't seem as if Court needed anything from anybody.

The rivalry with Court had always been one-sided, for Court had never tried to outdo Shawn. Yet once Shawn had come to an age where he'd realized he and Court were not just of different mothers, but of different temperament and outlook altogether, he had begun to hate his half-brother.

Shawn hated Court's self-assurance, and he hated Court's taciturn response when he would try to antagonize him. Most of all, he hated Court's relationship with their father, Sam Bannister. When Court was to receive his pilot wings in the Air Force, Shawn had had an angry fight with Sam, who had taken it for granted Shawn would go with him to Court's graduation. Shawn knew he could not bear to see his half-brother in his moment of accomplishment. He had gone on a three-week binge that had ended in a Paris jail for starting a fight in Maxim's, an exclusive Paris restaurant. When Sam had come over in an attempt to straighten him up, he had said the worst possible words of all to the rebellious Shawn: "Why don't you try to be more like your brother?"

Ever since that time, Shawn had spent most of his time and efforts doing the opposite of his goody-goody half-brother. While Court flew airplanes, Shawn drove motorcycles, expertly and with abandon. When Court got married, Shawn made international headlines by being the co-respondent in a divorce scandal involving a Greek tycoon and his young wife. When Court got posted to Vietnam, Shawn got hired by the antiwar *California Sun* to cover the war in Vietnam. It wasn't common knowledge outside of the editor's office, but Shawn had agreed to cover his own expenses if the editor would just hire him. The editor, no fool, had said, well, hell yes. And now, with his purpose more clearly defined, he could truly contribute to not just the *Sun*, but to mankind.

Shawn took the creaking elevator to his fourth-floor room at the Caravelle Hotel. He turned on the overhead fan, poured himself a glass of the tepid water from a vacuum jug, and for a few minutes stared out the window down on Tu Do Street. The crowd was thick with GIs surging from bar to bar, buying Saigon Tea for the bar-girls, looking for love by the hour, or minute. He was too tense to focus on the scene. His hand jerked when he heard the soft knock on the door.

Nguyen Tri smiled as he shook hands with Shawn. "It is good to see you again," he said. "You received your JUSPAO pass without any difficulty, I trust."

Shawn assured him he had the pass, directed him to sit on the wooden chair next to the small desk, and took a place near the window.

"First," Nguyen Tri said, "I want to tell you how we appreciate the hard work you and the other members of the *California Sun* are expending on our behalf."

"Wait a minute," Shawn interrupted, "what do you mean, 'we' appreciate, and 'our' behalf? Who is this 'we' you're talking about?"

Nguyen Tri smiled again, his face a study of genial watchfulness. He seemed to be measuring the American's capacity for information. He chose his words carefully.

"The 'we,'" he said, "is any right-thinking Vietnamese and peace-loving person of the world. We want this terrible war over sooner than you do. But we want to finish it ourselves. As you yourself have said so many times in your very excellent articles, this is a civil war. Foreign intervention is neither wanted nor necessary."

"We are the foreigners," Shawn said. Alexander Torpin had taught him all about this in Berkeley.

"Of course," Tri replied. "As you have so amply pointed out, and I quote one of your articles; 'The South Vietnamese must be left to settle their differences in a political manner, not in a war forced on them by American self-interest.' That was very well said, Mr. Bannister."

Shawn vaguely remembered the statement as one of many he had written in the stories he'd filed last year from Saigon. He rarely went out into the field. He was neither inclined to nor was he under pressure from the *Sun*'s home office in California to do so. They were content to have the famous Bannister name on their masthead as their man in war-torn Vietnam. They didn't care if he picked up the majority of his text from Vietnamese stringers at Givral's coffee shop or the Café Pagode, and from GIs on Tu Do Street for whom he bought drinks. He hadn't paid a lot of attention to his copy as he wrote. It had turned out he was a natural writer, and as long as his themes of antiheroes, antiwar, and antimilitary went along the lines and current trend his editor wanted, everybody was content. Text on battle scenes and true warriors was not in vogue; text about crazed GIs and bumbling generals was very much in demand.

"Yes," Shawn said to Nguyen Tri, "I remember those words."

"Do you believe them?" Tri asked.

"Sure," Shawn replied, his voice noncommittal. "I believe them. I wrote them, didn't I? Why do you ask?" He wanted to light up a joint. He had a feeling he knew where this conversation was going. For the moment, his time with Becky Blinn and Alexander Torpin seemed rather vague.

Nguyen Tri moistened his lips. "If you believe those sentiments, then you obviously would be of a mind to help save innocent lives. Innocent lives of Vietnamese, but more important, innocent lives of the young Americans who are forced to come here by a government that cares only for conquest." He studied Shawn. "You want to save lives, don't you?"

"Well, sure," Shawn said. He suddenly walked to his kit on the bed, and jerked open the straps. "Look, I hope you don't mind if I smoke."

"Not at all," Nguyen Tri replied. This was going better than he had expected. "In fact," he said, "I brought some very good cigarettes for you." He took a Marlboro fliptop box from a small black satchel, and handed it to Shawn. He opened the cover and sniffed.

"Smells like good shit," he said, and grinned. Alexander Torpin had obviously told Nguyen Tri all about him, Shawn thought. In seconds, he had a deep draft of Buddha's Burmese Best deep in his lungs. He slowly let it seep out. He sat on the edge of the bed and took another. Soon, he sat back against the headboard, his feet crossed at the ankles. He eased another long puff through his nostrils. Now he felt better able to handle this friend of Torpin's. It was all coming back; his revelations, his commitments.

"Okay, Tri," he said. "Sure, I want to save lives, but I gotta have a story to file, you understand?"

Tri grinned back and bobbed his head. "Yes," he said, "yes, I understand. How would you like an exclusive interview with one of the leaders of the Viet Cong underground right here in Saigon?"

Shawn Bannister sat bolt upright.

"Christ, yes," he said. "How soon can I get it?"

"Tomorrow morning," Nguyen Tri replied. "I'll pick you up in front of the hotel at seven-thirty. No camera," he warned.

Shawn's heart was pounding. "I'll be there. Christ, yes. I'll be there."

1600 HOURS LOCAL, MONDAY, 16 OCTOBER 1967
OFFICE OF THE SECRETARY OF DEFENSE
ROOM 3E880, THE PENTAGON
WASHINGTON, D.C.

☆

"I know I have my critics," Secretary of Defense Robert Strange McNamara said. He stood looking from his window over the Potomac River to the Tidal Basin. McNamara was dressed in a three-piece black worsted wool with narrow gray pinstripes. His impassive face looked as unlined and as animated as a blank computer screen. His rimless steel-framed glasses were spotless, and occasionally hid his eyes behind reflected light. The frames melded into his black hair combed straight back in the 1920s style, and held in place, it was rumored, by a substance called Staycomb. The person he was speaking to, USAF Major General Albert G. ("Whitey") Whisenand, stood in front of the Secretary's large desk. Whitey wore his Class A blue uniform. McNamara turned from the window to face him.

"Yes, I know I have critics," he repeated. "They say I am a power grabber." He tossed his head, eyes inscrutable behind his steel-rimmed glasses. "But knowledge is power. I provide knowledge. I provide them knowledge so they will have more power. Can't they see that? It worked so well at Ford Motors. I took control from the wasteful production people and gave it to the accountants. After all, the bottom line on the financial report is the only way to judge the efficacy of an operation, be it civilian or military. It takes knowledge to get that result. Total knowledge of input, throughput, and output. All that is important. That is from where power flows." He pursed his lips. "Can you see that point, General Whisenand? Can you see that I provide the knowledge that gives them the power?"

"Mr. Secretary, are you referring to the Joint Chiefs of Staff when you say 'they'?"

McNamara nodded in the affirmative. "Yes, I am. Of course. I have provided the Department of Defense with a planning-programming-budgeting system never before seen in the military hierarchy. Of course, to do so I have implanted civilian control. Napoleon is quoted as saying that war is too important to leave to the generals. I believe that. I also believe that budgeting is too important to leave to the generals." He made a stretching movement with his lips that he truly expected to be regarded as a smile.

"But I didn't call you up here to discuss budgeting, General. I want to show you something." He walked to an easel on a metal tripod. He flipped up a white cloth covering, revealing a big chart on poster board. A large graph had two lines snaking up: One depicted bombs dropped on the Ho Chi Minh Trail, the other showed supplies moved from North Vietnam to South Vietnam down the Trail. Both were plotted against a time line. McNamara tapped the graph with a pointer.

"When these two lines cross over, when the tonnage of bombs we drop is greater than that of the tonnage moved down the Trail, we will have begun to win the war," he said. "Numbers never lie. I want you to agree with this display, then we will take it over to the President."

Whitey studied the chart. "I agree with the graph," he said. The Secretary of Defense looked momentarily surprised, as if he had expected a different answer. "Now I want to show you mine." Whitey brought out his updated blackboard with the POW/MIA summary totalling 1,000 pilots lost and 1,700 airplanes destroyed. McNamara dismissed the board with a wave. "When compared under the statistics of the sorties flown," he said, "the losses are still within the mean of probability and therefore acceptable."

The Secretary was chauffeured to the White House in his black Lincoln Continental limousine. General Whisenand followed in a blue Dodge sedan from the Motor Pool, driven by an Air Force Staff Sergeant. They trooped into the President's office, where, without preamble, the Secretary of Defense began his briefing to the Commander in Chief.

"We are, I believe, turning the corner to victory," McNamara began. His eyes were alert and shining.

Robert Strange McNamara launched into twenty minutes of logistics figures, bomb tonnage, body counts, troops in country, and the myriad other particulars he could extract from his extraordinary memory. Flipping through charts, his excruciating details even covered how much barbed wire went into Vietnam, and how many written reports came out.

Toward the end, he brought out a chart depicting the reasons for sending more American troops to Vietnam. Whitey recognized the quantifying percentages as those advanced by a former assistant to McNamara. They were:

REASONS TO INCREASE TROOP STRENGTH IN SVN
70% for American prestige by not being defeated
20% for keeping South Vietnam free from Red China
10% for a better life for the South Vietnamese

His final chart was one he had shown Whitey in his office in the Pentagon. He traced the proposed meeting of the two lines of the Ho Chi Minh Trail showing when U.S. forces would start winning the war.

"Even General Whisenand agrees this is correct," he said, indicating Whitey. The President looked at Whitey, who spoke.

"No, sir, I do not," Whitey said.

"You did just a moment ago in my office," the Secretary said, with some irritation.

"Sir," he began, "I agree with the accuracy of the totals for bombs dropped, and I suppose the figures for tons of supplies moved down the Trail are accurate. What I do not agree with is your basic premise that we will start winning when the lines cross."

"But the facts are here, General. You cannot dispute facts," McNamara said.

The President looked from man to man as each spoke, as if he were at a tennis match. He enjoyed playing two people off against each other, figuring, often correctly, that it was a method of getting to the truth, the nut gut, as he called it.

Whitey faced McNamara. "Sir, with all respect for your efforts, I must tell you some facts. You say you like and admire facts. I have some facts that, I'm afraid, you will neither like nor admire." Whitey took a deep breath. "You are demanding statistics on pacification. Further you want to know the exact amounts of supplies moving down the Trail. You demand quantification of guerrilla activities. You demand after-action reports. You want to know tonnages of bombs dropped. You want body counts. All of these figures go into this graph and the others you just showed us. Mr. Secretary, I must tell you, you are getting garbage. These figures simply are not accurate. They range from outright lies to inflation and to duplication. The men in the field are pressed for figures. Regardless of what they are doing, they have to stop and fill out some sort of report you have ordered. So they do what any soldier in a battlefield condition does, they say anything to get headquarters off their back and the paperwork done. Then, at headquarters, the officers there don't want to be the messenger with bad news, so they pass it on, implying the information is accurate. Perhaps some even believe it is accurate. However, those who doubt and say the war is not going well are accused of negative thinking and are transferred out, often to the detriment of their career. You are manufacturing a corps of professional liars." Whitey felt he had worked himself into quite an exhibition of outrage. Yet McNamara seemed to ignore his accusations.

"Every quantitative measurement we have shows we are winning this war," McNamara said in a crisp voice to President Johnson, as if General Whisenand wasn't present in the office.

The President stood up and placed his hands, made into fists, on top of his desk.

"You've got to go back," he said in a loud voice, looking directly at Whitey. He walked around the desk to the fireplace, where he began pacing back and forth. He stomped his heels down hard as he made each turn. "I don't know what's going on over there. Hell, I don't even know what's going on over here. Everybody's lying to me. Get your ass over there, Whisenand, and find out the truth."

Whitey and McNamara avoided each other's eyes. Never the best of friends, and certainly at odds over policy, they had no intention of becoming co-defendants in the kangaroo court the President was conducting with his lashing sarcasm.

The President wasn't done. His anger was just igniting.

"It's that Fulbright and all those liberals on the Hill," he said, himself a liberal of great renown. "They're all yelling at me about Vietnam." He stopped and looked at the two men. "Why?" he asked in a voice made of gravel. He resumed his pacing. "I'll tell you why. Because I never went to Harvard. That's why. Because I wasn't John F. Kennedy. Because my Great Society program is accomplishing more than Kennedy's New Frontier ever did." He waggled his finger at the two men. "You see, they had to find some issue on which to turn against me, and they found it in Vietnam." He snorted. "That Fulbright, he joined the ranks of the dissenters. He was never satisfied with any President that didn't make him Secretary of State." He stopped pacing and walked over to the two men. He grabbed Whitey by the arm. At six-foot-three, he towered more than five inches over the general.

"You get over there," he said, "and—" He seemed to be looking for a mandate. McNamara supplied one.

"Give us your military judgment as to the prospects for a successful conclusion of the conflict in a reasonable period of time," McNamara said.

The President dropped Whitey's arm to face his Secretary of Defense. "Oh, my God, perfessor, I just want to find out if we're winning or losing," Johnson said. He shook his massive head like a lion trying to dislodge an ear mite. He walked away from both of them to the window behind his desk. He looked out over the lawn for a moment, then turned back to the room.

"There is one thing you ought to know," he said. "Vietnam is like being in an airplane without a parachute when all the engines go out. If you jump, you'll probably be killed, and if you stay in, you'll crash and probably burn. That's what it is." He fixed Whitey with a penetrating look.

"Get over there, Whisenand. I'll sign the orders personally. Find out if the goddamn airplane is going to crash and, if so, when."

16

☆

Nguyen Tri, in company with a Vietnamese driver in an old black Citroën automobile, was waiting for Shawn. He made no introductions. After a few blocks, Tri apologized, produced a piece of dark muslin, and said it was necessary to blindfold Shawn. From that point, it seemed to Shawn he was driven in circles around the city. He heard traffic sounds increase, then fade altogether, then sound again. He heard the rattle of boards as they crossed what sounded like rickety bridges. When they finally stopped, Shawn was helped from the car into what he guessed was an alley, the cement seemed gritty and trash-ridden under his feet. He was steered through a door that reverberated like cheap corrugated tin. They went into a room smelling of *nuoc-mam*, then he was led through another room, down some stairs, then carefully down a narrow ladder into a confined area that was cool and smelled of damp earth. They walked for several steps. Shawn felt the presence of walls close on each side. They pushed his head down to enter a room, and removed the blindfold. Tri showed him a small canvas-and-wood folding chair and he sat, facing a sheet of cheap cotton hanging from a line strung between the wooden walls. There were no windows. A bare light bulb hung from the cheap plywood ceiling.

"Welcome to the city headquarters of the Delta Two Battalion of the First Regiment of the People's National Liberation Front," Tri said. He stood next to Shawn. "You can understand our security precautions, I'm sure." He pointed at the hanging sheet. "Behind the screen is *Trung Ta* Nguyen Van Tung, that is, Lieutenant Colonel

Nguyen Van Tung. I am your interpreter. You may ask any question
you wish."

Shawn was caught totally unaware. It had never occurred to him
to prepare a list of questions. He thought quickly.

"Will you win the war?" he asked. Short, rapid-fire sentences rattled around the room like rifle fire.

"It is not a war, it is a political struggle to unify Vietnam against
foreign aggressors," Tri translated.

"But there are guns and bombs, and people are getting blown up
and shot," Shawn persisted. "That is war."

"The Americans are waging a war against the Vietnamese people.
It is a war they will not win," Tri translated.

"How do you know the Americans will not win?" Shawn asked.

"The Americans will not win because they have no stomach for
protracted conflict; they want immediate results. The Americans cannot win because they cannot impose their will on the hearts and
minds of the Vietnamese people, who only want a free country. It is
exactly as your revolution. You did not want a foreign power on your
land telling you to pay taxes and homage to a king thousands of miles
away."

Shawn did not wish to say that there was no analogy between the
English colonists of America, and the country from which they had
escaped persecution.

The question-and-answer session continued for another twenty
minutes. Then Van Tung went off on a long diatribe that Shawn had
decided was all a rehash of standard propaganda, worthy of maybe a
few lines. His mind wandered while the Vietnamese droned on. He
began figuring how he could capitalize on his personal experiences
of the underground visit. Maybe he could work in some heroic dodging of bullets or mortars. It was too bad no one was shooting in Cholon these days.

He was jolted out of his reverie when the Viet Cong leader asked,
through Tri, if he wanted to view an important attack, one that would
be decisive and war-changing; an attack that would make the fall of
the French-held Dien Bien Phu look insignificant by way of compar-
ison.

"Where? What kind of an attack? When? Viet Cong only, or in
conjunction with North Vietnamese regulars?" Shawn asked through
Nguyen Tri. Shawn was excited. This could be a big scoop. Maybe
he didn't need the money, but he did need the prestige and glory
that went with a major story.

"Colonel Nguyen Van Tung said the event will be soon," Tri said.
"Maybe in a few weeks. In the meantime, you can show your devotion to the cause—"

"Devotion to the cause?" Shawn interrupted. He stared at Tri. "I'm not devoted to any cause. What do you mean?" He was afraid he knew damn good and well what the Viet Cong colonel meant. Ever since the weeks with Becky Blinn and Alexander Torpin, he'd felt himself recklessly slipping into something quite dangerous. While there was a thrill to it like he had never before experienced, he wasn't sure of the outcome. His heart began to pound. He made a mental note to tell his accountant to shut off the money he sent Becky Blinn and her friends.

Nguyen Tri moistened his lips. "I am sorry, my new friend, I merely meant that since you strive to be an unbiased reporter, you are obviously devoted to the cause of . . ." he seemed to search for a word in his otherwise excellent English vocabulary, ". . . truth," he finished.

"Truth," Shawn repeated. "Okay, so I'm devoted to the cause of truth. I'll tell the story as I see it. Now, how do I show my devotion to the truth?"

Nguyen Tri said something to Colonel Nguyen Van Tung, who replied in a short sentence. "Write the story as you see fit of this interview," Tri said. "There is something else. We can speak of that on our way back to the hotel. Colonel Tung is busy, we must depart."

After Shawn and Nguyen Tri left the cave room, Colonel Nguyen Van Tung sat back and offered a cigarette from a thick blue package of French Gaulois to the man sitting next to him. The man, code-named *Than Lan*, the Lizard, was one of the top NVA men undercover in South Vietnam. The man waved the cigarette away.

"I do not smoke," Buey Dan said.

1415 Hours Local, Thursday, 19 October 1967
Hickam Air Force Base
Hawaii

☆

The early afternoon sun was painfully bright as the passengers disembarked down the mobile steps from the C-135. Whitey, as ranking passenger, was in the lead. After meeting with LBJ, he'd sent a back-channel message to CINCPAC, advising him of his arrival and asking for a meeting. He wore lightweight summer blues, and his ancient navigator's briefcase dangled from his left hand. With his right hand, he pulled a pair of jet pilot's sunglasses from an inside pocket of his tunic.

A USAF brigadier general who seemed familiar to Whitey saluted and escorted him to a blue staff car. They sat chatting while the driver retrieved Whitey's two B-4 bags.

"Yessir," the brigadier said, "I was one of the action officers in the Pentagon when you were in the Intelligence section."

Whitey remembered the brigadier then as an eager man who was always smiling and saying "can do." After a twenty-minute ride, he ushered Whitey into the office of the Commander in Chief, Pacific Forces, Admiral Sharp, on the Camp H. M. Smith facilities, and departed.

U. S. G. Sharp, Annapolis 1927, was a slight man with surprisingly broad shoulders. He had gray hair, a quick smile, and spoke with quiet articulation. His nickname since Academy days had been Oley. He wore the service white uniform with open collar. Had he so chosen, he could have worn all ten rows of his ribbons.

His huge office was furnished with a desk and conference table at one end, and a living room ensemble of light tan rattan furniture at the other. Considering the building was on a hill overlooking Pearl Harbor, the view was limited. The two officers sat facing each other across the rattan coffee table. A steward served tall glasses of iced tea. The two senior officers quickly disposed of the family inquiry niceties and got down to business.

"Whitey," the Admiral said, "your message was just a bit vague about the reasons for this trip. Are you permitted to elucidate?"

"Of course, Oley. It's quite simple, actually. The boss wants to know if we are winning or losing in Vietnam." Whitey sipped his coffee.

Admiral U. S. Grant Sharp looked at Whitey with some amusement. "Have you been reading my weekly message traffic to the Joint Chiefs of Staff regarding the air war portion?"

"Yes, I have," Whitey responded. "So I know that every week you request permission to hit the hard-core targets in North Vietnam."

"Let me tell you what I think about Washington and the White House," the Admiral said. His quiet manner gave no hint of the condemnation he was about to articulate.

"First off, when the government puts its military in a shooting situation, the American people want to know why; they want sound tactics; they want casualties kept to a minimum; and above all"—he pounded his fist on his knee—"they want to win." Admiral U. S. G. Sharp stood up.

"Regardless of that, Washington policy-makers have evolved and developed the policies of gradualism, flexible response, on-again, off-again bombing, negotiated victory—as if Ho would respond like a right-thinking Christian man—and cut and run." He put his glass down with a bang. His lower jaw came up like a bulldog.

"I'll go a step further. It's Johnson who has, himself, a personal strategy of equivocation. He blows hot and cold. He cannot make up his mind. He tries to apply the strategy of domestic policy and politics—consensus and compromise—to the battlefields of Vietnam, where firepower alone is the arbitrator. He has built his so-called strategy on faulty assumptions." Oley Sharp's eyes flashed. "He has not tapped the strengths of his country. His right-hand man, his architect, is the arrogant academician McNamara, who surrounds himself with civilian theorists who have no military background, either in uniform or, believe it or not, in classroom study. These men are brilliant statisticians, theoretical analysts, computer experts who scorn the military—the very core of the experience they so desperately lack. They have little use for what they call the military mind. They are second- and third-level political appointees with great authority who are not accountable, except to the man they work for. Let me tell you, Whitey, these men override, subvert, compromise, distort, and destroy opposing points of view. They follow their boss. McNamara has consistently discarded the advice of his military advisors. So of course his subordinates do the same." Although Sharp's eyes flashed throughout his diatribe, he neither raised his voice nor became shrill. However, Whitey noted, his voice did become as brittle and harsh as a nail scratching concrete. The Admiral continued.

"We have yet," he said, "to use air power to its fullest in Vietnam. I don't mean to say air power is the only or total key to winning this or any other war. Air power did not win World War Two, although we could not have won without it. The big Operation Strangle during the Korean War did not successfully cut the Red Chinese supply lines. But now, today, we have a large, professional force of Navy and Air Force aircraft that can bring this war to a faster conclusion with fewer casualties on both sides."

"Oley," Whitey said, "you are preaching to the choir. I am going to change the subject." He leaned forward. "Listen, I have some news for you. I don't know if it's good news or bad news. I do know it is very confidential news."

"There is very little confidential news about the war I don't know," the Admiral said with some tartness.

Whitey chuckled. "I know that. This is quite different. Johnson is going to get rid of McNamara."

The Admiral raised his chin sharply and studied Whitey's face through slitted eyes. "I can tell you aren't joking," he said. "Why and when? Did he tell you personally?"

"To answer in reverse order," Whitey said. "No, the President did not tell me personally. As an old intelligence officer, I'm ninety-nine percent sure it will happen. As to why: I suspect the protest movement has gotten to McNamara. I know the war has got to him—he has made eight trips to SEA so far—and probably even the statistics have gotten to him. I don't think he can last much longer. He was very petty in front of the Stennis committee. Kind of reminded me of the Queeg court-martial scene where the old boy bogs himself in details and recriminations. He seems obsessively precise. Once he actually asked them to stand by while he 'consulted his memory.' At any rate, I think he will be out of office . . . and very soon."

"Great Scott," Admiral Sharp said. "Won't that give the world something to say? The first American Secretary of War to be fired."

"They call them Secretary of Defense now, Oley, or haven't you heard?" Whitey gave a delighted chuckle. "But it won't come out in public that he is fired. It never does. McNamara will request retirement for ill health, or get promoted upstairs. Anything but fired." The steward entered and replenished the coffee in their cups.

"Break, break, new subject," Oley Sharp said. "I have been reading the classified test reports on that MiG-21 we got from the Israelis. Interesting. It's not as good an airplane as we had thought, is it?"

"No," Whitey said, "it is not. But there sure are a lot of them. The test report was made into a classified movie short titled *Throw a Nickel on the Grass*. We've sent copies to all the fighter wings. The film describes how the MiG-21 has poor forward and aft visibility, how the gunsight begins to fail when the pilot pulls more than four Gs, and how badly the plane behaves when a pilot wants to reverse a turn."

"What has definitely gotten my attention in the Hanoi area," the Admiral said, "is not how poorly the MiG-21 fights under certain conditions, just the opposite. The tactics and strategies are changing. The North Vietnamese pilots are becoming more aggressive, they are putting up more planes, and they are coordinating their tactics better among themselves as well as with the AAA and SAM rings around the target areas. They are hitting our guys much harder and smarter now than before. If they keep that up, we may well lose more airplanes," the Admiral concluded

"Wait until the press picks up on that," Whitey said. "I see trouble there and, ultimately, from public opinion. Which, by the way, LBJ is deathly afraid of."

"I agree," Admiral Sharp said. "We are not stopping the war in the south because we are not stopping the supplies up north, but we are losing more airplanes." He stood up. "I can see it now. The reporters will ask some poor guy at the Five O'Clock Follies why we are losing more fighters over Hanoi. And the poor guy will say it is because there are more MiGs in the air, and because they are more aggressive. The reporter will then ask, 'Well, sure, but why don't we just bomb their airfields and, since I'm asking questions, how come these little guys are beating big strong American men in aerial combat?' What do you suppose the MACV press man will say to that?"

Whitey gave a bitter chuckle. "He'll say, 'Because (a), we aren't permitted to strike their airfields, and (b), we haven't been training

our new fighter pilots well enough, because we don't want to take
the chance they may have an accident while they dogfight each
other.' "

Admiral Sharp nodded, a dour look on his face. "Yes, that's how it
will be, sure it will," he said in a voice loaded with sarcasm. The
admiral looked up, and sighed. "I haven't been much help, I'm afraid.
I'm sorry I can't give you a better picture." He stood up and paced
a few steps. "Are you sure you want me to give you an answer to
your basic question?"

Whitey nodded, lips drawn tight. He was afraid he knew exactly
what was coming. He was right.

"It isn't because of equipment problems, that can be solved. It is
because of the lack of national will. We *are* losing the war," Admiral
U. S. Grant Sharp, CINCPAC, said emphatically.

"It's a two-way street, Oley," Whitey said. "Congress can give the
people national will; or the people can generate it themselves and
pass it back to Congress. Neither is happening."

"That's correct," the Admiral said, "And so for the first time in our
history we are losing a war that should already be won."

17

☆

"It's only coincidence my name is George," Captain Richard C. Hostettler said from the podium, as George the gecko burped out one of his better "fuck you" soliloquies.

Hostettler was lying. He had never been called George. But, as one of the Intelligence Officers of the 8th Tactical Fighter Wing, his job was to get the crewmen he was about to brief for a combat mission alive and, if not happy, then alert. Little jokes never hurt. Nude girls on the slide projector, rousing marches on his portable tape recorder, imitations of how John Wayne or Lee Marvin would brief their Marine platoon before hitting Guadalcanal or Tarawa. Two days ago, he had hidden a whoopee cushion in the podium and pressed it in cadence with Colonel Crepens's footsteps as the colonel had walked across the stage. Crepens had slashed a ghastly smile, to show he was one of the boys. That evening, Crepens had appointed Hostettler to the career-broadening extra duty as Club Officer of the Ubon Royal Thai Air Force Base Officer's Open Mess. (The previous Club Officer, a nonrated lieutenant, had been shipped home early, a broken man. He simply had not been able to maintain the Officer's Club in the decorum and manner he had been taught at Hotel and Food Manager's College.)

Hostettler, Richard C., five-foot-ten, two hundred twenty pounds, former guard at West Point, former assistant line coach at the Air Force Academy, anticipated no trouble with his extra duty. A product of Plano, Texas, he also did a credible Mickey Mouse imitation.

There were twenty F-4s scheduled on the flight roster board. Four flights of four each, and one spare for each flight. It was a massive effort. Since the 8th was required to fly around the clock, usually only 10 or 12 F-4s were on each flight roster. The flight call signs were Rambler, Buick, Chevy, and Ford. The call signs had to be easy to pronounce and of significant difference so they wouldn't be confused in the heat of battle. Seventh Air Force said they were going to go random someday, but as yet hadn't got the computer working. Two flights were bombers, two were MiG cappers. Court got a chill of expectation when he saw that he was a MiG capper in Buick, Flak Apple's flight.

Hostettler pulled the first of four of his sideboards out from the wings. It was covered with a cloth flap. He pulled a sombrero from inside the podium, squared his already square massive shoulders, tugged at the waistband of his fatigues, rolled bowlegged to the front of the stage, and let go a moderately horrendous chili belch. (He made his own chili, and frequently downed two bowls for breakfast.)

"Thirty-seven millimeter," a lieutenant yelled from the assembled aircrew. "Naah, fifty-seven, at least," a captain said. "Yeah, 57 millimeter," two GIBs agreed, with some dismay. Hostettler's belches were measured in terms of the diameters of the various antiaircraft shells that were fired at the aircrews flying over enemy-held Laos and North Vietnam. He tried to make the size of his belch indicate the size of AAA fire the F-4 air crew would meet that day over the pre-selected target.

Hostettler nodded. "Okay, I'll buy that. Fifty-seven millimeter. How about this one?" He shoved his hat back and rumbled out a belch of extraordinary volume and substantial timbre. Before the troops could react, he blasted another of thunderous proportion. Some swore later they saw the walls reverberate and the curtains fly out slightly. The troops groaned.

"Oh, shit," someone said, "not eight-fives *and* one hundreds." Nobody disputed the caliber, least of all Hostettler, who turned around, bent over, and farted in generous and sonorous length.

"SAMs," his audience said in one breath.

"Now that you know *what*, I'll show you *where*," Hostettler said. He ripped the cover from the board. A three-page *Playboy* centerfold faced North Vietnam. Wolf whistles and cheers from the crew. "It's a hairy one," Richard C. ("George") Hostettler said.

He showed the pilots their target: The Canal des Rapides bridge that carried both the highway and the northeast railway running between Hanoi and China.

"This is a JCS target, gents," Hostettler said. "That means the Joint Chiefs of Staff have finally convinced the White House that destroying this truck and railroad bridge will significantly help stop the war supplies flowing south into South Vietnam."

"Now, that is brilliant reasoning for one target. Why in hell can't we take out *all* the fucking bridges?" a sardonic voice from the massed aircrew asked. Court thought it sounded like Partin.

Hostettler strode to the center of the stage. He stood at rigid attention. "Gentlemen," he said in a thick British accent, "ours is not to reason why, ours is but to fly and die." He resumed his briefing. There were, he pointed out, about 950 guns from 37mm to 85mm, in and around the immediate area of the bridge, which was well in the Hanoi inner air defense ring of an additional 3,600 guns and 225 radars. And there were SAMs.

"You know how mobile the SAMs are," he said. "They can be taken down or put up in less than twenty-four hours, search and lock-on radar included. So expect plenty of SAM launches."

He traced the ingress route, this time from the east over the water to the target, which was five miles north of the Hanoi area. Going into the Hanoi ring, in the Route Package Six area, was known as going Downtown. Of the 9,000 guns in North Vietnam, Hostettler explained, fully 6,000 were within the Hanoi 30-mile outer ring. That did not include the 156 SA-2 sites that could fire up to 100 surface-to-air missiles each, every day. The Russians supply them well, he said.

There was, however, no way to get an accurate count of the rifles fired at attacking planes. The estimate ran from one-quarter to one-third of a million. It was known that even female garment factory workers were issued rifles, usually Chinese-built 7.62mm (.30 caliber) rifles, that they hauled out when the sirens went off. They'd lay on their backs and shoot at anything that flew overhead: MiGs, F-4s, drones, even the International Control Commission transport carrying neutral dignitaries. If it was in the air, it was an enemy. Some young ladies and other workers suffered from lost eyes and other indentations, as the products of their weapons succumbed to gravity and returned whence they had originated at a great velocity.

The factory gunners claimed scores of planes a week. The North Vietnamese government did nothing to discourage such absurdities. They knew full well that just firing the guns was a morale-building and hate-strengthening device. In actuality, the third of a million or so guns averaged about one fighter aircraft per month. The 6,000 guns around Hanoi, that monthly exploded 25 tons of steel in the air, averaged 25 fighter aircraft per month. Neither the girls nor the gunners ever questioned why the American long-noses, the Yankee air pirates, didn't blast out of existence the means to bring such ample supplies of guns and ammunition to North Vietnam. They merely blasted happily away and claimed four times their actual count.

After Hostettler briefed the guns, he covered the safest bailout areas. Go feet wet if you want a Navy pickup. Go west, young man, to Laos, maybe stretch it into Thailand, if you want to be rescued by a USAF Jolly Green Giant helicopter. Feet wet was closest.

Hostettler drew imaginary pistols from his imaginary holsters and fired his fingers in the air.

"MiGs," his audience said.

"MiGs," Hostettler agreed. He pointed to the map. "You guys know where they come from. Bac Mai, Phuc Yen, Kep. And of course Gia Lam, just northeast of Hanoi. In fact, your target today is between Gia Lam at Hanoi and Kep farther up the rail line. You can't hit those air bases, though. That's naughty. North Vietnam might sever diplomatic relations with us." His sarcasm was not lost. The pilots booed and hissed at such an unfriendly reaction from North Vietnam.

Hostettler ran through the code words and two-letter identifiers for various activities and areas: Hotel Mike meant MiG CAP, Kilo Romeo stood for a divert to another target, Whiskey Victor for a MiG reaction, and so on for 53 other items. The pilots didn't have to memorize these codes. Hostettler handed out blue cards for their kneeboards, with all the information preprinted on them. A second card had frequencies for the radar sites, codes to set in their radar transponders when in certain areas, and other tactical frequencies for airborne command posts, ground sites, and secret rescue sites and helicopters. Each card was valid for only one day.

As soon as the pilots cleared the target area, they were to call College Eye, the orbiting EC-121D four-engined prop plane with warning radar on board. First word of successful, or unsuccessful, strikes and enemy reactions to the strike were relayed to College Eye by the code words on the blue card. College Eye flashed the information back to 7th Air Force via either Teaball in northern Thailand or Motel near the DMZ.

Soon, Hostettler's briefing was over. "Any questions?" he asked. he pointed to a lieutenant's raised hand.

"Yeah, George. You're the club officer. Is that no-booze bullshit still on?"

Hostettler winced. That was the one soft area he had yet to fix up. Colonel Crepens had been steadfast in his refusal even to consider reversing his prohibition order.

"Yeah," he said, "it is." He pulled his sombrero lower. "Tell you what, guys," he brightened. "I'll whomp up some good ole Tex-Mex hundert-proof chili for you special this afternoon." The pilots gave a mixed review of cheers and groans. Hostettler didn't care. He was giving information to men who were going on a mission from which a few might not return. He wanted to keep the scene light and as happy as possible, while impressing upon them what they needed to know.

Stormy, the weather briefer, was next. Cloud coverage in the target area could range from one half to full overcast, he said. Cloud bases about 4,000 feet, tops about 10,000 feet. Visibility in North Vietnam limited by clouds and haze caused by humidity. Late afternoon thunderstorms probable. Refueling area clouds were eight to ten thousand, scattered to broken. Condensation level starts at 33,000. That information was vital. Depending on temperature and humidity, the hot gases from a jet engine condense out water vapor into a miles-long streaming white arrow pointing to the originator. These arrows were called con trails. Once in the target area, however, the fighters never flew that high. They couldn't see the SAM launches or bomb with any accuracy from 6 miles up.

At lower altitudes, fighters make another trail, a fleeting one called a vortex trail. It occurs in certain humidity conditions. A high-G turn causes a sudden low pressure area over a wing, turning the water vapor into visible white streams coming from the wing tips or the wing roots of the airplane. Either trail brings unwanted attention to the offending aircraft.

When Stormy was finished, the strike commander, a major from the 435th Squadron, got up to brief on overall strike tactics.

"Today the collective call sign is Apache. Half of you are MiG cappers, half are bombers." The strike commander pulled out the maps and charts. "We're coming in from the water route," he said.

The Hanoi area could be approached from any direction, except north from Red China. The U.S. Navy always came from the east, because Task Force 77 was cruising east of the North Vietnamese land mass. The USAF frequently came from the south and southwest because that's where its bases were located. However, for the fighters, flying in the last couple hundred miles became a contest to find new ways to surprise the gunners. Rather than drilling straight across Laos directly into North Vietnam, which was the closest direction, the USAF strike forces frequently went feet wet. Feet wet was the call they used any time they flew over water, in this case the South China Sea.

Today the Ubon strike force was cutting across Laos and the DMZ on a northeast heading to meet their tankers over the water. Once tanked up, they would turn almost due north to just abeam of Haiphong. They would maintain Apache strike force integrity until they broke to the west to make for the target. At that time, the strike force would break up into individual flights of four. The two lead flights, Rambler and Buick, were the MiG cappers. Chevy and Ford were bombers. From there, the bombers were to dart inland to hit the bridge. The MiG cappers were to be a blocking force for the bombers, deflect attacks from the bombers, and kill any MiG foolish enough to press an attack. The F-105 Wild Weasel SAM killers would be in just ahead of the bombers. The TOT (time over target) for the Ubon bombers was one minute after the Thuds from Tahkli had attacked. The Tahkli Thuds were capped by F-4s from Da Nang. Egress was straight south to swing around Hanoi, then back east over the water. SAC didn't have enough tankers to have a second set available for a westerly egress. In case of bad weather, the alternate target was some easy, flat LOCs, Lines of Communications—the fancy word for roads, in Pack One, the relatively safe area just north of the DMZ.

The Apache strike force commander traced the altitudes and positions over water where the KC-135 tankers, call signs Tan and Purple, would hold oval orbits to refuel the inbound strike force. The crews copied the altitudes, radio frequencies, and call signs (always colors—Red, White, Cherry, Peach, and others, up to a possibility of twelve different tracks). The over-water tanks were always coded Tan and Purple.

"Last year," the force commander said, "the Thuds had fifty-six percent bomb-load jettison because of MiG attacks. These days, we put up you MiG cappers to drive away the MiGs so the bombers can go to work. Now, you guys who are carrying bombs today, you listen up. I know you'd rather go after MiGs, but the F-4 is also a good bomber, so today it's your turn in the barrel. Don't get antsy. Don't jettison your load just because someone calls out he sees MiGs. Jettison only if you actually have a guy making a pass at you from behind your three-nine line pulling lead, and the only way out is to dump your bombs. You'll get plenty of chances on future missions to be a MiG capper and go after your own kills." If you drew a line between the three and the nine on a clock face, with the airplane in the center facing twelve o'clock, you had a three-nine line. An aircraft behind that line could be in an attack position.

The strike force commander consulted his notes. "Base altitude today is 6,000 feet." That meant all references to altitude were added to the base reference. For example, thirteen thousand feet would be reported as base plus seven. He finished up by telling the troops to stay the hell off the radio unless they had something really important to say, like MiGs or Mayday, the international distress call. "Okay, Apache," he said in a quiet voice, "let's go get 'em."

"Wing, Tench-HUT," someone called, as Colonel Crepens walked onto the stage. "At ease, gentlemen," he said. "Please be seated." He stood behind the podium, and looked out over the audience.

"Men," he said, "I know it's a tough one today. But I know you are tough men." His gaze swept rapidly across each crew member. "Just remember, we of the 8th Tactical Fighter Wing want to be proud of each and every one of you." He assumed a steely-eyed expression. "When the going gets tough, the tough get going. And I know you are tough. Apache, let's go get 'em." He waved a fist in the air, then added: "But, remember, fly safely." While his audience pondered that bit of paradoxical advice, he strode off the stage. The strike force commander dismissed the aircrews.

The men arose with a low murmur of conversation to go to their own squadron areas for final briefings by their own flight command-ers. Court Bannister walked out with Flak Apple, the Buick flight leader.

"How many missions you got now?" Apple asked.

"Fifteen," Court said. "They were about half bombing and half MiG capping. A couple of the strikes were hairy. I've had two MiG en-gagements, nothing conclusive. Those damn things are so small. They dive away like minnows and we can't chase them, because we're too low on fuel. But most of the time we stooged around over the over-cast west of Hanoi waiting for MiGs that never showed up. I flew with Colonel Bryce most of the time after my theater checkout. But I'm still not assigned to a squadron. The Wing ops people are sched-uling me pretty much as they see fit."

There were four Phantoms and one spare in Buick flight, resulting in nine men following Flak Apple into the tiny flight briefing room, which was one of four in the 433rd Squadron building. In seconds the air was thick and blue with cigarette smoke.

"Gentlemen," Flak Apple began, "welcome to another opportunity to smite the enemy with superior American knowhow and technol-ogy. Anybody who comes back with an arrow stuck in his airplane will be severely chastised for flying too low." Chuckles and catcalls sounded from his flight members.

Apple quickly sketched on the blackboard how he wanted the mem-bers of Buick flight to position themselves. A standard USAF four-ship flight consisted of two elements of two ships each. Apple drew four ships, spaced like the four fingers of the right hand, minus the thumb. The middle finger represented the flight leader, Buick One; the index finger to the left was his wingman, Buick Two. They constituted the lead element. On the right side was his element leader, Buick Three, and to the right of Buick Three, his wingman, Buick Four. This was sometimes referred to as the finger-four formation.

"I'm Buick Lead, Bannister here is Buick Three." He listed the two men, young captains, who were the wingmen, Buick Two and Four. "Our job is to keep the MIGs off the bombers' backs. We deploy just south of the target area to block the MiGs coming up from Gia Lam, Hoa Loc, and Kep. Court, keep your element fifteen hundred feet higher, and position yourself up-sun from us with every turn. Wing-men, you fly forty-five degrees back, and five hundred feet out. Pro-tect your lead's ass." He pointed to the flight lineup. "Our load today is four AIM-9s, four AIM-7s, and the centerline gun with 1,150 rounds."

"College Eye will give you the radar words from their orbit to the west. The Navy radar coverage from some ships to the east in the Gulf is Crown."

He reviewed the visual signals they would use to maintain radio silence. Tap headset, hold up number of fingers for a radio channel change; drinking motion of thumb extended from fist to ask for fuel remaining, hold number of fingers up in reply to equal thousands of pounds; the HEFOE system for problems, one finger for hydraulic, two for electrical, three for fuel, four for oxygen, five for engine. Since there really weren't many ways to surprise the enemy. the system was rarely used except as a way to demonstrate radio discipline when flying to or from the target area.

"We'll take off single ship," Apple said, "at ten-second intervals, I'll come out of burner at 350 knots indicated airspeed, and throttle back a couple percent to give you a chance to catch up. If we're in the soup, hold a three-mile radar trail position. We'll join up on top of the overcast. We'll hit Lemon tanker over Laos at 20,000 feet, off-load 10,000 pounds each. Primary frequency is 229.2, backup is 234.1. We'll hit the same tank on our way home and take on 5,000 pounds. Over water, we'll top off with Tan and Purple tanks." He looked around the flight room. "We got eight pairs of eyeballs in this flight, guys, let's use 'em. Any questions?"

There were no questions. The men made their trip to the latrine for that last-minute nervous pee, then gathered in the personal equipment room to get their flight gear from their lockers and the parachute rack.

Court pulled his back-seater, Ev Stern, off to one side. It was the first time they had flown together. "We haven't had much chance to talk," he said to the young second lieutenant, a brand-new pilot. "But maybe that's okay. Tune the radios, set up the radar and the navigation gear, help me with the checklists, and call out the bogies. Outside of that, don't talk." The lieutenant nodded, his face a study of narrow-eyed coldness. "Oh yeah," Court said, "one last thing. If I say bail out or eject, and you ask 'what?,' you'll be talking to yourself."

The PE room was crowded with men getting prepared. Everyone already had his flight suit and boots on. They removed all personal items such as wallets or letters. They only identification each carried was his military ID card, his dog tags showing name, serial number, religion, and blood type, and the Geneva Convention card. This card was supposed to promote treatment in accordance with the recognized International Prisoner of War Conference held in Geneva in 1954. Since the United States had not declared war on North Vietnam, most pilots didn't bother with the card. There was absolutely no evidence a two-by-three-inch tan card had ever convinced the North Vietnamese to treat the shot-down pilot with anything resembling humane treatment. In fact, word was spreading, to be a prisoner in the Hanoi Hilton meant a lifetime of vile torture and death. As yet, the Department of Defense had not seen fit to inform the American public of this hideous fact.

Many crew members carried items of survival above and beyond what was in the survival kit attached to their parachutes. Extra silk escape maps (called blood chits), matches, lighters, cigarettes, were common items. Most pilots left their class rings and wedding rings in their lockers, many for sentimental reasons—they wanted a loved one to have them if they didn't come back—others because they knew a screw-up on bailout or during a parachute landing, where a ring could get caught in a projection, would tear the whole finger off. Conversely, other men had had rings and bracelets of gold made, because they thought they could use them as barter in an escape situation.

Flak commented on Court's olive-drab T-shirt. Then he noticed that Court's dog tags were taped together. "Now why in hell weren't we briefed on that?" he said. "Makes so much sense if you're sneaking through the jungle with an NVA patrol after your ass, not to have those tags jingling around."

"Got the idea from the Army," Court said. "Got the T-shirts from the Army clothing sales."

"Here's a trick you haven't seen," Flak said. He pulled out two cloth skullcaps and gave one to Court. "Soaks up the sweat from building up in your hair and running into your eyes." He gave a thumbs-up sign. "Say, how's that cowboy hat bird of yours doing? Got a name for it yet?"

"Sergeant Shanahan keeps it up," Court said. "Says it's his lucky bird. He's hit two jackpots on the NCO club slots since he took it over. And no, no name."

"Well, I hope you hit some jackpots. See you when we RTB," Flak said.

"RTB?" Court said with lifted eyebrows.

"Yeah, RTB. Return to base. This base. Ubon. See you when we come home."

It was still dark in the pre-dawn morning as the crew van, like a large open-backed bread truck with benches on both sides, delivered the crews to their airplanes. All along the wide concrete ramp, floodlights on tall poles illuminated the scores of revetments holding the large F-4 Phantoms. Huge, sparrow-sized flying insects rattled and banged into the bulbs. A Thai or two underneath tried to catch them, as they were considered great delicacies. Beyond the revetments, which disappeared in the shadows, were rows of light gray propeller-driven Thai Air Force T-28 aircraft.

As the van stopped at their airplane, each crew member climbed down, carrying a large bag stuffed with his helmet, gloves, and kneeboards with flight cards clipped to them. Each wore his G-suit, green mesh survival vest, holster with .38 and ammo, and several baby bottles full of ice, which would melt in the stifling heat by the time the pilot was ready for takeoff. A quick drink before takeoff and in the target area soothed many a cotton-dry mouth. After bailout in enemy territory, it was a life-or-death item, second only to a survival radio.

Each pilot carried three survival radios. One was an automatic beeper that was activated when his parachute deployed on bailout. It sounded an unnerving whoop-whoop over 243.0 megacycles, the radio frequency reserved for guard channel. The other two radios, RT-10s, were hand-held, and could transmit on guard channel or one other frequency. They were the size of two cigarette packs. One was inserted into the survival pack that was in the seat cushion of the pilot's airplane. The other he carried in his survival vest for easy access. A few enterprising crew members had a third radio in a G-suit pocket. Without a survival radio, there was absolutely no hope of a helicopter rescue if you were shot down in North Vietnam or Laos. Other rescue gear included large day–night flares, and a small red metal flare device the size of a fountain pen that could shoot a small red tracerlike flare 300 feet straight up.

Court Bannister and Ev Stern walked through the coolness to their airplane, F-4D, tail number 753. Court handed Sergeant Shanahan his helmet bag, and started the preflight without assigning any duties to Ev. Using his flashlight, he checked the general condition of the airplane, shook the missiles on their mounts, rapped the fuel tanks, peered up the twin tailpipes three feet in diameter, and looked at the Form 781 maintenance log the crew chief held out for him. There were no write-ups or discrepancies.

"Ready to go?" Ev Stern had silently followed him around during the preflight. He had made no comments about the white hat or the red star.

"No, sir, I'm not," the young man replied in a quiet but firm voice.

Court stared at him in the muted glare of the ramp lights. "You sick?" he asked.

"No, sir, I'm not. I just want to get something straight between us before we fly." His eyes glittered in the dark. His jaw was firm and resolute.

"I don't want to be in your back seat any more than you even want a back seat. I wanted the front seat, I wanted Thuds, I wanted F-100s, I wanted A-1s, I wanted O-1s, I wanted anything where I was the pilot in command. The Air Force just spent a whole shitpot of money teaching me how to fly, then they stuffed me in that goddamn pit." He pointed up to the back seat of the big Phantom. "Shit, that's what navigators are for. You think I like drilling around the sky with some yahoo in front that maybe never flew a fighter before?"

"I'm not exactly some yahoo that never flew fighters before," Court said.

"No, sir, I know *you* are not. But yesterday I flew with an ex-math prof from the Air Force Academy that hadn't been on his back since pilot training ten years ago. I had to recover the airplane for him when he went inverted in a cloud." He shook his head. "I guess I'm a little ticklish. So when you tell me to shut up and don't touch anything when we're going on a mission against MiGs, I just have to say something."

Court studied his GIB. "Okay, Ev," he said. "I think maybe I understand. I'm a little slow sometimes. Bear with me." He slapped Ev on the shoulder. "Okay, Tiger. Let's go kill some MiGs."

0945 HOURS LOCAL, MONDAY, 23 OCTOBER 1967
GIA LAM AIRFIELD, HANOI
DEMOCRATIC REPUBLIC OF VIETNAM

☆

Pod-Palcovnik Vladimir Nicholaevych Chernov stood in front of the blackboard with a piece of chalk in his hand. The board was full of swirling lines and little x's representing airplane positions. Toon and Van Bay sat at a table watching him. Chernov had just gone over the refinements of the new attack method. Victory Control would hold back SAMs and the big guns to better coordinate the MiG attacks. The MiG-19s would swoop down from an altitude above and behind the attacking Yankees; Chernov's MiG-21s would accelerate and zoom up from low and behind—called the deep-six position. Victory Control would keep him informed of the inbound progress of the enemy fighters. Each MiG-21 carried two heat-seeking K-13 missiles, two K-13A radar-homing missiles, and a 23mm gun in a belly pod. The K-13 was identical to the American AIM-9 Sidewinder; it was ten feet long and had a thirteen-pound warhead. Its range was not quite four miles. The radar missile was an advanced version of the K-13, and slightly larger. There were only 200 rounds for the 23mm cannon. When Chernov was satisfied they had absorbed as much as they could and would apply the new maneuvers, he dismissed the two Vietnamese.

He sat for a moment after they trooped out. He had been avoiding the Embassy and Ignatov by spending almost all his waking hours at the air base. Political Officer Ignatov was a serious threat, very serious. Why he seemed to have singled out Chernov wasn't particularly puzzling. He was a civilian *stukach*. Not of the military, he didn't understand that military men, particularly fighter pilots, had certain considerations that had to be satisfied or there would be no Party to protect. Being dedicated to a job one loved was one of those considerations. He checked his watch—time to leave that pig and his spiteful tyranny behind. He picked up his flight gear, and walked out the door.

An hour later, Chernov's three MiG-21s roared off from the Gia Lam runway, afterburners trailing flame, to intercept the inbound Yankee fighters and bombers. Each pilot had turned on his SRO-2M identification radar, allowing Victory Control to differentiate them from the enemy on their radar scopes. Chernov was leading, Van Bay and Toon were his wingmen. Their call sign was Khong Nam Bon, Vietnamese for 054, the three numbers painted on the nose of Chernov's aircraft. The MiG-17s and -19s were getting airborne from other bases to go to their intercept stations. Timing was critical. Although Chernov and his flight each carried external fuel tanks, they would have to jettison them before attacking. From then on, fuel was at a premium. Internal fuel in the MiG-21 was barely thirty minutes at low-altitude flying at best fighting speed.

"I have contact with Khong Nam Bon," Victory Control said.

"*Nhan biet,*" Chernov said in his terrible Vietnamese, trying to maintain the fiction no Soviet was airborne. The words meant he understood and acknowledged the transmission.

Chernov wore his standard Soviet Air Force VVS light blue flight helmet with built-in headset, visor, and fasteners for his oxygen mask on each side. The North Vietnamese pilots still wore their old leather flying helmets with built-in headsets under their wide, round, hard hat. Like American jet pilots, the microphone for their radios was built into the oxygen mask. All three pilots wore Soviet Air Force VVS issue flight coveralls and G-suits. Victory Control started feeding them intercept information as soon as their wheels were retracted and tucked into the gear wells.

Victory Control picked them up. "One flight mass, Thunderchief characteristics, situated west and heading easterly at six thousand meters, descending slowly." Victory Control paused, then transmitted. "One flight mass, Phantom characteristics, situated east heading northerly. Flashlight and Dart activated inner Goalpost ring." Goalpost was the code word for the ten-mile defensive ring around Hanoi, Flashlight was code for all AAA guns, Dart meant SAMs. Other areas of North Vietnam were code-named by sectors in a grid. Sector DI was the grid square over the Canal des Rapides bridge. Victory Control had to let its MiG fighters know when and where Flashlight (AAA) or Dart (SAMs) was active, so they would not be shot down by their own air defense weapons. Goalpost was always hot, and would shoot at anything. A senior air defense commander directed the air battle from his position in front of a large radar screen at Victory Control. Although the big search radars for Victory Control were above ground, the command post where the Air Combat Director and all the controllers sat was under 100 feet of earth.

"Has the enemy committed yet?" Chernov asked.

"No, Khong Nam Bon flight. Take up defensive orbit now."

Chernov signaled his flight to fall into trail behind him. He started a lazy left bank, throttle back to conserve fuel. He maintained an altitude of 150 meters, about 500 feet. Victory Control positioned eight MiG-19s east of Goalpost at 8,000 meters. The fighter director knew that the shipborne Crown radar would not see them that far inland. He also knew the radar carried by the approaching Thunderchief fighters was not good enough to discriminate and find his orbiting airplanes, neither the MiG-21s at low altitude nor the MiG-19s higher up. The F-105 was, after all, an airplane designed as a nuclear bomber and therefore had ground-mapping capabilities with its radar, not capabilities for aerial attack. In the air, it could barely differentiate a thunderstorm, much less an airplane. Conversely, the F-4, designed as an interceptor for the United States Navy, had a reasonably good air-to-air radar, and reasonably good ground-mapping radar; good if not overtaxed or exposed to too much heat and humidity.

The Apache strike force commander wheeled his mass of sixteen F-4s left to a heading of 342 degrees, and waggled his wings in the prearranged signal for Apache force to split up into individual flights. They did, and switched their radios to the strike frequency, which both the Thuds from Tahkli and the Phantoms from Da Nang were already using to strike the bridge.

The four flights split into prearranged positions.

Victory Control called Chernov. "We now see them. Steer for Grid Sector HI for positioning. Steer heading zero five zero, Khong Nam Bon flight. One Phantom mass is approaching from the east at 5,000 meters. This flight mass is splitting vertically; half is descending slowly, half remaining at altitude. Both flight masses headed toward Goalpost vicinity." Their altitudes were between 6,000 meters— 15,000 to 18,000 feet. These were the least dangerous altitudes to commence an attack.

"Understood, I am executing," Chernov said in his terrible Vietnamese. He swung his flight to the northeast, keeping low to avoid the searching American radar beams emanating from the Navy radar ship. He hoped his flight of three MiG-21s would be lost in the ground clutter that appeared on the screens of the Phantoms when the Americans searched in his direction. The radars in the nose of each F-4 in the inbound Phantom flight mass would be searching for the tiniest blip that meant a defending airplane. If they were spotted, Chernov knew, the escort elements of the attackers would try to place themselves between his MiG flight and the F-4 bombers they were trying to protect. From that position, the Americans would attack.

"Switches on," Chernov transmitted. The liquid nitrogen necessary to reduce the temperature of the seeker head of his missiles only lasted a few minutes, and had to be conserved. Although the K-13 was a copy of the American AIM-9 infra-red missile, it needed to cool its IR seeker head just before use. The American AIM-4 missile had the same problem. Overeager pilots switching it on too early lost the effect and their missiles ran wild. At that, the pilot had to be close to the heat source, the enemy tailpipe, and had to be sure the sun or ground reflection or a smokestack was not a better source of heat for the missile's "eye." Chernov didn't like having to remind his pilots of something he felt they should do automatically. Yet experience told him that in the heat of combat, men at war did strange things. Improper switch setting was a major concern. Better to lose radio silence than a missile that had been fired incorrectly at a critical time.

Flak Apple fish-tailed his F-4. Each flight member moved away from Flak who then pushed over and headed down. He would level out at about 4,000 feet above the ground, while Two, Three, and Four would stair-step up at 1,500-foot increments. They also spread out, putting 1,200 feet laterally between airplanes. As they pushed over, trading altitude for airspeed, their Mach meters showed they were flying at 95 percent of the speed of sound. On their radios, they heard the terse calls of the attacking Thuds and their protecting Da Nang Phantoms. Each Buick flight member put his weapons switches on.

Ahead, the sky was more clear than forecast. There were only some scattered cloud layers instead of the soupy mess usually encountered this time of year. They could see the Thuds diving to the attack, like runaway locomotives. They did not see the air battle farther west, where Victory Control had already steered the MiG-17s and -19s from Yen Bai and Phuc Yen behind the Thunderchief mass. Upon orders, the MiGs had swooped down from a higher altitude upon the Thunderchiefs. But Victory Control had vectored them down to the attack too late. The Thuds had pulled away from them with ease without jettisoning their bombs, while the Da Nang F-4s turned to intercept the attacking MiGs.

A rolling furball of fighter planes ensued west of Hanoi as the Da Nang Phantoms went after the MiGs, who did everything they could do to avoid getting involved in a maneuvering dogfight. When the Phantoms attacked, the less experienced MiG pilots pulled into a defensive circle—like that used by settlers' wagons when attacked by Indians—to cover each other. Any Phantom trying to break in ran the risk of the next MiG back in the wheel firing a missile at him. The MiGs could outlast the Phantoms, they had more fuel, and were close to their own bases. In a worst-case situation, they could even break for China, fifteen minutes' flying time away, where no American dare follow. The more experienced pilots had dashed successfully either to a base for fuel if they needed it, or to a reattack position if they didn't.

Near the target, Rambler headed northeast to screen for MiGs from Kep, a few miles up the rail line from the Canal des Rapides bridge. Flak took Buick flight to screen for MiGs from Gia Lam, southwest of the bridge.

"You got anything?" Flak Apple asked for the tenth time to his back-seater, whose head was buried in his radar scope.

"Negative," the young second lieutenant named Pete replied.

From the north, Victory Control steered the MiG-19s from Kep southwest toward the Ubon F-4 bombers. To the south, Chernov's flight stayed low. From nearly twenty miles away, he saw the inbound F-4s painted against the sky by their smoke trails. He smiled. His MiG was one-half the size, and made no smoke. They would never see him until it was too late. Chernov wanted to attack the bombers from the rear, so his heat-seeking missiles could easily find the hot tailpipes. But the bombers were rapidly approaching the bridge. He had no choice. He would have to make a frontal attack from below. He switched to his radar missiles. The on-board radar illuminated the target with pulses that bounced back to his missile. He told Khong Nam Bon flight to go radar.

"*MiGs, MiGs, ten o'clock low,*" Ev Stern yelled over the radio from Court's back seat, as his radar warning gear picked up the electronic emanations from Khong Nam Bon flight.

"Who's ten low?" Rambler shot back.

"Buick Three. Ten low from Buick Three," Court cut in, chagrined his back-seater had fouled up his MiG warning.

Chernov signaled Toon and Van Bay to drop their fuel tanks, engage their afterburners, and spread out for attack. He then gave instructions to Victory Control where to deploy the other MiGs. He might be an airborne flight director, but that didn't mean he couldn't fight.

"I got 'em, nine low. Buick Three rolling in," Court said. He punched off his fuel tanks, rechecked his switches to fire the radar-guided Sparrow, and rolled hard left and down. Buick Four, his wingman, did the same. "Go radar," Court yelled into the intercom at Ev. That meant he wanted to shoot a Sparrow head-on at one of the attacking MiGs. The heat-seeking Sidewinder, like Chernov's K-13 missile, was useless in a frontal attack.

Court had the dot of the gunsight reticle directly on the middle of the three climbing MiGs. Both planes were head-on, each splitting the air close to the speed of sound at a closure rate of 2,500 feet per second. They were four miles from each other. Minimum range for the radar missile was one mile. Each man had three seconds to acquire, lock, shoot.

"Lock on, in range, shoot, shoot," Ev said in a high register. This was his first air combat.

Court locked out the automatic sequence circuit of his fire control system. "Interlocks in" meant the fire control system would fire the missiles when its computer felt the logic was right. It would require nearly four seconds to settle down and tell the Sparrow it could launch. Court wanted the missile to fire the instant he squeezed the trigger, "interlocks out."

Chernov hissed in exasperation. Head-on, he could not see the plunging Phantoms. The bulletproof glass directly in front of him was too thick. And it was almost impossible to see the weak trace of his intercept radar in daylight on the small screen on his panel. Then the fire control system signaled his radar missile was locked on and ready to fire. He pressed the firing button on top of the stick, then immediately switched to his 23mm cannon.

At the same time, the AIM-7 Sparrow missile in the left bay of Court's F-4D dropped out of the well, but the rocket motor failed to ignite. It fell out of the sky, useless. By the time he sensed the missile had failed, he had one and one-half seconds remaining before collision. At the same time, a missile zoomed out from under the belly of the middle MiG and arced directly down out of control, disappearing from view.

Court savagely squeezed his trigger again and fired a second Sparrow. He knew it wouldn't guide, but he hoped it would go ballistic like a bullet and strike the MiG, or at least intimidate him. Then he sliced up and left, away from the MiG dead ahead. As he did so, he saw red golf balls spurting directly at him from the nose of the MiG. He had no idea what had happened to the unguided Sparrow he had fired at him. Court's wingman, Buick Four, hung desperately aft and inside his turn. Just then, Flak Apple rolled inverted, and saw the MiG-21 on his left turn after Court's Phantom.

When Chernov's radar missile failed, he grunted and switched to his 23mm gun and fired. Thirty-six of the shells punched through the air, like segments of one-inch steel rods. Just as quickly, he cursed and removed his finger from the trigger. He could not turn farther right sharp enough to keep his gunsight on Court's airplane. He paid no attention to the second missile from the enemy plane; he could see it wasn't locked on him. He told Toon to take the Phantom he'd just fired at, and pulled up to face the high Phantom, which was Flak Apple. Toon obeyed, and zoomed into a hard right turn after Court.

"Buick Three, you got one rolling in at your six," Flak yelled. His voice overrode the other excited calls in the air.

"Say again for Buick Three," Court transmitted.

"Check your—" Flak started and was cut out by a booming voice on guard channel. "SASSAFRAS, SASSAFRAS, SASSAFRAS. BASE PLUS SIX, BASE PLUS SIX. OMAHA, OMAHA, OMAHA. SASSAFRAS, BASE PLUS SIX, OMAHA."

Those code words on guard channel from College Eye blew everything and everyone off the air. No one could talk. It was almost worse then enemy jamming. Each pilot tried to remember what the fuck "sassafras" stood for that day. And what the hell direction was Omaha from Hanoi. And, Base was what? Fucking stupid. The MiGs knew where the hell they were. Why couldn't we be told in the clear?

"Jesus Christ, Cee Eye, shut the fuck up," someone snapped in the awed silence. Then the air went full pandemonium.

"Ford, break right, break right . . . Three's off . . . MiGs Rambler . . . MiGs north . . . I got him, I got him . . . get away, he's mine . . . shit, shit, I GOT ONE HAHAHA I GOT ONE . . . shut up and get another . . . at your six Buick Three . . . tally ho . . .

It was every man for himself. Flight integrity went by the board; wingmen desperately moved stick and throttles as they tried to follow their leader through six-G turns and zero-G rudder reversals, yet still look around to protect their own tails.

Over by Phuc Yen, after putting his bombs on target, a Thud sawed a MiG-17 in half with his 20mm M-61 Vulcan cannon.

Up north of the Canal des Rapides bridge, Chevy Four took three rounds of 30mm from a MiG-19 in his left engine. He shut it down and headed out to sea as Chevy Three blew the -19 off his tail with a Sidewinder. Chevy Four was last seen headed due east toward the Gulf. He didn't answer radio calls from his leader.

Rambler flight had split up, Lead and Two went after the MiGs chasing Ford flight. The UHF radio of Rambler Four went unserviceable in a hard turn, so no one heard his call to warn his leader a MiG-19 was rolling in on him. Undaunted, Rambler Four pulled into the MiG and hosed off a Sparrow in his general direction. The MiG-19 pilot ejected while the Sparrow was still 1,000 feet away. The missile missed the pilotless MiG by two hundred feet and flew another three seconds before self-destructing. The pilotless MiG-19 went into a diving spiral and crashed into the marketplace of a village east of the Canal des Rapides bridge.

Ev Stern told Court in no uncertain terms that a MiG-21 had rolled in on their tail. At that very moment, red golf balls started zipping underneath their turning Phantom. It was Toon.

"He ain't pulling lead," Court panted, racking it tight into a climbing turn. He banged both throttles outboard to engage the afterburners, which nearly doubled his engine thrust. He pulled up, rolled, unloaded, pushed down, and nosed after the MiG-21 flown by Toon. Court pulled seven Gs to try to stay with the turning MiG-21. He switched to Heat, unloaded his Gs so fast his feet flew off the rudder pedals, fired two AIM-9 Sidewinders, then immediately pulled the Gs back on. Both missiles flew under his nose and disappeared.

Without looking, he reached down and flipped his armament selector switch to Guns. He eased in enough back pressure to place his gunsight ahead of the MiG-21 flown by Toon, and felt the first nibble of the stall and snap that would spell departure, and a forced bail-out over enemy territory. He disregarded the angle-of-attack warning noise (a visual and audible stall warning device), shut Ev's warning yells out of his ears, and pulled the trigger activating the 20mm gun strapped to his belly. He saw sparkles as his rounds began impacting on Toon's right wing. Then he had to ease forward on his control stick to unload his heavy G-force as his Phantom started to enter a high-speed stall. He released the trigger, as his tracers started to arc under the MiG-21. He never saw that airplane again.

"Goddamn, Major," Ev Stern panted. "You try that again and I won't fly with you. You almost lost the bird. I don't fancy a stay at the Hanoi Hilton just because you want to make ace."

Court didn't trust himself to speak. He remembered his dad's warning about his motivation; and he remembered Flak's words about flying with GIBs. He and Ev Stern just had to work something out.

To the north, Flak and Chernov went around twice shooting at each other, neither scoring. When Flak discovered he was fired out, he accelerated away from the fight. Flak's wingman, Buick Two, never got in a shot. He had to work too hard to stay on Flak's wing.

Chernov in 054 didn't have enough fuel to chase them. He dove toward Gia Lam and found himself in a perfect deflection shot at an F-4 climbing out all by itself. He bored in and placed over fifty rounds from his 23mm cannon into the center of the F-4. It was as if the Phantom had never seen him. It went straight down, trailing a great sheet of fire and black smoke. Five minutes later, Chernov entered the landing pattern at Gia Lam, unscathed.

Over by the bridge, two Thud 750-pound Mk-117 bombs and one Phantom 1,000-pound Mk-83 bomb had impacted in the water close enough to the bridge to cause structural damage. The remaining 24 bombs cratered the approaches and blew holes in the water.

Of the 22 MiGs scrambled against the attacking Americans, 19 landed, 3 with heavy damage.

Of the 10 F-4s from Udorn, 9 returned. Someone reported two chutes fifty miles east of the target near Thud Ridge. All 16 Thuds made it out of the battle area. One Thud pilot had to recover at Udorn, near Laos, when his plumbing system wouldn't accept fuel from a tanker.

Of the 16 F-4s that had launched from Ubon, 14 returned. No one had seen or heard from Ford Four. Chevy Four, whose radio had been shot out, recovered at Da Nang on one engine. Chevy Three Bravo, Chevy Three's GIB, was taken to the base hospital with 37mm AAA fragments in his left arm.

The North Vietnamese claimed eight Yankee air pirates blasted out of the air, and no losses of their own. Seventh Air Force claimed two positive victories and one probable, and said one American airplane was missing.

1430 HOURS LOCAL, MONDAY, 23 OCTOBER 1967
MAIN BRIEFING ROOM, 8TH TACTICAL FIGHTER WING
UBON ROYAL THAI AIR FORCE BASE
THAILAND

☆

After the intelligence debriefing, the Apache strike force commander convened the remaining 28 members in the auditorium. Hostettler sat on a large supply case on one side of the stage and took notes. The major who had led the strike force paced the stage. There wasn't a sound from the audience.

"Pure cluster fuck," he said.

"Not for me, it wasn't," Rambler Four said. He had a wide grin on his face. Although official confirmation hadn't come back through channels from 7th Air Force in Saigon, enough pilots had seen the MiG-19 go down so that his kill was confirmed. His name was Chet Griggs.

"Excepting Griggs," the major said. "For an ATC puke, you done good," he said to Griggs. "You too, Bannister. You got a damage. Maybe Truncate will confirm a kill." Truncate was a clandestine listening post full of translaters who monitored North Vietnamese ground and aerial transmissions. "Then there's the rest of us. We didn't do so good." Most of the aircrew nodded. He pulled out a blackboard.

"Let's start with their side. What did the bad guys do right?"

"They got outta bed," a GIB lieutenant said. The major waited.

"Didn't anybody notice anything strange?" he asked.

"Yeah," Court said. "I did. I never saw a SAM or any Triple A over 23mm in size the whole time."

The MiGs were everywhere, they agreed, except for downtown Hanoi, where no MiGs ever flew, nor were they by the 23mm sites at the bridge.

"This has never happened before. Up to two months ago, we were bagging MiGs. We got thirty-two in April, May and June. Then they didn't come up for two months. Now it's only one for one. They're more aggressive, they're using different tactics, and they're coming in with more coordination. We've got to work up some new methods of our own before we go back up there."

The major drew a deep breath. "Okay," he said. "Now let's look at it from our side. Let's start from the top. What went wrong?"

"*I* got outta bed," the GIB lieutenant shot back. "The sun rose," another piped up. The major curled his upper lip.

"They knew we were coming," Ford Three said. The major wrote it on the board.

"Too many radio calls," someone said.

"That welded wing formation is too restrictive. It worked okay in props when things were slower. Now the wingman spends all his time hanging on to his leader, when maybe he should be looking around. That MiG-21 leader passed a potential kill off to his wingman. We should, too. I think the Navy is looking into this. They call it the Loose Deuce." Ron Olds had done away with welded wing. Colonel Delbert L. Crepens had brought it back.

"Hell, I'm not sure that's working, either," Partin called out from the audience.

Court and Flak sat side by side as the complaints mounted. The list grew; too many code words, too much chatter—especially on Guard—College Eye MiG codes useless, the F-4 engines smoked too much, not enough fuel, faulty gun cameras, and missiles not worth a shit. Finally the Apache strike force leader spread his hands.

"Okay, I hear you," he said. "Now let's look at the results." He made some quick sketches on the board. "One bird missing, one severely damaged, one man in the hospital, and all we did was shoot down one MiG and damage another. Piss-poor, guys. Piss-poor. Major Apple, you're the Wing Weapons Officer. What do you think?"

Flak Apple got up and walked up on the stage. He looked out over the audience, hands on hips. "How about it, guys, what's the problem? I want to hear it from you. How come we had such a bad day?"

No one answered. Hostettler stirred. "Major Apple," he said, and stood up. "May I propose a solution to the problem at hand?"

"Sure, George," Flak said, surprised. "But I didn't know we had a problem."

"Sure you do. The guys won't talk. You put fighter pilots in a big auditorium and they won't talk. Put them at the bar and they will talk your wristwatch off. So, *voilà*." Big "George" Hostettler leaned over and with a flourish, lifted up what he had been sitting on: a dummy packing case. Underneath were six cases of frosty Budweiser beer.

An hour later, Flak and the major had all the answers they wanted. They boiled down to three factors: bad equipment and bad tactics, multiplied by bad morale, equals bad results.

The bad equipment was the missile problem: Sparrows that fizzled, and short-range Sidewinders that could only be fired from the rear under perfect conditions. Flak would talk to the Sparrow technical representative in Saigon. New tactics could be experimented with right away—legally or not, the next flight, in fact.

The bad morale was a serious command problem: No wing commander in his right mind shuts off the booze. No one had a solution to that, except hang out more in the hootch bars, or go to downtown Ubon.

"There is one little thing more," the Apache force commander said. He shook his head. "We did not destroy the target we were sent after." He shook his head. "Our prime mission was not to kill MiGs. Our primary mission was to destroy an enemy line of communication, in this case a very important bridge, the Canal des Rapides bridge. Killing MiGs was ancillary to that little detail. Now we will have to go back and do it all over again. Think on that awhile." There was dead silence.

"Well, that was half our prime mission," Flak Apple said. "The other half was to make sure none of those Thuds from Tahkli were shot down by MiGs. We succeeded with that one ... with a little help from the Da Nang Phantoms."

The silence remained. Then someone noticed. "Hey," he said. "We haven't heard from George the gecko."

Hostettler looked very serious. He licked his lips. "I didn't want to tell you, guys, but Colonel Crepens had Base Engineering in here to trap and kill George."

1545 Hours Local, Monday, 23 October 1967
Gia Lam Airfield, Hanoi
Democratic Republic of Vietnam

☆

Vladimir Chernov and Toon stood at attention in front of Colonel Nguyen Van Huu. Toon's face was scratched and he had a bandage on his hand.

"What went wrong?" Huu hissed. "You assured me the new tactics would work. I sat in the radar control command post and saw how we lost many, many opportunities to defeat the Americans." He looked disdainfully at Chernov. "Real *Laitchik*, you, Chernov. Yes, I know they refer to you as a real *Laitchik*. What will your superiors call you when they find out that not only were you flying when you were specifically ordered not to, but that one of your men was shot down? Everyone fired out their missiles and cannon," he narrowed his eyes, "yet only one victory was scored by our airplanes. The one plane shot down by our ground guns is not important here."

Chernov decided not to bring it up that the luckless F-4 was his victory. And of course, Kirsanov had said he would be on his own. He regarded Huu calmly.

Huu was unlike most North Vietnamese men. He was a *métisse*, a mixture of French and Vietnamese. A product of the French Military Academy at St. Cyr, then the French Flying School, he was a direct man, used to having his way. He had learned to fly MiGs in Russia, and was frequently at odds with his contemporaries, who were now generals in the North Vietnamese Army. He looked at Chernov with angry eyes.

Chernov met his gaze. "Comrade Colonel, I must respectfully point out a truth to you. The imperialists did not destroy the target, the bridge over the Canal des Rapides. Even now, both rail and truck traffic flows across the bridge."

Huu regarded the Russian thoughtfully. Finally, he spoke. "Stand at ease, come over here." Huu walked from behind his desk to the low rattan table on which he maintained his tea set. He sat for a moment, then poured three cups. "Yes, Comrade Colonel Chernov, your point is made. And I know you are the one who downed the Yankee air pirate." He waved a hand to indicate that Toon and Chernov were to take a cup and be seated. "But, I must point out a truth to you. Regardless of what the propagandists say, we lost two airplanes in air battle today to the Yankees' one. You are leading a force with airplanes more maneuverable than the Americans', under a radar control they do not have, yet your kill ratio has not significantly improved."

Chernov noted Huu's use of the words "leading a force." It implied Huu accepted Chernov not only flying combat missions, but actually leading attack flights. He also noted Huu hadn't made any suggestion to ground him. Maybe Huu would be content with just castigating him verbally, here and now. If a report went to the Embassy, he would be through. Off to Chita. *Hara sho*, Chernov thought, I will do my job the best way I see to do it. If it means flying combat, I will fly combat. He knew he must choose his words to Huu carefully. At the same time, he had to tell him the Vietnamese pilots were not performing as well as they should.

"To continue truisms," Chernov began, "we must consider the Vietnamese pilots who fly so valiantly. These pilots are defending their homeland. If these pilots are shot down, they will be rescued and feted by their own countrymen. They do not face capture. So, Comrade Colonel Huu, is it not just possible they could fly a bit *more* valiantly? I myself know of one man, a MiG-19 pilot, who catapulted himself from his airplane before it was struck." Major Toon nodded in agreement.

"That man," Huu said, his voice scornful, "is even now locked into a hole in the ground to contemplate his cowardly ways. I intend to have him shot one week from today." He looked at Chernov. "You have identified a problem that is not entirely of our making. The training in Russia is not sufficient. My men are not as confident in their airplanes as they should be."

Chernov nodded. "That may be, Comrade Colonel. Yet the Soviet Union has allocated as many hours as it can to train men who are supposed to know how to fly before they get there. I myself have had students from your country who can fly only on clear days. They had never received any instructional flight time on how to fly by instruments in bad weather."

Colonel Huu did not speak. He sipped his tea, then slowly placed the cup precisely on the tray. "All right, Comrade Colonel Chernov," he said. "I will grant you four more weeks to continue to exercise your new attack plans."

"I need to be sure Victory Control will follow my orders," Chernov said. "Their timing is crucial to my plans."

Huu's eyes became mere slits. "They will obey, I assure you. But know well, that if your tactics fail to improve the ratio of enemy fighters downed, I will be forced to take action to have you replaced."

2030 Hours Local, Monday, 23 October 1967
Ubon Royal Thai Air Force Base
Thailand

☆

Still laughing and feeling good, Court and Flak took a beer and settled into their lawn chairs in the dark. When they had returned from the afternoon mission, they had been told that Truncate had verified Court's MiG-21. Court had jammed his Stetson on and, with the other MiG killer, bought the bar at the Officer's Club, the NCO Club, and the Airman's Club, as MiG killers were expected to do. There was some half-hearted talk about the booze restriction and chit system. Two tech sergeants solved that by putting the dozens of cases of beer Court bought into a Dodge carryall from the Motor Pool, and then handing them out in the parking lots next to the clubs. Ev Stern, who as Court's back-seater was also credited with a MiG, had not gone around with Court. He sent money along with another GIB to buy his share of the beer. Neither Court nor Flak drank as much as they wanted. Each had an early go the next day.

"Not bad, not bad at all," Flak said, "considering you never fought a MiG before. Too bad we don't have some at George to use."

"Right," Court said. "It doesn't do much good to fight an airplane with the same characteristics as the one you're flying. You need to fight a different kind, preferably a better one. At George, they should be fighting the Navy's A-4. It's small, maneuverable, and looks like a

MiG-21. For the matter, maybe we should be fighting our own T-38s. They're small and maneuverable, too. Point is, learning how to shoot down F-4s didn't do us much good. At least not yet. Who knows who we'll be fighting in the future? I hear there are some guys over at Nellis right now who are putting their careers on the line to improve our fighter-versus-fighter training."

"You'd think the Air Force would automatically want to set up the best training possible," Flak said.

"True," Court replied. "However, after that SAC General Sweeny took over TAC and introduced the management control system, things went to hell. Flying safety became more important than mission accomplishment. It got so bad I peeled out for a while and did some time as an instructor at Squadron Officer School. I remember one of my students from Luke telling me about the MCS program. He was a motor pool officer. Seems the year before, his boss had said the half-ton trucks would all drive a total of 228,000 miles. When it came time for the inspection a year later, they were about 16,000 miles short. Instead of getting a commendation for saving mileage, they stood not only to lose points for failure to make their goal, but to lose that much mileage from the next year's budget. So he put a shift of drivers on to drive two pickups round and round the perimeter road for a week. Made his budget allowance fall in line."

"Yeah, same thing worked with airplanes," Flak Apple said. "Lose an airplane to an accident and the wing commander would be at attention in front of that general explaining as if he were a cadet in front of the merit committee. Unfortunately, realistic training for air-to-air or air-to-ground has losses. So the wing commanders cut down on the realism and kept their jobs. Nonetheless, under MCS somebody always got fired."

"I know," Court said. "The wing commander on the bottom of the list, regardless of how well he had done. Management by fear. It made professional liars out of good men."

"And we have a lot of dead and captured fighter pilots in Vietnam because of that method," Flak said with great disgust.

"The trouble is, a lot of the current fighter wing commanders were brought up under that system," Court said.

Flak took a swallow of beer. "Yeah," he said. "About that GIB of yours, what's his problem?"

"Says I hang it out too much." Court took a pull at his beer can. "Hell, Flak, I was inside the envelope. You know, I was trained to make a living at stalling airplanes. Besides, in combat you got to hang it out if you want to do your job."

"I can fix you up with a new GIB," Flak said.

"No, thanks. I'll stay with what I've got. Maybe I should let him fly more." His Zippo flared and illuminated his face as he lit a ciga-

rette. "Starting tomorrow, I'll give him every other takeoff and landing. And refueling, hell, he can have *all* of those." He sank smoke
deep into his lungs. "Say, Flak, is it as bad as the debrief today said?
Are we really screwing up?"

"Considering we have so many new guys, no. In fact, we are beating the odds. Usually we lost about ten percent of the new guys in
their first ten missions over Hanoi. That's probably what happened
to Ford Four this morning. They just don't have SA yet."

A factor that old head fighter pilots had—situational awareness—
was sometimes referred to as SA. While indeed the manipulation of
the controls had to be as automatic as bike riding—the pilot merely
thinks where he wants his airplane to be and it goes there—a fighter
pilot has to have the ability to think in five dimensions. He must see
and move up and down, front and back, left and right. With that, he
must couple *real* time—where things are now—and projected time—
where things will be in the future. Then on top of visualizing where
the object, an enemy fighter, will be in the future, he must predict
the thoughts of the pilot of that fighter. Where does the enemy pilot
want his airplane to be? In an engagement, opposing pilots have about
thirty seconds of maneuvering before one starts predicting the other.

"We are running a little ahead of the game, though," Flak said.
"We've only lost one. And then there's you."

"Me? What about me?" Court said.

"You beat the odds. You didn't get shot down in your first ten
missions. In fact, oh fearless one, you have shot down some other
guy whose SA was tried and found wanting."

Court grinned. "Yeah, roger that."

"Tell you what," Flak said.

"What?"

"I'm fragged to attend a TAC fighter conference in Saigon this
Friday. I think you should go with me. I got a Phantom scheduled."

"Are you sure?" Court asked.

"Yeah. I need a back-seater and someone to carry my bags."

"Cotton bales, Apple. Remember the cotton bales."

"Okay," Flak said. "Walk then."

18

☆

Captain Toby G. Parker held his O-2A aircraft poised over the edge of the giant gunnery range east of Eglin Air Force Base in Florida. He sat in the left seat—the aircraft commander's seat. In the right was a check pilot who sat silent and observant. On the left windscreen at eye level were several short lines drawn in grease pencil to use as horizon reminders in a dive or for nose-high rocket launches. Toby set the firing switches for the two rocket pods he carried under the wings of the airplane. Each pod held seven white phosphorous rockets. He looked down on the ground at the tree line where he had spotted two trucks hidden by foliage. He had been on the scene for only eight minutes and was quietly proud that he had discovered the targets so fast.

He tightened the chin strap of his helmet to pull it closer to his ears, and adjusted his boom mike closer to his mouth. The shrieking whine of a dynamotor buried in the radio gear behind his head was a constant irritant and could hamper radio communications. He punched the microphone button on the control wheel to talk to the two inbound F-4s.

"Delta flight, I have a concealed truck park for you today. Target elevation is fifty feet above sea level, winds are from the south at four knots, altimeter setting is two niner eight niner, safe bailout area is two five miles due east."

Parker unkeyed the microphone for two seconds. It was not wise in combat to tie up the radio for more than a few seconds at a time. A call for help, sudden ground fire, or any of a dozen emergency transmissions might need to be made. Parker keyed again, and told

Delta leader where the ground fire was coming from, and from what direction to roll in and off the target.

The leader of the two F-4s in Delta flight acknowledged he had the information. Toby responded he was rolling in to mark the target.

Toby pointed his aircraft toward the ground in a steep dive, checked his airspeed, checked his dive angle on the horizon, adjusted for the light crosswind, and fired one 2.75-inch marking rocket. It shot out from under the wing with a bang, and impacted under the foliage exactly between the trucks. Toby pulled up to the left, looked back at his smoke, then radioed the orbiting fighters who were carrying racks of 33-pound practice bombs.

"Okay, Delta flight, hit my smoke."

The instructor pilot, a major, held a clipboard on his lap with several pages of TAC Form 88, titled "Individual Training Mission Grade." The fourteen categories of the grade sheet ran from Mission Planning, Ground Operations, and Preflight, through Navigation, Ordnance Delivery, FAC Procedures, and Emergency Procedures. There was room for other items such as Flight Discipline, Takeoff and Landings, and Radio Procedures. Before takeoff, the major had told Toby to pretend he wasn't there. Toby was doing just that. So far, the major had said nothing. Every time Toby made a radio call or a maneuver, or fired a rocket, the major made marks on the grade sheet.

The flight was Captain Toby Parker's final check ride for day flights as he neared the end of his Forward Air Controller course. If he passed this one, the remaining weeks would be taken up with night FAC training, cross-country flying, and academic studies.

Delta flight hit the billowing white smoke from Toby's rocket. When they were out of bombs, he called them in on strafe runs. They finished their runs and were cleared off range by Toby. As the morning passed, three more flights hit Toby's smoke as he placed Willy Petes at the proper places next to the fabricated targets on the gunnery range. If an FAC had to hit 100 meters north of his smoke, or 50 meters east, it meant he hadn't put his marking rocket exactly where he had intended. Sometimes, though, it worked out that the FAC saw an additional target in the area, then he'd give a distance and heading from his smoke. Other times, the smoke dissipated quickly, at which point the FAC would either put a new smoke in, or tell the strike flight members where to place their bombs in relation to the bomb dropped from the plane ahead of them. FACs hoarded their fourteen smoke rockets; they never knew when several new targets might crop up. But when they did shoot, the proudest call an FAC could make was, "Hit my smoke."

As the last flight departed, Toby checked out with the gunnery officer of Range 74. He headed south out over the water, then turned west toward the Brooks bridge, the initial point for landing on runway 36 at Hurlburt Field. The bridge spanned the water from Okaloosa Island to the coast of the Florida panhandle.

Toby flew at exactly 1,000 feet over the Gulf of Mexico. His air-speed indicator read exactly 140 knots. The sun was just beginning to bake the salt air over the blue water. The southern horizon stretched to shimmering azure, as moisture caused slight curves and bends in the light rays. On his westerly heading, Parker paralleled the island. Under his right wing, the sandy beach was a wide strip of the purest white. The Eglin Officer's Beach Club, scene of much panting and racing around, stood out like the cinderblock monstrosity it was. Yet, as thousands of pilots could verify, there was no greater place to fall in love . . . for a night, at least. Toby hadn't been back there to howl at the marlin since he'd first arrived.

Toby looked out each window, and behind, checking traffic. A few A-1 Skyraiders and O-2 aircraft were also headed toward the bridge checkpoint. Flights of F-4s roared off from Eglin Air Force Base. Toby was well under them as they zoomed to altitude. After he reported to the Hurlburt Tower that he was crossing the Brooks bridge, the major in the right seat spoke for the first time in two hours.

"Very nice flight, Parker," he said. "You're as good as everyone says. But you know, we didn't have time for any acrobatics. Let's see you do a loop with this old crock."

Parker didn't respond. He maintained his heading toward Hurlburt.

"Go ahead, loop it. This is fun time now. The test is over. You passed with the highest grade, all 'Fours.' " Toby didn't turn his head.

"Hey, Parker," the major tapped Toby on the shoulder. "Didn't you hear me? Let's see you do a loop." Toby checked his instruments and his position. He was lining up nicely for the traffic pattern. He made no indication he heard the major talking.

"What's the matter, Parker? Don't think you can crank this thing around? Maybe you're not as shit hot as I heard, after all."

Toby carefully cleared the area, bored straight ahead to the landing pattern at Hurlburt, and set the Oscar Pig down so smooth the tires didn't squeak. He taxied in and shut down. In the squadron building, the major listened to Toby debrief the intelligence officer. Afterward, he offhandedly told Toby he had made a good flight, and left the squadron area.

The major went directly to the office of the Director of Operations, a colonel, in the Headquarters of the Special Operations Wing that conducted the training at Hurlburt.

"Well?" the DO said, as the major walked in.

"It was as fine a flight as I've ever been on, Colonel," the major said. He was from the Standardization and Evaluation shop at the Headquarters of the Tactical Air Command in Virginia.

"Any deviations?" the DO asked.

"No, sir. Not a one. I tried to get him to play around, but he wasn't having any. He earned top grades in all phases. He's smart, sharp, and has a natural touch for airplanes. Too bad he's not in fighters."

"He's lucky to be in O-2s," the Hurlburt DO said. "If there hadn't been pressure from the top, he wouldn't even be in the Air Force."

An order had come from the USAF Deputy Chief of Staff for Operations (DCS OPS) in the Pentagon to TAC Headquarters, requesting special assessment of Captain Toby G. Parker. As a result, TAC had sent the major to Hurlburt to fly with him.

"We've got to take care of mavericks," the major said. "Someday they might become heros."

"Parker is already a hero," the DO said. "We just don't want him to become any more of a maverick. He has a bad reputation to live down. Funny thing, as many people as there are that want him out of the Air Force, they are even more who want him in."

"I know," the major said. "We've been tracking him. He's been right on the edge of disaster all the time. Parker has had a lot of publicity. So far it's been good."

"We can thank the Public Affairs people for that. They know who to talk to and what to say," the DO said.

"Too bad it doesn't work that way in Vietnam." He reached for the phone to tell the Deputy Chief of Staff for Operations in the Pentagon that Parker was sober, sharp, and still in the Air Force.

1600 Hours Local, Thursday, 26 October 1967
Room 422, Caravelle Hotel
Saigon, Republic of Vietnam

☆

For the tenth time, Shawn Bannister was studying the congratulatory cables when Nguyen Tri knocked on his door.

"Christ, Tri, just look at these," Shawn said after he let the Vietnamese in. Tri read several of the telegrams about Shawn's article on Colonel Tung and the VC in Cholon.

"Extraordinary in-depth reporting from other side," said CBS.

"Journalistic first," said AP.

"Pulitzer Prize material. More, more. Name your price," said the editor of the *California Sun*.

"They are very nice," Tri said. He nodded, delighted with Bannister's elation. He took a small newspaper-wrapped package from his satchel.

"Here," he said, "is a little present from a friend."

"I can get my own, you know," Shawn said. He unwrapped the

package of four Marlboro flip-top boxes full of expertly rolled Buddha's Burmese Best marijuana cigarettes with a hash kicker.

"Of course you can. Give these to your friends, if you wish," Tri
said. "It is a small matter. The big matter is the very excellent words
you wrote about the interview with the commander."

Shawn had titled the article "Why America Cannot Win in Vietnam." His interview with the Viet Cong commander had been
headline-grabbing material. Never before had an American inter-
viewed the famous Colonel Nguyen Van Tung of the First Viet Cong
Regiment, much less recorded his strategy on why and how the Viet
Cong would prevail. The junior Democratic senator from California
was so impressed, he had printed it in the *Congressional Record*. Because of the success of the article, the *California Sun* had come into
its own as a major antiwar newspaper.

Additionally, Shawn's thrilling account of his blindfolded trip
around Saigon, and into the dank tunnels and caves somewhere in
Cholon city, proved, it was editorialized, that the Viet Cong could
come and go as they pleased.

At the close of the article, Shawn hinted at another big story to
come from the same source.

For five days after he had written and filed the story, Shawn had
raced around Saigon on a nervous high. He'd gone through two and
three girls a day, and two and three packages of the Three Bees, as
he called Buddha's Burmese Best. Several TV newsmen had asked
for an interview with him. He'd given them one. To dress it up, he'd
worn a camouflaged tiger suit, complete with floppy hat. To empha-
size his complete and undying sympathy for the American troops,
he'd held an M-16. The interview hadn't gone as well as he had hoped.
The brash American TV reporters had thought him silly and fatuous
to be dressed like a combat warrior. Not one second of the interview
made the TV screens in the living rooms of the American people.

Shawn had also received a cablegram, more informative than congratulatory, from his godfather, Major General Albert G. Whisenand.
Uncle Albert, as Shawn had always called him, congratulated him on
the success of his article, but did not mention the content. Instead,
Whitey said he would be in Saigon for a MACV meeting later in the
week. He would leave a message at Shawn's hotel about meeting for
dinner. Shawn was apprehensive about meeting with his godfather,
whom he regarded as a shrewd and discerning judge of character.

"Yes, my American friend," Tri said, "your article was excellent.
Your colleagues, indeed, even your senator was pleased. You are tell-
ing the truth." Nguyen Tri smiled. "I know you have been very busy.
Have you had time to consider my suggestions about your next story?"

Shawn's jaw tightened. After Tri had removed the blindfold in the
car returning from the interview, he had talked about the American

presence in Thailand. Tri had told Shawn there were forty thousand American airmen stationed at seven air bases to support the bombing of Laos and North Vietnam. The American people hardly knew about it, Tri had said. He suggested Shawn might want to look into it. He could do so by spending some time near an American air base.

"Yes, but what of the big important attack Colonel Tung told me about?"

"Not yet," Tri said.

"Not yet. In the meantime, are you interested in the Laotian bombing story?"

"I'm interested," Shawn said. "It's for the story, right? No strings attached, right?"

"Strings attached? What does that mean?" Tri asked.

"I mean, you won't . . . ah, want anything from me, will you?"

"Want anything?" Tri repeated. "We didn't want anything from you before, did we? Why should we want anything now?" He laughed. "No, my friend. We do not want anything other than the truth. I know just the Thai village you should go to. I have a friend there who will help you find the truth."

"All right," Shawn said. "I might go. What's the name of the village?"

"Ubon Ratchitani," Nguyen Tri said.

0700 Hours Local, Friday, 27 October 1967
Commander's Briefing Room, 7th Air Force
Tan Son Nhut Air Base
Saigon, Republic of Vietnam

☆

Court Bannister and Flak Apple stood by the large urn at the coffee bar near the briefing room in 7th Air Force Headquarters. Flak sipped from his steaming mug. His face brightened. "Wasn't that something about all those geckos in Colonel Crepens's trailer?" After George had been killed, several lieutenants with a snootful had decided their wing commander needed to get to know geckos. They had bought 200-some for three baht each in the town of Ubon and let them loose in the good colonel's trailer. For good measure they had left hundreds of empty beer bottles as well.

"Take care of the troops, and they'll take care of you," Court said. "I hear Hostettler headed off the OSI and AP investigation Crepens wanted." He glanced at his watch. "Time to go."

They walked into the small auditorium and took seats. They were surrounded by fighter pilots from the four F-4 wings in Southeast Asia; two based in Thailand, two based in South Vietnam. The men chosen to attend the symposium were from the Operations and Plans section of their wings. The Director of Operations, 7th Air Force, a two-star general named Gordon Raimer, gave a one-minute welcoming speech, then left the stage. The next speaker, a colonel from Combat Operations, got down to business. He spoke in measured tones.

"Gentlemen, we have so many different air wars going on at the same time that even the communists don't believe it. Yet, in spite of the fact we have been at it three years now, there is no single manager. The White House runs the war up north through CINCPAC using USAF, Navy and Marine aircraft; the MACV runs the war down south using USAF, Navy, and Marine airplanes. I'm not going into detail on that at this time. Just know that it exists. Maybe someday we will have a coordinated air effort without restrictions." He looked over his audience of alert fighter pilots. "But I doubt it," he said.

He put a page on the viewgraph. "But, we aren't here to talk about restrictions today. First, I will give you the broad outline of the simultaneous air wars we are conducting, then we will narrow down to the problem we are here to discuss today." The viewgraph was titled

AIR COMBAT OPERATIONS

1. B-52s run by the Strategic Air Command (SAC)
2. Naval air war flown off the Task Force 77 carriers
3. Marine air war supporting Marine units
4. Army helicopter war supporting Army units
5. Close Air Support (CAS) missions flown for the Army
6. Interdiction in Laos against the Ho Chi Minh Trail
7. Strategic bombing in North Vietnam
8. Combat Air Patrols (CAPs) against MiGs in North Vietnam

"There are variations on these themes," he said, using a pointer. "The Navy does supply some CAS for the Army in South Vietnam; the USAF, the Navy, and the Marines do some CAS in Laos for the friendly Laotian troops, and the like. But our theme here today concentrates on Number Eight: MiG CAPs in North Vietnam." He put up maps depicting the MiG bases in Route Package Six.

"You must remember, our primary purpose up North isn't to shoot down MiGs. We do that to gain and maintain air superiority. Our primary purpose is to destroy strategic targets such that the North Vietnamese cannot send supplies and troops to South Vietnam."

Court raised his hand. "The MiG shot down today is not a threat tomorrow," he said.

"The target destroyed today is a target we don't have to hit tomorrow," the colonel replied. He pointed to a hard-eyed major who had also raised his hand.

"If the targets are strategic, why are we sending tactical fighters to destroy them? Why don't we send strategic bombers like the B-52 from the Strategic Air Command?" the major asked. The name on his flight suit was P. Combine.

The colonel pursed his lips. "Because," he began, "the B-52s are too vulnerable. We don't think the American public would stand for an airplane that big and expensive being lost to enemy action up north. Furthermore, world opinion wouldn't stand for big bombers blasting poor, tiny, defenseless, peace-loving North Vietnam."

"That sounds like so much horseshit," Court Bannister cut in. He stood up. "I thought SAC has all those magic whiz-bangs on their big birds. They've been saying for years they're invincible with all that electronic warfare equipment they have. That should make the '52 less vulnerable than the Thuds and Phantoms we're losing. And the American public doesn't seem to be particularly concerned that we've already lost hundreds of airplanes up north so far. So what the hell difference does world opinion make? They're against us now, and will be in the future, no matter what we do."

The colonel shrugged. "We only execute the frag down here at Saigon, we don't write it, much less argue about it. But I agree. It's a hell of a war where TAC airplanes are used on SAC targets and vice versa."

"Look, we aren't going to get the frapping Buffs," Flak Apple said. He referred to the B-52, as all fighter pilots did, with the initials for Big Ugly Fat Fucker. "Let's concentrate on making better what we do have. How about the Sparrow missile? Some won't fire, and those that do often can't hold a radar lock."

The colonel flipped a new viewgraph on the projector. "McDonnell Douglas is coming in with a modification to the AN/APQ-109 fire control radar on the F-4. The mod should provide a stronger signal bouncing off the bogey for the Sparrow to home in on. The Tech order should be in the field by the end of this week. Regarding the Sparrow motor, the company has a tighter, better-packed rocket motor due out that has longer shelf life and better reliability. The company tech rep is here today to talk about system reliability." The colonel motioned to a civilian sitting in the front row. "Mr. Bouk, I think this would be an appropriate time for a few words from you. Would you come up here, please?"

Ned Bouk, called Sailor since his days in the Navy as a gunnery officer, walked to the stage with jaunty steps. He stood a little under five-ten, had brown wavy hair, a fouled anchor tattoo on his left arm, and a toothy smile. Court thought he would look right at home in a third-rate used-car lot.

"Gentlemen, I am glad to be here," he said. "We are proud of our missile. The finest engineering, craftsmanship, and quality control have all come together to bring you America's finest air-to-air weapon. We believe in product reliability."

"Reliability. Well, then," the hard-eyed major named Combine said, "what I want to know is, which ones will fire, and which ones won't. Tell us, and we'll just *drop* those that won't fire on the bad guys, and *shoot* the others at them like we're supposed to."

Sailor Bouk looked at the major with dismay. He had been warned by his area manager to keep his mouth shut, and stay out of the limelight. "Gentlemen," Sailor Bouk soothed, "I can only tell you, lab test after lab test, and all the flight tests, proved our missile ninety-four percent reliable. No other missile comes close to that figure."

P. Combine stood up. His cotton flight suit was so worn it looked paper-thin. "Are you telling us it's pilot error? That we don't place our switches correctly?"

"Ah, well, maybe," Bouk said. The used-car saleman looked like he had just been served a summons by a city inspector. "Maybe also some of the pilots are firing too soon or too late, or out of the missile firing envelope. Or maybe the armament people don't store them well enough. Maybe the loaders don't connect a cannon plug correct. There are many things that can go wrong." Bouk smiled. He scratched his chin. "Tell you guys what—big beer blast at the O-Club tonight after the symposium. I'm buying. We'll talk about all this over there."

P. Combine snorted, and sat down. The remainder of the symposium was nothing more than a reiteration of the problems everyone had known about. The suggestions included getting more guns strapped on the Phantom, even some on the wing stations; more pressure on the contractors to improve missile quality control; less code words used by the College Eye control radar in the heat of combat; less rigid control from Seventh Air Force; and more autonomy for the individual fighter wings to develop their own tactics.

The colonel in charge of the symposium said he would get the notes typed up, and forwarded to Major General Raimer for his perusal. Copies would be sent to each attendee.

"What a big waste of time," Flak said as they walked out.

"I think it was just another of those square-filling exercises somebody high up wants so they can say they solicit feedback from the field," agreed Combine. His back-seater, a second lieutenant pilot, nodded his head in agreement.

"Notes to the Director of Operations don't do any good," Court said. "He should have been here in person."

"Do you really think so?" a senatorial voice said behind them. Court whirled. He recognized the voice. It was his father's cousin.

"Yes, sir," he said to Major General Albert G. Whisenand.

☆

Whitey Whisenand carried the four fighter pilots in his staff car to his private quarters, a snug, air-conditioned trailer with bedroom and sitting room. He said he wanted to hold a private symposium. At first, Flak Apple and P. Combine were suspicious as to just who he was, or whom he represented. Whitey said he was in theatre to study a few things. Talking to the lads would help, he said.

Court, so far, had not acted in any manner other than as a younger officer would act to a superior officer that he knew from somewhere. Court and Whitey had an understanding. No one knew Whitey was Sam Bannister's cousin. In uniform, neither referred to the other at any time except in an official capacity.

"I'm Whitey Whisenand. I'm from the office of the President of the United States," he began. He wanted to put these young officers at their ease. "When I'm in the White House, I represent you. When I am out here in the field, I represent our Commander in Chief. Any questions?"

There were none, so Whitey skillfully led them past their natural reticence in front of a general officer who was unknown in fighter circles. Had they been of an intelligence background, they would have known of his legendary feats since his days with the Bletchley bunch in England in World War II, and of his special operations after his F-80 crash in Korea. They had no idea he was one of the early advocates behind the U-2, SR-71, and remote-controlled drones that were flying over North Vietnam at that very moment gathering intelligence. Whitey charmed them, and soon they were easily rehashing what had been said with the colonel from 7th Air Force Operations at the symposium.

P. Combine launched a few choice words about problems with fighting the F-4. Mainly, he was unhappy with the missiles, and the front seat ejection system. The missiles were unreliable, he said. And, even though the pilot and his GIB might have just agreed on the intercom to eject from a crippled F-4, too many times the front-seater never ejected after his back-seater punched out. There should be a command ejection system for the back-seater, he said, so that when he ejected, the front-seater would be punched out automatically.

For the first time, Whitey spoke up. "MacAir is on top of all those," he said. He was referring to the McDonnell Douglas Aircraft Corporation, the company that manufactured the F-4 Phantom. "Modifications fixing those problems are well under way. They will be in the field very soon. Let's hear some more details about the Sidewinder and the Sparrow. What's the PK?" Whitey was asking for the probability of kill per missile fired.

"About thirty-seven percent, sir," Flak Apple said. "We lose about half from firing missiles out of the proper flight envelope, and the other half from malfunctions. Either the motor doesn't fire, or the missile won't guide, or the proximity fuse failed. One of our guys had a Sidewinder zoom about five feet over the canopy of a MiG-19 and not explode." He was not smiling when he told the story.

Whitey looked at the men. "All I can tell you about that is, you gentlemen are doing a great job with a Navy missile designed for high altitude, straight-and-level shooting against nonmaneuvering bombers." He flashed a rueful smile. "If we in the Air Force had been more on the ball, we would have a built-in gun in the F-4 and a more maneuverable missile. All I can say is, you've got the strap-on 20-millimeter cannon now. Soon the F-4E model will be out with a built-in gun. Later, better functioning derivatives of the Sparrow and Sidewinder will be along soon. Meanwhile, do the best you can." He pulled some soda cans from the refrigerator and passed them out.

"The other problem, sir," Flak Apple said, "is that we are restricted to staying close to the bombers we are escorting. The MiGs, especially the MiG-21s, are using new tactics that we can't meet, because we are too close to the bombers. We need to be spread out more so we can see them coming, and make an intercept before they get too close. The way we are restricted, we can't do that."

"Restricted?" Whitey said. "Restricted by whom?" he asked in a neutral voice.

"The Director of Operations for 7th Air Force, sir," Apple and P. Combine said.

Whitey nodded. He decided to change the subject. "What's this I hear about an aircrew revolt at Ubon?" he asked.

P. Combine guffawed. He was from Da Nang, where they had no such problem with a teetotaling fighter wing commander. Flak and Court exchanged glances.

"We can handle it, sir," Flak said. Whitey would have been surprised if Court or Flak had said more. Regardless of how bad your commander was, you did not talk about him when you were out of sight of the flagpole. If he was a menace, one could go to the Inspector General. Among themselves, fighter pilots cursed or praised their boss wherever they were, but only among themselves. Whitey was an outsider, and a high-ranking outsider at that. As much as Court and Flak would have liked to see Crepens fired, they would not talk about him behind his back. If they didn't have material for a formal complaint to be entered over their signature, they shut up. However, as far as Whitey was concerned, what they didn't say answered his question.

It was time for the aircrew to get to the flight line to reclaim their fighters from maintenance and fly back to their home bases. P. Combine's back-seater, a second lieutenant pilot, hadn't said a word the entire time. Almost as an afterthought, Whitey asked him directly how it was going.

"Not worth a shit, General," the second lieutenant responded in a deep voice. Whitey took a closer look at him. He was stocky with wide shoulders and black hair cut to little more than a dark fuzz on his skull.

"What do you mean?" Whitey asked.

"It's like this, sir. I joined the Air Force to fly. Not make like a bombardier or a navigator in the back seat of one of the best fighters in the air today. I want to upgrade to the front seat. But do you know what the regulations say now about upgrading?" Before Whitey could respond, he answered his own question. "They say I can only upgrade if I sign on for another year of combat. I ask you, sir, how the hell many times do I have to pay my dues?"

"Starting this very month," Whitey said, "we are shipping our first fighter-trained navigators over here. Ubon already has some. They will eventually phase into the back seats, freeing up some of you pilots back there. So hang tight, son," Whitey said, "this too will pass."

"General," the lieutenant said, "my active-duty commitment is up two years after this tour. If I can't get an assignment to the front seat of an F-4, I'm going to the airlines." On that note, the impromptu meeting broke up. It was midafternoon.

Whitey drove the staff car himself. He dropped P. Combine and his back-seater off first, and later managed to pass a few words with Court while Flak was preflighting their Phantom. They stood next to the nose of the big fighter.

"How's it going, Court?" Whitey asked.

"Fine, sir," Court answered.

"Your dad sends his best," Whitey said. "Says he'll write soon. He looks good. I'm seeing Shawn tomorrow. He's back here, you know."

"I know only too well," Court said. "His interview with that VC commander caused quite a stir. Everybody asks me about him. The whole damn world seems to know he and I are related. Two days ago, our public information people contacted me. They're worried he might come to Ubon and do a story. I told them I had no control over him whatsoever."

"How's the war going?" Whitey asked, changing the subject.

"What do you mean, how is it going? You're closer to that than I am. You know the big picture." Court saw Flak climb into the back seat. It was his turn. Court began zipping up his G-suit.

"Are we winning or losing?" Whitey asked.

"Now that's a hell of a question, Uncle Albert." The crew chief started the auxiliary power unit. The roaring hiss made Court yell into his uncle's ear. "We are winning. I mean, we *can* win," he shouted.

"*Can* win?" Whitey cupped his hands to Court's ear.

"Sure. Get your boss to turn us and the Navy loose on North Vietnam," Court said, and climbed up to the front seat of the big fighter. In moments, he had the big J-79 engines spooled up. The noise was deafening. He waved as his uncle watched him taxi out. Burners roaring, he took off, snapped the gear up, and turned to a northwesterly heading for Ubon.

"You and that general seem awful chummy," Flak Apple said from the back seat.

"He's my uncle."

"Sure. And I'm your aunt."

1930 Hours Local, Friday, 27 October 1967
Ubon Officer's Open Mess
Ubon Royal Thai Air Force Base
Thailand

☆

Early that evening, the two fighter pilots sat in the dining area of the Officer's Club. They had just finished the best meal in the house, the $5.50 steak, and were nursing coffee and 30-year-old cognac Court had smuggled in.

Flak pushed back from the table and sipped his coffee. "Ahh, that's how I like it, hot and black."

"I hear that's becoming the 'in' word now," Court said.

"What's that, *hot* or *black?*"

Court lowered his chin to his chest, and raised his eyebrows as high as he could.

"You're owling me," Flak said, then relented. "Yeah, right. It is. I'm not a negro anymore, I'm a black man." He sipped his coffee and sighed, and nodded his head. "Actually, I like it better. Some people used to slur their words, so that 'negro' came out 'nigra.' I don't much care for that. In D.C., at Howard, we didn't talk much about all that. Oh yeah, maybe a few wild-eyed types ran around yelling, but me and the other guys in ROTC didn't pay a hell of a lot of attention. We had our studies, some nifty girls, and good careers in the making. Some of us had money, some didn't, but that didn't make any difference. We all had something to look forward to." He took another sip.

"But those wild-eyed types, those bastards, are now burning down ROTC buildings on campuses all over the U.S., white and black. You ought to hear Chappie James go off on this. He'll brace any man, black or white, who pisses and moans about equality in or out of the Air Force. He'll brace him and flat out ask him if he wants to be a fighter pilot or a professional colored man. 'Choose,' he says to them, in that deep menacing voice of his, 'choose, because I only take fighter pilots in my outfit.' He'd say that to the enlisted troops too, it didn't make any difference. He only wanted guys around with the fighter pilot attitude. When you swear in, leave it, or stay the hell out."

Court could see Flak was getting a bit worked up. They both knew of and respected Colonel Chappie James, the black fighter pilot veteran of three wars. He had been the vice wing commander under Robin Olds, and the two had flown many combat missions together in F-4s from Ubon, calling themselves Blackman and Robin.

Flak took another sip of his cognac and sighed. "It wasn't like this just a few years back," he said.

"The cognac?" Court asked. "It's always been good."

Flak, imitating Court's earlier action, lowered his chin and raised his eyebrows.

"Okay, now you're owling me," Court said. "What hasn't always been good?"

"Getting served in the States. Even Las Vegas. Back in the mid-fifties, a black man couldn't even get into the casinos to play the machines, much less eat. When I was stationed at Nellis, I remember making a reservation on the telephone for me and a buddy at the Dunes as Lieutenant Apple. No problem that night until the waiting line wound down to the reservation desk. 'Must be some mistake,' the maître d' said when he saw us. We were in uniform. I said, You mean we can wear this uniform, fight and maybe die for guys like you, but not eat here? He took us to see the manager, who said the Air Force might be integrated, but we could understand that as yet the Dunes was not. Wasn't his fault, he said. Sure, I said, and asked for the telephone. Told him I was going to call my friend, the Nellis base commander, and tell him how badly his boys were being treated. That he'd put the Dunes off-limits and tell all the newspapers about it. He asked us to wait a minute and went out. Five minutes later, he was back, gave us the best table in the house and free champagne all night."

Court laughed. "Terrific," he said. "Who was the commander?"

"Hell, I don't know. I was just a dummy lieutenant trying to learn how to fly the F-86," Flak ended with a laugh. "What the hell. Growing up in the U.S. means that there are people out there who hate you just because you are what you are . . . be it black or rich, Jewish or Irish Catholic, whatever. Anything different from the bigot. There are some small-minded people out there who have got to think they

are better than anyone else. So it goes." He held up his cognac snif-
ter. "Bottoms up," he said, and tossed down the remaining amber
liquid. He placed the glass carefully on the table, and studied Court.

"You're not trying to prove something, are you?" Flak asked, his
eyes strangely veiled.

"What do you mean?"

"Hanging around with me."

Court stared hard. "No, goddammit, I'm not," he snapped. He relaxed a little. "You're a good guy, you're fun, and you're a good jock.
But that wasn't a nice thing to say, Major of the Air Force Apple."

Flak looked at Court. "All right, Bannister, Major, one each. Maybe
not. But I want to tell you something, so maybe you'll understand a
little more what it's like to be a black man."

Both men were getting to that stage in liquor consumption where
everything is terribly important, and all words intense and true.

"I want to tell you," Flak began, "it is a white man's system. Oh,
sure, there have been changes since the big war, when the Tuskegee
airmen proved blacks didn't have tiny brains and big thumbs. An
Army War College report said our brains were smaller than whites'.
Tuskegee was an experiment, you know, supposed to show a black
man couldn't hack it in a cockpit. Those guys proved a man of color
was also a man of courage and skill. Take the 332nd Fighter Group.
They flew fighters for bomber protection. Not one bomber under
their protection was ever shot down. Not one. And listen, the Tuskegee airmen shot down well over a hundred enemy fighters." Flak
nodded.

"Sure, it is better now," he said. "But it's still out there. At Del
Rio when I was a student officer, I couldn't get a room off base, not
in a hotel, no place. At Squadron Officer's School, I was a 'special
category.' My section commander had to tell the police if I was vis-
iting his or any other white officer's house in Montgomery." He
nudged Court. "You ever wonder why I'm such a shit hot good jock?"
Before Court could answer, Flak Apple said, "Because I'm a man of
color, and when you are a man of color, you got to be three times as
good as the guy who ain't. *Capiche?*"

Court nodded. The big man had just revealed a lot of himself.
"Thanks," he said. "Just thanks."

19

☆

If nothing else, each participant would take away with him a heavy metal ashtray made from the butt end of a 105mm howitzer shell. It was a gathering of the highest-ranking civilian and military officers seen in years. They were gathered in the small thirty-seat auditorium reserved for VIP conferences and briefing. The large room was in the MACV complex known as Pentagon East. The neatly laid two-story prefab metal office buildings snaked around in such a way as to provide five rectangular closed courtyards and one huge open courtyard. The ceiling was covered with a symmetrical array of acoustical tiles broken by banks of recessed fluorescent light tubes. Slides, films, charts, and maps brought for presentation were carefully logged in and out with the security clerk in the back of the room. The plush movie-theater chairs had been removed. In their place was a conference table long enough to seat twenty. Behind each conferee's chair (metal, steel gray, with armrest) was positioned another chair (metal, steel gray, without armrest) for an advisor. On the table in front of each position were three yellow legal-sized tablets (lined), six pencils (#2), and the polished copper-colored 105mm ashtray.

Most of the conferees had a younger officer seated behind them. Very few of the conferees had brought with them their deputies or directors of operations, for two reasons: someone had to stay behind and run the store, and a decision-maker wasn't necessary to back up the boss today. Today, the boss needed a storehouse of instantly available facts, because this conference had been called by COMUS-MACV, and who knew what questions he might ask. Each storehouse was neat, trim, and earnest. Many wore black horn-rimmed GI-issue glasses. All were low in rank, that is, captains or majors, with an occasional lieutenant colonel, because they could retain and recover facts faster than the higher-ranking—and older—officers. These men were going nowhere in terms of command positions, but they would always have a place on a staff . . . until their photographic memories and instant recall facilities began to fail. Or until they realized the role they played and got out of the service to become reasonably successful account executives or stockbrokers.

A few conferees, four out of the thirty-two, were quite conspicuous, because the seated symmetry was broken by the empty chairs behind them. Two, both air force brigadiers from Seventh Air Force, never thought to bring anyone along. Their attitude was that if they couldn't cough up a fact, it wasn't worth coughing up.

A third was a grizzled Army full bull. He was out of uniform and looked out of place, and was decidedly out of sorts because he had to attend one of these silly-assed bullshit sessions. The chair behind him was empty. Although he was the lowest-ranking attendee at the conference, he commanded more men than 90 percent of the Army officers present. He was the Commanding Officer of the 5th Special Forces Group (SFG), the one and only SF contingent in Vietnam. The CO slot called for a colonel, not a brigadier, yet he commanded the equivalent, in riflemen, of two divisions, which was the minimum size to make up an Army Corps—a unit commanded by a three-star general. Probably because the 42,000 riflemen in his command were Nungs, Montagnards, Cambodians, and Vietnamese; and probably because the 2,650 officers and NCOs that led these troops were all Special Forces, the United States Army didn't think the command position important enough to merit a general officer. If the truth be known, few general officers wanted anything to do with this bunch of unconventional and decidedly unkempt warriors.

The colonel wore neatly pressed jungle fatigues with his pants bloused into his boots. Opposite his jump wings and CIB stitched in black thread was his last name, Dall.

The other conferee with an empty chair behind him was Major General Albert G. Whisenand. He sat halfway down the far side, away from the lectern and stage. He was lucky even to be there. Only his orders signed personally by the Commander in Chief of the American Armed Forces had gotten him in the door. Even so, the Army three-star who provided executive services for COMUSMACV was upset. He had lost a clash with Whitey the year before, over Whitey's itinerary in Vietnam. At that time, under COMUSMACV's direct order to get a handle on the zoomie from the White House, the three-star had made up an agenda that would keep Whitey busy and in Army hands for his entire visit. Only when Whitey had assured him he was investigating USAF matters, not COMUSMACV's performance, had the three-star felt mollified and backed off with his schedule.

This year seemed a repeat of the last, only more dangerous. Whitey not only still worked at the White House, this time he had a piece of White House stationery signed by The Man that he was to be shown *all* courtesies—and that meant by ambassadors and four-star generals alike. Whitey, cherubic and slightly overweight, had decided it best not to wear a uniform. He might be construed as an Air Force spy, or partisan, or too friendly, or the dozen or so things the fear of a White House representative can generate. So Whitey attended the conference in civvies, looking benign, and beaming at all who looked at him. He wore tan slacks and a white short-sleeved shirt open at the neck. Most people glanced at him twice, because of the burn scars on his face.

He was a bit of a mystery man to the assemblage. He was not recognized as from the embassy, nor was he recognized as being with the Agency, nor AID or USOM, or any other civilian outfit that would employ an older man such as he. In a moment of mischief, Whitey had fashioned a name tag from a folded page of the yellow tablet and stuck it into his shirt pocket. The visible part read only his name, no rank.

There was general milling about before the official start of the conference. The hum of conversation was steady, occasionally punctuated by shouts of recognition or bursts of laughter. Four minutes remained before the convening time of 1600 hours. The lowest-ranking attendee, the Special Forces colonel, studied Whitey for a moment, then walked up to him with a broad grin. He was the same height as Whitey, but much broader.

"Whiz, you were dumpy in the company at the Point and you're dumpy now. Where did you get that permanent suntan on your face? And civvies. You a spook now?" Fred John Dall, "Bull" Dall, said. The two men grabbed each other by the shoulder, faces split in happy smiles.

"Well, well, Fred Dall," Whitey said with a broad smile. "I knew you were running in the woods someplace over here, but I never thought I'd see you at a headquarters conference. What are you on now, your second tour? What does Betty think about that? Damn, but I'm glad to see you."

Since no one calls "Tench HUT" at such an auspicious gathering, the two West Point classmates were still slamming each other on the back and asking questions without answers so fast, they didn't hear the discreet words "Gentlemen, the Commander," when General William Childs Westmoreland, COMUSMACV—Commander U.S.

Military Advisory Command Vietnam—walked into the room. Everyone popped to rigid attention and closed-mouthed silence except Whisenand and Dall.

"Ohh, shit," Bull Dall said under his breath, as he perceived what had happened. He nudged Whitey, who was in the middle of an answer about his Korean crash. The two men looked like a pair of schoolboys caught on the playground with dirty pictures as they drew themselves into a position of attention—chin in, thumbs along seams of trousers.

General Westmoreland, Westy to his friends and classmates, strode briskly toward the podium. He nodded at Dall and Whisenand, so obviously not standing at their assigned places. COMUSMACV was a handsome and erect man, well-built, six feet tall, with thick white hair combed perfectly in place. He had a broad face and wide-set eyes. He wore crisp ironed fatigues with only his name, his jump wings and CIB, and his four stars embroidered in black thread on the blouse. He stopped by the two officers.

"Bull, I'm glad you could make it. I know how you detest coming to Saigon except to visit MACSOG." He initiated a handshake with the Special Forces Colonel. He turned to face Whitey. His face creased into a smile.

"You are traveling in the best of company, General Whisenand," he said, cocking his head toward Bull Dall. "The very best." He smiled. "Welcome to the conference," he said, the warmth obvious in his voice. "Stop by my office before you leave the country, will you?"

"Thank you, sir. Yes, I'll stop by," Whitey replied, surprised not only that the general knew who he was, but had gone out of his way to let Whitey know it. General Westmoreland took his place behind the lectern and began his speech.

"Gentlemen, be seated, please. I appreciate your taking time away from your mission. Time is precious here, we never seem to have enough of it, so I'll be brief." He took his watch off and laid it on the podium. He really didn't need to do that, for he could speak at any length and, with an uncanny built-in clock, stop within seconds of the time he had allotted. Today, he used the movement to emphasis his respect for the time he was usurping from his audience.

"I consider the subject matter so vital to your knowledge that I wanted to present the material myself." He cleared his throat. "There has been much negative talk and rumor about our current situation here in Vietnam that has found its way into the press. It started with an article in the communist newspaper published in Hanoi, the *Quan Doi Nhan Dan*, the *Military People's Daily*. In it, Vo Nguyen Giap, the general in charge of the North Vietnamese forces, said his strategy had forced us to fight him in locations of his choosing, namely along the DMZ at places like Khe Sanh, and in the Central High-lands. This simply is not true. These border battles, in fact, were a significant success for American troops." He punched a button on the lectern. The lights dimmed as, one after the other, he clicked slides onto a huge screen. They depicted battle scenes, aftermaths with dead VC bodies and weapons booty, and appropriate maneuver maps.

"The enemy has not pulled us *to* the borders. Rather, he can only mount his large actions *from* the border where he has sanctuary. This means their major efforts are largely limited to the periphery of South Vietnam. Gentlemen, I believe the crossover point of the war is here—the crossover point where we are attriting the enemy faster than he can replenish himself."

He quickly explained a series of slides that showed how the ranks of the guerrillas were falling, how Viet Cong and NVA killed in battle had more than doubled since 1965, how the body count had risen to an average of 7,315 per month even during the rainy season, how communist forces had diminished from 285,000 to 242,000, and that "even just north of Saigon, the enemy units in War Zone D are having rice problems. Of the one hundred and sixty-three Main Force Viet Cong and NVA battalions, almost half—seventy-six battalions— were unable to fight due to disease, deprivation, desertion, and dis-may."

Westmoreland looked about with pride at the men assembled in the room. They were the ranking officers of all the services—Army, Navy, Air Force, Marine, and Coast Guard—under his command. He was giving them the ungarbled word, and they would take the word back to the troops for dissemination.

"In conclusion, victory is measured by control. Look at this chart, and it is the last." He chuckled as he stressed the word *last*. It was a pie-shaped chart.

"You can see," he said, "that the Viet Cong control a mere 17 percent of the population, another 16 percent are in the contested category, while 67 percent of the 17 million people in South Vietnam are in the cities, or located in relatively safe hamlets."

His eyes ranged his audience like search lamps, catching each man, making each think he was personally being taken into the confidence of COMUSMACV.

"Yes," he said with grave finality, "while there may be a final large attempt, we have reached the crossover point and we are draining the enemy. That is the message for you, and for your troops. It is the message for the press and for the world. I repeat, we have reached the crossover point, and are draining the enemy." He looked around. His expression implied his briefing was complete enough so that ques-tions weren't really necessary. However . . .

Bull Dall raised his hand. "Sir, we are at 525,000 troops now. Do you see any reason to eventually ask for more?"

"That is an option," General Westmoreland replied in a pleasant tone, "that I don't care to discuss at the moment." These "win" briefs had been ordered by LBJ when Westy was in D.C., and he was delivering.

1945 Hours Local, Friday, 27 October 1967
Carusso's Restaurant, Vo Di Nguy Street
Saigon, Republic of Vietnam

☆

"I'm glad you could make it this evening," Dall said. At Dall's insistence, Whitey had broken a dinner engagement with some Seventh Air Force people to spend a few hours with his old classmate. They ordered wine and picked up the conversation where they had left off earlier that day.

"Damn, Whitey, I wish I could say you are looking fit, but you're not," Bull Dall said, his own face lined, weathered, and well-used. In Army terms, he was ancient. He had been given the job as 5th SFG commander as a cap to a career that had started in the infantry in the thirties. Seconded to the OSS under Wild Bill Donovan in World War II, he had never really come back to the Regular Army. He had done a lot of clandestine work in Korea with Jack Singlaub and Heine Aderholt. Later, he'd worked with Sir Robert Thompson in Malaysia, quelling the Communist uprising.

"You're looking great, too, Bull," Whitey responded in a mocking tone. Dall had been a champion wrestler, weightlifter, and horseman at the Point. Whitey had been a real mover in track. Both men had been on the debate team, and both had finished in the top 10 percent of their class. Except for one reunion, they had lost contact when Whitey had opted to be among the men who had chosen the Air Force portion of the United States Army Air Force. Each knew the other's whereabouts from *The Assembly*, the West Point Alumni magazine, and from the military grapevine that easily equaled Ma Bell for speed of information transmission.

Each wore dark pants and sport shirts draped over their belts. Whitey didn't know it, but Bull Dall had a snub-nose .38 in a tiny belt holster. They sat in one of the six booths arranged around the floor tables of the restaurant. Robert, husband of the owner, Michèle, strummed a guitar from a stool near the bar. There were huge, round ceramic vases of potted palm varieties on the floor, and a profusion of hanging greenery around the discreetly lit dining room.

Bull tapped Whitey's arm. "I want you to meet some guys I think a lot of; Al Charles and Wolf Lochert. Since you want to know if we are winning or losing, and about the Ho Chi Minh Trail, I thought you should get to know them, to hear their thoughts and ideas. They're a couple of youngsters, but they have a lot of field experience and they'll tell you what's going on."

Whitey said he appreciated that, then asked Dall what he thought of the statistics General Westmoreland had presented at the conference.

Bull Dall laughed. "Let me tell you," he said, "where those friendly and unfriendly village control figures come from. They come from a computer that has been fed with so-called facts and figures under the HES—Hamlet Evaluation System. Every month, civilian guys in the provinces fill out thousands of computer program cards about who owns what part of the surrounding territory. That information is supposed to tell us who is winning."

"Didn't you believe COMUSMACV today when he said we were winning?" Whitey asked.

"Of course not," Bull Dall replied.

"Why not?"

"He might believe the stats, but I don't, because I think those guys who feed the computers are just juggling figures. The truth is, we got troops, but no executive leadership; we got tactics, but no strategy; we got force, but no commitment. We've got the sons of a half-million people here whose parents haven't the faintest idea why they are here. Pretty soon they are going to tell us to shit or get off the pot. They're going to say 'I want my boy brought home . . . but not on his shield.' "

"So?" Whitey said.

"So unless we get some grit in our people, and in our civilian leadership, this place is gonna go down the bloody tubes." After extensive combat in Korea, Bull Dall had picked up an international relations degree from Harvard with honors. He knew what he was talking about.

"Right now, the subject is military leadership," Whitey said.

"Sure. If we had the right civilian leadership we would have responsive military leadership. But I ask you, how can you lead somebody when you don't know where you are going?" He looked pensive. "Westy is one helluva guy. Did you know he turned down a third star when he was Superintendent at West Point? His exec, General Davidson, told me about it. Generals do that as often as the Pope says Mass in the Shiloh Baptist Church. The reason was, he would have had to leave the Point. He had things he still wanted to do there, so he stayed on and did them. He added electives in the courses for cadets, for one."

"He had to," Whitey injected. "The Air Force Academy was already doing that instead of forcing all the cadets to take just engineering subjects."

"You're right," Dall said. "Then he persuaded JFK to agree to double the cadet corps from 2,200 to 4,400."

Whitey laughed. "Yes, but remember, he also hired Paul Dietzel away from LSU to coach the football team. You know what a disaster that was." The two men laughed and finished off their bottle of Australian Hunter Valley red wine. Michèle, the hostess and owner, brought another. The two men were feeling the effects. They rapidly covered the many topics dear to their hearts.

"Something I've noticed among the faint-hearts in the officer corps," Whitey said, "is they seem to be adapting an attitude of 'screw it, if I'm not allowed to win, I might as well go for promotion.' I hate to admit this, but in the Air Force we are now writing an evaluation report on our officers over here every six months. That's twice as many as in peacetime."

"I don't believe the Army is any better," Dall said. "We ticket-punch. Get the right squares punched on your ticket and you can advance to the next step on the board." He made a wide, lopsided grin. "That isn't exactly what I have been doing, you will note." Bull Dall was referring to the fact that he was still a full colonel, and had been since 1943, when he had been one of the youngest full colonels in the Army. Considered a comer then, he had fallen out of favor as soon as he had thrown his lot in with the OSS and, later, with the Special Forces in the early fifties.

Whitey and Bull Dall had finished almost all of their second bottle of red when the two officers from MACSOG entered the restaurant. Broad and craggy, almost Neanderthaloid Wolf Lochert, and Al Charles, big and black; together they had all but routed most of the French diners at the restaurant. Wide-eyed, the diners were afraid the two Americans were Corsicans come to blow the place away over some drug-smuggling dispute.

Bull Dall introduced Whitey as an old West Point chum who had gone astray and drifted into the Air Force. He did not mention his rank. Wolf Lochert and Al Charles easily accepted him as one of their own. They listened impassively as Bull Dall told them Whitey was from the White House to determine the answer of a single question about the war in Vietnam: Is the U.S. winning or losing?

"I know about you, Colonel Lochert," Whitey said. "I read your classified report about the black market and drug ring the Provost General was involved in."

Wolf nodded, and made a sour smile. "It was not a thing I'd care to do again. I'm a soldier, not a cop, or a criminal investigator." He glanced pointedly at Al Charles, who had played rather loose with the sixth directive.

"That's right," Al Charles added. "That's the last time I'll put one of my men through something like that. Wolf wrapped up the ring in a matter of days. We have managed to keep it from the press that the suicide of the Provost General was related to the smuggling case."

"And that civilian Bates?" Whitey said.

"That slimy bastard Bubba Bates was still walking around. The court wouldn't accept my evidence that he'd recruited in and out of jail for the PG and his ring. That in itself wasn't a crime, they said. Bah, I should have strangled the little weasel. We've lost a lot of good GIs to stolen and black market weapons."

"He got off free?" Whitey asked.

"Not exactly," Wolf growled, trying to suppress a smirk. "I believe he was captured by the Vietcong on the Vung Tau highway." He drained a bottle of *Bière 33* Michèle had brought him. "They are a particularly nasty bunch."

Al Charles clapped Wolf Lochert on the back. "We are going to award this guy an Elmer for his acting. He and those guys from the First SF at Okinawa put on quite a show in front of the bar on Tu Do Street. Barely cost us a hundred bucks to pay the damage in the bar and to buy the guy a new shirt to replace the one he broke the blood pack on. When Wolf fired a blank from his Mauser, he smacked it with his hand. Had it taped to his chest. The MPs said it looked mighty realistic."

"Had to make sure I didn't punch him there and break it too early," Wolf said. "Had to make the blank myself. Cartridges for my 7.63 are hard to come by." He looked at Al Charles. "About my acting. Don't you mean an 'Oscar'?"

"No, Elmer. As in Elmer Fudd," the big man said.

"Aw," the Wolf said with feigned injured dignity, "you're just jealous." He turned to Bull Dall and Whitey, a serious expression on his face.

"You wanted to know who is winning. That's easy. We are. If I didn't think so, I wouldn't be here. I don't follow those fancy charts, or listen to those lectures. I know we are winning, because *I* am winning. The minute I can't win, I'll pull out and let somebody take my place who *can* win. Now, ask me if I think we can win better, or faster, and I'll say damn right we can."

"That's certainly laying it on the line, Wolf. What about you, Al?" Bull Dall asked.

"I'm like Wolf. I do my assigned tasks the best way I know how. I get my troops to do their assigned tasks the best way they know how. If we run into problems, we solve them ourselves. If we don't have the correct kind of supplies, I don't bitch, I or my troops go steal them. I leave all that high-level worrying to you guys. I just accept whatever mission you give me, salute, and go do it. That's what I signed up for. I remember that JFK said to bear any burden, pay any price to assure liberty. That's why we are here." He finished his bottle of *Bière 33*. "Also, like Wolf, ask me if we can do it better. I'll say, hell yes we can."

"What about the ARVN, the Army of the Republic of Vietnam?" Whitey asked. "Can they win this war on their own?"

"Not unless Prime Minister Thieu and his deputy, Ky, get rid of all the corrupt generals and civilian grafters," Bull Dall said emphatically. Wolf and Al Charles nodded in agreement.

"I have another question," Whitey said. "How can we not win?"

"You mean, how can we screw it up so bad we can't win?, don't you?"

"Yes," Whitey said, "that's what I mean."

All three men started to speak at once, then subsided. Al Charles spoke up, his black face earnest and intent. "We will lose if, one, the ARVN doesn't come around and take over, and two, we don't go north and cut their nuts off."

"Is that likely to happen?" Whitey asked.

"Isn't that where you come in?" Wolf Lochert asked in a flat voice.

Whitey leaned forward, a look of great interest on his face. "Given that we can't do that, what would you do different?" he asked Al Charles.

"Outside of South Vietnam, I'd cut the VC off from their supplies. I'd do that two ways. First, prevent Russia and China from supplying North Vietnam. The North Vietnamese are on their ass. There is no way they can supply the South on their own. Simultaneously, I'd bottle up North Vietnam in such a way they couldn't get supplies to the Ho Chi Minh Trail."

"I'm telling you, we haven't figured that out in Washington yet, Al," Whitey said in disgust. "We aren't allowed to seal off North Vietnam."

"Well, then," Al Charles said, "I'd bottle up the Ho Chi Minh Trail itself as it goes through Laos."

"How?" Whitey demanded.

Al Charles's black eyes gleamed. "Easy," he said. "I'd put a big force together to invade Laos and charge straight across northern Steel Tiger to Thailand to cut the Trail in half. In the meantime, because that size operation would take several months to put together, I'd put plenty of my people in Laos on the ground to find the supplies, trucks, and road equipment. Then I'd have them call in air strikes to destroy what they found."

Bull Dall looked at Whitey. "We do have some Shining Brass Trail watchers in place, but nothing on the grand scale Al wants." Shining Brass was the code name for the Special Forces Trail watch and Intel gathering teams in Laos for the last two years. "What would it take to get authorization for both of Al's ideas? Can you sell them to the President?" he asked.

Whitey leaned back and cocked his head. "Maybe. But that isn't enough. If McNamara didn't like it, he could bind DoD in small ways so that nothing would happen. Same with the JCS. If they didn't like it, they could drag their feet until the President forgot about it."

"What if I just went ahead and did it?" Bull Dall said.

"Did what? Invade Laos?" Whitey asked with a chuckle.

"Sort of. Just on a smaller scale. I'm talking about part two of Al's idea. Let's put some 'find 'em and fix 'em' teams in there. Some teams that will do more than just *watch* the Trail. They would call in air strikes. There is a lot of activity on the Trail now, I think it's picking up. If I start putting special teams in, can you arrange it so more air assets would be available to them?"

"Hell's bells, Bull, I'm barely on the NSC. I'm not a manager of air assets. I'm lucky to have a parking place at the White House," Whitey said.

"An SF man wouldn't have any trouble arranging assets," Bull Dall said, with silk in his voice.

"I though you zoomies all knew each other," Al Charles said, all innocent.

Wolf Lochert delivered the clincher. "I always thought fighter pilots did it better," he said.

Whitey Whisenand looked from face to face and threw up his hands. "Tell you what I'll do," he said. "I have to make the rounds with the people at Seventh Air Force who control all in-country air assets, then back to the people who control all the airplanes out of Thailand. I'll see what I can do and let you know unofficially."

Wolf Lochert's eyes lit up. "I want to be first to take a team in. I want to use HALO," Lochert said, eyes glittering. HALO was the term for a High Altitude Low Opening parachute jump to put forces on the ground undetected. They would leap from an airplane several miles high, tracking far away from the drop zone, then literally soar to the DZ by positioning their bodies like gliding birds. The other Army men nodded. They understood.

"HALO," Whitey said, impressed. "Okay, Wolf. I'll see what I can do," He looked toward the kitchen. "Now, how does a man get to eat around here?"

Bull Dall, who had frequented Carusso's before, called to Michèle to serve her best. She did. The four men ate, savoring every bite of the gourmet meal Michèle was able to provide. From the *escargots* to the *Coq au Vin*, from the *Cocktail de Crevettes* to the *Timbale de*

Veau Sous-Cloche Bergere to her *Soufflé Surprise* dessert, they ate with appreciative gestures and words. They also put away two more bottles of the red. The bill, with 15 percent service charge, came to nearly 13,000 piasters. Since Whitey had no piasters, he illegally paid his share in green: $42.00.

They finished the evening at the bar at House Ten, a Special Forces safe house. By the time they even thought of the curfew, it was three in the morning. Major General Albert G. Whisenand, Air Force special assistant to the President of the United States and member of the National Security Council for air power, spent the night with the three Army officers on the roof of the safe house doing in a bottle of scotch, each trying to outdo the others with rotten limericks. Ever true to the space age, Whitey won with his astrological scatological rhyme about the young man from Rangoon who tried to fart his way to the moon. Seems he flopped as a rocket, shit in his pocket, and died in a rectal typhoon.

0900 Hours Local, Saturday, 28 October 1967
Office of the Director of Operations
Headquarters, 7th Air Force, Tan Son Nhut Air Base
Republic of Vietnam

☆

"What did you think of the fighter symposium yesterday?" Major General Gordon Raimer asked Whitey Whisenand. Raimer had known Whitey since Command and Staff College days. As a major, Raimer had been a student of Whitey's, an eager but average student.

"Not much," Whitey said. His normally benign face was quite serious. "You should have been there to listen and answer the questions. You're the gentleman who directs operations, are you not? Those were operational people there, with valid operational complaints and suggestions. Maybe your representative didn't correctly interpret what was told to him. Maybe he didn't tell you everything he heard. You should have been there. Why should you get your input secondhand?"

Raimer stiffened. "I'm sure my deputy's notes are accurate and complete," he said.

"Gordon, you are missing my point," Whitey said, with some force. "You, you personally, Major General Gordon Raimer, Director of Operations, 7th Air Force, should have been present at that meeting. The way it was, all the aircrew knew was that they were only talking to some fellow from the staff."

"General Whisenand, with all due respect, you are the one who doesn't understand. The reason the aircrew were at that meeting was to discuss problems of fighting the air war in North Vietnam, specifically Route Packages Two through Six. We here at 7th Air Force have no control over the targeting that goes on up in those packages. It all comes to them from Washington via PACAF. I did not want the pilots to think they had my backing or approval for any of their new-fangled ideas to use on those targets. To avoid that, I felt it best not to be there." Raimer stood up.

"I am not talking targeting," Whitey said. "Neither were those pilots. They were talking deficiencies in some of their weapons, particularly the missiles. And they were talking about bad tactics against the North Vietnamese air defense system. If you can't help fix the problems in weapons and tactics, at least give them the go-ahead to solve them on their own."

"What would you have me do?" Raimer asked.

"First, let them use the gun more, and don't charge them with a missile fired out of parameters as a pilot-error misfire when it was used as a deterrent," Whitey said. "Second, they are the men doing the actual fighting. Let them devise their own tactics to fight the MiGs. No more dicta from your shop down here in Saigon. I've checked the backgrounds of your people. You don't have enough pilots who have been fighting up north and know what they are talking about. The few combat pilots that you have under your command are junior in rank and not listened to."

Raimer walked to the wall chart of Southeast Asia. He stood staring at it, his back to Whitey. His uniform was beautifully cut and pressed. "There can be no deviation from 7th Air Force policy and procedure," he said over his shoulder.

"Deviate? Great Scott, man. You are the man who *sets* 7th Air Force policy and procedure. They originate from this very office. You're the *Director* of Operations. Do some *directing*. You must loosen up. Can't I get you to change your mind? These are our men, trying to do a job, a bloody tough job. You can help them do that job better. They fight MiGs in the air with weapons that don't always work, and on the ground they fight the Rules of Engagement that don't always work. Now tell me why they should have to fight their own chain of command at the same time?"

Raimer turned from the map to face Whitey. "Why are you bothering about all this? As I understand it, you're here on a classified study for the President. Daily operational matters are not in your area of interest. You do your job, and I'll do mine. I cannot help you, General." He seemed glad to have a point with which to attack.

Whitey remained seated. He rubbed the back of his neck where the collar of his overstarched 1505 khakis had been chafing. He sighed. "All right," he said in a weary voice. He sighed again, and stood up.

"Major General Gordon T. Raimer," he said, with a voice suddenly edged with steel, "in accordance with the authority vested in me by the Presidential directive dated 19 October 1967, you are hereby relieved of command, effective immediately. You will remain in your quarters until further orders."

Five minutes later, Major General Albert G. Whisenand stood in front of Gordon Raimer's boss, the USAF four-star general commanding 7th Air Force.

"You did what?" Commander, 7th Air Force, barked.

"I fired that cowardly son of a bitch you had as a director of operations, and I'll fire any other son of a bitch who won't back up our airmen," Whitey said.

"Amazing," Commander, 7th Air Force, said bitterly. "For a two-star, you sure are packing a lot of weight. How high can you fire? Me, for example? Can you fire anyone on the JCS?" He shook his head in disbelief.

Whitey remained silent.

"No, I guess you can't answer that one." He made a wry face. "In all the twenty-five years I've known you, I have never heard you swear. Raimer has only been here two months. I didn't ask for him. He and Crepens over at Ubon were directed assignments. I wasn't consulted when I got him, so I suppose it's only fair I wasn't consulted when I lost him. He had a brilliant staff background, absolutely walk-on-water efficiency reports, and had been to all the right schools. He was considered three-, if not four-star material. Not anymore. Not after what you've done to him."

"It's not what *I've* done to him. It's what he has done to himself. There was one school he didn't see fit to attend. That's the one where they shoot real bullets at you. Somehow, he saw very little combat in the Big One, and none in Korea. And he is yet to fly one mission here in Vietnam. Stars are worthless if you don't use them for the mission and the troops," Whitey said. "By the way, why do you think Raimer and Crepens were given directed duty assignments?"

"I think it had something to do with people against the fighter mafia. I think the nonfighter conglomerate decided to convince the Chief of Staff the fighter mafia was too entrenched and that he should put some other people in command positions. Fresh blood, new ideas. Maybe one of the past fighter commanders was too popular. Something like that." Commander, 7th , leaned back in his chair. He stared at Whitey. "To press on before I get the can tied to *me*," he said, "what can I do for you?"

"Tell me if we're winning or losing this war," Whitey said.

Commander, Seventh, threw back his head and laughed. "Whisenand, you are something. Indeed you are. First, without consulting me, you fire my deputy because you think he is not fighting the war well enough. Then you ask me if we are winning or losing the very same war." He suddenly became very serious. "Are you asking me officially?" He held up his hand before Whitey could answer. "Because if you are, I'll tell you, of course we are winning, and I've got the statistics to prove it." He pointed to a series of four-foot poster-board charts. Whitey recognized the figures from the top chart as the same shown in General Westmoreland's briefing. Among other things, they summarized the fact that over 30,000 targets had been destroyed or damaged in North Vietnam so far in just this year of 1967.

"Do you believe those numbers?" Whitey asked.

"I do," Commander, Seventh Air Force, said in a subdued voice. "I do, because the definition of 'target' is not included on the chart. Let me tell you, Whitey," he said, warming to his subject, "to fill the squares demanded by the office of the Secretary of Defense, we and the Navy now consider swaying bamboo bridges and wiblicks, among other items of dubious value, as targets."

"Wiblicks?" Whitey echoed.

"Wiblicks," Commander, Seventh, repeated. "WaterBorne Logistics Craft. Read that as sampans, log rafts, and the like. That does not include real supply boats found in the harbors. While we are not allowed to hit *targets* of significant value, we are nonetheless required to produce *figures* of significant value." His face was a mixture of pain and disgust. "So you come in here and fire a guy for not prosecuting the war the way you think he should. Does it really make any difference?"

"You missed my point," Whitey said. "I didn't fire him because of the way he prosecuted the war. I fired him because he doesn't listen to his troops, who are on the firing line every single day. He refused to listen to and act upon feedback from the boys about tactics and equipment that make trouble. That's cause to fire someone in peacetime, not to mention during a war."

Commander, 7th, rubbed his eyes. "You're right. I guess I know that. Sometimes I get so wrapped up in what's going on right here in South Vietnam—my boss, Westy, is a four-star Army general who wants constant air support for his troops—that I may miss what's going on out of country."

Major General Albert G. Whisenand studied the four-star general sitting across from him. "Ideally, we should bomb the MiG bases, mine Haiphong harbor, and take out the rail lines from China. But we can't, at least not yet." Whitey sat forward. "Meanwhile, what if I got permission for more Special Forces teams in Laos to find and call in fighters on supply targets on the Ho Chi Minh Trail? And what if I got more fighters allocated to that mission? These are interim measures, I know, but wouldn't you get better results?" Whitey's face lit up.

The Commander of the 7th Air Force leaned back in his leather chair. "Whisenand, you truly amaze me. The last time I saw you, you were up to your IQ in intelligence work. Quite good work, I might add. Now you want to run a war. Been reading your Clausewitz, have you?"

"Clausewitz, Douhet, Sun Tzu, Marx, Hegal, Mao, Giap, and Ho Chi Minh," Whitey replied.

"Quite a list. No Che?"

Whitey laughed. "No, no. His stuff is to convince young American girls that cutting sugar cane for Castro is world-healing." Whitey became serious. "Ho needs to pull something off. Giap is getting impatient. You can see it in his positioning of sizable NVA troops in the south. He will want to take control of as much territory as he can, preparatory to something, maybe peace talks. Something is up. We need more intelligence from up north. At the same time, we need to be hammering the supply routes—if not the harbors and rail lines—both to stop the equipment Giap needs for his new NVA troops, as well as to let Ho know we know he is up to something."

"I'm limited, Whitey. I can barely send out my airplanes to hit the Trail in Pack One and Laos. You've got to talk to CINCPAC about targets farther north."

"I already have," Whitey said. "Oley Sharp is asking for the same thing I am. For a deep-water sailor, he knows what air power can and cannot do. Yet he doesn't have any more control over targeting in the Route Pack system than you do. It's up to me to convince the President we need to step up strikes up north and along the Trail. Based on our past conversations, I don't think I'll have any trouble."

"The JCS is helpless, I suppose," Commander, 7th, said.

"Yes, they are. Except for one thing," Whitey said.

"What's that?"

"They can resign en masse."

"My God. They wouldn't," Commander, 7th, said in consternation.

"It's the only weapon they have," Whitey said, "and they can't use it."

Commander, 7th, rubbed his chin. "No, I don't suppose they can," he said. "That would play right into the hands of the protestors, wouldn't it?"

"Yes," Whitey said, "it would. Deeper than that, the Chairman finally decided not to because he thinks such a move is too close to mutiny. And in the end, all that would happen is that they would all be replaced with people who would go along with the President and McNamara."

Commander, 7th, looked pensive. "Do you suppose Ike went through anything like this?"

Whitey chuckled. "No, I don't think so. President Roosevelt gave Ike a charter to win and left the details up to him."

"Well, I can still do a couple of things out here," the Commander of the 7th Air Force said.

"What's that?"

"I can tell my combat operations shop to listen to the boys in the field and to start authorizing some new fighter tactics."

"And more frags for Laos and Steel Tiger?" Whitey asked.

"Sure, as long as Oley Sharp goes along with it."

"He does," Major General Albert G. Whisenand said. "He surely does."

1300 HOURS LOCAL, SATURDAY, 28 OCTOBER 1967
ROOF TERRACE OF THE CARAVELLE HOTEL
SAIGON, REPUBLIC OF VIETNAM

☆

"Sure," Shawn Bannister said to his godfather, Albert G. Whisenand. "I remember very well the last time we were here. You were drinking scotch while forbidding me to light up a joint." He pulled deeply on a two-inch Triple B. The burning-rope smell hung heavy in the air. He wore his trademark brown safari suit.

Whitey stirred his ice tea. He wore light tan cotton trousers. His light blue sport shirt had a sweat vee down the back. They sat under the awning, away from the bar. His face, framed by his short-cut white hair, looked composed. The Saturday afternoon crowd was beginning to filter in. Newsmen, military officers, embassy people, contractors, salesmen—all men of heavy thirst crowded up to the bar, talking, laughing, gesticulating and downing, on the average, one shot of hard stuff every eight minutes.

"I want to talk to you about your article about the VC, Shawn," Whitey said.

"What's the matter? Didn't like it? Afraid it might be true?" Shawn's voice was just short of being contemptuous.

"Not at all. I believed every word of it. I believe that the commander gave you exactly the overall plan Ho Chi Minh has worked out. But I want to ask you something else. I think something big is about to happen. You hinted in your story you had knowledge of such an event. I would like you to tell me what you didn't write in the story." Whitey looked carefully at Shawn's eyes as he spoke. They appeared both wary and worried.

Shawn sat back, and laughed. "Uncle Albert, I do believe you want me to violate journalistic confidence."

"This is a war, Shawn. Americans, your countrymen, are being killed. Maybe you can save some of their lives. What do you know of a 'big event,' as you call it?"

"This isn't a war, Uncle Albert. This is a political struggle to unite North and South Vietnam. We Americans are the unwanted aggressors here. We are killing people to further our gains."

"That is pure communist claptrap, and you know it," Whitey said. He purposely kept his voice low.

"Maybe, maybe not," Shawn replied. "But I'm a reporter. My job is to get the news and report it, not violate a confidence or a source. Or take sides."

"There is nothing newsworthy about propaganda," Whitey said.

"I didn't say there was," Shawn replied. "But I am going to be invited back for the big show, and that won't be propaganda."

"The 'big show'?" Whitey said.

Shawn leaned forward. Finally, he thought, I am impressing this man. "The VC commander said it would be the most important attack of the conflict. One that would make the fall of Dien Bien Phu in 1954 look insignificant."

"When will this attack occur?" Whitey asked.

"He didn't say exactly. Soon. A couple weeks."

"Where?" Whitey persisted.

Shawn wagged his head. "I had the impression—I don't know why—it would be up north."

Whitey looked off into space. He shook his head. "No," he said, "I don't think it will be up north. Giap has already tried to cut the top from South Vietnam. It didn't work."

Hard-core NVA troops had tried to occupy the top of South Vietnam from Hue to the DMZ, but they had not been able to capture and isolate the whole area. In fact, the NVA had been decisively defeated at Ashau both by the Army and by B-52 Arc Light strikes that had wiped out thousands.

"Look, Uncle Albert," Shawn said. Whitey saw a muscle tic by his left eye. "I think I know what you want from me. You want me to spy for you, don't you?"

Whitey watched him carefully. "Yes," he said. "Will you perform a service for your country?"

Shawn licked his lips. His muscle tic became more pronounced. "Ah, this is rich," he said. "This is really rich." He leaned forward. "You want me to spy for a military organization I detest, against some people I happen to believe are right." He snorted. "You know I don't agree with what you are doing over here. How could you ask me to do such a thing?"

"Listen to what I just said." Whitey spoke with a sharp edge to his voice. "You could save American lives."

"Yeah, at the expense of the poor Vietnamese peasant who is just

trying to make it in his rice paddy against all you American killers."
Shawn sat back with his arms folded. He didn't try to disguise the
contempt he felt for his godfather.

"Shawn, you are being used by these people," Whitey said. He
tried not to show his exasperation.

"No, I'm not. You're the one being used. I have a choice. I don't
have to answer to anybody. I can stay or go as I see fit. You do not."

"You do have something to answer to, Shawn."

"Oh, yeah? Like what?"

"Your own conscience."

"Right on, Uncle Albert. And my conscience says that this is an
imperialistic war of aggression waged by the capitalists against a peace-
loving people for purposes of exploitation."

"You almost leave me speechless. That phrase is right out of
Hanoi . . ."

"So what? It's what I believe," Shawn interrupted.

"And for purposes of exploitation—ridiculous. Name one product
to exploit from here? Tin? Rubber? Not enough to warrant an office,
much less a war. Rice? We produce our own in Louisiana. No, Shawn.
You are being used by these people as a propagandist, and I think
you know it."

"Let me tell you, Uncle Albert, maybe I am being used by these
people, but I am doing it willingly. I'm doing it because I think I can
help stop the war by reporting it as it really is, not as you and all the
other military people would like it to be."

"This is a stupid and trite conversation," Whitey said. "Just tell me
you'll think about letting me know where and when the big event
will take place. Look at it as a reporting story. You'll be getting a
scoop on the other reporters. Tell me you will think about it."

"Sure, I'll think about it, Uncle Albert. But I can tell you right this
moment my thoughts will be that I won't do it." He was high now,
his eyes bright and shining. He had trouble focusing on exactly what
was going on. He looked down with pity at this sad old man who
thought he knew so much. "Don't you see, Uncle Albert," he said in
a soft voice. "It's all so simple. I mean it's really simple. The answer
is right there. Can't you see it?"

"The answer to what, Shawn?" Whitey said. He prepared to rise
and leave this disheveled young man he used to cuddle and bounce
on his knee. There was nothing more they could talk about.

"Why, the answer to everything, just everything. It's all so simple,
don't you see?" Shawn said. He sat loose in his chair, taking in the
universe with his expanded arms.

Whitey stood up. "Goodbye, Shawn. Any message for your father?
He is concerned you don't write." He stared down at his godchild.
Just how much of this do I tell Sam Bannister? he asked himself.

Shawn got to his feet. "Tell him everything is just fine with me. You can see that yourself. Everything is fine." He flashed his brilliant smile.

The two men parted: Whitey headed to Tan Son Nhut for his flight back to Washington; Shawn returned to his hotel.

Shawn Bannister unlocked the door to his room. His mind was muzzy. Maybe he should take up Whitey's offer. Maybe it would put him on to an even greater story if he could just play both sides properly. He was preoccupied with the possibilities his uncle's offer had opened up as he walked into the room. He involuntarily jerked as he spotted a figure by the window.

"How was the visit with your godfather, the general?" Nguyen Tri asked.

20

☆

For the last four days since the meeting at Tan Son Nhut, the 8th Tac Fighter Wing at Ubon had, in addition to the night missions, mounted morning and afternoon strikes and MiG CAP escort missions with no variation in tactics or targets. Entreaties for tactics changes from squadron commanders and from the wing tactics officers were not falling on deaf ears, they were falling on infertile soil. Seminar notes to the DO of the 7th Air Force notwithstanding, nothing had come down from the 7th Air Force. Number-crunching as taught by Robert Strange McNamara, the former Ford Motor whiz kid and producer of the Edsel, was Crepens's vogue. Those numbers and tables said the MiG pilots could not and would not come up with unusually bold and slashing attacks, because they had not done so in the past.

Colonel Delbert Crepens believed this theory—a good staff man always believed his boss without question. It really wasn't necessary for him to fly any missions over Hanoi. He had flown two bombing missions up there, and no MiGs had attacked his flights. Thus it was that Crepens had not taken it upon himself to authorize any deviation from the standard close-in escort for F-105 and F-4 bombers.

Without permission, Court and Flak had been easing their flights out to intercept the MiGs as early and as far away from the bombers as possible. Though they had been spotting MiGs well in advance, many were still getting through because they still weren't out far enough, and there weren't enough of the Phantoms. College Eye was starting to complain about the separation. The result was the bombers frequently could not hit their target, because they were forced to jettison their loads to defend themselves. So far, the MiGs had not remained in the area to fight. They had seemed content with forcing the bombers to jettison. No one had claimed any victories. There had been stories of a few particularly aggressive MiGs led by a pilot with an odd-colored helmet. As yet, however, no one had a clear sighting. Some of the Thud pilots wanted to know who the cowboy was when they saw Court's airplane. He had yet to answer.

Ev Stern had come out of his shell. Court had to restrain a smile one day when Ev told him that he was was becoming more "secure" with Court's flying. He felt like asking Ev why an Edwards graduate with two combat tours would not be "secure." But Court was pleased with him. Ev wasn't exactly at the experience level Court desired, but he had to learn someplace. Court figured himself as the best front-seater there was, so Ev could learn from him. Ever since the day they had shot down the MiG, he had given Ev every other landing and takeoff, all GCA approaches, and all the refueling hookups. Ev was trying valiantly to be the most proficient back-seater in the Wing, for a pilot, that is. The navigators were trying just as hard.

The daily early morning briefing began. Captain Richard C. Hostettler walked onstage looking unusually serious. He adjusted the microphone at the podium and looked out over his audience.

"Gentlemen," he said in measured tones, "I have an important message from Seventh Air Force. Because of its incredible content, I am going to read it direct to you." The audience went dead quiet at the unexpected severity of his voice. He began to read from a copy of a TWX message he held.

"Headquarters, Seventh Air Force, Message number 311920 Zulu. In the early morning of 30 October at 0220 hours local time, seismic sensors on the Ho Chi Minh Trail indicated large movements in strings nine through thirteen. At 0348 hours local time, the Bangkok Seismographic Center reported a reading of eight point three on the Richter Scale, the highest ever recorded, in the northern panhandle area of Laos near the Vietnam border in the Annamite mountain chain. The land formation in this high karst region is composed of limestone and calcium carbonate, which erodes easily and hence bares the karst to further exposure and resultant degradation. This composition is easily reduced by water and dynamic oscillation, such as produced by B-52 bombing, to a porous unstable condition, thereby weakening the rock substructure. At 0620 hours local time yesterday, a reconnaissance aircraft observed what appeared to be a large rift in the terrain running through

Mu Gia Pass that extended south through the Ban Phan
Op valley.''

Hostettler shook his head at the ominous implication of his last
words. The aircrew audience sat with parted lips and bodies unconsciously leaning forward to hear what came next.

"Due to bad weather, the reconnaissance pilot was unable to follow the phenomenon further. At 0940 hours
local time, a high-speed FAC in the Ban Karai region
descended through a break in the overcast and reported
a large section of the Dog's Head hill section had shifted
into the river at the Ban Loboy Ford area. Weather
closed in, preventing continued reconnaissance. As of
this moment, Special Forces ground team reports are
being collated. Seventh Air Force and the Blue Chip command post in conjunction with Air Force engineers from
the System Command concur that should this phenomenon proceed at the present rate, it will cause a situation inhibiting future USAF tactics. Current
prognostication indicates an 88 percent probability that
in the following 48 to 96 hours, 50 percent of southern
North Vietnam and related Communist-held portions of
Laos will detach itself from the Indochina peninsula
land mass and float into the Tonkin Gulf, thereby coming under U.S. Navy jurisdiction, hence releasing the
USAF from further participation.''

The audience, brows furled, sat stunned. Suddenly, Bannister, Flak
Apple, and several others burst out in wild guffaws. Then it dawned
on the rest that they had been had. The entire auditorium collapsed
into laughter that soon evolved into applause for the irrepressible
Hostettler. Men pounded each other on the back, and wiped helpless
tears from their eyes.

Hostettler stood—motionless, head tilted, a quizzical look on his
face—as the laughter subsided. Then he reached under the podium
for a paper bag. From it, he donned a serape and a new wide-brimmed
Mexican sombrero with tassels, before walking to the bedsheet covering the big target map.

"I will not reveal today's target," he said. "Your friendly strike force
commander has that privilege."

The strike force commander walked out on the stage, still grinning.

"Gentlemen," he said, "I am happy to report that starting today
we have some new and rather important targets." With a flourish, he
ripped the cover from the target map.

As soon as they saw where the arrows pointed, the already happy aircrew burst into cheers. Big red target circles had been drawn around three of the four MiG bases around Hanoi. A mixed strike force of Thuds and Phantoms was fragged for Phuc Yen, Hoa Loc, and Bac Mai.

"Somebody, someplace is wising up," the strike force commander said. Court and Flak winked at each other. Yet there was no red circle round the Gia Lam airfield. Regardless of the fact that MiGs regularly flew from there, Gia Lam was considered an international commercial airport and could not be struck.

"Now the bad news," he said. "In accordance with the frag order we have received from Seventh Air Force, we may only bomb the runway. We can only make holes in those long concrete strips. We are forbidden to hit either the revetments where the MiGs are parked, the hangars, or the headquarters building. To do so would be considered escalation. Furthermore, the only MiGs we can attack are the ones in the air."

The good humor of the aircrew disappeared immediately. Colonel Delbert L. Crepens took the stage as the strike force commander completed his briefing.

"We are under particular pressure from Seventh Air Force to strike these targets," he began. "I don't want any maintenance aborts. Unless the weather is down to the ground in the target area, there will be no weather aborts. Do you understand?"

"Colonel." All the heads turned to see Hostettler at the edge of the stage. He still wore his Mexican clothes. "Stormy said there might be a solid layer of clouds over the target areas. We were always told never to fly over or attack through an overcast."

Crepens eyed the intelligence officer. His lip curled. "We? I wasn't aware you were flying combat, Captain. Are you on the strike lineup?" His voice was thick with contempt.

Hostettler walked to the strike flight crew board. He carefully studied the call signs, and the positions and names of those flying.

"No, sir," he said. "I'm not. Neither are you."

Crepens looked startled. "Report to my office immediately after this briefing," he snapped, and stomped off stage.

The remainder of the briefing went as scheduled. The strike force commander had skillfully blended Hostettler's intelligence briefing with weather, armament, maintenance, and rescue. He went over the details for the F-105 Wild Weasel attacks on the radar and SAM sites just before the Ubon planes got there. The call sign for the entire strike force was Navaho. Individual flights were still automobile names.

☆

Court, as the leader of Packard flight, took his men to the squadron for a final briefing. He concluded his briefing with the remaining details of radio frequencies, lost communications, and emergency procedures, then said he wanted to talk tactics.

"The Phantom is not a difficult airplane to fly," Court said, "unless you start yanking it around. Then it becomes a whole new airplane, operating under a whole new set of aerodynamic principles."

"What do you mean?" Packard Four asked. He was a slender young captain with a dark crew cut.

"Do you know how to turn the airplane?"

"Of course."

"How?"

"Like any other. Some aileron, some rudder, some back stick movement. The normal bank and yank."

"Wrong. What do you know about turn performance parameters?"

"I know that there are four variables: Gs pulled, airspeed, radius of turn, and rate of turn."

"What are the other factors?"

Packard Four thought for a moment. "Well, there's structural limitations of the aircraft—you don't want to pull the wings off. There's the G-load on the pilot—you don't want him to black out. And stall speed. The more Gs you pull and the more you bank, the higher the stall speed."

"What does that mean?" Court asked.

"You don't want to get into a high-speed or high-g stall and fall out of the sky."

"What does that mean?"

"It means," the captain said, starting to feel exasperated, "that a steady-state turn requires that the vertical lift component be equal to the weight of the airplane and . . ."

"The horizontal lift component be equal to the centrifugal force," Court completed. "That's good slide-rule flying. But we must translate all that slipstick stuff into our feel for an airplane. It's not enough to know aero, thermo, fluids, astro, and all that mind-bending stuff. This is not the classroom now. If you've got to pull six or seven Gs when you're fighting an airplane, you're doing something wrong."

"That's heresy," Packard Four said, with a laugh.

"Not only that," Court continued, getting wound up, "a tight turn is primarily a defensive maneuver, not an offensive maneuver."

"Why?" the captain asked, then got it. "Because you're burning up airspeed."

"Exactly. You've got to keep your Mach up. And go vertical."

"Go vertical?"

"Exactly. Learn to love the vertical. Zoom up and roar down. No one else uses it. No one else knows how. They get into turning, bank-

and-yank hassles, each guy trying to get inside the other's turn. Didn't anybody listen to Boyd, that IP at Nellis who tried to teach energy maneuvering? Or Tanaka at George?" Court put his hands on his hips. "And don't be predictable. Turn with a guy for ninety seconds and he'll start predicting you. Turn with him for three minutes and he'll kill you. If you get into trouble, accelerate down and out of the fight. If you can't reattack, get away."

"No way," the captain said. "I don't run from fights."

"Stop talking like a Marine. There's no point in sticking your pecker down a gun barrel to pee on the bullet as it comes out just to prove you have balls. That's a one-time deal and they don't give out medals to peckerless pilots." Court pointed his finger like a gun at Packard Four. "Listen, if you don't have position and you can't gain it, if you don't have airspeed and you can't gain it, get the hell out of the arena until you can."

"That's not being aggressive," the captain said. "Everybody knows that to be a successful fighter pilot, to make ace, you've got to be aggressive."

"You wouldn't fight without ammo, would you? You wouldn't fight without fuel, would you? Advantage is everything. Get the advantage, that's what I'm telling you. And if you can't get it, get out, return to base to fight another day."

0815 HOURS LOCAL, TUESDAY, 31 OCTOBER 1967
ROOM 3S, SOI 175/32
UBON RATCHITANI, THAILAND

☆

Through his binoculars, Shawn Bannister studied the F-4s lined up in the arming area next to runway 23 at Ubon Royal Thai Air Force Base. There were six fighters heavily loaded with a mixture of bombs and air-to-air missiles. He quickly wrote down their tail numbers. Then he picked up a small booklet, and frantically scrambled through the pages looking for pictures to identify the ordnance hanging under the airplanes. He threw it down in disgust. He just wasn't close enough, the sun glare and heat shimmers were too strong, and the pictures in the poorly printed booklet Nguyen Tri had given him weren't clear enough to identify the bombs and missiles. Hell with it, he said to himself. He entered into his log just the number of bombs and missiles carried by each plane, not their type. They all looked the same. The bombs were olive drab with yellow bands around the nose, the missiles were long white things with little wings and rudders. Who cares if it's a five-hundred- or thousand-pound bomb. They all blow up, anyway.

He put on the headset attached to a small radio that was supposed to be tuned to the military control tower. He fiddled with the controls but was unable to get any sound.

Starting that morning, he had begun logging tail numbers and take-off times of the Phantoms blasting into the air. He was supposed to record which ones came back, when they came back, and if they had any battle damage. He was also supposed to match up tail numbers with the call signs as he heard them on his radio.

Souky, a Thai girl who spoke excellent English and seemed quite conversant on military flying matters, had met him when he arrived by train from Bangkok the night before. She had shown him to this room in a private dwelling, an old structure made of dark wood.

The room was small and cramped, and infested with most of the known species of crawling and flying Asian insects. There was barely enough room for the rough wooden table stained with decades of meals, and the wooden cot with a thin foam mattress. A mosquito net fell from a T-bar attached to the head of the cot. A long floor rag hung from one of the wooden pegs on the wall behind the door. As was typical with most Thai houses, the wide-open window had neither glass nor screen. Slung on hinges outside each opening were faded green shutters. An open bowl porcelain toilet was down the hall. It had to be flushed manually by dipping water from a large urn. Shawn had been warned by Nguyen Tri before he departed Saigon that location was more important than amenities.

Shawn was to familiarize himself with the cadence and tempo of F-4 operations from Ubon. He could take all the pictures he wanted through his long-range lens, but his primary job was to record and quickly report what he saw and heard. Tri had told him that the local contact, Souky, would collect his papers each evening.

"Wait a minute," Shawn had said to Nguyen Tri in Saigon three days ago, "that's not reporting. That sounds like spying. We have laws against things like that. I could get in big trouble."

"My dear American friend," Tri had said in a soothing voice, "do not concern yourself. The information is there to be gathered. There is no law against that. You are a very good reporter, who will merely be gathering the available information about American activities."

"The *California Sun* isn't interested in the tail numbers of airplanes that fly out of there," Shawn said.

"Perhaps not," Tri had replied, "but our newspapers, like the *Nhan Dan* in Hanoi, are interested. What difference does it make? You are a reporter. You report the truth." Nguyen Tri smiled. "I am authorized to tell you that if you report timely and accurate information, you will not only get an exclusive on any big attacks we may have in the future, you perhaps could earn a visa to visit Hanoi. There you could interview our leaders and photograph the conclusive evidence of the wanton and indiscriminate aerial bombing done on our peaceful country."

Based on those reassurances, Shawn had flown to Bangkok, then taken the late train to Ubon. Now, his first day on the job, he was uncomfortable, thirsty, and not at all sure he could sustain this effort very long. Maybe a few days, a week at the most. He had not slept well in the hot, airless room. Two thick triple B joints had eased the discomfort.

He flicked a bug with many legs from the radio and turned the switch on again. To his surprise he heard an American voice in the headset.

"Roger, Packard flight. This is Ubon Tower. You are cleared on and off with four."

0910 Hours Local, Tuesday, 31 October 1967
Airborne, Route Pack Six Alpha, Hanoi
Democratic Republic of Vietnam

☆

Court Bannister led Packard flight to the attack zone of the Phuc Yen MiG base. The frag order had called for all four of his flight to carry Mk-83 1,000-pound bombs with one-tenth of a second delayed fuse. The detonating delay was to allow the bomb to penetrate the concrete and plow deep into the earth before exploding. The idea was to dig a much bigger hole than a contact burst would. Flak Apple had consulted his charts, and what they really needed was the M-59 Semi-Armor Piercing thousand-pounder that could penetrate steel without breaking up. Only SAC had that bomb in its ammo dumps. Flak Apple had put a midnight call through to the SAC Command Post at Tan Son Nhut, requesting an emergency supply of the M-59s. "Sorry, we can't help you. Maybe next year when the paperwork gets squared away," was the best answer he got.

"So, okay, maybe they plan on sinking some Viet Cong battleships," Flak had said to the planning group he had gathered. We'll use our own bombs. By four in the morning, the armorers had each of the Ubon bombers loaded with 1,000-pound bombs, two Sidewinders, four Sparrows, and extra fuel tanks. The Phantoms would be taking off at maximum gross weight.

"Remember," the Navaho strike force commander said, "these targets are too heavily defended to stooge around for multiple bomb runs, like in the low threat area of South Vietnam. Remember the Pack Six motto: 'One Pass, Haul Ass.'"

The escort birds, those used for MiG protection, had the extra fuel tanks, a centerline gun for each element lead, and a full load of four Sidewinders and four Sparrows.

After takeoff and before entry into North Vietnam, all the Ubon birds loaded up with fuel from the Lemon tankers, and then they plunged northeast toward Hanoi. The time was just after nine in the morning. The weather in the Hanoi area was overcast at twelve thousand feet with scattered rainstorms.

Vladimir Chernov made wide slow turns in a low orbit from Gia Lam south a few kilometers to the Red River, then back again. He was serving both himself and his wingman up for bait, at the same time patrolling possible targets: the POL fields, bridges, and air bases east of Hanoi. Overhead, he had placed two MiG-21s in an orbit just under the overcast ceiling at 4,000 meters, twelve thousand feet. The two silver delta-winged fighters were all but impossible to see against the cloud cover. Well above the cloud cover he had positioned Toon to act as an airborne flight director. Toon was to supplement Victory Control by identifying aircraft type and mission—fighter escort or bomber. All F-105s were bombers, so among the F-4s Toon had to differentiate which were carrying bombs and which were designated as MiG fighters.

If any American was dumb enough to accept the bait, and roll in on Chernov or his wingman, the high element would be right on them with a height advantage. Had there been no clouds, they would have been up-sun, hence even more invisible.

The main task of Chernov's mission was to disrupt the bomber formations attacking the targets he was orbiting. In conjunction with Victory Control, he had other fighters scattered in high and low elements of two to make the slash-and-dash missile attacks on the bombers as they approached the target area. In no case were the MiGs to stay around and fight. The North Vietnamese pilots were simply too inexperienced. Besides, as Chernov had told them again and again, their job was not necessarily to shoot down enemy aircraft, their job was to prevent enemy aircraft from bombing targets. Privately, however, Chernov had told Toon, Van Bay, and Vong that if it looked right, stay and fight. They could always bolt for the sanctuary of the Chinese border barely twelve minutes' flying time away.

Court and Ev were tense and alert, all switches on, all systems up. Together, along with the Phantoms of the Navaho strike force, they bored into the Hanoi area.

There was bedlam on the radio strike frequency. SAMs were popping up through the Hanoi ring overcast, 85mm and 57mm flak was peppering the sky with black and orange, running-man-shaped bursts. Two Thuds and a Phantom had already been hit by antiaircraft fire.

The Thuds were limping back to the east. The Phantom trailed a long black spiral of smoke, then disappeared, falling sideways into the smooth white overcast. Two chutes floated off to one side. Their automatic beepers made unnerving whooping shrieks on guard channel.

Suddenly, the antiaircraft guns ceased firing, and the SAMs stopped rising up.

"MiGs, MiGs, six o'clock." New radio calls burst out, as three flights of MiGs sliced into the force from low and behind with tremendous speed. A sharp wingman had spotted them. They had popped up through the overcast under ground radar command by Victory Control, using advisement from Toon, the airborne flight director. Two flights of Phantoms moved to intercept, but were too late. Each MiG-21 fired two missiles at the rear of the bomber force and dove for cover through the overcast. One K-13 missile impacted in the tail section of an F-105, but failed to explode. Another flew up the left tailpipe of an F-4, exploding the engine and the fuel tanks in an instant. No pieces larger than the bombs themselves fell out of the giant fireball. "Jesus Christ," an awed voice said during the momentary hush. There were no parachutes, and no beepers. The strike force bore on, leaving the debris behind. The other four missiles arched harmlessly away and down from the strike force, trailing rocket smoke like giant fire arrows.

Court held his flight of four bombers steady, then took them down through the overcast. Each man held his breath at what might appear below when they broke out. At twelve thousand feet, they were in the clear from the clouds and into layer after layer of exploding flak barrages that filled the surrounding air with white, black, red-orange, and dirty gray bursts. Court's breath came in swift pants as he waggled his plane to spread the flight into attack formation as they sped toward the Phuc Yen MiG field.

Seconds later, Court spotted the northeast railroad line and the Red River confluence as his major visual checkpoints. "There it is, Packard, twelve o'clock low," Court transmitted. Two, Three, and Four rogered, their voices taut with excitement.

The airfield didn't look like anything shown on the black and white reconnaissance photos. Red laterite roads led to the field, pointing to the huge white concrete strips of runway, taxiway, and parking ramp in the green lushness of surrounding fields. Revetted MiG parking areas of black herringbone patterns butted up to the taxi strip. Scattered around the field in a seemingly random pattern was pit after pit of antiaircraft guns. They were all shooting. Red tracers seemed to arch up slowly, then gather speed, and suddenly seemed to change direction to zoom over or under Court's F-4. Clips of five and seven 37mm bursts made a thick dirty carpet at ten to twelve thousand feet.

Beneath that layer, thousands of white basketballs blossomed between six and seven thousand feet, as the rapid-firing 23mm shells exploded at their preset altitude.

Court had wanted to make an east-to-west run, coming from the sun, heading straight down the runway, and pulling off west toward the comparative safety of Thud Ridge. Now he and his flight had no choice. They had no chance to reposition once they were under the overcast into the thick antiaircraft fire.

In line abreast, they made their bomb run perpendicular to the runway, the worst possible approach for accuracy on the 150-foot-wide concrete strip. Running in down the length of the runway would have given the bombs the best chance of hitting the 6,000 feet of concrete, whether they fell long or short of the midpoint.

Each man had his armament switches set up. The proper mils depression for the type of bomb were set into his gunsight pipper. Dive angle, release altitude, and airspeeds were carefully monitored by front- and back-seater until the front-seater had to look only at the target. The GIB would continue to call out his airspeed and dive angle.

The flight stayed with Court as he pushed forward on the stick. It was a terrible way to dive-bomb. Usually, one rolls in, always pulling positive Gs. But they had popped out of the overcast too close to the airfield to spend the time rolling in.

They arced down, negative Gs causing dust motes and a map to float up to the canopy. The planes were in a staggered left echelon formation, with Court trying to stay in the proper release envelope of 70 degree dive angle, and 560 knot release speed. As they passed through 7,000 feet, each pushed the red button on top of his B-8 control stick when he brought his gunsight pipper up to the narrow concrete runway. Each of the four planes rippled off six bombs. The black-red bursts of the twenty-four 1,000-pound bombs started two hundred feet short of the runway, ran across the runway, and on into the ramp and hangar area.

Eleven bombs hit short (two blew up a small fuel dump), four cratered the runway, seven dribbled across the taxiway and ramp, destroying six MiGs, two streaked through the main hangar roof and exploded just under the slick concrete floor, blowing four MiG-21s into blackened bits of metal. Two Vietnamese and one Russian in the slit trench outside were killed by falling debris.

"I'm hit. Packard Four is hit," the aircraft commander of the last Phantom to pull up from Phuc Yen called out.

Court strained under the G-forces to look around. He was jinking and climbing toward the west. He looked back and spotted Packard Four trailing a long plume of white smoke. The ground fire had suddenly stopped. Court suddenly saw that a MiG-21 was closing in on his, burning number four man from behind. He pulled toward the MiG, and transmitted.

"Break west, Four. MiG on your ass. I'm in on him." He unkeyed for an instant, then came back on. "You're on fire, Packard Four," he said.

Packard Four answered in a rapid cadence. "Yeah. Every light in the cockpit is on. Left engine out, ahh, hydraulics crapping out." He had his hands full trying to find the correct combination of stick, rudder, and throttle setting that would keep his crippled bird not only in the air, but climbing away from the Hanoi air defense ring.

Court clearly saw the light blue helmet of the pilot of the MiG-21 as he dove on him from his altitude advantage. It would be an easy high angle pass. Court's Phantom was clean now, and maneuverable. No bombs, no fuel tanks—two Sidewinders and four Sparrows. There was, however, a problem.

"Can't get him, Major, we can't shoot the Sparrows," Ev Stern yelled from the back seat. "Our radar is tits up." Without radar, the Sparrows would not guide. Their Sidewinders could only lock on to the heat from the rear of an airplane where the engine heat exhausted. A front end shot was no good.

"Goddammit, I already know that. Shut up. I'm trying to bluff him off Four," Court said, high-keyed enough without his back-seater interrupting his concentration with the obvious. This was exactly why he didn't want another man in his airplane.

"Well, shee-it. Just tell me what you're doing, then," Stern said.

"And when we land, tell me where 'tits up' came from," Court said.

Behind him, Court's wingman rolled in behind to cover him. "I'm with you, Packard Lead," he cried.

Vladimir Chernov saw the F-4s rolling in on him.

"Send two of your aircraft to my sector," he ordered Toon on the radio. He had seen Court's flight drop bombs, so he knew they weren't carrying guns. He also knew that the only missile from Court's angle that could endanger him at the moment was the radar-guided Sparrow. He concentrated on his attack on Packard Four. He would check the F-4 diving at him. If he saw a missile fired at him, he was confident he had the energy to outmaneuver it. The sweep on his screen told Chernov his radar missiles had a good lock-on. He fired two of them in rapid succession at Packard Four. At the same time, Court shot all four unguided Sparrows right into the Russian's face. Chernov saw them flash out from under Court's wing, trailing smoke, headed in his direction like four horrendous torpedoes. He wracked his airplane toward the missiles, causing his radar to break lock on Packard Four, leaving the Russian missiles unguided.

"Packard Four, break left, break left," Court yelled over the radio. "You've got two missiles coming up at you."

"I'm damn near stalled now, Lead," Packard Four said. He tried to bend his Phantom around by lowering the nose to gain speed. He didn't have to worry. Without Chernov's radar to guide them, the missiles wandered off to the east.

"Glory be, how about that shit," Packard Four said, and resumed his escaping climb. He was still trailing smoke from his damaged left engine.

"Thor's balls," Chernov cursed. He saw the missiles fired by Court for what they were, Sparrows that weren't locked on, fired all together like a shotgun. In his mind, he congratulated the F-4 pilot for a clever maneuver. It was too late to return to his pursuit of Packard Four. He continued heading toward the F-4, Court's airplane, that had shot the missiles at him. He smiled. He saw two of Toon's MiG-21s dropping out of the clouds toward the same F-4. He switched to guns, and began to track Court's airplane with his 23mm cannon. They were closing fast, over 1,000 miles per hour. In a split second, Chernov was in range. He fired. Too late. Court had pulled straight up and rolled out keep Chernov in sight. Chernov would have to pull harder to keep his gunsight on the climbing Phantom. He couldn't make the sharp turn. Chernov engaged his afterburner to gain energy, at the same time rolling to one side to keep out of the firing line of the two MiG-21s from the upper orbit maneuvering to attack the Phantom. For an instant, he was almost parallel to Court's airplane. The two pilots looked at each other. Court saw clearly the light blue helmet and the number 054 on the nose of Chernov's MiG-21. Chernov saw the white hat painted on the side of the F-4 and the large letters WP on the tail. Chernov rolled away to attempt a reattack, while Toon's MiGs swept down. Though Chernov had high confidence in his "pupils," he wasn't entirely sure they wouldn't shoot because they didn't recognize a MiG-21 so close to an F-4.

"Two MiGs at six o'clock high, Lead," Packard Two called. Court saw Chernov roll away. He looked over his shoulder, saw the two attacking silver MiGs, then looked over to Packard Four being escorted out of the area by Packard Three. He estimated how many seconds he had before any of the MiGs would be in firing position against either him and his wingman, or against the departing Packards.

"Pull into the clouds, Three and Four, I'll fake these guys out," Court said. He blew his speed brakes out. "Hang on, Two," he told his wingman. At the same time, he engaged the afterburners on both engines. Although his airplane lost 200 knots in a twinkling of an eye from the big speed brakes, the engine thrust was building quickly.

The two MiGs, unable to check their speed, went roaring by like two silver darts. Court hosed his two Sidewinders at one, his wingman fired his two at the second MiG-21.

"Boards in," Court yelled at his wingman. "Unloading," he added. He retracted his speed brakes and pushed over on the stick. Dust rose from the floor and his feet tried to lift from the rudder pedals as he dove his F-4 almost vertically for a few seconds. His wingman, Packard Two, followed. With the speed brakes retracted, and the two engines in each airplane putting out 34,000 pounds total thrust, the two Phantoms went supersonic, causing two sets of sonic booms to crash down on Hanoi. The booms were lost in the terrific crescendo of antiaircraft fire pouring from the tops of hundreds of buildings within the city, and from the thousands of gun sites around the city.

As Court pulled toward the relative safety of the clouds, he looked for the two MiGs they had shot at. The last thing he saw before he zoomed into the cloud layer was one vertical thread of smoke and one parachute dropping down it like a fireman sliding down a pole.

Minutes later, he pulled on top of the overcast, and looked west for Packard Three. "There he is," he said to Ev.

"I don't have him," Ev said.

"Get him on the radar, eleven o'clock high for about twelve miles," Court said.

"No one can see an F-4 that far," Ev replied.

"I can," Court replied. "Do as I tell you. Get a lock-on."

In minutes, Court and his wingman caught up with Packard Four being escorted by Packard Three. They were slow, and barely maintaining their altitude of 27,000 feet. The radio was still cluttered. Court called his flight over to post strike frequency. They checked in.

"Two."

"Three."

"Hey, boss," Packard Four said, "the fire's out, but it's getting hard to handle, and I'm running out of fuel."

Court could see a streak of white vapor streaming out from under the belly of the Phantom. He was about to transmit, when a voice sounded in his headset.

"Packard Lead, this is College Eye. You have any words for us?"

"Stand by, Cee Eye, we've got a little problem here." He unkeyed for a second. "Four, what's your fuel level, and how are your hydraulics?"

"At this setting, maybe twenty minutes fuel. My PC One system is out. PC Two okay," Packard Four said. He had about twenty minutes of flight time remaining before his Phantom flamed out from lack of fuel. On top of that problem, his primary flight control hydraulic system was shot out. So far, his secondary system was holding up. Of course, he only had one of his two engines operating.

"Hold her steady, Four, we'll make it," Court said. He then called College Eye and gave him the code words for the successful strike, the MiG sightings, and the hit on Packard Four.

Court checked his TACAN against the Channel 97 site maintained in northern Laos. He estimated it would take thirty-five minutes to reach their post-strike tanker.

"What's your fuel now, Four?" he asked.

"Ten minutes," Four said. His voice low and measured.

"College Eye, get an SAR going," Court said, giving in to the inevitable. He had just asked for a Search and Rescue mission to be launched to pick up the crew of Packard Four when they bailed out. He could see they could barely get to the North Vietnamese border before Packard Four and his back-seater would have to eject from their Phantom.

"Ah, hello, Packard," a new voice came on the air. "Can you go Tiger common?" The voice was quiet and very calm.

"Hell," Court said into his mask. "What the hell is Tiger common?" He did not remember any brief about a Tiger frequency, nor was there any mention of it on his blue flight-data card.

"It's four three two point zero, sir," Ev said from the back seat. "But don't call it out. Switch to it. I'll hand signal the other guys to switch there."

Court manually switched his radio to 432.0 megacycles.

"This is Packard Lead on Tiger," he said, wondering just what he would hear. Two, Three, and Four had caught Ev's hand signals. They checked in.

"Roger, Packard. This is the old White tanker anchor here. I understand you gentlemen are a tad short on go juice. Just happen to have a few thousand pounds. You copy?"

"Good copy, White tanker," Court said. "Thanks, but we are too far from your position. My number four man is streaming fuel. He's going to flame out in about ten minutes."

"This old filling station is just down the road from you, Packard. Hold your present heading. Be nice, and we'll fix up your number four man."

"Major Bannister," Ev said from the backseat. "White tanker has left his assigned orbit point and is homing in on our radio transmissions. I'm searching with our radar right now. I'll have him in a sec."

"How did you know about that Tiger frequency?" Court asked.

"I talked to one of their guys at the Chao Phya Hotel bar in Bangkok. Their code name is Young Tiger. The Tiger common radio frequency is the same number as their squadron, four three two." Ev paused, then said, "Okay, steer left three degrees. We're forty-two miles away from him. He's almost at the North Vietnamese border."

"Christ," Court said, "if we can paint him, so can Hanoi." Once past the Black River and beyond Thud Ridge, all the outbound fighters thought they were safe. No MiG had ever chased them that far.

"Three," he transmitted, "get these guys to the White tank. I'm going to look around."

Three rogered. Court made a tight turn to the left until he was facing toward Hanoi. Because his search radar only scanned forward in a narrow cone, he had to be pointing the nose of his aircraft that contained the radar dish in the general direction he wanted to search.

"Contact, one o'clock level, thirty miles, and closing fast," Ev sang out.

"Warning, warning. You are approaching the border," Victory Control said to Vladimir Chernov. "Reverse your course immediately."

Vladimir Chernov had not planned on chasing an American airplane to the border. He was so low on fuel, he had already sent his wingman back to land at Gia Lam. He had one K-13 missile and eighty shells remaining for his 23mm cannon.

One more shot, he said to himself. I want one more shot at that tricky Yankee. When he had rolled away from Court in the climb, he had kept track of Court's airplane, then lost it when Packard flight had entered the cloud cover. Chernov was not used to being beaten, much less deceived by another pilot. He had described Packard Lead's last-known position to Victory Control, and asked for a vector to chase him. He checked his forward search radar.

"Thor's balls," he said in happy surprise. There was one blip moving toward him, but beyond was a huge blob that could only be a large American airplane.

"Victory Control, describe what is in front of me at one hundred kilometers," he transmitted.

"It is a Kay Cee One Three Five we have been tracking. It is far from normal orbit. You must reverse, Khong Nam Bon. Reverse immediately."

Chernov checked his fuel and his map. There was an emergency recovery base at Na San behind him. He could fly four minutes on this heading before he must turn back. The F-4 heading toward him showed clearly on his radar screen; behind him was the big KC-135 blip. He wasn't sure the airplane in front had the white hat, but he hoped so. Chernov hurriedly made his battle plan.

Court saw the MiG boring in. "I have a lock-on," Ev cried from the back seat.

"No good, I don't have anything to shoot," Court said.

"What are you going to do?" Ev asked. His voice had become calm.

"Gotta protect the tank, and the rest of the flight . . ." Court's voice trailed off.

The two airplanes streaked toward each other at a closure rate of nearly a thousand nautical miles per hour.

"My God," Ev yelled, "you're not going to ram, are you?"

"Just keep track of him," Court said. He strained and searched the sky in front. In seconds he had a visual on the approaching MiG. Court pointed the nose of his Phantom directly at the tiny dot as it rapidly grew in form and substance. He pushed forward slightly on the stick as the distant wings became discernible. They were six miles apart. Time seemed to slow down. Five seconds later, they were four miles apart, closing at 2,100 feet per second.

Chernov saw the F-4. He held his heading and altitude steady. Beyond the closing F-4, he saw a KC-135 and the three F-4s. One F-4, streaming smoke or fuel, was on the boom. He put his eyes back on the F-4 dead ahead. By feel, he switched to guns and pulled the trigger. His plan was to drive off the approaching Phantom with his gun, then pull up and lob his last heat-seeking K-13 at the four-engined tanker.

Court saw the slow red winking of the GsH 23mm cannon under the belly of the silver MiG. At first, the tracers curved down, falling far short. If he maintained the collision course, he would fly exactly into the stream of shells, and a half-second later smash into the MiG itself.

Chernov waited for the Phantom to open fire, either with a radar missile or a gun. He sat forward, hunched over his gunsight. At least I don't have to look behind me, he thought. These are the last Americans out. Suddenly, there was no time for anything. The Phantom filled his windscreen.

"We're merging," Ev yelled from the back seat, as he saw the enemy blip slide to the center of his screen. Then they were in Chernov's stream of shells. Court unconsciously leaned forward and hunched his shoulders as they streaked through the tracers. He barely registered the bang as one exploded on top of the fuselage.

"Madman," Chernov yelled into his mask, as he pushed violently forward on his control stick. The Phantom flashed past his upper canopy so close he heard the engines' roar and was tossed in the downwash. Dirt and debris flew into his eyes from the savagery of his negative G-force. His attack was broken. He didn't have the fuel to get back on course to shoot at the tanker. He eased back on the stick, and rolled left to head back toward his emergency recovery base. He looked across the radius of his turn. The Phantom was turning back toward the border. Chernov clearly saw the white hat painted on it. He realized then the pilot was out of ammunition and had once again duped him into losing a shot. He shook his fist as he turned for the emergency strip at Na San.

Court watched the MiG as he turned back to the border. He had an instant to register the blue helmet, then they were separated. Normal time resumed for Court. It came when he suddenly noticed the sound of his own breathing in his headset. It was rapid and roaring. He took a deep breath and held it while he rolled level to head for the tanker.

"Boss, we ain't got no fuel," Ev said from the back seat.

Startled, Court looked at the fuel gauge. He rapidly converted the figures. "About ten minutes," he said on the intercom.

"Less than that if we want to catch White tanker," Ev said. "I've got 'em on radar, twelve o'clock for fifty, same speed as us. We've got to pour on some coal if we want to catch 'em. If we don't catch up, it's hello jungle." Below was the dense, green, triple canopy of North Vietnam merging into Laos. Men had parachuted into there and never been heard from again.

Court pushed the throttles up to 95 percent. At that setting, they had seven minutes to catch the tanker, hook up, and be receiving fuel, before a flameout. With only a hundred knots of overtake speed to cover thirty miles, they would never make it.

"White, Packard Lead," Court transmitted.

"Packard, White. Go," the tanker pilot answered.

"Got a bit of a problem. Need gas in seven minutes or we flame out. Would take me double that to catch up. Check that the Packards with you are okay. If so, can you make a couple of three-sixties?" Court wanted White tanker to make two circling turns to give him a chance to catch up.

"Standby, Packard Lead."

"Packard Lead, this is Three. Four is leaking bad, so I've had him hang on the boom. He came off for a few minutes, so Two and I could fill up. We can do that again. So come on down to your friendly filling station."

"Starting a port turn, now, Packard Lead," White said.

They were now over Laos. From their position, it was forty-five minutes to Ubon. Ev and the White tanker navigator coordinated the turn by radio. They set it up so that White was rolled out, heading toward Thailand, when Court slid up under the boom.

At the last second, Packard Four pulled off to one side. None of the four Phantoms were more than fifty feet from each other as they flew formation with the big KC-135 tanker, a Boeing 707 converted to carry 100,000 pounds of JP-4 fuel that it could transfer at the rate of 6,000 pounds a minute. A sergeant, called the boomer, lay flat on his belly in a compartment under the tail. He had a thick glass port to look out and see Court slide his Phantom up to the boom. The boomer had hand controls to position the boom over the refueling port on top of the fuselage just behind the back seat of the F-4. Upon movement of a switch by the pilot, the door opened revealing the receptacle.

With easy expertise, the boomer plugged in just as Court slipped under the big tanker. He flipped the fuel transfer switch and got a red light. At the same time, fuel gushed like vented steam from a tear in the skin behind the refueling port.

"Bad news, Packard Lead," the boomer said. "You're pumping out as much as I'm pumping in." Court turned control of the Phantom over to Ev, and checked his gauges. A trickle of fuel was finding its way into one of the fuselage tanks. Not much, just enough to keep his engines running if he topped off every few minutes.

"I'm about out of gas again, Lead," Packard Four said. He was hovering in formation twenty feet to Court's left side. "I can give you maybe five more minutes," he added. His voice was calm and without inflection.

"Go override, boomer. Give me what you can," Court said.

"PACKARD, PACKARD, PACKARD. THIS IS COLLEGE EYE ON GUARD. IF YOU READ, COME UP POSTSTRIKE FREQUENCY." The transmission on guard channel was deafening. Court scrambled for his radio switch to turn off guard channel.

"You're getting max pressure and max flow, Packard Lead," the boomer said. His voice was as calm as a bored filling station attendant. Boomers were tough. The men chosen to occupy that critical position were carefully culled from hundreds who applied. They had to have nerves and hands as steady as those of the pilots they refueled. When asked by strangers what their job was in the Air Force, they reveled in saying they passed gas.

"Rodge, thanks," Court said. "Would you mind asking your pilot to answer College Eye and tell them our flight is with you." Sometimes, there were just too damn many people pestering the strike pilots for information.

"Will do, Packard Lead."

Court watched his main gauge creep slowly upward.

"At this rate, it will take us an hour to refuel. It just won't go into the fuel cell," Ev said.

"Okay, White tanker," Court transmitted. "Here's the problem. Packard Four and I will have to cycle on and off the boom, five minutes each, all the way back to base." He signaled a disconnect to the boomer, and pulled off to the right to allow Packard Four in.

"I got a copy on your problems, Lead," the aircraft commander of White tanker said. "Now listen to mine. We've off-loaded far more fuel than we were supposed to. If I tow you guys back to home plate,

I'll be giving you our own fuel, so we won't have enough to get to home plate." He was referring to his base of U Tapao, several hundred miles south of Ubon.

There was silence. Everyone knew that SAC had rigid rules and regulations regarding its tankers. Any deviation was grounds for a flying evaluation board at best, or a court-martial at worst.

"Ahh, what the hell," the pilot of White tanker transmitted before anyone could say anything, "can't let you guys punch out. Besides, I've always wanted to see Ubon by the Sea."

For the next two hundred miles, Court and his number four man alternated time on the boom.

Each man would slide into position, the boomer would hook up, then fuel would start flowing. From Court's airplane, it splashed out the hole just behind the refueling receptacle. From Packard Four, it streamed from the belly like smoke. They alternated fifteen times, neither man able to sustain flight more than five minutes without fresh fuel.

When they were in radio range, Court called the Command Post, call sign Wolf Pack, and told them what was happening: Two F-4s with battle damage, one KC-135 tanker low on fuel.

"Roger, Packard Lead," the SOF at Wolf Pack said. "We know all about you. SAC Advon has been screaming for their tanker, College Eye has been complaining you didn't check out with them, and Radio Hanoi says you killed a bunch of civilians in the target area."

"I don't think I'll land," Court transmitted.

"Aw, come on, Packard, you done *sierra hotel*. We got the champagne for you," the Supervisor of Flying at Wolf Pack said. He was a combat experienced major. *Sierra hotel* was fighter-pilot slang for shit hot.

"Ubon dead ahead for ten miles," Ev said.

"Packard Two and Three, break it off and land," Court ordered. "See you on the ground," Three said. The two escorting Phantoms peeled away for the landing pattern.

White tanker brought the two F-4s directly over the Ubon runway at 20,000 feet. From that altitude, any plane could make a safe flame-out landing.

"Packard Four, top off last, land last, make an approach-end barrier engagement. If at any time it doesn't look good, point it toward Chandy Range, and punch out," Court ordered. Because of his hydraulic problems, Packard Four was to lower the big hook under his airplane to snatch the cable at the end of the runway just as he touched down. His airplane would slam to a halt in less than one thousand feet. It would take the ground crew several minutes, that neither Court nor the tanker had, to unhook the crippled plane and get it off the runway. If he crashed on the runway, there was no place for Court and the tanker to go. Court, and the SOF, had to land the most damaged airplane last to ensure the runway wouldn't be tied up for his airplane or the KC-135. Court had also told Packard Four to bail out if the airplane started to act up.

"White tanker, you land first, but move it. We'll be on your ass," Court transmitted. The four-man crew of the tanker had no easy way to bail out. They had to be first down. Tankers didn't have ejection seats, just hatches to dive out of.

Court sucked up as much fuel as he could get in the time remaining, slid off the boom, and pulled the throttles back to idle to conserve fuel for his final approach. He started a slow, spiraling descent over the base to allow time for the tanker to top off Four, then land.

Packard Four slid under the boom, and took as much fuel as he could. Then he dropped off, and throttled back, a spume of leaking fuel streaming under his airplane.

The White tanker pilot pulled his four throttles back, put out his spoilers, and made one of the most rapid, spiraling descents he had ever made in his life. He racked the big tanker into a sixty-degree bank, let the nose drop, and plummeted toward runway Two Three at Ubon.

There were two sets of red and blue crash vehicles and ambulances waiting, engines running, fireman suited in silver suits. One set was at the approach end, another on the midfield taxiway.

Within minutes, White tanker was floating over the end of the runway. His main wheels touched with huge puffs of white smoke, he rolled smoothly down the runway and turned off. He was safe.

Five thousand feet behind him, Court Bannister touched down.

"Nice job, boss. My fuel gauges read zero," Ev said from the back seat. Halfway down the runway, both engines flamed out.

"Flameout," Court told the tower. "Turning off here." He used his excess speed to coast off the runway on to a taxiway just past midfield. He used his remaining hydraulic pressure to brake to a halt. The fire engines immediately surrounded him. Their foam turrets pointed at him looked like 37mm cannons. Firemen in their flame-retardant silver astronaut suits ran up to chock his wheels. Court and Ev unstrapped, and sat on the canopy rail to watch Packard Four land out of his flameout approach.

They saw the F-4 in a left turn from a very high base leg on to the final approach. Slowly, the angle of bank increased beyond what was necessary to make the turn.

"Hey, roll out," Ev yelled, in an unconscious effort to command the pilot to recover.

"He's flamed out," Court said. "I don't see the fuel stream anymore."

The airplane kept rolling slowly to the left. It had lost all lift, and was about to fall out of the sky. The rear canopy blew off, followed by an ejection seat trailing rocket flame and smoke. In quick succession, the front canopy blew off, then the ejection seat rocketed out parallel to the ground. By now, the pilotless airplane was inverted. The pilot fell toward the ground, still strapped into his seat. The parachute of the back-seater blossomed, the little stick figure underneath swung once, then plunged into the trees off the end of the runway. At the last second, the parachute of the pilot opened, and he too disappeared into the tree line.

The airplane continued its lazy roll, falling straight down, until it thumped onto the ground. A huge ball of dust and airplane pieces erupted, then fell back. There was no fire, because no fuel remained in the tanks. The battle-damaged flight controls had finally failed when the Phantom had flamed out. The approach-end fire trucks and ambulance raced to the crash site in the tree line.

Thirty minutes later, Court's flight and the crew from Packard Two and Three were debriefing with Hostettler. They were in a large room, where intelligence debriefers sat at individual tables and members of each flight gathered around. Every man had a cold beer in his hand. After particularly hairy missions, Hostettler always brought over a tub of ice and beer cans from the Officer's Club. So far he had gotten away with it. Crepens never visited the place, and of course no one snitched.

There were only six people from Court's flight at Hostettler's table. He had confirmed the two men from Packard Four were slightly beat up, but generally in good condition. At the moment, they were undergoing a check at the base hospital.

During their debrief, the men of Packard flight described the weather, the SAMs, the ground fire, the bombing of Phuc Yen through an overcast on such a miserable attack heading, and the flight home with their crippled airplanes pulled along by the valiant KC-135 crew.

Hostettler took notes and asked many questions. He was particularly interested in the MiG pilot with the blue helmet. He made several more notes on a separate sheet of paper, then started to close out the session.

"Last question," he said. "Did you see any MiGs hit or go down?" Everybody shook their heads no, except Ev Stern.

"I did," he said.

"Did what?" Hostettler asked, "See one get hit, or see one go down?"

"Both," Stern replied. "I saw one get hit, and I saw the same one go down. He was just south of Hanoi."

"Did you see who got it?" Hostettler asked.

"Sure," Ev Stern said. "We got it."

"We *did?*" Court said in surprise. "When?"

"Your second Sidewinder got him," Ev replied.

"Why the hell didn't you tell me?" Court demanded.

"You told me to shut up, remember?" Ev Stern said in a bland voice, a look of pure innocence on his face.

Court sat speechless, and an idiotic smile appeared on his face.

The word quickly spread around the debriefing room. "Hey, Court, Ev, shit hot," Flak Apple said. "I saw one smoked, but I didn't know you were the guys who got him. Nice job." Hostettler offered his congratulations, and punched Court on the arm. He shook hands with Ev. Back-seaters shared victories with front-seaters. The other flyers offered their heartfelt congratulations. Yet, down deep, each pilot knew that, given the right amount of luck and circumstances, he too would be able to shoot down one or more MiGs. There was a mild flare of exuberation, but the joy was tempered with loss among the strike force members. The score for the morning's work was three airfields bombed, two MiGs shot down, one MiG damaged, one Phantom downed by a MiG, two Phantoms destroyed by AAA, and two F-105s damaged.

Even Court, soon to be credited with his third MiG, remained subdued. The atmosphere wasn't at all like Bolo. Leadership and esprit had been very different then. But he did feel good about Ev Stern.

"You did a great job," he told him. "Sorry I snapped at you. It's taking me a while to get used to someone else flying with me."

Ev Stern merely nodded.

"By the way, what's 'tits up'?" Court asked.

"GIB talk. Means the guy or thing is flat on its back, out of it, kaput, busted."

Court laughed. "Okay," he said, "let's go find that tanker crew, and fill them up with some booze at the O-Club." Then he remembered the restrictions. "Belay that last order. We'll take them to the hootch bar," he said. He and his crew stuffed a few beers from the tub into the bottom pockets of their flight suits.

Before they could leave, the phone rang on Hostettler's desk. When he answered, Court could hear the voice crackling from where he stood. Hostettler yessired a few times, and hung up.

"Comes the bad news," he said. "It was Colonel Crepens. He sounded mean as a snake. Snarled the insulation right off the telephone line. He wants all of Packard flight in the main briefing room ASAP."

Court looked thoughtful. The others groaned. They were worn out, shocked by the crash of their number Four, thirsty for more beer, and in no mood for any word from the wheelhouse, other than they had done a shit hot good job.

"Buck up, guys, you did a great job today. C'mon," Court said. They followed Court to the briefing room in silence.

Inside, they found four men in flight suits—three captains and a tech sergeant—standing in a group. "Hey," Court yelled, "are you guys the White tanker crew?"

"That we are," one of the captains answered. With whoops and cheers, the six members of Packard flight surrounded the tanker crew. They pounded them on their backs, and shook their hands. In seconds, the beers were being passed around. Just as fast, the cans were empty.

"God, that tasted good," the aircraft commander said.

"About a case more, and I might feel alive again," the copilot said.

"You guys are real four-engined fighter pilots," Court said. "You did a hell of a thing out there. We'll get you all the beer you want."

Ev Stern nodded his head toward the podium. "Tench ... *hut*," he sang out. The ten men popped to attention.

"At ease," Colonel Delbert L. Crepens said from the stage. "Sit here." He indicated the front rows of seats below him. The men walked over and seated themselves.

Crepens stood next to the podium. He wore a perfectly tailored and pressed 1505 khaki uniform. His thin face was livid. His pale blue eyes swept over the men seated before him like small lenses recording the most offensive of sights. He pointed to the plaque mounted on the podium with the motto of the 8th Tactical Fighter Wing, *Attack and Conquer.*

"You have disgraced this insignia," he said. "You bombed an unauthorized site, and you used unauthorized refueling procedures with a Strategic Air Command tanker. Rest assured, this will be reflected in my endorsement of your efficiency reports."

He pointed to the tanker crew. "Although you men are not in my chain of command, I have been requested by SAC Advon to detain you here until another crew can be brought in to fly your airplane back to U Tapao. Consider yourselves confined to this air base."

He took a step forward, and placed his hands on his hips. "I don't know what you individuals—I won't call you men—thought you were doing today. Whatever it was, it was not taught to you in any Air Force school or by any squadron. The Rules of Engagement, the Air Refueling Regulations, and the placement of SAC tankers is done strictly in accordance with established procedures." Crepens began to pace the stage. "These procedures, these regulations, these rules, are all determined by men much higher in rank than you." He spun to face them. "And, I might add, much smarter than you. Certainly, they are men of judgment. You are not. By your actions today, you have not only jeopardized your careers, you have jeopardized the standing of the United States Air Force with the highest authority in

Washington—the White House. Furthermore, you have jeopardized the standing of this fighter wing." He pointed to Court. "Your decisions today as a combat flight leader in contact with the enemy seriously damaged the reputation of this Fighter Wing. Furthermore, you were responsible for the alcohol in the debriefing room. That is clearly illegal. I will not permit such a thing." He stomped his foot. His face was red and distorted with rage. "You hear me? I will not permit it. You and that crazy Hostettler will be punished as a warning to the others."

Before the stunned air crewmen could react, the side door to the stage opened. Hostettler leaned his head in. "Excuse me, sir, but we have a visitor." His face was inscrutable as he flung the door all the way open.

Commander, 7th Air Force, walked in, the four stars on his collar reflecting brilliant shafts of light. "At ease," he said quickly, before any one could call the group to attention. Behind him followed Hostettler, and the two pilots from Packard Four who had ejected. The front-seater had his arm in a sling. The back-seater had a badly scratched face and swollen eyes. They both wore the big grin crash survivors wear once the shock has worn off. The other members of Packard flight passed silent grins and thumbs up to them. They also passed "what's going on" eye rolls.

Commander, 7th Air Force, motioned Crepens to one corner. "Del," he said. "Take a break. Go on back to your office. My new DO is there rustling up some coffee. He's waiting for you."

"Certainly, sir," Colonel Delbert L. Crepens said. "May I add what a pleasure it is to see you here? And it will be good to see Major General Raimer again."

"Ah, Delbert," Commander, 7th Air Force, said very quietly, "Raimer doesn't work for me anymore. I sent him back to the States. He will be on the retirement list very soon. I have a new Director of Operations now, Major General Milton Berzin."

Colonel Delbert L. Crepens nodded thoughtfully, turned, and walked off the stage, placing his feet in front of each other as carefully as a man on a tightrope. He continued down the aisle and out the rear door, closing it softly behind him.

Commander, 7th Air Force, walked to the edge of the stage. "Hostettler," he barked. "Go tell Colonel Stan Bryce to come over here. Then go get some more of that illegal beer, and make sure it's ice cold." He sat down on the floor of the stage, legs dangling over the edge. The Packard Four crew took seats with the tanker crew facing the stage.

Colonel Stan Bryce, Director of Operations, 8th Tactical Fighter Wing, walked in. If he knew his boss was about to be fired, he didn't show it. The creases and lines on his face and the sweat stains on his flight suit indicated he had just returned from a mission. He had not, however, been in the Navaho strike force.

"Come up here, Stan," Commander, 7th , said. Bryce joined him on the stage. "Gentlemen," Commander, 7th, said to the men, "I present you with your new wing commander." There was silence, then applause rocked the auditorium. Not only was Stan Bryce popular, more important, he was coming to be regarded as a great combat commander.

Then Commander, 7th Air Force, a career fighter pilot, looked at the men facing him. He reached up, unbuttoned his shirt, and tucked his collar inside, hiding his four stars. "All right, gentlemen," he said, "let's talk."

By the time Hostettler returned with more beer, the men were talking. Court Bannister had described how criminally fatal it was not only to fly over a cloud layer covering enemy territory, but to actually attack through it. "There was no way we could have repositioned under the clouds to make our attack run lengthwise down the runway, without endangering the entire flight any more than it was," he said. "So maybe some bombs didn't land on the runway. The only way we could have prevented hitting the hangar would have been not to drop at all. In that case, we would have been too heavy to jink away from the ground fire. We would have been hit even more." Court could feel himself getting angry about the impossibility of the situation.

"Don't worry about hitting the hangar, Major. I get paid to take care of things like that," the general said. "Tell me about the rest of the mission."

Court described the withdrawal, and the extraordinary rescue performed by the crew of White tanker. He told how the pilot had held the big plane perfectly steady, even in rough air, and the boomer had never missed a plug-in.

"Write up each member of the White crew for the Distinguished Flying Cross, Hostettler. I'm awarding them effective today," the general said. "You've got plenty of witnesses." He winked at the tanker crew. "Forget this stuff about evaluation boards. No one is going to investigate a crew that saved two Phantoms and four pilots. Besides, your four-star boss owes me one, and it's time to collect."

"Sir," the tanker pilot said, "I think there is something else you should know. A MiG started to vector in on us, and Major Bannister took him head-on. His back-seater told me they didn't have anything to shoot, either. He got the MiG to fire wild, then run home. Could have been our asses."

"He did?" the general said, eyebrows raised. "Two more DFCs, Hostettler," he said, indicating Court and Ev Stern.

"Sir," Ev Stern said. "I guess you didn't hear it yet, but Major Bannister got another MiG today."

"Terrific," Commander, 7th, cried. "By God, you two had a helluva day. Tell me about that MiG," he ordered Court.

Court told him about the shoot-down that Ev had corroborated. Then he told him of the persistent MiG-21 that had tried to attack the tanker. The general nodded when he mentioned the blue helmet.

"A Western diplomat in Hanoi has reported that one of the Russian pilot advisors regularly flies with the North Vietnamese during raids," he said. "At Gia Lam, he once saw a Caucasian in a flight suit carrying a light blue helmet. Since that is the standard color for Soviet helmets, we may assume your boy is a Russian pilot. Is he any good, Bannister?"

"He's good," Court said. "Damn good." He looked the general in the eye. "But I'm better."

Commander, 7th Air Force, stared right back. "I'd expect nothing less," he said. He had a thin smile on his face. He motioned for Bryce, Apple, and Bannister to follow him to one side. He spoke to Bryce. "See that these two get scheduled for more MiG CAP missions than bombing. I want one of them to get the man in the blue helmet."

21

☆

The two engines of the battered C-123 transport spun to a halt as the cargo doors opened. Toby Parker stepped out into the hot sun and steamy humidity of the Da Nang flight line. Along with the other twelve passengers, he retrieved his luggage after the load master had removed the red net from the items stacked on the cargo ramp. The sun was so bright Parker had to squint behind his aviator's sunglasses. He was lean and tan. His blue officer's cap with the silver piping was crunched down at a cocky angle over his crew-cut hair. He wore a K-2B flight suit, with a patch showing he was an O-2 pilot who had been through the theater indoctrination school for FACs at Phan Rang Air Base 300 miles south of Da Nang. He slung his duffel bag over his left shoulder, picked up his canvas B-4 bag in his right hand, and walked to the Quonset hut bearing a "Passenger Terminal" sign. Next to the hut was the Base Operations building and the multi-storied control tower.

Inside, on the dispatcher's counter, Toby Parker found a small fly-specked typewritten sign over a black telephone with no dial. He read where incoming personnel for the 20th TASS were to ask for extension 2020. He did as requested.

Within an hour, he was in the office of Lieutenant Colonel Chuck Annillo, the squadron commander. Annillo was a dark, thick-shouldered man, who once had been the lead quarterback at Chapel Hill. He wasted no words.

"Parker, you have a lousy reputation. The word I get is that you drink too much and you have a bad attitude. I don't know if any of that is true and I don't care. All I care about is your performance in this squadron. I expect you to perform your duties in an outstanding manner. See that you live up to my expectations. Any questions?"

Toby Parker said no. He was somewhat taken aback by this fierce and fast greeting. Then Annillo stood up and told Parker to follow him to the intell section.

They went out the back door of the operations building, across the grassy compound where the Covey FACs held their barbecues, to the one-story concrete building housing the meager intelligence briefing facilities. The entire locality was in an old French compound next to the east runway. The Americans had tried with varying success to keep up the crumbling buildings that were succumbing to the all-pervading moisture and humidity of Vietnam.

Inside the building, Annillo led Parker to a floor-to-ceiling map of Vietnam and Laos covered by clear acetate. Next to the map was a large wall clock with the letter H taped on its front. The H, the eighth letter of the alphabet, meant Vietnam was eight hours ahead of Greenwich Mean Time. In Washington, the letter was R; five hours behind GMT.

On the map, a long north–south slab of Laos next to Vietnam was titled Steel Tiger. A thick black hydra extended from North Vietnam, growing more heads as it extended through the Steel Tiger portion of Laos into South Vietnam. Surrounding and on the hydra were hundreds of overlapping red circles drawn with a grease pencil. Annillo traced the hydra with his forefinger.

"This is the Ho Chi Minh Trail," he said over his shoulder, "and these red circles are the guns protecting it." He faced Parker. "Our mission here is different from those FAC units flying only close air support in South Vietnam. We do that, all right, but we also fly in Laos. Since that fact is still classified, we call the missions by the area code name, Steel Tiger. We have two primary responsibilities in Laos: find and call in air strikes on supplies being sent down the Ho Chi Minh Trail; and support Special Forces units crawling around the jungle on reconnaissance or pilot rescue missions." He pointed to a photo of the O-2 aircraft. "Our little Oscar Deuce," he said, "is a bit underpowered for the mission, but we make do. In another year or so, we will get the OV-10, a big turbo-prop that will fly rings around it." He slapped Parker on the back. "Let's go fly. I want to see what you can do."

Bewildered by Annillo's abrupt maneuvers, Toby followed him out the door. The colonel did not tell Parker why he, the squadron commander, rather than the operations officer, was flying with him, a new guy. It was because USAF Colonel Donald Dunne had called up Annillo from Tan Son Nhut Air Base near Saigon. Dunne, a staff officer, had once witnessed Toby's drunken antics in an officer's club and had filed his name away in his mind as an officer he wanted to cashier someday from the Air Force.

"Your new guy, Parker," Dunne had said to Annillo, "is a drunken bum. He doesn't belong in the Air Force. Watch him. The minute he makes a mistake, court-martial him and get him out." Dunne was on an extended tour in the combat operations command post called Blue Chip, located at 7th Air Force headquarters.

"With all due respect, Colonel," Annillo had replied, "it is true you are in my operational chain of command—you can tell my squadron where to fly and when. But you most definitely are not in my administrative chain of command. It would make no difference if you were; I will judge Parker myself. How he performs under my command is how I will rate him."

Parker and Annillo went to the personal equipment shop. Toby was assigned a hook with knobs, on which to hang his parachute, survival vest and helmet, and a locker for his other flight equipment. At no time had Parker said one extra word. An hour later, he was 15 miles east of Da Nang, rolling an Oscar Deuce in on a deserted rock poking up out of the South China Sea. Lieutenant Colonel Annillo sat in the right seat while Parker flew. He watched Parker's every move as he rolled in from several directions and dive angles on parts of the rock. Annillo threw problem after problem at Parker, who solved them quickly and with a flair, Annillo thought, found only in the naturally gifted pilots. Using grease pencil horizon lines on the side window, he taught Toby how to lob rockets from what might be considered a safe distance away from a heavy gun.

When Annillo throttled the rear engine back and said, "You have a failed engine," Parker calmly started to check his survival gear and said he would bail out. "Why?" Annillo demanded. "Because one engine isn't enough power to keep this airplane airborne with the two of us in it, and you outrank me," Parker replied. Although some stateside pilots had flown the Oscar Pig without parachutes to save weight, Toby Parker wouldn't consider such a thing even though the rear propeller posed a serious bailout problem. Unlike jets with ejection seats, O-2 pilots had only gravity to rely on. Annillo grinned, pushed the power back up to halt the gradual descent of the airplane, and said, "Take us back to Dang Dang. We'll refuel and rearm and go on a real mission."

1245 Hours Local, Saturday, 4 November 1967
Airborne in an O-2
Over the Ho Chi Minh Trail
Royalty of Laos

☆

"We are just abeam of Khe Sanh," Annillo said. "Tell Panama we are over the fence. Then turn starboard to a heading of 335 degrees for Mu Gia Pass."

"Panama, this is Covey Four One," Parker transmitted on his UHF radio to the radar unit on a mountaintop near Da Nang.

"Covey Four One, Panama. Go."

"Panama, Covey Four One is over the fence."

"Copy, Four One. Contact Hillsboro on Golf. Good day."

"Panama, Covey Four One going to Golf." Parker checked his blue card for the Golf frequency, dialed it in on the UHF, and checked in with Hillsboro, the orbiting Airborne Command and Control ship. Covey Four One was Toby's permanently assigned Covey call sign.

Hillsboro was a four-engined turboprop C-130 with the back end full of people and radio sets in a huge container called a capsule. They had maps and the frag order of the day, and enough radios to talk to the Pentagon if need be. (In fact, they often joked wryly about expecting their Secretary of Defense to announce on high frequency that he was personally taking over the frag for the rest of the day.) The nighttime orbiter was called Moonbeam. Their mission was to coordinate aerial functions: who could divert to where to handle what emergency, what FAC needed what strike ordnance to take out what target. Hillsboro did not have radar. That was the function of an airborne radar plane (College Eye), a shipborne radar boat (Crown), and many land-based radars (Invert, Lion, Brigham, Panama, to name a few).

"Say again your mission number, Covey Four One," Hillsboro asked. They couldn't find this call sign on their frag orders. "Four One is an unfragged orientation flight," Annillo said.

"Rodge, Four One," Hillsboro said. "Welcome to never-never land. Can you handle fighters if need be?"

Annillo nodded to Parker. "Roger that," Parker transmitted. In fifteen minutes, Annillo was showing Parker the karst and lush jungle around Ban Karai, one of the three passes that funneled supplies from North Vietnam through the Annamite Mountains into Laos. They flew at ten thousand feet in clear air. To the east, lazy fat cumulus were slowly building and spreading.

They orbited and watched as Covey Three Six put in an air strike of three Navy A-4s against a target under the jungle trees that produced only minor secondary explosions. Annillo pointed out the white puffs of 23mm and larger bursts of 37mm directed against the Covey FAC and his fighters. Through some very adroit jinking, no one took any hits and were soon on their way; the A-4s back to their ship, and the Covey FAC farther down the Trail, looking for targets of opportunity like a beagle sniffing a forest track.

"I see something back in the trees behind the strike," Parker said. He pointed a darker area out to Annillo, who pulled up his binoculars and studied the area. "It might be a truck or two," he announced. "Call Hillsboro for some air."

Parker contacted Hillsboro and said they had a fleeting target of two or more trucks at coordinates Whiskey Echo 331062.

Fifteen minutes later, Chevy flight, consisting of three F-4s from Ubon, checked in.

"Roger, Covey Four One, Chevy flight has mission number 1846. We are flight of three Fox Fours. We have twenty-four Mark-82 five-hundred-pound bombs and six cans of CBUs. We have you in sight."

"Roger, Chevy flight. Your target is two or more trucks. Target elevation is 840 feet above sea level. Wind is from the northwest at about ten knots. Altimeter setting is 29.97. There are 23 and 37 mil in the area to the immediate west of the target about three miles. Safe bailout area is back west to Thailand. Use your bombs first. Random roll-in. FAC is in to mark."

From ten thousand feet, Toby pulled the throttles back and rolled in to fire a 2.75-inch Willy Pete smoke rocket at the jungle canopy where he was sure the trucks were located. His rocket went exactly where he aimed, deep into the jungle. Several seconds went by before some wisps of white smoke drifted up and were quickly dissipated by ground wind.

"Chevy doesn't have your smoke, Covey," the F-4 flight leader chided.

Without looking at Annillo, Parker chose a clear spot to the south of the target, rolled in, fired one rocket, raised the nose of the O-2 slightly, and fired another rocket one hundred feet north of the first. He pulled up and broke away from the suspected gun positions and looked over his shoulder.

"Hit three widths of my smoke to the north, Chevy," he called. Since fifty or one hundred meters meant nothing to a fighter rolling in from three miles high at speeds over 500 miles per hour, the known visual distance between the two smokes was a common yardstick. Chevy used it. In four passes, Chevy flight put their bombs exactly where Toby had instructed. There were two large secondary explosions several feet apart, indicating they had blown up two trucks or two cargo caches.

Toby told them to save their CBUs, which are useless on thick jungle canopies, and cleared them off target. After giving them the coordinates, and their on- and off-target times, he told them their BDA (Bomb Damage Assessment) was 100 percent ordnance on target, two trucks probably destroyed, but no further BDA due to smoke and haze. At least telling a pilot he had 100 percent ordnance on target was something positive.

"Where did you learn that one?" Annillo asked. Until then, when they couldn't see anything, the FACs had merely reported there was no observable damage. That was not morale-building.

"Down south," Parker replied.

"With Phil Travers?" Annillo asked.

"Yes," Parker answered, surprise obvious in his voice. "How did you know?"

"I know a lot about you. Your old boss, Leonard Norman, is an old friend. I requested you by name after talking to him." He thumbed toward the east. "Okay. Take us home. You're checked out." Privately, Annillo thought Parker flew the mission as confidently as if it were his fiftieth, not his first.

1615 HOURS LOCAL, TUESDAY, 7 NOVEMBER 1967
AIRBORNE IN AN O-2A OVER THE HO CHI MINH TRAIL
ROYALTY OF LAOS

☆

Toby Parker felt better than he had in months. After his flight with Colonel Annillo, he had had three more local and combat area rides with the operations officer and two different squadron instructor pilots. None had said much, but all had given him outstanding ratings. He hadn't had a drink since that day four weeks before at Fort Walton Beach. Nor did he smoke anymore. He had been running and working out every day since. He felt confident, proud, and fit. Better, he decided, better than he had in years.

Now he was on his first solo combat FAC mission. It was a four-hour flight, during which he was to put in two preplanned flights at the Ban Karai Pass, then perform a Trail recce from there to Mu Gia Pass, 75 miles farther north. As was customary, he was to make a radio check with American troops at two locations, the Marines at Khe Sanh, and the Special Forces at Lang Vei, as he flew into and out of Laos.

Indeed, Toby felt better. So much so, in fact, he was belting out line after line of *Roll Out the Barrel*. He sang as he automatically checked all his engine and navigation gauges, and ran his finger along his map to correlate it with ground reference points. *We'll have a barrel of fun* ... engine oil and temp in the green, RPMs okay ...

We've got the blues on the run ... brown-green of Khe Sanh checkpoint and the Lang Vei SF camp ... *Zing boom terrero.*

At 1735, he was at 10,000 feet in the Ban Karai area. He oriented
himself on the 5,300-foot karst peak. He had checked in with Hillsboro, who had dispatched his first set strike planes to him. By 1815,
he had put in the two sets of fighters. The target had been a suspected truck park hidden under two layers of jungle canopy. No one
really knew where the coordinates on the 7th Air Force frag order
had come from—a ground team or agent, maybe. All Toby and his
two sets of fighters had stirred up was a lot of dust and splintered
trees. After the leader of the second flight heard Toby report no BDA
due to smoke and dust, he transmitted in a scolding voice that "If
that's all you can scare up for us, Covey, we ain't coming out to play
no more." "I'll do better next time," Toby had responded on his UHF
radio.

Now he was doing a road recce from Ban Karai to Mu Gia Pass.
This is my first time, he said to himself, I'll find something. He flew
the best he could with one hand on the control wheel and one hand
holding his binoculars. He let down to 7,200 above the ground, then
4,800. He never held a constant heading for more than ten seconds,
and constantly let his altitude drift up and down several hundred feet
to spoil a gunner's tracking solution. He swept the meandering segments of the Trail he could see, as it wound in and out of the jungle
and through several areas cratered so heavily by bombs it looked like
mosaics of a sandy moon. *We'll have a barrel of fun.* Several times,
he orbited over a suspicious area, looking for clues to enemy activity.
He was looking for objects in the shadows of karst overhangs, off-
colored foliage, dust, tracks: anything of a suspicious nature. Twice,
he went below 4,500 feet and drew long looping tracers from 23mm
guns hidden in karst caves. His teeth were bared and he hummed
his *Barrel* song over and over again. He only had twenty minutes
before it would be too dark to see anything, much less put in an air
strike.

When he saw it, he couldn't believe it. He swallowed and looked
again. There it was, partially hidden in shadows from a karst cliff. It
was a big beautiful ZIL-135 truck with a load capacity, he remembered, of ten tons, and it looked as if that much were on board right
now. He snapped his head away from his glasses and twisted his O-2
into an uncoordinated circle. He flew away from the truck and
climbed higher to get a better fix on the map of his location.

The face of the karst cliff ran north and south. Toby estimated it
to be three hundred feet high. The truck was under an overhang that
faced east. He was lucky to see it. The whole face was in shadow,
since the sun was behind it, descending in the west. The overhang
gave out to about forty feet of open area before the jungle started.

Old eagle eyes, he congratulated himself, and whooped. Yahoooo. EEhaahhh.

He called Hillsboro and said he needed air to put on a truck.

"You got a positive ID on that truck, Covey Four One?" the Hillsboro controller asked.

"Roger that," Toby responded. "Old eagle eyes is on the job." Toby gave him his mission number, the location of the truck, and a rendezvous point for the fighters off the NKP TACAN Channel 89.

"We'll get your fighters, Covey. How much play time you got?"

Toby was startled. In his excitement, he had forgotten he needed an hour and a half of fuel to get back to Da Nang. He quickly checked his gauges and computed how much loiter time—play time—he had remaining before he had to start back. "Zero plus twenty," he said. He had twenty minutes to get the fighters in, mark the target for them, and, hopefully, have it destroyed.

With eight minutes remaining, Pontiac, a flight of two Fox Fours from Ubon, checked in with four 500-pound Mark-82 bombs each.

"Sorry, Covey," Pontiac Lead transmitted, "we got diverted from striking another target. This is the best we can do before nightfall. Hillsboro told us about your truck. We're ready. Old eagle eyes, huh?"

"Roger that, Pontiac. Your target is one each large supply truck. Target elevation is 700 feet above sea level. Wind is from the west at five knots. Altimeter setting is 29.93. I haven't observed any ground fire in the area. Safe bailout area is west to Thailand. Make your passes east to west. The truck is under an overhang, so you will have to skip your bombs in. FAC is in to mark." Toby's voice was light and confident.

He rolled his O-2 up on a wing, pulled the nose around and down until he was heading toward the overhang. From this high angle he couldn't see the truck, so he walked two rockets up to where he knew it was hidden. He broke left and jinked away.

"Got your smoke, Covey," Pontiac Lead transmitted.

"Roger, you're cleared in hot, east to west with a north break. You'll have to press it a bit to get those bombs under there, then do some yanking and banking to get out," Toby said.

"Rodge. I'll make a damn near level run in, then pull up right smartly. Pontiac Lead is in, FAC in sight." All commands were in the clear. Things just happened too fast for code words. Intel had said there probably wasn't a VNF radio receiver and English speaker available, anyhow.

Toby orbited at four thousand feet over the run-in path of the two Pontiac Phantoms. They would pass well under him. He watched lead flash below him and saw two bombs detach from his belly to fly parallel toward the overhang, then the pilot pulled sharply right and up. His wingman, Pontiac Two, called he was rolling in.

"Cleared in, Two," Toby said.

As Pontiac Lead flashed over the top of the karst cliff, the whole world lit up. Stream after stream of 23mm from the top of the rock played out after Pontiac Lead; two streams reached out for Toby's airplane; three hosed level, letting their shells fall downward into Pontiac Two's run-in path. At the same time, clips of five and seven 37mm shells began to burst at 10,000 feet, effectively causing an overcast of exploding steel.

"Pull up, pull up, Two; break it off," Toby screamed into the radio.

"Lead's hit," Pontiac One transmitted.

"Jesus Christ," Pontiac Two said, as he yanked back and up. A tracer stream touched his plane briefly.

Toby felt a crash and a bang behind him and his cabin filled with white smoke and the sweet metallic smell of cordite. At the same time, his plane rocked sideways as he flew through three bursts of 37mm. Black smoke engulfed his plane for an instant and tearing metal shards ripped out most of the plexiglass from the right window. The airplane flew out of the bursts, nearly inverted, front and rear engines roaring. He wrestled with the control wheel. He could feel heat behind him and he smelled burning insulation. When he had the wings level, he let go of the controls and reached down for the 20-pound red fire extinguisher. As the plane started to fall off on a wing, he pulled the pin and shot it back over his shoulder with one hand and leveled the plane with the other. Then he looked back and directed the CO_2 stream into the wrecked radios where a 23mm had burst. The bulk of the radios had contained the explosion and the fire, which went out under the blast of the CO_2. With the fire out and the airplane under control, he scanned his instruments. All the needles on the gauges looked to be where they should be. He tried his radios. They were dead. He looked around for the fighters and saw absolutely nothing. Except for some residual and fast-dissipating white smoke, the air was as clear as if nothing had happened. He looked around and down in the karst region. There were no columns of black greasy smoke indicating an airplane had crashed.

Bewildered, he started an orbit at 10,000 feet off to one side, well out of range of the guns. "I've got to find my fighters," he said out loud. He saw nothing. He looked about in a panic. Where are they? Oh God, I've lost my fighters.

He stabbed at the radio control button on the control wheel again and again, as if he could force his shattered radios to work. Calm down, Parker. Calm down, he told himself. He reached under his parachute harness for the small radio in his survival vest, extended the antenna, and held it close to his lips. He cupped his hands in an attempt to deaden the roar of the slipstream tearing at the broken right window.

"Hillsboro, Hillsboro, this is Covey Four One on guard channel. Do you read?"

"Covey Four One, Hillsboro. We read you faint but clear. What is your status?"

"I'm okay. My radios are out. I'm using my survival radio. Where are my fighters? What happened to Pontiac flight?"

"Take it easy, Covey. They both took some rounds. Pontiac Two's back-seater is hit bad. Lead's okay. They are on their way home. They thought you had been shot down. Are you sure you don't have battle damage?"

"Just my radios and a smashed window. I'm headed back to home plate."

Suddenly, a very loud and angry voice blasted through the small speaker of the radio that Parker held to his ear.

"FOUR ONE, YOU DUMB SHIT. THAT WAS A FLAK TRAP AND MY BACK-SEATER WAS HIT. HE'S FUCKING BLEEDING TO DEATH. IT'S YOUR FAULT, YOU BASTARD."

"Easy, Pontiac Two," the Hillsboro controller transmitted. "Ambulance and crash crew are standing by at Ubon for you. Please leave guard channel and go to a discreet frequency. Break, break. Covey Four One, give radar a call every fifteen minutes on guard, so someone knows you're okay. Copy?"

Toby Parker mumbled he understood. He was stunned. He circled aimlessly for a moment. He fumbled for his binoculars and focused them on the karst overhang. In the failing light, he saw a fire where the truck had been. The bombs of Pontiac Lead must have touched it off, he thought. That was some satisfaction. But a flak trap? Then he realized there was something wrong with the fire. It was small and even, and gave off white smoke. A burning truck would have gas or diesel fuel and tires to burn red and emit gobs of black smoke. This was more like a wood fire.

"OH SHIT," he screamed at the top of his lungs. "SHIT! SHIT! SHIT!" He pounded his knee. I've fallen for the oldest trick in the books. I burned down a decoy set as bait in a flak trap. His eyes burned with bitter tears as he turned southeast toward Da Nang.

He flew, numb and mechanical. for several minutes. By rote, he checked his instruments. His mind duly registered that the engine instruments were satisfactory. The fuel gauge indicated he had just enough gas remaining to make it back to Da Nang. Little "off" flags had dropped over the gauges of the directional needle and the distance readout of his TACAN navigational radio. That's not important, he thought, mind in a haze. Damn little is important. Damn little.

Below him, long lances of shadow speared down from the jagged karst peaks into the green and brown jungle valleys. Ahead of him, towering pillars of cumulus clouds, dark at their bases where they protruded from the purple haze, rose as stately cathedrals to blaze majestically white as their tops caught the last rays of the setting sun behind him. They were early evening thunderstorms birthing themselves with the moist air being swept inland from the South China Sea. Scattered now, they would soon form a solid north–south line that halted at the Annamite mountain chain, presenting a massive barrier between the mountains and the air base at Da Nang. Even now, at this early stage inside of them, sixty-mile-an-hour vertical winds were causing so much air friction that charged particles were building more electrical energy than could ever been created by man. Already, tentative fingers of lightning were reaching from cloud to cloud. Soon, very soon, they would become giant discharges of fearsome power between the ground and the night clouds, and would rent the air with ear-splitting shock waves. Although any one of their destructive elements—the shearing and wrenching vertical winds, the megawatts of electrical power, or the vacuum left after a bolt of lightning streaked through the air—could tear an airplane apart, most airplanes were destroyed by being ripped asunder by the vertical winds. If a pilot tried to pass under a thunderstorm—their bases were usually at 6,000 feet—the driving rain and vertical wind shears would hammer the airplane out of the sky. More violent and wrenching things awaited the pilot who tried to fly *through* a thunderstorm. Pieces of him and his craft could be bounced aloft for minutes, maybe hours, before they were finally spit out. If a pilot flew too close to a thunderstorm, particularly near or under the roll cloud protruding from the top of the anvil-shaped cloud, the plane could be shattered by giant hailstones that had been formed by water droplets pummeled up and down in the belly of the storm, gathering size with each vertical movement like layers of pearl forming about a grain of sand.

The thunderstorms developed and matured even further during the thirty minutes it took Toby Parker to reach the turning point west of Khe Sanh. He had not heard Hillsboro calling him on guard channel, warning him to divert to Ubon because of the storms. He had long before turned off his survival radio and tucked it under a leg strap. If he had made his fifteen-minute call as ordered, he would have gotten the same instructions from Panama, the Da Nang radar site. None of the controllers figured he could make it to Da Nang.

It was dark now. Soon it would be pitch black. Even the sun no longer lit up the tops of the clouds billowing and towering miles over the tiny airplane. Toby Parker sat slumped in his pilot's seat, hands gripping the control wheel, feet on the rudder pedals. Although he had climbed to altitude to save fuel, and had leaned out the engines' fuel–air mixture to cut fuel flow, his airplane was still slowly climbing, a few hundred feet per minute. He had been taught to trim slightly nose up in combat. The theory was that in case a pilot suffered a hit and could not control his aircraft for a few minutes, it would climb rather than settle slowly to the ground. Had he been monitoring the flight instruments more closely, he would have noticed his gradual increase in altitude.

By time and distance alone, he had instinctively turned almost due east at the Khe Sanh checkpoint. Da Nang now lay one hour's flying time in front of him. There was barely enough fuel in the tanks of his O-2 for one hour and ten minutes' flying time. The air became more turbulent. His hands and feet manipulated the controls as unthinkingly as a person lost in thought strolling a rocky beach.

Soon the instruments on his panel were unreadable. He had been using what there was of the visual horizon to keep his wings level, and, he supposed, to maintain a constant altitude. He had glanced just enough at an interior compass to correct his heading. Ahead, continuous lightning flashing and dancing between clouds and to the ground provided just enough visual cues to keep him from losing all outside reference points as he approached the ancient mountain chain, climbing, climbing . . .

His head felt heavy. He stared straight ahead, oblivious to the roaring of the engines or the wind moaning and whistling through the broken right window. His mind was repeating over and over the words yelled at him by the angry Pontiac Two: "That was a flak trap . . . flak trap . . . my back-seater was hit . . . bleeding to death . . . bleeding to death . . . hit . . . bleeding to death . . . death . . . your fault, you bastard . . . your fault."

His mind pictured a pilot slumped in his harness, blood pouring from a wound in his chest. Suddenly, he saw the scene in the airplane a year before when his pilot, Phil Travers, had been gut-shot. Phil had moaned and thrashed and was about to crash the tiny O-1 airplane when finally Toby had had to hit him on the back of the head with his service .45 to quiet him down.

"I killed him. I killed Phil. Now I've just killed another pilot," Toby said out loud, in a voice lost in the cockpit noise. A violent crack-bang sounded, as a streak of lightning superheated the air when it shot past his left wing. The plane bucked and pitched, first lightly, then heavily, as small vertical wind shear shook it. The thunderstorm line was closer. Toby stared in trancelike fascination at the lightning display as he flew closer and closer. His plane had climbed through 14,000 feet. The engines were losing horsepower in the thin air. The airspeed needle slowly unwound toward the red-lined stall speed. Brilliant and dazzling flashes of light revealed his tiny plane to be flying toward columns and pillars that soared seven and eight miles above him into the night sky. His plane began buffeting more frequently, and with greater ferocity.

He began an unconscious chant: bleeding to death . . . bleeding to death . . . I killed them . . . I killed them. The wind whistle in the broken window dropped imperceptibly to a low moan as the airspeed fell off in the thin air. The air temperature, dropping two degrees per thousand feet of altitude, was now chilly as it swirled through the cockpit. Toby began an uncontrollable shivering. Someplace in the back of his mind, with curious detachment, he saw his tiny airplane entering the most gigantic of the thunderstorms, one that towered over 50,000 feet and was lit up inside with continuous lightning like a celestial cathedral. He saw his craft being flung up and up—until there was quiet and peace, and oblivion, peaceful oblivion. He began to feel very tired, and wanted nothing but to sleep.

"Hey, Tobes, old buddy, how ya doin'?" said Phil Travers from the right seat. Toby clearly saw his red hair and infectious grin in the almost continuous strobes of white light.

"Aw, Phil, Phil," he cried into the cockpit. The plane was bouncing, struts and other metal braces beginning to creak and pop.

"Hey, Tobes, old buddy. Like I always said, you gotta fly the bird, not let it fly you. Now, you ain't flying this here airplane."

"Phil," Toby cried again, "I want to sleep. Take me with you . . ." On the darkened panel, the airspeed indicator wavered just a few knots above stall speed. One more upsetting vertical draft and the plane would fall off into a diving spiral, or a spin.

"Come on, I taught you better than that. First you gotta breathe, then you gotta fly the bird. Breathe and fly. Breathe and fly."

The plane shuddered and tipped as a violent draft of air slammed down the right wing. Breathe and fly. Breathe and fly. The nose of the O-2 rose up almost vertical, then the airplane stalled and started down in a tightening spin. Toby, hands now in his lap, lay slumped in his harness, head rolling with the motion of the airplane. His eyes were closed, a look of great peace on his face. Lightning bathed the sharp karst peaks below with pitiless blue-white light. Breathe and fly, breathe and fly. The words meant . . . nothing. Breathe and . . . breathe and . . . breathe . . . The death spiral tightened. The wind whistle returned, rising in pitch.

"Come on, Parker," Phil Travers shouted into Toby's mind, "BREATHE AND FLY!"

As if with a will of their own, Toby's hands slowly crept from his lap. They fumbled with the side of the survival kit he sat on. There was a pop as he pulled a little green knob. He lifted a rubber tube and slowly moved it toward his face. Without opening his eyes, he pushed it into his mouth. The tube emitted a constant flow of pure oxygen.

"BREATHE AND FLY," Toby Parker shouted, and sat bolt up-right. He held the tube and sucked in the life-giving oxygen. In a split second his senses returned as the 100 percent pure oxygen flooded his starved system. Fully alert, he looked about, finally registering the danger in what he saw.

In the illuminated canyon, he saw enough reference points to know he was in a right-hand spin. He slammed in left rudder, at the same time shoving the control wheel full to the instrument panel. The plane groaned, as the spinning motion abruptly stopped and the plane screamed down in a dive, engines shrieking in overspeed. Toby snatched the throttles back and slowly raised the nose, mindful of not overstressing the airframe in the now turbulent air. He continued sucking on the oxygen. When the plane was under control, he eased the throttles forward, then flipped some switches up on the instrument panel, lighting his cockpit gauges. They faded into purple swirls as he was dazzled by successive brilliant flashes, and deafened by the continuous roll of thunder. He turned up the lamp clamped on his left to bathe the panel in a glare of white light that would override his flash blindness.

His mind almost froze in horror as he saw the altimeter needle. He was barely three hundred feet above the nearest karst. He slammed the throttles to the stops to climb away from the reaching teeth. He clawed his way back up to 9,000 feet. His head was clear now, and he no longer needed the raw oxygen. Outside, the air was all turbulence and flash and crashing rain as he turned the control wheel and pushed rudder to steer the bucking aircraft away from the storm barrier and toward a calmer section.

His mind was working now, taking in and processing data. Fuel level—low. Position—uncertain. Radios—still out. He picked up the survival radio.

"Panama, Panama, this is Covey Four One on guard. Do you read, over?"

He held the small radio to his ear and heard only the hissing of the UHF carrier wave.

"Panama, Covey Four One on guard. How do you read?"

". . . Four One, this is Panama. Read you weak and garbled. Squawk flash for identification."

The voice was faint but clear through the hiss. Toby reached down to activate the switch on his radar transponder that, if it was working, would throw out an extra burst of energy to light up the controller's screen in his sector. It was one of the few working electronic devices.

"Covey Four One, Panama on guard. We have a positive ID. What are your intentions?"

Toby almost laughed. My intentions, he said to himself, are to live. "Panama, my intentions are for you to thread me through the thunder-bumpers to recover at Da Nang as quickly as possible. I am at an emergency fuel state. You copy?"

"Four One, Panama. Steer one zero five degrees. We have you, and we have good paints on the thunderstorm cells. What is your fuel state?"

Toby checked his gauges. By leveling at 9,500 and leaning the two engines, he could stay aloft for fifty minutes.

"Five zero minutes remaining, Panama. Can you do me any good?"

There was a long pause before the Panama controller answered. "Sorry for the delay. Did a little calculating here. You have a nice west-to-east tail wind. Even zigzagging around the storms, we can have you over the base in forty-five minutes."

The controller knew what he was talking about. Everything worked. In forty-three minutes exactly, Toby Parker was on the ground, safely in a revetment, shutting his front engine down. The rear had quit from fuel exhaustion as he taxied in. The thunderstorms passed out to sea, muttering and grumbling. The bright ramp lights mounted high up on poles glistened on the wet steel planking of the fight line. Lieutenant Colonel Chuck Annillo waited for Toby in an open jeep.

"I told everyone to stay behind until I talked to you," he said. Toby could tell Annillo knew the whole story of the flak-bait truck. The Intelligence people at Ubon, or maybe Pontiac's squadron commander, had called Annillo to the phone.

"How is that back-seater?" Toby asked, afraid he knew the answer.

"Look, son," Annillo said, looking at Parker in the darkness, not moving the jeep. "Most anybody could fall for that trap. Especially a new guy. You're going to do just fine around here. Take my word for it."

"He's dead, isn't he?" Parker said.

Annillo nodded, a look of great compassion on his face. "Yeah, son, he's dead. Think you can live with that?"

Toby Parker's eyes glistened, but he straightened his back and lifted his chin. "Yeah," he said, "yeah. I can live with that. But it will never happen again. I'll never be sucked in again." He looked sharply at Annillo. "You still want me in the squadron?" he asked.

"You bet, son. Remember, I hand-picked you, and I don't pick losers." He slammed Toby Parker on the back, then dropped the jeep into gear. As he turned toward the intelligence shack, he thought of what he had told Colonel Donald Dunne down at 7th Air Force when

Dunne had demanded Toby Parker be court-martialed for dereliction of duty or criminal negligence or malfeasance, or whatever could be hung on him.

"How much you been shot at, Colonel?" Annillo had demanded.

"What does that have to do with this?"

"That's what I thought," Annillo replied. "You come up here and fly Covey for a couple weeks and then we'll talk further. Out." Annillo had hung up the phone, and Dunne hadn't called back.

22

☆

The President turned to face Major General Albert G. Whisenand. "You know why I keep you around, you piss-ant? I keep you around to see how long I can restrain from stepping on you. There is only one elephant here and you are looking at him."

Whitey's face flamed as he stood in front of Johnson's desk. "*Mister* President," he said in a voice edged in steel, "you are demeaning yourself and, more important, you are demeaning your office by talking that way. Furthermore, you are totally ignoring the information I am bringing to you from Vietnam. I went to Vietnam at *your* request to ask *your* questions and now you won't listen to the answers."

"You didn't bring the *right* answers," the President fumed. "Why can't you agree with Westmoreland—now he's a 'can-do' fella—and Rostow and Bunker? Listen to me, Whisenand, this is a war like no other. We have no songs, no parades, no bond drives and we can't win the war otherwise." He waved his arms. "Go get a colorful general, with his shirt collar open like MacArthur, to go over and argue with the press. We've got to do something dramatic." He seemed unaware of his previous tirade.

From behind his desk, the President drew himself up to his full six-foot-three height. "Let me tell you something else. It isn't just Vietnam, you know. I've got to deal with major military crises abroad and with social reforms at home. I've got race riots in Newark and Detroit. I'm trying to pass a tax surcharge to slow inflation. And now Westmoreland wants more troops, the Joint Chiefs and Oley Sharp at CINCPAC want more raids up north, I've got a Secretary of Defense going dovish on me, and"—he glared at Whitey—"you stand there and tell me we are losing the war in Vietnam." He stomped from around the desk and headed toward the fireplace. Halfway there, he turned back to face Whitey Whisenand. He was fired up again.

"This is not *my* war. This is not *Johnson's* war. This is *your* war. This is *America's* war. If I drop dead tomorrow, this war will still be with you." LBJ glared at Whitey as he spoke.

"Mr. President," Whitey began, not sure he was in control of himself, "you want solutions and strategies for winning the war, but you can't tell me what 'win' means. Do you want political stability in the South? Do you want them free from attack by the Communists from the North? Do you want to destroy the Communist North? If you cannot make up your mind what course to follow, how can you expect this country to make it up for you? You don't seem to have a plan, and the plan your commander in Vietnam has is faulty because you haven't given him a covenant to go out and win."

Johnson flared up. "Just what do you mean by that?"

After talking to the three Special Forces men in Saigon and, later, General Westmoreland again, Whitey had spent long hours with lower level staff officers in MACV and the Pentagon, and with analysts of the Central Intelligence Agency. He had come to a conclusion that was not flattering to COMUSMACV.

"I mean that General Westmoreland firmly believes he is, as he says, 'attriting' the Communist forces with his Search and Destroy method faster than they can replenish themselves. He is not. The fact that he is not can be proven. Because he is held back from all-out offensive operations, attrition is his only strategy and it is not working. The CIA will brief you at any time on the details." Whitey nodded. "Ho Chi Minh can sustain attrition. He welcomes attrition. Remember what his General Giap said about Dien Bien Phu. 'One hundred thousand to glory for this victory.' Ho will use attrition and world opinion, flamed by selected protestors, until we get tired and go home."

Whitey saw the President seem to sink into himself. "You have some lonely decisions to make, Mr. President, but you must make them. You wanted to be President. Now make some Presidential decisions. That's what you asked for, that's what you got, that's what you get paid for. Make some decisions."

Whitey could feel hotness rise in his cheeks. He continued. "I see it this way. Ho Chi Minh is betting we will lose public opinion in the States before he loses the war in the south; or we build a viable democratic nation in the south."

The President blew out a lungful of air. "All right," he said. "All right. You want some decisions; I'll *make* some goddamned decisions. We are not going to invade the North. That is final. But we will not stop bombing up there . . ." He held up a finger. "Yet I will still select the targets. In a nut-gut, I still want to make Ho's infiltration too costly, and I want to exert pressure on him to stop aggression in the South. That is what I want to do. And McNamara, he's got a new way of doing it."

LBJ gave a fleeting smile, and continued. "Yup, the perfessor, Bob, he's got this new thing called Igloo something. Maybe he doesn't want you to strike up north, but he wants you guys to drop sensors all over the Ho Chi Minh Trail. They're supposed to feed information to a big computer someplace over there in Thailand. You know the program?"

"Yes, sir, I do. Igloo White. The Air Force is to drop acoustic and seismic sensors, camouflaged as branches and twigs, along the Trail at precisely known spots. The sensors will pick up the sound or vibration of troops or trucks passing by and relay that datum to a computer in the USAF complex at Nakhom Phanom Air Base in Thailand. Based on the input, the computer will print out the location, direction, and intensity of what they have detected. From that printout, Blue Chip, the command post at Tan Son Nhut, can order air strikes." Whitey leaned back, his face without expression. "The system should be in operation in a matter of weeks. Total cost will be over two billion."

"Whitey," the President said, "when you get that blank look on your face, you're against something. What is it? Tell me the nut-gut of the Igloo stuff. Igloo . . . in a jungle. Who thinks up these names?"

"Mr. President, the names are from USAF computer codes. What I have against Igloo White is that one of our two basic premises is incorrect. Let's assume the first premise is true, that electronically the system will work. But the second premise, that the North Vietnamese don't know the system is there, can never be true. They will know, because every base that the launching aircraft fly from, whether in Vietnam or Thailand, is penetrated to one degree or another. Agents see and report what weapons the aircraft carry. They will know, because those on the ground will see American airplanes flying new patterns, very low and straight and level, while the sensors are being dropped. And they will see the Americans dropping new 'weapons.' In short order, they will find the sensors and figure out what they are for. Then they have three options: destroy them, move them, or feed in false information. It wouldn't take much to set up one truck to drive in a pattern all night to make us think a big convoy is there. Or, conversely, cover a microphone while a division passes by."

"So you don't think they will work?"

"That is correct, sir. I don't think they will work."

"But you think we have to beef up the strikes on old Ho's Trail, don't you?"

"Yes, sir, I do," Whitey said. He judged that the time was now. "I have a way to get the job done better," Whitey said, thinking of his conversation with Bull Dall and Wolf Lochert. He told the President about increased surveillance and the resultant air strikes in the Steel Tiger area. He told him that the air assets would be available with the concurrence of 7th Air Force and CINCPAC, and that COMUS-MACV must be asked for additional Special Forces input.

LBJ stood at the window for a long moment, with his hands behind his back. Then he turned and pointed his finger at Whitey.

"Here's how it is, from the beginning. I will let you carry on with Rolling Thunder, but under the same rules of engagement as before; you can't mine the harbors or permanently cut the rail lines. You can't attack airfields unless I say so. Maybe you're right about Mc-Namara's Igloo White line. Maybe it won't work. Based on what you just told me, I want you to tell the JCS to step up the bombing on the Ho Chi Minh Trail. I don't know where, yet. But I want you to get those trucks before Ho sticks 'em up my ass. Day and night, go get 'em. Seal that supply line of Ho's up like a polar bear's ass." The President walked over to a map of Southeast Asia pinned to a tripod easel. He moved his hand up and down Laos, the country that bordered Vietnam to the west. Long thick black arrows marked the Trail, where it came in from North Vietnam through the passes at Mu Gia and Ban Karai, then fanned south through the Laotian panhandle and on into Cambodia and South Vietnam.

"Where would you do it?" he said, slapping the palm of his hand on the Laotian panhandle.

Whitey pointed to the northern panhandle of Laos that included Mu Gia Pass. "Right here, Mr. President," he said. "Right here in this area we call Steel Tiger."

"Then that, by God, is what we do." He turned from Whitey to look at the map he had just touched. "Set it up, Whisenand. Set your plan in motion. But I want results, you understand? Bankable results. Or you, General Whisenand, will be reduced, retired, and railroaded out of Washington."

0130 HOURS LOCAL, WEDNESDAY, 15 NOVEMBER 1967
FORWARD OPERATING BASE NEAR BAN ME THUOT, II CORPS
REPUBLIC OF VIETNAM

☆

Based on Whitey's input and rationale, the Joint Chiefs of Staff agreed with the Chairman of the Joint Chiefs to increase American Special Forces activity on the ground in Laos, in conjunction with stepped up air strikes on the Ho Chi Minh Trail. Privately, they were apprehensive that COMUSMACV, General William Childs Westmoreland, would ask for more troops.

It took less than thirty-six hours in the Pentagon for the message to go out from Army DCSOPS (the Army Deputy Chief of Staff for Operations), to PACAF, to COMUSMACV, requiring increased Trail watching and the destruction by air of supplies thereon. General Westmoreland requested his operations people to take care of the request. Certain non-SF one-star generals, with happy approbation by some equally non-SF colonels, surreptitiously downgraded the command to a request for a feasibility study to be performed by Colonel Fred John Dall, Commander of the 5th Special Forces Group at Nha Trang. Unaware of the cabal, Bull Dall felt the study requirement was better than no increased Trail activity at all. He sent a lateral message to operations at 7th Air Force for a drop aircraft to be ready when requested by the 5th. PACAF and 7th Air Force prepared for extra air strike sorties into Steel Tiger.

In three days, Wolf Lochert had assembled his team and the training began. Their call sign was to be Dakota. He had with him two American Special Forces NCOs, Frenchy Roland and Dave Rhoades, and three Nungs, and the Vietnamese called Buey Dan. They were supported at a Forward Operating Base near Ban Me Thuot, 150 miles south of Da Nang, where a mission launch team helped them prepare. They went into isolation: signals and paper in, nothing out. They spent a week running in the woods and mountains nearby, getting to know the signals, the equipment, the mission, but most important—getting to know each other. Wolf explained their twofold mission:

(1) Determine if there were sufficient and suitable targets of opportunity for ground-controlled air strikes to merit increasing the number of Trail watch teams,
(2) Determine if indigenous Laotian natives could be recruited for an underground to convey shot-down aircrew to safety.

Just before sundown on the night of 14 November, they departed their FOB by helicopter and landed at Da Nang. Thirty minutes past midnight, they were airborne in an Air Force C-130. The Herky bird, as the crew called their thirty-ton Hercules transport, was powered by four turboprop engines of 4,000 horsepower each. The Herky bird could carry eighteen tons of cargo or 64 fully rigged paratroopers. Tonight, it took off with a total of thirteen men on board. It would land with only the five USAF crew members and the SF launch officer from the FOB, whose job it was to see the HALO team safely out the door over the correct area.

The seven men who were to free-fall into Laos sat in the rear of the plane on the pull-down canvas seats. Each man was loaded with sixty pounds of gear and two parachutes, one steerable ASP-1 back pack, and one chest pack reserve. Attached to the top of the reserve was an altimeter and a timer set in a curved aluminum frame. Each breathed oxygen from a walk-around bottle when the C-130 was level at 18,500 feet. Rather than decompress when it was time to jump, the plane flew the entire outbound leg of the mission without engaging the pressurization system. During the free-fall, they would breathe oxygen supplied under constant pressure to their masks from foot-long green cylinders that had a ten-minute supply.

The men were dressed in standard Army olive-drab jungle fatigues, with black spray paint creating uneven camouflage lines. The material of the Special Forces tiger suits had not proven as suitable for long-term jungle wear as the fatigues. They had cut the wide cargo pockets off the bottom of the shirts so they could be tucked into their pants. They had added pockets to their sleeves. They wore Nomex pilot's gloves, with the fingers cut out for the right hand. All had used a camouflage stick on their faces.

The fatigues were sterile; there were no rank or insignia tabs, nor were there any manufacturer labels. Nor did the men wear dog tags or carry any ID cards. Most of their gear came from a CIA warehouse in Da Nang. Even their packets of freeze-dried food were in unmarked plastic bags. This was a clandestine mission into a supposedly neutral country where supposedly no U.S. troops were operating. To maintain this fiction, there could be no identifying labels, tags, or cards. Of course, this meant that in case of capture the men could be shot out of hand as spies—all in accordance with the Geneva convention. There were also tens of thousands of North Vietnamese troops in Laos, even though Ho Chi Minh's people proclaimed daily there were not. Each Dakota man cheated to some extent. The Nungs carried joss sticks and pictures of a revered leader, Phuc Po. Roland and Rhoades each had small untraceable mementos: a lucky rock for Frenchy, an ivory Buddha for Dave. Wolf carried a picture of a green-eyed American beauty named Charmaine and a fragment of his first green beret, which had long since shredded (it was one of the early Canadian hats).

Buey Dan carried no visible memento. In his heart was hatred more than sufficient to see him through this, perhaps his final mission. He had conferred with his sector commander and with Colonel Nguyen Van Tung. They had learned of the new American plan to patrol and interdict the Truong Son trail, as they called the long supply. They knew that Lochert's group was really only a study effort. If it failed, then the whole effort would be finished. Buey Dan had been assigned to ensure that the study plan failed. The time had come for Buey

Dan to extract the blood revenge for which he had waited and bided his time ever since that *mui lo* Wolf Lochert had killed his son with a stiletto.

Team Dakota's sixty pounds of equipment was a mixture of radios, rations, weapons, ammunition, medical supplies, and clothes. Buey Dan carried two extra concealed items. Their weapons were all Sino-Soviet and East bloc manufactured, not only to maintain the fiction, but, more important, to avoid the distinctive sounds American weapons made in battle, thereby giving their position away. Among them was a Dragunov 7.62 airborne sniper rifle with a four-power PSU-1 scope. Their HALO headgear was a hybrid of a football helmet and a WWII leather flyer's helmet, complete with goggles. The oxygen mask was attached by pull-away tabs to each side of the helmet.

Frenchy Roland was designated the base man. This meant he would lead the others to the target area by being first out the door. Sewn to the back of his parachute pack was an electric wand that gave off a soft glow when activated by a switch on his reserve. It would go out when he deployed his parachute. Then he could activate another small light on top of his canopy. All men wore a tiny transistor radio taped to their helmets, set to a frequency that received a whistling chirp signal from a small transmitter that had been dropped into the target area 6 hours before by a fast-flying, low-level F-4. Using the aural null method, each jumper could track to the beacon if separated from the base man in the air or the team on the ground. The base man had a more sophisticated tracker with a needle.

The C-130 loadmaster gave the signal to the launch officer that he was about to lower the rear ramp. He activated the hydraulic mechanism, causing the huge slanting ramp to drop down from the roof of the fuselage to provide a big platform leading into the black night. Then it was three minutes to drop. By hand signals, the launch officer gave the well-rehearsed instructions to the stick of jumpers: stand up, activate the green oxygen bailout bottles, disconnect from walk-around oxygen, check each other's equipment, shuffle to the door. The three Americans exchanged thumbs-up and patted the Nungs on the back. They aligned themselves on the platform in jump formation, Frenchy outermost. Although the launch officer was attached to the airplane by a harness, he nonetheless wore a parachute. He caught the green light from the cockpit and gave the "Go" signal. In less than five seconds, the seven jumpers cleared the platform and dove into the darkness.

The launch officer gave the "Go Home" signal to the loadmaster, who relayed it to the pilot. He closed the ramp and cleared the engineer to pressurize the airplane. All crew members popped their ears as the pressure increased to an altitude equivalent of 8,000 feet.

The loadmaster, a stocky air force sergeant, took his mask off. "I wouldn't do that for all the money in the world," he said to the launch officer.

"I do it for $110 bucks a month, and I'd do it for nothing if I had to," the launch officer snapped. He was unhappy he hadn't been chosen for the mission.

Neither of the two men noticed the C-rations carton placed under the seat that had been occupied by Buey Dan. It contained four pounds of plastique fused to explode in fifteen minutes.

23

☆

Airman First Class Michael LaNew seemed more than happy to drink all the scotch his newfound friend would buy for him. The scotch—pronounced *su-cosh* by the Thai barmaids—at Tippy's ranged from rotgut to the unwatered best. LaNew was drinking the best in the bar—Cutty Sark—and feeling really, really good. And feeling really good was something he had to strive for, because, as he told his friend, he was an unhappy man. He had a right to be unhappy, he revealed. He was broke, several hundred bucks in debt, and suspected he had a dose.

Michael LaNew said he worked in the munitions shop in the 8th Tactical Fighter Wing. He let it be known that he didn't like his job (as a missile propellant specialist), his boss (Tech Sergeant Bob Crowder), the base (Ubon Royal Thai Air Force Base), or the United States Air Force. He did like booze and submissive Thai girls. He had, he said, three and a half years in toward a four-year hitch and he wanted the last six months to go as fast and painless as possible.

"An' it's a fucked-up war," LaNew said to his companion. He turned and blinked owlishly. "Wha's your name again?"

"Ah, my name is John. Listen, I got something a little better than this stuff. Let's go back to the hootch and we can light up," Shawn Bannister said. He had been drinking the sharp Filipino beer.

Michael LaNew looked indignant. He drew himself up to his full five-foot, nine-inch height. "Whaddiya, some kinda faggot or something?" He huffed and expanded his chest. "An' I don't smoke no dope, ya got that, huh?" He poked Shawn on his breastbone with a stiff forefinger.

"Okay," Shawn Bannister said, pushing the man's hand down. "So yeah, I smoke a little dope. But I'm no faggot, anything but. I like girls, and plenty of them." He waved his hand at the half-dozen or so slender Thai bar-girls in the room. They all had flawless bronze complexions, dark lively eyes framed by long black hair, and wore one-piece miniskirt shifts and sandals.

LaNew looked appreciatively at the girls. "Ain' they cute? Now thas some real sweet stuff."

Shawn saw craving on the airman's face. "Listen," he said, "what say we get a couple and take them to my hootch. My treat."

"Show me yer ID," LaNew said suddenly.

"What for?"

"Show me yer goddamn ID. I wanna know who the hell you are before I go anyplace with you." LaNew's eyes were red and slitted.

Shawn thought quickly. He had to take a calculated risk to reel in this fish he needed so desperately. "Okay, sure," he said, and pulled out his wide traveler's wallet from the left front pocket of his safari suit. He made a point of thumbing through the several American hundred-dollar bills and the red Thai hundred-baht notes. Finally, he produced a battered Nevada driver's license and handed it to LaNew. His MACV journalist's accreditation card was in his other pocket, along with his press card from the *California Sun.*

LaNew squinted at the card. "Sez 'Shawn,' not John." He looked up. "Wha' the hell is yer name? How do I know yer not a commie spy or from OSI or the Air Police or sump'n?"

"OSI?" Shawn said. He was stalling for time, as he tried to assess the best way to get this man's confidence. He had been hanging out at the bar several nights a week for the past two weeks, trying to make friends with the airmen and aircrew who hung out there. So far they all had been very cliquish and had not let him in. He had found he had to trim his hair to the shorter military style.

"Yeah, OSI," LaNew said. "You know, Office of Special Investigation. They're allas messing roun' with us." He had forgotten his question about Shawn's name.

Shawn laughed. "No, I'm not a commie spy or from the OSI." He took a chance. "I'm a journalist. I'm always looking for a good story." He stared LaNew in the eye. "A good story is worth a lot to me."

LaNew's eyes grew piggy and slitted. "Oh yeah?"

"Yeah," Shawn Bannister said. "And money is no object."

"Oh yeah?" LaNew said, and crossed his arms. "Prove it."

1345 Hours Local, Tuesday, 21 November 1967
Room 3S, Soi 175/32
Ubon Ratchitani, Thailand

☆

"Yes, Mr. Shawn," Souky said three days later, "they say they are very happy with the article you wrote for the *Nhan Dan* newspaper." She wore sandals and a knee-length shift of light green Thai silk. She carried a white plastic shopping bag with red Thai lettering on it. She had already given Shawn Bannister a large sack of Buddha's Burmese Best.

Shawn Bannister didn't want to light up just yet. He had his feet up on the plank desk, facing Ubon Air Base through the open window. Sweat ran in rivulets down his bare chest. He stubbed a cigarette, reached down to an ice chest, took out a bottle of Tiger beer, and popped the cap with an opener. He wiped the opening with his hand and took a long pull. He swung around to face his Thai contact.

"It's the first time the fact those missiles misfire so much has been reported, isn't it?" he said. "And did they like the part about the number and type of bombs that go out from here each day? And the fact I included all the call signs in my article? They liked all that, did they?"

Shawn Bannister had finally figured out the pilot and control tower jargon and how to recognize the bombs and missiles carried under the dozens of Phantoms that thundered off the runway each day. From bar talk, he had learned that the AIM-7 and AIM-9 missiles suffered from humidity and short shelf life, causing rocket motor and guidance problems.

He coupled those bits of information, with what he had learned by listening in on other conversations at Tippy's Bar. Then he had written a long article for Souky to give, along with photos, to the newspaper people from North Vietnam with whom Nguyen Vo Tri had arranged contact. He had taken the pictures through the window with a 300mm telephoto lens on his Nikon 350. As a hedge, he had also sent a copy of both the photos and the article to the *California Sun*. The copy he had sent to the *Sun* he titled *Secret War of the Air Force*. It would be two or more weeks before he would hear from the *Sun*. In less than 36 hours, he had heard from Souky that the Hanoi newspaper people were very happy.

"They like your report on the airplanes, Mr. Shawn, yes. Very much," Souky said. She regarded him with soft eyes from under her black bangs. Shawn misinterpreted the look. He took a pre-rolled marijuana cigarette from a tin box and lit up.

"Well, that's just great. Now it's time to celebrate." He went to sit next to her. He buried smoke deep in his lungs before slowly letting it out. "Have one," he said. He stroked her knee with one hand and put the other on a small breast.

Souky stiffened and pressed her lips together. With that one motion, she lost her shy Thai female look. Her face looked hard and speculative, as if she were a street vendor trying to decide just how far to pluck the brash tourist. Then she realized what she had done and tried to soften her face, and her voice.

"Mr. Shawn"—she put a hurt look in her eyes—"do not get angry with me, but I . . . I do not do those things." Souky twisted her body away from him. She was lying. She had been a top agent of the CPT, Communist party of Thailand since her early teens and would do anything, use her body—even cooperate with the Vietnamese—to bring down the monarchy in her country. She had been recruited as a schoolgirl in a terribly poor northern Thai province by the CPT, trained in revolutionary tactics in China, and now functioned in whatever capacity the CPT desired. She had used her body before and, in all likelihood, would again. That didn't mean she liked it. She was thankful it was not now necessary. This American was already hooked for Party use through his own excesses. "I do not want," she said, pushing his insistent hand away. "I do not want."

Anger flitted across his face. He was not used to being turned down by girls, regardless of who they were. Certainly not some back-country slut like this. Shawn grasped her arm. "Well, then tell me what the hell you do want. How do you fit into all this? What are you doing acting as a contact for the Viet Cong or the North Vietnamese, or whomever? You're not in the newspaper business. What *do* you want?"

In a lithe move, she slipped out from under his hands and stood up. "Oh, Mr. Shawn, it is not what I want. It is what *they* want. And they want more. More articles about the airplanes."

"More?" Shawn echoed. He slammed his fist on his knee. "What the hell for? I've already done the article they wanted. How about my visa to Hanoi? When can I go up there? And what about the big story?"

Souky looked blank.

"Oh, I don't know, Mr. Shawn. I don't know about visa to Hanoi, or big story." She pronounce it "suh-torry." "They just tell me to tell you they want more. Maybe then you can go to Hanoi."

"Who are *they*?" Shawn said. "Who are your local contacts that tell you all this? I want to talk to them." The scowl on his face framed his mouth with inverted half circles.

"Please," she said. "I must go now. You do not need to be interested in these things. You write good articles. Write more. I will contact you in three days. You must write more." Before he could make a move, she was out the door.

His scowl deepened. He drew heavily on the fat marijuana cigarette, and stared without focusing through the window at the Ubon
runway. Planes were taxiing out, engines whining in the distance like
giant insects. Others, landing on the parallel runway, had white drag
chutes wagging and spinning behind them.

A thought, a questioning, started to surface in his mind. Where *do*
I fit into all this? What *am* I doing here? His thoughts ranged out and
back. Then he shook his head, and refused to pursue the self-
questioning. He didn't like the conclusion that would so obviously
follow. The conclusion that he was no longer a reporter. The conclusion that he was sliding into the murk and fog of . . . he couldn't say
the word. He put it all out of his mind.

To erase his thoughts, he stood up and stared hard out the window.
He focused on the Phantoms. They looked deadly and warlike. Un-
bidden, a picture of Court Bannister seated in one of those planes
formed in his mind. He saw his half brother sitting there in his flying
clothes and helmet, oxygen mask swinging free as he talked with
somebody on a ladder to the cockpit. It became clear that that someone was their father, a smiling Sam Bannister. Shawn's upper lip
drew back. He stood more erect, his chest swelled. His scowl slowly
disappeared, as his famous grin appeared. He nodded. It was clear
now. I'm just a reporter doing what reporters do, he said to himself.
And reporters gather intelligence information. He nodded again,
question resolved.

He hummed happily in a tuneless buzz and pulled out his radio
and binoculars from the chest. He began to write what he heard and
saw with sharp, stabbing motions. The wide grin never left his face.

1930 Hours Local, Tuesday, 21 November 1989
Coordinates WE77244543
Royalty of Laos

☆

The storm had broken over the cave holding Wolf and his team.
Thunder echoed through the steep pass like massed cannon fire.
Sheet lightning strobed the karst mountains and green jungle fronds
in eye-searing sheets. The heavy rain sounded like dozens of freight
trains roaring through the night. Inside the tiny cave, Wolf and Roland, two Nungs, and Buey Dan were reasonably warm and only
slightly damp. They were holed up at the western lip of Mu Gia Pass.
The entrance to the cave was concealed with large interwoven tree
leaves and palm fronds, which kept the rain out while providing cover.
Rhoades and a Nung were on sentry duty. Inside, they had arranged

ponchos and rucksacks around a depression lined with rocks they had scooped from the sandy cave floor. Burning chunks of the putty-like C4 explosive heated tea and a freeze-dried soup. The heat had burned some of the humidity from the air. The tiny blaze also provided just enough flickering light for the occupants to see. Seven days had passed since their night jump into Laos. This was their first night not sleeping in the jungle.

"This is real living," said Frenchy Roland. He leaned back against his pack and took another sip of the strong Chinese tea.

Wolf Lochert looked up from the small green booklet in which he was writing. "Just don't get used to it," he growled. "This is a one-night stand. If it weren't for the rain, we'd still be in the woods. And tomorrow, rain or no rain, we're going back in the woods." He gestured with his pencil and returned to his writing.

"Of course, it would be nice if we could build a real fire and dry us and all this stuff out," Roland said. All their gear was damp and spongy and moldy. Constant rubbing and oiling kept their weapons ready.

"Yeah, and the NVA and spotters from the road-repair teams would be on us in a heartbeat," Wolf said. He gave a final stab at the pad and tore a sheet out and gave it to Roland. "Get this off when the antenna is dry." The outside antenna wire for the PRC-25 was wet and grounding out. Besides being a medic and a demo expert, Frenchy Roland was a communications specialist.

The seven men had parachuted in with seven radios: four PRC-25 FMs, and three pocket-sized RT-10 USAF survival radios that transmitted on guard channel. One PRC-25 had been damaged beyond repair on landing and had been kept for parts. Two of the other three had been acting up. The '25s were the size of two shoeboxes stacked on each other and yielded good ground-to-ground jungle comm up to about 10 miles. It also provided excellent ground-to-air results if the airplane overhead carried FM equipment, which fighters did not, but most liaison and support aircraft did. The team carried a booster which, when coupled to a PRC-25 using a long-wire antenna, increased the range considerably, though the resultant power drain was hard on the batteries. The RT-10s were half the size of a cigarette carton and were for last-ditch communications with any aircraft under emergency conditions that was within line of sight.

Team Dakota made radio contact three times a day with friendly forces: a brief "we're still alive" check-in every twelve hours via PRC-25 with airborne USAF command posts, and a situation report once every 24 hours with Group Headquarters at Nha Trang, using the boosted PRC-25. To reach Nha Trang, radio site Hickory, hidden on a Laotian mountaintop called Eagle's Nest, relayed the messages from

Wolf's team and others operating in Laos. The team had been shocked the second day out when Hickory had relayed that their C-130 drop plane had never made it back to Da Nang.

The sheet Wolf handed Frenchy Roland contained the 24-hour sit rep for Nha Trang. Using the one-time pad code, it told the commander of the 5th Special Forces Group that their location was WE77244543, all team members were healthy, they would be moving northeast to the border of North Vietnam at first light, and that southbound traffic on the Ho Chi Minh Trail at night was as heavy as the San Diego freeway at rush hour. It ended with the statement "Negative White Hat," which meant they had sighted no American captives or signs of shot-down crewmen trying to escape and evade.

Over 120 Americans had been downed in Laos; although many had been picked up, scores had been killed in the crashes and 40 or so were thought to be captured. Several sightings had been made of bound POWs in the Sam Neui area way north of Mu Gia, but rescue attempts had ended in disaster. It was a known fact that if the USAF Jolly Greens or the Navy rescue helicopters didn't get over the downed airman in fifteen minutes, his chances for rescue diminished immensely.

So far, Wolf's information had resulted in only five air strikes in the six days they had been in the field. The problem was not finding targets, it was getting the information to the airborne command posts—code-named Hillsboro during the day, Moonbeam at night. The PRC-25s had not been putting out full power. Frenchy said maybe they had a bad lot of batteries.

When they did get through, it went very well. Hillsboro could process the strike request in minutes. Then an airborne forward air controller would be over the target area to control the strike; within fifteen minutes, strike planes would be rolling in. Commander, 7th Air Force, while delivering his part of the bargain—the airplanes— was wondering why Team Dakota didn't use more air. As it was, Team Dakota could have used five times as many airplanes over the six-day period, if only their radios had worked better. There was no chance of a resupply for a team buried this deep under cover.

Wolf looked at his watch. Time for the 2000 hours radio check on the PRC-25 with Moonbeam. He crawled to the cave mouth, told Frenchy to cover the tiny blaze, and poked the whip antenna of a PRC-25 through the opening.

"Moonbeam, Three One Five, radio check," he transmitted. He used a predetermined three-number set each day that involved the day of the month, time of day, and whether he was transmitting under duress or not. Moonbeam answered on the third try.

"Three One Five, Moonbeam, faint but clear. Any activity?"

"Negative. One Five out."

"Moonbeam out."

The team in Laos kept their radio transmissions to the minimum, not only to save battery power, but because it was known that the NVA had triangulation equipment.

Outside, Rhoades and a Nung maintained a watch. Because of the 3,600-foot elevation and the down-slope of the karst, there was no rotted base vegetation clinging to the mountainside. The trees were widely spaced and formed only a single canopy. They sat under trees twenty feet outside the camouflaged cave mouth. Rhoades faced downhill, the Nung looked up the slope to the lip of the crest. Water dripped off their floppy jungle hats onto the rubber groundsheet each had wrapped about him. Each kept one eye pinched shut with his fingers to save his night vision during the rapid lightning flashes. Besides an assault rifle with a taped muzzle, each carried a knife, water, and ammo pouches on his web gear, and grenades in their pockets. Their bulky harnesses and rucks were secure and dry in the cave. When the roar of the rain would slacken, they could hear the grind and chugging of straining engines, as supply trucks made their way south along the canyon floor of Mu Gia Pass.

Roland poked the burning C4 as Wolf crawled back into the circle of flickering light, and he leaned back against his ruck and glanced at his watch. He and a Nung were to relieve Rhoades in two hours. He rubbed his eyes.

"We could sure have used more fighters," Roland said, and yawned.

"Particularly at night," Wolf said. "Even the few we got in the day has made them start to slow down, but night traffic is something else. I think hundreds of those trucks are moving on the Trail at any given time after dark. I wish there was a way to conduct night strikes." He turned to the Vietnamese. "Beedee, you been awful quiet this trip. You feeling poorly?"

Buey Dan shook his head. "No, Thieu Ta, I am well. It is the rain perhaps." He kept his eyes averted.

Wolf leaned back and closed his eyes. Roland slept, face to the dirt wall. The two Nungs were asleep. Buey Dan stared into the tiny blaze. He imagined himself taking the stiletto from his pack and driving it in the belly of bulky Lochert, just as the *mui lo* had done to his son. Imperceptibly, he shook his head. First he had to sabotage the mission slowly so that the Americans at the headquarters knew this method did not work. Then, when that was so, he would destroy the whole team, Lochert last . . . slowly.

Activity on the night shift in the frag shop at Seventh Air Force Headquarters increased as the daily quota of strike messages from CINCPAC were decoded.

24

☆

Hostettler had been up since three in the morning preparing his briefing from the sheaves of coded teletype strike orders from Tan Son Nhut. He felt good. Life had improved considerably under Colonel Stan Bryce. He no longer had extra duties as veterinary officer, postal officer, mess-hall inventory officer, or voting officer. He smiled. The troops would like today's lineup, he knew. They didn't mind hanging it out if the targets were worthwhile.

It was now three weeks since all the elements had fallen into place to allow Court Bannister and Flak Apple to go into the air together on a combat mission. Before that, the two majors had flown daily missions in North Vietnam and Laos, but always in separate flights. Court had flown all positions, from number Four to Lead, as he gained experience. He now had sixty-two missions and was strike-force commander-qualified.

The Russian pilot had been up and had scored, they had been told, but always at a time and place where Court or Flak had been on the ground. The USAF frag order was so insistent on raids in the Plaine des Jarres and increasing strikes on the Steel Tiger portion of the Ho Chi Minh Trail in Laos, in addition to North Vietnam, that Court and Flak had been able to arrange only two training flights together. Flak had flown combat with Colonel Bryce several times, both as leader and wingman. Bryce had finally assigned Court to Flak's weapons shop as an assistant tactics officer. Today, Court and Flak would be in the same flight of four.

Commander, 7th Air Force, was told by Blue Chip that Packard flight, a flight of four Phantoms headed for North Vietnam, had both

Apple and Bannister in it. He sat back in his thick brown leather chair behind his desk and remembered his conversation with them three weeks ago, when he had replaced Crepens with Bryce. Not for a moment did he wonder why he hoped Courtland Esclaremonde de Montségur Bannister of Albert Algernon Apple would be one of the two men who would nail the Russian pilot. He knew why he wanted them to score. Along with the Army and the Marines, the USAF was suffering some bad press. Either pilot—Bannister because his father was famous, or Apple because he was black—would get favorable headlines if he could make a spectacular shootdown. He was a little upset that they hadn't been more on the Ubon schedule for the northern missions, where the chances of spotting the Russian pilot were good. All of his fighter pilots, he knew, would give up the next two promotions and five years of flight pay to shoot down a MiG, double that if it was flown by a Russian. Not that his boys hated Russians; it was just that they would be far more worthy opponents. In fact, he thought, I'd like a crack at one myself.

Thirty-two F-4 crewmen—the Comanche strike force—assembled to hear Hostettler give his usual outstanding briefing. The frag order called for sixteen Ubon F-4s to strike a POL (Petroleum Oil, Lubricants) dump near Hanoi—big cheers—eight to be loaded with Sparrows, Sidewinders, and the gun for MiG capping—bigger cheers. Hostettler gave the final Wild Weasel information and the briefing was over. It took 48 minutes. There were no spare aircraft or pilots. The heavy ops tempo didn't permit it.

Then Colonel Stan the Man Bryce bounded onto the stage. He was a well-built man, six feet tall, with sharp gray eyes, an aggressive upthrust chin, and he played a mean game of handball. He had lifted all the bar restrictions and occasionally drank a beer or two with the boys. He had been flying missions about twice a week, usually leading a flight or an element. He liked flying with men of experience such as Flak Apple. He had too much paperwork on his desk to do any of the pre-planning, he had told Flak, so he'd just given him his flight card and told him to keep him out of trouble. Stan Bryce always flew with one of the three most experienced back-seaters in the Wing. The consensus was that he might be just a tad too eager to be a rough, tough combat commander. Exuberance unbalanced by skill could lead to trouble.

"We've got a great target today," Bryce said. "The Hanoi oil tanks, and you are just the guys that can get it. It's a JCS target and the big eye is on us. That's just fine, because you guys are good, very good. I know you're good and you know you're good." He paused, hands on hips, and seemed to look at each man. "I know you can lick anything up there. You bombers will take the tanks out, and you MiG cappers will take the MiGs out, and we'll all be back for beer call."

He looked around, then gave an upraised fist boxing motion. "LET'S GO DO IT, COMANCHE," he shouted. The aircrew cheered. This was more like it. He held up his hand for silence. "One last thing," he said in a quiet voice. "Don't do anything stupid. I want to see you all back here for beer call. Don't anybody get hurt."

Court and Flak, with their back-seaters and the four men flying the other two F-4s in Packard flight, rode out together in the blue crew van to their airplanes. Ev Stern was with Court. They were very comfortable together now. Court was even letting him take off and land the Phantom every other mission.

The eight members of Packard flight filled the two wooden bench seats with their bulky gear and helmet bags crammed with maps and charts and kneeboards. Their twelve-pound survival vests hung on them like green mesh flak jackets. The morning coolness had fled the flight line the minute the sun rose up over the revetments. The wing-men weren't aware that they had been specially chosen the night before from a pool of ten put together by Court and Flak. They knew something was up, because Court and Flak had told them in the briefing they would have one final word to say at the airplanes. They all got out of the van, sometimes called the bread truck because it had the same general outline, and stood by Flak's airplane. Flak Apple was Packard Lead today. He and Court had been alternating Lead the few times they'd flown together.

The eight men stood in a loose circle, each garbed in a light cotton flight suit, a heavy canvas G-suit with rubber bladders, a heavy sur-vival vest (covered by a parachute harness) worn unsnapped until in the cockpit, a webbed belt with holstered gun (each to his own) and cartridges. Each man wore a crushed blue ball cap with their squad-ron insignias and straight-framed aviator's sunglasses. Court had taken to wearing his Stetson whenever he was assigned 753, his F-4, which was often. Sergeant Shanahan would carefully guard the hat for him, then hand it to him when he returned. When he wasn't scheduled to fly an airplane other than 753, he left his Stetson in the locker room. He always wore his red, white, and blue Mike Force scarf from his Bien Hoa days. Although the men wore their scarves around the base and in the squadron, they would take them off and put them in their helmet bags before takeoff. They had good reasons for doing this; the scarf could tangle on something during or after a bailout, and they might provide a clue to a captor as to where the man was from. The North Vietnamese would find out soon enough, using the rope tor-ture, but there was no point in giving anything away. The scarves would be destroyed with the helmet bag in a crash.

On their feet they wore thick wool socks and either standard GI jungle boots or black Air Police boots. Strapped to each man was a K-bar knife and 150 feet of thin nylon strapping attached to a lowering device for exiting tall tress from hung-up parachute canopies. Crammed into G-suit pockets were extra survival-radio batteries, small and large flares, water flasks, extra tracer ammo for their gun, an olive-drab towel to use as a sweat rag, and a spare survival radio. Under their flight suits, everyone now wore light cotton shorts and foliage-green T-shirts. Only new guys wore white. On their harnesses they hung two baby bottles fresh from the freezer compartment of the squadron refrigerator. They would suck on them on the way out as the ice melted even before they took off. The eight members of Packard flight ranged in age from 24—a new back-seater from Lafayette, Louisiana—to Flak Apple, who had been born 36 years ago in Washington, D.C. Between the eight of them, they totaled over 10,000 hours flying time, all of the time in training and in fighters starting at Nellis outside of Las Vegas and Luke at Phoenix. There were no ex-MAC or SAC in this flight. It simply wouldn't have been fair. They just would not have had the years of fighter flying required to make the actual manipulation of the controls of the twenty-five-ton Phantoms as effortless and as automatic as riding a bicycle. Nor did they have SA—situational awareness.

And there is an additional demand on the experienced pilots. The flight lead had to control from two to four airplanes; the strike force leader was responsible for as many as 48. This was not a place for a man whose previous pilot duties had included making coffee, and whose pilot chair could slide back and forth but not eject.

"Listen up, guys," Flak Apple began his final words to his flight, "there is one each blue-helmeted Russkie up there stooging around Hanoi, that one of us is going to nail today. Whoever is in position gets the shot. That goes for you wingmen, not just me and Court." The two wingmen, young captains with over eighty missions each, made wide grins of approval. Flak looked at the GIBs. Their faces were so smooth-shaven and their hair cut so short, Flak noted, that they looked like doolies at the Academy. "You guys help your front-seater and we'll all be back at the bar in a few hours. Don't do anything different today," he went on. "Just do what we've been teaching you. Spread out and stay alert."

Flak and Court had introduced the spread, line-abreast formation. They had picked it up from the earlier MiG killers, who were now trying to get the tactics accepted by the USAF and put into the training curriculum. It was quite different from welded wing, where a wingman tacked on to his leader and tried to follow him through every gyration in the book, and some not in the book, as leaders pushed the envelope with their big Phantoms. Often as not, the wingman was so intent hanging on that he lost his ability to look around. The new formation assumed that everybody was combat-proficient and didn't have to fly wing because of inexperience.

In addition, they were flying with the new electronic countermeasures pod now. The spacing not only enhanced the search pattern, it enhanced the masking the QRC-160 pod provided.

Major Flak Apple looked at each man. "Let's go get 'em," he said in a quiet voice. They turned toward their airplanes. He hung back for one last word with Court. Assuming the aggressive stance of Stan the Man Bryce on the stage, he waggled a finger. " 'Don't anybody get hurt,' " he said, rolled his eyes, and strolled to his F-4. That was not a statement a leader should make to his troops before a combat mission.

Court and Ev Stern made an exacting pre-flight then patted the white hat. It had brought them through a lot. Sergeant Shanahan had already been over 753 with his critical eye and fingers. Yet he did not begrudge the walk-around made by the two pilots. He wanted pilots to walk around his airplane and look everywhere, because by God they weren't going to find the smallest item misaligned or out of tune. He was proud of his bird and his ability to make his bird fly, and he wanted his pilots to know it.

Next to each airplane was a large, yellow, self-powered cart, about the size of a Volkswagen. It carried a small jet engine, which supplied air under pressure to the engines of the Phantoms, and electrical current to power the systems while they did their pre-start cockpit checks.

Once the exterior check was completed and Court's hat carefully stowed, Shanahan and his assistant crew chief mounted the yellow metal ladders with Court and Ev, and helped them strap in. Each pilot placed his hands on the canopy rim and the front bow to ease himself down into his seat, which was already occupied by a seatpack full of survival gear and a backpack full of nylon parachute. The entire seat, with pilot and his gear, weighed 470 pounds and could be rocketed up with a 14-G push to no less than 180 feet above the ground from an unmoving airplane and still have a functioning parachute shot out from the backpack. The rocket seat was made by the British company of Martin-Baker. Sir James Martin had thrown a party at the Dorchester in London two years before in honor of the first 1,000 successful ejectees. He was a very popular manufacturer, even without his parties.

Shanahan and his assistant helped each pilot attach himself to the craft by two hoses (one for oxygen to his mask, one for pressured air to his G-suit), three wires (radio headsets and microphone to his helmet), survival pack clips, lap belt, shoulder harness, and two calf garters to keeps his legs from flailing about during a high-speed ejection.

Court clipped his kneeboard to his right leg and donned his helmet, snapped the oxygen mask in place, and pulled on his gloves.

"How do you read?" he said over the intercom to Ev Stern in his back seat.

"Loud and clear," Ev replied.

Court went through his pre-start cockpit checklist. It contained 37 items, ranging from generator control switches "On" and rudder pedals "Adjusted," to fuel boost pump checks and missile control panel settings. In the rear cockpit, Ev performed 33 checks.

Court began the engine start sequence.

"How do you read, Chief?" he asked over the intercom to Sergeant Shanahan, who stood to the left of the big Phantom wearing giant earpieces and a cupped microphone strapped to his face like an old gas mask.

"Loud and clear, sir. Ready to start," Shanahan said. Court gave him the windup signal with his left forefinger. Shanahan motioned his assistant to open the air valve. The little jet engine wound up to a shriek and the 12-inch flex tubing leading under the aircraft to the right engine, writhed like a giant black and yellow snake, then steadied, rigid with pressure. At 10 percent RPM, Court depressed the right ignition start button with his right hand while advancing the right throttle with his left. He released the button, as the exhaust gas temperature showed a rise, and he felt a rumble deep in the airplane. When the right-hand RPM gauge climbed through 45 percent, he signaled Shanahan to disconnect the air and pull the thick black electrical cable. With practiced motions, the assistant crew chief switched off the air and the electrical current, then scrambled under the belly of the big Phantom to disconnect the tube and cable.

In the cockpit, Court checked his RPM as it stabilized at 65 percent. He monitored the engine and hydraulic gauges approaching the green markings on their dials, to check at a fast glance that all was well. He noted low fuel pressure during the start, which meant he had the latest engine modification of the cool-start fuel-control cams to prevent overheat. He put his generator switch on, and repeated the sequence to start the left engine.

Next, Court went through the 15-step before-taxi check, which included checking his radio and navigation gear. Finally, in conjunction with Sergeant Shanahan, he cycled the hydraulic systems.

"Speed brakes," Shanahan said.

"Cycling," Court responded, as he thumbed them down, then back up after Shanahan inspected them.

The two men went through the same routine with the wing flaps, the aileron, elevator, and rudder flight controls, a stabilizer augmentation device, and the takeoff trim to position the big elevator slabs. Finally, Court signaled Shanahan to disconnect and pull the wheel chocks. The crew chief did as requested, then stepped back, came to a ramrod-straight position of attention, and gave his pilot a very spiffy salute. Court responded, then each man gave the other a thumbs-up.

As Court advanced the throttles to move the big jet from the revetment, he and Shanahan stared for a moment into each other's eyes, in the glance reserved exclusively for those who fly and their crew chiefs. It had been so since the first Nieuport and Fokker had taxied out on grass. It happened among the good ones. They knew each other. If one could check, it would probably prove out to have been the same look given between squire and knight before battle. The look from the pilot was an affirmation of trust that his crew chief had done all there was, and then some, to ensure his plane was safe for flight and combat. The return look from the crew chief was his bond that he had done so. It was understood that the pilot would use the craft to the utmost of his ability for the purpose intended. Were either man pressed to acknowledge this intimate exchange, he would scoff and change the subject. But God help the man who maligned the chief or the pilot in front of the other. This is how it is among the good ones.

The big Phantom was now ready to do what 1,900 people had spent seven months in a building longer than three football fields in St. Louis, Missouri, building it for: to fly and to fight.

The four Phantoms pulled into the armament area near the runway, and stopped parallel to the rest of the Comanche airplanes. The pilots kept their hands outside the cockpit in plain view of the master sergeants who ran that portion of the mission. One false move, stray voltage, or pin pulled at the wrong moment could lead to catastrophe. Three years before at Bien Hoa, many airmen had died and several planes had been destroyed in the arming area due to a faulty move.

The only in-cockpit movement permitted was when a missile specialist held a flashlight a few feet in front of each Aim-9 heat-seeker. A moveable eyeball in each seeker head followed the heat from the light bulb as it was rotated to the limits of the missile's scanning view. In the cockpit, each pilot moved his missile switch and listened to the tone, as the seeker element of each missile growled out an urgent tone that it had a lock-on.

In moments, all the airplanes at Ubon had their release. They sat, lined up, waiting for clearance onto the runway. "Button up," Court said to Ev Stern. Each man lowered the big clamshell canopy over his head to chunk down onto the rails next to his shoulders, then pushed the locking lever home. Court had to ensure that both engines were at idle, so that excess air pressure didn't prematurely inflate the canopy lock seals, forcing a false lock. The "canopy unlocked," lights went out. They could feel in their ears the cockpit pressurize.

"Let's do the doughnuts," Court told Ev. Each pulled a grease pencil from his sleeve pocket, then positioned his head in the normal attitude of combat flight, that is, slightly forward and head up. On either side of the canopy, at the ten o'clock and two o'clock positions, each drew a small circle around their view of a pre-selected object at a distance of 1,000 feet. In the air, whenever either pilot wanted to put the eyes of the other on an object too small to point out readily, and he had the time, he would position his doughnut over it. They inscribed their doughnuts, and were soon cleared onto the runway.

After Court taxied onto the runway as Packard Three, he and Ev Stern began their challenge-and-response-before-takeoff litany. Ev called out the checklist items, and Court responded with his action.

"Stab aug."

"Three on."

"Flight controls."

"Free and clear." Court moved the stick to all corners.

"Trim."

"Two units down, set for takeoff."

"Canopies: canopy closed, light out," Ev continued the litany.

"Closed and out," Court responded.

"Seat armed." Ev moved the lever to arm his ejection seat.

"Armed." Court did the same.

"IFF."

"On." Court activated a device that would give coded signals on demand to radar controllers.

"Pitot heat."

"On." Court turned on the heater for the external probe that measured air pressure and velocity.

"Left engine check."

"Checking." Court manipulated the throttle from idle to high RPM and back down again, checking gauges, acceleration, temperatures, and pressures. At high RPM, Ev looked out at the big slab of metal ramp next to the giant air intake for the engine. It moved as more air was demanded. "Left ramp okay," he told Court. They did the same for the right engine.

"Wing flaps."

"Half down." Court positioned the lever.

"Anti-skid."

"On."

"Fuel transfer switches."

"Normal and outboard."

"Warning lights."

Each man took one last look around the cockpit. There were no warning lights illuminated.

"Shoulder harness," Ev said, reading the last item on the before-takeoff checklist.

"Locked," Court said, and looked out at the other three airplanes.

Packard flight was lined up on the runway in a staggered manner such that no exhaust and jet blast impacted the other. At takeoff thrust, with both afterburners roaring like smelter stacks and burning 40,000 pounds of fuel each per minute, the gas the engines generated left the exhaust nozzles at 3,000 degrees and a velocity twice the speed of sound. Twenty feet back, the temperature was still 1,600 degrees and the velocity 1,100 miles per hour.

As Packard Lead, Flak Apple gave the windup signal to his wingman by rotating his right forefinger. Court repeated the signal to his wingman. By making as many signals as possible by hand waves and head nods, the pilots did not clutter up the radio. However, any attempt to preserve radio silence that might give them the edge of surprise had long since gone by the board. There were simply too many ears and eyes in the loop that started in the frag shop at Tan Son Nhut and extended to tankers and airborne control ships, as well as the fighters. The only surprise a strike force could mount was a last-minute turn after a feint toward another target.

Court gave the signal, then ran his throttles up to the stops. He held his brakes for a second, as he and Ev did a last-minute check, then, with a head nod to his wingman, he released his brakes. With another head nod, he moved both throttles outboard to engage the afterburners. With that motion, the eyelids at the tailpipe of each engine opened wider, as raw fuel sprayed into the burners was ignited, providing 75 percent more thrust. It was wasteful of fuel, but it accelerated a heavy airplane off the ground to climb-out speed in a hurry. Some heavily loaded airplanes couldn't get off the ground without AB. The afterburners could only be engaged after brake release, because their combined thrust was so great they would skid the airplane along on locked wheels.

There were more checks to perform, even as they were rolling down the runway. Certain systems had to be fully engaged and operable; oil, fuel flow, boost, exhaust temp and nozzles had to be checked; airspeeds had to be met at precalculated distances; nose-wheel rotation and aircraft lift-off speeds had to be adhered to. Ev called the inlet ramps fully retracted. The 25-ton Phantom accelerated from zero to 200 miles per hour (which Court read as 175 knots on his airspeed indicator) in 22 seconds and covered one mile of runway. They passed go–no-go speed (141 knots), refusal speed (158 knots), nose-wheel lift-off speed (165 knots), and at 172 knots the Phantom lifted off the runway. After a few seconds to make sure they were going to stay airborne, Court raised the gear, then the flaps. In seconds, they reached 350 knots, the speed at which the flight leader comes out of burner. Court, as did the other three flight members, came out of burner at 400 knots to give him a rapid overtake. Flak made a right turn to head out over Laos toward the Gulf of Tonkin. All three ships joined on him in close fingertip formation in less than three minutes. Flak checked them over, then fishtailed his airplane as a signal to spread out as they began the climb to 28,000 feet.

The men relaxed in their cockpits and took a few seconds to flex and limber themselves from the strain. Using his radar, Flak stayed in a three-mile trail with the flight in front. His flight, Packard, was the fourth in the strike force stream of four flights. The other MiG CAP flight was in the number two position.

The plan was to cut across Laos and South Vietnam just south of the DMZ, refuel with Tan tanker over the water, then head north-northwest toward Hanoi and Pack Six. They would make a feint at Vinh, halfway up the coast to Hanoi, then another at Nam Dinh, before swinging into the POL complex four miles west of Hanoi. Split-second timing was required to get in just as the Weasels were pulling off the local defenses.

What they didn't know was that, the night before, a flight of four MiG-21s had been ferried to the small airfield near the town of Vinh. *Truncate*, the highly secret listening post, knew of the move and had so informed *Green Door*, the small USAF intelligence branch buried in an unmarked room in 7th Air Force Headquarters. The branch chief of *Green Door*, a lieutenant colonel career intelligence officer, decided the very timeliness of the information made it impossible to pass on to the operators. To do so would reveal to the operators, that is, the Navy and Air Force crewmen who might be flying that day, that the U.S. had a method for real-time voice interception and interpretation in close proximity to North Vietnam. And that, *Green Door* knew, was a highly classified, eyes-only secret that he was charged with keeping. Keep it he would. He decided to wait 48 hours before passing the news of the deployment of four MiG-21s to Vinh.

0915 Hours, Wednesday, 22 November 1967
Temporary Shelter Mot Tam
Airfield Vinh
Democratic Republic of Vietnam

☆

Pod-Palcovnik Vladimir Nicholaevych Chernov gave his last bit of advice to Toon, Van Bay, and Vong before they walked to their waiting MiG-21s. They were under a canvas overhang slung from a concrete bunker. The air was stifling and dusty. The ancient French hand-cranked telephone had just passed the words that a big American air armada was heading toward Vinh and maybe points north. Intelligence said they were twelve bombers and maybe as many as eight fighter-configured Phantoms from Ubon. Chernov was allowed to try his over-water intercept that might allow him and his MiGs to jump the Americans outside of their radar coverage. They had flown down from Gia Lam to land just at dusk the night before. Toon had led the flight, so that Chernov did not have to make any transmissions in his execrable Vietnamese.

"They will not be expecting us," Chernov said. "Although I don't think their radar coverage reaches this area, we cannot be sure. We will go in low, then split into two flights of two and attack the tail-end flights. Toon, you and Vong attack the second-to-last flight. If we have the advantage of surprise, and the kill envelope is correct, shoot all four of your missiles. I will lead Van Bay to do the same to the last flight. If we do this correctly, we will score four to eight kills." He grinned at the three pilots gathered around. Only he was sweating in the heat. "This day will be victorious," he said. "I am confident we are prepared and ready to kill the *khi dot*," he said, using the North Vietnamese slang "big monkey" for the Americans. We had better, Chernov thought to himself. Or it's off to Chita for me.

Sixteen minutes later, they were streaking low over the water ten miles off the coast, nearly upsetting fishing sampans as they headed on a southeast track to intercept the Americans. Using code words, the local radar site, Triumph Control, told them that radar had tracked the Americans at their eleven o'clock position forty kilometers away at 9,000 meters and closing. Chernov, flying number three, rechecked his armament switches. Each airplane had four missiles: two heat-seeking K-13s, two radar missiles, and one 23mm GsH gun with 200 rounds.

Chernov was tense and alert, but confident. His plan had been working. Since his talk with Colonel Huu four weeks ago, his MiG-21 force had scored seventeen victories. Of those, Toon had three in fourteen intercepts, and he had two in eight intercepts. The remaining victories were divided among Van Bay and the other pilots. In one week, Comrade General Kirsanov was due back for another visit. With luck, Chernov would have another late-night session with him. This time, in view of his success advising the North Vietnamese Air Force, he intended to ask forcefully to remain here, because it was combat and combat was where his heart lay.

Streaking low over the water, Chernov's flight was invisible to the forty Phantoms flying 5 miles above the ocean. The cone-shaped search system of the radar in the F-4 searched forward and slightly up and down, but could not paint the MiGs hidden in the ground clutter. Neither Crown up north nor Panama to the south at Da Nang could paint Chernov's MiGs. Triumph Control, however, had an excellent display of both their Migs and the Americans on its screens.

"Eleven o'clock high at 32 kilometers. Advise you start your acceleration and intercept," Triumph transmitted to Toon and his flight.

"Executing," Toon responded, and signaled the other pilots. All four men engaged their afterburners, accelerated beyond the speed of sound. As the Americans passed overhead, they planned to zoom up to engage the last two flights of the American fighter stream.

Court was the first to spot them. "Packard, we got four MiGs," he said over the radio, in a surprised voice. "Eleven o'clock low and climbing."

"I don't have them," Flak Apple said. "Dodge, you got the MiGs?" Dodge was the second flight in the stream. He preferred Dodge to go after them, because he wanted Packard to go on the prowl in the Hanoi area for the MiG driver who wore a blue helmet.

"Negative," Dodge Lead replied.

"Are they in an attack curve, Packard Three?" Flak asked. "I still don't have them."

"Affirmative," Court replied.

"If you got 'em, you take the lead," Flak responded. There was no hint of disappointment in his voice. A MiG was a MiG was a MiG. Better one in the air than two on the ground. Even if he had to relinquish the lead.

"Packard flight, this is Three," Court transmitted in response to Flak's command. "I got the lead. Check switches on. Comanche, Packard is engaging." Court rolled up on a wing, preparatory to diving to the attack. He knew they were enemy, because no friendly forces would come from that direction. If there had been any doubt, he would have to move the flight into a position where they could positively identify the airplanes as MiGs. More than one Navy A-4 attack aircraft had been shot at because, to a nervous pilot, it resembled a MiG-21 at a distance.

"Good hunting, Packard," the strike force commander said. "Comanche, stay loose. Move your eyeballs." The Comanche strike force moved away from Packard flight, as Court led them down the chute toward the four climbing MiG-21s.

"Jettison tanks ... now," Court transmitted. "Double-check those switches."

Four sets of 375-gallon drop tanks tumbled off the wings of the Phantoms and flew back as the airplanes picked up speed in the dive. Each pilot rechecked his AIM-7 Sparrow switches first. This would be the best missile in a head-on attack, since it was radar-guided. Only after the Phantoms were on the tail of the MiGs could the infrared Aim-9 Sidewinders pick up and track a heat source. Court told Ev to leave the interlocks out, so he could fire a missile each time he depressed the pickle button. At that, a direct frontal attack by a radar missile was chancy because of the fast closure rate and the small frontal area reflecting radar energy from the attacking plane.

Chernov and Toon had practiced their climbing attack. Usually, it was from the rear and they were not spotted. This time, they had been seen, because Triumph had positioned them for a lead collision course, not a stern attack. To make it worse, the Americans were hidden in the morning sun.

Chernov swore as he alternately raised and lowered his sun visor. The phosphorous sweep of his R2L forward-searching radar was very dim and required he look down into a small hood. He had to raise his sun visor or he couldn't see the presentation at all. When he looked up out of the cockpit in the quadrant where the Americans had been reported, he had to lower his visor. Finally, by holding his thumb in front of him at just the right distance to block out the sun, he saw the American fighter stream. Then his eyes picked up the attacking Phantoms heading right at them. He had first seen the smoke smudge from the engines. Then they appeared as tiny as four specks of dust on his canopy.

Chernov transmitted to Toon. "They are in the sun. Four of them coming at us."

Toon knew what to do. They had practiced the maneuver for just such an event. "Split," he commanded. He pulled his plane sharply left and upward and his wingman followed. Chernov did the same, turning sharply to the right and up, and his wing man followed. They made their turns about forty-five degrees to the attacking flight path and never took their eyes off the four Phantoms that were growing in size every second. Their bent wings and drooping tails made them look like misshapen birds of prey diving on their target. When the time was right, Toon would give a command and the four MiGs would reverse course and catch the attacking Phantoms in a pincer movement. It was a basic fighter maneuver.

"Defensive split," Court transmitted to Packard flight. "Flak," he said, abandoning proper radio procedure in the heat of battle, "you take the northern two, I'll take the southern element. You got a visual on them yet?"

All four airplanes had the MiGs on radar, and now they were picking them up with their eyeballs. Court had had them in sight since he'd first spotted them at 22 miles. He was one of the few pilots blessed with phenomenal eyesight, and he used it to great advantage. His back-seaters became instant believers when their radar picked up the target at the range and azimuth he said it was.

"Roger," Flak sang out, "radar and visual." Because the MiGs had turned into their split, they were at an angle that presented more surface for the radar as well as the eyeballs.

Court checked his position. He could probably get one of the two MiGs below, but his wingman, Packard Four, had a slight advantage.

"Okay, Packard Four, take him, I've got you covered," Court transmitted and slid back to protect his new leader. "Tally ho," Packard Four said as he dove in.

"Giving away MiGs, Major?" Ev said. "Surprise, surprise." Court grunted.

"Missile away," Packard Four shouted, signaling he had fired a radar-guided AIM-7 Sparrow missile. One of the twelve-foot-long missiles dropped from its well in the fuselage of his Phantom. In less than half a second, the rocket motors of the 450-pound missile ignited with a gush of bright red flame longer than the missle itself. One and a half seconds later, the missile accelerated through Mach 2, leaving a streaming trail of thick white smoke etched across the sky as clean and pure as engraved crystal. The white smoke rippled and the beam-riding missile bobbled, as it checked the sides of the radar pencil beam from the radar dish in the nose of the Phantom. "Here's another," Packard Four said, as he fired again.

Chernov and his wingman, Van Bay, saw the first missile speeding in their direction. Chernov pulled up sharply, followed by Van Bay, and waited for the missile to start up after them. It did not. A circuit in its computer logic burned through, allowing the missile to track out to infinity. It would soon fall out of the sky. But the second missile, fired when the MiG was climbing, arced up immediately and came down toward Chernov's wingman with an inexorable certainty that sent him rolling into a screaming dive. Van Bay looked back. In the split second he had remaining to live, he knew he could not outmaneuver the homing missile now splitting the air at four times the speed of sound and heading directly at him. The 66-pound warhead exploded on contact, fragmenting a tight drum of continuous rod stainless steel wrapped around it into 2,600 fragments. The MiG-21's fuel and engine blew an instant later in a big dirty yellow fireball.

To the north, Toon was heading toward the fighter stream, hoping to lob some missiles at them from astern. He had lost the initial advantage, but was sure he could outrun the two F-4s that had dived toward him. He was too far away to see the number four man in his flight, Van Bay, be blown out of the air.

"I'm heading north after this guy," Flak said. Court turned his head quickly and saw Flak and his wingman arc up and away toward the two northern MiGs. He turned back to concentrate on the remaining MiG-21 in front of him. Below, he saw the debris spinning out of the black cloud caused by Packard Four's second Sparrow blowing the MiG-21 apart.

"Yahoo," Packard Four shouted.

"Okay, Four," Court transmitted. "I've got the lead. Nice shooting." Shit, he said inwardly, I probably could have gotten that MiG.

"What the hell," Ev exclaimed from the back seat as they watched Chernov's MiG. "Where's he going?"

Chernov had pulled his airplane up, then over Court and his wingman. In a flash, he was hidden in the sun and had height advantage. He instantly reversed course and triggered off two of his K-13A missiles. The first bobbled, then set on course toward Court's airplane. The second fell off the rail without igniting. Chernov looked carefully ahead of his one operating missile. He could easily see when the plane it was heading for should start an evasive maneuver. The only correct direction would be a climbing turn to the northeast, followed by a diving turn to the south and west once Chernov's missile committed to following the Phantom. Chernov kept his course, his radar still illuminating the Phantom, until he knew the missile could track the last mile alone. He turned his airplane south a few degrees and held his finger ready on the trigger for his 23mm cannon. When the time was right, he planned to squeeze off a long burst, seemingly into empty air. If the Phantom pilot did what was expected, he would fly into the burst.

"I've got it, I've got it," Court said to Ev. "No sweat."

"Okay. Boss," Ev said, confident now in his front-seater's prowess.

Then Court's wingman slid close to Court's airplane. He hadn't intended to. In trying to keep his position, as well as follow the enemy fighter somewhere in the direction of the sun—maybe he'd get two today—he'd had an instant of purple sun-blindness. His back-seater had his head buried in his scope, trying to break out a blip to the west, and didn't note the sliding action of his airplane.

Ev Stern, looking over his head and upside down now, as Court came over the top preparing to jink down and away from the missile tracking him, saw the belly of their wingman, also inverted, sliding up toward them, as fixed on course as a freight car on rails. Although both planes were tearing through the air at hundreds of miles an hour forward over five miles above the earth, the relative speed between the two was less than ten miles an hour. That made no difference. Neither pilot saw the other. Ev, hanging from his straps in the back seat, saw it all. He acted immediately, doing two things at once.

He snatched at the control stick with his right hand and the mike button on the throttle with his left. As he rolled and pulled the airplane away and down from the rising Phantom, he punched the button and yelled over the radio.

"BREAK DOWN, PACKARD FOUR, BREAK DOWN, BREAK DOWN."

Packard Four reacted instantly and pulled back sharply on his stick and, rolling into a turn, flew directly into Chernov's bullet stream aimed at Court. Seven of the 23mm shells, eight-inch slugs of high explosive, ripped along the wings and into the canopy, blowing the pilot's head into a mass of bone and pink tissue. The same shells disabled the rear ejection seat as they tore into the engine. The back-seater hammered only twice on the canopy before the left engine exploded, blowing his upper torso clear of the disintegrating airplane.

The missile tracking Court's airplane lost lock as he started south in his planned escape maneuver, but managed a re-lock the instant Ev pulled their Phantom away from the imminent collision with their wingman.

Yet Chernov's K-13 missile could not completely turn the corner with Court's airplane, so it did what its proximity fuse was pro-grammed to do when it passed within 33 feet—it exploded.

Most, but not all, of the fragments of the 13-pound warhead spun harmlessly into space from the spherical blast. A handful of cold rolled steel fragments zinged into the rear canopy and struck Ev Stern in the left arm and neck. There was a loud bang as the air pressure was lost through the holes. The air from the lungs of both pilots ex-hausted in a gasping rush. The white vapor of condensed air swirled around both cockpits once and was sucked out the holes. Court's and Ev's maps and cards from their kneeboards were sucked off and dashed about the cockpit. Air rushing by the holes emitted screeching whistles.

Court was shocked and confused, but knew he had to keep a G-load on the airplane until he could find the attacking MiG.

"Ev," he yelled into his mask, "Ev, are you okay?" He couldn't understand the mumble he heard in response to his cry. "Put your oxygen on a hundred percent," he called back to Ev. Although the oxygen system automatically supplied the required amount of oxygen mixed with ambient air upon demand, full oxygen under pressure would help Ev fight the rapid decompression and his injuries, what-ever they might be.

Court eased up on the G-load to look back over his left shoulder for the plane that had fired the missile. He saw the MiG, coming around in a hard left turn, maneuvering to fire another missile or his cannon. He also saw the pieces of Packard Four's airplane tumbling down far below.

"Ev," he called again into the intercom, "I'll get you out of here. Hang on." His only chance to clear the area was to accelerate down and away from the fight. He rapidly rolled level and jammed the control stick forward to lower the nose and unload. Above the cockpit noise, he thought he heard Ev scream. He slammed both throttles outboard for a few seconds of afterburner to gain enough airspeed to pull away from the MiG-21. He saw that his heading would take him on the most direct route across North Vietnam and Laos into Thailand and Ubon. In the back seat, metal fragments grated on Ev Stern's clavicle as the plane moved, and dark blood from his left subclavian vein oozed through his flight suit and drenched his survival vest.

Eight minutes had passed since Court had first called out the MiGs; five and a half minutes had passed since the first missile had been fired. Comanche strike force was now well over 100 miles to the north. Sixty miles behind them, Flak Apple and his wingman had zoomed up and were about to gain the advantage over Toon and his wingman, Vong. The fight between Court and the MiG had taken them 30 miles southwest of Vinh.

In his cockpit, Vladimir Chernov was sweating, but beginning to feel more confident. He had been pulling and turning and now, in just a few more degrees of turn, he would have the F-4 Phantom again in his sights. He was sure the last missile he had fired had caused some damage, because he had seen pieces and a smoke wisp stream from the Phantom after the explosion. Triumph Control could give him no vectors, since the blips of the two aircraft were so close. Triumph did tell him that Toon was now seventy-five kilometers to his northeast, still fighting.

As happens in the speed of high altitude combat, neither man knew who the other was. Court had not been close enough to see Chernov's light blue helmet, nor had Chernov seen the hat on the nose of Court's Phantom. Each man was consumed now; Chernov on his kill, Court with escaping.

Court pulled his throttles out of afterburner as his airspeed indicator shot through Mach 1.5. He looked back and could just make out Chernov coming out of his turn and lowering his nose to catch up. Chernov's short-range missiles were useless over four miles, and his 23mm cannon was useless over half a mile. Court estimated they were six to eight miles apart. He had time to escape. Ahead he could see the terrain of the flatlands give way to the lush green of the rising mountains of the Annamite chain. He knew he was going fast enough so that the fuel-critical MiG-21 would give up the chase. He checked his engine gauges and his fuel. Everything was functioning normally, but he did not have enough fuel to make it to Ubon. No matter. Once away from the MiG, he would tap a tanker. He called to Ev once more, but got no answer.

Chernov had advanced his throttle into the afterburner range to catch the escaping aircraft. His fuel was low, very low. He could only fly a few more minutes away from Vinh before he would have to reverse course. Then he remembered; there was a small strip at Tan Ap used for propeller aircraft. He quickly checked the map on his kneeboard. Tan Ap was ahead and slightly south of their current flight path. It was a short strip, 1,700 meters, and he would have to do some fancy flying, both to get in and to get off again after he refuelled. But he could do it. Chernov did some rapid figuring, and calculated that if he conserved his fuel, he could chase this enemy all the way to the Laotian border and still have enough fuel to land at Tan Ap. He grinned in his mask. He planned on shooting the damaged Phantom down long before the border. He pulled his throttle back enough to save precious fuel, but still gain on the enemy Phantom.

Twenty minutes flying time to the north, Flak Apple had rolled out on the rear of Toon's wingman, Van Bay, and pumped an AIM-9 Sidewinder up his tailpipe. He had been so close, small pieces of the exploding MiG had gone up his left intake. Now his left engine was grinding and only delivering half-thrust. He was at 12,000 feet.

"Damn," Flak told his wingman, "I've ingested some stuff. Left engine going out. Got to head west. Cover me." Toon saw Flak's airplane emerge from the explosion of the MiG-21 and correctly surmised what had happened. He circled back. Triumph Control said they were within effective slant range of the Thanh Hoa antiaircraft emplacements. Toon told Triumph the altitude of the enemy Phantom. Flak's wingman slid in between Toon and Flak's damaged airplane. He saw Toon abruptly pull up and to the north.

"Hey, Packard Lead, he's pulling off, he must be out of ammo," the wingman said. He rolled out level on a heading to parallel that of Flak. At exactly that moment, five 85mm antiaircraft shells from the Thanh Hoa battery detonated in front of and to the side of Flak's airplane. In a second, it was engulfed in a long sheet of flame. The speed of his Phantom force-fed oxygen to the fuel fire, so that, until the plane began to tumble, the sheet of flame was white. The backseater ejected out of the wreckage immediately.

Inside Flak's cockpit, it was all violent tumbling and heat from the flames, as the Phantom spun through the air, rapidly breaking up. Then the entire aft section separated, taking the engines with it. The forward section was flung free. Flak's head was smashed against the canopy, then he was crammed into his seat from a crushing force of ten Gs, as the cockpit section tumbled over itself and began to fall straight down. Flak was barely conscious as his hands grappled for the handle between his legs. He found it with one hand and tugged, then passed out from the shock of the rocket ejection. The Martin-Baker seat had suffered no damage and performed as advertised.

"Mayday, Mayday," his wingman called, knowing they were too far away for a rescue effort to be sent in. "Mayday, Packard Lead, an F-4 is down south of Thanh Hoa."

He set up an orbit off to one side as he saw first, one, then, after a horrifying pause, another parachute blossom open. He couldn't get any closer. The Thanh Hoa battery was firing full out in his direction. When he saw Toon set up for a pass on him, he turned into him, fired his last two Sparrow radar missiles, and turned southwest to Laos and Thailand. "We got him, we got him," his back-seater yelled, when he saw a wing blown off Toon's MiG.

Flak came to, hanging in his parachute 4,000 feet in the air over a small village. His left arm hung numb and senseless. His face felt funny. He reached up with his right hand and felt around. His helmet had been blown off. He could not see out of his left eye. He felt only mush and flapping things. He put his right hand on his riser and looked down at his left arm. He groaned when he saw white bone sticking out of his shredded sleeve. He fumbled for a minute with his survival vest with his right hand, until he realized he couldn't open anything until he was on the ground and out of his harness. He looked around. On a hillside several miles to the north, he saw the white of a parachute just disappear into the jungle. He looked down. He was dropping toward a stream next to a small village of brown-thatched huts next to a palm grove. He distinctly saw villagers running toward him as the ground rushed up, and he saw no more.

Chernov, satisfied with his fuel burn, moved his throttle forward a notch and began a slow 500-feet-per-minute climb. He was still gaining, but wanted an altitude advantage on the F-4 in front of him. He checked his armament counters. He had two KA-13 heat-seekers, and 80 rounds of 23mm cannon shells. It was important he get this American. This shoot-down would make his fifth recorded victory, and that put him in the ace category that the Western world saluted so highly. Not since Russians had advised and flown with the North Korean Air Force in the early fifties had a Russian airman made ace by shooting down American airplanes.

"Ev, can you hear me?" Court repeated several times to his back-seater. He pressed his hands against the sides of his helmet in an attempt to block out the screeching howl of the shattered canopy. He couldn't tell if Ev was talking or not.

"Tap the stick twice if you hear me," he commanded. He felt the stick jerk slightly under his hand. "Okay," he said. "Twice for yes, once for no. Are you wounded?" He felt two faint jumps in the stick. "Bleeding?" The stick jumped twice. "Lots of blood?" The stick jumped twice more. "Can you put a tourniquet on it?" There was no response, then the stick made one feeble jump.

"I'll get you home, Ev. Just hang on," he said over the intercom. Then he had a horrible thought. He was slowly climbing his plane to get to an altitude where he could save fuel. They were passing through 22,000 feet, more than double the altitude where oxygen was required. "Oh God, Ev. Does your oxygen mask work?" There was one very faint tap. The metal fragments that had torn into Ev's body had first severed his oxygen hose and microphone cord. He could hear, but he could not transmit.

Court immediately pushed the nose down. He had to get to a lower altitude so Ev Stern could get enough oxygen with each breath to stay conscious. He knew he would burn more fuel, but he had no choice. "Ev, Ev. I'm sorry," he groaned into the intercom. "We'll level about fifteen thousand. Can you still hear me?" He felt two faint jumps in the control stick.

He switched to guard channel on the radio and called for help.

"Hillsboro, Hillsboro, this is Packard Three on guard, do you read?"

"Packard Three, Hillsboro. Go to Golf frequency."

"Haven't got the blue card," Court said. Court's kneeboard cards with all the frequency codes had disappeared in the rapid decompression of the missile hit. "The cockpit's a mess. I'm fifty miles north of Mu Gia Pass and I need a tank. I'm about out of gas and my backseater is wounded." He spoke rapidly.

"Roger, Packard Three. Can you come up two two eight decimal three?" Although Packard Three had a valid emergency, the controller wanted to keep guard channel open for the other emergencies he knew were coming after a big strike.

"Roger, two two eight three, switching," Court transmitted. He reached down to the right console and dialed in 228.3 on the UHF radio control head. After hearing the tone that indicated the channel change, he called Hillsboro. Hillsboro had no radar. They exercised command and control by using radios. Therefore, they could not warn the pilot of Packard Three that there was a bogey twelve miles on his tail, low, and slowly closing.

"Hillsboro, Packard Three. You copy, my back-seater is wounded and I need a tank?" Court's voice was normal now. His oxygen mask covered the sound of the slipstream tearing at the holes in the aft canopy when he transmitted.

"Roger, Packard, I copy. Stand by." Court's controller keyed in the master director on his console. He was told where and when the C-135 tanker would be available.

"No sweat, Packard," the controller told Court. "Blue tanker will be waiting for you near the NKP TACAN. He'll give you precise vectors when you get closer."

"Okay, Ev. You copy that?" Court said on the intercom. He checked his fuel, then looked up. He thought he could see the green peaks of Mu Gia Pass in the distance. "We'll make that tank in just a few minutes. How ya doin? Gimme a tap." He felt the stick move ever so slightly.

Chernov was at 5,500 meters, about 18,000 feet. His R2L radar, as short range as it was, told him he was twenty kilometers behind his prey. He needed to be within seven kilometers, less than four miles, to fire his two remaining heat-seeking missiles. He noted he was now 500 meters above the American. He rechecked his missile switches and pushed forward on the control stick. With his height advantage, he didn't need the fuel-consuming afterburner to gain speed. He planned to build up to nearly Mach 1 as he plunged deep into the American's six o'clock position. Then, out of sight, and with a speed advantage, he would trigger off both heat-seeking missiles and be ready to follow up with a gun attack. He noted with satisfaction that the sun was still behind him, giving him further protection in its glare.

Since the days of bi-winged fighters made of wood and fabric, the basic lesson had been to hide in the sun, stalk your enemy, then shoot him in the back. No one gave up an advantage like that for some misunderstood, mythical idea of chivalry. Generally, a fighter pilot only thinks of chivalry when he is out of ammo and his opponent is not.

Court rechecked his fuel and his position for the tenth time. He had twelve minutes of flying time left and estimated he was ten miles from Mu Gia and sixty miles from Blue tanker. His true airspeed was 480 knots. That made it easy to calculate that he would have a spare three minutes to locate the tanker and get on the boom to receive fuel. He was apprehensive but not worried about getting the fuel. As long as he stayed alert and did not give in to mind-numbing panic, they would be all right. "Real soon, Ev, real soon," he said in his microphone. He felt two faint but reassuring taps on the control stick.

Chernov's radar display showed a 280-kilometer-per-hour overtake speed as he leveled 300 meters below and six kilometers to the rear of the F-4. He reached down without looking and turned on the switch to send the refrigerant moving to cool the seeker heads of his two K-13A missiles. In seconds, they both emitted electronic tones, indicating they were charged and had locked-on to a heat source. Chernov kept his gunsight centered between the twin tailpipes and listened to the tone increase in pitch, as he flew his plane closer to the origin of the heat. By feel, he again rechecked his firing circuits and fingered the firing button on the control stick. The tone in his headset reached an almost unbearable shriek that brought nothing but pure joy to Vladimir Chernov. He pressed the firing button once, then again.

Ev Stern had his head back against the headrest of his ejection seat. He felt nauseated and cold. Waves of pain that would increase, then subside, then increase again, throbbed in his left shoulder and hand. With his right hand, he had unhooked his lap belt to free his shoulder harness. Then he had reached up, undone the chest strap of his parachute, and rummaged around under his survival vest inside his flight suit, trying to find a hole to plug, or a vein or something to pinch. He found nothing except grating pain and huge waves of nausea as he pushed and poked. He had given up trying to find the vein or artery that was bleeding so badly. Now he sat holding his left hand, with his right in his lap. His head was back and he thought of Jan and the picnic they had had before he'd left the States for Ubon. He had joked wryly about maybe getting checked out in the front seat once he had shown he could hack it in the back. She'd said she didn't care, just come back to her and Tommy. Ev had no trouble picturing Jan holding little Tommy. Then he saw a flicker.

Chernov watched the missiles streak clean and unerring toward the enemy Phantom in front of him. The smoke from their rocket motors drew clean white arrows to the nozzles of each missile. Chernov had fired them from a range of two miles, they had accelerated to Mach 2, they would impact in less than 4 seconds. He had already flicked his selector switch to cannon in case something went wrong. But he knew it wouldn't. The American plane flew along as steady as an airliner. What Chernov was alert for was not so much an evading maneuver on the luckless American's part, but the need for a cannon attack if the missiles failed, or—more likely, and he hoped this would be the case—the need to make a rapid roll and pull to avoid the debris from the exploding American fighter when his missles impacted.

In Ev Stern's field of vision were the three rearview mirrors attached at the 11, 12, and 1 o'clock positions of his canopy. He saw a flicker again, a crisp spear of white, and knew exactly what it was.

"Break left, break left," he screamed against the canopy noise, already knowing that Court couldn't hear him; and instantly, without conscious thought or direction from his brain, his right hand slammed the control stick to the left, and he slumped as total pain stunned him into unconsciousness.

Court's first mental reaction was to think the control system had somehow ruptured and was causing wild inputs. His first physical reaction was to put pressure against the stick movement. As he did so, the pressure gave way in such a manner that he knew Ev had done it. He looked back over his left shoulder as he increased back pressure. All this flashed through his mind and was resolved so quickly, he had no trouble spotting the incoming missiles and pulling even tighter to break their tracking solution. At the same time, he engaged the afterburners, knowing he had to have the extra thrust or die.

Chernov saw the Phantom break into the twin paths of the missiles at the last split second, and marveled at the control of the pilot as he pulled his own plane straight up to dissipate his overtake speed, and rolled as he climbed to keep the American in sight. *Hara sho,* he grunted against the G-force, as he saw the white hat on the nose of the camouflaged Phantom.

Court instinctively clawed for altitude as the two missiles zoomed by and detonated as the distance circuits in their proximity fuses sensed closure disparity. The booms were too far away to do more than sprinkle pieces of steel against the tough skin of the Phantom. As Court rotated during his climb, he saw the attacking airplane—it was a MiG-21. He could see the pilot inside the cockpit as the MiG floated lazily over the top of the vertical maneuver. Court was able to get off one wild snap shot with his gun, before he too had to ease the nose of his fighter over the top of the looping maneuver.

Chernov unloaded his airplane as he came down and slammed the throttle into afterburner range. He had not expected the Phantom to follow him so far up the climb, and had almost stalled trying to rise higher in the sky. He raged again at the poor rearward visibility, as he shot through the speed of sound, then pulled abruptly back up again to reengage the American. He searched and finally spotted the American Phantom fleeing west, now almost to the karst of Laos. He checked his fuel. Barely enough. He gritted his teeth, left the afterburner engaged, and shot after the elusive enemy.

Court saw him coming. He couldn't get another ounce of speed from his airplane. He only hoped he could make it out of North Vietnam past Mu Gia Pass into Steel Tiger, where he and Ev could bail out with a fair chance of a Jolly Green rescue. Hopes of reaching Blue tanker had died when he plugged in his burners to avoid the MiG attack.

Court clenched his teeth. He couldn't fight, he could only flee straight ahead for the comparative safety of Laos. He looked back and saw the MiG boring in. "Don't be predictable, don't be predictable," Tanaka, an instructor at George, had hammered at him. He could make one last-ditch maneuver that might throw his attacker off. When he saw Chernov roll in on him and the fire start to come from his belly and the round red cherry balls start toward him, he pulled back on the stick as hard as he could and at the same time jammed in right rudder. The heavy Phantom snapped and stalled in a horizontal corkscrew maneuver that dissipated 300 knots of airspeed, effectively stopping it dead in the air. At the same time, he squeezed the trigger of his 20mm cannon. Even though Chernov snatched back on his stick, it was too late. He zoomed by, straight into the stream of 20mm shells erupting from the gatling gun slung under the belly of Court's airplane.

Time froze for Court at that second. He saw the sparkles of his cannon shells erupting all over the fin and tail section of Chernov's

MiG as it clawed for altitude. He actually saw the gushes of smoke, then flame, spew from the individual holes, then combine into one big torrent as the thin metal skin gave way and the engine started to break up and spit out pieces trailing long red ribbons of flame. Court rolled high and to the left in a half barrel roll that put him parallel to Chernov's climbing MiG. It wasn't a zooming climb, just the momentum of their maneuvers carrying them up at a lazy rate, Court a hundred feet or so higher than Chernov as they topped out, with the MiG starting to fall off on a wing. In slow motion, Court saw the canopy separate from the MiG, then a blast of flame as the ejection seat shot out from the airplane. Fascinated, and still in slow motion, Court pulled his Phantom easily around and down, all the time watching the enfolding drama of the ejection. It occurred to Court that if he had not passed off the other MiG that day to his wingman, he might be an ace now. He saw the pilot fall free of the seat and start to fall through space on his back, legs apart. Then a pilot chute whipped up from behind his head, pulling a cable and a long streaming length of white that slowly blossomed into a fully opened parachute. The pilot swung down beneath the chute and hung there. Court saw him slowly raise his hands to the risers. His light blue helmet stood out quite clearly.

He lost sight of the descending parachute as he turned the airplane away and lowered the nose to gain airspeed.

"Ev, Ev. I got him. I got him," Court said over and over to his back-seater.

Then he turned back toward Laos and Steel Tiger. He was very slow, barely 250 knots. The man in the parachute appeared between him and the Laotian border. Court stared, fascinated, as the parachute drifted down directly in front of him, down through the range circle and center pipper of his gunsight. He was astounded to feel his lips draw back. The trigger under his finger was still hot. One twitch and his foe would be forever vanquished. The pilot was facing him. Court saw him reach inside his upper harness and withdraw something. Then he realized the man had pulled a handgun and was shooting at him.

Chernov yelled at the Phantom driving directly at him. He pulled the trigger as fast as he could on his revolver, knowing it did no good, but thinking maybe just one round would impact the windscreen and kill the American pilot who had shot him down. He was furious, and in a full battle mode, ready to kill. At the same time, deep in his mind, he was aware of his mistake. He should have felt that same fierceness as he'd bored in much too complacently to finish off the American from behind. He had fallen for one of the most basic of fighter maneuvers—the high-G barrel roll. The last round snapped out of his gun. With dawning horror, he realized the Phantom pilot

was not going to shoot him with his cannon but was going to run
him over with his airplane. He drew his arm back, prepared to throw
the gun at the last instant, in a futile gesture of defiance.

Suddenly, Court realized that, unless he pulled up, he would hit
the helpless man or collapse his parachute. He jerked back on the
control stick and rolled several hundred feet over the top of the parachute. In his haste, he pulled harder than he intended and the big
Phantom slopped upside down and quit flying. At the same time,
both engines unwound as quickly as if the throttles had been stop-
cocked. Instantly, Court jammed his left hand toward the restart button, but knew as he did so it was a useless motion. A look at the fuel
gauges confirmed what he knew to be the truth; the airplane was out
of fuel . . . and stalling.

They were two miles in the air, out of fuel, out of airspeed, falling
straight down toward the green and brown of Mu Gia Pass.

"Mayday, Mayday, Mayday. Packard Three Alpha and Bravo bail-
ing out over Mu Gia. Bravo is wounded." He transmitted the message
on guard channel once more.

"Ev, we gotta get out. Brace yourself, I'm going to pull the handle,"
Court spoke rapidly but clearly into the intercom. He braced himself
and pulled the yellow-and-black D-ring between his legs to start the
ejection sequence that would get them both out of the dead Phantom.

The rear canopy shot off the falling Phantom, followed instantly
by the rear seat rising out of the cockpit on a column of fire. It was
barely clear when the front canopy flew off and the front seat rocketed out on its pillar of flame parallel to the ground as the Phantom
nosed straight down.

Court's parachute was pulled open by a lead slug shot from a drogue
gun less than two seconds after his seat had left the cockpit. The
opening chute snapped him from the seat just after his shoulder harness and lap belt automatically released. He fell sideways until he
reached the end of the risers and swung down under the canopy.
The chute immediately started oscillating, flinging his body first one
way, then the other, like a pendulum under a giant clock.

Without conscious thought, his Special Forces jump training took
over. Timing it just right, he chinned himself on the risers away from
each oscillation. After two dampened swings, he hung down straight.
He reached down and pulled his orange survival knife from a G-suit
pocket. He reached up as he had been taught and cut four lines going
up to the parachute canopy to better steer the chute. After that, he
pulled the handle to release his seat survival pack to dangle from a
thirty-foot lanyard. Then he looked around. Below and to his left, he
saw the white of Ev's parachute. The canopy hid the figure underneath. Court couldn't tell if he was conscious or not. The fact that

the chute was open told him nothing, for it had been activated as automatically as his own.

Below him, toward the south where it was all black karst and lush green jungle, he saw the spilled canopy of a parachute hung on a tall tree like a long white-and-orange ribbon. That would be the Russian pilot.

He estimated he was about five thousand feet above the trees. The green jungle stretched for miles in all directions except south, where it culminated in the mountain pass that funneled traffic from North Vietnam into Laos through Mu Gia Pass. He could see clearly the untouched brown road that stretched from North Vietnam into Mu Gia. He saw light truck traffic on it that was backing up just short of the Laotian border, preparing for the run down the Trail that night. It was barely eleven in the morning. By nightfall, he knew, there would be hundreds of trucks ready to plunge south.

He unzipped a pouch of his survival vest and took out his survival radio. He extended the antenna and transmitted: "Mayday, Mayday, Mayday. Packard Three Alpha and Bravo are down north of Mu Gia Pass. Alpha is okay, Bravo is wounded." He repeated the call twice more, but heard no response.

He could see his drift would take him to the north side of the pass. He started pulling on his southernmost risers to slip the chute in that direction. He would pass near, but not directly over the Russian's parachute. He looked back over his shoulder in the direction he had last seen Ev's parachute. He froze. He was enough to one side to see Ev's body hanging slumped in the harness. His chute was drifting almost directly onto the road. Then he heard faint popping noises and realized that figures on the road were shooting at his back-seater. He could just make out Ev's canopy collapsing as his body fell into a small clearing near the road. It was quickly surrounded by small figures with rifles. Some looked his way and started to shoot.

He pulled harder on the risers, trying to slip more to the south, where he could see a hole among the tall trees. His heart almost stopped as he looked down and could see he was very close to the jungle top. He remembered his training. He made a conscious effort to put his feet together, bend his knees slightly, cross his arms over his face and hold the inside of the risers. He forced his eyes to the horizon so as not to anticipate the impact. He smashed into the top layer of branches of a thick grove of trees just short of the clearing.

Time did not slow down. He heard and felt crashes and branches breaking, and his body seemed to be hurtling in stops and starts toward the ground. There was one torso-wrenching jerk, as his chute snagged further, then gave way. Wrapped in the risers, it seemed he fell forever until there was nothing.

25

1415 Hours Local, Wednesday, 22 November 1967
Mu Gia Pass
Royalty of Laos

☆

Court felt the pain first. He felt his chest had burst open, and maybe his stomach. He wasn't sure where he was or what had happened. I must be in the Vette. I've crashed. Then he knew that wasn't right, because . . . because he remembered his fight with this MiG and the bailout.

"Ev," he cried. "Ev." He struggled to get up and fell back, gasping with the hot searing pain that renewed itself in his chest. He lay panting, his eyes closed. He felt the sun hot on his face. But he had seen Ev. Ev was right over him. Ev was here looking at him. He forced his eyes open against the glare of the sun. He squinted. Someone was standing, framed by the sun, looking down at him. "Ev," he said to the figure, relieved. "Ev, get your radio out. Call in an SAR."

"Only you Yankees carry radios," said Vladimir Chernov.

Chernov stared down at the fallen pilot. He looked so . . . normal. He looked, Chernov thought, like one of us. This wasn't what the agents of the dark forces were supposed to look like. He had seen the movies. The Americans were fat and ugly, and had little pig eyes.

It all came to Court Bannister in a sudden awareness. He clawed for his gun. Waves of pain shot through his chest. His holster was empty.

"Very good gun," Vladimir Chernov said. His accent was thick. "Very" came out "wery." He brought his right hand into Court's view. It held Court's .38 revolver.

Fighting the pain, Court felt for the bulky pocket of his survival vest where the survival radio should be. The vest was gone. All the pockets of his flight suit were unzipped and empty. He moved his legs. They felt sore but operable. Groaning from the pain in his chest, he pushed himself to a sitting position. He saw the other man had unhooked his harness and his G-suit for him. All his equipment was laying spread out on the ground next to him. The survival seatpack had been opened and the contents placed on the ground in an orderly fashion. Court saw that the wrappings of the various packs had been opened and the contents examined. He looked around. They were at the edge of a clearing at the base of several tall trees. Court saw his risers snake up to the nylon of his parachute that was streamered up through the branches. He looked at the man standing over him. He wore Court's green mesh survival vest. Under it was a powder blue flight suit.

"Do you have a blue helmet?" Court asked.

"You fly Phantom with white hat?" Chernov countered.

"Yes."

"From where?"

"I'm not supposed to tell you that."

Chernov looked puzzled. Then he brightened. "Ah, no. Not airfield. I already know. 'WP' on tail of Phantom, that American base Ubon. I want to know where in airplane you fly?"

Court understood. "From the front seat," he said.

"You make good trick," Chernov said. He peered at Court's name tag. "Bann-as-tarr. Good trick, Bann-as-tarr." He seemed relaxed.

From his sitting position, Court made a lunge for the Russian's hand with the gun in it. Chernov easily stepped back, and Court flopped to the ground, a groan escaped his lips.

"Ho," Chernov said. "Bad trick, Bann-as-tarr. Bad trick. I could kick easy." He waved the gun. "I could kill easy." He squatted down, just out of range of Court's hands or feet. Court lay on his back, faint with pain.

"Give me some water and some of those pills," he croaked. He pointed to the water tins and the aspirin package from the seatpack. The man kicked them over to where Court lay. He opened a pint tin, drank half, swallowed four aspirin, then finished the tin.

When Chernov saw what was in the tins, he opened one and drank deep. "Ahhhh," he said, wiping his mouth. "Good."

"Are you Russian?" Court asked.

Chernov laughed. "No, *Amerikanski*. I am from Cal-for-na."

"Sure you are," Court said with a grin. "How come you speak English?"

"Every Cal-for-na speak English, yes?"

"You fly a good airplane," Court said.

"Ah. And *you* fly good airplane, *Amerikanyets*. How much you fly? How many hours you have? You shoot any MiGs before me?"

"I have about two thousand hours," Court answered. He didn't think it smart to tell the Russian that he had shot down three MiGs.

"How much money?"

"How much money? How much money what? How much does the airplane cost? What do you mean?" Court asked. His head was clearing.

"In week," Chernov asked with exasperation. "How much money you make in week?"

Court snorted, then grimaced with the pain. "That's a stupid question."

"Have auto?" Chernov asked. He looked genuinely interested.

"Hey," Court said. "You're supposed to be asking me military questions. Sure, I have an auto."

"What auto? Ford? You have Ford?"

This is crazy, Court thought to himself. "No, I have Chaika limousine. All us Russians have Chaika limousine."

Chernov threw back his head and gave a great laugh. Then he looked very shy for a moment, as if he were asking an embarrassing question. "The hat on your airplane," he said. "It is, ah, *cowboy* hat, yes?"

Court laughed. "It is a cowboy hat, yes. You speak good English."

"Hah, so do you. Speak Russian you?"

"*Nyet, tovarich,*" Court said.

Chernov laughed. "Yah, you Bann-as-tarr *Amerikanyets* I like. You good pilot. Next time I beat. We meet ..." He stopped, his face turned serious. He drew back and motioned with the gun in his hand. "There be no next time. You are prisoner. Maybe you shoot me down now, but I capture you now." He did not smile.

Court stared at him. He saw a man with light brown hair and blue eyes, probably a few years older. The man had thin lines extending back from his eyes, a smooth brow, and curved lips that looked as if they wanted to smile a lot.

Then reality returned in a rush. This was war. This wasn't hands-across-the-border crap, this was hands-in-the-bear-trap if I don't kill this guy and get the hell out of here. Court made a mental search of his own body. What do I have that I can use as a weapon, he asked himself. Not a fucking thing, he answered himself a second later. This Russian puke has it all.

Then they both heard the warbling sound of a police whistle, faint but clear through the jungle from the direction of Mu Gia Pass. Court had been told the North Vietnamese Army used whistles to signal to each other. Troops were obviously headed up to where they had seen the parachute come down. They already have Ev, now they want me, Court thought. He rolled over and came to a position on his hands and knees. He bit off the groan that sprang from his chest.

He heard a new noise, from the opposite direction of the NVA whistles. It was the faint hissing and whooping sound of a big helicopter in the distance. His heart jumped. The SAR was on. A big Jolly Green rescue helicopter was moving into the area. Mixed with the sound he heard the deep roar of the big prop engines on the A-1 aircraft escorting the Jolly Green. The sound seemed to grow stronger and sing through his body. Life and energy flooded into him. His brain cleared and became purposeful. He knew he was going to go toward that sound, regardless of what might happen.

He sat back on his heels and looked up at the pilot in the blue flight suit. Wearing the USAF survival vest, he looked like any American pilot. Court clenched his teeth and rose slowly to his feet. The pain seemed far away now. He felt almost lightheaded, even slightly euphoric.

He was still facing the Russian, who held the gun on him.

"I am going now," Court said very slowly and evenly, enunciating every syllable. "I am going now. If you want to stop me, you will have to shoot me in the back." They stared hard at each other, each man with a set and determined mouth. Holding the Russian's eyes until the last instant, Court turned and started out from under the trees into the clearing. He walked slowly toward the sound of the SAR. He put each foot down with a deliberation as careful as if he were walking barefoot on broken glass. He could feel the muscles in his back tense. He thought of his dad, then of Susan Boyle. They'll never know, he thought. They'll never know how I died, or where my body is.

"Bann-as-tarr," Chernov said quietly. Court did not turn. He felt the hair on the back of his neck rise as the skin on his scalp contracted.

"Bann-as-tarr, you will need this." Chernov's voice was sharp, almost harsh. He spoke in the manner one speaks to an undisciplined soldier.

Court stopped. His legs felt wooden. In slow motion, he turned and looked back. Chernov motioned with the pistol toward the survival gear spread out at his feet.

"Take." His voice was definitely angry now. He stepped back and motioned again with the revolver. Court walked to the seatpack, squatted facing the Russian, and began putting water tins and the two survival radios into his flight suit pockets. He hesitated, then tossed a tin of water to the Russian who deftly caught it.

"They torture, Bann-as-tarr. Pig fucking bastards torture. Worst is Cuban. Ceballos. Cannot give you to Ceballos." Chernov felt angrier than at any time in his life. When this American pilot had groaned and struggled to his feet to walk away, Chernov had again seen the defiant American navigator, that Bomar, being tortured. "Cannot give you to Ceballos," Chernov repeated. But he was angry, very angry. Shooting down American fighters was one thing; capturing a pilot was something else entirely. What a feat—to actually capture an enemy pilot. Ignatov would have to give him the best possible of all Party evaluations. He would be set for life. He shook his head. Angry and sad at the same time. "Cannot," he said with finality.

He stood looking down at Court, who was packing his survival gear. The whistles were getting louder behind him.

"Maybe . . . I go with you." He looked thoughtful for a moment, then he laughed, his face clear now, the anger gone. "But no. I go back. We fight again, yah? I am Chernov, *Pod-Palcovnik* Vladimir Nicholaevych Chernov. We fight, or maybe we drink." Still holding the pistol, he waved his hands in a *comme si, comme ça* gesture.

Court looked into his eyes. The bond was instant. There was no war, no enemy. Here were two champion fighter pilots who had just fought a superb battle. Court moved to offer his hand.

Something hit Chernov's chest with a wet, smacking sound. He went down like an empty sack at the same time a snap sounded from across the clearing. Court dropped to the ground and stared in horror at the body of the man who had just told him his name was Vladimir, his animated face suddenly slack and lifeless. Bright red blood began to ooze through the fabric of the American survival vest and through the flight suit from the hole in the Russian's chest.

The sound of the helicopters suddenly rose to a crescendo. Two A-1s dove and roared, their cannons spitting, over the clearing toward the direction of the shot. Suddenly, small arms and heavier machine-gun fire erupted at the aircraft from the North Vietnamese troops who were pouring into the clearing. Mixed in with the gunfire was the sound of whistles and yelled commands. Court suddenly realized the cracking sounds he heard were made by bullets being fired at him. He crouched lower, and quickly stuffed some of the survival packets into his flight-suit pockets and prepared to scuttle into the jungle. His breath came in short desperate pants, and his heartbeat was so heavy he thought his chest was going to burst. Adrenaline overrode the pain in his ribs. He looked at Chernov, and grabbed the gun from his lifeless hand. At the last minute, he noticed the blue scarf around Chernov's neck, tugged it off, and poked it into his knee pocket. Still on his hands and knees, he backed into the jungle thicket, heart thudding.

The canopy and vines closed over him as if he had backed into a cave entrance. Even outside sound seemed muted. He felt resistance behind him and turned around as best he could in the narrow confines. Sweat began to stream down his face and chest. He didn't feel the punctures or hear the rip as three spines as big and hard as ten-penny nails, from a squat broad-leaf plant, tore across his back. Staying low, worming his way forward on his elbows, he inched along one of the many small game tunnels crisscrossing the thicket. The shouts and whistles faded quickly in the dense, rotting growth, but he knew the enemy troopers would very quickly find his blundering path into the jungle. He didn't have time to stop and call the rescue team on one of his survival radios.

Overhead, Sandy Low Lead, the pilot of the big prop-driven A-1 fighter, radioed Crown what he saw as he pulled up over the clearing.

"One man is down, I think the other is in the jungle southeast of the clearing. I have negative radio contact with either man. We're being shot at bad. I don't want the Jollys in there until we suppress the fire and make contact." Sandy Low Lead unkeyed for a second, then transmitted: "Packard Three, if you read, come up guard channel, beeper, or key your mike."

If the enemy were too close to hazard a voice transmission, a downed crewman could depress the mike button twice on his survival radio to signify he was alert and listening. Or he could turn on the beacon switch of his RT-10 radio that would transmit an eerie whooping call on guard channel.

"Packard Three, if you read, come up guard channel, beeper, or key your mike." There was no reply.

Higher up, at 8,000 feet, Sandy High Lead and his wingman orbited, waiting to be called in to lay ordnance and tear gas, if necessary, on the enemy while the pickup by a Jolly Green, a giant HH-53 helicopter, took place. Each A-1 carried four 20mm cannons, and 8,000 pounds of assorted weaponry. The HH-53 Jollys—the first in the theater—had door gunners firing 7.62mm gatling guns to protect themselves.

The Jollys carried a hoist on an arm on the right side of the craft to let down a cable with a heavy device like a lead plumb bob to penetrate the jungle. Three narrow metal seats unfolded down like flower petals from the device. A strap held each person in place as they were lifted up. The PJ—the pararescue jumper—usually went down with the penetrator to assist the rescue. PJs, all NCOs, were the most decorated men of the war.

But the Jolly Green helicopters were extremely vulnerable, as they hovered motionless for the long minutes necessary to winch up a downed crewman. Usually a second Jolly orbited in the distance to back up the first, while the Sandys protected them both. However, without radio contact or a confirmed visual sighting, there would be no rescue. Court Bannister had none of these; he was neither seen nor heard.

The advancing Vietnamese found Chernov and, from him, Court's clear path into the thicket. Upon command, two men stripped off their pith helmets and load-bearing harnesses, grabbed their SKS rifles, and wormed into the heavy growth. Others probed Chernov's body, while one spoke on a radio. He stiffened, electrified at what he heard. *"He is Russian, protect him,"* he barked to his soldiers. *"Take him to the base camp. Carefully, you idiots, carefully,"* the leader said.

Creeper vines caught at Court's arms and legs, and thorns scraped him as he wriggled through the tiny game path. He hoped he was safe, at least for a little while, in the thicket which rose up as huge as four or five boxcars piled on top of one another in the dense jungle. He slowed his frantic flight and stopped, and lay panting as he fumbled for a water tin. He didn't find it. In a panic, he ran his hands down his flight suit. He lay too flat to see what condition it was in. Fluttering and searching, his hands found tear after tear. Without the thick mesh and canvas of his survival vest to hold them, he had lost the heavy water tins. What he did find in his remaining pockets, he pushed forward in front of his face: a thick K-bar hunting knife, a package of bandages, a waxed packet of matches, only one of his two survival radios, his .38 revolver, and Chernov's blue scarf. His whole flight suit was now dark and soaked. In an awkward, cramped motion, he shifted his head to wipe the grime and sweat from his face on his sleeve. The air was thick and stifling as he studied his meager findings, which rested on the ground barely five inches in front of his eyes. He rolled over on his back and wrapped the blue scarf around his forehead, then he grasped the RT-10 radio and extended the antenna up into the tangled foliage over his head. He turned the small black wafer switch from OFF to STNDBY. The next two positions were TRANS/BCN and TRANS/VCE.

". . . voice or beeper. Packard, do you read?" Court quickly covered the miniature speaker with his hand to muffle the noise. The two NVA eighty feet behind him heard, and squirmed faster, homing in on the signal.

Court unwrapped the tiny earplug that silenced the speaker as he plugged it into the set. He keyed the mike button twice.

"Packard, Sandy. That you?" The tinny voice of the A-1 pilot sounded in Court's ear.

"Roger," Court whispered into the mike built into the small radio. "Packard Three Alpha here."

"Authenticate with the code of the day," Sandy Low Lead demanded. More than one radio had been used by an English-speaking decoy.

Court's face contorted. "Oh fuck, I don't remember."

The Sandy pilot noted the anguish in the voice he heard. "Name a team in the NFL," he said.

"Oh fuck," Court whispered, his mind a whirl. "Redskins," he finally blurted.

"Where they from?"

"Unh, ah . . . D.C." Court put his head on his arm. This can't be happening to me, he thought.

"Packard, is your Bravo with you?"

"Negative. He went down on the road. They already got him."

"Okay, Packard. Can you give me a flare?"

"Negative. I don't have any. I'm in the bottom of the big thicket at the south end of the clearing." When Court finished transmitting, he heard a rustling, and looked down between his boots.

Three feet down the tiny tunnel he saw the shaved head of the first crawling Vietnamese soldier. He reached back for his revolver, held it in two hands between his legs, and fired twice. Both .38-caliber bullets made small blue holes where they entered the smooth skull. The head ballooned slightly and dropped the few inches to the tunnel floor. Court heard a muffled yell in Vietnamese that seemed to come from behind the soldier. He couldn't see the second man frantically trying to bring his rifle to bear past the body. It was impossible, the jungle too thick, the path too small.

Court grabbed his equipment, frantically pushed off with his feet and scrambled down the path, pumping his way on his elbows and knees, oblivious of the clutching vines and scraping thorns, or of the noise he was making.

For thirty minutes he inched and squirmed down the game trail. Heavy sweat stung his eyes, nearly blinding him. He took an occasional swipe with his sleeve, and plunged on. He was panting heavily, and making noises in his throat as he exhaled. He felt cramped, and contained. Jolts of claustrophobia confused and panicked his mind. The jungle was a big green monster and he was a trapped worm in its stomach that would soon be torn apart and dissolved.

Suddenly, his head popped out from the bottom of the thicket at the edge of a glade full of elephant grass and bamboo groves. Although the effect calmed him, he felt like an accident victim peering up from the bottom of the wreckage at a tranquil scene. He stayed still for a moment, then wormed himself out of the thicket, and lay at the base, gulping air. He needed to slow his mind down and take stock of the situation.

He sat up and began to check his body through his torn flight suit. The scratches were starting to burn like tiny trails of fire. The pain from his ribs pushed into his consciousness. He moved his arms and legs, and felt himself. Nothing broken, he concluded. He snorted, as the thought of his being tossed around in a concrete mixer full of pins and rocks flashed into his mind.

He sat back for a moment and tried to concentrate on what his next move should be. He had hardly begun to sort things out when he heard a noise and froze, his heart beating wildly. It came from behind him, from the thicket. Someone was coming. He scrambled to his hands and knees, then to his feet, and dashed away from the thicket toward cover on the other side of the glade. He was within five feet of the far green wall when the ground suddenly gave way and he dropped into a hidden sinkhole in the porous limestone. His world turned blazing white, then black as a tomb.

1445 Hours Local, Wednesday, 22 November 1967
Airborne in an O-2A
Over the Ho Chi Minh Trail
Royalty of Laos

☆

Toby Parker, call sign Covey Four One, wheeled his O-2A over the karst seventy miles south of Mu Gia Pass. He had relieved Covey Three Five barely ten minutes before, and circled and soared now, jinking constantly, as he searched the Trail below with binoculars. He had flown several missions in the weeks since Pontiac Two had been killed attacking the fake truck under his control. Although Toby had been gloomy and morose, he had not touched a drop of liquor. Instead, he had worked out in the makeshift gym at Da Nang, lifting weights and studying Tae Kwan Do from a senior NCO, until he could fall into exhausted sleep each night. Though Chuck Annillo had been supportive and flown him as much as possible, he hadn't tried to penetrate Toby's withdrawn manner. He felt his job was to keep the brass off Parker until the young captain could work it out himself. Parker's newfound dedication and great ability as a pilot was enabling him to do a fine job as a new FAC, and Annillo was sure his spirits would pick up.

Toby heard a call from Hillsboro. He let the binoculars hang from the cord around his neck and answered.

"Hillsboro, Covey Four One, go."

"We've got an SAR going north of Mu Gia. You're closest. Get up there. Enroute contact Dakota on Delta Kilo. Tell them we've got one, maybe two down in their AO. Pin Dakota's position. We may need them for a snatch." AO meant Dakota's area of operation.

"Roger. Covey Four One headed to Mu Gia. Dakota on Delta Kilo." Toby spun the O-2A to a northerly heading, then opened his thick checklist binder for the codes of the day. In the cryptic letters, he read where Dakota was a team on the ground for road watch and pilot rescue. Fox Kilo was the day's code for the frequency 32.6 on the FM radio.

"Dakota, Dakota, Dakota. Covey Four One, Covey Four One on Fox Mike. Do you read?" After three calls, Dakota checked in.

"We read you, Covey. What's up?"

Toby consulted his checklist. "Dakota, authenticate Golf Tango."

After a moment Dakota replied with the correct words. "Bravo Delta. What's happening?"

Toby gave him the code words for the coordinates of the Mu Gia Pass area, and asked how soon they could get to that location where there was an aircrewman in trouble. After two minutes of map study, Dakota replied.

"Covey, Dakota. About forty-eight hours. Sorry 'bout that."

1530 Hours Local, Wednesday, 22 November 1967
Commander's Office, 7th Air Force
Tan Son Nhut Air Base
Republic of Vietnam

☆

At noon that day, Commander, 7th Air Force, had heard the news that Bannister and Apple were down in enemy territory. Now he sat at his desk listening to the afternoon briefing by his Director of Operations, Major General Milton Berzin. He had named Berzin—a stocky man in rumpled khakis—as the replacement for Raimer, whom he had sent to a supply post in disgrace. Commander, 7th Air Force, sat in his chair, both hands flat on the desk in front of him. He looked like a thoughtful and contemplative man who was about to push abruptly to his feet. And that was just about how he felt. He was responsible for 70,000 airmen and pilots, and 1,500 airplanes on twenty bases in South Vietnam and Thailand. He also had operational control over 400 more airplanes based in the Philippines, Okinawa, and Guam. He took two, sometimes three briefings a day on both in-country and out-country combat activities.

Now he was impatient. He wanted the latest news on Bannister and Apple. What had happened? Did they get the Soviet pilot? Couldn't have, they went down too far south. Did a rescue unit already pick them up? What about their back-seaters?

Milt Berzin was using his pointer on a situation map propped on an aluminum tripod. It was the last of today's in-country briefing series. The map was marked with blue and red grease pencil showing friendly and enemy positions, and long black lines showing aerial routes into the Dak To area, where a large battle was raging between

NVA regulars and American paratroopers of the 173rd Airborne Brigade. The paras were winning a significant battle.

"General Peers says the final assault on Hill 875 will be tomorrow
morning. He says his aerial resupply situation is okay, but he wants
to make sure he has the priority on all the fragged and unfragged
close air support airplanes we can give him, starting at first light."
Berzin looked expectantly at his boss, his bristly eyebrows drawn together.

"It's been laid on for a long time, Milt. See that there are no
glitches. Give me hourly reports." Berzin nodded. He began the out-
country briefing.

"The Team Dakota action is not bringing in the success rate we
anticipated. So far we have lost one C-130—you recall the one that
dropped then failed to return—and the team has put in only about
twenty percent of the strikes we anticipated. There is talk by MACV
of calling off the operation." Neither man knew the name of the
Dakota team leader, Wolf Lochert; or that a team member planned
to kill him.

"No word at all on that C-130, Milt?"

"No, sir. No radio calls, no beepers, no wreckage." With only a
handful of C-130s in the theater, the loss of even one was of great
consequence.

Berzin flipped another chart forward. He pointed to a spot on the
Ho Chi Minh Trail next to the Vietnam border near Lang Vei and
Khe Sanh. "The FAC, Covey Four One, reported traces of PT-76
enemy tanks here, but the Intel people have downgraded the probability to zero."

"Why?" Commander, 7th Air Force, asked.

"First off, because the NVA has never brought tanks down the
Trail, and secondly because Covey Four One's credibility is suspect.
He recently called a strike in on a phony truck set up as a flak trap."
Berzin paused. "I think you should know Covey Four One is Parker,
Toby Parker, General."

"Oh, yes. The captain with all the attention from the Pentagon. I
remember being briefed about him. Air Force Cross, Purple Heart,
drinking problem."

Berzin nodded, turned over another chart, and resumed his briefing. "Twenty-five F-105s from Korat and Tahkli struck the northeast
rail junction on the morning go. They reported seventy-five percent
bombs on target and eighty percent of the target destroyed. Twenty
Ubon F-4s and sixteen from Udorn . . ." He stopped as he saw a
full colonel from the Blue Chip command post stick his head in
the door.

"What's the latest on the Ubon shoot-downs?" Commander, 7th
Air Force, asked.

"Sir, we lost three Ubon planes with five crewmen missing," the colonel said.

"What about Bannister and Apple?"

"Sir, Major Apple went down just west of Dong Hoi. His wingman saw one good chute. As yet, no one has come up on the radio, so we don't know if it was Major Apple or his back-seater. Major Bannister went down near Mu Gia and has not been picked up. We had radio contact with him, but now we've lost it. His back-seater fell into enemy territory and was captured. A third F-4 is missing."

"Did anybody get that Soviet?"

"Yes, sir, we think Bannister did. But the only word I have so far from Major Hostettler on the scramble phone is that Major Bannister and the MiG-21 shot each other down. It's kind of a vague story so far, but it's possible Bannister was with the Russian pilot on the ground."

"How so?"

"Hostettler interprets the initial on-scene reports as three pilots down in the Mu Gia area. That could mean one F-4 and one MiG-21 shot down. He's pretty certain Bannister's back-seater parachuted into the hands of the NVA, and that Bannister was with the Russian in a clearing when the first Sandys arrived. Bannister came up on guard shortly after, but we lost contact with him almost immediately."

"What's the status of the SAR?"

Berzin consulted his note pad. "There are two Jollys on orbit, four Sandys, plenty of fighter cover, and a Covey enroute to the area. The Covey FAC says Team Dakota reports it can be on scene in forty-eight hours. They are our backup in case the pickup goes sour. And it might."

"What's the enemy situation?" Commander, Seventh, asked.

"Bad, sir. They're all over the place. The Sandys are keeping their heads down, but they have a couple fourteen-point-five triple A guns down along the Trail that just about reach up there. The Sandys don't want to blast anything until they pinpoint Bannister's exact location."

"Who is the FAC?"

"Covey Four One, sir."

"Oh, my God."

1600 Hours Local, Wednesday, 22 November 1967
Airborne in an O-2A
Over the Ho Chi Minh Trail
Royalty of Laos

☆

"Hillsboro. Covey Four One is approaching Mu Gia." Toby Parker saw with grim clarity the sharp karst mountains rising from the dense junglelike black shoals in a green sea. He had a visual on the orbiting Jolly Green helicopters and the A-1 Sandys.

"Covey Four One, Hillsboro, contact Sandy Low Lead on Lima Lima."

Toby read the correct UHF frequency for LL on his kneeboard. "Sandy Low Lead, Covey Four One inbound."

"Roger, Four One. Orbit west a few miles. Familiarize yourself with the site. We're getting low on fuel. We've lost contact with the guy on the ground. The bad guys are all over the place. Doesn't look good."

Toby did as he was told. He orbited a mile west at 7,500 feet, and studied the ground with his binoculars. He saw the rising karst, the thick lush jungle with its triple canopy, and the tiny clearing where the rescue attempt had been aborted.

An hour later, Sandy Low Lead called Toby.

"Covey Four One, that's it. We're bingo fuel and have to cut for the home patch. You've got ten more minutes of daylight. See if you can make contact with Packard Three and pinpoint his position. Moonbeam will relieve you when the sun goes down. We've done all we can ... which wasn't shit. Good luck." Anger and frustration had tightened the Sandy's voice to a thin scratch. No Sandy wants to leave the scene of an incomplete rescue. They get mean and want to punch things out.

The main Joint Search and Rescue Center was set up in Saigon. They worked with the Rescue Control Center at Da Nang, and Compress, the Rescue Command Post at Nakhon Phanom Air Base, Thailand. The USAF men were part of the Aerospace Rescue and Recovery Service. They coordinated and integrated both USAF and Navy rescues. Compress had the action because NKP was the rescue unit closest to Mu Gia Pass. The senior duty officer called the Rescue Center in Saigon on the hotline.

"About Packard Three—we can't get anybody out before dark, and tomorrow the weather's gonna be dog shit," he said.

"Seventh Air Force is hot to get him pronto. You know you have on-scene clearance for any kind of fog you need." Fog meant CBU-19 or CBU-52, which was plain tear gas or tear gas mixed with napalm. Authorized by MACV Directive 525-11, fog was considered a component of combat power. It was, however, used sparingly and only on special occasions, such as making a rescue. So far, the newsies hadn't caught on.

"Listen, we want to get *all* the guys out pronto. We just don't have night or bad weather capabilities yet." Compress cleared the line.

"Any Packard read Covey Four One, come up guard or beeper. Packard, come up guard or beeper," Toby had made the calls on guard channel every five minutes. There had been no answer. He had ten more minutes of orbit time before he was bingo.

"Covey Four One, this is Moonbeam, how do you read?" The C-130 ABCCC was settling in orbit for the night.

"Loud and clear, Moonbeam. I've had negative response from Packard."

"Any ground activity, Covey?"

"Negative. The bad guys aren't visible in the clearing anymore, and nobody is shooting at anybody right now."

"Okay, Covey Four One. Moonbeam is on station. You're cleared off station. Break, break. Packard, if you read Hillsboro, come up guard or beeper."

There was no answer. It was dark now. The sun had set.

26

☆

His eyelids fluttered as water began to drip on his face. Dirt and rotted fungus clotted his hair and smeared the left side of his head. With a start, Court Bannister opened his eyes. Like wisps of lake fog blowing away, the fuzziness of his mind cleared. Full awareness came slowly. He moved an arm, then a leg. He was cramped and full of sudden pins and needles as he moved his limbs. He realized he lay at the bottom of a hole of some kind, his left arm under him, both legs jammed against the crumbling dirt wall. He moved his right hand in front of his eyes and wriggled his fingers. He touched his face. He pushed up and freed his left arm. The pain spurted anew as blood rushed through his pinched veins.

I've been captured, he thought. Best I don't let them know I'm conscious. He spent long minutes slowly and silently moving his body and limbs to more comfortable positions. The pain of the pins and needles subsided as the low and constant ache of every muscle and joint throbbed into his consciousness. He bit off a low moan as he struggled to kneel and peer over the lip of his hole.

The hole was small, and partially covered with vines and leaves. He realized it was raining, heavily and noisily, but the covering had been protecting him. Then full awareness came from his cracked lips and swollen tongue. He grasped leaves and licked the water, quickly picking them up and discarding them as he lapped up the moisture. Then it dawned on him—there was no lid or grate over his hole. He peered out. All he saw was the rotting surface of the jungle floor extending out two or three feet in each direction, until it faded under scrub plants and rotted detritus. Then he remembered fleeing the thicket and crashing into the hole late in the day. Was it yesterday? He looked at his watch, and slowly realized he had spent the night—or maybe longer—in the sinkhole. He vaguely remembered waking up and nodding off many times. But where were the NVA soldiers?

If the soldiers had finally gotten through the thicket, he reasoned, they never would have seen the hole unless they stepped in it. They must have gone farther down the mountainside looking for his tracks.

Then the skin on his forehead tightened as he realized that not only was the weather terrible, there were no sounds of airplanes. That meant no rescue attempt until it cleared up. He reached for his radio. On his chest he found only tatters and hanging pieces of his torn flight suit. Reaching down farther, he discovered his knee pockets had been ripped off. In a leg pocket he found the K-bar knife. On his wrist was his issue watch. Even his .38 was gone. Chernov's blue scarf had fallen down around his neck. There was nothing else in his pockets. His mouth went dry as he scrambled around the hole, frantically digging with his hands for the radio that meant life or death. It wasn't there.

He made a conscious effort to stop moving. All right, he said to himself, calm down. There are other things to be considered here.

He looked down and realized the pit was filling with seeping water. He took the scarf, scrunched farther down into the hole, and soaked up water to wring into his mouth until his stomach bulged. Then he stood in the pit like a soldier in a foxhole and looked around. The jungle was close and comforting. The rain sounded like a thousand shower sprays beating on big drums. Even as he listened, he could tell the intensity was diminishing. He crouched and arranged the wide fronds over the top of the hole. Something wriggling fell to the bottom of the pit. Soon the rain stopped, and the jungle became silent and steamy.

Court poked his head out of the hole and cautiously looked around. There were no immediate signs of activity. Then he heard a hissing noise, and a faint click near his head. His heart jumped and he felt his lips draw back in terror. Immediately his mind signaled what the noise was; his radio. He grabbed it and put it to his ear. There was nothing except the faint hiss of static. He looked around again, then spoke quietly into the built-in mike.

"Anybody read Packard Three Alpha?" He couldn't tell if the radio was transmitting or not. Being on all night wouldn't deplete the dry battery too much, but transmitting caused a heavy power drain. He waited a few minutes and transmitted again. This time he got an answer.

"Packard Three Alpha, Packard Three Alpha, this is Hillsboro, read you faint but clear. Save your battery. I'm going to ask a few questions, you think about them, then answer."

The controller aboard Hillsboro pulled out a copy of the private data he had received that morning from his Intel officer that each pilot fills out before he flies combat. It contains the answers to questions only the downed man could know: wife's maiden name, name of first dog, type of car he owned, and the like. Whatever the crewman felt comfortable with. The questions had to be simple, so that he could easily answer correctly while under extreme stress. More often than not, a man missing for more than twelve hours was captured, and his radio was used as a flak trap, hence the quiz. Hillsboro asked a series of questions. Court thought out the briefest answers possible, and replied.

"White sixty-seven Vette. Sam. My watch works okay. Negative flares. I'm maybe five hundred feet south from the clearing in a covered hole. No sign of the bad guys, but they could be hiding."

"Roger, old buddy. We affirm your answers. Look, the bad news is the weather is delta sierra, and due to remain so all day. Down to the trees. The good news is some friends are coming to visit." Hillsboro unkeyed for a moment, then continued. "The second bad news is you got to give me a thirty-second hold-down now, and every twenty minutes for the next hour. We don't know exactly where you are anymore, so we need a fix on your position. If you move, we got to do it again. So get set up." He unkeyed for a long moment, then transmitted. "Start hold-down . . . now."

Court held the transmit button on his radio for thirty long seconds as ticked off by his watch. He knew Hillsboro was using their AN/ARA-25 UHF/VHF homing device to get a cut on his position. Using four cuts from different positions would pinpoint his location close enough to vector the ground team to within a few hundred meters of him. Over the next hour, Court gave three more hold-downs. At the end, he couldn't even hear faint static. There was a chance the battery would revive enough after a few hours to send a feeble signal. All Court could do now was wait, and hope he wasn't discovered and forced to move. He made himself as comfortable as he could in his muddy hole. To keep occupied, he started using pieces of his torn flight suit and the scarf to set up a water filter. He debated eating the leeches he found. He had learned in survival school they had protein—just like maggots. A turn of his stomach said no. He wasn't that hungry—yet.

0900 Hours Local,
Friday, 24 November 1989
The Mu Gia Pass Area
Royalty of Laos

☆

At one time, before Special Forces training, Dave Rhoades had been nearly as wide as he was tall. Now he was thin and as gaunt as a marathoner. All the Caucasian Dakota team members were gaunt. They had sweated and worked off about 5 percent of their body weight during the nine days they had been on the ground in Laos. For this leg, Rhoades was leading. Wolf Lochert climbed at the tail end of the seven-man team. Each man took his place as point, then worked back to tail-end Charlie. Point was rough because it meant breaking trail through the thickest of Asian jungles where gains were measured in meters, not kilometers. The men were never more than four feet apart as they made their way in line, up the steep side of a karst ridge toward the position they had been given for the downed American flyer.

Wolf glanced at his watch. In two minutes, Rhoades would call a compass break. He pulled up the olive-drab sweat rag around his neck and wiped his face. Exactly on time, the hand signal was passed for a break. No one smoked. They talked in whispers. Even though the jungle face was mere feet or inches away, all the men faced outward in a herringbone pattern before squatting to rest. Each took a sip of water from their water bags. Both point and tail-end Charlie checked their compasses. So far, so good. Rhoades had a Nung strip off his gear and shinny up a tall bamboo for a fix. He came down shaking his head. Too much tree, he said in Chinese patois, meaning the canopy prevented him from seeing any prominent features.

Wolf took the phone from the PRC-25 and called Hillsboro.

"Hillsboro, Dakota. You copy?"

"Loud and clear, Dakota. What can we do for you?"

"We need some help here. I'll give you two hold-downs on the RT. Give me a steer to our passenger."

"Roger, Dakota. Hillsboro listening out."

Wolf held the transmit button on the small survival radio for thirty seconds, then released it. Five minutes later, he repeated the process. "You got that, Hillsboro?" he said on the PRC-25.

"Got a rough cut, Dakota. You're nearly all the way up the Phou Toc Vou karst. Go over the crest holding about zero two five degrees. A Covey FAC will be on station in an hour orbiting west. Give him a flash, and he'll give you a better vector once you're on top."

An hour and a half later, Dakota crested the 4,700-foot Phou Toc Vou karst, the eastern peak of Mu Gia Pass. They went over the crest

on their bellies, slipping and sliding in the vines and scrub. Wolf gave
the radio to Roland and told him to tell Hillsboro he was flashing.
Rhoades and the Nungs moved into a guard position. Wolf pulled out
his five-by-three-inch survival mirror and started flashing to the west.

Buey Dan stood to one side, weapon and eyes on the alert down
the karst. He wasn't sure what Wolf had in mind, but he knew if
there was an evacuation, he would cut the long-nose and his companions down as they boarded the helicopter. Then he would grenade the helicopter.

After ten minutes, Covey Three Two came up on the PRC-25 radio
and said he had a good fix on the Dakota flashes. "Steer zero eight
two for about three hundred meters. That will put you at the clearing
where your package was last seen. Best I can tell, he is five or six
hundred feet southeast of that location."

Wolf told Covey Three Two he estimated it would take three hours
to reach the clearing, another hour or two to make contact, depending on the density of the jungle, the weather, and the probability of
enemy contact. "Good luck, Dakota," the Covey FAC told him.

Buey Dan, as point, found the first booby trap just after high noon.
He had been on his knees, slowly moving his hands like a swimmer,
feeling for trip wires when he found one. It was rusty and ancient,
and he knew he had somehow led the team onto an old jungle path,
unused and long overgrown. He conferred briefly with Wolf, who was
behind him. Time was running short. Downed pilots were perishable
products, normally not able to sustain themselves long in the jungle.
Covey Three Two had been replaced by Covey Four One. He had
said the weather was forecast to go bad again. Rhoades and Roland
came forward. The four men crouched over Buey Dan's map and
compared positions as to where each thought they were, and finally
agreed.

"I think we should stay on this old trail as long as it goes in the
direction we want," Wolf said. "But the only way we are going to
find the closest path to the package is for the FAC to get a fix on
both of us, then give us a steer." The others agreed.

Wolf made contact with the new FAC, who said his call sign was
Covey Four One. "Get a flash from us and from the package and
give us a steer," he commanded.

"Roger, Dakota," Toby Parker answered. He thought the voice
vaguely familiar, but gave it no further thought. A Nung shinnied up
a suitable tree that topped the canopy and started flashing at the
droning O-2 plane off to the west.

Toby dropped down to 7,000 feet. That put him only 2,500 hundred feet over the tall karst. He saw the glint from a spot in the jungle
canopy, fixed it in his mind by triangulating it with several distinctive
trees and rock outcroppings, and marked his map.

"I have a good fix," he told Dakota on FM. He gave them a steer in the general direction of the package, then switched to UHF Guard channel to call Packard Three Alpha.

Court Bannister was so stiff he could barely move. His fingers were wrinkled and white from the constant moisture. To keep busy, he removed his boots for the third time and massaged his feet. His toes looked as shriveled as his fingers. He wrung out his socks and put them back on, then checked his watch and found it was time to turn on his radio. Moonbeam had said to listen but not transmit for three minutes on every even hour. Through the night, the controllers had talked to their downed pilot trying to cheer him up with progress reports, jokes, and snatches of music. They had no way of knowing if the signals they sent out in the night air were heard.

Though the signal was weak, Court had received the messages. He had checked the luminescent dial of his watch, then turned the radio on as instructed. He had felt his eyes sting when one controller said a certain man at a certain base had a hot bowl of chili waiting for him. He knew he could not have made it through the night in his hole without the hope and cheer given by the tinny voice through the earpiece. It was twelve noon, time again to listen. The heat and humidity covered the glade and the hole like a wet carpet. Insects hummed and crawled. He turned on the radio.

". . . is Covey Four One. Packard Three Alpha, this is Covey Four One. Do not acknowledge, do not acknowledge. I need a fix on your position. I understand negative flares. Give me a flash, repeat, give me a flash. I'll jazz my engines for you." Toby Parker banked into a left-hand orbit, and moved his throttles back and forth a few times to let the man on the ground know where he was.

Ah shit, Court said to himself. His inventory was no better than yesterday. Nothing to flash with. The mirror was back with the survival gear by Chernov's body. Even the blade of his K-bar knife was black. He'd have to light a fire and put damp green leaves on it and hope the smoke would clear the trees. He pulled out the waxed packet of matches. Then with sudden inspiration, he opened the package of bandages. They were dry. He grabbed the radio, "No mirror, smoke. No mirror, smoke," he transmitted. When he heard no static on receive, he knew the battery had faded to zero output during his transmission. He turned the set off, hoping the battery would rejuvenate itself enough so he could at least hear the FAC's instructions.

He cautiously poked his head above the rim of the hole just enough to look around. Seeing nothing, he pulled himself out and set about finding a suitable place and some dry wood to get a fire going. Under an opening in the canopy, he tore the grass out of a small circle and laid the stalks aside to use as smoke producers. He opened the bandage package and fluffed up the olive-drab gauze. Over the pile he placed small sticks he hoped were dry enough to burn. He used a rock he had dried to light the first of his dozen kitchen matches. It sputtered and went out. One by one, he tried four more that left nothing but the acrid smell of sulphur in the air. Relax, he told himself. He took a deep breath, and tried three more matches. They sparked and spit like miniature fireworks, but failed to ignite. The ninth match lit with a feeble glow. Quickly, Court moved it to the cloth, but the sudden motion extinguished the flame. He swallowed and bundled the remaining three matches in his fingers. He held the rock next to the base of his fire pile, struck all three matches at the same time and, in the same motion, plunged them into the cloth. The sulfur streamed and flared and stunk. A wisp of flame ran up the side of the cloth as the fuzz burned off, then a corner of one of the bandages lit with a tiny beacon of hope. Cautiously, holding his breath for fear of extinguishing the tiny flame, Court poked other portions of the bandages toward the small blaze. They lit in turn and reinforced the heat to light off other bits of the gauze. Soon he had a three-inch flame spreading up though the small sticks. They began to swell and sizzle. Moisture oozed from the ends, then small jets of steam. Thin smoke began to swirl up from the sticks. Court could see they weren't as dry as he had thought. He started to fan the fire and blow on it. The sticks weren't catching. They bubbled and bloated like hot dogs on a grill, but didn't flame. Court looked up. The thin stream of smoke was rising in the still dank air toward the canopy a hundred feet over his head. He looked down at the fire. The flames from the gauze bandages weakened as they glowed like incandescent screens and turned to ashes. He knew the fire would die. There was nothing dry to add.

Ah God, he moaned. One last chance remained. He carefully sprinkled grass on the fire and ashes, hoping against hope there would be at least a small burst of smoke for the FAC to see. The diameter of the smoking pile was less than a foot. He blew against the ashes, trying to increase the heat. His eyes burned and he choked as he inhaled, but a gush of smoke started up toward the hole in the jungle canopy. He grabbed the radio and turned it on.

"Smoke, smoke, smoke," he transmitted. He held the button down and kept transmitting, knowing if there was any juice at all left in the battery, this prolonged transmission would exhaust it fully. "Packard Three Alpha sending smoke, smoke, smoke, smoke ..." He kept it up for several minutes, knowing full well if the first few words didn't get out, he was doomed to find his own way out of the jungle. With anguish in his eyes, he looked up through the opening in the green canopy at the tiny patch of blue sky that represented freedom.

Toby Parker caught the word "smoke" twice then the transmission faded. He had been looking in the area where he expected the flash from the mirror. He saw nothing. Then he knew what the man meant. He stopped jinking and turning, and dove at full throttle toward the area to the east. To do so he had to cross directly over the pass at Mu Gia. Up to now, he had been protected by orbiting behind the lip of the western ridge, where he could see across to the eastern plateau where Dakota and Packard where located.

Toby was surprised the guns did not open up the minute he was exposed. There were scores of 37mm and 23mm zippers down there that could drop a 500-knot Phantom from a mile away. He had three minutes of spine-crawling exposure before he cleared the eastern ridge line and was safe. His mind worked on the phenomenon as he furiously searched the terrain barely one thousand feet below. Then he knew what it was. The operators of the big guns were under great fire discipline, waiting for the SAR they knew would take place. They were after bigger game than one lonely Cessna O-2 with just a single crew member.

He scanned the terrain below. It all looked damningly similar. An unbroken green carpet of foliage that hid all the secrets. Then a blur caught his eye. No, not a blur, rather a fading of the green. Smoke. It was the thinnest of smoke, faintly lightening a small portion of the dense green. He nearly tore the wings off in his haste to turn toward what he had seen. He never took his eyes off the spot as he banked his airplane, advanced the throttles, and started a descent. Then he had to flick his eyes away and quickly back to make sure it was there. He got closer. Definitely smoke, not mist, too hot for mist, too sunny. It was smoke. He roared over the spot and pulled up and called to Dakota on FM.

"Dakota, Covey Four One. Steer zero eight seven degrees for about one hundred meters. I have smoke there. I think it's our package." Wolf rogered and started his team on the new vector.

The first shot sounded fourteen minutes later, then a fusillade. Soon a light machine gun joined in. The team, unable to withdraw, dropped into a defensive herringbone, but did not fire. Wolf was surprised and puzzled. The portion of the jungle they were in was tangled and thick, forward visibility nil. Then he realized that no bullets were impacting around them. The NVA soldiers were close, but instead of ambushing the Dakota team, they were shooting small arms at the Covey FAC. It was ragged fire, and undisciplined. Must be the search troops, Wolf reasoned. Out looking for the downed flyer, they were potting at the low-flying O-2. Their leader, probably a corporal, would have to answer to the commander of the main air defense unit that controlled all antiaircraft fire along this section of the Ho Chi Minh Trail. The shots died as the plane droned away.

Wolf crawled forward to confer with Rhoades and Roland, and to check the map. They decided the enemy ground troops were between them and the American. To skirt them would waste time and probably could not be done with any great accuracy. Besides, they could easily run into flankers. Each spoke in turn, then they agreed on a plan. Wolf crouched over the radio, holding the map on his knee.

"Covey Four One, Dakota."

"Dakota, Four One, go."

"Here's how it is, Covey. There is a contingent of NVA between us and the package. They shot at you with small arms and a light mg as you made that last pass. If you can drag the same spot to keep them shooting, we can move a hell of a lot faster covered by the noise, find them, and take them out. Then we'll locate our man and have him ready for pickup. Acknowledge."

"Dakota, Covey Four One acknowledges. Get set up. I've a few phone calls to make first, then I'll come down and make the passes."

Toby pulled up, relayed the message to Crown, and said he thought the SAR effort could recommence. The weather looked acceptable, and should hold for the next few hours.

Crown called Compress, who scrambled the Jollys and the Sandy and Hobo A-1s from Nakhon Phanom, and the first flights of the fragged fighters from Da Nang, Ubon, and Task Force 77. Over one hundred USAF and Navy planes were apportioned this day for the rescue of one man. Such an immense response was nothing new. Every combat aircrewman knew that massive efforts would be expended to get him out were he shot down. In turn, each crewman was willing to lay his life on the line to rescue another. There was a tightly woven net among these men that did not allow anyone to go it alone.

After talking to Crown, Toby flew back to the area where Wolf had said the NVA was shooting at him. He had a dilemma he wasn't sure how to handle. He was the only man who had exactly pinpointed the location of the downed pilot. He knew which tree on which ridge line next to what karst was where the Jolly should lower his penetrator. The jungle was so thick and impenetrable that should the Jolly hover just fifty feet away, the man most probably could not find the device for several hours. Were Toby to be shot down, this precious information would be lost. If another FAC were on site, or a Sandy, Toby could fly over the site, dip a wing and say "there." Or fire a marking rocket well off to one side and vector them in to the rescue site from the smoke.

He finally pushed the throttles up. The project at hand was to get the NVA firing. If he was shot down, well, Dakota knew where the survivor was. He dove toward the solid green mass of jungle.

When he heard the noise, Court's eyes widened. He froze. He was shocked how near the firing was when the O-2 roared overhead. With dawning horror, he realized the shooters were right outside his hole. He remained still, and tried to assess the situation. His radio was out, so he could only surmise what was happening. Since the O-2 had passed so close, he figured his position was known. Remembering what the FAC had told him about some friendlies on the ground, he decided all he had to do was stay put until someone showed up. With enemy troops all around, there was precious else to consider as an option. He simply had to wait, and hope for the best. He slowly and carefully twisted some water into his mouth, and eased back against the mud wall of his hole. He wished he hadn't lost the .38.

For thirty minutes, Wolf Lochert led his men toward the sound of the firing. While the general area was marked by the turning and twisting O-2, the final assault would be made on the noise from each individual weapon. Since the FAC had stayed in one area so long, Wolf had to assume the NVA knew there was an American on the ground nearby, and that more NVA search troops would soon be flooding the area. There would be some delay, because the new men would have to climb up the steep karst from the valleys through which the Trail twisted and wound its way.

They came upon the first shooter sooner than expected. He had been inserting a new magazine when Wolf crept around the huge roots of a giant tree. Wolf didn't want to risk a shot—his weapon wasn't in good position anyhow—he had to use the knife. Like an attacking snake, he launched himself toward the man, releasing his gun on the ground with one hand, while jerking the handle-down K-bar from the scabbard taped to his harness with the other. The Vietnamese died with only a slight gurgle. Wolf lay flat on him for a few seconds before moving. He could feel the warm blood from the dead man's throat spreading over the front of him. He made sure he was unobserved, rose to his elbows and knees, and backed up around the tree. Rhoades covered him with his Swedish K. On their stomachs, the two men peered around the base of the tree to assess the situation.

They saw a rectangular glade maybe forty feet by eighty. Scrub bushes and grass rose up from twelve inches to four feet. There was no secondary tree growth making a first or second canopy. The top of the glade was formed one hundred feet overhead by the branches and crowns of huge trees. Their ten-foot thick trunks rose from the ground like mammoth pillars. Their branches did not meet over the center of the glade, providing an open circle roughly ten feet across. A few hundred feet in the air, wide of the opening, the obliging Covey FAC was orbiting just outside the narrow field of fire. Wolf wondered who Covey Four One was. He would put him in for some kind of medal when he got back. Every few minutes the daring pilot would dart his O-2 across the opening, causing the troops to open fire. Wolf estimated fifteen to twenty NVA were in the glade. He was sure they were green; they had no hope of hitting the plane, as they fired straight up, like men shooting up a chimney at a swallow as it flashed past the opening.

Using hand motions and whispered commands, Wolf told his team what he wanted each man to do. In general, it entailed encompassing most of the glade in a horseshoe formation. Upon signal, they would open fire at the enemy in such a manner the men on the sides of the horseshoe would not be shooting at each other. Rhoades and Roland would be stationed at the heel of each side. They would function as a combined blocking force, and would pick off whatever enemy tried to scramble out of the killing zone. Wolf pointed to his watch and said the attack would commence in twenty minutes. Everybody had damn well be in place. Silently, with precise movements, each man crept off to his assigned post. Toby Parker, Covey Four One, dragged the circle. The enemy was getting smarter. They held and timed their fire, so that he started taking hits toward the rear of his ungainly craft.

Wolf's attack plan was basic and simple—with one major exception. Someplace hidden in the grass was an American who might panic and stand up once the assault commenced. This required each man on the Dakota team to be on special alert. They were, after all, here to rescue the man, not rack up an NVA body count.

Wolf started the attack by opening fire with his weapon. Before the second round had exited the barrel, his team members had opened up. The Nungs on his left and right alternately fired and heaved grenades. Rhoades and Roland had it easy, dropping the surprised NVA with well-placed bursts of three rounds. Buey Dan, on the right of Wolf Lockert, sighted and fired bursts that narrowly missed the NVA soldiers, but passed dangerously close to Roland. He was in fact trying surreptitiously to take out the white men, one by one. He had decided to implement his plan of narrowing down Dakota to a manageable force that he could wipe out. Then he would kill Wolf Lochert as slowly and painfully as he could. An NVA soldier popped up from the grass on one knee with his AK pointed directly at Wolf Lochert. Buey Dan dropped him before he could pull the trigger. This was not the way he wanted the big nose barbarian to die.

"Nice shot, Beedee," Wolf said, himself killing two fleeing soldiers with accurate three-round bursts.

In less than five minutes it was all over. Wolf estimated over a dozen enemy dead—there was no time to count—and he had one Nung wounded in the foot. Time to find the package and get him extracted.

"Packard Three," he called out, "Packard Three, we're your friendly delivery service. You call, we haul. You ready to go home?"

"Over here," Court Bannister sang out from his hole in the ground. He didn't think it prudent to rise up out of nowhere in a battle scene amidst a bunch of men with hair triggers.

"Stand up, show yourself," Wolf commanded. He saw a movement near the center of the glade, then stared at the apparition that rose from the ground. "Man, you look like you just crawled over half of Laos," he mouthed.

Court Bannister's flight suit hung in tatters around his neck and chest, showing the long red scratches from the spines and thorns. What wasn't torn was wet and muddy. In his right hand he held his K-bar knife, in his left was his survival radio. He looked around. He saw two men in camouflaged jungle fatigues emerge from the jungle and start to search the bodies of the dead NVA. Two more poked gun barrels from the bushes. Two squatted and took defensive positions with their automatic weapons, one was talking on a radio. The seventh, a stocky man holding a camouflaged assault rifle, beckoned.

"Come on, pilot," the man bellowed above the uproar. "Get your ass in gear. That Jolly will be down in two." He motioned with the rifle for Court to hurry toward him.

Court rose and started walking toward him, pain forgotten for the moment. As he drew up to Lochert, he looked around, his mind taking in what he saw. The Nungs were eying him and smiling. A tall Vietnamese crouched nearby.

For the first time, Court focused on his rescuer. "Wolf Lochert," he said. "My God, but I'm glad to see you."

"Bannister," Wolf said in surprise, "you should have stayed in Las Vegas."

"I should have stayed anywhere but here." He looked around and caught the eye of Buey Dan, who looked away.

Wolf noticed Court's look at the Vietnamese. "That's Buey Dan. Been together a long time."

Court nodded. "I guess we better get the hell out of here."

"Yeah, I guess," Wolf said with a bark of sardonic laughter, "*you* better get out of here."

The sound of a helicopter burst suddenly into the clearing like a passing freight train. Two Sandys zoomed overhead, firing at nearby targets. Dave Rhoades looked up from the radio. "Your taxi, sir. But you better hurry. The Covey FAC says there's bad guys swarming up the side of this here karst."

"Get a couple of Nungs and set up a defense," Wolf commanded. Then he crouched and, running, led Court toward the roaring hiss of the helicopter turbine engines. Sporadic firing sounded from behind them. Wolf took an RT-10 from his pocket. "What about your back-seater?" he asked Court.

"He was badly wounded. I saw him go down by a road about five miles north of here. They got him the minute he hit the ground."

"Anyone else down in this area?" Wolf asked.

Court hesitated. "No," he said. He thought about Vladimir Chernov. "No one."

Wolf looked at Court, his face expressionless. "Hillsboro said there might be a Russian pilot down around here."

After a moment, Court answered. "Yeah, there was. He was saving me from an NVA patrol when they killed him. He was letting me go. Said he didn't want me tortured in Hanoi."

Wolf Lochert was silent for a moment. A look of pain flashed across his face and was gone in an instant. The big helicopter was seconds away.

"If the situation were reversed," Lochert said, "would you have let him go?"

Court hesitated. "No," he said. "I'd have brought him in."

"Why?"

"We don't torture. Besides, I think he wanted out."

Wolf nodded, and held the transmitter to his lips. "Covey Four One, Dakota. I have Packard Three Alpha. He's ready for extraction. Copy?"

"Dakota, Four One copies. Are you declaring a Prairie Fire?" Prairie Fire was the code for a team requesting emergency extraction.

"Negative, Covey. Just your everyday run-of-the-mill pickup." He unkeyed the transmitter. "We're not going anywhere, just you," he said to Court. "No point in letting the gomers know that fact by transmitting in the clear. We still have work to do down here."

"You're not going out with me?"

"Negative. We've got a lot more to do down here besides evacuating just one pilot." Wolf Lochert looked at his deployed team. "We're going to disengage and get back to work."

Covey Four One answered Wolf's last transmission.

"Roger, copy, Dakota. The Sandys are working the area over now. The Jollys will vector in on your flare. This is Covey standing by."

They heard the approaching helicopter. Wolf took a day–night flare from his ruck and shot it toward the opening.

"Tally ho the flare," a new voice said on the RT-10. "This is your Jolly. We're coming in. Now give me some smoke."

Wolf took Court's day–night flare, popped the smoke end, and tossed it into the clearing.

"I've got red, Dakota," the Jolly Green pilot said.

"Roger, red," Wolf transmitted.

In the remaining seconds as the Sandy pilots worked over the perimeter, cannons hammering, the huge Jolly Green HH-53 zoomed over the opening and hovered on the six-bladed rotor powered by two shrieking turbine engines. The red smoke was sucked up, then spat out in looping whorls by the 72-foot blades. A PJ started down on the penetrator through the opening in the canopy. Another Jolly hovered high and out of sight.

"On your way, Bannister," Wolf said. He saw Buey Dan near the spot where the PJ would touch down. "Hey, Beedee," he yelled above the roar of the engines. "Get over here. We're not leaving with these guys." The Special Forces colonel turned back to Court and shook hands. Then Court ducked and ran to the penetrator. He was still carrying his gun and radio.

Once on the ground, the PJ—hooked by his harness to the penetrator—pulled Court onto one of the folding seats and snapped the safety harness around him. Then he tilted his head back and gave a thumbs-up signal. In seconds, they were winched aboard the helicopter. Nose down, the helicopter sped forward, then rose like a runaway elevator. Court clutched the door frame and looked down to see the last of the Nungs melt into the jungle away from the shattering blasts the Sandy pilots were putting on the side of the karst. The view dwindled and was lost in featureless green.

The PJ turned to Court and shouted over the noise. "No one else down there? No one else that needs a helping hand from the friendly Jolly Green Giant?"

Court looked out the open door at the brown and green karst sliding by. He heard again the anguished cry of his wingman that Flak was down; he saw Ev Stern's body fall on the road; and he saw Vladimir Chernov drop like a poled ox. The fact he had shot down his fourth MiG meant nothing. He took out the blue scarf.

"They're down there," he said, "but it's too late. Too late," he repeated, with infinite sadness in his voice.

27

☆

Milt Berzin shot into the office of Commander, 7th Air Force. His usual calm demeanor was interrupted by the excitement evident on his rugged face.

"Sir, we got Bannister out. Hostettler just called on the scramble line. He was a bit vague, but it appears Bannister is okay."

"What do you mean, 'vague'?"

"Well, Hostettler said Bannister started slugging down mission whiskey on the Jolly Green and hasn't been too cooperative on the debriefing. Doesn't seem all that happy about getting his fourth MiG. He said something about talking to the pilot and that the Russian somehow saved his ass."

The Commander of the 7th Air Force thought for a moment. "Tell Colonel Bryce to rig it so Bannister can fly down here tonight . . . no, make that tomorrow, on the Scatback courier. I want him to brief me personally on all this."

"Yes, sir, I'll do that," the colonel said. "Ah, sir, there's one more thing you should know about Bannister and Ubon."

The Commander nodded. "Go ahead."

"Major Bannister's brother has been picked up by the OSI in the town of Ubon for soliciting classified material and passing it on to the North Vietnamese. They had been on to him for some time. Special Agent LaNew made the collar when he sold him some phony missile documents."

0730 HOURS LOCAL,
SATURDAY, 25 NOVEMBER 1967
T-39 ENROUTE FROM UBON TO TAN SON NHUT AIR BASE
REPUBLIC OF VIETNAM

☆

Court Bannister rested his head against an oval window in the small USAF passenger jet. He stared down without really focusing. From seven miles up, there wasn't much to see: some scattered clouds, brown and green angular patterns of Thai rice fields; later, silvery waterways and miles of flooded spots of the South Vietnam delta region. He had had a lot to drink the night before, and his head softly pulsed and throbbed to the beat of the two jet engines as they phased in and out of synch with each other. He wore his 1505 khakis with open collar, major's oak leaves, senior pilot's wings, para wings, no ribbons. Underneath his shirt were several layers of rolled gauze and tape to keep his cracked ribs stable. The dull pain pulsated in cadence with his headache. Salve on his back and legs eased the tightness of the deep scratches. They had just started to fester when the flight surgeon had cleaned him up at the Ubon dispensary. In his pocket was a light blue scarf.

There had been a great turnout late in the afternoon the day before at the Ubon flight line. Returning a rescued pilot to his home base was a big event—certainly in the life of the pilot. As profound, to some, as a religious rebirth. The big Jolly Green helicopter had swooped low making its victory pass before settling down like a giant mother hen. The entire fighter wing had turned out with jeeps and flight-line vehicles parading colored smoke. There was loud recorded military parade music, and cases of champagne. It wasn't that the war was called off for these events. The turnout was by those who had already flown or who weren't flying that day. They could afford to drink. In the distance, heavily loaded F-4s were blasting sound and flame as they struggled into the air, while others were alighting like weary birds, empty and spent.

A loud cheer had gone up when Court had dismounted from the big camouflaged helicopter, moving slowly and stiffly, helped by the PJ. Colonel Stan Bryce had met him and motioned others to take Court's gear as it was passed down. Court was already fuzzy from the aftershock and the Johnny Walker the PJ had slipped him. Hostettler quietly noted the blue scarf in Court's hand.

"Great job, great job," Stan Bryce had yelled into his ear. "Hillsboro passed the word you got a MiG. One more and you'll be the first ace." Bryce put his arm around Court's shoulders as the base photographer worked his big Graflex. Bryce got him into the lead jeep. Hostettler pulled out a clipboard and his USAF Mission De-briefing sheet. "I know you ain't going to make it to Intel, old buddy."

Court answered the questions as best he could, as Colonel Stan Bryce led the procession honking and yelling twice around the base. After two hours in the Club, Court used Hostettler's shoulder to make it home. Later he had awakened in severe pain and hobbled to the hospital, where he was given a sedative and some wrapping when the cracked ribs were discovered. The flight surgeon had chewed Court only slightly for not stopping by to get the required post-crash physical.

Now, across from Court on the T-39 Scatback, sat Colonel Stan Bryce, effervescent, greatly pleased one of his boys had tied the high-est MiG record of the war so far. Only Colonel Robin Olds had downed four MiGs. Colonel Bryce had had a long telephone conver-sation with Commander, Seventh, about what should await the United States Air Force's latest hero when he landed at Tan Son Nhut.

Behind Court sat Colonel Peter Wysocki from Air Force Intelli-gence. He had flown up from Tan Son Nhut on the Scatback that morning to pick up Bannister, and wasn't pleased with the results. He was sure Bannister was holding back information needed to com-plete the six-page form titled *Foreign National Contact—Soviet.* For some reason, Bannister would offer no proof to back up the report from Truncate via Green Door that a Soviet pilot was missing and presumed down. Or that Bannister had not only shot him down, but had actually talked to him.

The T-39 swooped down and made a circling approach to Tan Son Nhut, then lined up on final approach. It flew lower and lower over the thousands of jammed-together wood-and-thatch shacks cross-hatched by narrow ditches of gray sewage, passed the airfield bound-ary, and touched down with faint tire squeaks and smoke puffs.

"Sir," the aide to Commander, 7th, said, "Major Bannister's plane is taxiing in." They departed his office next to MACV headquarters.

"Are all the arrangements made?" the Commander asked as they climbed into his staff car.

"Yes, sir. Welcoming committee, public affairs, civilian journalists and TV crews, podium, carpet, and band." The aide leaned over the front seat and showed him a box and a tube of paper tied with a blue ribbon. "Here's his Silver Star, Purple Heart, and citations to go with them."

The four-star commander of the air war leaned back and thought of Bannister. I hate to do this to you, son. But that's part of the game. Seventh needs a hero, the USAF needs a hero, even MACV can use one. And right now, it's your turn in the barrel.

Through the oval window, Court spied the crowd in front of the operations building. I wonder who the wheel is, he thought to himself. He looked away, then back, as the T-39 headed for the spot. His ears flamed as he realized it was for him.

"Oh shit hot, shit hot," Bryce said. "Look at that. We're famous."

"If that's really for me, I'm not getting off this airplane." Kee-rist. Court Bannister frowned and glowered so heavily he looked like a furious pink gargoyle. His bowels rumbled. Less than 24 hours before, he had been drinking contaminated water.

Guided by the lineman with wands, the T-39 coasted gently toward the yellow parking dot. The nose bobbed slightly as the pilot braked, and the two engines whistled a down note as they unwound. Sunlight sparkled from the four stars on the collar of the commander and from all the other stars on the collars of the 7th Air Force and MACV dignitaries gathered by the portable podium. The cameras were poised. Idle chatter ceased as the silver passenger door cracked open. Exactly as it swung downward and the steps appeared, the bandleader gave a stroke with his baton.

The booming notes of E.E. Bagley's *National Emblem* crashed across the flight line. The music rolled over the crowd and beyond, causing flight-line mechanics to stop and look and think of the monkey as the flaring brass and heavy drum thumps got all jangled up, reverberating in and out of the fighters revetements. The brassy music flooded into the gaping door of the little passenger jet.

Inside, Major Court Bannister, face hidden by glare, stared through hostile eyes out the oval window at the reception. He didn't move.

The music swelled.

All eyes remained focused on the open door.